EUROPE
NORTH AFRICA
& THE NEAR EAST
circa 1474
Peter McClure 1997
0 20 40 80
English miles
N
KHANATE OF
CRIM TARTARS
Sea of Azov
Straits of Kerch
Kerch
Qirq-yer (Chufut-Kale)
Mankup-Kale
Baçi-Saray
Caffa (Feodosiya)
Soldaia (Südäk)
Cherson
Alushta
Gurzuf
Cembalo
Simiez
Alupka
GOTHIA
Black Sea
Novgorod
Volga
(Ledil)
Vladimir
Moscow
Viazma
Riazan
Smolensk
Minsk
RUSSIA
Volga
KHANATE OF THE GOLDEN HORDE
TARTARY
Aral Sea
Don (Tanais)
Saray
Dnieper
Astrakhan (Citracan)
Oxus
Kamenets
Dniester
Tana (Azov)
Caspian Sea
0 100 200 300
English miles
Ochakov
Sea of Azov
ABKHAZIA
KABARDIA
Derbent
CIRCASSIA
Caffa
Kutaisi
Sukhumi
Gori
Tiflis (Tblisi)
Baku
Black Sea (Euxine)
Fasso (Poti)
Rioni
GEORGIA
Asterabad
Trebizond
ARMENIA
Mt. Ayrarat
Erzerum
Tabriz (Tauris)
Tehrān
Pera
Constantinople
Lake Urmia
Bursa
Kharput
Qom (Koum)
Diarbekr
TURKEY
PERSIA
Yazd
MESOPOTAMIA
Spaan (Isfahan)
Smyrna
Tigris
Baghdad
Aleppo
Antioch
Euphrates
Shiraz (Siras)
SYRIA
Nicosia
CYPRUS
Famagusta
Damascus
Gulf of Persia
Jerusalem
Gaza
Alexandria
Cairo
Nile
Mt. Sinai

ALSO BY DOROTHY DUNNETT

The Game of Kings

Queens' Play

The Disorderly Knights

Pawn in Frankincense

The Ringed Castle

Checkmate

King Hereafter

Dolly and the Singing Bird (Rum Affair)

Dolly and the Cookie Bird (Ibiza Surprise)

Dolly and the Doctor Bird (Operation Nassau)

Dolly and the Starry Bird (Roman Nights)

Dolly and the Nanny Bird (Split Code)

Dolly and the Bird of Paradise (Tropical Issue)

Moroccan Traffic

Niccolò Rising

The Spring of the Ram

Race of Scorpions

Scales of Gold

The Unicorn Hunt

To Lie With Lions

The Scottish Highlands

(*in collaboration with Alastair Dunnett*)

Caprice and Rondo

The House of Niccolò

Caprice and Rondo

DOROTHY DUNNETT

ALFRED A. KNOPF *New York* 1998

THIS IS A BORZOI BOOK
PUBLISHED BY ALFRED A. KNOPF, INC.

www.randomhouse.com

Originally published in Great Britain in slightly different form by Michael Joseph Ltd., London, in 1997.

Library of Congress Cataloging-in-Publication Data
Dunnett, Dorothy.
Caprice and Rondo / Dorothy Dunnett. — 1st American ed.
p. cm. — (The house of Niccolò)
ISBN 0-679-45477-2
I. Title. II. Series: Dunnett, Dorothy. House of Niccolò.
PR6054.U56C36 1998
823'.914—dc21 97-49458
CIP

Manufactured in the United States of America
First American Edition

For Annabella Charlotte Dunnett

The author wishes to express warm thanks to the Centralne Muzeum Morskie, the Polish Maritime Museum of Gdańsk, source of much of the known information about the seamaster Paúel Benecke, and possessor of an elegant scale model of the actual *Peter von Danzig*. The kind help of the museum's staff and librarian, Bożena Świderska, was invaluable in recreating the Danzig of half a millennium ago.

Perhaps it should be added that Hans Memling's historic painting, *The Last Judgement*, remained in Gdańsk, and is on public view there.

Characters

November 1473 – January 1477
(Those marked * are recorded in history)

Rulers

* England: King Edward IV, House of York
* Scotland: King James III, House of Stewart
* France: King Louis XI
* Burgundy: Charles, Duke of Burgundy, Count of Flanders
* Pope: Sixtus IV (della Rovere)
* Venice: Doges Nicolò Marcello, Pietro Mocenigo, Andrea Vendramin
* German Emperor and King of the Romans: Frederick III
* Portugal: King Alphonse V, nephew of Henry the Navigator
* Muscovy: Grand Duke Ivan III Vasilievich, Autocrat of All Russia
* Scandinavia: Christian I
* Poland and Lithuania: King Casimir IV Jagiello
* Bohemia: King Wladyslaw, son of Casimir
* Hungary: King Mathias Corvinus
* Moldavia: Stephen III The Great
* Ottoman Empire (Istanbul): Sultan Mehmet II
* Mameluke Empire (Cairo): Sultan Qayt Bey

House of Niccolò

Nicholas de Fleury, former governor of the Banco di Niccolò
Szalec Jelita, his servant

VENICE BANCO DI NICCOLÒ:
Gregorio of Asti, lawyer and director
Margot, his wife
Jaçon, their son
Egidia (Gelis) van Borselen, wife of Nicholas de Fleury
Jordan (Jodi), their son
Clémence de Coulanges, his nurse

Pasque, his former nursemaid
Captain Cuthbert, his Scottish master-at-arms
Raffo, his 'groom'
Manoli, 'servant' to Clémence
Tobias Beventini of Grado, physician

LOW COUNTRIES: HOF CHARETTY–NICCOLÒ, BRUGES:
Diniz Vasquez, director, nephew of Simon de St Pol
Mathilde (Tilde) de Charetty, his wife, step-daughter of Nicholas
Marian, their daughter
Catherine de Charetty, Tilde's unmarried younger sister
Father Moriz of Augsburg, chaplain and co-manager
Govaerts of Brussels, management, Bruges and Cologne
Jooris, agent in Antwerp

GERMAN COMPANY:
Julius of Bologna, notary and director
Gräfin Anna von Hanseyck, his wife
Bonne, her daughter
Brygidy, her maid
Petru, her guide
Friczo Straube, company agent in Thorn
Sinbaldo di Manfredo, company agent, Black Sea

MERCENARY COMPANY:
Astorre (Syrus de Astariis), mercenary commander
Thomas, deputy to Astorre
John le Grant, engineer, gunner, sailing-master

PERIPATETIC:
Michael Crackbene, shipmaster
Ochoa de Marchena, former sailing-master on African voyage

Duchy of Burgundy

DUCAL HOUSEHOLD AND ARMY:
* Charles, Duke of Burgundy and Brabant, Count of Flanders, Holland, Zeeland, etc.
* Margaret of York, his wife and sister of King Edward IV
* Marie, daughter of Duke Charles by previous wife
* Bastard Anthony of Bourbon, natural brother of Duke Charles
* Baudouin, bastard and half-brother of Anthony
* William Hugonet, lord of Saillant, Chancellor of the Duchy
* Jean de Rubempré, sire de Bièvres, governor of Lorraine
* Niccolò de Montfort/Gambatesta, Count of Campobasso, Italian mercenary leader

* Jacopo Galeotto, Italian mercenary leader
* Philip de Croy, comte de Chimay, company commander
* Josse and Jean de Lalaing, Burgundian captains
* Matteo Lope de la Garde, Portuguese physician to the Duke

BRUGES AND GHENT:

* Anselm Adorne, Baron Cortachy, Conservator of Scots Privileges in Bruges
* Jan Adorne, his oldest son, a lawyer in Rome
* Katelijne (Kathi) Sersanders, Adorne's niece
* Robin of Berecrofts, Scotland, her husband
* Mistress Cristen, her nurse
* Anselm Sersanders, her brother, Adorne's nephew
* Arnaud Adorne, Adorne's second youngest son
* Agnes von Nieuenhove, his wife
* Dr Andreas of Vesalia, physician and astrologer
* Louis de Bruges, seigneur de Gruuthuse, Earl of Winchester, Governor of Holland
* Marguerite van Borselen, his wife
* Tommaso Portinari, Medici manager in Bruges
* Hans (Henne) Memling, Rhineland artist settled in Bruges
* Jehan Metteneye, host to Scots merchants in Bruges
* Stephen Angus, Scots agent in Bruges

VEERE AND MIDDLEBURG:

* Wolfaert van Borselen of Veere, Count of Grandpré, 'cousin' of Gelis van Borselen
* Wolfaert van Borselen, his son
* Charlotte de Bourbon, Wolfaert's second wife
* Anna van Borselen, their daughter
* Paul van Borselen, bastard son of Wolfaert

DIJON/FLEURY:

Enguerrand de Damparis, friend of Marian de Charetty's sister
Thibault, vicomte de Fleury, maternal grandfather to Nicholas, and brother of late Jaak de Fleury of Geneva
Brother Huon, his nurse
Ysabeau, younger sister of Josine, first wife of Thibault

The Vatachino Company

Martin, broker, merchant and agent
* David de Salmeton, former agent

Rome (*including Papal Legates*)

* Father Ludovico de Severi da Bologna, Patriarch of Antioch and Papal Legate to Persia
Brother Orazio, his clerk
* Marco Barbo, Cardinal of San Marco and Papal Legate to Germany, Poland and Bohemia
* Prosper Schiaffino de Camulio de' Medici, Collector for the Apostolic Camera in England, Ireland and Scotland
* Cardinal Philibert Hugonet, brother of Chancellor Hugonet of Burgundy, and employer of Anselm Adorne's eldest son Jan

Poland

* Paúel Benecke, Danzig privateer, captain of the *Peter von Danzig*
* Malgorzaty, his wife
* Elzbiete, his daughter
Gerta his mistress, tavern-keeper in Thorn
* Filippo Buonaccorsi (Callimachus), royal secretary, exiled Italian poet and scholar
* Nicolao Lipnicki, his servant
* Filip Bischoff, Danzig merchant
* Elzbiete Gerber, his wife
* Barbara, one of his daughters
* Jerzy Bock, Elder of the Confrérie of St George; Bischoff's brother-in-law
* Johann Sidinghusen, Danzig merchant, part-owner of the *Peter von Danzig*; father-in-law of Bock
* Tidemann Valandt, Danzig merchant, part-owner of the *Peter von Danzig*
* Heinrich Niederhof, Danzig merchant, part-owner of the *Peter von Danzig*
* Elizabeth Habsburg of Austria, Queen of Poland, second cousin of the Emperor Frederick
* Wladyslaw, King of Bohemia, her eldest son
* Kazimierz, * Jan Olbracht, * Aleksander and * Zygmunt, other sons
* Jan Długosz, royal tutor, national historian, canon of Cracow
* Jan Ostrórog, royal tutor, political writer, Castellan of Poznan
* Archbishop Gregory of Sanok, Primate of Poland
* Thomas Halkerston, Scots merchant in Danzig
* Stephen Lawson of Haddington, the same
* William Simpson, the same
* James Lauder, the same

Germany and other Hanseatic League

* Emperor Frederick III of the House of Habsburg
* Archduke Maximilian, his son
* Heinrich Castorp, merchant of Lübeck

France and Lorraine

* René, Duke of Anjou, Count of Provence and titular King of Naples and Sicily; father of former Queen Margaret of England
* René II, Duke of Lorraine, grandson of King René
* Bernard de Moncourt, seigneur de Chouzy, kinsman of Clémence de Coulanges

Scotland

ROYAL HOUSEHOLD AND NOBLES:
* James Stewart (Third of the Name), King of Scotland
* Margaret, daughter of Christian I of Denmark, his Queen
* Mary Stewart, the King's elder sister
* James, 1st Lord Hamilton of Kinneil, her second husband
* Robert, Lord Boyd, father of her first husband
* Alexander Stewart, Duke of Albany, the King's brother
* Margaret Stewart, the King's younger sister
* James Stewart of Auchterhouse, Earl of Buchan (Hearty James), half-uncle of King James

IN EXILE:
Jordan de St Pol, vicomte de Ribérac, lord of Kilmirren, formerly royal adviser and merchant in France
Simon de St Pol of Kilmirren, his son
Henry de St Pol, son of Simon's late wife Katelina van Borselen, sister of Gelis

MERCHANTS AND OTHERS:
* Archibald of Berecrofts (Archie), Canongate merchant
* Robin, his son, husband of Katelijne Sersanders
* Isobella (Bel) of Cuthilgurdy, neighbour to the St Pols of Kilmirren
* Andro Wodman, merchant; former Scots Archer in France
* Euphemia (Phemie) Dunbar of Haddington Priory, daughter of George, Earl of March
* William Roger (Whistle Willie), Court musician
* Thomas Cochrane, master mason
* Thomas (Thom) Swift, Edinburgh merchant

* Andrew Crawford, Edinburgh merchant
Richard, his son
* John Bonkle, merchant
* Andrew Haliburton, merchant

The Duchy of the Tyrol

* Sigismond, Duke of Austria and Styria and Count of the Tyrol
* Eleanor Stewart, his wife, aunt to King James of Scotland

Venice: Colonials and Diplomats

* Caterino Zeno, envoy to Uzum Hasan of Persia
* Martin, his clerk
* Violante of Naxos, his wife, niece of Uzum Hasan's Christian wife
* Pietro, her legitimate son
Nerio, exile from Trebizond, her unacknowledged son
* Catherine, widowed Queen of Cyprus
* Marco Corner, sugar-grower in Cyprus, her father
* Fiorenza of Naxos, his wife, mother of Queen Catherine and sister of Violante and Valenza
* Josaphat Barbaro, Venetian envoy to Persia; former consul at Tana
* Ambrogio Contarini, Venetian envoy to Persia
* Father Stephano Testa, his chaplain and secretary
* Augostino Contarini, his brother, *sopracomito* to Barbaro in Cyprus
* Francesco Contarini, Venetian governor of Albania
* Paolo Ognibene, Venetian envoy to Persia
* Bartolomeo Liompardo, Venetian envoy to Persia

Genoa: Colonials and Diplomats

* Antoniotto della Gabella, Genoese consul at Caffa
* Oberto Squarciafico, Treasurer for Genoa at Caffa
* Christoforo, Governor of Soldaia

Florence & Bologna: Colonials and Travelling Professionals

* Arnolfo Tedaldi, Medici agent in Poland
* Nicholai Giorgio de' Acciajuoli, Greek-Florentine nobleman
* Rudolfo Fioravanti degli Alberti ('Aristotele'), engineer
* Andreas, his son
* Pietro, his pupil

Gothia and Black Sea Circassians

* Isáac, prince of Mánkup and Gothia
* Aleksandre, his brother and successor
* Abdan Khan, Circassian leader of Gothian armies
* Marta, Circassian housekeeper in Fasso

Muscovy

* Zoe/Sophia Palaeologina, wife of Grand Duke Ivan III and niece of the last Emperor of Constantinople
* Ivan, her stepson
* Maria, Grand Duke Ivan's mother
* Andrew, Grand Duke Ivan's brother
* Boris, another brother

Dymitr Wiśniowiecki, fur trader

* Metropolitan Philip

Brother Ostafi of the Trinity Monastery of St Sergius

Brother Gubka of the same

* Marco Rosso, Grand Duke Ivan's envoy to Persia

Persia

* Uzum Hasan, prince of the Turcoman Horde of the White Sheep, and chief ruler in Persia
* Theodora, his wife, daughter of John, Emperor of Trebizond, and aunt of Caterino Zeno's wife Violante
* Hadji Mehmet, legate of Uzum Hasan

Tartars

* Mengli-Girey, Khan of the Crim Horde, Qirq-yer
* Karaï Mirza, his constable
* Eminek, brother of Mamak, the late Tudun (Tartar Governor) of Caffa
* Sertak, son of the widow of Mamak
* Akhmat (Mohammed), Khan of the Golden Horde, Saray

Ottoman Turks

* Sultan Mehmet II of Istanbul/Constantinople
* Gedik Ahmed Pasha, his Grand Vizier

Cairo

* Sultan Qayt Bey, Circassian Mameluke
* Father Lorenzo, Greek Orthodox steward and Treasurer of the monastery of St Catherine's, Mount Sinai

Imam Ibrahiim of the University of al-Azhar, Cairo

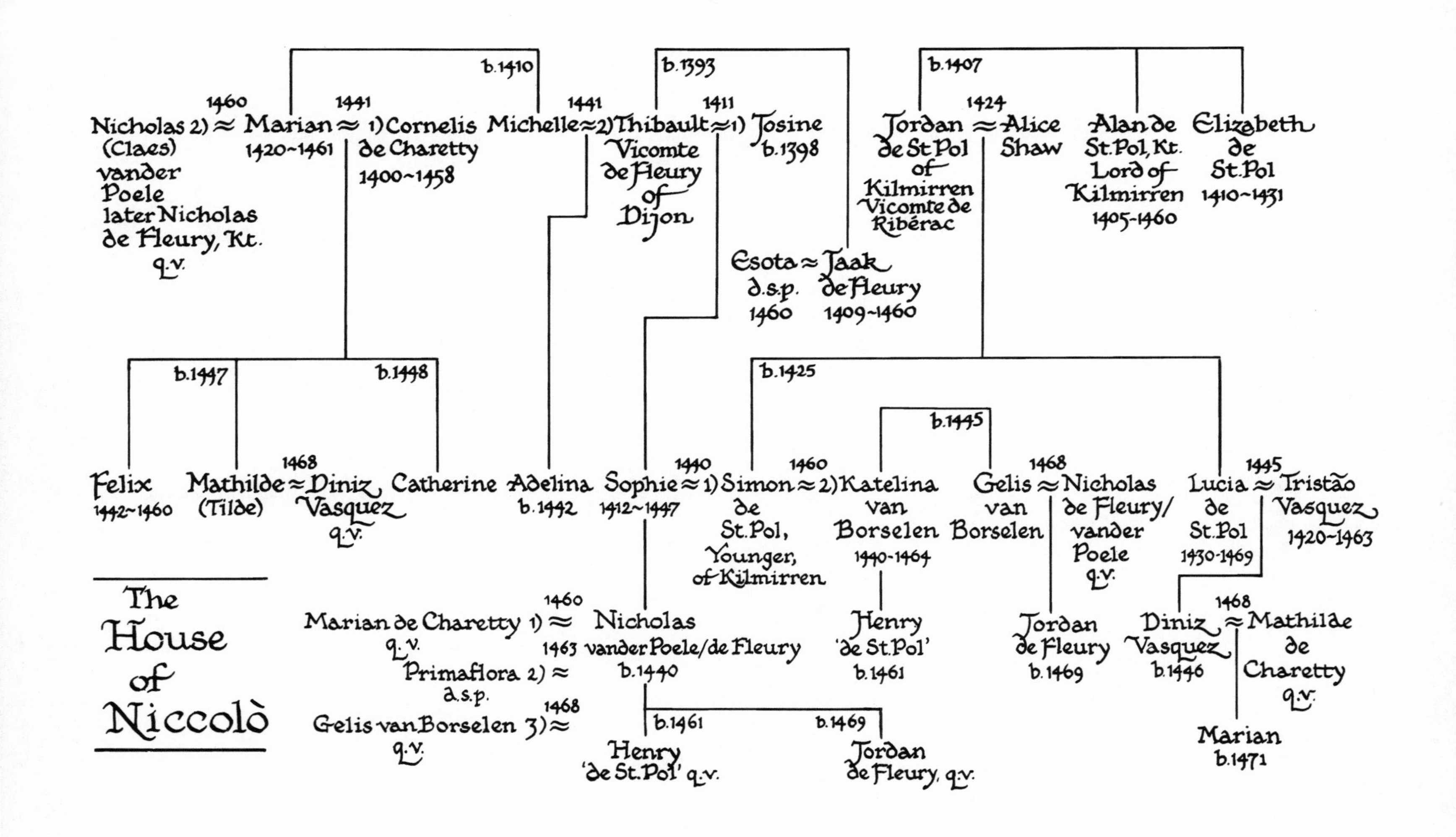
The House of Niccolò
b.1410
b.1393
b.1407
1460
Nicholas 2) ≈ Marian ≈ 1) Cornelis
(Claes)
vander
Poele
later Nicholas
de Fleury, Kt.
q.v.
1420~1461
de Charetty
1400~1458
1441
Michelle ≈ 2) Thibault ≈ 1) Josine
Vicomte
de Fleury
of
Dijon
1411
b.1398
Esota ≈ Jaak
d.s.p.
1460
de Fleury
1409~1460
1424
Jordan ≈ Alice
de St Pol
of
Kilmirren
Vicomte de
Ribérac
Shaw
Alan de
St.Pol, Kt.
Lord of
Kilmirren
1405-1460
Elizabeth
de
St.Pol
1410~1431
b.1447
b.1448
b.1425
b.1445
Felix
1442~1460
1468
Mathilde ≈ Diniz
(Tilde)
Vasquez
q.v.
Catherine
Adelina
b.1442
1440
Sophie ≈ 1) Simon
1412~1447
de
St.Pol,
Younger,
of Kilmirren
1460
≈ 2) Katelina
van
Borselen
1440-1464
1468
Gelis ≈ Nicholas
van
Borselen
de Fleury/
vander
Poele
q.v.
1445
Lucia ≈ Tristão
de
St.Pol
1430-1469
Vasquez
1420~1463
1460
Marian de Charetty 1) ≈
q.v.
1463
Primaflora 2) ≈
d.s.p.
1468
Gelis van Borselen 3) ≈
q.v.
Nicholas
vander Poele/de Fleury
b.1440
Henry
'de St.Pol'
b.1461
Jordan
de Fleury
b.1469
1468
Diniz ≈ Mathilde
Vasquez
b.1446
de
Charetty
q.v.
Marian
b.1471
b.1461
b.1469
Henry
'de St.Pol' q.v.
Jordan
de Fleury, q.v.

INTRODUCTION

THE ELEGANT WORKING out of designs historical and romantic, political and commercial, psychological and moral, over a multivolume novel is a Dorothy Dunnett specialty. In her first work in this genre, the six-volume "Lymond Chronicles," suspense was created and relieved in each volume, and over the whole set of volumes; the final, beautifully inevitable, romantic secret was disclosed on the very last page of the last volume. "The House of Niccolò" does the same.

The reader of *Caprice and Rondo*, then, may wish to move directly to the narrative for a first experience of that pattern, with a reader's faith in an experienced author's caretaking; the novel itself briefly supplies the information you need to know from past novels, telling its own tale while completing and inaugurating others. What follows, as a sketch of the geopolitical and dramatic terrain unfolding in the volumes which precede *Caprice and Rondo*, may be useful to read now, or at any point along the narrative, or after reading, as an indication of which stories of interest to this volume may be found most fully elaborated in which previous volume.

VOLUME I: *Niccolò Rising*

"From Venice to Cathay, from Seville to the Gold Coast of Africa, men anchored their ships and opened their ledgers and weighed one thing against another as if nothing would ever change." The first sentence of the first volume indicates the scope of this series, and the cultural and psychological dynamic of the story and its hero, whose private motto is "Change, change and adapt." It is the motto, too, of fifteenth-century Bruges, center of commerce and conduit of new ideas and technologies between the Islamic East and the Christian West, between the Latin South and the Celtic-Saxon North, haven of political refugees from the English Wars of the Roses, a site of muted conflict between trading giants Venice and Genoa and states in making and on the take all around. Mrs. Dunnett has set her story in the fifteenth century, between Gutenberg and Columbus, between Donatello and Martin Luther, between the rise of mercantile culture and the fall of chivalry, as the age of receptivity to—addiction to—change called "the Renaissance" gathers its powers.

Her hero is a deceptively silly-looking, disastrously tactless eighteen-year-old dyeworks artisan named "Claes," a caterpillar who emerges by the end of the novel as the merchant-mathematician Nicholas vander Poele. Prodigiously gifted at numbers, and the material and social "engineering" skills that go with it, Nicholas has until now resisted the responsibility of his powers, his identity fractured by the enmity of both his mother's husband's family, the Scottish St Pols, who refuse to own him legitimate, and his maternal family, the Burgundian de Fleurys, who failed his mother and abused him and reduced him to serfdom as a child. He found refuge at age ten with his grandfather's in-laws, especially the Bruges widow Marian de Charetty, whose dyeing and broking business becomes the tool of Nicholas' desperate self-fashioning apart from the malice of his blood relatives.

Soon even public Bruges and the states beyond come to see the engineer under the artisan. The Charetty business expands to include a courier and intelligence service between Italian and Northern states, its bodyguard sharpened into a skilled mercenary force, its pawnbroking consolidated toward banking and commodities trading. And as the chameleon artificer of all this, Nicholas incurs the ambiguous interest of the Bruges patrician Anselm Adorne and the Greco-Florentine prince Nicholai Giorgio de' Acciajuoli, both of whom steer him toward a role in the rivalry between Venice, in whose interest Acciajuoli labors, and Genoa, original home of the Adorne family. This trading rivalry will erupt in different novels around different, always highly symbolic commodities: silk, sugar, glass, gold, and human beings. In this first novel the contested product is alum, the mineral that binds dyes to cloth, blood to the body, conspirators to a conspiracy—in this case, to keep secret the news of a newly found deposit of the mineral in the Papal States while Venice and her allies monopolize the current supply.

Acciajuoli and Adorne are father-mentor figures Nicholas can respect, resist, or join on roughly equal intellectual terms—whereas the powerful elder males of his blood, his mother's uncle, Jaak de Fleury, and his father's father, Jordan de Ribérac, steadily rip open wounds first inflicted in childhood. In direct conflict he is emotionally helpless before them. What he possesses superbly, however, are the indirect defenses of an "engineer." The Charetty business partners and others who hitch their wagons to his star—Astorre the mercenary leader, Julius the notary, Gregorio the lawyer, Tobias Beventini the physician, the Guinea slave

Lopez—watch as a complex series of commodity and currency maneuvers by the apparently innocent Nicholas brings about the financial and political ruin of de Fleury and de Ribérac; and they nearly desert him for the conscienceless avenger he appears to be, especially after de Fleury dies in a fight with, though not directly at the hands of, his nephew.

The faith and love of Marian de Charetty make them rethink their view of this complicated personality. Marian, whose son was killed beside Nicholas in the Italian wars, and whose sister married into his family, is moved towards the end of the novel to suggest that Nicholas take her in marriage. It is to be platonic: her way of giving him standing, of displaying her trust in him and his management of the business, and of solacing him in his anguish. Once married, however, she longs despite herself for physical love, and Nicholas, who owes her everything, finds happiness also in making the marriage complete.

That marriage, however, sows the seeds of tragedy. The royally connected Katelina van Borselen, "characterful," intelligent, and hungry for experiences usually denied a genteel lady, has refused the vicious or vacuous suitors considered eligible, and seeks sexual initiation at the hands of the merry young artisan so popular with the kitchen wenches of Bruges. Against his better judgment, Nicholas is led to comply, for, however brusque her demands, she has just saved his life in one of the several episodes in which the St Pols try to destroy him. Two nights of genuine intimacy undermined by mismatched desires and miscommunicated intentions culminate in Katelina's solitary pregnancy. Unaware of this, Nicholas enters his marriage with Marian, and Katelina, alone, fatalistically marries the man in pursuit of her, the handsome, shrewd, and fatally self-centered Simon de St Pol, the man Nicholas claims is his father. Sickened at what she believes is Nicholas' ultimate revenge on his family—to illegitimately father its heir—Katelina becomes Nicholas' most determined enemy.

VOLUME II: *The Spring of the Ram*

Simon de St Pol, the overshadowed son of Jordan de Ribérac, husband of the bitter Katelina, father of the secretly illegitimate Henry, has clearly had his spirit poisoned long since by the powerful and malignant de Ribérac, and is as much pitied as loathed by Nicholas vander Poele, who sees in Simon something of his own deracinated brilliance. Looking to find a sphere of activity where Simon and Nicholas can no longer injure each other, Marian de Charetty, now the wife of Nicholas, persuades her husband to take up an exciting and dangerous project: to trade in Trebizond, last outpost of the ancient empire of Byzantium.

It is less than a decade since Sultan Mehmet took Constantinople, and several forces of Islam—Mehmet's Ottomans, Uzum Hassan's Turcomans, Kushcadam's Egyptian Mamelukes—ring the Christian outpost while delegates from the Greek Orthodox East, led by the very earthy and autocratic Franciscan friar Ludovico de Severi da Bologna, scour the Latin West for money and troops to mount still another crusade. With Medici backing and Church approval, Nicholas sets out for Trebizond to trade as Florentine consul, bringing his skilled mercenaries as a show of support from the West—a show that will soon turn real as the Sultan moves against the city more quickly than anyone had anticipated.

Nicholas' rival, and in some ways alter ego, is the gifted, charming, and amoral Pagano Doria, trading for Genoa, gaming with Venice's Nicholas in a series of brilliant pranks and tricks which include, terribly, the seduction of the thirteen-year-old Catherine de Charetty, one of Nicholas' two rebellious stepdaughters. Pagano, who is secretly financed by Nicholas' enemy Simon de St Pol, has invited the adolescent Catherine to challenge her stepfather, and no pleas or arguments from Nicholas, her mother's officers, or the new figures joining the Company—the priest Godscalc and the engineer John le Grant—can sway her.

In Trebizond, Nicholas deploys his trading skills while he assesses Byzantine culture, once spiritually and politically supreme, now calcified in routine, crumbling in self-indulgence. Nicholas must resist the Emperor David's languidly amorous overtures while he takes the lead in preparing the city for, and then withstanding, the siege of the Sultan. The city, however, is betrayed by its Emperor and his scheming Chancellor, and Pagano Doria suffers his own fall, killed by a black page whom he carelessly loved and then sold to the Sultan. Nicholas has willed neither fall, yet has set in motion some of the psychopolitical "engineering" which has triggered these disasters, and he carries, with Father Godscalc's reflective help and the more robust assistance of Tobie and le Grant, part of the moral burden of them.

The burden weighs even during the triumphant trip back to Venice with a rescued if still recalcitrant Catherine and a fortune in silk, gold, alum, and Eastern manuscripts, the "golden fleece" which this Jason looks to lay at the feet of his beloved wife. A final skirmish with Simon, angry at the failure of his agent Doria, ends the novel abruptly, with news which destroys all the remaining dream of homecoming: Marian de Charetty, traveling through Burgundy in her husband's absence, has died.

VOLUME III: *Race of Scorpions*

Rich and courted, yet emotionally drained and subconsciously enraged, Nicholas seeks a new shape for his life after visiting his wife's grave, establishing his still-resentful stepdaughters in business themselves, and allowing his associates to form the Trading Company and Bank of Niccolò in Venice. Determined to avoid the long arm of Venetian policy, attracted to the military life not precisely for its sanction of killing but for the "sensation of living through danger" it offers, Nicholas returns from Bruges to the war over Naples in which he had, years before, lost Marian's son Felix and contracted a marsh fever which revisits him in moments of stress. When he is kidnapped in mid-battle, he at first supposes it to be by order of his personal enemies, Simon and Katelina; but in fact it is Venice which wants him and his mercantile and military skills in another theater of war, Cyprus.

The brilliant and charismatic but erratic James de Lusignan and his Egyptian Mameluke allies have taken two-thirds of the sugar-rich island of Cyprus from his legitimate Lusignan sister, the clever and energetic Carlotta, and her allies, the Christian Knights of St John and the Genoese, who hold the great commercial port of Famagusta. Sensing that, of the two Lusignan "scorpions," James holds the winning edge, Nicholas agrees to enter his service. He intends to design the game this time, not be its pawn, but he doesn't reckon with the enmity of Katelina, who comes to Rhodes to warn Carlotta against him, or the sudden presence of Simon's Portuguese brother-in-law Tristão Vasquez and Vasquez's naïve sixteen-year-old son Diniz, all three of whom do become pawns.

Nicholas is now the lover of Carlotta's courtesan, the beautiful Primaflora, whose games he also thinks he can control, and he recognizes a crisis of countermanipulations brewing between Katelina and Primaflora. Only at the end of the novel, after Katelina's love/hate for Nicholas has been manipulated to bring Tristão to his death and Diniz to captivity under James, after Nicholas and Katelina rediscover intimacy and establish the truth of their relationship, after a brilliant and deadly campaign waged by Nicholas for James has brought him to ultimate tragedy—the siege of Famagusta which he planned and executed has resulted, without his knowledge, in the death of Katelina and the near-death of Diniz, trapped in the starving city—only at the end does Nicholas fully admit even to himself that much of this has been planned or sanctioned by Primaflora, intent on securing her own future.

In the end, too, the determinedly rational Nicholas gives vent to his rage. Punishment for the pain of the complex desires and denials in his private and public history cannot be visited upon the complex and only half-guilty figures of his family or his trading and political rivals and clients. But in this novel, for the first time, he finds a person he can gladly kill, the unspeakably cruel Mameluke Emir Tzanibey al-Ablak, whom he fatally mutilates in single combat while James, unknown to him, has the Emir's four-hundred-man army massacred in a preemptive strike carrying all the glory and damnation of Renaissance kingship.

Like Pagano Doria, like Nicholas himself, Primaflora is a "modern" type, a talented and alienated "self-made" person. Unlike the other two, Nicholas has the memory of family in which to ground a wary, half-reluctant, but genuine adult existence in the community. At the same time, however, he avoids close relationships: he has established the Bank of Niccolò as a company, not a family. But, resisting and insisting, the members of the company forge bonds of varying intimacy with Nicholas, especially the priest Godscalc and the physician Tobie, who alone at this point know the secret of Katelina's baby and carry the dying woman's written affirmation of Nicholas' paternity.

Nicholas' only true intimate, however, is a man of a different race entirely, the African who came to Bruges as a slave and was befriended by the servant Claes, who first communicated the secret of the alum deposit, who traveled with him to Trebizond to run the trading household, and to Cyprus to organize and under Nicholas reinvent the sugar industry there. His African name is as yet unknown, his Portuguese name is Lopez, his company name Loppe. Now a major figure in the company, and the family, he listens at the end of the novel as both Nicholas and his new rival, the broker of the mysterious Vatachino company, look to the Gold Coast of Africa as the next place of questing and testing.

VOLUME IV: *Scales of Gold*

For those who know the truth, the deaths of Katelina, Tristão, and Tzanibey, the brutal forging of a new monarchy for Cyprus, even Nicholas' alienation from and reconciliation with young Diniz, have stemmed from honorable, even noble motives. But gossip in Europe, fed by de Ribérac and St Pol, puts a more sinister stamp on these events. Under financial attack by the Genoese firm of Vatachino, the Bank of Niccolò undertakes a commercial expedition to Africa, which young Diniz Vasquez joins partly as an act of faith in Nicholas, while Gelis van Borselen, Katelina's bitter and beautiful sister, joins to prove him the profit-mongering amoralist she believes him to be. They are accompanied by Diniz' mother's companion Bel of Cuthilgurdy, a valiant and razor-tongued Scottish matron who comes to guide the young man and woman and ends up dispensing wisdom and healing to all; by Father Godscalc, who desires to prove his own faith by taking the Cross through East Africa to the fabled Ethiopia of Prester John; and by Lopez, whose designs are the most complex of all. Through Madeira to the Gambia and into the interior they journey, facing and eventually outfacing the competition of the Vatachino and Simon de St Pol.

Like everyone but the Africans, both companies have underestimated even the size, let alone the cultural and religious complexity, of Africa: no travelers in this age can reach Ethiopia from the East, and the profits from the voyages of discovery and commerce recently begun by Prince Henry the Navigator are as yet mainly knowledge, and self-knowledge. There is gold in the Gambia, and there is a trade in black human beings which is, as Lopez is concerned to demonstrate, just beginning to take the shape that will constitute one of the supreme flaws of the civilization of the West. There is also, up the Joliba floodplain, the metropolis of Timbuktu, commercial and psychological "terminus," and Islamic cultural center, in which Diniz finds his manhood and Lopez regains his original identity as the jurist and scholar Umar; where Gelis consummates with Nicholas the supreme relationship of her life, hardly able as yet to distinguish whether its essence is love or hatred.

On this journey, Godscalc the Christian priest and Umar the Islamic scholar both function as soul friends to Nicholas, prodding him through extremities of activity and meditation that finally draw the sting, as it appears, from the old wounds of family. Certainly there is no doubt of the affection of Diniz for Nicholas, and surely there can be none about the passion of Katelina's sister Gelis, his lover. As the ships of the Bank of Niccolò return to Lisbon, to Venice and Bruges, success in commerce, friendship, and passion mitigates even the novel's first glimpse of Katelina's and Nicholas' four-year-old son Henry, molded by his putative father, Simon, in his own insecure, narcissistic, and violent image.

On the way to his marriage bed, the climax and reward of years of struggle, Nicholas is stunned by two blows which will undermine all the spiritual balance he has achieved in his African journey. He learns that Umar—his teacher, his other self—is dead in primitive battle, together with most of the gentle scholars of Timbuktu and their children. And on the heels of that news his bride Gelis, fierce, unreadable, looses the punishment she has prepared for him all these months: she tells him how she has deliberately conceived a child with Nicholas' enemy Simon, to duplicate in reverse—out of what hatred he cannot conceive—the tragedy of Katelina. As the novel closes, we know that he is planning to accept the child as his own, and that he is going to Scotland.

How Nicholas will be affected by the double betrayal—the involuntary death, the act of willful cruelty—is not yet clear. There is a shield half in place, but Umar, the man of faith who helped him create it, is gone. Nicholas' own spiritual experience, deeply guarded, has had to do with the intersection of mathematics and beauty, with the mind-cleansing horizons of sea and sky and desert, and with the display in friend and foe alike of the compelling qualities of valor and joy and empathy: the spiritual maturity with which he accepts the blows of fate here may be real, but he has taken his revenge in devious ways before. More mysteriously still, the maturity is accompanied by a curious susceptibility he cannot yet understand, a gift or a disability which teases his mind with unknown events, unvisited places, thoughts that are not his. As much as his markets, his politics, or his half-hidden domestic desires, these thoughts seem to draw him North.

VOLUME V: *The Unicorn Hunt*

Thinner, preoccupied, dressed in a suave and expensive black pitched between melodrama and satire, between grief and devilry, our protagonist enters his family's homeland bearing his mother's name. Now Nicholas de Fleury, he comes to Scotland with two projects in hand: to recover the child his pregnant wife says is Simon's and to build in that energetic and unpredictable northern backwater a new edifice of cultural, political, and economic power. Nicholas brings artists and craftsmen to Scotland as well as money and entrepreneurial skill, making himself indispensable to yet another royal James. But are his productions there—the splendid wedding feasts and frolics for James III and Danish Margaret, the escape of the king's sister with the traitor Thomas Boyd, the skillful exploitation of natural resources—the glory they seem? Or are they the hand-set maggot mound, buzzing with destruction, of Gregorio's inexplicable first vision of Nicholas' handsome estate of Beltrees? Is Nicholas the vulnerable and magical beast whose image he wins in knightly combat—or the ruthless hunter of the Unicorn?

The priest Father Godscalc, for one, fears Nicholas' purposes in Scotland. Loving Nicholas and Gelis, knowing the secret of Katelina van Borselen's child, guessing the cruel punishment which her sister has planned for Nicholas, the dying Godscalc brings Nicholas back to Bruges and extracts a promise that he will stay out of Scotland for two years, and so remove himself from the morally perilous proximity of Simon, the father-figure whom he seeks to punish, and Henry, the secret son who hates him more with every effort he makes to help him. Nicholas agrees, and turns to other business, mining silver and alum in the Tyrol, settling the eastern arm of his banking business in Alexandria, tracking a large missing shipment of gold from the African adventure from Cairo to Sinai to Cyprus. These enterprises occupy only half his mind, however, for the carefully spent time in Scotland has confirmed what he suspects, that the still-impotent Simon could not in fact be the father of the child whom Gelis has in secret borne and hidden, and who, dead or alive, is the real object of his quest. In a stunning dawn climax on the burning rocks of Mount Sinai, Nicholas and Gelis, equivocal pilgrims, challenge each other with the truth of the birth and of their love and enmity, and the conflict heightens.

The duel between husband and wife finds them evenly matched in business acumen and foresightful intrigue, tragically equal in their capacity to detect the places of the other's deepest hurt and vulnerability. But Nicholas is the more experienced of the two, and wields in addition, or is wielded by, a deep and dangerous power. One part of that power makes him a "diviner," who vibrates to the presence of water or precious metals under the earth, his body receiving also, by way of personal talismans, the signals through space of a desperately sought living object, his newborn son. The other part of the power whirls him periodically into the currents of time, his mind aflame with the sights and sounds of another life whose focus is in his name, the name he has abandoned—the vander Poele/St Pol surname whose Scottish form, Semple, is startlingly familiar to readers of the Lymond Chronicles, Dorothy Dunnett's first historical series.

The professionals Nicholas has assembled around him have always tried to control their leader's mental and psychic powers; now a new group of acute and prescient friends strives to fathom and to guard him, from his enemies and from his own cleverness. Chief among these new friends is the fourteen-year-old niece of Anselm Adorne, the needle-witted and compassionate Katelijne Sersanders, who finds some way to share all his pilgrimages as she pushes adventurously past the barriers of her age and gender. The musician Willie Roger, the metallurgical priest Father Moriz, and the enigmatic physician and mystic Dr Andreas of Vesalia add their fascinated and critical advice as Nicholas pursues his gold and his son through the intricate course, beckoning and thwarting, prepared by Gelis van Borselen. In the endgame, as Venetian *carnivale* reaches its height, this devoted father, moving the one necessary step ahead of the mother's game, finds, takes, and disappears with the child-pawn whose face, seen at last, is the image of his own.

Yet there is a Lenten edge to this thundering Martidi Grasso success. Why has Nicholas turned his back on the politics of the crusade in the East to pursue projects in Burgundy and Scotland? Who directs the activities of the Vatachino mercantile company, whose agents have brought Nicholas close to death more than once? Have we still more ambiguous things to learn about the knightly pilgrim and ruthless competitor Anselm Adorne? What secrets, even in her defeat, is the complexly embittered Gelis still withholding? Above all, what atonements can avert the fatalities we see gathering around the fathers and sons, bound in a knot of briars, of the house of St Pol?

VOLUME VI: *To Lie With Lions*

Nicholas de Fleury goes from success to success, expertly operating large structures by the nice application of invisible pressure, as the craftsmen do in the miracle plays in which he has from time to time taken part. Within the theatre of family he has produced the convincing illusion of harmony between himself and Gelis, his estranged wife, for the sake of their beloved, acknowledgeable son Jodi. Within the circus of statecraft, where the lions of Burgundy and France, Venice and Cyprus, England and Scotland, Islam and Christendom stalk and snarl, the Banco de Niccolò wields a valued whip. Its *padrone* is a cosmopolitan, virtually stateless man, intellectually drawn to the puzzle of history in the making, but not visibly compelled by the roots of race—although, to be sure, some of his enemies think him motivated mainly by the passion of revenge on his own family.

Free now to enlarge and complete projects in the small, unsteady country of Scotland—which the priest Godscalc, half guessing his intent, had compelled him to abandon for two years—Nicholas carries out two *coups de théatre* which have consequences and resonances unexpected by their designer. He spends ruinously of his time and the kingdom's money on a nativity play whose single performance, a glory of thought, feeling, and art which makes transcendence of all its illusions and momentarily unites its fractured community, hints at the strength and value of the wounded spirit who has devised it. And he mounts a merchant expedition to the fish-fertile waters of Iceland, whence he lures and bests his old rivals the Adornes and the Vatachino company, as well as a new one, the Danziger pirate Pauel Benecke.

Sharing this adventure are Kathi Sersanders and Robin of Berecrofts, a Scottish youth whose courage, and desire to break free of the bounds of his sturdy mercantile heritage, bring him to the magnetic Nicholas as an admiring squire. Together they explore the new world of the north, learn from the hardy generosities of the Icelanders, and, transformed in the end from actors and designers to spectators, experience in awe and humility Nature's own nativity play, the re-creation of a continent in the double explosions of Katla and Hekla, the volcanoes of Iceland.

Nicholas' well-wishers will need this glimpse of his humanity. For in the matters he controls, Nicholas' plans are coming to dark fruition. Gelis has a climactic announcement to make—she has won the war between them because she has secretly been working for years for the Vatachino. But Jorden de St Pol, whose painfully rebuilt career in France Nicholas has undermined once again, brings a devastating illumination: Nicholas knew of Gelis' connection with the Vatachino and skillfully played with it; further, all his projects in Scotland, from the nativity play and the Iceland expedition which brought him a barony, to more secret investments of the bank's and the country's money in worthless mines, poisoned grains, and debased coinage, were meant in fact to financially wreck the country whose gentry, the St Pol/Semples, had terrified and rejected Nicholas' mother, and Nicholas himself, thirty years before.

He has carried out this plan because he could: he could not draw back from it because it was his. In this final spectacle, the work of an angry child, of an obsessed artist, even his friends believe they see the death of Nicholas' soul, and desert him. Stunned by his own dire success, Nicholas agrees with them: as the novel ends and the abandoned and pitiless banker allows himself to be carried East by the newly ascendant emperor of Germany, he seems ready for burial. Or, possibly, resurrection.

If he seeks his grave, there is no lack of deadly alternatives available: the perils of ruthless private enterprise with pirates like Paúel Benecke, or of the ever-beckoning Eastern Crusade which was the dream of another of Nicholas' mentors, Cardinal Bessarion, now dead, and the latter's hairy acolyte Friar Ludovico. If there is to be a renewal of spirit, there are incentives to this as well. The alienated but still beloved family of Gelis and Jodi, who are still endangered by the St Pols. The now-engaged young people, Kathi and Robin, who remember stubbornly that the Machiavellian Nicholas did, after all, momentarily desert his Scottish plans and the Scottish King James, whom he did not love, to go, tragically too late, to the side of the Venice-threatened Cypriot King James, whom he did love. The handsome and exasperating Julius and the Countess Anna, his loving and beautiful wife. Or perhaps renewal will be triggered by a more mysterious set of forces, crystallized in the mystics and astrologers drawn to Nicholas and in the sometimes devastating shafts of foreknowledge through which Nicholas seems to be excavating the buried trauma of his own nativity.

Judith Wilt
Boston, 1997

Part I

POLONAISE

Chapter 1

THE WIND BLEW from the north, from Siberia, and the clatter of hail on his shutters woke the captain. He had only been in bed for an hour, but land noises disturbed him. He grunted, considered, then dragged on his robe and, without taking a lamp, made his way to the leeward side of the villa. He had built this one only last year, and put in a brick chimney-wall: warmth from the stove below mellowed the air and his mood, although his throat was wrung dry, and he was still wearing his wrinkled day shirt and hose, as when he had dropped — or been dropped — on his bed. The sleeping rooms creaked and groaned as he passed them: his house was always full. Only the single chamber, as he half expected, was empty; the door ajar, the window unshuttered. Through it he could see a paring of moon, coarse as pomegranate. He walked over and looked down below, at the blood on the snow. Then he looked beyond his gates, at the city in which his fine house was set. At the walls, the watchtowers and the icy huddle of dwellings, above which reared the stiff-necked herd of her churches, scanning the west. Danzig, at four hours after midnight in the deep cold of January, 1474.

There were others awake. Beneath the congealed thatches there glimmered jointed hair-lines of light, fine as lettering. A squat figure, forced by the wind, plunged across a cake of pink light and disappeared. Here, the alleys were snow-filled and crooked. In the New Town, there were more lamps than shrines. In the New Town, the streets built by the Knights drove across and down to the river like prison-grilles, their crowns rutted and black with wheeled traffic. The Knights, the bastards. He was still celebrating Danzig's victory over the Knights. Everyone was celebrating.

Within the room, the quality of the air underwent a change. He smiled. He said, his back to the door, 'So, how was she?'

'Whetting her claws,' Colà said. He was the only man known to the captain who could move as silently as himself, despite his height. They engaged in these exercises sometimes, stalking one another, testing, deceiving. It was part of the return the captain compelled from his guests. In winter, a seaman required to be entertained. *Der harte Seevogel,* Tough Seabird, they called him.

Colà said, 'Is there some problem? You need a friend to help with your buttons?' He had picked up tinder, and was lighting the lamp by his bed. Paúel closed the shutters and turned.

'I was contemplating the scene of the slaughter. You look as if the girl got to you first, then the father.'

Colà blinked. His eyes were like pewter platters, and his real name was not Colà. The captain knew what it was, and had called him by it throughout the campaign in the north, where they had met. Then, after the better part of two years, a merchant's train coming in from the west had insisted on bringing their friend to the guild hall, even though they had only just met him in Lübeck two weeks ago — such a lively, remarkable fellow was he. Name of Colà z Brugge. A one-time merchant who had decided to let his business go hang and see the world. And Captain Paúel Benecke, looking up at this bland, bristle-chinned figure, had said slowly, 'Oh, yes? Decided to give up your business?'

'Yes,' had said the newcomer meekly.

'And come to Poland?'

'Why not?' had said the big man in a reasonable voice. 'I could see, from the little experience I had, that its people needed advice. Some hints about etiquette. A touch of help as to manners and culture. A bit of —'

Here, he had been forced to desist by the pack of genial, hard-fisted arms that rose and fell on him: it had evidently happened often before, and he accepted it amiably. When, at last, the two were alone, the captain had set himself to pin the newcomer down in another way. 'So, what's the point of all this? Of course they will find out who you are. You have an agent here, haven't you?'

'Straube, yes. He's gone to Portugal for the winter. Oh, they'll find out,' said the man they called Colà. 'But they'll also know by the time he comes back that he isn't my agent any more. I've retired from my company.'

'Why?' had said Benecke. He remembered trying to kill this man once. He remembered that the first time they met, this man had broken his arm, and later his leg.

'Why do you think?' the newcomer had said.

Benecke considered. So far as he knew, the fellow had been good at his job. The business had prospered. If he'd cheated, he hadn't been found out. That left only women. There had been two: a harridan of a wife, so he'd heard, and a little virgin who thought she was a boy. That is, there had been a lot more than two, but none spoken of seriously. The captain said, 'I think you just wanted some fun. But since you ask, I'll guess you killed the wife and raped the little girl-brother Kathi. I liked her,' said the captain with a catch in his voice. 'If you've raped her, I'll kill you.' They were both, by this time, quite full of ale.

'You think you could?' Colà said; and ducked as the captain got out his knife. Someone took it from him quite soon, and they settled to drink again. Eventually Paúel had to ask. 'So what happened?'

'You weren't far wrong,' Colà had said. 'The wife flung me out, and the girl married somebody else. So I thought I'd get out.'

'So why here?'

'I thought I'd get out to where somebody owed me a favour. Are you busy this winter?'

The captain sat up. 'You want a job?' There were no jobs in winter. Danzig was sealed in by ice. There would be no ships in the port until March.

'No,' said Colà. 'Or not until spring. Or not until I decide where I'm going. I just want to pass an entertaining winter with my inferiors.'

Ten minutes later, picking themselves up from the snow outside the Artushof: 'They'll never let you back in,' Benecke said.

'Yes, they will. Anyway, you started the fight, and they'll forgive you. Do I get a bed?'

'No,' had said Paúel Benecke. 'You'd spoil my winter complaining about your women.'

'I shouldn't,' said Colà.

'You'd get into bed with my women.'

'Of course,' had said Colà. 'You couldn't stop me. That's why you don't want me to come.'

That time, no one separated them, and it was three days before either of them could talk without lisping. Colà had been living in his house ever since, and Danzig would never forget him, nor would Paúel Benecke. He would never have to forget him. He was going to keep him in Danzig for the rest of his life. Despite the blood on the snow.

Now he said, 'So where have you left her?'

'Never mind. Anyway, she's not yours, she's mine. I got a doctor to see to the boy.'

'I thought his arm was going to come off. You ought to be chained up and put in a lazar house.'

'Come on,' Colà said. 'I'm going to tame her. Then I'm going to sell her to you.'

'Before or after you pay me for your lodging?' Paúel Benecke said. He gazed with fascination at the scratches all over the other man's neck and arms. He said, 'What if she's diseased?'

'You're worried?'

'No,' said Benecke. 'But I'm thirsty, and the look of you is spoiling my thirst. Good night, fool.'

He left, slamming the door. You found a man you could enjoy winters with, and he still behaved, at times, like an idiot. In their first weeks together, he had discovered it. Ingenuity, yes; lunacy even, to a degree — those were acceptable, those were what the merchants from Lübeck had enjoyed. But these escapades led by Colà were suicidal.

Three weeks after he came, the situation had come to a head over the bison hunt. Then they had been out of the city, travelling over snow to the forests, with their dogs, their nets, their spears and arrows. Colà had learned, God knew from where, that the beasts were enraged by red cloth, and had brought some. It had ended with the death of two men, while Colà cavorted round one of the animals in snow-crusted boots, whirling the fabric round his fur hat and calling and whistling.

It had been funny, all right. In the midst of the extreme danger that threatened them all, it was still funny to see the big man addressing the bison in prose, song and verse, while two thousand pounds of massive beast lowered its horns and skittered backwards and forth, its eyes red as lamps and the snow flying in clods from its coat as the cloth whisked about, almost touching. Then a dog got tossed in the air, and a man; and after the second man died, Paúel gave the order and they all ran in with their spears and took the beast, to the risk of their own lives. Paúel had led the party that harnessed the big man to a sledge and whipped him back to their lodge; he ran them into a tree on the way, and was arranging to hang Paúel with the harness when they got hold of him again. They were none of them sober.

That was close to being all right. Winters were spent in rough play and rough punishment. But when they were back home, and had broken the news to the two men's wives, and had the bison taken off to be jointed, Benecke had got hold of Colà and sat him down by the stove and said, 'Stop it, or get out. I'm not sick of life yet. Neither were my two lads.'

'I'm culling them for you,' Colà said. 'I thought it was a tough life at sea.'

'Some seamen need to be tougher than others,' Benecke said. 'He was a pilot, one of those boys. But I notice they're all the same to you, anyway.' He waited. Then he said, 'Why don't you want to go home, my big man? Perhaps you are more of a poltroon than any of us.'

A moment passed. 'That's unlikely,' said the other man. His gaze had fallen on his own arms and hands: a bloody rut on one forearm ran into another similar gouge long-since healed. 'The bolting Bonasus,' he said thoughtfully, 'whose fart can cover three acres, and set a whole forest on fire.'

'What?' said Benecke.

'A classical allusion. Ignore it. I mean that I am staying; I wish to stay; I have no immediate plans to get rid of you, unless you start preaching three times a day, in which case your own men will drown you before I do. Is there no ale, or are you drinking nothing but buttermilk now?'

And from that time, although their pastimes had been wild enough, they had been tempered with some sort of reason. The ritual of girl-hunting played its part as the winter progressed, and days became heavy and dark. Then, the young gallants would assemble their sleighs and bowl their way over the snow in a sparkling chain, bearing pasties and sweetmeats and flasks from one great timber *dwór* to another, and bringing out pretty captives, smothered in furs, to be returned flushed at dusk. Every red-blooded man enjoyed that, and the homeward course through the snowfields by night, when flickering brands danced in the void, and the throb of deep voices in harmony was matched with the far, surfing trill of the bells.

Colà had, it seemed, learned some sort of lesson. And even today, although he had been reckless, it had not been quite without reason, the exploit he had proposed. The boy's hurt could not have been avoided. Unless, of course, they had been more sensible still, and killed instead of bringing back their beautiful captive. But only Colà would propose to tame a live lynx.

The captain went to see him while he was at work in a half-empty warehouse. A cage had been made, and the big man was hunkered quietly outside it, speaking at intervals. He had some meat on a stick. His voice, of an exceptional richness, kept the rhythm and cadence of song; Benecke could not make out the words. When the speaker broke off at his step, Benecke gave way to a bellow of mirth. 'Crooning, by God! Are ye taming it or giving it suckle?'

Colà jerked up his chin. Squealing, the animal flung itself back, its ruff stiff. The bars thrummed. Paúel waited, loosening his shoulders, his hand hanging close to his dagger. The would-be tamer, instead of whirling about, thoughtfully brought up the rod and, detaching the meat, dropped it inside the cage without speaking. Then he rose and turned mildly. His face, though manufacturing anger, held the vanishing trace of another, less likely expression. Behind, the cat glared, a growl in her throat.

'A woman would be easier,' Benecke pointed out.

'Some women,' said Colà. His composure, if lost, had returned. 'What is it?' Recently, he had become more observant.

The rest of the warehouse was empty. Benecke said, 'Do you know that they say you are a spy?'

'They?'

'At the Artushof, the taverns, the wharves. They say you are an agent of Germany, planning to bring the Knights back.'

The Order of the Teutonic Knights, once so holy, had just been prised free of Danzig. Danzig and all her wealthy cluster of satellite towns was now part of Royal Prussia, and hence Poland. The King had come once to Danzig.

Colà laid the bar on his shoulder. He said, 'Well, I'm not. Haven't they noticed the agents of Germany, watching me? The King's agents as well. I don't mind. I'm not going back. I'm betraying no secrets, stealing no business. They'll see.'

'You could pass secrets on,' Benecke said.

'In winter?' Every movement was noticed in winter. From a bustling, free-flowing port, Danzig in winter was a snug Germanised town, its few foreigners remarked on and counted; its astute, inquisitive gaze, its rumbustious merriment all turned in on itself. Because it was winter, Danzig had had time to study Colà and reach an opinion. That it liked him was something quite separate.

'In spring,' said Benecke. 'There's to be a Burgundian mission passing through Poland in spring. Someone you know. The aristocratic uncle of your married, seraphic virgin, and a patriarch sent by the Pope.'

Colà's eyes were sharp as the cat's, but bigger, and grey. 'Why?' he said. And then, 'Because of what you did? Because you seized a Burgundian ship and its cargo?'

'Among other things.' Paúel Benecke gave a prosaic answer to a prosaic question. He was a pirate. That was his career. He was a sea-borne mercenary leader of skill and renown, whose highly paid interventions might change the fate of a crusade, or a duchy, or a group of powerful towns like the Hanse. He sailed under letters of marque, empowered by kings, and his booty paid for cropland, and castles, and villas.

The coming summer might turn out to be different, for the Hanse war with England was ending. But there would be other quarrels; other vindictive men who wished to hire their own bullies. Next summer, unless some idiot babbled, this maniac Colà was going to agree to turn pirate and join him. Paúel said, 'So keep clear of these envoys, I'd say. Or men will assume you are passing them secrets.' He made a considering pause.'If you ask me nicely, I might even rescue you. You could come south in the spring, and help float my grain down to market. None of us conscious for weeks.'

'Are you certain a mission is coming?' Colà said. But he was surely convinced because, as he spoke, he gripped the rod like a whip and threw it, hard. It cartwheeled twice, giving tongue like a tocsin. The lynx, her pointed ears flat, ricocheted round her cage, squealing.

Benecke said kindly, 'You've undone all your good work. Go and croon to her.'

The other man did not even glance over. He said, 'No. You were right. Get some keeper to train her.'

JINGLING ITS WAY ROUND the shores of the Baltic, the cut-price Mission to Persia intended to enter Danzig in March, having been entertained on its way by the civic leaders of Lübeck, Wisenar, Rostock and Stralsund, and survived the unstinted goodwill of their clubs.

The two leaders were not, of course, unknown to their hosts. Every merchant who had conducted business in Bruges remembered the courtly Anselm Adorne, envoy now of the Duke who ruled Flanders. Others, wincing, had met Adorne's unforgettable companion, the Papal and Imperial Legate. The Patriarch of Antioch had been this way before. Indeed, the unsavoury sandals of Father Ludovico da Bologna had tramped every byway in Europe, raising gold to fight Turkey. Between them, this powerful pair represented the three richest lords in the world, and their retinue, anywhere else, would have been gorgeous. But here, instead of silken banners and servants, soldiers and sumpter wagons of silver and mattresses, the train of the mission to Persia consisted of a number of packmules, eleven stoutly dressed men and, on sufferance, Anselm Adorne's twenty-year-old niece and her bridegroom of three months.

The presence of Katelijne Sersanders and her very young husband had not been part of Adorne's plan. Barely married, newly settled into a delightful small house of her uncle's, Katelijne herself had been equally far from contemplating an immediate journey. Then, on the eve of the mission's departure, Ludovico da Bologna had trotted his mule into Bruges and, before so much as calling on Anselm Adorne, had banged on her door to congratulate her on her marriage.

The Patriarch was over sixty years old, and he and Kathi Sersanders had known each other, off and on, for four years. Skipping out to receive him, Katelijne recognised in his manner the same sardonic detachment which had always coloured their dealings. To say she liked him meant nothing: she liked almost everyone. It was a pity that her uncle, tied to the Patriarch for the forthcoming mission, felt differently.

In the meantime, however, she had to admit that she was desperately pleased to see the old ruffian for reasons which Robin would share. She began, however, by laying meat and water before him, the first essential when entertaining Ludovico da Bologna, and only after that did she send for her husband. When he arrived he was scarlet, and she had to pull him down beside her for fear that he would start firing questions at once. Last winter, a man they both knew had vanished. And the last person for certain to see him, so far as they heard, was this priest.

Typically, if the Patriarch noticed their anxiety, he ignored it.

Instead, devouring his chops, Father Ludovico put some questions himself. So why, girl, had she decided to marry? And to a Scots lad? (Well, Robin, you've done well out of this, haven't you?) The Patriarch supposed it was because of the gossip: she should never have gone to Iceland, of course, with de Fleury. But there it was, and he supposed they'd do as well as any other silly young couple. Then (switching subjects as Robin showed signs of exploding), how was her uncle? Stiff-necked as ever? Looking forward to five years on the road patronising the natives?

'You'd better find out for yourself,' Kathi had said, kicking Robin. She didn't mind putting up with the Patriarch. She had learned patience the hard way, as maid of honour at the Scots Court, where she had come across the great mercantile family of Berecrofts, and her good-hearted Robin, of the fair hair and fresh skin and compact, athletic build (silly young couple, indeed). Her uncle, elegant aristocrat that he was, approved of her husband. Adorne, although his home was in Bruges, maintained close connections with Scotland, and had been honoured with land by its King. It was land he would not see for some time.

She knew he didn't mind that: after the death of his wife, Anselm Adorne had wanted this mission. Certainly, he disliked being leagued with the Patriarch, whose identical remit he saw as an insult to his own ducal lord. The Patriarch, on the other hand, was engaged on his own private scheme for mustering aid against the Ottoman Turks, and didn't care what Adorne thought, or indeed the Pope, or the Emperor he was supposed to be working for. Ludovico de Severi da Bologna made use of anybody he could find, including brilliant bankers who abandoned their families and vanished.

Further propitiated by beef and dumplings and pudding, the priest was quite ready to talk, in the end, when Katelijne, lady of Berecrofts, carefully opened that particular topic. 'Where's Nicholas de Fleury of Beltrees? Ask the Emperor. I left them both at Cologne in November.'

Robin glanced at her. He was still flushed. He said, 'But M. de . . . But my lord of Beltrees isn't in Germany now. That is, he can't be working for anyone now. He has nothing to offer.'

'De Fleury? Why not? He hasn't got a Bank any more, but he could advise. He could spy. He'd need to, wouldn't he? He has no income, or none that I know of.' The Patriarch lowered his tankard of water. A touch of grease swam on the top.

Robin said, 'But where would he be, if he couldn't work for the Emperor? You were with him. Didn't he tell you his plans?' He sounded angry, for Robin. The Patriarch remained calm.

'No, he didn't. One, he was sick. Two, he didn't mention he was about to disappear. Three, I don't know what he's done to make you so nervous. He had caused, it would seem, some catastrophe, but whatever it was, I can't see our busy friend overwhelmed by remorse. No. He'll have an uncomfortable winter, and get himself a job in the spring. He may even think he can come back and start again.'

'No!' said Kathi.

'Really? As bad as that? People would learn what he had done, or his friends would be compelled to denounce him? Torture, lopped limbs, execution? You wouldn't like to tell me what he *has* done?'

'No,' said Robin. 'But he knows he can never go back. No one would stand for it. And his wife and son would be dragged into it too. All the same . . .'

'Yes?' said the priest. He put down his spoon. 'All the same what? I must go.'

'Take the tart,' Kathi said. Her hands with her new rings felt cold.

'All the same,' Robin repeated, 'I wish I knew where he was. Can't you make a guess?'

'If you have a napkin. Now that is kind,' said the priest. 'Can't I guess what? Where Nicholas is? I don't need to. Wherever it is, I'll find out before we get beyond Poland. Every friar in the land is looking out for him. And if you want to know where he's going, I'll tell you that, too. To Tabriz. Because that's where I shall be sending him.'

At last, Robin looked at his wife and Kathi drew a short breath and spoke with no patience at all. 'And you imagine he'll go? Has Nicholas de Fleury ever done what you told him before?'

'No,' the Patriarch said. 'But his friends have never flung him out before, have they? What else should he do?'

She sat, watching him lick and holster his knife, and then proceed, with some deftness, to parcel up the thick, sticky tart. He got out his satchel. Robin said, 'If Kathi's uncle allowed it, would you mind if I came on this mission?'

The priest got to his feet, satchel in hand. 'To Persia? Really? Through Poland, round the Black Sea, across the land of the Crimean Tartars, south through Georgia and into Tabriz? My dear boy, what a glutton for travel!'

Robin was not put off by mockery. 'Not so far. At least I hope not so far. To wherever M. de Fleury has stopped.'

'And what good will it do if you find him? You'll hand him pretty notes from the child, and he'll pine, or come back and be killed.'

'It is not for him,' Robin said. 'It is for me.'

The Patriarch's eyes, under their spirited brows, relaxed their stare. He said, 'Well, that's frank enough. I tell you what, then.' Father Ludovico bent and lifted his satchel. 'Adorne may not agree. But I'd take you to hunt for de Fleury. You might shame the brute into repentance. He needs to take a look at what's happening in Caffa. He needs to be frightened into doing God's work in Tabriz. You come and tell him, my boy.' And baring a set of frightening teeth, he departed.

. . .

ALONE WITH ROBIN that night, Kathi returned again to the argument they had been having all evening, and which she knew she would win in the end. 'If you go, so do I. Nicholas won't forget what he has done, but you might.' She spoke wryly. Despite what the Patriarch rightly called *the catastrophe*, she could not expect Robin to throw aside years of hero-worship; to dismiss this unpredictable, this extraordinary man who would choose, if he felt like it, to risk his own life for theirs, and yet would destroy, they now knew, just as wantonly.

'You think he should be induced to go east?' Robin said. 'For the sake of the Patriarch and the Church? Into a porridge of Ruthenians and Tartars and Mongols, Turcoman bandits and Turks who have four wives apiece and eat horses?'

'He might enjoy some of it,' Kathi said. 'Look. He has a life to fill. It may as well have a purpose.'

'And Nicholas is supposed meekly to go wherever the Patriarch wants him?'

'I think,' said Kathi, 'that would be unrealistic. I think the Patriarch's pushing, not pulling, and he wants you as his floppy-eared beater. You're supposed to flush Nicholas out, and drive him painlessly east, at the trot.' She gave an involuntary shiver.

Robin moved, and was still. They had an arrangement; or rather he had, with himself. Kathi put her hand into his. She said, 'We'll go together. I'll speak to my uncle tomorrow . . . My bed looks very cold. Who will warm it?'

IT WAS NOT EASY, that interview the next day. Departure was close, and Anselm Adorne was preoccupied with the needs of his journey, and of the family, grown and half-grown, he was leaving behind. Also, his travelling companion the Patriarch of Antioch had called, unacceptably late and no more agreeable than he had ever been. When Kathi found him, her uncle was grim.

Katelijne Sersanders of Berecrofts might look like a child half her age, but she thought and felt like an adult. In asking her favour, she was conscious of the factors against her. Her abundance of energy (her uncle could say) was deceptive, and her health fragile. She should be settling to marriage, as Robin ought to be fostering his grandfather's business. And lastly, of course, it was outside common decency that Nicholas de Fleury should claim her thoughts or her time. Deceived by the man whom he had watched growing from boyhood, Anselm Adorne was attempting to forget de Fleury, and so she must, too.

Despite all of that, Kathi Sersanders sat by her uncle's desk and put her proposal, and hard man though he could be, her uncle gave her the courtesy of a hearing. A just magistrate, a Flemish–Italian merchant prince with generations of Genoese nobility behind him, Anselm Adorne had not lightly given in, either, when his niece had proposed to marry young Robin. But he was fond of her, and he respected her judgement, and Scotland had offered security. Or so it had seemed to him then. So now, Adorne said, 'It is Robin, not you, who wants to find and speak to de Fleury?'

'I shouldn't stop him,' she said. 'Robin was his page, then his squire. He can't forget. He needs to speak to Nicholas; to satisfy himself over what has happened.'

'And you?' her uncle asked.

She had not been dazzled, like Robin, by the compendium of assorted delights which made Nicholas at first sight so winning. She had been a critical admirer, a fellow lover of music and, latterly, unexpectedly, a friend. Until the catastrophe. She said, 'Now I think Nicholas is best left alone.'

'Certainly, that would be my opinion,' her uncle observed. He did not elaborate, but he was thinking, she knew, of his task. This mission would be thorny enough, without inviting more trouble. Resentful of Adorne, Nicholas might be stirred, if resurrected, to find ways of obstructing the mission. And while he was free to impugn whom he wished, Adorne's hands were tied. For what Nicholas had done had not been made public, and would not be, for the sake of his victims.

She said, 'I want this for Robin, not myself. Nicholas may never appear. He may not want to be found, or he may not be where the Patriarch thinks. I don't intend to wander for ever, but I do want Robin to feel that at least he has tried. And if Nicholas is still alive, I can't believe that he would harm you. Although, of course, no one can be sure.'

'No,' her uncle said. He paused. 'You would not think of letting Robin travel without you?' Then, as she looked at him in silence, he answered his own question. 'No.'

She wondered if he understood, and thought that he probably did. If Robin went, she must go, and not simply because they were newly united. The truth was that she would be twenty-one in November, while Robin was three years her junior. Soon, the difference would fade, and they would live the span of their lives as contemporaries, lovers and friends. But first, they had to secure the form of their union.

It had never been her ambition to wed. She would not have done so, had she not seen within this sweet-tempered man all the promise of just such a future. But, wise as Robin was, it was for her, in these first weeks, to shape from intangibles — dreams, thoughts, sensations — the image of the marriage that they were going to have. She was not alone, for he was aware of it, and helped her as he could. There was a precedent.

Adorne said, 'I am not sure that it is wise. But I trust your good sense, and I would not have Robin waste his life mourning a scoundrel. Come with me, then. Let Robin satisfy himself, if he must, and bring you back to your own home, and your own life. Nicholas de Fleury has had his chance, and is worth no one's pain now.'

Chapter 2

In Danzig, as the Mission approached, the captain communicated his plans to remove Colà, for a time, to the country. Colà, although compliant, had howled. 'I didn't know you had a wife!'

'I have to have one,' said Paúel Benecke sourly. 'Or I couldn't be a *schep-herr*. It doesn't mean anything.'

'So I've noticed,' said Colà, still wheezing. 'But she doesn't live on the Vistula?'

The captain had decided, some time ago, not to risk sending Colà up the River Vistula. He didn't want Colà going south or east. He didn't want Colà going anywhere except the near vicinity of Danzig, to which he would return when the Mission had gone. He had sent his wife Malgorzaty a bribe. Regard it as an investment.

He should have known it wouldn't work. He survived the dubious pleasure of a single day's ride, with Colà at the top of his form, imitating every voice in the Town Hall, and then they rode through to the yard of his house to find the snow trampled deep by unknown horseshoes. The next moment, they were dragged from their own mounts, and their arms pinioned behind them. Colà objected, and was disciplined. The captain gloomily did as he was told. Their captors were Malgorzaty's grooms. And standing before him was another familiar figure, six feet tall with a billhook over its shoulder. 'Hello, *tatko*. Come on, you,' said Paúel Benecke's daughter Elzbiete.

'Madame,' said Colà obediently, and followed her into the castle. Benecke wasn't invited. It was snowing, and none of his wife's men would speak to him.

He was sitting drinking hot ale in the gatehouse when Colà emerged with Malgorzaty. They were much the same height, the chief difference being that Colà was clean-shaven. He looked like an owl, with both dimples showing, and compressions of powerful brown hair distorting the shaggy rim of his *kolpak*. Malgorzaty said to the captain, 'He's too bright for you. Take him back to Danzig.'

The captain got up. 'He doesn't want to go. I explained.'

'But *they* want him to go,' said his wife, jerking her head. He was being invited indoors, to the stockroom, where he was not surprised to find some indignant soldiers he knew from the Town Hall. He knew whose they were, and he understood perfectly well what had happened. The bitch had let slip to the magistrates that Colà was escaping from Danzig, and then had held up his pursuers, while she had a good look at Colà herself.

And of course, the big man and she had got on. Despite which (or because of it), she had decided to hand Colà back to the Danzigers, instead of letting him vanish with Paúel. Malgorzaty thought that Colà would be a waste as a privateer, when the Danzigers could sign him into a guild, and marry him to somebody's tall, spinster daughter. Once, that is, they knew whose side he was on.

The captain wondered if Malgorzaty knew that there was a girl with the Mission. He hadn't told Colà. With Colà away, he would have had a good chance with the little once-virgin Kathi. He still had a good chance. He had money.

Infused with natural optimism, Paúel Benecke set off with his guard back to Danzig, his grinning companion beside him, and behind him the glare of his womenfolk, their folded arms solid as fenders. '*Der harte Seevogel*. Tough Seabird!' jeered his wife.

BY THIS TIME, twelve days out of Bruges, the Ducal, Apostolic and Imperial Mission was halfway to Danzig and splashing into the large port of Lübeck, carrying with it a silent Adorne, a blithely truculent priest, and the self-effacing persons of Kathi and her husband, contriving at all costs to be useful.

Given that to agile minds, most journeys are delightful, this one had so far been less so. They did not see much of Adorne. For him, at each stop in their chilly itinerary, the daylight hours were crammed with meetings, disputes and discussions to do with trade between Burgundy, Bruges and the ports in the league of the Hanse. Frequently the Patriarch would intervene, referring to the discomforts of hellfire, and the nuisance it would be if the Ottoman armies came marching through Germany. Finally, as if that were not bad enough, there was the Paúel Benecke business, which forced Adorne to display the full weight of Burgundian anger in every miserable place that had dealt with the stolen cargo. The trail meandered over half of Europe. Every town in the Hanse seemed to have a share in the plunder, and lied about it, coolly, to his face. Adorne had disliked all he heard of Paúel Benecke from the moment their affairs crossed in Iceland. The dislike was mutual.

In Lübeck it was the same; and after the meetings were over, the merchant societies, as was usual, politely sent to claim Adorne as their guest. His niece was not invited. It was by accident, therefore, that one of Adorne's hosts arrived early to collect him one evening and, waiting, chatted to Kathi. Heinrich Castorp was the richest merchant in Lübeck; the King of Denmark (he said) had once pledged him his crown for a loan. He had also resided in Bruges for nine years. It had been a long time ago, but Heinrich Castorp still recognised a French–Flemish accent when he heard it. So he came to mention the companionable fellow who had passed through to Danzig this winter, and now spent his time, so they said, raising hell with that rascal Paúel Benecke. Name of Colà. Her uncle might know him.

'No. I'm sure he doesn't,' Kathi said. The Patriarch was out. She could hear Robin breathing. Then her uncle came downstairs and he and the Lübecker left. They were to watch a special performance at the exclusive club of the Cirkelselschop where the Burgundian envoy would be offered, and would successfully drink, fifteen tumblers of wine. She turned to Robin, and smacked her hands shut in traitorous triumph. Then she gave a sniff.

Robin said hoarsely, 'Nicholas. It must be. Of course it is. Christ, what shall we do? He's with *Benecke*! Your uncle won't let us see him.'

'We don't tell him. Benecke is crazy,' Kathi said. She and Robin had met him in Iceland. Benecke had courted her. Benecke had asked her to go with him to Danzig. She had no qualms at all about Benecke, she was worrying so much about everyone else.

She sniffed again, and this time Robin looked at her. Then he took her shoulder and shook it. He said, 'You didn't believe it. You said he wouldn't do anything stupid, but you didn't really believe it.'

'I did,' she said. She felt weak.

'But we ought to make sure,' Robin said with sudden decision. 'Look. There's a club of cod-fishers here, the Bergenfahrers. Someone asked me to come. They allow women. We could both go and see what they know. Oh goodness, *I* knew he was going to be all right.'

They went and ate pickled herring, and Robin sang, when he was invited, and drank, to Kathi's admiration and alarm, as much ale as Adorne ever managed of wine, and with equal aplomb. There was gossip about people they knew, and Robin encouraged it. There were men who took fish into Bruges, and traded with the Banco di Niccolò; who had corresponded with Julius, its agent in Germany, and knew of his beautiful wife. But inquisitive Julius of the unfettered conscience had not passed through here yet, nor discovered, clearly, that the convivial Colà had another name. No one had, so it seemed. The cod-fishers sang, stamped and drank but had nothing to say of the sociable stranger. As the night wore on, the atmosphere thickened, and the reddened faces of Rolf and Hermann and Hanke reminded Kathi of others, swaying, gleeful, in fleets of small vessels off Iceland, while the smoke in her throat was that of a mountain about to explode. The greatest spectacle ever conceived, by a Master no man could ever compete with.

It was because of Iceland, she knew, that Robin retained, unconfessed, that ultimate, ineradicable belief that the gleams of virtue in Nicholas could be coaxed into constancy; that one day he should be, through and through, what he seemed. Now all the early illusions had gone, but Robin, struggling to comprehend, would not be satisfied until he had found him.

They never spoke of what had happened to Nicholas: how he had taken his powerful Bank, and using it to obtain credit in Scotland, had plunged both the Bank and the country into near-ruin for the sake of a family feud. Kathi, numbed by the scale of the damage, would not herself have done what Robin was doing. To her mind, Nicholas now had to devise his own road to salvation. To pursue him simply burned the brand deeper; reiterated that he could not go back. Which was what the Patriarch wanted, of course.

IN DANZIG, Paúel Benecke sulked in his house, peaceably warded by the Town, who permitted him to go where he pleased, so long as it was not outside the walls, or any spot where he might find himself holding an unsupervised meeting with the Burgundian Mission.

Colà was in Danzig as well, but lodged in the palatial mansion of an Elder of the Order of St George, and escorted wherever he went. Danzig did not propose to lose either man in advance of the Mission.

Naturally, neither was allowed to send messages out. It did not prevent messages from slipping discreetly inwards in cowls, packs and satchels. For a while, so approached, Colà did nothing. Then he roused himself to draw up a plan. Finally, without taking more than he came with, he made a smooth and successful exit over his chosen part of the walls and, crossing the ice of the ditch, made his way through the stiffened snow of the suburbs to reach the frozen swamps of the country beyond. He had only six miles to walk, and moved quickly.

It was still daylight when he reached the monastery of Oliva, with its twin-towered basilica and its massive outbuildings and farmland and parks. They were looking out for him. The gates were opening as he approached, and a pair of horsemen rode up, with some squires. He saw the Florentine badges before they addressed him. 'My lord of Beltrees?'

'You are mistaken,' said Colà dryly. He spoke, as they did, in Tuscan.

'Naturally,' said the spokesman a little quickly. 'But you intend to accept, I trust, the hospitality of the abbey, and we should be happy to show you the way.'

He let them lead him to the Abbot's wing of the monastery. He had been there often, and knew where the guest-quarters were. Every Cistercian priory held to the same plan; although here the little river was put to much greater use than in Scotland: the wheels of the wool-beater, the tanner, the miller thudded and creaked; and he could hear the axe-blows of the monks trimming the ice. They had already cleared the pathways with shovels and oxen: a task seldom necessary in Haddington. He encouraged his mind, as ever, to dwell on such comparisons. Nothing should be unthinkable.

In the guest-parlour, the man who rose to greet him was not, of course, Arnolfo Tedaldi himself, Medici agent from Florence, royal banker and wealthiest of all the Italians in Poland. This man was his kinsman Filippo Buonaccorsi, one of the more notorious of the Western World's political refugees. Or, if you were more interested in his physical presence, a decorative man still in his mid-thirties, whose high cheekbones and long, curling hair merely acquired extra piquancy from the spectacles perched on his nose.

Colà squinted at them. 'You got them,' he said.

'Better than the first pair. Caeculus no longer. Wait. Don't move. So this is Ser Nicholas de Fleury, writer of informative letters. Rumour has not lied.'

'Rumour?' said Nicholas de Fleury. He waited, exchanged a handclasp, and sat down. He had been corresponding for a long time with this man, in the knowledge that Buonaccorsi could influence the expansion of trade east of Germany. Now that Colà's interests had changed, he had hoped to avoid or at least postpone a meeting. It was inconvenient that the man had travelled north especially to see him, but at least it would get the matter out of the way.

Buonaccorsi had reseated himself slowly opposite. 'We have a mutual friend, the charming youth Nerio, who sends me word of you. But I take nothing at its face value. Childhood playmates do not mature to the same measure, like plums. Those who meet only through letters may mistake a slight tilth for common ground.'

'You wish to harrow,' Nicholas remarked. He set himself to be patient.

The Italian considered. An elegant hand lifted and removed the nose-hold of the spectacles. 'I know, I think, what I should find. A layer of Plato, a drill of Aristotle, some pockets of Horace and Homer. A generous mould of mathematics, astrology. Some evidence of divining, and Greek of the Trebizond kind. But also the mushrooms, perhaps, of illusion. An interest in home and family, rilled in tribes, but easily abandoned. A taste for luxury, without the application to sustain it. A mountebank's fondness for disguise, pretending to hide under a nickname when none can fail to know his identity.'

'All you say is true, Maestro Callimaco,' Nicholas said. 'Who would befriend such a person?'

The man nicknamed Callimaco was smiling. 'You, I trust,' said Filippo Buonaccorsi. 'How agreeable to find one's conceits not only understood, but indulged. And in Teutonic Danzig, that bastion of the literal-minded.'

'I have no objection to Danzigers,' Nicholas said. His patience had slipped a little, and he felt no urge to retrieve it. 'Nor has your King, I should think. Some of them have advanced him large loans.'

'My lord Casimir knows what he owes them. But others, he fears, are less concerned with the future of Poland than with their own fortunes from commerce, or piracy. I am not sure where your sympathies lie?' Buonaccorsi had switched to Latin halfway through the sentence, adding, 'Unless you object?'

'I do not object. Must I have any preferences?' Nicholas said. He used Louvain Latin, being buggered if he was going to bother with the Tuscan variety. He was increasingly aware that a winter with Benecke had unfitted him for this sort of thing. Servants had come in, and were placing platters before them. There was a smell of fresh bread, and almonds, and fish. Trout, from Oliva's own lake. With lovely sauces. With personally chosen lovely sauces.

Buonaccorsi said, 'You have closed your business in Scotland. You have withdrawn from Venice and Flanders, although your Bank continues, I am told, in the hands of its managers. You were the Duke of Burgundy's agent, then the Emperor's. You may still be working for either or both. Or you may have determined to stay idle, or to select another base for your talents. If you wish to stay in Poland, we cannot help you unless we know your intentions.' He didn't specify who *we* were.

'Before the Mission arrives,' Nicholas said. A hand over his shoulder poured wine, and he sat without touching it. He felt himself becoming annoyed.

'Naturally, Ser Niccolò. Or, if I might . . . ?'

'Please.'

'Naturally, my dear Niccolò, we are all aware that the members of this embassy are well known to you. Perhaps you have corresponded with them over the winter. Perhaps you feel that you must take their part. I believe you even grew up in Bruges with the Medici manager who is suing poor Benecke.'

Tommaso, we should have booted more sense into you when you were young. 'You are a friend of the Medici,' Nicholas said, smiling a little.

'And you of Paúel Benecke,' said Buonaccorsi. 'But few of us are free to act as we would wish. The King, valuing Burgundy, would not refuse reasonable reparation for this cargo, but the merchants of Danzig feel differently.' He paused. 'My wish is that you had come directly to Thorn or to Cracow, and had won the King's trust. An informed mediator is honoured by both sides. It could have been your role for the future. Among others.'

'Living in Cracow?' Nicholas said. He tasted his wine, and reluctantly set it aside.

'Living wherever the Court is, or at any other centre of excellence. I do not need to recite names to you. You know who is here; we have exchanged letters about them. I believed at one time that you wished to meet them.'

'And now they would like to meet me?' Nicholas said.

Buonaccorsi looked at him thoughtfully, through long-lashed, myopic eyes. 'I suspect I am receiving a refusal. No, I cannot flatter you with the names of those who would have wished to meet you: they do not know you well enough as yet. Yes, this approach on their behalf is chiefly for national and commercial ends, although not only for those. I have not referred to pleasures other than those of the mind, but they are there to be had. Not that I have anything against the customs of Danzig.'

'I'm glad,' Nicholas said. 'I find they suit me well enough. You may be reassured: I am not interested in the Mission, and it is unlikely to be interested in me. I find my imagination has been fired by the classical pleasures of seafaring. Theseus. Ulysses. Paúel Benecke. I thought I might go to sea with Paúel Benecke.'

'I am sorry,' said Buonaccorsi, without haste. He displayed no disapproval, other than sedately returning, in his next words, to the vernacular. 'I heard your departure was sudden, but I thought we might still find . . .'

'Common ground,' Nicholas said.

The other man laughed. 'Quite. But if your difficulty was a simple one, then perhaps I might still help. Was it over a woman, for example? According to my little Nerio, your lawyer Julius has an exceptional wife.'

'Anna? No. That is, she is exceptional, but not my reason for leaving.'

'So something more novel. You planned to murder the Pope?' said Filippo Buonaccorsi.

Nicholas smiled. 'Nothing so ambitious or so bold. I chose to end a family feud, and then leave.'

'I see. Was it mortal? The family feud?'

'Am I an assassin? Of course not: how crude. How can the quick satisfaction of murder compare with the effects of a well-designed war?'

'And this, do I take it, is why you are estranged from the Mission? The Patriarch of Antioch will feel bound to denounce you?'

'He might, if he knew anything of it. My activities are not public hearsay. I left because I didn't wish them to become so. And, although I thank you, I am not in any difficulty.'

'So you do not expect to see Anselm Adorne, or the Patriarch?'

'I have no plans to meet them. On the other hand, if they enquire, it might be difficult to deny I am in Poland.'

'Where men know you as Colà?'

'And also as Nicholas de Fleury of Bruges. I left a note under that name with the Council to say that I am here, at your invitation, in Oliva.'

'I see,' said the other. He replaced the spectacles on his nose and looked mildly through them. 'And I understand, I suppose. You are inviting King, traders and pirate to compete for your services. And also Burgundy and the Emperor?'

'I have removed myself from both,' Nicholas said. 'And I am spying for neither. As for the rest, my preference is, as I mentioned, for Benecke, but I should also like to have freedom of movement. Nicknames outlive their uses.'

'Naturally,' Buonaccorsi agreed. His hands, freed, were reflectively tented. 'A life at sea. A surprising choice. Of course, you have your mathematics. Navigation and the stars: you may explore some new realms of the mind. They say diviners can discover drowned men.'

'They discover the coins in their purses,' Nicholas said. 'And, speaking of salvage . . . I hoped I might be allowed, before I went, to look at the altar-piece.'

'The altar-piece?'

'Henne Memling's "Last Judgement". It came with the last of Paúel Benecke's — appropriated — cargo. The Abbot won't admit that it is here. You might persuade him.'

'I haven't been shown it myself,' Buonaccorsi said. 'Didn't you see it being painted in Bruges?'

'Everyone saw it,' Nicholas said. 'Everyone was in it, just about. The Saved and the Damned. Henne got all his drink free on the strength of it. I just wanted to check something for myself.'

'What?' said the Italian presently. The painting, on the Abbot's wall, was gigantic; the gold glowed; the throng of nude figures gleamed.

'It doesn't matter. Tommaso Portinari. I've found him. I can die happy now. I wonder if these are for me?'

He had turned his head to the window, from beyond which could be heard the minor tumult of horsemen arriving. He was probably right. These would be the emissaries of the eminent councillors, merchants, shipmasters and members of the Confrérie of St George: the bluff

Bischoff and Bock for example, and Sidinghusen and Valandt and Niederhof of the syndicate that owned Benecke's ship. All men who would prefer the former Colà z Brugge to merge his interests with those of Danzig, rather than those of Casimir its nominal lord. If de Fleury were returning to Danzig, he would now be able to do as he wished. He had been approached by the King, and had not accepted.

Filippo Buonaccorsi did not escort his guest to the door, nor attempt to view those who came to remove him. It was not his purpose, or the King's, to challenge the merchants of Danzig. He presumed that they knew that Nicholas de Fleury was not attracted to them, but intended to partner the privateer Benecke. It would still be, on the whole, to their benefit. He thought of his own chequered past in Rome and Florence and Venice: the passionate militancy, the flaunted follies, the dangerous plot (de Fleury had smiled) from which he had barely escaped with his life. His habit of learning had saved him.

This man, of whom he had expected much, had refused such a path. Buonaccorsi wondered what had produced, in reality, so drastic a change. But then, the cause hardly mattered. Men either dealt with adversity, or did not.

Chapter 3

In April that year, the winds which had sealed off the mouth of the Vistula backed at last to the west and, overtaking the Three Princes' Mission, the fleets of the Baltic united at Danzig, there to jostle and bob, awaiting their clients the grain rafts: the winners of the annual race down the Vistula with the fruits of the broad Polish cornfields.

Because the Mission travelled by road and arrived, by intent, on the Sabbath, its ears and eyes were spared the immediate impact. It heard, in the clear, biting air, only the battling clangour of church bells and the crackling tread of the welcoming cortège, followed, as they entered the city, by the dutiful salutes of the citizens. Only when riding down the wide street to their lodging did Kathi glimpse through the portals ahead the wharves of the little Mottlau, Danzig's river, and the second, watery city that dwelled there.

Not all the inhabitants of Danzig lined the streets, or gazed in curiosity or annoyance through their expensive glass windows. Some had climbed the tower of St Mary's, the better to follow the foreigners' progress. Two, especially at home on the wharves, had joined the freightermen in the holy of holies, and were standing on the towering, topmost floor of the Crane, where the timbers creaked in the wind, and the cable, even when bound, muttered and snored as if at any moment the mighty hook would come thundering down to ganch all the men on the jetty and raze the mast from the ship lying beneath it. Paúel Benecke said, full of anticipation, 'Here they come.'

The man he now thought of as Colà did not immediately answer. You could see little as yet: a line of plumes, the glint of cuirasses; a quantity of large velvet hats and cloaked shoulders. Benecke said, 'They're putting them into the royal apartments. Windy as hell, and first thing tomorrow, all the noise of a seaport. I see the Franciscan. Is that Adorne, with the chequer? And another chequer of sorts — it must be his nephew.'

'It isn't his nephew,' said Colà.

Benecke pursed his lips and shaded his eyes. 'You're right. It isn't. It's the little lad who came with us, Robin something. But with Adorne's chequer? How odd!'

'He's married to Adorne's niece,' Colà said.

Benecke shot him a sparkling glance. Then he returned to surveying the riders. He said, astonished, 'It's the girl-brother Kathi! The maid in the fur hood is Kathi! She married that *infant*?'

Colà got up. 'Why, does it make you ache in the joints? His voice has broken, so far as I know. I have to tell you that old women prize youths: they are indefatigable.'

'You should know?'

'I should know.' The cavalcade had disappeared; the show was over. Men moved and joked, and began to clatter down the steps of the Crane, Colà among them. He said, over his shoulder, 'So why have the two of them come?'

'For you,' said the captain immediately. He frowned. Colà had turned off from the steps, and had vaulted down to the pair of wheels, fifteen feet from top to bottom, that worked the machinery. When Paúel reached him, he had stepped into one and was seated, clasping his knees, between the rungs where men usually paddled. The wheel, which was made fast, rocked a little. Benecke stepped up-wheel and sat himself facing him.

Colà said, 'They don't know I'm here. I think they want to call in some favours from you. That pair saved your carcass in Ireland.'

'After you'd half killed me,' said Benecke, frowning more deeply. The wheels occupied the vaulted roof of a passage through to the wharf. People walking below heard his voice and peered upwards.

'But you've forgiven me that, and your wife wants me to marry your daughter. So what do we do?'

Benecke thought. He knew when to pay no attention to Colà. He also suspected that his duplicity had been discovered. He had known that the little Kathi was coming. Below, six familiar caps walked through to the plankway and someone blew for a boat. He waited till they had gone. Ice was forming again at the edge of the water, and the opposite granary quay was quite white. The wheel trembled beneath him. Colà, his expression in shadow, was gently rocking the wood with his spine. Benecke said, 'If you break the shackles, the whole drum will run. Ever seen that happen?'

'Yes, in Bruges. Do you think you've got the only God-damned crane in the world? But that time, I was jiggling it harder. You were saying?'

'I was going to mention the Council. They wouldn't want you to upset Adorne. And they wouldn't want me to interfere with the law. To me, there's only one thing to do. So let's do it.'

'Break the shackles?' said Nicholas de Fleury. He helped himself up, balanced, swung, and launched himself down to the slush of the passage-way. Then he stood, grinning, while Benecke, with resignation, did the same. He changed direction on landing, and so escaped the vicious swipe that was meant to spin him over and into the water. Colà had guessed, all right, that something had been kept from him.

A COMPANIONABLE FELLOW, the Lübecker had said, *who now spends his time raising hell with Paúel Benecke*. That was all Kathi knew, but it was sufficient.

The day after the mission's Grand Entry to Danzig, Katelijne Sersanders, lady of Berecrofts, left the splendid lodging they had been given at the Green Bridge and made her way to the great florid home of Filip Bischoff, there to eat marzipan and drink Malvasian wine with his second wife and two of his daughters, together with a selection of the women of Danzig.

For a century and a half, the Teutonic Knights had ruled Danzig, and it was not long since they left. The merchant families who had taken their place were, many of them, the same as those who had served the Knights as factors and agents, and their customs and tongue were still German. The husbands of these women knew every town of the Hanse, had lived in Veere and in Bruges, were familiar with London and Leith, Perth and Aberdeen, the Bay of Biscay and Brittany. Despite the hearty, disarming chatter, Kathi had to remember that they knew as much of her family as she did; and would wonder why she had married whom she had married, and what she was doing here. She would be regarded, of course, as her uncle's spy.

Nevertheless, she was also a source of information and entertainment and they were not, she found, malicious in their enquiries as a Venetian, for example, would have been. They talked of her home town of Bruges, and their husbands, and invited her to trust them with any gossip attached to the members of the Kontor, the council of Hanseatic merchants living in Bruges. How could it be healthy, to demand that honest men live as monks, without their wives to console them? And such wine, such fabrics, such jewels, they said, could be bought for nothing in Bruges! Katelijne's betrothal ring was passed round, then her earrings, then one of her shoes and a sleeve. They spoke admiringly of her handsome young husband — and Scottish, not Flemish: how important his father must be! They sought to compare German and Flemish wedding-bed customs, and exchanged reminiscences about the performances of their own husbands under the eyes of the statutory witnesses:

Did he pretend to do something, then?

Oh, the rogue, no: he pretended to pretend, but all the time . . . ! The thumb-marks next day!

It was all comfortable, coarse and not unfriendly: the feminine equivalent of the Bergenfahrers. A little flushed, Kathi collected her wits and replied as cheerfully and uninformatively as she could. Fortunately, there was no one else to be embarrassed: Robin was at the Town Hall, where the Council and Jury were receiving my lord Anselm Adorne and the Patriarch on the first full day of official meetings. The morning was wearing away before she managed to enquire where Paúel Benecke lived.

She had asked Barbara Bischoff, one of the daughters, but a different girl remarked, 'Why? Have you met him?' The speaker was built like a bison, and was eight inches taller than Kathi. Barbara giggled.

Kathi said, 'I met him in Iceland with Nicholas de Fleury, Lord Beltrees. Or Colà, he calls himself now.'

'Did they share you?' enquired the young woman.

'Elzbiete!' the girl Barbara said.

'No, my brother and Robin were there, and Lord Beltrees, of course, was still married. You know Lord Beltrees?' Kathi said with exquisite nonchalance. 'Under both names?' The conversation about her was dwindling.

'Colà z Brugge the madman, of course. Everyone knew who he was: they all kept quiet, for they thought he was spying. You say, *was still* married?' said the girl.

'To a lady called Gelis van Borselen. They have separated since, and await an annulment. I hope he is in no danger,' said Kathi solicitously. 'I know that Captain Benecke owes him his life.'

'I should not thank Colà for that,' the young woman said. 'Paúel Benecke is a black whoring rat.'

Through a chorus of screams, Barbara patted the girl's brawny arm while explaining to Kathi: 'Paúel Benecke is her father. What she says is quite true. Did you want to meet Colà? Nikolás of Fleury, as you say?'

Kathi swallowed. She said, 'I should like to surprise him.'

'That can be arranged,' said the thoughtful bass of Elzbiete. 'So, tell us what you know of Nikolás, Colà. Does he keep extravagant mistresses, or does he make do with inexpensive bought favours, as here? Was his wife, Gelis, frigid? Is he a vigorous man, and well made, as they say? Is he depicted in the great painting at Oliva?'

'None of his wives was what you'd call frigid. What great painting?' said Kathi, slow for once.

Someone coughed. Bischoff's lady wife said, 'A picture of men, unsuitable for unmarried girls. You do not need to reply. Give me a few hours to arrange it, and you and Elzbiete may surprise our wicked Colà z Brugge before supper.'

'Wicked?' said Kathi.

'In charm,' said Barbara's stepmother. 'In the extent of his charm, and his escapades. Look how Elzbiete is bewitched. And now, of course, our girls can command a good dowry.'

Someone else coughed. 'That's nice,' Kathi said, and smiled at Elzbiete.

WHEN HER UNCLE and Robin returned, Kathi was sitting alone, half undressed, in her room. With dusk, the din outside her windows had reduced itself to the constant tramping of feet, and the roar of men's voices in song or obscenity. Danzig was well provided with ale. Then a door banged from inside the house, and she heard her husband's light voice, and the velvet timbre of her uncle's polished German. The Patriarch, it seemed, was not there.

In a moment, Robin would leap upstairs to find her. She did not want that. Her gown lay by her bed. The opulent ladies of Danzig had already examined, in silence, its meagre proportions: she had always been small, with the slight, wiry build of a child. Her eyes were hazel, not blue, and her hair plainly brown, against the flaxen bounty of Elzbiete's, for example. She smiled, thinking of Elzbiete, and then did not smile. The drunken voices had risen outside. *Does he make do with inexpensive bought favours, as here?* She dressed and walked down.

Anselm Adorne was angry. Even now, alone with his niece and her husband, he would not burst into speech, but the grooves in his cheeks were bitten deep, and the brows above his eyes, normally amused, or detached, or quizzical, were heavy and straight. Since his wife died he had not touched a lute, or written verse, or laughed aloud. The mourning ought to be over, and Kathi knew that it might have been, but for something else he could not forget. Also, Margriet's family had traded in Danzig — not that the Danzigers would allow that to affect them. Kathi said, 'What happened?'

It was the usual problem: the Danzigers' unshakeable determination to preserve their trade at all costs: even against the interests of their fellow Hanse cities. And against the Danzigers' single voice, the divided one with which Anselm Adorne had to speak. On behalf of the Duke of Burgundy, a threat to clear the Hanseatic Kontor out of Bruges, unless he obtained the trading concessions and the redress for the ship that he demanded. And in private, from Adorne's well-liked and respected fellow burghers and office-holders in Bruges, the brief to promise anything, do anything, so long as the Baltic trade came to Bruges uninterrupted. And all, of course, had come to focus upon this stupid case of Paúel Benecke and the *San Matteo*.

'It sailed under a Burgundian flag,' Adorne said. He recited it, as if she were a jury. 'It had been Italian-built, with its consort, to go on Pope

Pius's Crusade, and when Pius died, the Medici leased the two ships from the Duke, who had not paid for them yet. This voyage was one of their regular trips between Pisa and Flanders. Both ships had a Florentine crew: one was captained by a Strozzi, and one by a Tedaldi. They left Flanders freighted for Florence, but also intending to stop at Southampton to pick up English wool, and to sell a consignment of alum from Tolfa worth forty thousand gold florins. Because the Hanse towns were at war with England —'

'In reprisal for their unlicensed fishing in Iceland,' Kathi said.

'— in reprisal for Iceland, I agree. Because there was a war, Paúel Benecke and his *Saint Pierre de Rochelle* —'

'His *Peter von Danzig*,' Kathi said. 'Or *Das Grosse Kraweel*, if you prefer. It's outside the window.'

'I have seen it. It carries over three hundred men. It intercepted the Burgundian ships and boarded the *San Matteo*, killing thirteen Florentines and wounding a hundred before making off with its whole cargo, including all that intended for Italy. The cargo has now been divided up and sold, despite Tommaso's appeals at Hamburg and Utrecht, despite the promises made to the Duke that none of the Hanse cities would handle it. They all have.'

'And the *Peter*'s owners and crew all got shares of the booty,' Kathi said. 'Their daughters are expecting fine dowries. Paúel Benecke made himself a fortune, but the ship wasn't his.'

'Of course not. He did the killing. He's disappeared. The men who did own the ship were a syndicate from the Confrérie of St George. Valandt and Niederhof and Sidinghusen. Three of the very gentlemen who are attending the Town Hall and entertaining us so very pleasantly at the Artushof. Who are proposing, if I am not mistaken, to continue to delay us without profit, even though I have letters to present to the King, and every day the year is advancing . . . They make no bones about admitting what happened. It was justified: it was an act of legitimate war; the *San Matteo* was in English waters; if anyone is to blame, it is the English. They even admit to the two altar-pieces.'

'Tommaso's is at Oliva abbey,' Kathi said. 'You wouldn't get in, but they might let me see it, if you wanted.'

'Is it? How do you know?' Her uncle stopped pacing.

Kathi said, 'I thought I had a lot to tell you, but you seem to know it all. I've been with Paúel Benecke's daughter all afternoon.'

'Kathi?' Robin said. She had felt his eyes on her, anxiously, throughout the recital.

Adorne said, 'You've . . . ? My dear, I am sorry. I have been thoughtless. Sit down. Tell us what has happened.' He took her to a chair, and sat down beside her. 'Now.'

She began with the conclusion, which was all that mattered. 'Elzbiete, Benecke's daughter, thought she knew where he was, and we looked for him. Nicholas has been with him all winter, and she thought I should find them together. But as you already know, Benecke has gone, and Nicholas with him.'

'Where?' Robin said.

She shook her head.

'Why?' her uncle said. 'I should have thought Nicholas would brazen it out. Unless he thought that I, like himself, would break my promise. There are two Scots ships in the Mottlau, and plenty of traders in Danzig.'

She did not answer. She knew that. One of the chief events of the deadening, deafening misery of the afternoon had been Elzbiete's insistence on visiting the Dominican church of St Nicholas, its ancient red brick visible from the shuddering ground where eighteen millstones thundered beneath the half-open book that was the roof of the Knights' mighty legacy. The Knights might have been banished, their castles razed, their trade usurped, but what remained, as with Rome, as with all the great military societies, was the skeleton, still intact, of their efficiency, evidenced in the voices and eyes of the councillors who had dealt smilingly with Anselm Adorne that afternoon. Three generations ago, a Walter van Niederhof had been one of the best overseas agents of the Teutonic Knights; as a Henry von Allen had factored for them in France. The Knights had gone, but the trade of Danzig was still in practised hands.

Paúel Benecke had not been in the Order's great mill, although they had searched all seven storeys for him. Nicholas, of course, might frequent the church of his name — except that she discovered, too late, that this was the church of the Blackfriars commonly used by the Scots, who possessed here their own special altar. She had said, 'Elzbiete, I'm sorry. M. de Fleury would not have come here.'

At which a priest, turning round, had said, 'You speak of Colà? Why, Fräulein, we know him well: he spoke often to our Scottish friends here, these latter days. Our wicked friend, this lady's father, first brought him. Is he well?'

The priest did not know where Colà was. They went to the market, pushing between vendors and buyers, storytellers and small gambling circles, stalls of second-hand clothes and worn furs and chipped clay pitchers. They crossed the sweet-water river, which the Knights had made into a canal, and rounded the shore to the smoking fires of the first of the boat-yards. Over there, amid the din of saw and hammer and voice was where the *Saint Pierre*, now the *Peter*, had first been brought, and her fine Breton caravel planking faithfully copied. This was the home yard of the *Fleury*, now loading salt and wine, so Elzbiete said, in

Bourgneuf. 'But it does not belong to Colà now, but to some woman called Anna?'

They returned to the wharves where the immense *Peter von Danzig* was now moored. Once the wonder of the whole western world, the caravel was itself dwarfed by the sky-piercing bulk of the Crane. The hook was crawling down on its cable: above Kathi's head, through the din, she heard the creak of two wheels and, peering up through the gloom, saw the great wooden roundels turning, and the plodding feet of the men who empowered them, their outstretched arms gripping the rims. Seeing them, the four men had looked down and bellowed salacious pleasantries. 'Animals,' Elzbiete had said.

They had intruded, against custom, into the Artushof, and found a drunken feast in one room, and a group of men gambling in another. In the Town Hall there was a trial, with people shouting. Last of all, they had gone to the elaborate house of a merchant. It was there that they learned that Colà had been there, but that the good captain had come and removed him. Where? No one knew.

Kathi, lady of Berecrofts, said to her uncle, 'I think they may have gone because Benecke thought we should entice Nicholas home. And I think Nicholas may have gone to please Benecke. The *Peter von Danzig* is a privateer. And they expect Colà to join them this summer.'

She did not say, even to Robin, what else she thought. She did not repeat Elzbiete's stories of how Nicholas had spent the winter, or her unbelievable, her sickening quotations from Nicholas, followed by the questions they inspired.

Old women prize youths: they are indefatigable. ('So, Katarzynka, what crone's bed did he take?')

Never trust blacks: they are vermin. ('Did some servant steal from him, then?')

'And why, Katarzynka, do you say his wife is not stupid and prudish, when Colà has described her to Paúel as both, and her son as a bastard?'

That had been just before Elzbiete and she parted company at the end of the long, fruitless search. Elzbiete had begun to express her regrets. But Kathi, her perceptions rubbed raw by distress, suddenly exclaimed in a low voice, 'You knew! You knew from the beginning that Nicholas — that Colà had gone.'

And Elzbiete, pausing only a moment, had said in her most reasonable voice, 'Well, Katarzynka, yes. But my father would be sorry if Colà left Poland.'

There was such a difference of height that Kathi had to strain to look up, as if she were trying to convince God of her innocence. She said, 'But we don't want him back. He couldn't go back. I want to persuade him to stay here in Poland. Elzbiete, tell me. Tell me, where is he?'

Elzbiete gazed at her, frowning. 'He can't go back? Why?'

'Because of something he did. I can't tell you what, but your father would approve, I am sure. A great coup. The biggest act of piracy you could imagine.'

'So he is rich? He has been ransoming prisoners?'

'No. You don't sell vengeance, you buy it,' Kathi had said bitterly; and recovered. 'So will you tell me? Please, where is he, Elzbiete?'

And Elzbiete had looked at her in silence and then had said, 'With my father. My father will write. He writes a good hand, and can decline and conjugate too. Then, if he allows, I shall tell you.'

'Without telling Nicholas?'

'If you like. You still want to surprise him?'

'That is one way of putting it,' said Kathi.

But she revealed none of that to her uncle. To Robin, later, she said, 'Benecke thought we'd take Nicholas home. I think I've convinced his daughter we shan't. If we're lucky, her father will send for us. Not my uncle, but us.'

'Why should he?' he said. They were in their bedchamber, and he was standing, fully clothed, at the window.

'Because he wants me,' Kathi said. 'And he has discounted you. He thinks you aren't really my husband.'

Robin turned. She could rely on him, always, to understand her. Youth and crones. She thought of what else went into that delicate equation. She thought of Marian de Charetty, who had fallen in love with her apprentice, who, from love and from pity, had married her. She studied, with furious affection, the young man before her who was the age now that Nicholas must have been then. Robin of Berecrofts had long guessed, before she had told him, that she was not a sensual being; that bodily pleasures meant little or nothing; that all her joy came from the mind. He had entered open-eyed into this marriage, feeling his way, never intruding, always controlling, as well as man could, the surging impulses of the blood. And she, fallen silent that first night at the sheer comeliness of him, unclothed, had made an equal pact with herself and with him, to give him all that she could, and nearly all that he could want. Only, always, she made the first moves.

As now, when she said, 'And of course, he must be right. Or why else are you standing there clothed?'

Once he was with her, he could not always be gentle, nor did she want him to be, but studied how to bring him to deeper fulfilment; to realise the great urge that overwhelmed him. She learned too, how swiftly young hunger returned, and how to welcome and satisfy it. Working with him, she took a craftsman's delight in his quickening breath, his moist skin, his clenched eyes wet, sometimes with tears. Then he was her child. The rest of the time, they were equals.

. . .

A WEEK LATER, when no word had come, and Anselm Adorne was still held fast in Danzig, Katelijne Sersanders left her husband and, accompanied by a group of Teutonic ladies, rode out from the west gate of Danzig to visit the abbey of Oliva.

The church was tall, echoing and unusually narrow. The cloisters were like all other cloisters. The Abbot, although warned beforehand, seemed about to repudiate the arrangement. 'The Confrérie have made me its custodian. I am not supposed to display it. Especially to . . . ' And he had glanced distractedly at Kathi.

'My lord, she knows it's here. Her uncle knows. Everyone knows. Does your lordship suppose we are about to help her carry it out of the country? Now, when the grain is about to come in, and you need all the advice you can get about taxes?' The lady of Filip Bischoff could threaten.

The Abbot said, 'Of course. I see your point. If Cracow knows, all the world knows, I suppose.'

'Cracow? The King? The King has been told that the painting is here?' asked Frau Bischoff.

'Presumably so,' the Abbot replied. 'When his sons' tutor was sent here, and saw it. And the other young man.'

'His sons' tutor? Signor Buonaccorsi, the scholar, was here?'

'Callimaco,' said Kathi to the air. 'He attempted to murder Pope Paul, my uncle says. He used to live in Murano. Zacco helped him in Cyprus. He went to Constantinople, and tried to hand Chios to the Turks.' She looked at the Abbot, who was old enough to think thirty-three young. She said, 'Signor Buonaccorsi was here, my lord, to look at the painting?'

And the Abbot said, 'No. I have already said. He wished to meet the foreign merchant with whom he had been corresponding. Colà. Nikolás. The surname escapes me.'

With whom he had been corresponding. 'De Fleury,' Kathi suggested. She heard the tremor in her own voice. 'The King sent this gentleman to meet M. de Fleury?'

'Colà,' said one of the ladies. 'We knew as much. Did we not mention it? Colà received an invitation from the Court, but refused it. We found it most gratifying. There is nothing at Court for a merchant. Danzig is the place for a merchant.'

'Or a pirate,' Kathi said. A conversation came into her mind. Tedaldi. One of the patrons of Callimaco was the Medici agent Tedaldi, chief of the Florentine merchants in Poland. The *San Matteo*, with its Florentine crew and its Florentine cargo, freighted by the Florentine Tommaso Portinari, had been commanded by a Tedaldi. Before, that is, it was captured by Paúel Benecke, with the loss of thirteen dead and one hundred wounded and the dispersal of all its cargo, including the great altar-piece by Hans Memling, which she was now about to be shown.

The King was interested in Nicholas, but Nicholas for some reason had rejected him. The meeting had been arranged in Oliva, where the painting was placed. The King might be under considerable pressure from his Italian colony to defy the Danzigers and hand back the Italian cargo. All these things her uncle needed to know. At the same time, of course, she would not have been allowed here unless everyone wanted her uncle to know them.

Kathi said, 'So, my lord, might one see this magnificent work?'

It was a magnificent work. She had seen it before, or most of it. Angelo Tani and his wife on the back of the flaps, and then the triptych itself. The rainbow. The Elect, with Duke Charles curly-headed among them. And the Saved. And the Damned.

She couldn't see Nicholas among either. He was probably somewhere in limbo. She did see someone else whom she knew. Tommaso. Tommaso's neat coiffeured head on top of someone else's limp body, kneeling piously in the pan of some scales.

It beat Sixtus. It beat Pope Paul's successor, who provided his wealthier guests with ex-cathedra gold pots in the close stool. Despite everything, she found herself pink with foolish amusement.

Elzbiete saw it. She said, 'Were you looking for someone?'

'Yes,' said Kathi. 'I've found him. I can die happy, now.'

Chapter 4

DURING THE DAY, he was sober: he had to be. During the night, he was more often sober than not, according to his own choice. When the day came that Paúel Benecke ruled the habits of Nicholas de Fleury, then would life become ludicrous.

On the face of it, this was merely a race. The plains of Poland yielded their crops in the autumn, when the great highway of the Vistula might be low, and the shipping roads of the Baltic were closing. The grain came to the river, and waited. In spring, the world's fleets came to Danzig. Last summer, fifty had sailed out in April, bound for Flanders and Holland and Germany. Through the summer, there might be a thousand ships more. They came for grain, and for copper and timber. The great estates sent their corn to the riverside granaries, and men like Paúel Benecke floated it north on rafts a hundred feet long and nearly thirty feet wide which were worth more in themselves than the corn, for the rafts were made of the mainmasts of caravels. Other craft, small and big, came as well, often manned by their owners: tenant-farmers and smallholders. And whoever reached Danzig first received most for his wheat, oats and rye, and his timber.

He had wanted to do this, even before Paúel had wrenched him away from the Mission and Danzig. It reminded Nicholas of Iceland, of which he often spoke entertainingly. It amused the flotilla: his remorseless mimicry, his scathing tongue, until he turned it on their masters, their institutions, themselves. And even then, they brought themselves to put up with it for, like the Icelanders, they had been locked in their houses by winter and would seize on any diversion.

But that was by night, when the concourses travelling the river would arrive at their next loading-port and, mooring the rafts to the quays, would leave their dogs or their guards by the silos and surge bellowing into the taverns. Or sometimes, as dusk overtook them, they would come to rest on some hospitable shore where the country people would flock down to serve them, bringing black bread and sausage and cheeses, and frothless ale by the cask, and this season's new batch of whores. Then the gambling and fiddling, the high-jumping dancing and singing would continue long into the darkness, until the most energetic lapsed into sleep.

Some rivermen, desperate for an advantage, tried to run the river with lanterns by night, but not many, and none could keep it up for long, however many polemen they carried.

That was why Nicholas never drank during the day. He had a reluctant respect for the power of the Vistula, this shining, swift-running highway which swirled through the fabric of Poland for six hundred miles to the sea. He had a respect for its dark, savage currents, and for the shifting white sand of its shoals. The men who manned the great rafts, poles in hand, provided the power and the strength, and dragged up the single unwieldy sail when wind and river might briefly co-operate. But it was the river pilots who were kings on the water; whose orders were law; and who rode their rafts with their steering-oars and their bodies, like men bounding downhill through snow, heeling out of one stream and slipping into the flow of the next, pitching safely aside from the watery glare of a shoal, even though the rafts lurched and juddered and bucked, and the timber groaned in the rush of the water. Sometimes even skill wasn't enough, and a raft would strike and, bursting asunder, would send whirling downriver a pack of half-submerged logs: random, lethal. The rafter name for these, *wilki*, meant 'wolves.'

Daytime was better than the night. You fought the river by day, and if you lost, you lost to the river. To lose by night in a brawl would be pitiful.

In the few days they had sailed, Benecke had been pleased to be complimentary. 'You have the knack. You could learn the river in a couple of seasons.'

It was not true. Generations went into this skill, and every stretch of the bank had its experts. Nicholas had observed that much at least, even though they hadn't come the whole way, but had picked up the fleet in the middle, after four days' hard riding from Danzig. Benecke did not say whether he owned the raft that he boarded, or the rye that he took from the granaries: he had a share very likely in both. The raft was one of the biggest; a *marktschiff* built like a box, with room for over a thousand bushels of grain and twenty men, including sailors and steersman and cook, and Paúel Benecke and a discarded banker. It possessed some primitive shelter, to which they could retire from the wind and the rain, and where Benecke continued, if allowed, with the interrogation that had been going on all through the winter. Sometimes Nicholas humoured him for a time. There was something he wanted from Benecke. He had lost some gold, and rather thought that Benecke had heard something about it.

It was never too hard, in any case, to answer Paúel's questions. 'Tell me again about Anselm Adorne,' he was saying. 'Do you still think you know why he's here?'

Nicholas produced a long groan. 'You know why he's here. He has to wave a flag on behalf of the Medici: the Duke of Burgundy owes them a fortune. Bruges wants him to sort out its trade; and he'll have a little mandate, I'm quite sure, from Scotland. And when he's finished in Poland, all his masters would like him to keep the Pope happy without actually going on crusade. Hence the trip to comfort the Christians in Caffa, and the further trip to prod Persia into helping them, too. Anselm Adorne has a lot of friends in the Levant.'

'Genoese friends,' Benecke said. 'Caffa is a Genoese colony. Do you trust him? He tried to usurp the Hanse trade in Iceland.'

'He succeeded,' Nicholas said. 'He bribed the Danish officials. And someone in Danzig kindly helped him by delaying the ship they were building for me. And, as you know, I got a ship anyway. We all like it when you fall out among yourselves in the Hanse, because it adds so much to the business opportunities. What are you trying to get me to say?'

'I'm trying to get you to tell me why you're here. They say it's because of a feud that went wrong.'

'What a stupid idea,' Nicholas said. 'If it had gone wrong, I shouldn't be here. And if it had been against Anselm Adorne, he'd be dead. You owe me some money.'

'I bloody don't!' Benecke said.

'You will, when you've taken this wager.'

'You don't have any money,' Benecke said. He had never said it outright before. 'What could you do if you don't come with me?'

'Start another feud,' Nicholas said. He picked up the bowl that Benecke was eating from and threw it and its contents into the water. 'What would I do if I did come with you? Piddle about the Baltic in convoy like a shopkeeper? The war's over.'

Benecke breathed through his nose. Beneath the week-old black beard he was yellow. He said, 'Learn who your friends are. You need money.'

'Not all that much,' Nicholas said. 'What do you think I'd do if I did come into money? Buy a fine *dwór* in Cracow and sit in it? I didn't go to Cairo or Scotland or Iceland because I needed money. Your trouble is that you've got access to a bloody great ship and nothing interesting to do with it.'

Benecke's colour had returned. He said, 'So what would you do if you had money?'

'Tempt me,' said Nicholas. 'What could you devise that needs capital no one else would offer you?'

There was a pause. 'I could go to Iceland again,' Benecke said. 'Paid protection as well as cod-fishing. Or I could move further south. You can do things without letters of marque. There are rich men always willing to pay.' He stopped. His eyes, which were black, were glittering. He said, 'I was right. You want fighting.'

'Yes, but not on a diet of whale blubber. Why don't you put together a programme? You're the professional pirate. I don't mind providing the brains.'

Benecke picked up Nicholas's bowl and threw it outside. They were both on their feet in enjoyable anticipation when the raft hit a new eddy and tilted; someone roared, and the discussion came to a halt for the moment.

They arrived at the crowded jetties of Thorn, built like all the busiest ports on a bend of the river. Benecke didn't try to penetrate the massive line of red walls, but stayed and transacted his business among the cabins, the warehouses, the cranes, the baths, the stews of the foreshore, with the ruins of the Knights' castle at one end and the monastery and church of the Holy Ghost sterilising the worst of the carnal excesses, Nicholas observed, at the other.

On the slopes of the opposite bank stood a castle, to which the Court was shortly shifting, they said, from Lancisia. Anselm Adorne might already be here, with his letters of credence, which was why the captain had lodged on the foreshore. The captain wished to spare Colà speech with Adorne, and Nicholas did not mind being spared. Benecke had not yet put into words his own plans for the summer, but was preparing the ground by making sure that Colà never went thirsty. Nicholas, who understood his dilemma, fully appreciated his sudden good fortune, but still got drunk only at night.

So that his movements would be known to someone, he had sent his usual letter, which Mistress Clémence would receive in three weeks or perhaps longer. He had also sent a note to the Patriarch. It was amusing, in its way, that the only two people who were not in the slightest degree repelled by his treachery were his priest and his notary. Although he couldn't even say that, strictly speaking. The Patriarch, although unremittingly predatory, was not in fact his personal priest and Julius, although still serving the Bank, could not now be viewed as his lawyer. He had no staff. He had no one. He was free.

Nicholas wondered if it were true that Anna had confirmed her part-ownership of the *Fleury*. If it was, she was welcome. He could hardly claim it. His share belonged to the Bank. He dreamed that night of Anna, as he often did; and lay awake for a time after that, wondering where she was, and whether she was tired of being married to Julius. But however disappointing Julius in action might be, he was rewarding to look at. They made a magnificent pair, as once he and Gelis had done. But nothing lasted for ever. He reached for the flask, always there, and emptied it thoughtfully.

It was Robin who pointed out that Adorne ought to be told, when Benecke's daughter arrived with the news they were waiting for. Kathi admired her new husband's character, but sometimes regretted his lack of low cunning.

Now they knew where Paúel Benecke was, they could have slipped off without telling anyone. The house was frequently empty. The Patriarch shuttled between Royal Prussia and Royal Poland at will, and might stay with bishops, courtiers or his fellow Franciscans for several days at a time, if they happened to keep a good table. Periodically, too, her uncle found himself carried off to endure an unwanted few days of hunting, fishing, and feasting in the country homes of the Danzig élite, while negotiations ground to a halt. Everything that a Danziger did for his King was rewarded with land: villages and lakes, fishing pools and forests and ferries were showered upon him. A good German merchant in Danzig might own whole streets of houses and gardens, granaries and baths, lucrative facilities on the wharves. They were rich, and enjoyed being hospitable. With Adorne away, pale with frustration, there would have been plenty of time to escape from the city and make for this mysterious spot towards which (Elzbiete would have them believe) her father and his unsuspecting friend Colà were solemnly engaged in propelling a raft.

At first, of course, Adorne had forbidden them sharply to go. Kathi had allowed Robin to plead his own case, and had been taken aback at how well he did it. Her uncle himself could not move; the merchants here had him at their mercy until he obtained some agreement. But Kathi had made friends with Paúel Benecke's daughter. And Paúel Benecke, in a way, held the key to the dispute over the *San Matteo*. To see him might be advantageous.

'I don't understand,' Adorne had said. 'You expect Benecke to admit to acting outside the law?'

'Not in public,' Robin had said. 'But he might just drop us a hint, if the Danzigers' case is less than perfect.'

'Why should he?' Adorne had said.

'He's reasonably safe. He was an employee of the syndicate, and they'll protect him. His daughter says he wants rid of us all so that he can go into business with Nicholas.'

'And his daughter is helping him?'

Robin had cleared his throat. 'We aren't sure what part his daughter is playing. Or his wife, for that matter. But it seems worth the risk, sir.'

She would never have expected Adorne to agree, but he did. She thought he did it for Robin. It did not occur to her that he might have done it for her. She hadn't supported this scheme to find Nicholas.

Soon after that, she found herself riding south, with Robin and Elzbiete Benecke and a very small escort, some of them drunk. Kathi turned up her eyes, and Robin grinned, for he was happy as well.

THE TEUTONIC KNIGHTS' CASTLE of Mewe was one of their chain of forts perched on the Vistula, each within signal-fire range of two others. In Mewe, as elsewhere, the domination of the Order had recently come to a gratifying end but, unlike elsewhere, the square, red-brick castle had not been razed or much tampered with. The private privy cubicles with their neat *toleta* planks had all crumbled, but the stables and internal courtyard were useful for horses and wagons, and the tower and two of the wings were used to store grain. The best chambers had been commandeered by the officers of the castle's small, perpendicular township, who were also petty landowners and members, some of them, of the Confrérie of St George.

Elzbiete had avoided such properties on the way south, which was why they had bypassed Rudolf Veldstete's fine farm and made the forty-mile ride in one day. Although strenuous, it was not a penance in May. For once, the weather was dry. To begin with, they had the pleasant company of the Mottlau and the Radunia, so cleverly engineered by the Knights, who had been good for one or two things, Kathi sometimes thought, especially when she considered latrines. It was not until after their circumvention of Dirschau that Kathi saw the mother river itself: the mighty Vistula, broad as a lake, with a dim line of trees and white sand on the far bank. Then she noticed the swaying flats and glossy swirls of its currents, dredging their own fickle channels. Hence the need to sail in the spring, when the river was brimming and swift from the Carpathian rains, and before the low waters of June and July. Hence you sailed, even though last autumn the rains had not come, and seagulls stalked on the water, and men sat and fished from the sandbanks, which rose all around them like opening graves.

For all the fortune of Poland flowed north on the river: the slithering grain and the unwieldy timber; the long tulip-barrels with their wax and their dull lumps of ore; the glittering hunks of sheared pitch; the faggots of gnarled iron bars and the bundles of stinking blond cable. A challenge, to vigorous men. A challenge to headstrong, irresponsible men like Paúel and Nicholas.

The travellers from Danzig arrived at the high ridge of Mewe just before dusk, when the rafts were already coming in on the broad shining curve of the river, small in the distance as woodlice, lumbering the water below like great turtles. Elzbiete was impatient to move, but Robin and Kathi stopped in silence to watch as the sun sank and the lights began to prick and ripple below, and the water brought them the thin, fluctuating clamour of voices: greetings, laughter, curses, the barking of excited dogs and even the screaming of children, for half the populace of Mewe was making its way down to the strand. The other half was up at the castle, preparing the wagons of grain or setting up the trestles within for the paperwork. Obeying Elzbiete at last, Adorne's niece and her husband rode downhill past the church and the market to the handsome house where she had promised them a night's lodging.

The woman who was called by her servant to greet them was handsome, too, and extremely hospitable, as could be judged from the laughter within, and the smell of ale, and the clinking of tankards. She and Elzbiete kissed. Robin said, 'Excuse me, but this is . . . ?'

'A tavern,' said the woman in German, smiling at Elzbiete and then returning the smile, with appreciation, to Robin himself. The German was accented with Polish. 'You don't object? Of course, I do not offer bed-space, except when Paúeli's friends want to set down their mattresses. Have you seen him? Is he here yet? And Colà?'

'Ah! You have had your eye on Colà. I heard,' said Elzbiete prosaically. 'And was Colà fortunate, Gerta?'

'Not with me, although your father was most generous, I believe, all through the winter. He likes to share with his friends.' She turned, and laid her arm round Kathi's thin shoulders. 'But you are new-married, I'm told, and are not interested in such talk, with this young Adonis to sweeten your pillow. Shall I show you your chamber? Take off those cumbersome clothes. I shall send you a tub. Rest a while. And when you are ready, you will join us at table. We had a pig killed just last week.'

Upstairs, they were shown to their chamber. An elderly woman, winking broadly, dragged in an immense splashing tub, and left after lighting their candles. There were no visible towels. Kathi sank in a chair, her arms dangling. Robin, his head in his hands, gave way to a pent-up explosion of laughter. 'She must be Benecke's mistress! Does his daughter know all of them?'

'It depends how many there are. I don't know about conjugating but he certainly didn't learn how to decline. Oh, *Nicholas*!' she said to the air.

Robin also had sobered. 'I know. Kathi . . . I can't imagine how it will be, but I think I'd like to see him before you do.' He looked at her in the fond, earnest way that so disarmed her. 'You bathe, if you want to, and rest. I'd like to go down to the rafts now, before anything.'

'Before *anything*? No, it was a joke. Despite Gerta's opinion, forty miles on a horse doesn't sweeten your pillow.' She paused, frowning at the comatose tub. 'You think Nicholas is coming to this house? He may not.'

'Yes, he will,' Robin said. 'Not because of the woman, but because he would think this is the last place Adorne's party might come. And Benecke will bring him here, anyway. He wants us to meet.'

'He wants us to collide,' Kathi said. 'He wants us to behave so repellently that Nicholas will never go home. Robin? Don't go.'

'Why not?' said Robin, approaching. He added, helpfully, 'I'll undo your laces.'

'No! Don't touch me!' said Kathi.

She saw him jump, fear and concern darkening his eyes. Then he drew a sighing breath, as he heard what had caused her to say it. First Gerta's voice approaching the door, with its half-German accent. Then two men's voices in true staccato Polish, fierce as the rattle of kettledrums.

One of them belonged to Paúel Benecke. 'So there's your damned room, but you have to pay for it, *towarzysz*. If you can't, it's the rafthouse, or Gerta. And Gerta is softer.' The door opened.

A man walked in whistling, and stopped. It was Nicholas.

He was six months older, that was all. He had fled in November, with a physical wound which must have hampered his travelling, and had since spent a violent winter, in which everything had been neglected but sport. His hair, thick as copra, was uncut, and his fingernails black. Like Benecke, he was unshaven, half his face furzed with dull yellow. One could understand all of that, on a raft. He had not, certainly, pined: anyone interested in anatomy could admire, if they wished, the structurally perfect interleaved muscles of his bare arms, his chest and his abdomen within the sleeveless waistcoat, the *delia*, that was all he wore with his leggings. And all the lines on his face were still laughter-lines: below and outside his large, winsome eyes; between nostril and nose; the ineffable dents in his cheeks. Even the lines on his brow were the marks of vivacity. The face of a man devoted to entertaining the world, and himself. The face of a retired clown, who had chosen one face now to live by, and who had cut himself off from his past. There were no scars on his hands.

He spoke at once, in hilarious German. 'My dears! Shall I go out and come in again when you're naked?' Paúel Benecke, also bearded, ducked past him and pranced towards Kathi.

'. . . the wrong room?' Gerta's voice could be heard saying, without much conviction.

'Oh no, the right room,' the new Nicholas replied in a clear voice. 'But nothing was happening. They wouldn't perform? Or couldn't perform? Or didn't want to get wet? How are you, Mistress Berecrofts? And the young Master?' He had settled propped by the door, in the manner less of a faun than a satyr.

'They're thirsty,' said Benecke. 'Gerta, wine for us all. Perhaps Colà would like you and Elzbiete to join us?'

'Another time,' the new Colà said. 'Ah, the Herod-Baba Elzbiete. Nightingales are not born from owls. She brought our devoted young couple from Danzig?'

'We asked her to bring us,' said Robin. He was standing.

'And are we not glad!' Benecke said. 'My little Kathi!' He bent and kissed her on the mouth, his sinewy hands on her shoulders. He smelt unwashed and looked raffish, as the new Nicholas did, but thin and tough as she remembered. She sustained it calmly, although Robin moved a shade nearer. Colà did not move at all. After all her difficulty, in the past, in accustoming herself to his first name, she had begun almost at once to see that this was a man also called Colà. He seemed to be studying Robin.

Robin spoke to him. 'We were hoping to talk to you alone.'

'Were you?' Colà-Nicholas said. He stepped aside, making way for a tray to come in, borne by the same grinning woman as before. She set down tankards and wine, and departed. Nicholas returned to the door, but not to close it. 'You won't get rid of Paúeli now. Enjoy it. Good night.'

Paúel Benecke turned, jug in hand. 'And where are you going?'

'Downstairs. I came to this place to eat.'

Paúel put the jug down. Kathi said, 'Why don't we all go downstairs and eat?' She no longer felt tired. She felt feverish.

Robin said, 'Would you mind that?' to the new Nicholas. He paused and then added, 'We don't want anything from you.'

'Of course you do. You are a messenger of divine admonition,' Colà-Nicholas said. 'And I am the Judas of the Paschal, with my light about to be snuffed in a sack. *Nie pozwalam,* my friends.'

'I wish to rule, and I will not let anyone pick my nose?' Kathi quoted.

He stopped, at least. He said, 'People try, on occasion. So this is merely a courtesy call? You are on your way to Tabriz, to persuade Uzum Hasan to fight his fellow Muslims in Christ's cause?'

'I thought we were on our way to eat,' Kathi said.

He lifted an impatient shoulder and turned, and she followed him down to the common room, with Robin and the pirate behind her. The room was warm and stinking and full of bibulous men, some of whom Benecke and Colà-Nicholas knew. They had spent the winter, after all, roving the countryside. Elzbiete had disappeared. Gerta set a board before them, and food, which Kathi found suddenly welcome. Fright had given her an appetite. Robin said, 'So tell us about bear-hunts.'

All the information about bear-hunts was in fact imparted by Paúel Benecke, with ample illustrations from recent misadventures. He followed with other stories, none of them flattering to his companion, and frequently mentioning women. Colà-Nicholas occasionally commented, and occasionally turned to contribute to quite different conversations taking place within earshot elsewhere. Robin kept his head, and sustained some part of the talk in his quiet way, but Kathi soon dropped out in order to watch, and to agonise, and to think. After a while Nicholas noticed it.

'Regretting you came?'

Robin said, 'She didn't want to come. It was my idea.'

'But you don't want anything. So why? Why is he here, Paúel?'

'He was anxious,' Benecke suggested. 'He thought I might have cut your throat, or you might cut your own. He was afraid you might murder Adorne, or upset his embassy —'

'You don't say!' the new Nicholas said. 'Whatever would make him think that?'

'— or start another business which would rival the old one. Or he might have wanted you to come back. Perhaps what you did has been forgiven. What did you do?'

So Benecke didn't know. It was what Kathi had been afraid of, that Benecke knew. She heard Colà-Nicholas swear at him casually, and then return his attention, without answering, to Robin. 'The man has a point. It occurred to me, when I saw you, that I might just come back. Poland is fit for no one but Poles and I've done everything really worth doing. I'd be better off going back to Scotland.'

She saw Robin grow white, and she put her hand on his arm. Heads turned; Nicholas had not spoken quietly. Now he glanced round and turned back to Paúel. 'Really,' he said. 'I'm tired of teaching you all. You can't build, you can't sail, you can't even make wheels go round as well as mice do. I'm going to go back and re-open my house. Take up the Bank again. Look for my snivelling little wife and her bastard . . . What were they called?'

Robin's colour had begun to come back. Kathi took her hand away, shaking her head. Benecke had got to his feet. So had a number of other men in the room. Colà said, 'Who's going to argue?'

The men were grinning. No one had taken him seriously. He had spoken out of pure malice, with all the authentic ring of those brutal remarks which Elzbiete had quoted. There seemed no topic now that was sacred. Now he had vilified everything — everything except, so far, the person he had mentioned even to her only once, and whose name was already blackened. But then, he had not had cause recently to speak of his parents.

Everyone had risen. The promised brawl had degenerated into good-humoured badinage, and the tavern's clients, their meal over, seemed inclined to wander out of doors, where the night was cool but not cold, and still dry. The sound of drumming pricked in the distance, and the wail of bagpipes, and the scratch of a fiddle. Benecke said, 'There's a party down by the rafts. Why not come? If it's to be Colà's last night, we should give him something to remember.'

Robin went off to bring her a cloak. Benecke retired to the yard. Kathi spoke fast to Nicholas. 'Jodi misses you, but he has Mistress Clémence and Dr Tobie, and he's well. We brought nothing from him, in case you thought we were taking advantage. We really didn't want anything. Just to see how you were.'

'And God has two wives,' he said. 'Why did you come? I know Robin's great bleeding heart, but you? Because you're still training him?'

'That is wicked,' she said.

'But true. Here he is, with your shawl and your slippers.'

They walked down to the beach, and she could not bring herself to speak to him on the way, because he was the only man there who was sober. She thought, then, that she had plumbed the worst of it.

Chapter 5

AT FIRST, she had Robin; and it was warm inside her cloak, sitting close to him, and they were able somehow to extract enjoyment from it all because they were both young, and had by now learned to partner each other through a great many exciting occasions, as well as imposing and tedious ones. Below the castle, the land that sloped down to the river was part watermeadow, part cobbled pathways which led to the jetties. The impromptu party was spread over the foreshore and dunes and had spilled, much of it, on to the vast swaying walkway formed by the rafts. The rafters themselves were mostly on shore or in the taverns, but the families of Mewe with their baskets and lanterns settled themselves shouting on the extraordinary craft, or made themselves seats on the bank, round the crazed red and blue light of the braziers, and got up and danced every time the musicians stopped drinking. Then, as they got tired, they sang.

Benecke had gone to check on his raft, accompanied by Nicholas. She did not want to discuss Nicholas. Especially she didn't wish to treat him as a subject of strategy. She had begun to say so to Robin, but had broken off while negotiating his name. Robin had said, 'Think of him, if you want to, as Colà. But call him Nicholas. He mustn't forget who he is.'

She hadn't answered. For that was the trouble. To the last red-hot wire of the armature, Nicholas knew who he was. All he had once tried to forget, he had now embraced. Not to assimilate, but as an infill of rubbish; a different form of insulation, that was all. And he didn't care, now, who else suffered.

The singing drew her mind from her thoughts, being discordant and cheerful and coarse. Robin began to join in. The water lapped the shore and suckled the rafts. Something splashed. A pair of children, scuffling with a stick, hit a ball into the dunes and she handed it back, rubbing sand from her eyes.

Tzukanion. A game played by horsemen, and children. A dangerous, elegant game played on a long, sandy shore by two riders in magnificent doublets, one in crimson velvet, the other in pleated black silk. The athlete, the acrobat: Julius the lawyer, and Nicholas de Fleury, the Chevalier Highmount. And then, the moon high over the estuary, they had made music: they had exchanged the wonder of fantasy for a wonder of a different kind; and Nicholas had been led by a master through the door he had now shut and locked. *He carries keys in his head.*

The same melodious voice spoke, here and now. 'Poor eager Willie and his Tenebrae service. Do you remember our first meeting, lady of Berecrofts? How old were you then, Robin? Five?'

'It was six years ago,' Robin said.

Nicholas laughed. Then he said, 'I've brought Herod-Baba to sit with you. Then Paúel wants to take Kathi off and seduce her. The raft is over there, at the end. I'll show her the way.'

'I'll take her,' said Robin. He rose, and so did she.

Kathi looked at him, and then up at Colà. She said, 'What does Paúel want?' Once, cold sheepskin pressing her cheek. Once, his hands in friendship, holding her safe.

He said, 'To winkle out of you the reason I'm here. To persuade you to leave me alone before something happens.'

'To me?' Kathi said.

'It's not impossible,' said the new Nicholas. 'But Paúeli generally prefers to take out his annoyance on men. So how is your uncle?'

'He didn't want us here either,' Robin said. 'As I've said, the whole thing was my idea. So let me tell him. We know you mustn't go back.'

'That's a challenging statement,' Nicholas said.

Kathi said, 'Don't start again. Robin, stay. Let's get this over.' And walked away from the firelight with Colà.

The noise receded. The river ran black and broad on her left, the bed of raft-lanterns flickering. On her right, the wind rustled the grasses and at the foot of the castle, loud as ducks, the frogs had begun their night's inflatable choir. 'Tenebrae,' Nicholas said.

She said, 'Is there nothing left that is bearable?'

'Debate it with Paúeli,' he said. 'While having in mind the handy phrase I just used. *Nie pozwalam.* Or a quick, simple *Nie*, if you're pressed.'

He sounded not just indifferent, but mocking. She rounded on him. He came, slightly surprised, to a halt. She said, 'And is there nothing at all, Nicholas, that you want to ask me? Nothing that matters about anyone else? Shall I give you a bulletin? Do you know that your wife has now taken your place? When you vacated the Bank, Gelis offered to help finance Gregorio in Venice, so that he could run the house as her partner. In Bruges, Diniz has done much the same. As well as managing the branch, he has bought it. It means that two parts of the Bank can survive.'

She was blocking his way. She could see him stir, but not his expression. He said, 'You see, you did want something from me. A tear, a shiver, a flush, a shade of distress, of remorse? Something to music, perhaps?'

She was tempted, but didn't pursue it. She said, 'A single question would have been a good sign.'

'About Gelis?' he said, walking round her. 'But, *aspettate e odiate,* Gelis always survives, as you've shown. A really good business brain. I should know, since I taught her.'

He had resumed walking on, and she followed. She said, 'She could have stayed with your rivals. She's left them.'

'*All* of them?' Nicholas said. 'Martin? Simon? Poor darling David? Perhaps I should introduce David to Buonaccorsi's friend Nerio? Or perhaps they are already acquainted, from Cyprus. Do you think Nerio could be my son or my daughter? No. Whatever his sex, he's too old.'

She knew Nerio. He was half Greek, and a year older than she was. She spoke shortly. 'He couldn't be your son. He's far too good-looking.'

'He had a good-looking mother. Did no one tell you I slept with Violante? Wife of Zeno of Venice. Nerio's her by-blow. Here's the raft. Paúel?'

She looked at Nicholas. A slow-swinging lamp in the dark lit his face. It was indifferent still, with a hint of impatience. Throughout, nevertheless, he had avoided her eyes. Now he called again, 'Paúeli? Here is your ex-virgin brother. Show her over the silos and bring her, *mulier intacta,* back to her husband. Farewell in Christ.' He waited to see Benecke hand her aboard, then moved away.

After two paces, he turned. 'Where's the watchman?'

'Drunk. I kicked him on shore. Colà, stay.'

'No.'

'I meant you to stay.'

The dialogue reached Kathi as she walked inboard over the raft. It was only thirty inches in depth. They had laid matting over the timbers. There was a neat hooded cabin in front, and a larger one for the crew nearer the back. She went into the smaller. Benecke's voice, by the shore, was still calling. 'I meant you to stay. Three of us. You know you . . . '

She couldn't hear the end, or the reply. She was not yet uneasy; merely weighing the advantages of opening these topics with two men instead of one. There was a pair of rolled mattresses and several boxes which doubled as seats; she sat on one of them. With the lamp lit, it was attractive enough, with a plank spread with platters of sweetmeats, and a flask of wine gently rolling from its hook. There was nothing she remembered as belonging to Nicholas. Benecke stooped and came in. 'He wouldn't stay. We'll have to drink all the Gascony by ourselves. So, tell me: what has happened since Iceland? Or would you rather hear the real story of the *San Matteo*'s capture?'

It was what her uncle needed to know. She postponed, while he told it, all the questions she longed to put for herself. The account took some time, because Benecke often diverged into this anecdote or that of a mildly scurrilous nature. Indeed the saga of the *San Matteo*'s fate became extraordinarily muddled, so that she frowned into her wine, trying to make sense of what she was hearing. The cabin had become very warm but, instead of removing the brazier, her host sat down beside her and, encircling her in a friendly way with his arms, unpinned her cloak to make her more comfortable. His fingers, which had a familiar griminess, then slipped further down to the laces of her bodice and set to untying them. The air on her skin began to feel cool. This, added to a hazy recollection of distressing Robin on this score quite recently, made her objection tender rather than vehement. 'All the same,' Kathi said, 'I don't think you should do that. It's too public.'

'But you like it,' said whoever it was. She was not even sure if it was the same person.

It was not something that Robin would say, although it was sometimes true. It was not true at the moment because, overwhelmed by the weariness of the day, she was going to disappoint him. It was why she had induced him, lovingly, to leave her the initiative. *Because you are still training him?* It had been cruel, that remark. 'Dear little Kathi,' someone said. 'You need a real man. Two real men.'

And then she seemed to be on the ground; and something was being done, as well as being said, that was utterly foreign to Robin. And now Katelijne, dame of Berecrofts, wrenched her head sideways and started to scream.

The weight on and beside her disappeared. The whole raft tilted, throwing her on her side, her arms clasped round her body. Footsteps thudded. The man or men whose leap aboard had shaken the raft began to run towards the hut where she lay, cannoning into the man or men who had just left her. She could hear herself shrieking. As she struggled to rise, a whole group crashed backwards into the cabin beside her, all of them shouting or squealing. More shouting came distantly from the shore, and the sound of many feet running. The lamp rocked above her and someone, throwing himself to her side, began to lift her into his arms, talking in a quick, murmuring monotone all the time. The hands embracing her shoulders alarmed her, and she struggled. Then she saw that the man carrying her, his tears falling, was Robin. A voice said, 'No, *not* that way, my dear one. And *do* keep her face covered.'

The speaker was Nicholas. The lamp, swinging, glared upon his impatient face and the grinning mask of Paúel Benecke. Both were dishevelled. About them was a struggling mass which, confusingly, included some complaining women. Two she didn't know. One was Gerta. She felt Robin stop, with a gasp. Then he turned aside, furling her cloak high about her, and holding her close carried her away from the blaze of the lamplight. Except that, as she now noticed, the blaze did not come from the lamp but from the brazier, overturned in the stampede, and now casting its translucent red embers across a deck composed of three thousand square feet of prime timber. Then the cabin caught fire, and the real screaming began, as men and women fled from it. She looked up at Robin, but he seemed not to care.

BY THE LIGHT of the blaze, Robin found a place in the dunes to conceal her. She was still as limp as a child. Sometimes a person woke with the mind of a child, after a shock such as that. He was not weeping now.

He wanted to take her away, but the shore was lit like a pageant, and swarming with Benecke's crewmen, thundering down to rescue their vessel. On the raft, the cabin burned like an oriflamme, and all the flooring beyond was alight: the fiery lines of the logs were regular as the ridges of spring in-field planting.

Berecrofts, and all his love, and his hopes.

He wrapped her in her own cloak, and his own, and smoothed her brown hair back from her face. Her eyes were huge in the shadow. He watched the fire, holding her. Against the wall of light, men were fighting. No, men were swinging buckets over the side and emptying them into the fires. The water spewed out gleaming like fish, ruddy with the light of the fire, the puny, man-crafted fire. Kathi moaned and he hushed her as he watched. Then he saw that he had not been mistaken. On board, and now on shore, regardless of the fire and all that was happening, two men *were* fighting. And the two were Paúel Benecke and Nicholas.

He couldn't ignore it; he couldn't pretend it hadn't happened: he had to go. He wrapped the cloaks again tightly about her, murmuring in distraction, and got to his feet. 'I shan't be long. I'll come back. I'll come back directly.' Then he ran, his hand on his scabbard.

At first, the heat drove him back. They had cut loose the neighbouring rafts and, commandeering small boats, were flooding the big craft with water. The centre was still alight, radiating heat on to the foreshore. Beyond its reach, the way was packed with spectators. Some were shouting advice to the fire-fighters. Others, turning away, formed part of a shifting audience cheering a different cause. Colà and Benecke, displaying their short tempers and their prowess yet again, in the way that turned a normal man cold.

No one attempted to stop them. The raft might be on fire, their future livelihood might depend on both that and the life of the captain, but a fight was a fight, and must be permitted to reach its conclusion. Someone exclaimed, 'All that over a woman! Would you believe it?' And someone else cried, 'But what else did these two ever fight about?' Robin heard them. They all but mentioned his wife, whose honour was his to defend. He threw himself forward.

Before he had taken two steps, rough arms pinioned him hard, and an admonishing voice was addressing him. 'Hold there! Don't you see there's a fight?' Beside him was the woman called Gerta, shaking her head in mock despair at his folly, even as her eyes darted back to the fighters. He saw the anxiety in them. He ceased struggling.

She had cause to be anxious. He had seen brawls. He had seen professional fights, and men wrestling for wagers. He had never seen deliberate, all-out fighting of the kind he was witnessing, in its last stages, now.

Now, their faces swollen, suffused, streaked with blood, two men fought toe to toe in short bursts of energy, kneeing, pummelling, elbowing, crashing to the ground and rolling over and over, before they scrambled upright again. Once at least they had plunged into the water, although the pulsing heat had already half dried their hair.

You could see, on their bare upper bodies, the other tracks of the battle. There were the marks of impromptu weapons: the gouge of a marline-spike; the scarlet weals raised by a lash. They both bore burns in glistening patches, and the pitted imprints of scorching-hot grain. Both were limping; both were breathing explosively, grunting when the blows fell. The blows fell like the quarry mallets at Fontainebleau. *Pif, paf, pouf:* hard rock; softer; here it is crumbling. There was something wrong with Benecke's arm. He saved it by kicking Nicholas, which brought them both down again, with Nicholas this time at a disadvantage. Robin saw his teeth close on his lip. Then he looked up, and caught sight of Robin.

No message passed. Nicholas drew a shuddering breath and, having filled his lungs, held it. The movements he then embarked upon were quite few, and to achieve them required an extraordinary concentration, it was evident, of his will and his strength. Robin did not see what they were. There was a sudden jerk. Benecke screamed. Nicholas broke free and, rising, lifted his hand. For a moment he held it quite still. Then he chopped it down on Benecke's neck.

Paúel Benecke slumped, his body collapsed, his head rolled to one side. Nicholas stood where he was, one hand holding the other. The privateer did not move. After the first moment of shock, the spectators began to surge forward. Robin broke free and went with them, pulling his knife from its sheath. He passed Nicholas and stood over Benecke with the rest, looking down. Nicholas said, to no one in particular, 'So finish him off.'

Someone said, 'He's still breathing! Tough little bastard.' Nicholas walked away, handing himself off other men's necks and shoulders until he was clear of the crowd. He didn't look round.

Before Nicholas spoke, Robin had been going to do just what he suggested: puncture the throat of an unconscious person; kill the prey another man had delivered. Now, slowly, he put his dagger away. His eyes ached, and his body. He turned. Beneath white clouds of steam, the last of the fires crackled and hissed on the raft, and water flowed in and out, where the coaming had gone. The smell of toasted rye and burnt wood was chokingly strong: at least the bastard would pay through his purse. The bastard. The bastards.

Kathi was half-sleeping still on the bank, but Elzbiete was now kneeling beside her. Elzbiete said, 'She was raped. Are they dead?'

'I haven't been raped,' Kathi said, with excessive gentility. 'I don't know who it was.'

'They drugged her wine,' Elzbiete explained. 'He has done it before. And have you killed your friend, Colà?'

She was addressing Nicholas, who had appeared from the darkness and was standing looking down, as he had looked at the felled body of Benecke. He didn't answer. It was not obvious how he had found them, unless by some primitive instinct: he looked detached from mankind.

Elzbiete spoke again, with greater distinctness. 'Colà? Is my father dead?'

He heard that. 'He ought to be. I think not.'

'Now you have to fight me,' Robin remarked. 'Or explain exactly what happened.'

Kathi frowned. She said, 'Nicholas didn't touch me. He wouldn't.'

'Well?' said Robin. He, too, had to look up to Nicholas. His voice was steady; the tears of shock gone.

Nicholas said, 'Are you asking me to deny it? You will have a long wait.'

Elzbiete said, 'Tell him, Colà. Tell them both. Katarzynka, it was Colà who sent for your husband, and for Gerta and her friends. It did not save you, but no one can ever be sure you were there.'

'And the fight?' Robin said.

'Over Gerta, they claimed. Men would remember it. She was flattered.'

Gerta had not been flattered, Robin thought. She had watched the two men as he had, and had expected one of them, as he had, to die. The death of Paúel; the death of a witness.

Kathi sat, looking up at him as he looked down on her. Her face was clearing: she had begun to understand what was happening. She was going to be all right. There was a trampling behind: the captain's men were taking Paúel off, no doubt to be tended at Gerta's. Kathi spoke to Elzbiete. 'Go with your father.'

Elzbiete looked at her in surprise, then pressed her fingertips, in welcome, on her shoulder. 'He deserved it,' she said. 'You could come back to the house. I know my *tatko*. He will respect Colà, although of course he will hate him as well.' She eyed Nicholas. 'You should sit. I shall go and see that Gerta knows what is needed. The raft will take time to repair.'

Robin said, 'We are not staying under the same roof as Paúel Benecke.'

'Then I shall find you somewhere else,' Elzbiete said. She walked away, and Robin followed and stopped her. Kathi could hear his voice, asking careful questions: about Gerta, no doubt; about Nicholas.

Nicholas was still here. Kathi shivered. Above her, Nicholas suddenly swayed and instinctively, Kathi shifted aside, until she saw he had regained his balance. His gaze, caught by the gesture, fell to rest on her sheltering hands, then travelled reflectively upwards. His eyes, open and clear on her face, were for a moment those of someone she recognised: the creator of marvels, the rare singer, the trusted friend. The man for whom — *Emmanuel!* — the silver trumpets had spoken in Holyrood.

He said, 'Kathi?'

She let herself gently back, the better to see him. She knew what he had guessed. 'Yes. I think so,' she said. She lay, watching him examine and nurture the thought, slowly, tranquilly, as if tending a brightening spark. Her cramped heart stretched; her burdens dissolved into gossamer. She said, presently, 'No one else knows. I want to be sure.'

He did not speak, but rested his eyes on her face, with a kind of abstracted contentment. Robin and Elzbiete were talking still. Kathi said, 'Take my hand and let yourself down. I won't let you fall.'

He blinked, rousing. 'Now that,' Nicholas said, 'is altogether too big a claim.' He took the hand she extended, but paused. 'No. I should go.'

She said, 'You must speak to Robin.'

'But not tonight,' Nicholas said. 'You are not supposed to be here.' He studied their hands, then gently rolled her fingertips in his own and returned them to her, looking into her face. He said, 'I should have killed Benecke.'

She said, 'No. He didn't succeed. It was as much your fault as his.'

He was silent.

She said, 'You let him think he understood you.'

'He does,' Nicholas said.

'But you still wanted to kill him.'

'It's how we live,' Nicholas said. Then he said, 'It's not how Robin lives. He would have died.'

She had long since realised that. She didn't answer. Her thoughts, beginning with Robin, travelled elsewhere.

Nicholas gathered himself, preparing to leave. She did not expect any more words; but his mind, his echoing mind, had followed the same path as hers.

'I am so glad,' he said.

Chapter 6

'YOU MUST SPEAK to Robin,' she had said. But of course, what she meant was the opposite.

That night, she could do nothing more. The opiate clung to her eyelids. By the time Robin carried her to her bed, she was too sleepy to ask where she was going, and had no recollection of arriving in the secluded house Elzbiete had found for them. When she woke in the morning, she was nestled within the hollow of Robin's bare shoulder and he was lying awake, his eyes heavy.

Her deep affection for him overwhelmed her. She said, 'I've made you numb from top to toe. I'm so sorry.'

His head turned quickly, and stopped. He said, 'I wish you had. I've been such a fool.'

'I don't think so,' she said. 'May I say something lofty and priggish? I was proud of you yesterday.'

He closed his arm round her a little, resting his chin on her head. 'I don't think Nicholas was.'

'Nicholas makes mistakes,' she said. 'He didn't know about the drugged wine. He didn't expect Benecke to misbehave, and if he did, he expected me to call much more quickly. And then he had no way of warning you that he was about to turn the whole thing into an orgiastic inferno.' *He was on board all the time,* Elzbiete had said. *He stopped Benecke. He tipped over the brazier.*

'And he fought. It was my place to fight,' Robin said.

'But that would have given me away. I expect you to fight for me every other time,' Kathi said. 'I shall insist on it.'

His eyes closed, on a smile. She knew that was not all he had been thinking of. Like herself, like Nicholas in his self-imposed limbo, he must be grappling with the implications of the wretched thing that had happened, and the best means to deal with it. It came to her again that, if Paúel Benecke was not dead, it was because Nicholas had seen what it would lead to. Or that he did not really dislike him. Or that he had other plans, which he did not intend to give up.

THAT MORNING IN MEWE, the Patriarch of Antioch rode in early from his overnight lodging and made his way up to the castle, from which he looked down on an empty foreshore tenanted by one blackened raft, pulled up out of the river and surrounded by the bent backs and flailing arms of a carpenter's work-team. The officials of Mewe made light of it. 'A carousal that got out of hand. Paúeli was always a devil for ladies.'

'Paúeli? Paúel Benecke?' The Patriarch, accepting a sausage, set it up for his thumb and his knife.

'And the big fellow, Colà. You won't see either of them in the chapel this morning. Came to blows over Benecke's women and beat each other to pulp.'

'What women?' said Father Ludovico, posting a roundel of pig-meat. The landowners of Mewe were always flattered when the Patriarch patronised them on his regular visits to Poland and his constant travels to and from Court. Nevertheless, there were times when they felt he might have attended, at least, to his tonsure; washed the frenzied grey and black hair that covered his neck, his powerful torso, his fingers; and repaired the snagged gown and the disgusting sandals. The groom he travelled with was as unkempt as himself. Only the poor Franciscan monk who did his bidding was neat as a good secretary should be.

The councillor of Mewe said, 'Oh, the usual. Gerta, Benecke's mistress, and her friends. You'd think he'd be careful, with his own daughter staying in Mewe with the Burgundians. But Elzbiete knows her father just as well as the rest of us.'

'I suppose she does,' the Patriarch said. He laid down the sausage and picked up a tankard of water. 'But Anselm Adorne must have a strange idea of the customs and culture of Mewe. Is he still here?'

'He never came. He's still in Danzig. It was his niece and her husband who came. They knew Colà and Paúeli in Iceland. It's my belief,' the councillor said, 'that this Adorne of yours sent them to find out what they could about the *San Matteo*.'

'That sounds likely,' said Father Ludovico da Bologna. 'But he's not my Adorne, and you'd better not suggest that he is, if you want to be welcome in Bruges.'

He belched, and tapped himself ruminatively with his fist. 'So Katelijne and her husband are here, and a few other people who, by the sound of it, could do with some spiritual counselling. I can see a hard day's work ahead for a conscientious man like myself. Is that a hare roasting? Why don't you kneel, and I'll say a few Parcias till it's cooked, and then an Adoremus, perhaps, just to crisp it.'

. . .

NICHOLAS HAD SPENT the same night in Gerta's tavern, sharing Paúel's sleeping quarters, and jointly submitting, with noisy alarm, to the brusque ministrations of Gerta herself, the ostensible cause of the battle.

It was the talk of hilarious Mewe, and the first thing Robin heard when, leaving Kathi that morning, he set out to find Nicholas. Restored now to his own, sober senses, Robin understood why it was necessary to keep up the fiction. He could not, himself, have stayed in the same building as Benecke.

Gerta greeted him in her own room. 'You've come to find out how they are? Here is Colà, come to see me, and on his own feet, so that you may know he's not dying. And Paúeli? Well, he is a very bad patient, who thinks, like Colà, that the best solace for everything is strong drink. You come and see Paúeli when you have finished with Nicholas.'

Robin said, 'I have to thank you.' He did not look at Nicholas, who had risen.

Gerta turned at the door. Her eyes were not smiling. She said, 'You would thank me best by taking that man away. He is bad luck.' The door closed behind her.

Nicholas, in the full picturesque panoply of blackened abrasions, purple bruising and misshapen swellings, certainly brought bad luck to mind. He had saved Kathi, but he had also endangered her. He had attacked Benecke to conceal what had happened, taking the onus from Robin. But he had also meant to kill Paúel for himself. Mixed with the breath-taking generosity, as ever, was the madness of vengeance, sometimes cold, sometimes hot, which had brought Nicholas where he was. And had brought Robin here, to Poland, where he had exacerbated the ill, not assuaged it.

Nicholas said, 'It was a good idea to come. This needn't take long. How is Kathi?'

'She slept well. She understands everything, and so do I. I am here, sir, to apologise,' Robin said. 'I was . . . upset. I would trust you with my life, and with Kathi's.'

'That might be misguided. But if I ever harm you, it will be solely through ineptitude, like last night's. I am sorry. And of course, it will not happen again, for we shall not meet again. When are you going back to Danzig?'

'We shall not meet . . . ?'

'Today, I should suggest. And what will you tell Adorne about Kathi?'

Robin was silent. Then he said, 'If I tell him the truth, he will report Benecke, and they will have to punish him.'

'I have punished him. They will hang him,' the other man said.

'They can do no less. Attempted rape of the niece of an accredited envoy? He will be condemned after a trial, naming Kathi. The merchants will then discover, to their amazement, that the pirate Benecke was wholly unauthorised when he took the *San Matteo*; that the kingdom cannot be blamed nor, of course, the cargo recovered, since he disposed of it all. Alive, Paúel Benecke is valuable. Dead, he can be safely repudiated. And Kathi suffers.'

'Adorne is her uncle,' Robin said. 'Surely her family ought to know.'

'He is His Excellency Anselm Adorne, Baron Cortachy. He must act, if you tell him. What would men think of him later, if they found that he knew and did nothing?'

Again, Robin was silent. Nicholas, propped in a chair, did not move. Robin walked to a stool and sat down. He said, 'Word might get out anyway.'

'How? The women know, but they don't want to imperil their Paúeli. And sweet Paúeli himself . . .' Nicholas paused, and then said, 'Wait here.'

He got up and walked out as if everything hurt. It probably did. Robin waited. When the door burst open, he jumped to his feet, his hand at his belt. Then he saw that Nicholas stood in the passage, gripping a doubled-up man by his shirt-neck. Then he pitched the man forward and came in, slamming the door.

Paúel Benecke hit the floor with his strapped arm and pushed himself up with the other, screaming a string of obscenities at Nicholas. His head was held to one side, and his neck was padded with linen and clay. He was drunk. Nicholas said, 'Penitential prostration. So. Go on. Benecke, look at that man.'

'I'll kill you,' Benecke said. He sat, where he was, on the floor.

'You won't get the chance. Look at that man. You tried to rape that man's wife. He's going back, now, to tell the Danziger Council. Apologise to him, or you're dead.'

'You apologise to him.'

'I beg your pardon?' Nicholas said.

There was a knife in Benecke's hand. Before Nicholas could touch him, the captain had thrown it. Nicholas dodged, and then they were at grips with one another again, crippled though they were. For the first time, Robin realised that Nicholas, too, had been steadily drinking. Robin said in a low voice, 'Stop it. Nicholas, stop it.'

'Do you apologise?' Nicholas said.

'Yes!' Benecke howled.

'You never touched Katelijne Sersanders, and you will deny it if anyone says that you did?'

'Yes!'

'And you understand that you will do everything in your power to make this man happy, and Anselm Adorne happy, and help the embassy obtain what it wants, or he'll tell the world what you've done, and you'll hang?'

'I understand,' said Paúel Benecke sullenly. Blood had burst through one of his bandages.

Nicholas looked up at Robin. 'Well?'

Robin said baldly, 'I am satisfied. We don't tell Adorne, or anyone else.' He paused. 'What are you going to do?'

'What we were doing,' Nicholas said. He had reseated himself, with difficulty, in the chair with a back. 'Taking the raft down to Danzig.' Benecke, lurching to his feet, had gone to pour himself wine.

Robin said, 'Together?' Then after a moment, 'Then we shall meet.'

'I don't think so,' Nicholas said. 'You're going to collect the rest of your embassy and get on your travels at last. To Thorn and the Black Sea and Tabriz in Persia. You *are* going on?'

'I don't know. Perhaps. But Adorne couldn't leave. They wouldn't let him move until they'd reached an agreement.'

'They'll let him move now,' Nicholas said. 'You'll be out of Danzig before I get there.'

'And after that?' Robin said. He felt cold.

'After that, you go south, and we stay and start our new season's sailing,' Benecke said. He turned round, his black bristles dripping, waving the flask. When Nicholas nodded, he filled up two tumblers.

'Together?'

'Why not together?' said Benecke, astonished. 'Don't you think we get on well together? He can't quite kill me; and so far, I can't quite kill him. You don't need a Bank to be rich.'

'I thought you needed a war,' Robin said. 'You're talking of going to sea?'

'I'm talking,' Benecke said, 'of running the first truly international force of seagoing mercenaries. My seamanship, Colà's fancy for numbers. Any job, provided the money is right.'

Robin was silent.

'What's wrong?' Nicholas said. 'Have you some other suggestion?'
'No,' said Robin at last. 'It is none of my business.'

TELLING THE STORY later to Kathi, Robin held nothing back, and she listened, gazing out of the window. She was already packed to return. At the end, she said, 'I thought he would join us. I was sure he would leave Benecke.'

'No. When Nicholas didn't kill him, he tied himself to him. There is no future in it. They will die from drinking, if nothing else.'

She knew as much, from Elzbiete, who had come to see her that morning to do what Gerta had done: to ask her to persuade Colà to leave Paúel and go home. But she could not do that. She was as powerless there as any of Benecke's forceful circle of women.

'We thought,' Elzbiete had said, 'that perhaps you and Colà were lovers, and he would give up his new plans to follow you. Or that my father's bad conduct would drive you all away. But . . .'

At which point Kathi had interrupted. 'Elzbiete? Who prepared the drugged wine?'

And the girl had flushed before saying, 'Gerta has a stock of these things. Also a drug which makes a man ill if he drinks. I would give you some if you took Colà away. We wish to be friends with you.'

'I'm sure,' Kathi had said drily. 'But we can't take him back home, and he doesn't want to go to Tabriz. So how do you persuade him?'

'A woman?' Elzbiete had said.

Kathi looked at her, and thought of Gelis van Borselen, and wondered how to deal with this. In the end, she said, 'He has a beautiful wife. He can't go back to her, but I think he finds it hard to forget her. Until he does, no one else would have much chance.'

'But he does not need to marry. A mistress would serve. What kind of girl does he like, Katarzynka?' Elzbiete had asked.

Kathi looked at her a trifle wildly. 'How would I know?' The ideal woman for Nicholas? She considered the question, intrigued. Someone beautiful, which poor Elzbiete was not. Someone clever, amusing, experienced. Not a virgin. Not an older woman again. Dark, perhaps, since Gelis was fair. Childless, or without close attachments to children: he would not want to displace Jodi. Someone he could trust, and feel safe with, and who would put up with his mistakes and stand up, too, for herself. Not the daughter of a hard-drinking wild Polish captain.

Kathi said, 'Elzbiete, I have no idea what he likes, except that it probably doesn't exist. He's had his share of the world's beauties. He was married once to a courtesan. It would take a lot to surprise him, or hold him.'

Elzbiete had thought. Then she had said, 'I do not know who would suit. But you must find him one, as my mother went out and found Gerta. A sick man can be healed by a woman.'

She had a high opinion of Elzbiete's good sense, but had not mentioned this conversation to Robin. She did, however seek his advice.

'Do you know that Nicholas wanted some information from Benecke, which Benecke was holding back?'

'Was he? What about? I shouldn't think he'll get it now,' Robin said. 'They may be partners in business, but Benecke isn't going to do Nicholas any favours at the moment.'

'That's what Elzbiete said,' Kathi said.

'Elzbiete? She knows what it was?'

'Yes. She didn't tell me this time. But I think she would, if I pressed her.'

'And what good would that do?' Robin said.

'I don't know. But failing a quite exceptional Gerta, I would snatch at absolutely anything,' Kathi said, 'to keep society safe from a second Tough Seabird. A pair of leg-irons. A contagious disease. An attack of religion.'

Robin stared at her. He said, 'We might just manage that. I was going to tell you. Father Ludovico's in Mewe.'

'So there you are,' said Father Ludovico, skipping over the wet-beds and sitting down on an outcrop of stone. He peered round at the man already sitting there. 'You're lucky to have a set of strong teeth. Benecke's lost so many now, he'll have to resort to a liquid diet, I shouldn't wonder.'

'You've seen him,' Nicholas said.

'He tells me you're going to be pirates together. Your early promise fulfilled. Why did you write to me, then?'

Below them, the renovated raft, somewhat smaller, was in process of being refloated. To the right, dim in the distance, more rafts could be seen coming in. Paúel Benecke was going to be far behind in the race. Nicholas said, 'I'd forgotten that we didn't get on.'

The Patriarch grunted. 'I haven't time for this rubbish. You thought you might come to Tabriz, then you found the two children were coming as well. That's quite a nice little marriage. You're jealous?'

'Naturally,' Nicholas said.

'Well, thank God that's a lie. What else are you lying about? Benecke said you were speaking of returning to Scotland.'

'That was different. That was a joke,' Nicholas said.

'I imagine it was,' said Father Ludovico.

Nicholas looked at him. The Patriarch said, 'Yes, I know why you had to get out of your business. I made the Berecrofts boy tell me. As sins go, it marks a significant peak. But then, I never thought you would be satisfied by a little cheating, or a few simple betrayals and murders. It took an original imagination, I must say, to use your Bank to create such pure misery. Holy Father of Pity, sit down. I swore not to tell. Can't you take the word of a priest?'

Nicholas remained standing. He said, 'Of a priest? You're a timber merchant's son from Bologna who became a priest by a fluke.'

'And who are you then?' the Patriarch said. 'An apprentice of eighteen, who never grew up. You wrote me a note, an idle letter from an idle man choosing a pastime. What about, you thought, a journey to the Shah

Uzum Hasan in Tabriz, some good company, some interesting fighting, and perhaps a permanent post with some money in it? And along with it, some holy grease to slide you in past St Peter?'

'You have it exactly,' said Nicholas.

'And then you thought, No, it would be more amusing to sit in a boat and play robbers. Which is just as well. I have nothing to offer you. *Whoever is unsupported by the Mystery of Love shall not achieve the grace of salvation. Whoever shall cast love aside shall lose everything*. Track down these quotations one day. God doesn't sell forgiveness, neither do I. I don't care what you've done, and I wouldn't waste my time trying to save you. I want you as much as I want the soles of my sandals: they get me where I want to go, and I'll throw them away when they're done. I don't suppose that is water?'

'No, it isn't,' said Nicholas. 'But it's empty.' He threw the flask aside and sat down.

'You did that last time,' the priest said. 'When your first wife died, and I got you out of Bologna. I nearly made you a man.'

'That wasn't you, it was Violante of Naxos. You got me out of it,' Nicholas said, 'and I ended in Cyprus.'

'And you regret it? The time after that, you agreed to fight for Uzum Hasan against Turkey. Then you reneged. So would you have come if Adorne's party weren't going?'

'No,' said Nicholas. He said it too quickly.

'Brain getting sluggish?' said the Patriarch. 'No, I wouldn't stop Adorne going. I don't need to. And yes, you'd have been more use than Adorne. You know Muslims. I could do with your opinion of the trading future of Caffa. And Uzum trusts you. You don't have an army any more — Oh, I know about Astorre and the rest. But you know a lot about guns, and about war. And you wouldn't have got wet, in Persia.'

'What do you mean, *you don't need to*?' said Nicholas.

'Why are you asking? You're not going. Benecke won't get much for his timber, will he?' the Patriarch said. 'Late, and patched up with spare splits. I don't fancy that bit over there. So, you'll be in Danzig in a few days, and boarding the *Peter* soon after that. I'll tell Julius.'

Nicholas, succumbing to, and emerging from a deep pang of nausea, recalled why he hated Ludovico da Bologna so much. He said eventually, 'Julius? I thought he was in Cologne.'

'No, no: I've just left him in Thorn with your agent. His wife is with him, the beauteous Anna. They were planning to come up to Danzig to see you. And, of course, to see Adorne and his niece. That was a pity,' the Patriarch said discontentedly. 'A nice marriage. But she would have made a good nun.'

'Who? Anna?' said Nicholas.

He spoke automatically, and the Patriarch replied with a broad snort of amusement, getting up. The Patriarch said, 'Well, I wager *that's* sent you back to drinking water.'

BY THE TIME that the big raft was ready to leave, you could say that, of all the people implicated in Nicholas de Fleury's short visit to Mewe, one at least emerged from the mayhem with a sense of profound satisfaction. Battered, broken and bruised, balked of his conquest and forced to grovel to the Flemish child and her husband, Paúel Benecke was helped on board that afternoon with his privateering and personal career arranged, at last, as he wanted. Now Adorne's niece and the boy were on their way north, taking his disapproving bloody Elzbiete with them. Now he had renewed his attachment to that fine woman Gerta. Now Colà and all his assets were to sail with him on the *Peter von Danzig*.

Filled with ale and contentment, the captain sat with the steersman in the sunshine, waiting for Colà. It did not even alarm him too much to see a couple of mules and three poor-looking pedestrians descend to the jetty, and discover that the Patriarch of Antioch was stepping on board, with the object of demanding a passage to Danzig. Now and then, Benecke had nursed a concern that Ludovico da Bologna might damage Colà's instinct for adventure. Now, with Paúel himself in the party, it was more likely that Colà and he would frighten the life out of the disgusting old brute. Benecke grinned through swollen lips at the Patriarch, and showed him where he could sit and stow his frayed baggage.

The Patriarch, looking about, nodded to the men who were crossing themselves and enquired if Herr Benecke would like a departure prayer, one that mentioned the current off Ostaszewo and the sandbar at the Mottlau junction. Herr Benecke replied in the affirmative, adding that he thought Nikolás de Fleury, when he arrived, would especially appreciate it.

'Ah!' had said the Patriarch. 'Then I'll say the prayer, and you can leave. He isn't coming.'

The captain felt his face growing hot. The last time he saw him, Colà had been no drunker than he was, and still walking. Colà had no reason for staying in Mewe, unless he had secret designs upon Gerta. This was more likely to do with the girl Katelijne. Colà had wanted her: maybe he'd got her for good, with Elzbiete's diligent help. Maybe he'd gone north with Katelijne and her complaisant young husband. The captain enquired, breathing heavily, if this were the case.

The Patriarch had pulled out a Gospel and was riffling the pages, releasing a staccato odour of onion followed by a closing gasp of fried goat. 'Oh, no, no, no, no,' he said. 'That little girl? No, no, no. He's going to Thorn, after the other one.'

'Thorn?' The town of Thorn was where the King came. Where the

Court came. Where Callimaco came. Where Colà had previously elected, with good sense, not to go. Where, in the course of its travels, the entire mission, led by the Patriarch and Adorne, would be arriving. Colà had inexplicably changed all his plans and, without informing him, had gone south to Thorn . . . 'after the other one'.

'What other one?' had asked Paúel Benecke after an interval.

And Father Ludovico da Bologna had answered him with unstinted good cheer. 'The Gräfin Anna, of course. That black-haired German beauty who married his notary Julius. Anna and her husband are in Poland on business. Now Nicholas knows, he's going to meet them in Thorn. I was to tell you.'

'What were you to tell me?' said the captain softly.

'That you weren't to wait for me,' said Colà's voice. 'But I thought I'd better see you myself.'

Paúel Benecke stood. Colà was looking down from the edge of the jetty, bare-armed and broad, with his contusions clear in the daylight. You could see the older marks, too, from all the other times: from the bear-hunt; the wrangle outside the Artushof; the scuffle they'd had over that girl. Paúel said, still speaking softly, 'Come aboard.' His crew, grinning, were gathering round him.

'And have them punch me until I agree? You won't persuade me that way.' Colà spoke gently as well.

'Maybe not. But it would please me a good deal, and men would see what it means when you try to make a fool of Paúel Benecke. Or,' said Paúel levelly, 'they could quite as easily join you up there.'

'Well, of course. But think of all the sailing we'd miss. I can't join you just now, but later, or next season, we could still do something together. Iceland? Africa?'

Paúel Benecke gave a faint, distorted smile. The movement he made was quite slight, but as he made it, fifty men leaped from the raft-edge to the jetty and laid hands on Colà, who resisted querulously for a moment, then gave in. Paúel Benecke emitted a laugh. Then he stretched up his good hand, for something was pricking his neck under the dressing.

It was the priest's eating-knife. Benecke started to turn. The priest's powerful arm bent round his chest, and the knife-point dug deeper. 'Tell them to let de Fleury go and come back,' said Father Ludovico da Bologna peaceably.

It was ridiculous. The man was an idiot. And in any case, priests didn't kill. Benecke, no longer smiling, began to make the crooked, disabling move that would free him, and unexpectedly yelled. Fresh blood gushed down his neck. The priest said, 'Tell them.'

He told them. The men on the jetty hesitated, then, freeing their captive, began to scramble back on to the raft, their expressions ranging from amazement to cheerful derision. 'That's right,' said the priest. He still gripped both Benecke and the knife. 'And now tell them to cast off and get away. And no turning back, and no reprisals, or you'll blubber in Hades. I show God's mercy to imprisoned spirits, but I have this free hand with flesh born in corruption.'

Shaking with rage, the captain heard himself giving the orders. His eyes never left Colà. He said, 'Sheltering beneath a priest's skirts.'

'Have you sniffed them?' Colà said. 'I didn't know he'd do that. I didn't need to come here. You gave me a good winter, and I tried to give you the same in return. We will sail. But I can't do it now.'

'I don't believe you. Why?' Benecke said. They were already moving out into the river.

'Why am I going? I'll tell you some day.'

'Don't trouble. You're right. I'm not in the mood to exchange confidences either. Go off and kill yourself without me.'

The raft jerked, turning into the current, and the priest's knife jabbed deeper in sympathy. Benecke yelled. The priest, viewing the space which now existed between the raft and the bank, withdrew his arm, and then the knife, which he wiped on his robe and resheathed. Benecke lifted his fist.

Colà, on shore, called for the last time over the water: '*Krzywousty!* He's the Patriarch of Antioch! They really would hang you!'

And, of course, they would. He had to let the old man sit down, the stupid priest whom he and Colà had been going to make fun of. He was going to have to take him to Danzig. He was going to have to sail without Nicholas de Fleury.

Benecke stood, his kerchief pressed to his wry neck, and voiced his opinion of Flemish bastards and *bougres* of Italian priests in a way that would have earned him excommunication, had not Father Ludovico found himself temporarily occupied with his satchel. But secretly, the captain was not quite so angry. Colà had come, risking something, to tell him himself. And one day, surely, they would terrorise the sea lanes of Europe together.

Chapter 7

On Thursday the nineteenth of May, Anselm Adorne, Baron Cortachy left Danzig to lead his Mission of the Three Princes to Thorn. With him rode two Danzig councillors whose task was — of course — to smooth the way of the ducal ambassador, to oversee his reception in Thorn and to make quite sure that nothing happened detrimental to the interests of Danzig. Thick-set, hard-drinking and voluble, Jerzy Bock was related by marriage to Bischoff, whose second wife had been so hospitable to Kathi. Johann Sidinghusen, elderly part-owner of the *Peter von Danzig*, was even more insistently affable. Adorne suffered it all with civility. He was on his way to Thorn, knowing that Nicholas de Fleury would have arrived there before him.

Until recent years, Adorne had thought of Nicholas, if he thought of him at all, as his protégé. Only gradually had it become apparent that Nicholas, grown, was a man of exceptional ability, whose genius for finance and trade brought him to vie for the same markets as Adorne himself. Adorne had accepted the challenge with equanimity, as a good merchant should: giving no quarter and expecting none. But he had also learned, as the years went by, that the whispers about Nicholas were probably true. Other men, suspecting injustice, fought it in the open. Nicholas met it underground, by devious channels that ended in ruin and death. Especially the death of his own closest relatives.

It was because of his family — the dead mother, the foolish husband who repudiated her — that Nicholas had done what he had done in Scotland. Now, barred from the West, Nicholas was here — looking for power; perhaps looking for vengeance against those whose trust, at last, he had destroyed. Adorne had never believed that Nicholas would waste his time at sea.

The success of his mission mattered a great deal to Adorne, the more so that he was alone and the future of his house lay with him. He was uneasy about Nicholas de Fleury, and hurt, although he would not admit it, that his young Kathi seemed more concerned over the wretched man than over himself. He had felt relief, therefore, when Katelijne and her husband returned unharmed from their visit to Mewe, even though their encounter with Benecke had produced no advice, good or bad, that affected the affair of the *San Matteo*. And from what Robin volunteered, nothing seemed to have emerged, either, from their foolhardy encounter with de Fleury, except that the man had convinced them that he did intend to spend the summer at sea. Adorne had hoped it was true. From Kathi's face, he guessed that the meeting had been a disappointment and, on the whole, he was glad.

Then, a day later, the priest had arrived, like a thunderclap in a play, and everything changed. Unkempt, unwashed and reeking of fish, Ludovico da Bologna had tramped in from the wharf and, throwing himself on a brocade cushion, had announced casually that Benecke was back in Danzig and about to set off with the fleet on his own. The Baron Belchtrees was not going with him. That is, de Fleury had changed his mind in midstream, and was making his way south to Thorn.

With Ludovico da Bologna, all news sounded dire, and he had perfected a style of delivery that Adorne found excessively irksome. He had not therefore immediately replied; nor had Katelijne, although she sat up as if roused by a drumbeat. It was left to Robin to exclaim, 'Ser Nicholas has gone back to Thorn? But, Patriarch, why?'

'Nostalgia. Curiosity. Lust. His lawyer Julius is in Thorn, with that fine-looking Countess, his bride. Nicholas wouldn't miss that,' said the Patriarch. 'You'll see him, most likely, when you arrive. I should have told you. My lord of Cortachy, you have to leave Danzig immediately. I have word from the Kanclerz. The King is coming to Thorn in ten days. If you want an audience, you have to go there.'

'And you?' Adorne had said after a moment. 'Or have you perhaps seen King Casimir already on your travels?'

'Me? Hardly,' the Patriarch said. 'He's been in the south with his sons. If you want to find out what's happening in Poland, there are more interesting people to talk to than Casimir. So can we tell the Council we're leaving? I've sent a messenger south. There'll be a house and free food and entertainment: ambitious countries look after envoys. When the Holy Roman Emperor Sigismund visited Berne, he was given a three-day group pass to their brothel. I saw his letter of thanks. Casimir married his granddaughter.'

They had lived for over four weeks in Danzig and the Patriarch had provoked him throughout, travelling where he pleased when he pleased, and ordering the embassy as it suited him. Adorne said, 'I am sorry, Father. I understand that you think we should go, but the talks here are still in progress.'

'And they'll still be in progress at Christmas,' the Patriarch said.

'Talk isn't going to get you any further; only a shift in policy is going to do that. Sign the points of agreement. Give them an ultimatum over the rest. Then leave it to the lawyers. They'll send you your answer to Thorn.'

'And if they don't?' Adorne said. 'We have to reach Tabriz before the summer is over.'

'Get to Thorn. See the King. Worry about all the rest of it later,' the Patriarch said. 'Are the young people coming?'

The young people had become unaccountably silent. Then Katelijne had said, 'Yes. If my uncle will have us.' And, coming round to Adorne's chair, had knelt. 'Never mind about Nicholas. Leave him to us. What can we do for you next? You brought us, and we are determined to help.'

Her voice was earnest; her face reminded him, in its innocent glow, of his wife. Touched, Adorne made to say so, but was not given time to reply. 'And so you shall,' had said Ludovico da Bologna in his ripest voice. 'So, my dear child, you undoubtedly shall.'

'And so, my dear child, you undoubtedly shall . . .' In private, Robin was a good mimic. He addressed his wife: 'Didn't that strike you as sinister?'

'He meant it to. Nicholas is the Patriarch's property, so do as you're told. Never mind that,' Kathi said. 'The point is that dear Master Julius and the Gräfin have achieved the impossible and induced Nicholas to change his plans. Why, do you think?'

'She's pretty,' Robin said. Until the recent unpleasantness, Kathi had been intrigued to discover, he had taken a lenient view of this aspect of Nicholas.

She said, 'Anna is much to be admired, but I don't think he has rushed off to . . . to ravish her. Perhaps he wants scraps of news, or to send some.'

'Or the company of Master Julius?' Robin said. 'A sporting friend from the past, who won't condemn him, as the rest of us do? Perhaps Julius will be another Paúel.'

'No,' she said. As a rule, she abstained from discussing Nicholas de Fleury; it was a mark of their joint anxiety that they were doing so now. 'No, I think it's the opposite. Paúel was a source of punishment: that was why Nicholas joined him. And I don't think that's changed. So why suddenly the soft life at Thorn, with tolerant friends who might even admire him?'

'I don't know. I'd like to think that I know. Because it is another kind of punishment?' Robin said slowly, surprising her once again. For, of course, he was very probably right.

Later, thinking about it, she found herself thankful, despite everything, that Nicholas was going to Thorn. There, he would be among people of worth who might persuade him, this time, to accept office. Unless, of course, the Patriarch got his way, and Nicholas was somehow forced to come with them to Persia. But her uncle would never allow it. And if the Patriarch were to insist, she thought that her uncle would break his oath, honourable man though he was, and broadcast the truth about Nicholas.

She was among the few who knew what it was, and in general, she tried not to think of it. Now, sitting alone, she brought out and re-examined, for herself, what Nicholas had done.

It was six years since they had all gone to Scotland: Nicholas de Fleury to found a branch of his Bank, and Anselm Adorne to foster Scots trade with Flanders. They had worked and lived in Scotland, all of them. Her uncle had lost a child there, and found some good friends. Nicholas had won the fickle affection of the juvenile King and his kindred, and had endeared himself — open-hearted, entertaining, galliard — to the musicians, the merchants, the architects with whom he spent his work-time and his leisure. He had effortlessly won Robin's love, and the respect of his family. He had befriended and was trusted by the King's lonely sister. Nicholas was a Knight of the Scottish Order of the Unicorn, and so was her uncle. Her uncle had a Scottish barony and so had Nicholas, granted in gratitude by the King.

Her uncle had repaid what he was given by wise advice and good service to Scotland and to Burgundy. Nicholas had repaid it, in blind pursuit of a family feud, by deploying all the power of his Bank to bring about the ruin of Scotland; to carry out a programme of faulty projects and massive debt-creating commitments that would eventually beggar every person he had pretended to befriend, and leave the kingdom shorn of defences. And all the time the King and his advisers, suspecting nothing, had heaped him with rewards and affection.

They still suspected nothing. Nicholas himself had closed the Scottish branch of his Bank and withdrawn all his assets. The effects of what he had done were not yet obvious, or could not be traced directly to him. Nor could they be repaired, so that there was no object in compromising the integrity of the Bank or of his wife by disclosing them. So Kathi's uncle had agreed: as long as Nicholas left the Bank, and held no controlling post in any business venture in Western Europe, he would keep silent. It had been a painful decision.

For Kathi, too, disentangling the justification for such a piece of methodical destruction had been a slow, sombre process, owed to Robin as much as to herself. No normal man would bring down a nation for the sake of a petty vendetta, however deep the injustice. No ordinary man, indeed, could have done it. The concept might have sprung from pure evil. It might be impelled by something less grand: by waves of uncontrolled spite, as events from the past could suggest.

To explain it otherwise, you had to understand how single-minded Nicholas was, and the ferocious powers of concentration that he possessed, as anyone might see who had watched him divining. Kathi could not excuse him, but she thought she did understand. He had wished to cast before his contemptuous family and his obdurate, untouchable wife a masterpiece of organisational planning; a demonstration of what he uniquely was capable of that could raise or dash nations. And, entranced by his creation, he had disregarded everything else.

Ludovico da Bologna desired Nicholas to join his papal legation, and perhaps some sort of redemption lay there. But although the Patriarch might wish Nicholas to go, her uncle did not. Her uncle, conscientious, bereaved, did not deserve the extra strain of deciding the fate of the man who, to him, had once been the wayward, innocent, beguiling boy Claes, apprentice of Bruges. Nicholas must stay in Thorn, and must be kept, if possible, from meeting Anselm Adorne. His relations with the Patriarch he must manage for himself.

Lying awake that night, Kathi reached the conclusion that she and Robin should never have come. They had done little good, and it seemed to her that she had failed in her one wretched role, that of protecting her uncle and Robin from Nicholas. But although they should not have come, there remained one moment to relive and remember. She lay and thought of it now: of the fragmentary exchange in the flickering dark which suggested that, against all appearances, the gleam was not beaten out, that a trace of the friend she'd once had was still there.

But then, she was not present at Mewe when, three days before, Nicholas de Fleury had stood on the jetty and watched the raft with Paúel Benecke leave, bearing all his freedom away, along with the shadow of Colà.

WHEN THE DECISION to leave Mewe was made, no one alive but himself could have judged what it meant to Nicholas de Fleury, and no one was better placed to conceal it.

The raft gone, he did not have to think very deeply to decide his next moves. If Julius knew, then the whole of Royal Prussia would be aware that the seigneur de Fleury was coming to Thorn. Accordingly, the seigneur might — and did — take his time over the eighty-five miles of road and ferry which lay between the two ports.

The marks of his injuries faded. Riding at ease; crossing and recrossing the river at leisure between Marienwerder, Graudenz and Kulm, he hired a servant and made certain adjustments to his wardrobe. It cost him the last of his aiguillettes and most of his small store of winnings. He was a good gambler, and he cheated (as the Patriarch had observed) when he had to. Then, on a fresh day in the middle of May, groomed and barbered, booted and gloved and mounted on a remarkably fine-looking horse, he presented himself at the Kulm Gate of Thorn and, passing over the bridge, made straight for the lodging of Anna von Hanseyck and Julius, her husband. His face was quite calm.

Thorn was half as big as Danzig, and a fifth the size of Bruges or London or Ghent. But it had been built by the Knights, and the wealthiest of its ten thousand inhabitants lived, as in Danzig, within a grid of tall narrow houses whose south-sloping streets led to the quays through the thick river-portals. The heart of Thorn was in its central square, which held the red four-square bulk of the building which was at once Burgh Hall and palace and prison and, facing it, the inevitable Artushof of the Confrérie of St George. In the serried houses lining the square lived the nobles and merchants of Thorn and the royal and civic officials, cheek by jowl with the tailors, barbers, candle-makers and drivers who served them. And because the Knights were not long gone, and their Teutonic thoroughness survived everywhere, the city walls, the high towers and the moats were trim and well kept, the streets impeccably paved, and the houses, new-built since the fighting, presented a façade of paint and gold and ceramics that blinded the eye in strong sunlight, and glowed underfoot like church glass in the rain.

The house of the German agent Friczo Straube was painted red, black and white and was two windows wide, standing hunched between neighbours on the eastern side of the square. The Straube coat of arms was fixed over the portal, together with the arms of his visiting clients, one of which belonged to the family Hanseyck. Not that identification was necessary to a man who had received written reports from this address for six years. Now Friczo Straube would presumably be reporting to Julius. Nicholas did not own the Bank any more.

The square was excessively crowded. A fish market was in full cry at one corner, and a spate of hammering from the centre indicated that a podium for something — an execution, perhaps — was being erected before the Burgh Halls. Dogs barked, children screamed, seagulls shrieked overhead and, at the top of a fine flight of steps, the Straube door opened, and Julius stood in the entrance. 'I saw you coming,' Julius said. 'It was either you or the Archbishop of Gniezno. Is that your man? Tell him the stable's round at the back, and come up. You're not staying anywhere else. I can't wait. I want to hear everything.'

He looked the same: the vigour, the bonhomie, the bronzed, classical head with its oblique eyes. Nicholas would have thought him alone but for the scent, which he remembered from Bruges, from Augsburg, from Trèves. Anna, the blackhaired Anna of his dreams, leaned there, behind Julius, studying him.

'You have been fighting,' she said. 'You arrogant man, when will you learn? Oh, come in, come in. I see we shall have to find someone to look after you.'

HIS CHAMBER, high at the back, overlooked the garden and was normally in use as a storeroom: it was only through Julius that he had obtained it. Straube's house was crowded with visitors, and the welcoming meal had been served convivially below, with little chance to do more than exchange gossip. In any case, Nicholas was no longer a client, and Straube believed what he had been told: that having established his Bank, de Fleury had withdrawn his share and departed to enjoy it. Throughout the meal (a calf's head with a full set of teeth) Straube could be seen eyeing Nicholas. Behind the disapproval lurked a flickering hope. Julius might run a business well enough, but de Fleury had created an empire; and with the right agent, might do so again.

His thoughts were easy to read, and to ignore. You couldn't ignore Julius and Anna, interrogating Nicholas in their private room later. Not that Anna pressed him for answers. Anna sat still in her plain, fine-seamed gown without jewels, her hair veiled, her grape-coloured eyes moving from himself to her husband. Her second husband. Bachelor Julius had met this young widowed Countess and entered upon passionate marriage just over a year ago, long after his friends had despaired of him. Nicholas, nine years his junior, might boast that he walked off and founded a bank. But Julius of Bologna was happily married.

Julius also knew far, far too much, and was bursting, as ever, with joyous and indiscreet malice. 'What a bloody fool you were, Nicholas! But only the company knows, and the Adornes, and they're too pious to go back on a promise. You do have the devil's own luck. I heard all the Scots merchants in Danzig were fawning over you, and you sent them a barrel of ale. I hope they thanked you.'

'They couldn't speak,' Nicholas said. He had expected this, and so dealt with it.

'Well, I hope they made the most of it. Although you look prosperous enough. I'm surprised. Laid hands on your African gold? Or got something else salted away?'

'How did you know?' Nicholas said. Neither guess was correct. The gold in question had been waylaid by the Knights of St John, who still had it, or believed that they did. And he had nothing now salted away, barring the money that guarded his son and his wife. But very few knew about that: least of all his son and his wife.

'All the same,' Julius said. 'You've had a winter to play. Funds won't last for ever. Here's something I wanted to put to you.'

Nicholas half listened to what followed, since he could have guessed most of it. He was being offered, of course, a share in Julius's branch of the Banco di Niccolò, refounded as a Polish–Imperial company. The capital would be put up by Julius and Anna; Nicholas would bring his experience and the goodwill of the Emperor Frederick. Nicholas ought to face the plain fact that men would speak out if he worked in the West, while Julius didn't mind what he had done.

Nicholas wondered how much money Anna had. Julius would have some, of course. After his suicidal triumph in Trèves, Nicholas had resigned his shares in the Bank: some to his son, the rest to his partners. The latter had used them as he intended: Diniz his step-son to take over the business in Bruges, with Father Moriz to help him; Captain Astorre and John le Grant to make his mercenary troop fully independent; and the lawyer Gregorio to run the Banco di Niccolò in Venice with (according to Kathi) the help of Gelis, his wife. Whatever else that might do, it should improve the health of the Venetian business: Gelis had acquired half his fortune when he married her. And now Julius had spotted, of course, the opportunity that existed — not through the blocked road to Cathay, but in the broad, fertile lands east of the Oder.

Julius was going on. 'We heard you turned down Callimaco. You should have let him explain. Poland needs every skill that you've got: your divining alone would refill your coffers. And when Duke Charles gets what he wants and rules Germany, you can go back to Burgundy with a solid reputation behind you and your old sins forgotten. Keep in touch with Gelis, why not? And the little one. You'll be back in Bruges and Antwerp and Venice one day.'

'And in Scotland?' said Nicholas encouragingly.

'Well . . .' Julius began. He looked doubtful.

Anna laughed and, stretching across, touched her husband with her knuckles. 'You still don't know when he is joking. Go and get us some wine, and give him a chance to think it all over.'

Julius left them. Nicholas watched the door close, and then met Anna's astonishing eyes. Her regard was as direct as a man's. She said, 'I should feel more apologetic about Julius if you didn't know his enthusiasms so well. His heart is set on this scheme. I am sure that you find it disagreeable: it must remind you of Scotland. If you did steel yourself to agree, your success would be brilliant, of course. But it isn't fair to hold out false hopes. I believe it is too soon to judge whether you would ever be allowed back in Burgundy. Forgive me for saying so.'

'Not at all,' Nicholas said. 'You know what happened. I drained the reserves of my Bank to finance a private vendetta. They think I might do it again.'

'Would you?' she said.

'If you have to ask,' Nicholas said, 'I rather think that it would be unwise to employ me. But I expect you will manage perfectly well on your own. How is your daughter?'

Sudden questions seldom disconcerted her. 'Bonne is well,' she said, smiling a little. 'There is a fine school at her convent, and the priest is teaching her Greek. And your son? It must be hard not to see him. How old is he now?'

Nicholas withdrew his eyes from the throng outside the window. 'A year or so short of learning Greek: Jodi is five. But there can only be six years between my son and your daughter. There might be a place for another sort of contract between them one day. What do you think?'

She caught her breath. Her pale face had flushed. 'Would you give it your blessing?' she said. The words were French: sometimes she used a mixture of French and Flemish with him and with Julius.

Nicholas said, 'I know nothing but good of young Bonne. Jordan would not object. And by marrying Julius's shares to my son's, we should have reconstituted two parts of the Bank. A blessing all on its own, don't you think?'

'I'm sorry,' Anna said. 'I thought you were serious.'

'I thought I was, too,' Nicholas said. 'But sometimes I delude myself. Is Julius serious?'

He watched her slowly relax. 'About things that matter,' she said. 'He was a good friend to you, when you were young.'

'Did he tell you that?' Nicholas said.

Her mouth quirked a little. 'Of course. But other people say so as well. The greatest pair of practical jokers in Flanders, I have heard. Nicholas . . .' She paused. 'He misses you. I know this scheme is wrong, and it doesn't tempt you. But if there is any part of it that you like; or if you can think of a better, would you tell us? Don't reject him and leave. Give him a few days of your time. You won't regret it.'

'I should like to stay,' Nicholas said. 'In fact, I was hoping to stay, if Herr Straube can continue to lodge me. It is only fair to tell you that there have been other offers, all of them promising.'

She said, 'Then it depends, doesn't it, on what you want. Adventure? Money? Fulfilment?'

'Expiation?' he suggested.

She was silent. Then she said, 'Julius would tell you it isn't necessary. That your demonstration of what one man can do was more extraordinary than the damage it caused.'

'And you?'

She said, 'I see the marks on your face. And I think that you will dig your own grave if you are left alone very much longer.'

'Do you? Anna, my dear,' Nicholas said, 'you must have a very low opinion of my resources. Who on earth have you been living with recently?'

They looked at one another. She said, 'Of course. I am sorry. I was treating you as a child. I live with Julius; and he does take a long time to bring wine.'

Then Julius came, and Nicholas excused himself presently. The first encounter was over.

She was all that he remembered, and more. Back in his room, her scent stayed with him still. Nicholas walked to the window and stood. He wondered how long he had, before Adorne descended on Thorn. A week, little more. The King was coming to Thorn, and Adorne had been advised to be there by Pentecost. With the Patriarch. With Katelijne. With Robin.

Put yourself in the other man's place. He had done that. He was fairly sure he knew what to expect. He was back in the vice. The Patriarch would not approve, but there was a certain grim pleasure in reviving the arts which had led in the first place to his success. Success, that implacable foeman of virtue, as someone had once observed.

IN THORN, the summer rains started early that year. Usually, the wet month was June, but the heavens giddily opened just before Pentecost, filling the streets with loquacious torrents and clouding but not improving the river, whose sandbanks and shallows made even short crossings a penance. The rafts had long since gone north, and the river would continue to shrink. The people of Thorn, throwing their rubbish into the ruins of the departed Knights' castle, reminded one another of the great final days of the war, when the grain rafts had gone north in convoy, with the King's warships and cannon escorting them.

That was Casimir for you: a careful King who looked after his own in the matter of taxes. Thorn was pleased when the King came to stay, in spite of the expense of preparing the Burgh Halls, and decorating the churches and streets, and painting the ferries. Even when he proposed to lodge at his castle on the opposite bank, they were tolerant, for all his audiences, of course, would be held in the city; and the town would fill up just the same with surplus courtiers and petitioners. Also, of course, the boys sneaked across. Casimir had thirteen children, and some of them were always about, with their tutors and dancing masters and nurses. Thorn was a lively place then. It was lively even before the Court arrived, or the princely delegation they said was coming from Danzig. One of the reasons why it was lively was the high spending of Friczo Straube's clients.

Julius had always enjoyed making an impression. His social ambitions, carefully monitored, had been one of the assets of the Bank in the days when he controlled the Casa in Venice, and his marriage had given him cachet in Germany. His name therefore was already familiar in

Poland, and Herr Straube's recommendation did the rest. Invitations poured in.

On the first morning, he had found Nicholas resistant. 'Who are they?'

'One of the old Cracow families. I've done business with them in Cologne. They want to meet you. All right, you'll need to mind your manners and dress up and shave, but their castle will be really worth seeing.'

'I mustn't piss on the hangings, or blow my nose into my hat?' Nicholas had complained. 'You'll have to tell me what to do. I've been in Danzig all winter, fishing from a hole in the ice.'

Anna was smiling. She had warned him that Nicholas might be difficult. To begin with, Julius had thought she was wrong, for the conversation over the morning ale had been all that he had looked forward to. Expertly quizzed over Scotland, Nicholas had obligingly described how he had divined gold where there was none, and had brokered loans that could never be repaid. He brushed aside Julius's good-natured strictures on the harm he had done to the Bank, adding that Julius hadn't seen Gelis's face when she found out. It confirmed what Julius had already been told: that by this success, Nicholas had won some sort of contest in Trèves with his wife.

Julius, setting aside the details for future dissection, had repaid these confidences with a helpful précis of all that his former colleagues were doing while avoiding, under instruction, any mention of the same Gelis and her young son. The reuniting of Nicholas with his family, he quite agreed, was Anna's province. His intelligent, beautiful Anna upon whom the gaze of the gallant Nicholas so often dwelled, to the amusement of her new husband. For Julius knew that, however ardently he might try, Nicholas could never steal Anna's affections.

At the same time, Nicholas was right in suspecting his motive for this week of superior junketing. The wealthier merchants of Poland and Germany were impressed — over-impressed — by the intimacy between Julius and the former banker Nicholas de Fleury of Beltrees, and made certain assumptions about the future. Julius would be the last to deny them and Nicholas, so far, had not done so. Nicholas had still to make up his mind, but meantime acceded, for the most part, to the grandiose schemes laid before him, in which Anna nearly always took part.

The week that followed was not free of incident. In elevated company, Nicholas might not take a red cloth to a bear-hunt, but he did lead an unwise attack upon elk which nearly speared Julius in an area which, at the very least, would have ended his effective contribution to the marriage-bed. The following day, riding in a highly competitive relay race, Nicholas nearly fell to his death, taking Anna down with him. It was a miracle that neither was injured and Anna, thereafter, was debarred from rough sports. It saved her at least from the wolf-baiting in the moat when, after a vast drunken dinner in someone's magnificent *dwór*, Julius and Nicholas were both carried out, gored and spluttering curses and laughter.

'You both drink too much,' Anna had said to her bandaged husband that night. 'I know you are happy in his company, but he cannot partner you if he is disabled or dead. Let me speak to him again.'

Julius agreed, out of guilt. He often spoiled her quiet, logical plans through lack of caution, he knew. He had accepted, eventually, her view that Nicholas required looking after, and that this would best be achieved by bringing him to reconciliation with his wife. She would do nothing so crude as to suggest it to Nicholas outright. Reporting early progress to Julius, she had remained wryly determined rather than hopeful. Nicholas did not seem to mind when she mentioned how Gelis had abandoned her defiant post with the opposition after her husband's departure and, against all expectations, had carried her private fortune and the business secrets of the Vatachino to the Venice branch of the Bank, where the lawyer Gregorio had welcomed her. '*Welcomed* her! The bastard!' Nicholas had apparently remarked cheerfully at this point; but with so little engagement that he had remained perfectly amenable when Anna steered the conversation elsewhere.

The next time, when she spoke of his son, Nicholas had neither encouraged nor discouraged her, which Anna had supposed a good sign. 'I told him all I knew about Jodi in Venice: about the dog and the bird and his swimming, and how he could shoot with a bow. He didn't speak, but he listened. The little boy had sent him a poem, and when I held it out, Nicholas took it. He didn't hand it back, or show disgust, or dislike. He loves them both still — he must do. If we persuade him to stay, he will send for them.'

It had seemed to bode well, but when Anna called on Nicholas later that evening she found that, although his candles were lit, he had departed to spend the night elsewhere, in the manner no doubt of the Emperor Sigismund at Berne. Then, leaving, she had noticed the charred heap on the platter, which was all that remained of the child's loving, laborious missive.

Julius had been sympathetic. 'Nicholas was humouring you. I suspected as much. Look, don't worry. If he hates his family, that's up to him.' Julius was not entirely sorry, himself. He was not attracted to Gelis.

Now, however, several extremely vinous days later, he agreed with Anna that something more ought to be attempted. Since Nicholas was seldom in his chamber, they chose to tackle him during a hawking expedition, conducted over the extremely lush land of a party so rich and so noble that all conversation was conducted in the third person. The birds were superb, and the hounds tender-nosed and well taught. The silver bells shook, and the light silks and cuffed gloves and great jewels shimmered and glowed and gleamed in the sun. At midday, carpets were spread under trees for refreshments. Nicholas arrived and, sliding down beside Julius, provided the opening himself. 'You'd better know: I've just mentioned to Anna that my marriage is being annulled. One should not live in the same basket as a snake. It will take some little time, but for all practical purposes, I am a free man. You wouldn't like to let me have Anna, siren of sirens?'

'No,' said Julius happily. 'Also, you've to stop swilling wine. I hope she told you.'

'She did, but I'm not married to her,' Nicholas said. 'And not even allowed to receive favours. Therefore I shall succumb to *diabetica passione* all by myself, and you will drink water. Tell me about Bonne.'

Julius was first startled, then peeved. 'You know about Bonne. Anna's daughter.'

'I know she has a daughter, natural, adopted or prematurely installed by some well-plotted design of the Graf's. I need to know more, if Jodi's to marry her.'

Julius sat up. 'What?'

'Your wine has spilled. Anna doesn't seem to object. But it's a long way ahead: he's still young. Who is Bonne's father?'

Julius gazed at him. 'I thought you knew. You just said. The Graf Wenzel, Anna's late husband. Anna's mother told me herself. Bonne was born to Anna in Augsburg while Wenzel's first wife was still alive, and Anna's parents looked after the baby. Then, when Wenzel married Anna, he adopted their love-child.' He paused, and said, 'She is illegitimate, but you couldn't fault her bloodline. But, Nicholas? She is eleven, and Jodi is five?'

'I'm not suggesting that we draw up contracts yet,' Nicholas said. 'You and Anna might have a daughter yourselves. Come to think of it, what's the delay?'

Julius supplied an acid answer; Nicholas laughed and rose, saying something, and that, Jesus be praised, was the end of it. Julius had no desire to dwell upon the delay. Anna's failure to conceive continued to be a surprise and a disappointment to her husband. Naturally, he hoped for an heir, but that was not quite all. In the various theatres that made up his life, Julius preferred the occasional exquisite performance to the predictable and diligent routine. When Anna bent over and touched him, smiling, at bedtime, he responded, of course, but not at once. Yet he had no real complaint, my God no. He was the envy of every man he met. And while they awaited their child, she was his.

Before the repast was over, Julius did however find her and draw her aside. 'Nicholas spoke to you about Jodi and Bonne?'

Her lips parted. 'I thought he was teasing. Does he mean it?' In the open air, she had never looked lovelier, with the colour roused in her skin and her eyes glowing and brilliant as lapis. Serious conversation suddenly appeared idiotic. Nevertheless, he persevered.

'Unless we have a daughter,' Julius said. 'And, of course, Gelis might not agree.'

'To a van Borselen–von Hanseyck betrothal? I think she might,' Anna said gravely. 'And I suppose Nicholas might really be serious. He is leading a dangerous life, and you have been his mentor for a long time, and the only person who hasn't rejected him. Is that why?'

'I suppose so,' said Julius. He felt perplexed. 'He's never said this before.'

'He's never been so isolated before.' Her brow wrinkled. 'But what should we do? The boy is charming, of course, but his parents are parting, and Nicholas has nothing to leave.'

'Or not yet,' Julius said. 'A lot may happen. Perhaps the annulment won't take place. Or we have a child of our own. But you of course must decide about Bonne. You know what is best.'

He felt discomfort, as always, about Bonne, firmly lodged in her convent because Anna would not burden him with the presence of a thin, sullen child who had outgrown her strength. Anna's daughter might not want to marry. She might want to become a nun, for all he knew. Anna said, 'You are always so kind about Bonne. Let us wait and see. There is no hurry yet.' Shortly afterwards, they all left for home.

Julius's saddle-girth broke as they approached the town moat at full gallop, and he was cast rolling and tumbling among the pounding hooves and yelping, slavering hounds. Nicholas was the first to help him up and he was able, cursing, to remount. He had been lucky. And it was the last mishap between that day and Thursday, the day when Anselm Adorne rode into town with his married niece and the Patriarch and the Danzigers, followed almost at once by the King.

Chapter 8

Blessed as Anna von Hanseyck was not, the Burgundian Ambassador's niece participated in his ceremonial entry to Thorn, deeply thankful that it wasn't timed for the morning. Kathi was sick in the mornings.

She had told Nicholas that she wished to be sure, and now she was. She had not told her husband. It was fairly typical, she thought, that the first high-water mark of her family life should be disrupted by a riverside brawl. The Danzigers had gone to stay at the Artushof. Dismounting at the handsome house they'd been allotted next door, she observed that Robin looked grim, the Patriarch smug and her uncle superbly composed. Of course, the papal nuncio was well known: his voice exploded in sonorous syllables from a raceme of tonsures, birettas and mitres. But Anselm Adorne, too, was acquainted with some of these officers. He was accustomed to occasions of state. And he was here to conclude at least part of his mission: to present and have answered his Duke's personal message to the King. The King who was arriving tomorrow, and who might, among other things, overrule decisions made or not made further north.

Before nightfall, she had found out where Nicholas was. Ludovico da Bologna had informed her, taking her up to the top of the house and pointing out the Market Square she had just left, its bunting obscuring the vacant trestles and stalls and the arched entrance of the vast quadrilateral edifice at its centre, where the Mayor and Council would receive the King, and the King would receive Anselm Adorne and his Mission this Pentecost. The rain poured down, and a sodden triangle flicked in the wind, striping a passing dog yellow. The Patriarch said, 'You are facing north. Half the merchants and most of the officials of Thorn stay in the residences lining this square. Look to the east, to the right of the Halls. The agent of the Banco de Niccolò occupies one of those houses. It is tall, narrow and painted red, black and white. You can see it from here.'

'And Nicholas is staying with him?' she said. The lower windows were tall enough to give a good view. It was like one of the thinner houses of Bruges, except that it had a wooden awning over its door, and its doorstep, spreading outwards and sideways, formed a narrow stone apron upon which, presumably, the inhabitants sat when it wasn't raining. There was a simple balustrade round it, and steps led down from that to the street. Most of the houses had similar shelters or balconies, some of them of wood. There were cellars beneath them. She added, 'It's very near.'

'You don't see that as fortunate?' said the Patriarch. 'Adorne isn't going to let you or your young master visit there, or you'll upset his relations with Thorn. And de Fleury would be shown the door if he tried to come here, as would our handsome Julius, for supporting him. The wages of perfidy. So guess who will come, once her servants tell her that Adorne has stepped out of the house?'

'Don't you want to see him?' Kathi asked.

'Nicholas? No. I can wait. And yes, I know what he's done. A foot-soldier of Satan, and a fit tool for any man's hand.'

'I'm sure you are right. So why do you really think he is here?' Kathi said.

'Why ask me? You didn't like my first answer. The woman Anna might suggest something different. Or he may simply have fallen out with Paúel Benecke. If so, you might even know why.'

She returned the Patriarch's stare without answering. He was absently massaging his chest through his habit. She said, 'A foot-soldier of Satan. But you would use him?'

'God would use him,' the Patriarch said. 'If I am to make one parchment Bible, I need the skins of three hundred sheep.'

'But you don't consult the sheep,' Kathi said.

'I don't need to,' said the Patriarch patiently. 'They do what they're told, and go directly to Paradise.'

ANNA VON HANSEYCK presented herself quietly at the door the following morning, rather earlier than her hostess would have chosen, but with otherwise impeccable timing, for Kathi was alone. The Burgundian and papal ambassadors, with Robin in attendance, were in the process of being formally received in the Burgh Halls opposite, and it was Adorne's understanding that they would remain to welcome the royal party when it arrived. Kathi hoped that he was right.

Robin had called Julius's wife a pretty woman, but many women were pretty without possessing the qualities that made the Gräfin so singular. In build, she was slim and well proportioned, but the clear bright skin against the profusion of charcoal-black hair was more Irish than

German, and her principal features were not these at all, but the steadiness of the violet-blue eyes and her tranquil manner, touched with amusement. She was intelligent. Kathi who, without being vain, knew herself to be both quick-witted and mature for her years, yet recognised that here was a calm, a gentle detachment she would never possess. Fortunately, Robin had both, and lent them to her, as once he had tried to serve Nicholas.

Anna was younger than Nicholas, and considerably younger than her second husband. Indeed, her marriage to Julius represented, in Kathi's view, a mystery only to be accounted for by the blindness of passion. At any event, in the year that had followed, Anna had made her husband's circle her own. Consistently deft in her relations with Nicholas, she had also made friends with his wife and their child. Seemingly, these warm-hearted relations continued, even though Anna knew what had happened in Scotland. Kathi wondered if Anna, more subtle than Julius, had come to share his hearty tolerance, or would look harder and further, seeking the middle road between that and rejection. She hoped so. Kathi did not hold the illusion that she or anyone else could or should direct the future of Nicholas. But Paúel Benecke's daughter had observed that he needed a Gerta, and that was Kathi's view also. More accurately it was Kathi's view that Nicholas needed a wife, and preferably the one he was losing. In the meantime, almost anyone of good sense would do.

It was therefore with some approval that Kathi heard her visitor's first words on the subject, once the friendly preliminaries were done, and Anna was sitting divested of her wet cloak, her hands restfully folded. 'Katelijne, I want to ask your advice about —' She broke off and laughed. 'I'm sorry. It is natural to you, but I still feel it a presumption to call him Nicholas.'

'Try Colà,' Kathi said. 'Or Nikolás, maybe. He's had so many names that he'd answer to anything, really. What about him?'

'Two things only,' Anna said. 'He is the last person to want to be managed: I am only afraid of doing something wrong. Julius would like him to join our part of the Bank, working east of the Oder. Would this be good? As you know, he has a great deal of energy . . .'

'Most of it currently going in the wrong direction. Yes, it would be good,' Kathi said. 'Unless he chooses to work in Poland on his own account.'

'Would that be better?'

'It's too early to say, and none of us could influence him anyway. Julius might as well ask him.'

'I thought so,' Anna said. 'I know he cannot go back, but I thought it might keep one channel alive, between Nicholas and his friends and his family. I had this hope — you will think it far-fetched — that he and his wife might be reconciled. But now I am not so sure. That is the other question I have.'

'I see,' Kathi said.

'No,' said Anna swiftly. 'I have asked you too much. We should not be discussing these things. Forgive me.'

It was her perception, as always, which was so disarming. Kathi said, 'I did hesitate, but you are right: it's important. I feel as you do. Until this happened, I thought they would spend the rest of their lives together, he and Gelis. Robin thought so as well. If he had had his way, we should have come to Poland weighed down with gifts and messages and tales of Jodi's prowess. Thank God we didn't.'

'Tell me why,' Anna said. Her voice had changed.

Kathi gazed at her, frowning. 'Oh dear,' she said. 'You see, it would simply have made matters worse if he hated her. And if he didn't —'

'It would have reminded him of all he had thrown away,' Anna ended. 'I am a fool. I am a miserable, unthinking fool. He sat as if listening to every detail I told him about the Bank, about Jodi, about Gelis. He said nothing much. I had a feeling sometimes that he was thinking about something else, but he didn't stop me. He accepted the paper with the little boy's poem. Only, afterwards . . . '

A poem from Jodi. Kathi felt sick. She rose and walked across to pour wine, her back turned. She said, 'What happened then?'

'He set fire to it,' said Anna steadily. 'I found it later that evening, in ashes. Does he love them?'

Kathi stopped pouring. *My snivelling little wife and her bastard.* She said, 'To hear him, no. I can't tell you what to believe. But if I had no love for a child, I might discard what the child sent, but I shouldn't burn it as if it would infect me. Don't you think?' She collected herself and turned.

Anna sat where she had left her, motionless except for a glimmer under her lashes, like mist on the curve of a glass. Kathi set down the wine and went to sink down beside her. 'But you weren't to know what was best. Anna, he is a grown man who has to learn discipline. If you hurt him, he deserved it. And whatever he may feel about Gelis, nothing can be resolved unless she changes her mind. Perhaps she will. I haven't seen her since Trèves.'

'Nor have I,' Anna said. She dragged her palm over her cheek. 'This wasn't my intention. I'll go.'

'Have your wine first. I don't know the answer to your questions,' Kathi said. 'I'd say, give him work if you can, but don't be disappointed if he throws it over quite soon. The point is that he must come to decisions, not us.'

Anna looked up from her cup. 'Julius says that your uncle would never take Nicholas to Tabriz. But perhaps that would be best?'

'Not for my uncle,' Kathi said.

'Nor for Julius,' said Anna. 'How well organised we should be without menfolk.'

'And how dull,' Kathi said, cheering up. She had heard Robin's voice.

Later, when Anna had unobtrusively left, Kathi ran downstairs and found herself in the midst of what anyone else would have called a celebration, but her uncle referred to as an expression of cordial optimism. He had been received by the city. The magistrates had not asked him to welcome the King, but trusted that he would attend, as civic guest, the Pentecostal Mass at which the King would be present on Sunday. Thereafter, as a matter of course, the Chancellor's office would communicate a day and a time for his audience. It was done. Soon, he would have completed his mission in Poland, and they could set out for Tabriz.

'Where is Father Ludovico?' asked Kathi.

'At the Franciscans'. The Marienkirche. They've got pickled oysters,' said Robin. She loved Robin.

Later, having heard most of the story, he said, 'You approve of Anna. I'm glad. Do you think she might talk to Gelis some time? Persuade Gelis to come here, and bring Jodi?'

Kathi thought of the burned poem, of which she'd said nothing. In the past, Robin had undergone more for Jodi's sake than she had. Kathi said, 'I suppose Gelis might agree to come, one day. Or the boy, with his nurse, or Dr Tobie. But not now. It would be the worst possible time for it now, when Nicholas has just publicly repudiated them. He is not fit for his son, not at present.'

'So what can we do?' Robin said. Beneath the reasonable tone, there was anguish.

'Nothing,' Kathi said. 'Nothing directly. Now, we leave it to Anna.'

TO THIS PLAN, Nicholas de Fleury had no objection. Since he had access to the front as well as the back windows of Friczo Straube's house, he was able to discern what might have escaped Julius: that Kathi and Anna had met. He thought he might mention it to Julius, in the interests of friendship.

Their strenuous attention, at the time, was being given to the current *Zielone Świątki* or Green Festival, a happy blend of church and pagan spring ritual which had begun with flower-gathering in the country and would end in bucolic riot the day after Pentecost Sunday. As esteemed guests of the nobility, Julius and his former padrone performed their flower-gathering at one remove, alighting at various handsome *dwory* containing various handsome women who took part in the feasting and in the languid dances that followed, plaiting circles on the late evening turf while servants passed by with barrows of greenery. Some of the servants were slaves, black or Tartar. They looked well dressed and fed, and were presumably grateful for their good luck.

Anna was not present, nor was the Mission, which was being entertained by the Town. The Court remained over the river. The itinerary of the Patriarch was not known, although he had sent an unexpected message to Nicholas, in the latter's well-known role as a master mechanic: he was wanted to fix up a dove in the Marienkirche. It didn't seem much. And Nicholas, who could recognise the inevitable, whether emanating from the Patriarch or the Third Person of the Trinity, had promised to do it.

But that was for tomorrow. Now, he sat on a rug made from wolf fur and viewed his temporary host's rolling domain, and silk-clad guests disposing themselves upon it. A dwarf dressed in velvet was turning somersaults. 'That reminds me,' Nicholas said. 'What did Kathi think about all your schemes? I didn't know you liked lampreys?'

'*Neun Augen,*' said Julius complacently, stirring the dish at his side with a finger. 'Nine eyes. German. I'm getting to like German food. Fish in white vinegar. Puddings. What do you mean? I haven't seen Kathi. We agreed to leave her and her uncle alone.'

'Oh,' Nicholas said. 'Yes, of course you did. So what else do you recommend beside lampreys?'

Julius's oblique eyes had become slits of suspicion. 'Wait a moment. Has Kathi been spinning some tale?'

The late sun slanted over the meadow, and sleek limbs gleamed, and jewels burst into radiance. Nicholas had pushed his hat back from his subversive brown hair and large, shining eyes. He said, 'It's all right. You know what women are. I saw Anna go into the house when Adorne was away. I expect they talked about puddings.'

'They probably talked about you,' said Julius sharply. 'Not that Anna could say very much, since you haven't honoured us with your decision. I can't wait about the whole summer.'

'I didn't ask you to,' Nicholas said. 'Although I was grateful for the introductions. Why don't you go home and I'll send you a letter? I expect to decide fairly soon. I'll probably have it decided for me tomorrow. You don't want to come and help me sheet up the Holy Ghost for Father Ludovico?'

They went home early that night, and Julius didn't join him for their evening session as usual. But next day, when he went off to the Marienkirche, Julius went with him.

OF THE EIGHT CHURCHES in the double city of Thorn, the Franciscans had built their humble offering to the Blessed Virgin Mary in one of the best positions, next to the monastery they had established when the town was founded over two centuries previously, and behind the present Burgh Halls. Eschewing the vanity of a high tower, the monks had contented themselves with a pair of small spires on top of a Gothic monolith containing two mighty aisles and a nave eighty feet high and painted inside and out with everything from geometric three-colour patterns to graphic Bohemian scenes from the Gospels. There were tall stained-glass windows, a prodigious altar and flowers and stars on the vaults. Father Ludovico was eating dinner in the cloisters but came to greet Nicholas and Julius at once, wiping his hands. 'Well, kneel,' he said.

They knelt.

'Right. You see that hook at your feet. There's the other. There's the pulley. There's where the other hooks used to be. But when we fix the dove there, it doesn't work.'

It was supposed to swoop down from the roof to the altar. Nicholas got to his feet, intrigued if unshriven. 'Where is the bird?'

'Here.' The Patriarch proffered a bundle. Inside a napkin was a half-eaten pullet. The Patriarch blessed God's left toe and disappeared with it back to the cloisters. Julius, his head tilted back, said, 'I'm not going up there. Are you going up there?'

'I need someone. There's scaffolding,' Nicholas said.

'And there's lunacy,' Julius retorted.

'Then I'll take someone else. Father Ludovico?'

'Now, there's an idea,' Julius said. The Patriarch had just re-entered bearing the dove, a ponderous object in sleek silver-gilt. It looked new and expensive. Nicholas said, 'Is this the same weight as the last one?'

'So that's what's wrong,' said Father Ludovico.

It took a while to assemble the new chains and brackets and wheels, and by the time that was done, the Patriarch had found a smith and his apprentice who were perfectly prepared to do all the work on the scaffolding except that, by that time, a number of spectators had arrived and *sotto voce* wagers had already been laid on the Flemings. The Patriarch, who otherwise had been violently opinionative throughout, expressed nothing but indifference when, in place of the smith, first Nicholas, then Julius ran up the ladders that led to the top of the chancel arch. His confidence didn't surprise Nicholas: Father Ludovico knew precisely what each of them was capable of. It did surprise him that, having contrived this encounter, the priest had failed to talk about anything at all but the bird. Then he put his mind to it, and thought of a reason.

It was this distraction, perhaps, which made him careless. Or the fact that he had drunk rather too much rather too often in recent days. Or the further fact that Julius, feeling cross about Anna, had transferred his annoyance to Nicholas and, as soon as they were working aloft, began to lecture him about Gelis.

'Forget her lovers: what do they matter? Get her to bed; give her your best and she'll forgive you. Then you can think about going back to Bruges — even Scotland. Adorne's fifty. He could drop dead in Persia. The niece and nephew won't give you away. And you never did try to apologise to Diniz and Tobie and Gregorio. What are the grounds for annulment, anyway?'

'A flaw in the contract,' Nicholas said. The nail he was hammering broke, and he fished out another.

'What flaw?' Julius said.

'I don't know. They haven't found it yet,' Nicholas said. 'Will you hold that bloody thing *straight*?'

'Then how do you know —'

'Because lawyers will do anything if you pay them enough.' The piece of wall he was working on crazed, and the second nail dropped. He stared at the wall, then took out the last half-dozen nails and stuck them into his mouth like short straws.

'You'll have to move further along,' Julius said. 'I'll hold you.' His hand, approaching with sudden intimacy, removed the nails from between Nicholas's lips. 'I'll keep these, you'll swallow them. Would you like me to talk to her?'

'Yes, if you'll let me entertain Anna.' There were so many people below that falls of grit dispersed soundless as dew. He could see the spectators quite clearly, inscribed by the south-facing windows with sinuous figures in cobalt and carmine; a solitary dazzling ray from a hole in the glass was bothering the flesher collecting the bets. Nicholas could not hear what his audience said, and they could not hear the conversation he and Julius were having: it was between the stars and themselves.

'Try it,' said Julius. 'I told you, that patch of wall is no good. If you don't want to stretch, then we'll have to wait till they fix some more scaffolding.' He leaned over the rail at the edge of the platform, shouted down an instruction and squatted down with his back to the rail-post. 'So why not write to your wife?'

Nicholas studied the wall; identifying three new possible sites and computing, effortlessly, the variations each would require, having regard to questions of weight, angle and speed. He said, 'All right, I'll write to her. I'm hungry. Aren't you hungry? Let's go down.'

Julius created a negligent barrier with a robustly shaped calf attached to an elegant ankle and foot. 'Before anyone comes? You have to show them where to put the new nails. So what's wrong, then, with poor little Jodi? Suffering Christ, why burn the little brute's message?'

Nicholas turned his head slowly. He could see Suffering Christ from where he stood, as well as St Andrew embracing his own bit of carpentry.

In a voice of freezing surprise he said, 'I needed a spill.' He and Julius stared at one another. Nicholas said, 'Where's all this rubbish from: Anna? You wouldn't notice poor little Jodi if you were driving a wagon-train over him.'

'Neither would you,' Julius said. 'That's what women are for. What do you think you are doing?'

'Climbing over and marking the wall,' Nicholas said. He had a piece of charcoal in his hand. 'And then I'm going to break your leg and walk down to my dinner.' There was a reasonable ledge within reach of the scaffolding and he was under the impression that he was sober.

He arrived on the ledge. Julius scrambled up to the rail and said something. The noise from below increased quite a lot. Steadying himself with one hand, Nicholas viewed the wall, and leaning, scrawled two crosses, each in its appointed place, and sidled along to complete the third. Then he turned and began to come back and stopped.

The sun had moved. The ray of pure light was now focused on the dove, which hung upside down from its temporary harness and, revolving, flashed its blinding light into his face. The Third Person of the Blessed Trinity Disapproves. His foot slipped. Nicholas saw, dimly, the handrail over which Julius was leaning. He saw the platform of planks it surrounded, and their supports. He saw the system of timber and ladders below. He launched himself outwards into space and caught the end of a beam and held on with both hands, his body swinging, his feet seeking a purchase as shouts rose from below and Julius yelled. He saw that Julius was yelling because the shock of his arrival had dislocated the posts holding the rail, throwing Julius downwards as planks began slipping around him. A stanchion, hurtling down, struck Nicholas on the shoulder and neck so that he swung, his arm numbed, and half fell. Below, the spectators had scattered, baring the small, distant tiles of the floor. He made a great effort and, lunging, found a tenuous toehold and a desperate grasp for one hand that brought another clatter of collapsing planks, and Julius's blundering body down with them.

Once, Nicholas had saved Robin, hanging one-handed like this. Now, Julius could do nothing for him. Julius, passing hand over hand, slipping, falling, clutching, was himself dashing down from the rock, down from the mountain, down from the stars as the dove would come, but not to rest in the dovecote of its master.

Curiously, the dove still shone in Nicholas's eyes, as if wherever he fled, the blaze of its anger would seek him. Yet despite the glare, there were some things he saw very clearly. He saw the vivid polyptych of the High Altar, the crucified Thieves wrapped, legs and arms, round their scaffolds. He saw a stately canopied chair and a chessboard. He felt, rather than saw, something he could not describe: something that filled him with anguish, and love, and unspeakable yearning. He was still clinging, forgetful, when the structure he was holding collapsed, his holds forsook him, and he fell.

For those moments, at least, his mind cleared. He heard the screams. He saw that Julius was safe, caught and lodged just below him. He saw the tiles of the floor rushing towards him and thought of a chute, and a cry, and something he would never now say. But all that was already lost to him, in any case. Then he struck and found, swaying, swaying, lurching and swaying, that he was in a net.

Chapter 9

SHAKEN, SORE but alive, Nicholas de Fleury missed both the Pentecost Mass and the revels that followed on Monday, although Julius conveyed himself with caution to both, as a good merchant should. The dove, according to Anna, had turned in an impeccable performance.

It was the first sensible conversation they had held since she had received him from the awed hands of the Polish Franciscans, who perceived the net as a donation by Bóg, rather than a consequence of the Patriarch's distrust of poor timber. Of the night that followed, Nicholas remembered little but a sequence of extraordinarily sensual dreams, from which he woke in some discomfort to find the house empty but for his servant, and the square packed with jewelled mitres, cloth of gold and white satin, with golden crosses and high swaying canopies and the hats and silken shoulders of the nobility, all assembling for the procession to church. Behind them somewhere, he supposed, would be Julius and Anna, with Straube and his household. Somewhere else, not too far from the royal party, wherever it was, would be Anselm Adorne, his niece and his nephew. And the Patriarch, of course.

The vestibule hall, two storeys high, did not appeal to him, so he installed himself instead at the window of one of the small hanging rooms at the front, where there was a seat and, he found, a recess offering a small keg of ale and some wine. He sent Jelita for a cup, then dismissed him. By then the chanting had begun, and the incense rolling inwards was making him queasy. He shut the window and, his gaze on the square, poured his wine and began to think through what had just happened. After a while, he made out the figure of Anna. Much later, he saw Kathi and Robin. They both looked happy, on their way to a Christian blessing. Some sects incinerated children as soon as they were born, and made Communion-bread from the ashes. And then, presumably, ate it.

A long while after that, someone touched his shoulder and he found that it was Anna herself, smiling, still in her cloak. He saw it was raining again. He said, 'I was asleep.' The flask was empty.

'So I saw,' she said. 'Come back to your room. The dove did very well, and so did Julius.'

In his room, he pulled himself up on his bed while she sat on the edge of it, studying him. She said, 'Don't worry. I'm not going to preach. I know this wasn't a drunken Benecke prank, but men are going to wonder, in time, if that is all you can do. Maybe it is. But I don't want Julius to take that path.' She paused. 'May I suggest something? I went to see Katelijne of Berecrofts, and I think that you should do the same. Julius also agrees, now he understands. Her uncle, of course, shouldn't know, but I am sure that she would be willing to meet you, if you wanted. You do like her?'

The damp had brought a single strand of black hair to her shoulders, and her eyes were the colour of hyacinths. He said, 'Did you look after me last night?'

Her smile deepened. 'Jelita was there most of the time. Julius didn't mind. You did nothing to be ashamed of.'

'What a pity,' he said.

Her smile remained: amused, mild, understanding. *And I think that you will dig your own grave if you are left alone very much longer.* Anna, Anna, Anna: how did you know?

He said, 'I think a great deal of Kathi. I would see her, of course, if you suggest it. But isn't she leaving almost at once, with Adorne?'

'He hasn't had his audience yet,' Anna said. 'The King didn't come to the city. He was indisposed, and heard private Mass in the castle. His officers can't properly arrange for Adorne to present his credentials until after the holiday. Then he will leave, and Kathi and the Patriarch with him. And Robin, of course. So there is time.' She paused. She said, 'I admit I am not being entirely altruistic. Julius thinks, and I agree, that you will not make up your mind until you know Adorne's plans, as well as the Patriarch's.'

He noticed that, when she was serious, her upper lip curved like a child's, and was naturally tinted, like her cheeks, with a child's rosy colour. Her gown had been dyed, very expensively, in two shades, and its fine lapels met, as befitted a lady, without sinking into the hollow below. Despite that, and the discreetly lined bodice with its custodial seams, he did not need to be told that, unconfined, her breasts were full and tender and round, and that under the swell of her ribs was a small, silken waist. Like Gelis, Anna would always be womanly, whether a maid or a wife. Kathi, whatever her state, was only her own, sexless self. Nicholas said, 'Then arrange what you like. I don't mind.' His eyes, drifting downwards, had closed, and he was aware of a hazy contentment.

He said, 'What did you give me? A *schlaffdruncke*? Something from an apothecary?'

Her voice was like a nurse's: amused. 'Something from Kathi,' she said.

There passed six curious days, during which nothing happened. The square emptied of clergy and filled again with officials taking over the leases of their houses as the hierarchy of Crown Poland made themselves available, for business and pleasure, to the magistrates and office-holders of Royal Prussia and the influential citizens of Thorn. The King and Queen made a ceremonial visit to the Burgh Halls, addressed the magistrates, were feasted and, instead of occupying their usual apartments, returned to the castle. Adorne, although he waited all day, was not summoned.

In Thorn, Friczo Straube's house, shaking off the post-festival languor of Tuesday, resumed its normal brisk pace of business. Julius, recovering quickly, returned to treating Nicholas with his usual mixture of irritation and camaraderie, after a moody few days in which he tended towards outright aggression. And Nicholas, excusing himself from country sports, had filled his days with sedate engagements in town, drinking ale in some cellar, or playing cards or dice in the Artushof where, as Julius had particularly mentioned, he found a friendly welcome from the Scottish merchants in town, some of whom — Simpson, Lauder, Halkerston, Stephen Lawson from Haddington — he had already spent time with in Danzig. At other times, if it wasn't raining, he would sit with Straube and his household outside his front door on the terrace, drinking wine and chatting to friends who came to lean over the balustrade, or step down with a client to unlock the door of the stockroom. On occasion, Anna would sit with him.

He knew that Adorne was still here, although he had taken care not to meet him. He also knew, as did all the town, that the promised summons to Court still delayed. On Tuesday, the King was still indisposed, and on Wednesday he was burdened with overdue business. On the day of the civic reception, through some oversight, foreign merchants were not invited to the banquet, and on the following three days the King felt constrained to remain in his castle. The only delegate who enjoyed unrestricted access was the Papal and Imperial Nuncio, Father Ludovico da Bologna, who trotted through the square on his small mule almost daily, on his way to the ferry with Brother Orazio. He did not stop at Herr Straube's, and indeed had made no attempt to communicate since the accident of the dove, which suited Nicholas very well. Nicholas waited, and on Monday morning his messenger came: a black-clad, youngish man named Lipnicki, who wished to know whether Pan Nikolás was free to take refreshments with the lady who sent him.

The sun was shining, for once, and although the wind was high and the clouds had an untrustworthy appearance, the merchants of the Artushof had set aside that afternoon for a contest of crossbow and sword of the kind at which Julius shone. He had already been threatening to go, whether Adorne was to be present or not. Now, at least, Kathi would know Adorne's movements. He might be with the King at the castle. He might already be planning to leave.

In any case, Nicholas was very conscious that this would be the last occasion on which he and Kathi would speak together in Poland: perhaps the last occasion in life. He had not been entirely sure, when Anna suggested it, that he wanted this meeting. There was too much about it that was difficult. It couldn't repair what was irreparable, and might end by making it worse. But since Anna had asked it, he did not want to refuse. He would not admit to more than that: he could not afford to.

He walked away with Lipnicki, having left a message for Julius. The man — a superior servant? A clerk from the Artushof? — led Nicholas over the square but, instead of turning towards Adorne's house, walked between the booths and stalls of the market and directly through the main doors of the Burgh Halls. Nicholas had been there before often enough. The cellars, reached from the outside, were where men like himself gathered to drink. Here, the inner courtyard was an extension of the market, although more exclusive. On the right were the stalls of the bakers, and on the left, the cloth halls of the merchants. Ahead, long and low as were the other four sides of the square, was the building which housed the great hall, and the apartments used by the King when he came over the river.

Since the Court was lodged in the castle, it was a surprise to see, ranged before the far portal, a guard of fully armed men wearing the livery badge of the Jagiellonian. It was more of a surprise, as his guide stepped across, to discern that the arms of the Habsburgs appeared also. Lastly, as he reached the royal portal in the wake of his leader, it was with quite a different sensation that he saw step from the doorway to greet him a man, an elegant, short-sighted man he had last seen in Oliva.

'Welcome, *Panie Bracie,*' said Filippo Buonaccorsi. 'I hope you will forgive us. My serene lady could not flout protocol openly. I am sure you understand.'

My serene lady.

It was not Kathi he had been summoned to meet: it was the Queen.

THE PAINTED CHAMBER into which he was shown held no surprises: the tapestry had been commissioned by King Casimir through the Banco di Niccolò in Bruges, and the carpet and one of the chests had been found and conveyed by Gregorio from his headquarters in Venice. Most of the silverware had originated in Germany, ruled by the Queen's second cousin, the Emperor Frederick, and some had been bought through the Florentine company of the Medici, whose agent, Arnolfo Tedaldi, stood among the group of gentlemen at the Queen's side. Many of these were Italian and one was Venetian: Caterino Zeno, the husband of Violante of Naxos. He was smiling.

Nicholas bared his head and knelt, bending his neck. *'Meine Königin.'* Latin was the language of diplomacy; Italian was the language he hoped for; German was the official language of Cracow. She answered in German. He rose and stood facing her, one hand at his breast, while she examined him.

Elizabeth of Austria, Queen of Poland, was little older than he was himself, but the birth of thirteen children had lent a certain opulence to her frame, and the robe of linen interwoven with red and gold thread was splendid but bulky. Her face was Habsburg, with the heavy jaw and congested nose he had last seen in the younger face of the Emperor's son Maximilian. But she also had the fine eyes, open and lustrous, of her family, and a roseleaf skin set off by the precious scarf which covered her hair and her throat. Below, she wore a necklace trembling with pearls, and pearls edged the tight cuffs under her oversleeves. All the men in her presence were handsomely dressed, and her own ladies were silk-gowned and comely. Not only a learned woman, then, but a secure one.

He knew her to be adept in Italian because she had stayed at the court of the Emperor, in the days when his secretary was that golden poet and future Pope, the idol and model of Callimaco. You might almost say that the shadow of the late Pope Pius lay over this meeting. It was for his aborted Crusade that the *San Matteo* had been built, and it was by his decree (later regretted) that Fra Ludovico da Bologna had become Patriarch of Antioch, in which capacity he was now present in Thorn, representing both the current Pope and the Emperor. How loyally he was representing either master was as questionable as the degree of accord between the Queen and her second cousin. One day, their heirs would compete for the Empire.

Nicholas stood, accepting her scrutiny, and betraying nothing but deference. Callimaco, delicate as a carving at the Queen's side, watched him also. It had always been possible, from the moment Nicholas came back to Thorn, that he would receive a royal summons: it was one of the reasons why he had delayed making decisions. Now suddenly he was here, squarely placed on a board quite as complex as any of those from which he had been driven. He experienced, distantly, a flicker of interest: another game, another puzzle, another project. Nicholas, his voice gentle, said, 'Madame, how may I serve you?'

Someone knocked on the door. The Queen turned her head and Callimaco, without spoken orders, crossed the room and admitted a well-dressed nobleman in his mid-thirties who doffed his hat, bowing, and ushered in his companions. There were four of these, all fair, all bright-eyed and handsome and ranging in age from, he guessed, sixteen or so down to seven. Nicholas did not need to be told who they were, although the Queen introduced them: 'Kazimierz, Jan Olbracht, Aleksander and Zygmunt. Four of my sons.'

The eldest, of course, was not present. The eldest, Wladyslaw, was King of Bohemia. And the nobleman with them was the scholar Jan Ostrórog, who had graduated from Bologna five years after Julius did, and who had just been awarded a lucrative post by the King. The Queen said, 'You were asking how you might serve me, and I shall tell you. My sons are here to learn. You will be seated, and then you will tell us your view of the Kingdom of Scotland, and how it is ruled, and what advances it has made towards prosperity. For, although we have persons of many nationalities in our kingdom, and quiz all that we may, we seldom have men who have touched, as you have, on the central trade and monetary affairs of a country. You do not object?'

He did object. He could not say so. He said, 'Illustrious lady, I am no longer a banker, or even a merchant.'

Her voice was dry. 'You would not be here if you were. You have been in this kingdom for six months. You may wish to stay longer. I desire you to look at the country you have left, and compare the two. Tell me about coinage. The King of Scotland saw fit to debase his silver? Why was this thought to be necessary? Does he not forbid the export of precious metals? And how does he mine those he has?'

Poland, stretching from sea to sea, was the largest country in Europe; Scotland one of the smallest. He thought at first that he was betrayed: that someone — Adorne? — must have named him, and mustered a list of all the destructive policies which he had launched. Then, as the questions continued, he saw that this was not so; that he was the subject of a purely intellectual enquiry which ranged over all those subjects, economic, financial, industrial, which were of common interest, and which included matters of much wider import, from the relations of the King to his subjects to the relations of the King to the Church. Ostrórog in particular had been amused. 'At least you forced through your Archbishop, bravo! We have had a Primate for nearly sixty years, and for more than ten, all abbots and bishops have been appointed by our prince without reference to Rome. Not that there is not more to be done. And tell us, the King has no standing army, and his only seamen are merchants? What does he do when he would go to war?'

He answered them pleasantly, and illustrated his points with anecdotes which made the boys laugh. He was used to covering up and could deal, with relative ease, with questions from a Tedaldi or a Zeno. He was less used to being trapped into philosophic discussion by men who had known Cardinal Bessarion as well as Pope Pius, and were familiar with the thinkers he had heard speak in Trebizond. Nor could he escape, as he usually did, by appearing ignorant. He had corresponded for a long time with Filippo Buonaccorsi, and whatever deductions Callimaco had made, he had passed to the Queen. That was why, as she said, he was here. He was unattached and potentially useful. He was being given a test, based on his knowledge of a small country whose dissection would alarm no one except, as it happened, himself. And he was performing for an audience of four princes, the future kings of this realm, who, again as it happened, were children. He knew how to make them laugh, because he knew about children. He had two.

He began to feel very tired, and was conscious of relief when the Queen, intervening, signalled that the discussion was over and conveyed to him her thanks, and those of her absent husband. She hoped that, with the help of her servants, my lord of Beltrees would continue to relish his stay in her country. Everyone stood. Nicholas kissed hands and began to retreat. Jan Olbracht, who was not in awe of his mother, caught Nicholas at the door and said, 'I heard great tales of the Ferrara wedding. Was it true that they heaped snow under the awnings, and blew cool air into the party with bellows?'

'So I believe,' Nicholas said. 'It didn't come cheap. They filled the rooms with silk flowers from France, and there were four tablecloths to each table, one for each course, and the servitors changed costume to match. Why, my lord? Are you marrying soon?'

'Jan Olbracht!' said his mother.

'Not today, at least,' said Jan Olbracht with a wink, and slid off.

'No, indeed,' said the voice of Caterino Zeno, close at hand. 'Aged fifteen, and three mistresses already, to my knowledge. If you are as thirsty as I trust you are after that heroic performance, I propose that we retire in the direction of the cloth halls, collect some amiable company and descend to the cellars to discuss nothing that is not liquid or frivolous. Do you agree?'

He agreed, since it was necessary. He had never known Caterino Zeno to be frivolous. His wife was another matter, or had been.

THE BEER CELLARS were packed with courtiers and with wealthy citizens waiting for the noon downpour to cease, but Venetian foreigners had their own table at which Zeno and his party were welcomed, and where conversation took place in that peculiar tongue, with its slovenly affectations, which might confound even Italian eavesdroppers.

Not that, to begin with, the talk strayed far from the orthodox: Cracow scandal, local women, and home news from Venice. Twice, Nicholas had to watch what he was saying: once when Gelis was mentioned; and once when the talk turned to Cyprus. Neither reference was serious. He expressed mild gratification when complimented on his wife's brilliant work for the Banco di Niccolò in Venice, and merely nodded when Zeno referred to the failed revolt against his young niece Queen Catherine in Cyprus. Neither was news, and he thought it extraordinary that they should have expected to read something in his face.

That said, he was mildly interested to learn that the Venetian branch of the Bank was still known by his name, and wondered why. It would suit Venice, of course, to have him safely back, making money for the Republic with his brilliant wife. As for Cyprus, the bond between himself and its late King was no secret. Privately, he had rejoiced when the murderer of Zacco's small daughter Charlotte had been killed. But the rebellion had failed, and the Queen's legitimate son would now become a proper Venetian — a spectacle that Zacco, at least, had been spared.

Becoming tired of the subject of Cyprus, Nicholas got to his feet, lifted his newly filled humpen and offered a toast, waving his hat in the Polish fashion: 'To the Kingdom of Cyprus, where three things are good and cheap: *il sale, il zucchero e le puttane!*'

Zeno drank it, wearing a smile. Then he proposed another: *'Kochajmy się!'* — Let us love one another. Then someone thought of another toast, and another. It was harmlessly restful. And there was plenty of wine: six pots within reach for the eight of them.

That was the frivolous part. Much later, alone by his side in the privy, Caterino Zeno said, 'You hold your drink well.'

'I am sorry,' Nicholas said.

'Don't apologise. We are expected to talk, you and I.'

'Oh? Expected by whom?' Nicholas said.

'By Ludovico da Bologna, for one.' Zeno retied his cords, and watched Nicholas prepare to do the same, with no particular haste. Zeno added, 'You enjoyed life on the rafts?'

'Do I like the company of rough men? Yes, of course. I prefer women, but they don't come on rafts.'

'I heard differently,' Zeno said. He paused. 'You know that our precious Buonaccorsi's mistress has married this year? Everyone is sorry. You see his influence on the young princes. Luxury in the home, in the bed, at the table.'

'And a certain amount of learning as well,' Nicholas said. Since Zeno didn't move, he leaned on the wall. No one came in. The rain had stopped.

Zeno said, 'That is why the Queen indulges him; indulges old Długosz, Ostróróg, all the boys' tutors. The boys are to grow up wise and lettered, as Casimir was not. The magnates of his day saw to that.'

'The King is said to be wise,' Nicholas remarked.

'He has his mother's temper, but yes. Thirty-four years have taught him to rule. He was soldier enough to throw out our white-cloaked knightly friends, and has wit enough to know which allies to cultivate.'

'Certainly, he has had good advice,' Nicholas said. 'Barbaro, Liompardo, Contarini, Ognibene. Four different sets of Venetian ambassadors passing this way in a matter of months, quite apart from yourself.' He shifted. The smell was terrible. He supposed Zeno thought this important.

'Naturally. Venice is at war with the Turk. She is Poland's buckler, as the Church is her sword. There have been papal envoys as well. Barbo for one, and the sadly maligned Maestro Laetus, on his way to and from Moscow. It was necessary for both gentlemen, of course, to be kept apart from the prized Callimaco.'

Julius Pomponius Laetus had been sadly maligned for the same things as Filippo Buonaccorsi and, for that matter, King Zacco of Cyprus. Nicholas, eyeing his immediate surroundings, said, 'It is true. People do talk. You haven't mentioned Adorne and the Duke of Burgundy. Are these not also allies worth keeping?'

Zeno smiled and began to walk to the door. 'The Duke has other uses at present for his troops and his money. When he makes promises, no one believes them, and when he makes threats, Poland knows that his own merchants will quietly modify them. As for Adorne, he and his family are still Genoese by investment and instinct. They send sons to the Knights of St John, another military order. Uzum Hasan does not trust them.'

'But you had a successful stay at the Persian Court. They received you in bed together, they say: Uzum Hasan and your aunt Theodora.'

Opening the door, Zeno smiled once again. 'It was an assertion. Despite the superior fruitfulness of his Kurdish and other wives, Uzum Hasan (he would point out) does not deny his bed to Theodora the Christian. The death of Zacco has shaken him, naturally. Since his great success, he has suffered some reverses, and can be irritable — he sent home the envoys of Poland and Hungary. I was luckier.' The cellar was virtually empty. The contests must have begun. Zeno stopped at a table and turned.

'I have done what I could with Uzum. Now I have to go home and report to my princes. And you? Will you stay here, beguiled by the good Master Julius, or seek the joys of a royal appointment, and the everlasting friendship of Callimaco? I could understand it. War against the Turk might seem uncomfortable by comparison. But are you so cynical now that you are not stirred by a gamble? Yes, you could die. Yes, Uzum might lose. But if he were to win, what rewards would he and Venice not give to those who have helped him?'

'Such as good business opportunities, of course?' said Nicholas thoughtfully. 'Yet it does no harm, I notice, to be Genoese. Our friend Prosper de Camulio seems well thought of in Rome.'

'That is true. But he has never been sent to the Levant. The wealth of the Levant is for others to exploit. I have here a . . . consideration.'

'It looks like money,' said Nicholas with interest.

'It is money. The purse comes from the Senate. It is to fund any journey you may make through the Tartar khanates to the court at Tabriz. I am empowered to give it you now, even before you make your decision.'

The purse was heavy. Nicholas weighed it in his hand. He said, 'I may not be too cynical as yet for a challenge, but Tabriz seems to have saviours enough. Perhaps I should wait until Anselm Adorne and the Patriarch have finished there.'

The eyes in the button face glanced about and returned with a considering look. Zeno said, weighing his words, 'I should like to think that Adorne might not succeed in reaching Tabriz. The lord Uzum Hasan is uneasy. A Genoese voice at this delicate stage might, in my view, endanger the whole Venetian alliance. I am not alone, I am sure, in that view.'

It was like the old days: plan and counter-plan, filament crossing filament. Nicholas said, 'Perhaps you are right, but it is too late to stop Adorne now. He is presenting his letters. He is ready to leave.'

'He has not presented his letters. The King set out from Thorn this morning, and the Queen left the building when you did. The princes will appear, for form's sake, at the games, and then they, too, will leave.'

'Adorne will follow,' Nicholas said.

Zeno shook his head. 'Not without a safe conduct which, sadly, the King has not thought to provide. And no one knows when the King may return: perhaps not even this year.'

'And the *San Matteo*?' Nicholas said. 'Has the King made any ruling?'

But, of course, the answer was no.

Zeno talked. Nicholas watched what he could see of the house over the street where, for twelve days, Anselm Adorne had attempted in vain to see a King who did not wish to be seen. There was no sign of activity. Adorne might not give up; he might set out for Tabriz despite everything. Or he might respond to the rebuff by returning to Danzig at once, to the merchants who might cede, in time, to his claims and give him some small success to report back to the Duke. Nicholas had known Adorne for most of his life, and had fought him for part of it. In business, the older man had given no quarter, and had treated him, seven months ago, with freezing contempt. He did not care what Adorne did, but he found that he did not wish Kathi to leave before he had seen her. He would send her a note.

He thought of something else. 'The Patriarch? Where is the Patriarch in all this?'

Zeno broke off what he was saying. He said, 'Physically, he is, or was, with the King. Whether he continued with him, or called back to Thorn,

I do not know. And in every other sense he stands as he did: as the legate of the Pope and the Emperor, on his way to Tabriz by way of the Black Sea and Caffa. He is, of course, well known to the King and is acceptable to Uzum Hasan, as you are. In his case, there are no complications.' He made an agreeable pause. 'You may find he has left you a message.'

'Then I should probably return and look for it,' Nicholas said. 'You are going to the games?'

'To entertain. The Confrérie have invited me to conclude the day with a display. It is nothing: a little mounted archery in the Persian style. You would not care to join me? I have a short bow you could use.'

'Today, you will have to forgive me,' said Nicholas. 'But Julius is the man you should ask. Go and speak to Julius, if you have spare bows.'

They parted outside. He had been asked for no promises. He had been given money. He took the chance, politely, to send his regrets to Violante, and Caterino Zeno assured him that he would convey her husband's affectionate greetings to the lady Gelis in Venice. Nicholas assumed that Gelis could deal with that, if he could. The sun was shining as he crossed the square, and the vendors were unwrapping their stalls. He made his way, thinking, past baskets of berries and mobs of lacquerred radishes big as plums. The painted houses stood upside down in wide puddles, and pigeons drank from their windows. Beside the steps to Straube's house, a man stood awaiting him.

'Now it is my turn,' said Callimaco. 'Pray come in. I shall not keep you long and, as you see, you do not have far to go. I am living here, between the house of Copernicus and yours.'

Chapter 10

A MEETING WITH Callimaco had been inevitable, and Nicholas saw no point in avoiding it. As his host pointed out, he had no distance to go. Only, before he climbed the parallel steps, Nicholas took a moment to check that no message from Father Ludovico had come, and to dispatch Jelita with a message for Kathi. Then he went next door, to make himself available to Filippo Buonaccorsi.

The two houses were very alike. In this, the wide public room on the first floor overlooked the long garden, like Straube's, but was otherwise unremarkable except for those few objects which the lessee had clearly brought here: a writing-box inlaid in Florence, a globe, a painted chest, a ewer with a trailed handle and a set of Murano glass goblets. The man Lipnicki filled them. Compared with that of the Burgh Halls cellar, the wine was ambrosia, and Nicholas could not bring himself to refuse it. He thought, then, that the day was within his control.

Callimaco was wearing a robe of dun-coloured taffeta, and a single jewel, and his spectacles. His hair was like Zacco's. *Kochajmy się*. Outside, speaking in Polish, he had *waszmośćed* Nicholas in the third person, but now he used the Italian of his Siena countryside. 'Have you been told that I may molest you?'

'Caterino Zeno, it is true, is not a sensitive man. But then he is trying to propel me into the arms of the Tartars and Uzum Hasan. It surprised me that the Patriarch left without helping him.'

'He has not yet gone,' Callimaco said. 'Nor has Adorne, but he will. Adorne was a bad choice: I agree with Signor Zeno, if for different reasons. The Duke sent Lord Cortachy to lodge a public complaint with the Hanse, or be seen to be doing so. He made him envoy to the Levant on a whim, to please Adorne himself, whose name is known there, and as a sop to the Pope and Milan. But how could he ever succeed? Venice has always been able to promise Uzum more than anyone else, and it is Venice whom

Uzum and the Great Horde will favour. Then, if Uzum conquers the Turks, it is Venice who will benefit from the flood of renewed trade, and who will take control of the alum mines. That, of course, is Zeno's interest. You will have guessed.'

He had guessed. He knew, also, what Callimaco's bias was. Zacco, too, had hated the Genoese. Nicholas said, 'I should tell you that I have been given a bribe. Or a non-returnable gift. Or perhaps even a pension. I have taken it, but I am not yet committed.'

'Whatever it is, the King would offer more,' Buonaccorsi said. 'If your commitment is for sale.'

'Why?' said Nicholas. 'Why not allow someone else to pay me to advise Uzum and what is left of the Horde, and help free Poland from all these threats?'

Callimaco leaned back in his chair, his long-fingered hands embracing his glass. 'Because, Niccolò, this country has been torn to pieces by mercenary troops over the years, and we have had enough. Our delegate to the Council of Constance denounced crusading as contrary to God's will. It amuses you. But we are the base for every Western attack: against the Muslim, against the pagan, against those of Orthodox faith. Destroy the Turks, and the Grand Prince of Moscow will immediately appear on our frontiers. Ally with Moldavia, as we are doing, and how far will Stephen's ambition finally take him? And what of the Mongols? Listen to Father Ludovico when he talks of the khans' friendship, and listen to me when I tell you that the Tartars from north of the Black Sea plunder us daily and always have done so: they will fight for anyone, and will join with the Turk or the Russian or Uzum Hasan as it suits them. And because these nomads are not ambitious for land, the Western princes see no need to give us protection.'

He paused. He said in a calmer voice, 'We are a buffer state, and our friends are as dangerous to us as are our enemies. So Casimir does not fight, Niccolò. He prevaricates. He conciliates.'

'He disappears,' Nicholas said.

'Oh, yes,' said the other man. He rose, crossing the room. The folds of silk, falling loose, smelled of something sweet. When he returned, it was to hold out some papers. 'You read ciphers. You once encoded reports, I am told, for the Medici.'

Nicholas received them, and the pen and ink he was given. He was beyond, now, feeling merely intrigued or annoyed. It was true that he had a natural facility for everything appertaining to numbers: for ciphers and navigational calculations, for mathematics and gunnery, for astronomy and, of course, music, which he had denied himself for seven months. An aberration he would soon overcome.

The codes were not simple and he sat, head bent, working on them while the other man watched. These were not trading reports. He saw almost at once that they were copies of secret dispatches, mostly between Venetian agents, but some involving Florence and Rome. They were all very brief. He translated them silently, for himself, and then, laying them down, picked up and drank off his wine. He said, 'So much for Adorne.'

'As you see. Zeno and his colleagues have written to all the princes of the West, warning them that Adorne's embassy would be disastrous. The Duke cannot afford to let him go to Tabriz, any more than the King can afford to admit Benecke's piracy. And meanwhile, Venice is promising the world to Uzum, and to you, while secretly half her ambassadors are suing the Sultan for peace. If you go to Tabriz, you become another part of that false Venetian promise, that is all. That is why you were paid.'

'To do that, or to go back to Venice. A place on the Great Council, and full control of the Bank, with my wife.'

'You may want that, of course. Or you might prefer to stay here, and send for your family. Niccolò, may I speak?' Nicholas waited. The other man hesitated, and then went on. 'It seems to me that something has happened, and that this change of career and of country is not by your choice. Am I right?'

'I have not complained,' Nicholas said.

'No. You took some time to recover. When you came to Thorn, I saw it as a sign that you had done so: an indication that you had resolved to rebuild your empire.'

Again, he stopped. Again, when Nicholas did not speak, he went on. 'I thought I knew you from your letters, even though all you claimed to seek was information for your Bank. Some men work for a cause; many achieve as much or more through ambition alone. With you, I thought it was first one, then the other. Now I think it is neither. I cannot see your purpose in life.'

'Because there is none,' Nicholas said. 'You have just defined freedom.'

'For an adult? I have just defined mediocrity,' Buonaccorsi said.

Their eyes met. Then Nicholas laughed. He said, 'The happy mean. Why despise it? You still thought me worth buying.' The wine had been left on the table. He rose to lift it and found it set aside from his grasp, and the other man standing beside him.

Callimaco said, 'Of course I will buy you. You will always be bought, because you will always be worth something to others, even as you become worth less and less to yourself. Dare to aim for what you want. Dare to fail.'

'Dare to succeed?' Nicholas said. He moved away and sat down, without the wine. The weariness had returned, and some of the anger.

'Ah,' said Callimaco. He also turned and after a moment sat down.

He said, 'If you are afraid of success, then you are fighting the wrong wars. There are men who could advise, some of them in Poland.'

'Ludovico da Bologna?' said Nicholas. 'Or perhaps an astrologer? You know what the late revered Pope Paul thought of astrology?'

'*That* is one of your fears?' the other man said. His voice had changed. 'Why? Because of some other man's prophecy, or because of something you yourself have experienced? I know you have witnessed one of the great mysteries of this world. Benecke has spoken of Iceland.'

'Then you know as much of Iceland as I do,' Nicholas said with finality. Through the open window a faint, hoarse sound swelled as he spoke. Beyond the walls of the Old Town, the games were under way. Time was passing. Adorne was leaving, and he had to see Kathi. He said, 'I must go. You have been frank, and I value it. I shall give you an answer. But first, you will agree, I must find and talk to the Patriarch.'

'I could find him for you,' Buonaccorsi said. 'It is not in my King's interest, but I could arrange for you to see him, for a fee.' A mild irony entered his voice. 'It is a fee you will experience no embarrassment in paying. Lipnicki!'

The black-clad secretary appeared. 'Maestro. He is here. I shall bring him.'

Nicholas rose. Illogically, he expected to see enter the coarse, bulky form of the Patriarch. Instead, there came the short figure of a fair-haired boy-child of about seven.

'The prince Zygmunt,' Callimaco said, 'expressed some eagerness to witness a master diviner at work. I have told him you are such a person, and that one day, when he is grown, he may hold silver coins from the mines you have found. Meanwhile, all he asks, as I do, is a demonstration of your art. You will allow us?'

Nicholas, making his bow, was simply pondering how best to refuse. Perhaps, trained astrologer that he was, Callimaco already knew what he was asking, and even that Nicholas, since he became Colà, had forsworn both the pendulum and the rod. The child spoke before him. Employing the charming Polish usage, the child said, 'Will my dear lord not do us this favour?'

'Sire,' Nicholas said. 'I am sorry. I have no pendulum with me.'

'But I have,' said Callimaco, and took from the breast of his robe a cameo set in a ring.

The stone was Greek, Nicholas guessed; pale and heavy, and carved in the likeness of a child's face. It was warm from where it had been, and the thong on which it was threaded was scarlet. Nicholas held it.

Its owner continued, in that deceptive, mellifluous voice: 'Let us sit by the window. This is a divine gift we practise, and God's air should breathe upon us as it is done. My lord prince there. My lord Niccolò at his side. And I shall sit here. Now the stone hangs from its cord on my lord's finger. What do we wish it to tell us?'

'It cannot speak!' cried the boy.

'Oh, it can speak,' said Callimaco. 'How else will it tell us what you have hidden?'

Nicholas, watching the cord, felt the other man's gaze as a weight. The child's voice rose and fell in delight and excitement. Zygmunt had concealed a purse. Pan Nikolás was to divine where it was. 'Now! Please! My dear lord!'

'I am sorry,' Nicholas repeated. He met Callimaco's eyes.

Callimaco said, 'Perhaps my lord is tired. We understand. But tell the prince what might happen, were the pendulum to speak?'

A child should never be denied; his curiosity quenched. A child. A vulnerable child. Nicholas said, 'To find something of yours, sire, I should touch you. Then I should ask the pendulum questions. This is not my stone, so I do not know how it answers. With mine, it swings from one side to the other if the answer is yes. For no, it gyrates.'

The boy said, 'It is raining. Ask it if it is raining.'

It was raining. The downpour pattered on the trees outside the casement; the haze of water rose from the ground. Nicholas watched it, his head turned, and felt the thong stir. The boy screamed, 'It is moving! It is moving from side to side!'

It was true. He felt it before he gave it, at last, his attention. The swing was polite, moderate, unemotional. Is it raining? It is.

'Now find my purse!' said the boy. 'Ask it. Please, Pan Nikolás! Please? Is it in this room?' And taking Nicholas by the arm, he lifted the broad, adult hand that was free and laid it, palm down, on his own young, bony shoulder. His eyes were not grey but brown, and full of expectation. *Where is maman?*

He did not need to formulate any question at all. Of its own accord, as the boy cried out, the pendulum began to move in a slow circle. *No.*

'Is it in the hall? Is it in the hall?'

No. No. The loop, revolving more briskly, rasped his finger.

'Is it on the roof? Is it in the privy? Is it in the cellar?'

No. No. No! 'Keep clear,' said Filippo Buonaccorsi, his voice curt. 'It is rising quite high.'

It was rising quite high. It was describing a full circle now, and increasing slowly in speed. The small, pale face at the end of its cord made a whispering sound.

The boy's face was red. 'Is it in the kitchen? Is it in the dairy?' Whirr, whirr, went the stone. Under the cord, the diviner's hand wore a rough inflamed ring pricked with blood. It was painful. Beyond the snarl of the ring, Nicholas could see the scholar's large eyes and curling hair and ascetic face printed with growing alarm. 'Is it in the garden?' shouted the boy.

And *NO!* screamed the ring, just as Nicholas flung out his free hand and stopped it.

The prince said, 'But . . .'

'Sometimes,' said Nicholas, 'it is sick, and does not speak the truth. I am sorry.' He spoke with difficulty.

Zygmunt said, 'Then it couldn't find silver. The purse *is* in the garden; I put it there. It didn't know. It can only tell if it is raining.'

Nicholas kept his fist closed, the ring burning his palm. He said again, 'Sire, I am sorry. It is not the ring's fault, but mine. Some day it will perform for you. Let someone recover your purse.'

'I shall do it myself,' Zygmunt said.

He rose, and Callimaco rose with him. Lipnicki came, at a sign, to the prince's side. The boy said to Nicholas, 'It was not your fault. Such things happen. It was probably the fault of the purse.' He left with the secretary. Nicholas straightened.

Callimaco said, 'What was unleashed?' His face was a little pale.

'Anger,' Nicholas said. He remained standing, the cord and ring crushed in his hand. After a while he said, 'It knew what its real errand was. It was being asked the wrong questions.'

'Ask the right one,' Callimaco said. 'Or do you lack not only wisdom but courage?' Then he stopped speaking, as Nicholas opened his hand, and let the cord unfold from his finger.

The face in the stone was a sweet one. He wondered where Callimaco had found it: in Constantinople, perhaps. He wondered, fleetingly, what else Callimaco might have brought back from Turkey. The ring hung, passive, waiting. The anger, he well knew, did not reside in the stone; the grief, the anger, the despair. He said, 'No.' And even as he spoke the word, the ring started to move. Its first essay was short. In the second, it stretched out as far as the wall.

Callimaco said, 'It is swinging, not circling. Nikolás, it answers you yes. What did you ask it?' Faint from the garden, there came the sound of the prince's high voice.

'I don't know,' Nicholas said. He had asked it nothing. It had lifted the question, he thought, like a print from his mind, and was forcing on him an unwanted answer. Yet if he were ever going to get rid of anything — music, anything — he had better start doing so now. He said, 'Would you allow me to borrow this, and try somewhere else?' He paused. 'I shall tell you what happens.'

'I think,' said Callimaco, 'that you have already paid what you owe. Go. I shall find Father Ludovico for you. Then you may bring me your final decision. Look. It swings for you still.'

Nicholas caught it and left, walking unevenly. He felt like a cripple. He felt as he had on the raft, fighting Benecke. The house next door was empty: Friczo Straube and his lodgers were attending the games. Advancing experimentally, Nicholas stopped inside the hall. Looking down, he opened his hand and, attaching the cord to his finger, painstakingly let the ring hang. It began to swing gently; its pulse leading away rather than towards the wall common to the two houses. He had guessed correctly. This was where it had wanted to come.

As soon as he started to move, he was made aware of the difference. The ring wasn't whipping him this time. This time, all its fierceness subdued, it seemed full of an earnest solicitude, nudging, prompting, swaying, circling demurely. No, I do not wish to go through to the stockroom. Yes, this is the way I wish you to turn. Yes, I wish you to climb. No, I do not wish to go to the reception-room, to Herr Straube's chamber, to the other guest-room, to the granary. Yes, again I wish you to climb. This is the place. This is the door. Go into this room.

It had brought him to his own chamber.

He stood inside the door. The cord shook itself suddenly. An end to pretence. The ring gave a harsh whisper. No more need for blandishments. He knew now what was going to happen; but he was not a minion, an echo. He would determine when and where he would cede. He stood in the doorway and, drawing on all his remaining strength, hurled his contrary demands, the will of the diviner crossing the will of the pendulum: self against self. You want me to go to the window? The candleholder? The cupboard?

He was punished for it. This time, the answers were physical. The circling stone started to rise. The childish face, stony, smiling, passed his with increasing speed, its hiss changed to a snore. The cloth was snatched from his hand, and the ring, smoothly hurtling, seared the air with its rebuttals. *No* to the desk. *No* to the bed. *No! No! No!* to the prie-dieu. His wrist ached, with refusing to name what it wanted.

He went there, in the end. In the end, he said, in his mind, 'To the table?' And the stone pulled him there; converting itself, in a great convulsive leap, into the pendulum that answered him, *Yes!* Then it fell, and hung dangling, like the arm of a fighter which has just delivered the ultimate blow.

It had brought him to nothing very much, you would say. Made free of the whole country of Poland, the whole of Thorn, the whole of Friczo Straube's fine house, the stone had brought him to nothing more sinister than this table, upon which rested a flat pewter dish, stained with black.

Nicholas stood. He was still standing when someone addressed him. The voice was quite near. 'Pan Nikolás?'

Jelita, his servant, submissive as ever in his long coat and cap and soft boots. He was in the room. Perhaps he had been there for some time. He spoke once more. 'My lord?'

Nicholas moved. He felt very stiff. He remembered being in a great haste about something. To find and talk to Katelijne while everyone was occupied at the games. His hand was sticky with blood; he saw the man looking, alarmed. Nicholas said, 'It's all right. The lady of Berecrofts. Did you find her?'

'I came to tell you, my lord. She has gone to the contest with her husband and uncle. The merchants invited them. The Baron Cortachy is to leave Thorn, it appears, and the merchants wished to do him particular honour, not desiring him to think badly of them in the future. So they say, my lord.'

Nicholas gazed at him, vaguely surprised by the unaccustomed loquacity. He seemed to remember that Julius and Zeno were to attend the same gathering. Propriety would presumably prevent an explosion, and the presence of Anna would be conciliatory. He could not, at the moment, bring himself to think about it. He said, 'Then I may see the lady Katelijne when she returns. There is no need for you to stay. Perhaps you would like to see the sport yourself.'

'Everyone is going,' the man said. 'Thank you, my lord. Everyone wants to be there for the show Signor Zeno is to give at the end. Not being a friend of the Genoese, he'll likely perform some great feats, so they say, just to flaunt the superiority of Venice. They say Signor Zeno is a great man with the Persian bow. Very dashing.'

And then, at last, Nicholas realised that something was being conveyed to him. He said, 'What do you mean?'

The man looked abashed. 'Why, nothing, my lord. Only they say that the Baron Cortachy and Signor Zeno dislike one another, and tempers might be lost. That is all.'

'And you think I should do something about it?' For once, he was unconditionally disagreeable.

'I am sure I don't know, my lord. Except that my lord knows them both. And an accident is always bad business, and harms trade for the foreigners that are left.'

'I am sorry for them,' Nicholas said. 'But not perhaps quite sorry enough to go into battle on their behalf.' He noticed that someone had refilled the wine-flask.

'No, my lord,' said Jelita, and bowed.

'And before you go,' Nicholas said, 'take this platter. It is filthy, and should have been cleaned.'

The afternoon took its predestined course. The archers of the Confrérie of St George, pleasantly replete from their meal at the Artushof, lethargically competed against one another in the charming meadow which currently formed their arena. Pole shooting, target shooting, distance shooting engendered a few disputes and a good deal of loyal endorsement from wives and parents. It rained, causing a short intermission. The sun shone, upon which the bows came out again. The royal princes, who entered and won two competitions, were plied with sweetmeats and talked, shrill and croaking, together. Robin kept clear of them. It was bad enough trying to look happy. The wretched day was almost complete, release was almost at hand when, amid the shouting, the drumming of hooves, the screams of the triumphant contestants, the little prince Zygmunt sprang to his feet, drawing Robin's attention. The boy was watching a belated arrival: a rider who materialised unattended, and then guided his horse to the far end of the arena where, having rested his gloved hands on its neck, he paused and looked hazily round.

Robin said, *'Kathi.'* And Katelijne Sersanders, at this low moment in the lowest of days, lifted her eyes with misgiving and trained them, with rising anger, on the distant, disruptive person of Nicholas de Fleury.

FOR KATELIJNE, lady of Berecrofts, the misery had started that morning, with the message which confirmed all her uncle's suspicions. The King had gone. His official audience was cancelled. And it now became clear that it had never been the King's intention to receive the Burgundian embassy. Whatever the excuse — affairs of state, illness, a family crisis — the effect was an insult. To Anselm Adorne, experienced diplomat though he was, it was a humiliation he could not forgive. He had begun by refusing, point-blank, the Confrérie's repeated invitation to be their guest at these games. It had been Jerzy Bock, spokesman for the Danzig merchants and a St George's Elder himself, who persuaded him to agree. 'They wish to show that their esteem is not tainted by politics. Royal Prussia will be your friend, whatever Royal Poland may do.'

So Adorne had come, bringing his entourage with him, but leaving no instructions to pack. He had been obdurate. If the King wished to move, Anselm Adorne would follow.

'How can he be so blind!' Kathi had wailed to Robin.

'He is not blind. He has been slighted. He needs to recover. Give him time,' Robin had said. Robin was usually right.

Even so, the subsequent day had been miserable. The ceremonial ride to the ground had been disrupted by showers, the horses bucking and flying amid the rods of water discharged from the roof gargoyles. The street gutters flooded. Every other man told her, as men will, of the great plans to drain the moat and build a summer hostel for the Confrérie; but meanwhile they had to ride over the drawbridges and through the suburbs and past the watermills and the breweries to the edge of the vineyards, where the archery ground had been laid out.

This was simple enough, consisting of an oblong of grass upon which had been set a shooting-mast, a series of wands for field archery and, distantly, a mud wall on which targets had been fixed. Beyond that, there was space for flight shooting. There was a grassy bank on either side for the spectators, each fronted by a row of benches under an awning. The Confrérie officials occupied one of these, with her uncle and the Danzig merchants beside them. On the other was the palace party, consisting of the three youngest princes with their household officials and servants. The other foreign representatives, such as the Florentines, were seated some distance away. They had kept their distance, too, in the procession: no one wanted to catch the Burgundian infection. The papal nuncio, who had also been invited, was missing. The Patriarch had been with the King, they were told. The Patriarch, abandoning them, was possibly already on his way east and south to Caffa, and to Tabriz.

It had seemed merely an aggravation of all they were suffering when, once they were seated, their nearest neighbour proved to be Julius of Bologna. Adorne had barely responded to his bow, and had conveyed coolness, rising, when his German wife Anna approached. But no man with blood in his veins could long withstand that level, deep gaze. 'My lord, may I speak for my husband? He wished me to say that we have nothing but friendship for you, and hoped you would forgive us our loyalty to a still older friend, Nicholas de Fleury.'

Kathi, listening, thought how fortunate Julius was, and felt a surge of love for her uncle who, taking the girl's fingers in his, did not hesitate. 'Gräfin, of course. It is not for me to say where your husband's loyalties should lie. I know you have been kind to my niece.' And, making a space, 'Will you give us your company for a little?'

She sat as he asked, her eyes holding his. She said, 'There is something else. It has become necessary for Julius to settle a dispute in the Genoese colony at Caffa. It is between his branch of the Bank and the notary of a man who is dying. Of course, we shall not travel at the same time as you — we have to move fast, and at once — but it is not impossible that we shall meet when you come. We should try not to trouble you.'

And her uncle, after a moment's silence, had looked into those wonderful, dark blue eyes and said gently, 'You need have no fears. As it happens, my own journey is in doubt. The King has left Thorn, and all my plans are suspended. Even if de Fleury were with you, our paths would hardly cross.'

Anna's eyes were wide with concern. She answered, half automatically, 'Nicholas? Oh, we expect him to stay, working for us, or the Queen. But do you mean it, my lord? The King has gone! What will you do?'

The solicitude of a pretty woman worked its charm. Adorne's face softened. He said, 'There are various possible courses. One cannot quite brush aside an accredited ambassador. But none of that need concern you.' Then he paused. 'You say de Fleury may work for the *Queen*?'

It had startled Kathi as well. Beside her, she could feel Robin's stillness. The Gräfin said quickly, 'You hadn't heard? Then I may be quite wrong. But he spent the morning, I'm told, at the Burgh Halls with the Queen and Callimaco and the Venetian envoy. Someone claimed that money changed hands. Julius hoped he might choose to work with us, but others, of course, could offer more. My lord, might I bring Julius to speak, once the shooting is over? He has always admired you, and would not wish to be estranged.' She turned a little. 'Kathi and Robin would not mind?'

Kathi shook her head, hearing her uncle agree. She did not mind. This winter, however shallow his motives might be, Julius had stood by Nicholas de Fleury, as he had many times in the past. He had upheld him at Berecrofts five years ago, when a young woman died in the ice of a dark Scottish river, and Nicholas had been blamed. Anna, she thought, had a right to learn some of that, if not all.

She knew a little already, and Kathi answered her questions as the guild's heralds blew their flourish, and the contestants strode out, and the long, worthy succession of archers began to take shots at the papingo. Speaking like this, as she seldom did, it was clearer than ever to Kathi how much of Nicholas's character could be explained by his birth; with the repudiation of his mother by Simon her husband, and by Simon's subsequent vicious vendetta. She thought that Anna, too, might begin to interest herself in the enigma, even though she said very little, and that was mostly about Gelis, whom she admired. How had Gelis van Borselen come to marry a landless man born out of wedlock? Perhaps Nicholas had hoped to prove his legitimacy?

Kathi stared at her, and then fell back on modified discretion. 'You'd have to ask Julius. It would have been a good match, of course, if he'd been Simon's son. He would have had lands and a title in Scotland, and another title in France: his maternal grandfather was the vicomte de Fleury. But I rather think they married for love.'

And Anna had laughed and said, 'I think there is no doubt about that. She is ravishing. But there is a son, and I wondered if, for his sake . . . Kathi? May I confide in you?'

Kathi glanced round. Their voices had been low, and were now further drowned by the roar as someone brought down the second-last bit of the parrot. She saw without surprise that the marksman was Julius, and that Robin's seat now lay vacant beside her. Men. She turned back. 'I don't know very much about Nicholas.'

Anna said, 'I should never want you to say more than you wanted. But I am a little bewildered. Nicholas has asked if, one day, his son might marry my daughter.'

'Bonne?' Kathi said. Only the fastest of wits kept her voice level.

'Or, perhaps, any daughter Julius and I might have. I feel,' said Anna wryly, 'rather like Gelis's family must have felt at her betrothal. Of course we are fond of Nicholas too, but I wish I could see his future more clearly. If I ask you about him, that is why.' She broke off. 'That is all I wanted to say. Look! Robin is going to shoot!'

Kathi gazed at the field, her eyes blind. She realised that they were blinded not only by amazement but by the bulky forms of two men who had just arrived in front of her uncle. One was familiar: a servant from their own house in Thorn. And the stranger accompanying him was a courier whose travel-stained dress bore the badges of Burgundy. The stranger knelt, and her uncle took the packet he proffered.

It was wrapped in wax cloth, which he opened. Kathi saw that the papers within bore a seal, which looked to her like the great seal of Burgundy. Adorne's fingers hovered over it. On the field there was a roar of approval for whatever Robin had done that she would now never see. Under the awning, heads had turned, including those of Jerzy Bock and Jan Sidinghusen. Word was flying from one end of the ground to the other. *Charles of Burgundy has rushed a letter to Anselm Adorne, his ambassador. Will you take a wager on what it says? No?*

The courier stood. Adorne looked at the half-open packet in his hands. Anna rose and, glancing at Kathi, tactfully withdrew to her seat beside Julius. Kathi watched Adorne unfold the missive and scan it. His face flushed, and then patchily drained. Presently he refolded it and spoke to the courier, who turned with his conductor to leave. The President said, 'It is not bad news, I trust, my dear lord?'

Adorne looked at him. 'News, certainly; but nothing that need disturb so gracious an occasion. Pray do not concern yourself. I shall deal with it later.'

Kathi closed her lips, which had parted. She heard behind her the happy bustle of Robin's return, qualified as he realised that something had happened. The President, displeased, watched the courier leave and then, excusing himself, rose and walked to the edge of the field. The foot competitions concluded, and the preliminary announcements for the prize-giving began, after which there would take place the closing demonstration.

Adorne, collecting his papers, leaned over slightly and gave them to Robin. 'Perhaps you would take care of these?' His look, unmistakably, invited his niece and her husband to read. They did so together, at speed, crouched over the small, black angular letters as if they were chicken bones.

Charles, Duke of Burgundy to the most excellent Anselm Adorne, Baron Cortachy. It has come to our notice that . . . We are seriously displeased to learn . . . We assume that by this time you will . . . Nevertheless we cannot contemplate that . . . It is our command therefore . . .

Kathi looked away. Beside her, Anselm Adorne sat unmoving, his gaze on the field, his patrician profile betraying no emotion. Behind him, the murmurs continued. Before him, with laughter and shouting, announcements and awards were under way. Under Kathi's hand, the cutting phrases covered the paper. She could hear Robin swearing continuously under his breath, and compelled herself to read to the end.

It is our command therefore that you depart from the Court of King Casimir, and that, laying all other matters aside, you return to this country at once, leaving the papal nuncio and the envoys of the Republic of Venice to represent us in Persia. We repeat. Whatever you have or have not concluded, you are to return to our presence at once.

It was then that Zygmunt jumped to his feet, proclaiming the arrival of the one unprincipled man who embodied all the alien interests that had brought this about: the friend of Polish princes; the tool of the Patriarch; the past associate of the Venetian envoy. The child's welcome was for Nicholas de Fleury who, from the way he was sitting his horse, had just completed a long, liquid, and highly profitable morning in and about the marketplace — any marketplace — and was now making his way, at leisure, to where Caterino Zeno awaited him with a smile.

Robin said, 'Christ God,' and abruptly disappeared. Anna, her colour high, was grasping the arm of her husband and Julius was actually standing, his handsome face lit with glee. Beside her, Anselm Adorne was quite silent. Kathi felt her upper lip shorten, and told it to stop. She said to her uncle, 'We could go.'

He did not even look at her. 'Of course we cannot go,' he said. 'Or at least I could not. You may, of course. I would not have you treated with dishonour.'

He was not speaking of Nicholas. He was speaking of his recall, and all it implied. She said, 'This is not dishonour. It is expediency. The Duke knows he can trust you to do what is right; even to sacrifice your own pride for his sake.'

'And Tabriz? And Caffa?' he said. 'And all my kinsmen — your kinsmen — holding their own in an ocean bordered by Tartars and Turks, in the land of the Crimean Khan? Am I to abandon them and their hopes, and allow the Genoese to be driven from the peninsula because of *expediency*?'

Kathi said, 'We could go in your place, Robin and I. Julius is travelling to Caffa.'

'Julius?' Adorne repeated. He looked round, but Julius too seemed to have gone.

'He wouldn't harm us. He's interested in trading, not war. I know we are inexperienced,' Kathi said. 'But there are men who are familiar with the Black Sea and would advise us. There are consuls, interpreters, guides who would help us pass to Tabriz. We would bring back a report for the Duke.' She paused, feeling breathless. 'Whatever happens, the Duke will be in your debt. You will not lose by it.'

'You are confident,' her uncle said. 'Look at the man whose whim has ruined a nation, and see how he has lost by it.'

She stared at the field. They were rearranging it: setting up the marks for fast shooting from horseback; the targets, the wands. The central barrier had gone, and the archers' mast wore a ball, not a bird. To one side, grooms were arriving with horses and weapons: a bunch of short curling bows and their quivers. A group of three well-dressed men walked into the arena, where they fell into discussion with the President and some of his officers, and then separated. The tallest of the three, in a fine pleated pourpoint and jacket, was Nicholas. The second, covered in cloth of silver, was the Venetian envoy. The third, distinguished by his figured red velvet, was, astonishingly, Julius of Bologna. His wife, gazing at him from the pavilion, wore an expression of exasperation and anxiety which exactly matched Kathi's own. She had just signalled Anna to join her when, with a thud, Robin returned.

He said, 'He won't recognise me. I can't get near him. Sir, they're going to ask you to take part, and it isn't fair. You ought to withdraw.'

In adversity, Adorne could be both collected and patient. Now he said, 'Robin, I can hardly do that. What are they going to ask, and how will it be unfair?'

But it was too late for Robin to answer him. As the question was asked, the President returned to his seat, bringing with him the last person a dismissed Burgundian ambassador would wish to see: Caterino Zeno, with his glossy black hair and his sallow face round as a button. He was already equipped for his display: his left forearm, as he bowed to Adorne, was sheathed in an elaborate bracer of embossed leather, and the thumb ring on his other hand was of jade. Gifts from his wife's uncle, no doubt, like the bow chased with gold, and the great sheaf of eagles' wing-feathers that his servant held in their quiver, a snow leopard's tail furled round their stems.

Foreign rubbish, Kathi diagnosed bitterly. Persian rubbish, such as Meester Nicholas de Fleury and probably Meester Julius of Bologna had been trained to handle in the Levant, as Zeno had in Tabriz. And now they were being brought into use to ridicule the Burgundian ambassador. The former, the unwanted Burgundian ambassador. And even as she formed the thought, Zeno spoke — not in Italian but in loud and creditable Polish, addressing her uncle.

'My lord, forgive me. I have usurped your position, thinking that the King's jealous love would prevent him from sparing you to us. We know you must hasten to Persia, but we also know your reputation for chivalry. The President and I beg you to do us the honour of leading us in this, our small demonstration of horseback archery with the small bow. A round at the mast, a round at the butts, a round of flight shooting, and then some trick work together. My lord is familiar with all this, of course.'

He knew enough Polish by now to understand the gist of what was said. He also knew its intent. Her uncle answered, in Italian, 'You flatter me, sir. The short bow is not my weapon. I have some skill at straight shooting, that is all.'

'But that is all you require,' said Caterino Zeno. 'Leave the last phase to us, but give us the pleasure of sharing this skill with the guild. I have a bow you may use. It will serve you well at the mast and the butts and perhaps you would demonstrate a flight shot to end with. That is all we ask. Pray agree!'

Anselm Adorne had suffered one public humiliation. He would not show cowardice by trying to evade another. He said, 'Trick archery I must leave to you. But yes, I should be glad to open with you in a display of the other kind, so far as is in my power.'

Anna was biting her lip. Robin growled. Kathi wondered what he had expected to say to Nicholas when he arrived. Perhaps to ask him not to take part, or to accept Robin as his squire, or to allow Robin to shoot alongside him. But Robin had rarely used the short bow. A first-class archer, as her uncle was, could wield it, as he had said, in straight shooting. He had excused himself, reasonably enough, from the other kind. But to save his face, and his reputation, he must excel at what he did.

They had not expected him to agree. Kathi saw the President's surprise, and Zeno's mischievous grin, and the air of weary resignation with which her uncle rose, shed his splendid robe, and followed Zeno on to the field in the white shirt and sleeveless pourpoint and hose that emphasised his flat shoulders and still-supple waist, his fair, whitening hair curling round his neck under his deep velvet cap. Her lips compressed and her stomach rose into her throat. She excused herself and stepped quickly out, seeing Robin's glance of surprise as she went.

Some time, she would have to tell him, but not now. Not until her uncle had agreed to send them both to Tabriz; and perhaps not even then. She wondered, while being sick, if Persians were good at midwifery. She wondered, with angry impatience, what had gone wrong this time with Nicholas, and at what point even Robin would see that nothing more could be done, and give up.

It started to rain.

Chapter 11

By the time Anselm Adorne made his entry into the field of the Confrérie of St George at Thorn, every man in the ground knew that he had failed in his mission, and had been recalled by the master who sent him. His intention, alone and against odds, was to deliver a performance that would remind them, when he had gone, that he was Genoese, and Burgundian, and a knight who remained loyal, no matter what his lord chose to demand. Honour required him to demonstrate moral and physical courage against three perfidious men, two of whom had cause to harm or remove him. What he had not expected was that the elements, too, would be his enemy.

There had been a time when rain won or lost battles. It still happened. When, long ago, the gods had given immortality to the man who waterproofed the first bow, they had not ensured that the recipe was infallible. At Crécy, in the war against England, the shrunken strings of the Genoese crossbowmen had earned them the contempt of both sides. It was not by coincidence, Adorne knew, that the strings and weapon loaned him by Zeno were not proofed. The rain which he now felt on his cheek might fade away. If it grew worse, he could expect accuracy for a short time, but that was all. He did not make a complaint. There was mockery enough in the occasion: in the ceremonial ride into the field, two by two, the Venetian at his side followed by de Fleury and his lawyer. De Fleury who had inclined his head with drunken languor when they met, and smiled in conspiratorial greeting at the man Julius. The applause itself was a sham.

The bow served him for the first shot at least, which had to be taken, moving, on horseback. The mast was a hundred and twenty feet high, and the ball that topped it was much harder to hit than the papingo, which he had carried off with his crossbow so often at the St Sebastian meetings in Bruges. Then he had been shooting on foot; but he was a first-class horseman, with strong nerves and an accurate eye. He circled, once, twice, and then shot. Against the dark sky, the golden ball burst into bright flying fragments: the unfeathered dove. The rain beat on his back. The crowd applauded as he cantered to the side, and Julius took his place as the fresh ball was hoisted.

The bow of Julius, one could guess, had been proofed, and the hundred-pound pull was no trouble to a stalwart man trained by the Bank's own mercenary captain. An exuberant combatant, Julius was never the most guarded of performers: his first arrow glanced off the post; and his second made Nicholas duck. The third halved the ball, and his audience, disarmed by his unselfconscious good humour, cheered as he trotted back, grinning. Caterino Zeno took his place.

The rain was now becoming unpleasant. At this late stage, there was no question of closing the games; those who could not tolerate it had left, and the rest, used to brief soakings, simply pulled up their hoods and huddled closer. The water ran down Zeno's magnificent cloth of silver, drenching the two splendid white plumes in his hat and rendering brighter still the gold, the silver, the turquoises of his quiver, and the shining, safely waxed strings of his bow. His horse, twirling, frisking, curvetting, was foreign as well, and Zeno rode it with the short stirrups and forward-leaning seat of the Persian who is trained from birth to ride without reins. As he set to circle the mast, gaining speed, he tossed the bow into the air and caught it.

'Charlatan!' Robin muttered, watching.

'But also a marksman, I'm afraid,' observed Anna. Since Julius's competent performance, she had shown herself willing, in a resigned way, to comment. And she was right about Zeno. Having put his small speedy horse through its paces, the Venetian set it into a gallop and, riding faster and faster, rose in the stirrups to shoot. He hit the ball. But he made the shot backwards, over his shoulder. Then, amid uproar, he cantered back to take his place by the other three.

Adorne saluted him, as did Julius. Nicholas did not go quite so far. It was a feat, even if the Venetian used his own horse and bow; even if he wore, strapped to his bow-hand, the ivory trough which, by extending the draw of his arrow, added valuable power to its cast. He was a citizen of the Republic, and it was his duty to promote it. The next moment, de Fleury rode out unsensationally on his borrowed mount, equipped with his borrowed quiver and bow. The string was proofed. There was no excuse therefore for his failure, three times over, to shoot an arrow anywhere near the gold ball. One of the shafts, descending at random, came close enough to cause his three partners to scatter. The third time, the drum beat his recall and, frowning, he trotted over to Zeno, to a chorus of good-natured catcalls. 'Messer Caterino, who makes your arrows?'

'Messer Niccolò, who brews your ale?' said Caterino Zeno.

. . .

'. . .THAT WAS DELIBERATE,' Kathi said to her husband. The awning mumbled and spat: the rain was heavier. Robin and Anna exchanged glances.

Robin said, 'I was close to him just now. Kathi, he hasn't been drinking water.'

'It's not only that,' Anna said slowly. 'Is it?'

Kathi gave her a comradely look, and silently congratulated the Divine Bounty which had produced someone who could apply her mind to Nicholas without becoming instantly revolted. She said, 'No, it isn't, although he's pretty sodden as well. I shouldn't necessarily trust him an inch, but those shots were deliberate.'

'I don't see why you think so,' Robin said. He sounded exasperated. Kathi slid her hand into his.

It attracted one of Anna's wry, glinting smiles. 'I am afraid,' she said, 'that Julius is the worse for drink also. What are we to do with them?'

ON THE FIELD, his shoulders soaked, Adorne narrowed his eyes at the butts. His hair streaked his cheeks, and the grass churned under the hooves of his horse. Soon, the whole stretch would be mud. He was fortunate, being the first man about to dash across the width of the field, loosing his arrows. Or fortunate in the matter of foothold. Upon the range of distant targets to his left, the white of each bull's-eye was exactly the size of a crown: he was supposed to hit them while galloping, and his soaked string was useless. His mount continued to fidget, disturbed by the incessant manoeuvres of Zeno's short, deep-chested animal at his side. Behind Zeno was Julius and here, on his own right, was de Fleury. It enraged Adorne that, through no fault of his own, he was about to seem as incompetent as this unspeakable knave. The unspeakable knave, leaning over, said, 'That's a good bow.'

'It's wet,' said Adorne. He spoke shortly. The trumpets blew to announce the next phase, but Zeno's horse was still displaying its rider's skill and its mettle.

'All the same,' de Fleury said. He leaned over further. Unbelievably, before Adorne could stop him, his opponent had snatched up his weapon and carried it back to his own knee, causing his own horse to start. Next, grinning, de Fleury flung up his shirt-arm and plucked off his hat with a flourish, upon which his horse faced about and showed signs of evacuating the field. The trumpet blew a second time, and someone shouted his name. Adorne exclaimed, 'What are you doing, de Fleury? Give me my bow!'

It came, thrown into his hands, and he raised it, breathing quickly in anger. Then he saw that this was not his own bow, nor any of Zeno's providing. What he held was a small unadorned weapon of horn, wood and sinew, expertly proofed, and designed, Arab-style, to accommodate its own *majrā*: the trough which, like Zeno's, added length and power to each pull.

Adorne said, 'But this is yours.'

'Loaned me,' said Nicholas. 'Use it. Keep your shaft to the right.' Adorne stared at him. The field quietened. He heard his name called again. Anselm Adorne drew a short breath. Then, leaving his reins, he lifted the bow, and flung his horse into motion.

To cross the field at full gallop was a matter of moments. Twisted in the saddle, Adorne shot — once, twice, thrice — at the distant white coins, and, slewing round at the end, heard the three roars, and saw the flag lifted three times. With a strange weapon, out of a turmoil of angry surprise, he had delivered three shots in the white. Flushed and panting, he sat in the saddle and gazed over the field, where his fellows were set to perform.

He hardly heard the reception for Julius, who managed two out of the three at quite a spectacular speed. He did hear the shouting for Zeno, for it greeted a performance as good as his own. But the rest of his attention was fixed on the distant figure of de Fleury, who remained, awaiting his turn, with Adorne's useless bow in his hands. Except that it was useless no longer, for in those few moments aside, he had seen de Fleury begin, with powerful hands, to replace the wet string with the dry one from inside his hat. On horseback. And on a short bow with a hundred-pound pull.

But brute strength and long practice were one thing, and the sober concentration required by a feat such as this, on a thrice-churned field, were another. De Fleury pounded cheerfully across, occasionally sliding, and shooting carelessly and fast into every place on the bank but the white, after which, laughing, he tossed up his bow as Zeno had done, and caught it in cheerful contrition. Arriving, he did not even look at Adorne, and the latter, the borrowed bow outstretched, let his hand drop. He did not understand, but he could not deny he was grateful.

Zeno, accompanying Nicholas to the line for flight shooting, was in a sardonic mood. 'You should have kept your splendid bow. Where did you get it from? And having acquired it, why give it away?'

'Well, you saw,' Nicholas said. 'Even when I had it, I couldn't do anything. It was the wine *and* the beer, I suppose. I think I'd better leave the long distance to you, and save myself for the rest.'

Zeno had laughed, and Julius, overhearing, had punched Nicholas on the side and remarked that he didn't think he had anything left that was worth saving. Then Julius turned round and joined Zeno and Adorne at the line, and the last of the envoy's ordeals began: the round in which each man had three chances to shoot as far as he could. It was not a competition, and there were no prizes to be had, but honours between Genoa and Venice were at present even, and Anselm Adorne wished to change that.

He still had the bow. He had, more than the worth of the bow, the furious determination inspired by de Fleury's inexplicable act. Adorne's first two shots were both fine, but the last was brilliant, travelling straight and hard for well over four hundred yards. Even Zeno was unable to match it, never mind Julius the lawyer. Anselm Adorne had finished by holding his own, and even by creating a record.

Shaking his fellow performers by the hand, returning to bow to the President and, amid acclaim, to retake his seat, the Burgundian envoy could be satisfied. He had represented his master. He had completed the programme he had set himself, and had emerged unharmed, and with credit, as something better, at least, than a disgraced ambassador.

He was conscious, of course, of his debt. Quitting the field, he had returned the bow to its temporary owner with a curt question. 'Why?'

And the dark-rimmed, unhealthy grey eyes had glanced at him with something almost like amusement, while Nicholas de Fleury had said, 'Isn't it obvious? So that I shan't be blamed when you die.'

Then the princes left, and there remained only the exhibition of trickery. The Venetian and his pair of Persian-trained acolytes would surely enjoy displaying that.

Seen from the President's pavilion, the little extravaganza that followed was pleasant enough. Their anxiety removed, Adorne's companions could even admire the dexterity with which Caterino Zeno, twisting and turning between the lines of fine wands, would aim and strike each one from one angle or another; how Julius, acrobatic on his high-prancing horse, would run beside it and leap in and out of the saddle and then, racing parallel with de Fleury, would toss over and re-toss his weapon, each man shooting with first one bow, then the other. Lastly, in unison, the two performed the feat de Fleury had already demonstrated and unstrung and restrung their bows at the gallop, while controlling the beasts without reins.

Watching them, Anna spoke slowly. 'I wonder how often they have done that before. They are reading one another's intentions.' And she added, half to herself, 'I didn't know.'

'Perhaps they, too, had forgotten,' Kathi said. She viewed the two laughing men, and Caterino Zeno, who was not laughing. She had seen

Nicholas ride. She had seen him swim with a horse in the sea, and slide with one into a chasm of ice. She had heard from Dr Tobie of the games in the Meidan at Trebizond, where the hooves danced on cedar flour instead of thick mud, but where, nevertheless, Nicholas had been pitched to the ground. He had looked, arriving today, as if he had had just such a blow, and had tried to drink his way out of it. Then it came to her where she had seen that look before. She said aloud, 'He has been divining.'

'Nicholas?' said Robin sharply. The field shooting had finished, and now they were about to end, as they had begun, with the papingo: this time the proper parrot in wood, with its five sections to be shot down, leaving the last and smallest core for the victor.

'This is a country of silver and copper,' Anna said. 'I suppose his skills are worth a great deal, unless they exhaust him. You say that they do?'

'He has recovered now,' Kathi said. 'If you call that kind of behaviour a recovery.' Her eyes were on the field. The three riders, bows prepared, had taken their stance at intervals round the base of the mast. Receiving their signal, they had begun to set their horses in motion. As they gained speed, they fixed their gaze upwards, to the papingo at the top of the mast. For this time, they were to hit it at will, and as often and fast as they were able, until all the parts had been pierced and brought down. The rain beat on the contestants' dirt-smeared features and the upturned faces of the spectators, and frothed on the grassy mud. The awning rattled and boomed, so that Anselm Adorne had to lift his voice when he spoke.

'I am a little concerned. They have no protection.'

Jerzy Bock leaned over. 'They are good marksmen.'

'Even so. Shooting from all sides at once, it is dangerous. The arrows hit and rebound. We are safe enough, but they are not.'

But even as he spoke, a roar proclaimed that Zeno, his smile fixed, had repeated his own earlier feat and, shooting in reverse, had brought down the first part of the parrot. Then immediately, a second roar and a shout of laughter greeted the fall of a second part, brought down by Julius in an extraordinary shot which not only speared the wood, but caught it with a second arrow before it dropped on the ground. Then Julius himself yelled, for Nicholas, lowering his bow, had abandoned shooting the papingo in favour of firing his arrows, one after the other, around and sometimes into the upturned hooves of Julius's horse as it galloped, mud flying, before him, while Julius wildly attempted to bring it back under control, cursing at the top of his voice. The crowd hooted and Robin, his face brilliant, said, 'What about *that*!'

'I don't know about *that*, but Zeno is going to shoot Nicholas if he doesn't begin to take this seriously,' Kathi said. And just as she spoke, everything happened.

Zeno, his face showing his impatience, lifted his bow and released first one and then a second arrow into the papingo and then, taking a third, increased his speed until he had overtaken both Nicholas and his victim, coating them with mud in the passing. Nicholas spluttered, clawing mud out of his eyes, and Julius, yelling, brought his horse cantering back into its circuit and prepared to aim at the papingo again. Zeno, now on the opposite side, launched an arrow. Nicholas, his face still masked with mud, armed his bow and lifted it to do the same, just as his horse lost its footing.

Four arrows flew. One, from Zeno, whizzed straight for the papingo. The second, from an ecstatic Julius, crazily split Zeno's arrow in half. The third sprang, as his horse fell to its knees, from the short bow of Nicholas. And the last emerged, already singing, from somewhere at the edge of the field, and was not shot by the contestants at all.

The last arrow, which was a featherless bolt from a crossbow, soared over the field and clubbed the central pole of the spectators' awning under which Adorne sat, bringing down the rest of the frame and causing the cloth to empty its heavy burden of water over the broken timber and struggling people below. Anna was knocked to the ground.

The arrow ejected by Nicholas drove through the air with great force, and striking Julius, bored clean through his body.

Zeno set his horse at the crowd, and identifying the rogue with the crossbow, shot him dead.

In the field, Julius cried out, dropping his reins. His body inclined, remained caught by one foot, and then toppled finally on to the ground. Nicholas, brought crashing down by his horse, scrambled to his feet and stood still, his face ghastly. In the pavilion, Adorne, bruised and soaked, flung debris out of his way and began lifting canvas and shards to locate Kathi. Robin, doing the same, found and helped Anna, who had injured her shoulder. Kathi was discovered dazed where she had been thrown, her pallid face powdered with dust. Opening her eyes, she saw her uncle and Robin and finally Anna, risen with blood on her arm. Looking up at the tatters above her, Kathi said, 'Someone sneezed?'

Robin snorted, his eyes very bright. Her uncle knelt. Anna, dropping beside him, was exclaiming. 'Kathi? Are you all right? Is the baby all right?'

'The . . . ?' said Robin slowly.

'What?' said her uncle.

Anna looked up, and then down to catch Kathi's grimace. She bit her lip. 'I'm a fool. You hadn't told them,' she said. 'Oh, my dear, I'm so sorry. I guessed; I thought everyone knew.' From shock and distress her eyes were filling. Adorne stooped and, lifting her, steadied her shoulders.

Kathi said, 'They were going to have to know some time. Don't worry.' She spoke automatically. Her gaze on Robin, she was trying to rescue the moment, to recreate it, to exchange, without words, all the things that should have been said, for the first time, when she told him. Reading his eyes she knew, suddenly, what he, too, was trying to say, and would say when they were alone. But for the moment, he simply dropped to where she was and took her in his firm, enveloping embrace, and she found herself crying as well.

It was then that they heard someone calling for Anna.

Nicholas, standing straight-backed by the rigging of the mast, watched Adorne approach, helping Anna over the uneven grass. She wore a scarf round her shoulder and arm. By then, the horses had gone and there was a ring of people about Julius's body. One of them was a physician. Zeno could be seen at the edge of the field with the President, examining the corpse of the man who had brought down the pavilion. There was no doubt, of course, about who had brought down Julius. They were kind enough to say that it couldn't be helped, in the rain, with his horse falling and the arrow already sprung. Anna came up and looked at him and cried, 'What have you done?'

What have you done! Night, and an icy river outside Berecrofts, and an old woman's voice flinging the same bitter words at him over the still body of someone else who did not deserve to die. If there was justice, this was justice. Nicholas looked at the beautiful woman Julius had married and replied, 'I have killed him.' Then the violet eyes turned from him and she walked slowly to where her husband lay, the slanting eyes closed, the shapely limbs slack, and the careless, life-loving spring of wilful enjoyment all stopped.

Nicholas found that Adorne was standing beside him. Adorne said, 'I have spoken to those who saw it. It is not your fault. I am sorry.' He paused. 'You suspected there would be an accident to the awning? You said something of it.'

He had more than suspected; he had known. Jelita's masters had made sure of that. Poland disliked Genoa and dared not offend Venice, but there were limits.

Nicholas said, 'It will be hard to find the truth, now that the archer is dead. You were not hurt? Robin and Kathi?'

'Are also unharmed. I would not have spoken to you as I have,' said Adorne unexpectedly, 'if you had been the worse for wine. But no man in his cups could have made those hoof-shots as you did. Your friend did not lose his life through your failings, but from mischance.'

The rain fell. Nicholas, finding a stay from the mast at his side, ran his fingers along it and kept it. Adorne, after waiting a moment, moved off towards the little tableau around Julius's still body. Nicholas shut his eyes. It was Anna's voice he heard next, soft and clear above the beat of the rain. 'Wait! Wait! He is breathing!'

Adorne said, 'De Fleury? Are you there? He is alive!'

Nicholas heard him. Although his hearing persisted, his brain and his sight had become disconnected. His grip slackened. The cable rasped through his palm, and the ground tilted below him. He did not realise that he had fallen, and was lying, like Julius, in the mud.

IT WAS GIVEN TO Robin to shepherd Nicholas home, once the field had been cleared and the fit of dizziness had sufficiently passed.

Glancing at him from time to time as they rode, his former squire made no attempt at conversation. He had already said all that was necessary: a quick assurance that Master Julius still lived; and a word to explain that Nicholas himself was to stay at Adorne's house, to leave space for the sick man at Herr Straube's.

'Adorne wouldn't wish that,' Nicholas had said.

'He suggested it,' Robin had answered. That was all that had been said.

Robin was thankful for it, and guilty because he was thankful, with two-thirds of his mind singing with the news he had just heard. He thought of Kathi's face, looking at his, and felt again a pang of mild anger at Anna's thoughtlessness. It would mend itself, as soon as Kathi and he were alone. Meanwhile, it was easier to be here than in her company, and forced to be speechless. They were to have a child. He was to have the joy, all his life, of Kathi's child.

Remorsefully, he looked again at the closed face beside him, but was too wise, now, to blurt out encouragement. *Now you have both of us,* he had said, brashly, to this man by the river at Trèves, and had seen Kathi's glance of warning too late. For what had happened today, he had no comfort to offer. He had never had such an experience, although he knew it could happen in battle: the spurting arrow, the gaudy sword-stroke that severed the life of a friend. It was probable that Julius would not survive. Of course, there would be no recriminations. Everyone had seen the horse stumble. Everyone knew how long the two men had been together, in Bruges and then with the Bank. Robin grieved for Nicholas, without knowing what to say that would help.

It meant, of course, profound changes even if Julius survived. Julius could not now go to the Black Sea and Caffa. Nicholas might well stay in Thorn and work out his penance by presenting his talents to his company. And of course, there were other plans now overturned that he had scarcely as yet had time to think of. Kathi's uncle was returning not just to Danzig, but to Flanders. And the offer so lightly made by his niece was no longer valid. Robin and Kathi would not now be calling at Caffa, or taking Lord Cortachy's place at Tabriz. Kathi would return home with her uncle, and Robin with her, to await the . . .

His horse jerked, and Robin hissed under his breath and then steadied it. Something had dawned on him. Kathi had known she was pregnant when she had made the offer to travel to Tabriz. She had wanted to go. And that was why she had not immediately told him.

Nicholas said, 'Are you all right? Is Kathi all right? I'm sorry, I should have made sure.'

His face was still colourless, but not quite so closed. Robin took a quick decision and said, 'She's more than all right, sir. It has been a better day for us than for you. I have just heard the news: she's with child.'

'You've *just* heard?' the other man said.

Robin, puzzled, remembered again what had annoyed him. He said, 'Anna blurted it out. She'd guessed, which was more than I did. But we are so pleased.'

'And so am I,' Nicholas said. 'It is what I would hope for you both. It doesn't know how lucky it is.'

And Robin laughed, alight with joy. For he thought no one as lucky as he was, with the first child, hoped for by them both, on its way so painlessly and so soon. And he had been lucky to find in his wife a friend who had become increasingly his great and sole love, while keeping also, despite everything, his regard for this man who had shaped his young life.

Robin rode beside him in silence to the square, where grooms took their horses, and where he showed Nicholas watchfully into the house by the Artushof, there to surrender him into the hands of the house steward, who had already, it seemed, received his orders. The lord was recommended to accompany him to his room, and to rest there.

Obedient to the decree, Nicholas had paused to thank Robin, and to send a message to Kathi. He still looked and moved like a sleepwalker. Robin thought that Adorne had been kind in sparing him the need to face them all, for the moment, at any rate. Or perhaps Kathi had thought of it first.

At his side, the steward said, 'I was to tell you, Pan Robin. The lady of Berecrofts is waiting for you.'

HOURS PASSED. Awakening in an unfamiliar, candlelit room, Nicholas searched his memory for the reason, and found it. He also retrieved a vague recollection of drinking something which felled him with sleep. It had a familiar after-taste. Subsequent to that, evidently, he had been undressed and left covered in bed. But this time, there had been no voluptuous dreams.

The voice of Ludovico da Bologna broke upon his right eardrum. 'Are you sick because you hit him, or because you missed him? Now you can come to Tabriz.'

Nicholas forked himself into a sitting position.

'Just a pleasantry,' the Patriarch said. 'Certainly you are not wearing a hair shirt, I observe.' The bulky figure in the uncertain light was demoniac; the pectoral cross thick as horse-armour. He had asked Callimaco to find the Patriarch for him, and here he was; when now there was no conceivable purpose in meeting.

Nicholas said, 'It was an accident. How is Julius?'

'Still alive,' the Patriarch said. He lifted his cross on its chain and used it to rap Nicholas on the finger. 'The little girl said you'd been divining, and she hadn't even seen that. I hear you gave the Queen some excellent advice on how to rule Scotland. What a helpful person you are. And now you may multiply your good works and show penitence for your bad in one stroke. Come to Tabriz.'

'I might have done,' Nicholas said. 'But surely not now. Not until Julius has recovered, if then.'

'You would let his poor lady go to Caffa on her own?' the Patriarch said.

'Anna?'

'They were both to have travelled there with young Berecrofts. Now Julius cannot go; nor can the boy and his wife. I myself must leave at once. But whatever the fate of the unlucky Julius, his wife must travel to Caffa as soon as she may. And what better reparation could marksman make to his target,' the Patriarch said, 'than to assume the protection and care of his wife?' He waited, staring from under his brows. 'God forgive me, are you sick for some reason? Shall I send for your man?' His eyes mocked.

'Why must she go?' Nicholas said. It was an effort.

'Business. She will tell you herself, if you propose to give yourself the trouble of calling tomorrow. If he is dead, I shall stay for the Mass. He deserves that much, poor fellow.'

He rose to go. Nicholas could think of nothing to say. The Patriarch said, 'Make your mind up. It is overdue.'

The door shut. On the bed, Nicholas doubled up over tight-folded arms, and started to shiver.

JULIUS WAS STILL ALIVE the following morning. Nicholas crossed the square and was admitted by Straube's servant, who took him up to the sickroom. A tapestry had been hung to keep out direct sunlight, and Anna's face looked lily-white in the gloom. There was a physician by the bed, and a monk in an apron mixing something at a side table. The scene was an old one, threadbare in its familiarity: only the man in the bed — Godscalc, Zacco, Bessarion — seemed to change. Now the strong bare shoulders, the sunken face were those of Julius. His eyes were open.

Anna rose and, taking Nicholas by the hand, brought him round to the bed. She said, 'I'm sorry. It wasn't your fault. I was too shocked to think.' (*What have you done?*)

'Well, you were right. I had shot him,' Nicholas said. Below him, there took place, remarkably, a faint widening of the patient's lips. 'And not before time,' Nicholas added, responding to it with a tentative smile of his own.

'You were always a bloody bad shot,' Julius said in a whisper. Then he shut his eyes, and the doctor signalled that he should go.

Anna followed him out, and he did not know whether to touch her or not. He said, 'I am so very sorry. What do they say?'

Her eyes today were less violet than black, and stained underneath with her vigil. She said, 'They are not sure, but there is hope. They say it will be a week before they can be sure. Will you stay until we know?'

'Of course,' Nicholas said. 'Did you think I would walk out?'

'He jokes,' she said, 'but I know he would want it.' She frowned. 'We have taken your room.'

'It doesn't matter,' he said. He had had an interview with Adorne, stiff and cold in the Artushof. The Burgundian party was leaving, and the Danzig merchants with it. If Pan Nikolás wished, he might take temporary occupation of one of their rooms, with a bed for his servant. Thorn wished him to stay; the Danzig merchants still had hopes of him. So had the King. Jelita had transferred his belongings already. Adorne, receiving his thanks, had made it clear that he proposed to maintain the distance between them. He had not seen either Kathi or Robin this morning, and the Patriarch had gone out.

To Anna, Nicholas said, 'Is there anything I can do? Anything at all?'

She looked up at him. Then she said, 'Later, perhaps. Nothing just now, Nicholas, except perhaps to pray. He must mean as much to you as he does to me — perhaps more. You have known each other for a long time.'

He left quickly, but Callimaco caught him as he ran down the steps. 'How is he?' He listened. He said, 'It was my bow. I feel as if I had killed him myself. You were not accustomed to it.'

'I was perfectly used to it,' Nicholas said. 'And I was and am grateful. Whatever happened was none of your doing. But now, if I stay, my duty must be to Julius. I shall have to make my apologies to you and to the King and, I suppose, to Signor Zeno.'

'He has gone,' Callimaco said. 'Come in. You look as if a glass of wine might not come amiss. He has gone to Hungary, where they will knight him and make him great promises, which they will not carry out. But I think he knew you would not go to Tabriz.'

Nicholas followed the Italian into his house, and stood in the hall. He said, 'Who fired the shot that brought down the pavilion, and why? Zeno killed him.'

'No one knows,' the other man said. He pointed to a chair, and clapped his hands for a servant. 'It was a murder attempt. The supports of the awning had been tampered with. It only required one shot by that bolt to bring it down.'

'But against whom?' Nicholas said. Now he had the wine, he wasn't sure that he wanted it. He sat nursing the cup.

'Who knows? Someone with a grudge against the elders of the town? Against the Burgundian party? Against the rich foreign merchants of the Artushof? They will investigate,' Callimaco said, 'but I doubt if anything will be found.' His robes, as he took his seat, fell in graceful folds to the floor, and his fingers holding the wine were long and supple. He said, 'I am more concerned over you. Will you talk about it?'

'I made a mistake,' Nicholas said. 'I can, I think, draw the necessary conclusions without too much help. But I thank you.'

'The sick man can recognise and heal his own ailment? It is possible. It is not what I meant. (You are not enjoying your wine?) We spoke of the fire-mountains of Iceland.'

'You spoke of them,' Nicholas said.

He was ignored. 'You are acquainted with the natural sciences, with the phenomena of the earth and the mathematics of the stars. You have experienced different customs, different climates. You have been exposed to prophecy: you have lent yourself, through the art of the pendulum, to forces you do not understand . . .'

'I brought —'

'You brought my cameo. In my turn, I thank you, but I do not want it. You have made it yours. It obeys you.'

'It is the other way round,' Nicholas said. 'But I didn't come —'

'You didn't come for such questions, or to assuage your guilt or your grief. You came, I think, for what I was about to offer you. To discuss what has happened, and to place it in relation to other events.'

'What has happened? The fall of the awning?' He was being stubborn.

If he was being stubborn, the other man, this time, was being deliberately wilful. Callimaco said, 'I dream of writing a book. I had hoped, if you had stayed, that you would discuss it with me. It would contain all the themes I have mentioned. It would provide a context for the event you have not described: the discovery that one has deprived a friend of his life.'

The audible thud as the arrow entered the firm chest. The muddy, lustreless stain from which trembled and swelled a body of glistening scarlet. Once, they said, Callimaco had proposed to kill a man, in cold blood, for a principle. Nicholas said, 'You will have to write your book without me.'

He received a long scrutiny. At length: 'You are under no obligation,' said the other. 'There may come a time when you think differently, and I shall still be here, I suspect, with the book as yet unwritten. You did however make me one promise. What did my cameo tell you?'

Whoever is unsupported by the Mystery of Love shall not achieve the grace of salvation. Whoever shall cast love aside shall lose everything. 'Something I already knew,' Nicholas said, 'but had tried to forget.'

'Something painful. Shall I say I am sorry?' Callimaco said.

'No,' Nicholas said.

'Because you deserve pain? Or because it has restored to you something of worth?'

Nicholas rose, and laid down his cup. Buonaccorsi, taking his time, did the same. Since Oliva, Nicholas was aware, the other man had changed in his perception. It was not enough, not nearly enough to urge him to confide. Nevertheless, he did consider the question, and answered it under his breath. 'Both, I think,' Nicholas said.

Nothing more of significance was said: he had taken his stance, and Callimaco had accepted it meantime. They parted with the light embrace warranted by their strange paper friendship, which had been replaced by something hardly less fragile. Making his solitary return to the place where he now lodged on sufferance, Nicholas found it empty of all but house-servants. Adorne and his family were out taking their leave of their hosts, as were Sidinghusen and Bock. He did not want to see them. He particularly did not want to meet the Patriarch yet. But standing there at his window, looking across at the bustling market, beneath the booming tower of the squat Burgh Halls, he was conscious, as seldom before, of being entirely alone.

Chapter 12

WHATEVER ADORNE'S opinion of Julius, it was not in his nature to leave Thorn without calling on Anna, to discover what she might need, and how her husband was faring. Kathi went with him, and stayed longer so that, alone, Anna could talk to her freely. She considered her brave. Listening to Anna, she thought of the contrast of her own night in Robin's arms, wrapped about by new joy, while Anna might never know that comfort again. Yet Julius's wife bore no grudge against Nicholas. 'They are like children, careless with drink, wild with excitement . . .' And she had rubbed a hand over her face. 'It is my only fear, that when Julius recovers — and he *will* recover — Nicholas will still be here, unregenerate, and the mischief will start all over again.'

'He will want to help you,' Kathi said. 'He will do anything you wish, after this. He could be of great use in the business.'

'I know,' Anna said. 'And Julius would like that, of course. If only Gelis were here!'

Kathi gave a wry smile. 'You think she could control either of them?'

'The household could,' Anna said. 'Remember the poem? That was the smoke of self-sacrifice, not the indifference it might seem. Your conscienceless friend is passionate about at least one person, his son. With that small boy to rear, Nicholas would do nothing rash. From what I have seen of his nurse, Mistress Clémence is wise with adults as well as children. And perhaps even Dr Tobias would come. Robin says that he and Nicholas have fallen out and become reconciled in the past.'

'Perhaps he would, but Gelis wouldn't,' Kathi said. 'And without her consent, he could never see Jodi. In any case, he isn't ready for Jodi, and Jodi shouldn't have to act as his crutch. Nor should anyone else. Perhaps, if he hadn't alienated them all, they would come and restrain him for a while, but it never seems to last long: he breaks away and does something unforgivable yet again. He has to learn on his own.' She broke off, hearing the bleakness in her own voice. 'Which isn't much help to you. I'm sorry, but I don't think you are going to separate Julius and Nicholas that way.' She wondered, as she spoke, why they were talking of a difficulty that might never materialise; and realised that this, of course, was why they were talking. It was unthinkable that Julius was going to die.

Anna said, 'If Nicholas were legitimate, would Gelis feel differently?'

The hum of the market came through the closed windows. Women's voices spoke outside the door, and a clatter of pewter as something was carried upstairs on a tray. Kathi said, 'What do you mean? If there were a superior title for Jodi, would Gelis feel bound to repair the marriage? I don't think so. I think that her personal association with Nicholas matters more than anything else ever could. But does the question even arise? I thought his bastardy was proved by default.'

'But if someone were to show otherwise?' Anna said. 'You once mentioned a vicomte de Fleury. There was a man of that name in a monastery on the Montello, in the March of Treviso, north of Venice. Julius heard of him. He said your uncle had a brother buried there.'

This was true. She looked at Anna in astonishment. Jacques Adorne had spent two years with the Carthusians, and died there, a monk. On his way home from Venice three years ago, her uncle Anselm had taken his eldest son Jan to the grave, leaving Kathi in the nearest town to await them. Neither had spoken of this. She took a moment to think. Then she said, 'Was the vicomte a very old man?'

'I don't know. He may have been. He had no powers of speech and was quite helpless, Julius was told. He may even be dead. But Gelis could find out,' Anna said. 'As you go home, you could send and tell her.' From sleeplessness, her eyes were large and strained: she talked as if she were discussing the most important thing in the world. And then Kathi remembered that, if Jodi and Bonne were to marry, it might well be just that, for Anna. Her lover and husband might never recover, but she would secure a future for the fatherless Bonne.

Kathi crossed the room and, sitting, put her arm round Anna's shoulders. 'He'll get better,' she said. 'And we'll keep these two villains apart, whether we have Gelis to help us or not. But don't underrate what Nicholas offers. He can help you: he has a genius for business. And you might even come to help him. He needs a regulator. And Robin and I shan't be here.'

'You are fond of him,' Anna said gently.

'I used to be,' Kathi said. 'Half of me, I suppose, hasn't stopped. The rest has suspended judgement: that's Flemish caution for you. But he has taken this accident badly, and that's a good sign, I suppose. Force him to stop and think, and not to escape sideways any more. I confide him to you.' She halted and said, 'Yes, I'm fond of him.'

'I wish you were staying,' Anna said.

. . .

THE DAY WENT ON, and Julius lived. In the house of the Burgundian envoy the horses and packmules were assembled, and bags and crates and baskets appeared in the hall. Adorne interviewed and rewarded his servants, aided by the two Danzigers and Robin. Kathi went and tapped on a shut door. Nicholas opened it.

'You are leaving,' he said, and jerked the door wider. She entered, with care.

This was not the histrionic Nicholas of Mewe, with his wounding tongue and his single problematic relapse into tenderness. It was not, either, the crass intruder of yesterday's games, where he had saved her uncle from ignominy — but only because it suited him, or so he had said. This was not even the person who, encouraged by Anna, had earlier sent to ask Kathi to see him. This man, wearily inviting her into his room with something almost like hatred, was demonstrating that he did not want to encounter any soul from his past, and especially a friend. She sat, and he said, 'I have some wine, unless it is drugged.'

And, having no wish, as it happened, to pursue that, she jettisoned her qualms, crossed her ankles, folded her hands and gazed at him critically. 'Ludovico da Bologna?' she said. 'He always could produce this effect. Did he ask you if you meant to kill Julius?'

He opened his fingers and let drop the wine-cup he was filling. He did it quite deliberately, under her eyes, and she watched the cup roll and dent, and the spilled wine grow bald and begin to outline the tiles of the floor like a Teutonic town grid. 'Which means that he did,' she concluded equably. 'And perhaps you actually did give way to a sudden urge to get rid of Julius who, I agree, can be quite atrociously insensitive. So you shot him, and are now seized with terror, wondering what next your devil is going to allow you to do. Or . . .'

She paused, and he took his hand away from the hour-glass he had just turned upside down, having refrained from dropping that, too, on the floor. 'That is not very polite.'

'I am sorry,' he said, with no appearance of it. He remained standing. She resumed speaking, her voice as bland as before.

'Or perhaps you were simply drunk, or exhausted from divining — why did you so foolishly agree to do that? — and it has left you feeling as frightened of yourself as we are of you? I should like a glass of wine,' she added, 'if Jelita could bring you some more. Do you know what his name means?'

He blinked. For a moment, what she was attempting hung in the balance. Then he cleared his throat. 'He goes by the noble name of Bowel. Sally Jelita, I call him. Raging Bowel.'

He went to the doorway and called the man, allowing Kathi to blow her nose quickly. As he came back she said, 'They like intestinal jokes. They call watermills farters.'

'He is a spy,' Nicholas said. 'Jelita. A palace spy.'

She looked at him. 'You didn't warn us.'

'He was and is spying on me, not on you. You had nothing to lose. Adorne never had a chance anyway.'

'Why not?' she said.

'Because, obviously, I am in collusion against him. Hasn't your uncle already told you?'

'He said it was possible. He mentioned a few others with motives and influence, but I expect we could discount all those,' Kathi said. She noticed that her fingers were white, and unclasped them.

'Julius may die,' he said suddenly. The tone of his voice was a rebuke.

'But you didn't mean to kill him,' she said. She waited.

'Of course I did,' Nicholas said.

Her heart ached. He moved restlessly, once, and then stopped. His gaze turned to the door.

Kathi said slowly, 'Is *that* why you do what you do?'

'What do I do?'

He was still watching the door. Sally Bowel. His profile looked grey. Steadily, she gave him answer. 'Commit perpetual follies, to deserve perpetual punishment?'

He turned. For a fraction of time he looked into her eyes. Then a dimple slowly appeared and, with a stifled sound of amusement, he set to his desultory pacing again. 'No one has accused me of being crazy before. A life dedicated to misery? Really?'

'People feel guilty,' she said. 'Sometimes with cause, sometimes not. Sometimes they don't even know why, because they don't want to remember. Anna would never believe you'd harm Julius.'

'Will you tell her?' He was looking at her.

She took her time. 'No. You won't do it again. But you weren't really thinking of Anna, were you; only of Julius and yourself?' She broke off. She said. 'You should try to see behind all that self-possession. Anna is kind. She cares, like Bel. You do like her?'

'I like Bel,' he said. 'I'll take your word about Anna. You are saying I ought to confide in her?'

He hadn't said he didn't like Anna. He must have noticed how lovely she was. He hadn't had, as yet, much chance to discover anything else. Then she remembered something promising, in that respect anyway. 'You must like her,' Kathi said, 'if you want Jodi to marry her daughter. Or perhaps you were just tormenting Julius and never meant it at all.' She wished he would sit down.

Suddenly, he did. 'She told you? And you disapprove because of Jodi's youth? But it isn't more than a suggestion. It would unite two parts of the Bank. Gelis would first have to agree.'

She was relieved. She said, 'Anna would help. She would do anything to see you together with Gelis.' She hesitated. 'She told me about Montello.'

He stopped breathing. She saw it. Then he said, 'What about Montello?'

'Julius heard that the vicomte de Fleury — that your grandfather was being nursed in the Carthusian monastery there. One of my uncles died in the same place. It's just outside Venice. Jan went there with his father three years ago. I didn't know the connection. I don't think Uncle Anselm did either. But you did?'

'Yes,' he said. 'Naturally, he had to be paid for.'

She wished she had never opened the subject. She said, 'Anna thought Gelis ought to be told. She thought the old man might throw light on your . . . You might learn finally the truth of your birth. But you must know all he could tell you already.'

'No. I have never spoken to him,' Nicholas said. 'No one has. He is paralysed. There is no point in Gelis or anyone else visiting him, even with the lure of becoming mother to the next landless and penniless vicomte de Fleury. I'm sorry. You and Anna have clearly discussed the matter in depth.'

'I thought you would want it for Jodi,' Kathi said sharply. 'I heard about the poem you burned.'

The door opened. 'You did?' Nicholas said. Jelita came in and, receiving permission, crossed and prepared to pour out fresh wine.

Kathi hid her hands in her sleeves. She said, 'Anna told me. It wasn't hard to guess why you did it.'

A tray appeared, and she took a cup from it, as did Nicholas. Jelita bowed and departed. A few moments before, she had tried to joke about his name. Before the door had time to close, Nicholas had again disposed of his wine with a flourish, but this time down his throat. After that, he lifted the wine-flask, and refilled his own cup. Hers was untouched.

He said, 'There is poetry and poetry. Posterity, I assure you, lost nothing in that piece. Indeed, this time' — he emptied the goblet once again — 'not even the ashes complained.' The grey eyes, returning, contemplated her. 'Will two cups be enough? What else did you want me to tell you?'

He had guessed, although Jelita, bringing the wine-flask, had not. The drug this time had been light; enough, she had thought, to smooth this parting, and to give him ease afterwards. She had not expected confidences, although he had made her some without wine, and what he had withheld then, she suspected he would withhold now. She began, none the less, by simply repeating his last words. '*This time, not even the ashes complained?* What happened the other time, Nicholas?'

He answered with no hesitation, slurring slightly. The readiness itself was a mockery. 'Gelis once burned a toy and it screamed. She wanted to stop me divining where Jodi was. But of course, even ash is enough.'

He stopped, lifting a self-admonitory finger. Then he unfolded his other hand with the cup. 'Shall I drop it again? Now you can guess all that happened.'

'Don't,' Kathi said. She could guess. Destroying the poem, he must have thought it was over; the single agonising effort to make bearable the unbearable loss. But then he had found himself divining for Zygmunt, and the hungry spirit had abandoned the lesser child in its burning desire for a trace of his own. Eternal folly. Eternal punishment. She said, 'You want to see Jodi again. You want Gelis. You aren't really indifferent to Whistle Willie, to Tobie, to John. Use your brain.'

'I did,' he said. 'Look what happened.'

She was exasperated. 'Then take advice.'

'Anna's?'

'If you are going where she goes. Or you have talked to Callimaco.'

'The hyacinth of Cracow.'

'All right. But a learned man with a circle of sages and writers and artists who speak the same language as you. Nicholas, you see how they are struggling to find a new régime after the Knights. They have to teach these young boys how to rule, and keep their frontiers safe against all their neighbours. You could advise them.'

He was lying back in his chair, his eyes closed and both dimples showing. 'Redeeming my soul after ruining Scotland?'

'If you like.' She wanted to groan.

'Or ruining Poland? I might.'

'Of course,' she said. 'If you can't control your own whims, then you might. In which case, you had better go off to Tabriz with the Patriarch, and give Jodi up. By the way, if he loses his mother, what then?'

'Bel would take care of him,' he said. 'Or the van Borselen. Or you and Robin might, if you would. But you will have your own.'

'If need be, we should make him our own,' Kathi said. Looking at him, she found herself swept by inappropriate pity. She said gently, 'You were not much older, were you, when your mother died? How did she die?'

His eyes were still shut. He had been seven years old, she had heard, when his grandfather had sent him to Jaak de Fleury. De Fleury and his wife had since been killed, and the grandfather ruined. The paralysed grandfather who had to be paid for.

Watching him, the closed eyes, the closed face, Kathi thought of her own mother, lost early to illness, but leaving her daughter and son tended and happy under the tutelage of their godfather Anselm Adorne. Nicholas had exchanged his mother's home for something much harsher, had heard his mother reviled as a whore and repudiated by Simon, her fine Scottish husband. Small wonder that it had led to this: talents squandered, friendships in ruin, love cast away. And now, by the depth of the silence, she realised that she had asked a question of greater weight than even she might have guessed. How did she die, Sophie de Fleury, when just a year older than this, her second and only living son?

'You don't want to know,' Nicholas said, as if she had repeated her question. He opened his eyes. 'I should make you drink your own wine.' Curiously, his face, although hollow, was serene. He added, 'Or would you then give birth to Endymion? Robin wouldn't mind. I have never seen a sane man in such a state of ecstasy. Have you chosen a name? Robert? Archibald? Anselm?'

The wine had worked, she saw, as she intended. He would sleep when she had gone. She said, smiling, 'Or Margriet or Katelijne or Louise. Or what do you think of Aerendtken?'

'Ask the Patriarch,' Nicholas said. 'He'll tell you to wait till it's ripe, and then boil it through twelve Ave Marias. Oh Christ, I'm going to sleep and I haven't said what I wanted to say.'

'Then say it,' she said. She rose and came to him, sinking down by his chair, and trapping his hand in both her own before he could stir. 'What was it?'

'I am sorry,' Nicholas said. 'That was all. I am sorry. I am sorry.'

She swallowed. 'I think you ought to be. But show me, don't tell me. Show Anna. You have a great deal to make up to Anna for. Nicholas?'

He opened his eyes.

She said, 'I have something to tell you. Nicholas!'

He smiled, his eyes closing again. 'Tell me tomorrow. *Kochajmy się,*' was all she caught.

Having brought him the respite, it seemed unfair to attempt to disrupt it. She kept his hand for a while, contemplating the broad palm and strong fingers that could both preserve life and take it away. She wondered if he would adopt her advice, or even remember it. She thought that she would knit him a glove with two thumbs, if he did. She gave him back his warm hand and walked away, turning at the door to scan him for the last time. He was wholly asleep by then, and no longer smiling.

SHE DID NOT TELL HIM the next day, or ever, for that night Julius sank, and Nicholas spent all its hours by his bedside, silently watching with Anna. Then, when the sky paled and the house-signs creaked in the dawn wind, it was young Berecrofts who came to Straube's door to say that the Burgundian envoy was leaving, and would presently call. Robin was standing alone in the hall when he heard the measured tread on the stairs, and saw that the man coming towards him in the half-light was Nicholas. He looked grey, as Kathi had said. Robin said, 'Sir? They say he is still holding on.'

'He is strong,' Nicholas said. 'Adorne is coming?'

'He wanted to see you.' Robin looked at him in distress. 'Kathi and I wanted to stay. I meant to go with you.'

'I know. You meant well, but it might not have been worth it. As it is, Kathi seems to think I should remain and rehabilitate Poland, in my customary manner.'

Robin felt himself flush. He said, 'It was one choice we both knew you had. Or to help the Gräfin with her business, here or elsewhere. Kathi felt you might think she favoured one course over the other. She gave me a letter.' He held it out.

In the growing light, he could see nothing but mockery. Nicholas said, 'She suddenly realised she had compromised the entire future of Royal Poland and Royal Prussia by exposing both to my volatile nature? Let me see.' And he took the letter across to the lamp, where he opened and read it at a glance. He looked across. 'You know what this says?'

'She told me,' said Robin. 'She tried to tell you herself, but . . .'

'But she had misjudged the dosage. You will have to watch her,' Nicholas said. 'You may find you are conducting your entire family life from your bed. Will she drug the children, do you think?'

He had been awake all through the night by the bed of the man he had shot, perhaps killed. The words were random. Robin said, 'I wish we could have helped. You may be better without us. Listen to Anna. We could write to you, if you tell us where you are. And if you have any . . .' His voice faded.

'Messages? No.' Nicholas was burning the note. The light hardly reached under his lids. 'Does anyone else know about this? Apart from Elzbiete and Paúel and, I suppose, the semi-bereaved Anna? Yes, certainly Anna. This longing to have her appointed my nursemaid.' He looked up from crushing the ash. 'Doesn't anyone worry in case I take Anna, too, on to a raft?'

Robin sank his teeth in his lip. Then Nicholas flung down the platter and said, 'Kathi was right to keep me speechless. You can't possibly understand. All I can say is what I said to her. I am sorry. Go away. Expect nothing. But believe that I am sorry.'

Robin had begun to move forward, saying something, when the main doors clattered open and men began to come in, escorting Kathi's uncle, come to take his leave of Herr Straube, and visit the sick man and his wife. And, briefly and finally, to part from Nicholas de Fleury of Beltrees.

It did not take long. Formal words were exchanged, ending in bows. Nicholas was a disgraced man in exile, who had betrayed the Burgundian trust in a country of moment to Adorne as well as himself. He was the man who, very possibly, had engineered the Polish rejection which had led to Adorne's recall. Against that, his gesture in the sports field had very probably been no more than the act of self-interest he had called it. If Adorne were returning in anger, then at least his niece and nephew were also withdrawing unharmed from the orbit of this extraordinary man, in whom charisma and evil were so fatally mixed.

Adorne left, and Robin clasped hands and followed him. Nicholas watched them both out of sight.

JULIUS LIVED THROUGH all that day and the next. On the third, Nicholas returned to the empty house that had contained Anselm Adorne, his young married kinsmen and the two sobered Danzig councillors, and was visited by the Patriarch of Antioch, also preparing to leave.

'So!' said the priest. 'You've had your mind made up for you, I hope. Caffa and Tabriz.' The energy vibrated into the room, released by the impending journey, rocketing papal and Imperial commands into the ether. He paused. 'What's the matter? The man's recovering. The girl will set out on her own. You'll follow me with her. You'll try to bed her, if I know you.'

'You don't mind?' Nicholas said.

'You won't succeed. She's as capable as you are, behind all those pretty manners. I don't know why she ever married that fancy lawyer: you may have done her a favour,' said Ludovico da Bologna. 'So why not come and enjoy yourself?' His words, although encouraging, were accompanied by a perfunctory glare.

Nicholas found he wanted, rather feebly, to laugh. He straightened. 'Might I have Callimaco as well?'

'Don't be cheeky,' the Patriarch said. 'Make your plans. Hire your horses. Lay out all Signor Zeno's good money. I'll tell Uzum Hasan to expect you. You might get to climb into bed alongside him and all his four wives.'

'Father,' said Nicholas. 'How can I resist?'

He meant it, in a distorted way. He did not say that of course he was going to Caffa: the decision was long ago made, and he was already well ahead with his plans. City of Tartars and Christians, set in blue waters, and hanging with vineyards and fig trees, cherries and peaches; its fields heavy with corn and its houses scented with flowers and the warm smell of ripe watermelons . . . Caffa in summer, with Julius's beautiful wife. How could he resist?

And especially how could he resist, now that he possessed Paúel Benecke's secret: the piece of sea captain's gossip that the bastard had jealously kept to himself all through winter, despite Colà's cajolery? Of course Nicholas de Fleury was going to Caffa, my dears.

Kochajmy się.

Et non est qui adjuvat.

Help me, for I have no one, now. And right and wrong are the same.

'Nos,' BEGAN THE DOCUMENT. Kathi read it, skipping the hard bits.

Nos proconsul de consules oppidi Dantzig in Prussia . . . We the governor and councillors of the city of Danzig in Prussia —

'— *attestamur quod reverindissimus pater et dominus Ludovicus, sacrosancte apostolice sedis orator et nuncius, ac patriarche Antiochensis* . . . attest that Ludovico da Bologna, papal nuncio —

'— *et eneroso domino Anselmo Adournes milite, domino de Corthuy, consilarii, ambassadore et cambellano serenissime Karoli* . . . and Anselm Adorne, Baron Cortachy, councillor of Duke Charles of Burgundy. . .

'— *absolvit* —

'— whom he acquits.

The word that mattered. The niece of the *enerosus dominus* stopped, sniffed, and scrambled at speed through the rest:

'— of the charge and management of his Mission to the Prince Casimir, King of Poland . . . produced as evidence certain letters patent . . . but left behind at the Court of the aforementioned lord in the city of Thorn . . . who by no means appeared and was nowhere seen, as we are informed by the sufficient witness of Jerzy Bock and Johannes Sidinghusen, our delegates to the general assembly of deputies. *Idcirco, in fidem huius et testimonium, secretum nostre civitatis presentibus est subappensum.*'

And the seal hung below the two signatures. The affirmation, written today and witnessed in the winter assembly room of the Town Hall in Danzig, that Anselm Adorne had carried out the commands of his Duke to the best of his ability, and that no blame attached to him for his failure to present his Duke's letters to the King of this land.

Katelijne Sersanders closed the scroll and gave it back to her uncle and Robin, who had brought it. No one spoke. They were in their familiar noisy lodging at the Kogi Gate by the Green Bridge in Danzig, with the busy waters of the Mottlau outside their windows, and the last, bitter phase of their mission was now complete. King Casimir, having received no demands, was absolved from providing excuses or promises. And Danzig, left unconstrained, had replied with polite dismay to Adorne's charges.

Piracy? Surely not. Nothing more than a dispute between merchants which, in extremity, might be settled by the normal processes of civil law. The Medici — Tommaso Portinari himself would recognise the justice of this. Tommaso Portinari, whose likeness now hung, not in obscurity in the monastery at Oliva but blatantly, on the altar of the Confrérie of St George in St Mary's Cathedral in Danzig. Henne Memling's greatest work had arrived, with a pirate's help, where it was to remain.

There had been some small successes. Questions of trade had been ironed out, concessions made, arrangements reached, friendships formed. Communication with Bruges and Burgundy would henceforth be easier for a while. But nothing could compensate for the rebuff by the King and the Confrérie or — more wounding for Adorne than either — the recall which meant he would never travel the road his ancestors had taken, down the great rivers and over the steppes and the mountains to where his coat of arms decorated the frowning towers of castles, and he could make or stop wars with his letters, as his ancestors had done with their swords. If lost now, the opportunity would never be vouchsafed him again.

That afternoon, as the business had reached its conclusion, Kathi had made her own pilgrimage through the town, along the clamorous wharves and below the creaking wheels of the Crane, up the broad market street past the Artushof; over the ground trembling with the force of the *Ordensmuehle*. Past the church of St Nicholas, from which a cheerful Scots voice issued to hail her, and into the cathedral with its great astronomical clock, telling the phases between wars.

She called on the houses she knew, and sat in the shade of their orchards, where once she had trodden in snow, and related all the gossip of Thorn. All of them wished to know about Colà. All were surprised at the news, although none could match the intensity of her own relief, when she first heard it. 'He is going to Persia! And escorting a young married woman for part of the way! Would her husband not object?'

She explained about the Patriarch, whose household Anna would join. She explained about Julius, now slowly recovering, but was vague about the source of his hurt. It should not have surprised her, calling on Elzbiete, to find that Elzbiete already knew.

Paúel Benecke's daughter had lost none of her bulk, nor her forthrightness. Hugging Kathi in welcome; exclaiming in rapture at the news of her forthcoming child, Elzbiete was uncompromising in her opinion of Nicholas. 'Of course, he shot the fool to have the wife for himself. She is the woman who bought half his ship, but hasn't yet paid for it? My father would have done just the same. But you are not displeased? The story I told you has helped? We agreed that Colà should leave, and even that a woman might coax him. Maybe you chose the woman yourself?'

'He knew her already,' Kathi said. 'And it isn't quite as you think. She'll take care of him.'

'Like Gerta,' said Elzbiete.

'Yes. No,' Kathi said. She laughed. 'Just accept it's a good thing. What about your father?'

'What about him? He is on the high seas, stealing something, no doubt. He was angry with Colà; then he set to planning what they will do when he comes back. Will he come back, Katarzynka?' Elzbiete said.

'He might come back to Poland, but I don't think he will sail with your father. I think that is over,' said Kathi. 'Your father will find someone less wild.'

'He liked Colà,' said Elzbiete. 'They would have killed each other, but he liked him. Now he will die of drinking instead.'

THAT NIGHT, lying still in his arms, Kathi touched Robin's cheek. 'I don't want to leave Poland.'

'You must.'

'Of course. I know.' They had talked for a long time of the coming child. Thinking of her own childhood and Robin's, of her uncle's pride and love of his family; thinking of what Nicholas had undergone, and of what Elzbiete had told her of her father — abandoned, brought up at sea, condemned to search all his life for a companion — she had realised that she must bear her child at home; that she had been wrong to think of anything else. Then she thought of her answer to Elzbiete's question. Nicholas would not rejoin Paúel Benecke, she had said.

She thought that was true. The winter of desperation was over, and something must now take its place. Fate was carrying Nicholas where the Patriarch always intended to have him, and Christendom might get some good of it by mistake. She knew, as well as the Patriarch, that he had chosen to go for no spiritual reason. The Patriarch would assign the credit to Anna, but it was Elzbiete who had supplied the real lure: the secret that Kathi herself had sent Nicholas. The whispers about some lost gold, and a Spaniard, and a trail that led to the pirate haunts of the Black Sea around Caffa.

He might find his gold. He might create a merchant empire in Caffa, Circassia, Trebizond. He might settle in Poland. He might never find wealth, but still discover a purpose. And at least the journey itself would separate him from the dangerous life he was living. Although time had taken care of some of that. Benecke had gone, and Julius would lead no one astray for a while.

Robin was stroking her arm, his cheek on her shoulder. He treated her breathlessly now, as if she would bruise under his touch. She ran her fingers lovingly over his skin, to give him leave. She said, 'Julius. We'll have to tell Gelis. Shan't we?'

His head moved. Then he said, 'You don't really think he meant to kill Julius?'

She said, 'He sometimes loses control when he's goaded. He blames himself afterwards.'

'I know he blames himself,' Robin said. 'It was his fault, and he was trying to say so. But he wasn't upset when it happened. They were *laughing*.'

'So we tell Gelis it was an accident?'

His hand had moved lower. He said with sudden half-genuine annoyance, 'How did Gelis get into bed with us anyway?'

After that, because she had invited him, everything became rather pleasant and serious. But before her thoughts turned away, her mind heard again the drugged cry that contradicted all Robin's fine theory.

'I am sorry,' Nicholas had been driven to plead, although not to her. 'I am sorry. I am sorry.'

Not to her; for he had not used her tongue. He had spoken in the language of Homer, and of the great poet-librarian of Alexandria whose follower he had known, it seemed, for so long. He had reverted to the speech of the ruined empire to which he was returning, and of the man, also lost, in the end, who had belonged there. It was their forgiveness he had asked for, not hers.

Part II

CIRCASSIAN CIRCLE

Chapter 13

ARRIVING IN VENICE that summer, Caterino Zeno paid an enjoyable visit to his wife Violante, a lucrative one to the Doge and Senate whose servant he was, and lastly, with the mixture of opportunism and malice for which he was noted, directed his barge to the Bank called Ca' Niccolò where, landing, he enquired for the lady Egidia van Borselen of Beltrees. He was amused, lingering in the ornate marble hall, to hear from somewhere behind and outside the competing voices of very young children.

The message, conveyed to the counting-house, was received by Gregorio, the Bank's long-time director. He did not immediately take it to his new partner. Instead, withdrawing to assume his lawyer's silk robe and black cap, he took a moment to think, while sending to have the man taken aside, and offered a dish of fruit and some wine.

He needed to think, if Zeno had brought news of Nicholas de Fleury. For eight months now, by silent consensus, he and the others struggling to uphold the integrity of the Bank had taught themselves to envisage Nicholas as not only departed but dead, his ostracism regretted only by his army captain and Julius, neither of whom had any particular grasp of business morality, and by his son, who was too young to understand.

The arrival in Venice of Nicholas's wife and son Jodi had taken place in December, just as letters of warning about Nicholas were arriving from Trèves. Gregorio had greeted the beautiful Gelis with extreme caution verging on panic, and had been confused but relieved to see his own wife receive her with sympathy. Margot knew Gelis better than he did, and he trusted her judgement. And then, to reassure him a fraction more, it turned out that Gelis had come with the company doctor. Tobias Beventini might have turned his back for good upon Nicholas, but he had reached other conclusions about Gelis. 'She was obsessed. She forced him to compete against her in business, and she feels responsible for the way he elected to win. She wants to help put it right.'

Gregorio thought of his letters. He said, 'I understood she was selling his plans to his rivals.'

'She secretly joined them,' Tobie had said. 'She told Nicholas that to his face on that bloody day of reckoning between them at Trèves. She did it to win their God-awful contest and found, when they'd finished tearing one another to bits, that she'd failed because he was more ruthless than she was. At any rate, she's not likely to try it again. After what he did, she left Nicholas, and she couldn't return to the Vatachino if she wanted to. As it is, she's done the opposite. She's written down all their trading secrets for you, and she's willing to invest her own money to replace something of what Nicholas squandered. If you want, she'll stay and help with the business. She's had some experience.'

'I know she has,' Gregorio had said. 'But might she not want to use it to finish the Bank, as she has finished with Nicholas?'

And Tobie had listened, his cap dragged off and his balding scalp gleaming, and had said simply, 'She is offering a large sum of money. Take it. Make no promises. And see what she does.'

And what she had done was prove herself, bit by bit, to be almost as able as Nicholas. She could deal with the minutiae of running a company — she had shown as much in the short spells she had already spent in their branches: with Julius in Cologne, Diniz in Bruges, Jooris at Antwerp and here in Venice with himself. She had displayed it, there was no doubt, with Father Moriz and Govaerts during the term of the Bank's stay in Scotland. And what she had done for the Vatachino was evidence of another kind.

It was apparent also that she was a strategist: that rare person who could absorb and analyse current events, and construct from these a policy for the future. She did not have Nicholas's instant comprehension of numbers. She did not have his imagination: the intuition that took the facts and drew from them some project so unlikely that only Nicholas could have thought of it. But she was, she proved over and over, prodigiously gifted, hard-working, and beyond every doubt trustworthy in all that she did. And all those hours when she was not in the bureau, or representing the Bank in the Republic, she was to be found with her son and his nurse.

Venice had learned to admire her. Gregorio himself had eventually accepted her, with the others' approval, as a working partner of his Bank. And from Margot his wife he knew that the joint household was running in harmony and that, one day, even the nurseries might blend. His own son was nearly three, but Jodi was three years older than that, and had found himself separated from a father to whom, Gregorio had been astonished to discover, he seemed to have been deeply attached. The best remedy for that was the constant attention of his mother, which for the first time, perhaps, he now had. Soon the memory of his father would fade and then (said his excellent nurse) he would welcome a small friend such as Jaçon.

The Bank was slowly climbing the path to recovery. Nicholas's wife and his son had found a haven. The ugly wound left by his perfidy had been forcibly stanched and bundled out of sight, and the small group of folk he had deceived, now scattered, were methodically remaking their lives. And now Caterino Zeno had come to disturb them.

Well, thought Gregorio, let him come. Six months ago, it might have been different. But now, surely, they were secure. He settled his gown and was calling a servant when Gelis herself appeared at the door of his chamber. She said, 'They tell me Caterino Zeno has called.'

She looked composed. She had always been slender, and for a few weeks in the winter had appeared sufficiently etiolated to cause Margot anxiety. Then she had regained her strength, and was now much as he remembered her when she and Nicholas had become lost in the ecstatic affair which had led to their marriage. Gregorio had never quite known how Nicholas achieved his legendary successes with women. But it was clear to him how this pale golden girl had become his wife: the surface coolness did not always conceal what lay beneath.

But now, she heard him in silence and then said, 'He will have news of Nicholas, and wants to see how we receive it. Shall I see him alone, or will you come and support my performance?' Her eyes were sea-blue, and smiling.

Gregorio said, 'It may be bad news.'

And Gelis looked at him and said, 'But we have already had all the bad news, have we not?'

HOWEVER SPLENDID HIS DRESS, or skilled his barber, or devoted his masseur, a man who has spent nearly three years in the Levant will bear the mark of it for many weeks after, never mind one single day. Caterino Zeno, springing to his feet as his quarry entered the room, had the weatherbeaten skin and nervous energy of a traveller who, even yet, has not shaken off the need to be wary; but his eyes, scanning Gregorio and his fair companion, were bright. It was Caterino Zeno's cleverness, his curiosity and some would say his cheerful heartlessness that made him such an excellent ambassador for his city.

He thought again, kissing her hand, what a lovely woman Gelis van Borselen was, and that she would not long remain single, even in this uxorious household under the good Gregorio of Asti and his suspicious regard. Her marriage with de Fleury had failed, one supposed, because of the undoubted misconduct on either side. It occurred to Zeno, sitting, to wonder whether she suspected that de Fleury had been the lover of his own exquisite wife Violante. He himself was reasonably sure, but had not pushed Violante into admitting it. She had given him his legitimate heir, his handsome young Pietro, and he had his own compensations — a pretty daughter, for example, born in Georgia three years ago. Violante had said nothing of that, any more than he did of Nerio. They lived in a civilised world.

Now, he gave himself the pleasure of delaying his news, asking first after the lady's child, and Gregorio's family, and the fortunes of the Bank, now it had divided under its managers. Responding freely to questions, he described with attractive modesty his years in Persia at the warlike Court of the Turcoman prince, and the successes he had achieved in the name of the Lion of St Mark, for this dear Republic, so generous to all those who helped her. And finally, he related how he had returned — with such travail! through such danger! — by way of the Kingdom of Poland. His news from Poland, indeed, was the occasion for his trespassing thus on their hospitality. But someone had to be told. A double tragedy. And who would have guessed?

Surprisingly, it was the lawyer, Gregorio, who paled. The girl — the woman, she was in her late twenties — had weighed him up sooner, and, dropping her eyes to her lap, had shown no immediate sign of alarm. Only at the end, looking up, she spoke before her companion could do so.

'Some deal has failed to go through? Any other tragedy, I feel, would have been reported to us by now.' The man Gregorio had glanced at her.

Zeno said, 'I fear you are wrong, and I am the harbinger. The lord of Cortachy will hardly have made his way back to Flanders as yet, whereas my report will be released by the Senate tomorrow. I wished to warn you beforehand. I do so with the greatest reluctance.'

He treated the woman to a sensitive pause and saw that he had made an impression at last. None the less she did not exclaim, but merely spoke in a taut, level voice. 'Are you saying that Anselm Adorne has changed his mind about going to Tabriz?'

'Changed his mind? No. His mission has failed,' Zeno said. 'The King found himself unable to receive him, and your own Duke wrote to demand his recall. You will hear no doubt from Bruges. Duke Charles has decided that to send Adorne to Tabriz was impolitic, and Adorne has agreed to return.'

She had flushed. 'On Venetian advice.'

'And that of others. The lord your husband was of significant help.'

'Nicholas was in Poland?' the lawyer Gregorio broke in. He was still pale. 'What was he doing?'

Zeno released a delicate sigh. 'What was he not doing? I am sorry, madonna, but you must know your husband: his love of drink and riotous living. Tragedy was going to come of it: something much worse, madonna, than crazy contests and rich, idle women, such as Paúel Benecke pushed in his way all through the last winter. When Benecke left, it seemed that all might be well. We talked, as I said. De Fleury commended himself to the Queen and her sons, describing to them the proper management of Scotland. But the rot was there, the tragedy was preparing from the moment your former colleague arrived. Your lawyer friend Julius.'

Again, it was the man who responded, his voice as sharp as his nose. Gregorio was not renowned for his looks. 'Julius was in Danzig?'

'Thorn. All of this happened in Thorn. Ah! Herr Straube does not, of course, report to Venice now?'

'He works for Julius. But Julius, of course, writes from time to time, and no doubt we shall hear from him. So?' said Gelis. 'Apart from the Burgundian Mission, where was the tragedy?'

'Julius will not write to you, madonna,' said Zeno sadly. 'Your Maestro Julius is dead, killed in public before the eyes of his wife and the merchants of Thorn. Another *San Matteo*, you say! Another international incident, requiring the attention of princes? No, for your Maestro Julius was slain by a man of his own kind. By your husband, madonna. By his former patron, M. Nicholas de Fleury.'

Predictably, it was the lawyer who jumped to his feet. 'I don't believe you.' The young woman sat motionless, her eyes large. The man Gregorio spoke again, a little more formally. 'I am afraid I find this hard to believe. How and where is it supposed to have happened?' And finally, after a pause, 'Did they come to blows? Was M. de Fleury the worse for drink?'

'Yes,' said Caterino Zeno in a soft voice. 'I am afraid he was. But they did not quarrel, at least. There was a contest. They had bows. M. de Fleury's horse slipped, and his arrow misfired. He was not imprisoned or called to account: the shooting was clearly an accident. But a tragic one for your friend and his wife.'

'Anna?' The woman opposite him moved at last. 'What happened to Anna?'

Caterino Zeno conveyed deep regret. 'The details I do not know: you will hear them from Anselm Adorne. But the last word I heard was that the Gräfin, courageous as you are, had determined to carry on her husband's business, and was leaving for the trading marts of the Crimean peninsula. Our friend Nicholas de Fleury, they say, proposed to accompany her.'

This time it was the lawyer who flushed. 'You find that strange? That Nicholas should give a woman protection?'

'Not at all!' said Caterino Zeno, laying down his wine glass and rising. 'It is what I should expect, except that, of course, a former Venetian banker might require more protection in the Peninsula than he can give. No. I came in friendship to tell you the facts before others hear them. You will have cause to be glad, perhaps, that you and your Bank are no longer tied to de Fleury or Burgundy. You will not even require, I suppose, to consider the fate of the Cologne business, as that will descend to the widow and her young daughter.' He viewed the lady sympathetically, his head to one side. 'Have I distressed you? Please forgive me.'

The lady rose. She said, 'You have done what you came to do, and we shall no doubt receive the full story in due course, from the other participants, as you say. I am not sure that I understand why the Gräfin and M. de Fleury are both leaving Poland?'

He gave a gentle shrug, while retaining his expression of sympathy. 'The lady's company had urgent business in Caffa where the Genoese live and trade, as you know, by courtesy of the Tartar and the Turk. And M. de Fleury, I suppose, had excellent reasons for leaving. That is, my Senate had expressed, in concrete form, their hopes that he would travel to Persia, and use his special skills to press their interests, as I have done, with Uzum Hasan. It is perhaps all for the best, provided he is discreet in passing through Caffa. I escaped with my life, but Venetians are not welcome there: indeed, men have been forbidden to shelter them. A temporary matter of local politics, you understand.'

The lawyer said something. He looked disturbed. They were moving to the door, all three of them, when it creaked and hopped open. Caterino Zeno looked down to meet the penetrating grey gaze of a brown-haired child of about six who stood, one hand upstretched to the latch, the other clutching a paper. 'Ah,' said Caterino Zeno paternally. 'So this is the young lord your son. How like his father he is!'

The child, its regard switched to its mother, said nothing. It was the mother who surprisingly knelt, and put her arm round the boy and said, 'Here is a visitor, Jodi. No, it is not Papa, but you will make your best bow to him.' And after a tremulous moment, the child Jodi obeyed, and the Venetian envoy to Uzum Hasan was able, gravely, to leave.

'Bastard! Bastard! Bastard!' said the staid Gregorio wildly as soon as he had gone.

'We shall get the truth from Bruges,' Gelis said. 'That was not the truth.' But the boy looked up at her face, his own crimsoning, for the arm that gripped him was trembling.

IT WAS TRUE that the Burgundian Mission had been recalled, for the news was all over the Rialto next day, mixed with the latest reports of the Duke of Burgundy's political and military blunders on the borders of

Germany. There was enough to perturb the money markets, without paying attention, as yet, to the rumour that the German version of the Casa di Niccolò had lost its director: opinion had it that the company would continue under the widow, or amalgamate with Antwerp or Bruges. Gregorio spent the morning in conference with his officials, discussing what precautions to take and drafting communications to Diniz and Moriz and Govaerts in Flanders, for although the branches might now be separate, they were not rivals. Information was the lifeblood of banks, and the wider network, on which Gregorio depended, was managed by Gelis. Today she had remained in her room and, although he missed her, he did not send to hurry her, for he shared some of her helpless anger, mixed with distress. Julius was dead — the infuriating, life-loving colleague and friend who had run the Venice Bank for so long, and who had found in Germany autonomy and a happy marriage at last. And all they had found intolerable in Nicholas was now miserably reinforced by this news. For even though much of what Zeno said might be untrue, the picture he had painted of Nicholas in tribulation was painfully accurate. They had seen it happen before.

Then, at noon, when Margot came in and they broke off, gladly, to think about dinner, the courier had come to the landing-station with his satchel from Danzig, in which, brought by expensive relay, there was a letter from Katelijne Sersanders addressed to the lady of Beltrees.

Gregorio had taken it, and then, after thought, had asked Dr Tobie if he would deliver it to Nicholas's wife in her room. For this, sent before Kathi left Danzig, would surely contain for Gelis's eye the true account of what had happened in Poland. And Tobie, to whom his young Kathi was dear, was the best person to be at hand to interpret it. Also, he was a physician.

He was away for a long time. The household ate, with Margot, subdued, at the head of the table and Gregorio at its foot. The low, sensible voice of the nurse conversing with Jodi filled the spaces between the stilted talk of the clerks, and the nervous scraping of platters. Then, suddenly, Gelis came in, and the men raggedly stood, while Mistress Clémence finished what she was saying, her voice placid, her eyes on the doctor.

Gelis looked at them all. She had dressed more formally, you would say, than was her habit: her fair hair swept under the rolled brim of a pale satin hat; her light, narrow gown girdled with gold. She stood, one hand on the back of the master chair Gregorio had vacated, and spoke as a man would have done: a merchant among merchants.

'You've heard the rumours. I now have better news directly from Danzig. Meester Julius is not dead. He has been injured in an accident but, although badly hurt, is recovering. His wife waited to be sure he was out of danger, and has now gone to do business in Caffa, with the help of the Patriarch of Antioch, who is to fulfil Lord Cortachy's mission at Tabriz as well as his own. Lord Cortachy is returning home, that is true, but he has managed to complete some successful contracts with the Danzigers: I have details here. And lastly, his niece and her husband are coming home also, for a very good reason.' She looked across smiling at Margot. 'The lady of Berecrofts is with child. I think we should drink to that, and the other news. Goro, bring out the wine.'

He had begun to fetch it already. She sat down, the room ringing with relieved voices. She had not mentioned her husband but, for the moment, nobody cared. Julius was safe, and so was his wife, safely chaperoned by Ludovico da Bologna, of whom Zeno, of course, had said nothing.

The voice of Jodi said shrilly, 'What child is Kathi with?' and then broke off as someone chuckled. Mistress Clémence bent over and whispered; then, rising, drew the child from his chair and, curtseying, led him from the room. His voice faded. Tobie, who had not taken his seat, also left the room quietly. When Mistress Clémence presently emerged from the nursery alone, shutting the door, she found him waiting for her.

'He is jealous. He misses his father,' she said.

'Nicholas has gone to Caffa with the woman,' Tobie said. 'It would have been better if Julius had killed him.'

'You don't mean that,' said the nurse. 'The priest is with them, in any case.'

'When did that ever stop Nicholas?' Tobie said.

'Come into my parlour,' Mistress Clémence said, and opened the door.

She did not curtsey or address him with ceremony and had not done so for some time, but he never thought of the omission, any more than he had noticed when it began. To an outsider, they were two professionals, nurse and doctor. To themselves, it was the same.

He had grown to trust her in Scotland, once he had become accustomed to her tart speech and tendency towards boldness. She had proved quick-witted at Trèves. Since his birth, she had been an excellent nurse and a stern but fair mentor to Jodi. Tobie believed that the woman had had a fair understanding of Nicholas, and supposed that the revelations of the previous winter had been as much a blow to her as they had been to himself. When Nicholas's wife had reacted as she had done, daring to take up the business in Venice, Tobie had been impressed, rather than sorry for her, and had decided, since the company needed a doctor, to return to his old role.

Since then, he had seen a great deal of Clémence, who was now Jodi's only nurse, and who also gave her services, in her neat, angular way, to Gelis, Margot, or any who she thought required or deserved them. She was athletically thin, with a depressed Gallic nose and globular irises black as obsidian: he had never seen her brows, never mind her hair, both of which were permanently concealed under a hood of impeccable white linen. Her ankles were the finest he had ever caught sight of, to the extent of being disturbing. The doctor was in his early forties, and reckoned her to be ten years younger perhaps. It was at this stage of their acquaintance that, not so long ago, he had received his real blow: he had discovered Mistress Clémence by chance in a rival office, selling information for money.

The Bank in question had connections with Bruges, which was why he was there. Curiosity and a chance-open door led him to glimpse the woman ensconced in a chair, handing over a document to a clerk who, in return, took out and passed across a purse full of coins. Transfixed, Tobie had seen that the woman was Clémence. Completing, in a daze, his own business, Tobie had reasoned that the treachery must have started in Flanders, after Nicholas went, and was now being continued in Venice. He thought of all his own confidences, and the nurse's apparent record of loyalty to Gelis, and felt ill. When the nurse left the Bank, Tobie had waylaid her on the small dock outside. She had flushed.

'Well?' was all he had said.

And she had sighed and said, 'Dr Tobias. Well, I am glad it was not some fool who would jump to conclusions. I see I must trust you.' Turning the tables was a speciality of hers.

So they had retired to a little churchyard she knew, where they paid for two stools round a brazier and ate hot chestnuts out of a napkin, while she reduced him to the dimensions of Jodi. And yet that was unfair, for she did not expect him to have guessed that Nicholas, leaving, had sent to make a pact with her, and had sworn her to silence. She described it and ended, 'So, as he asked, his wife and child have been protected. You have seen Jodi's groom Raffo, and Manoli, my servant. The Lady pays them: I was allowed to select them. They are highly trained soldiers. They would not have dreamed of taking these posts without the extra gold I am permitted to draw upon.'

'Nicholas left it behind?' Tobie had said. When talking to Clémence, he had jettisoned, some weeks ago, the formal name of her employer.

'He deposited it afterwards. There was a time,' said Mistress Clémence, bursting open a chestnut, 'when M. de Fleury hoped to send for his son, but then changed his mind. He knew, no doubt, his own failings too well. Now the money is being spent wholly to guard the child and his mother.'

'Against what?' Tobie had said. A pang shot through his jaw and he stopped chewing. She put out a palm and, astonished, he emptied his mouth obediently into it. She disposed of the sludge.

'You eat too many sweet foods. You will end your days sucking up gruel. M. de Fleury's disaffected family, I understand, are still exiled in Portugal. It is probable, I suppose, that his present fears concern the rival firm, the Vatachino. The Lady worked for them, and has now transferred her allegiance to your Bank.'

It was possible. Since Nicholas's disappearance, the Vatachino had been singularly quiet, even that member of it who had already tried and failed to kill him in Cyprus. Since he had had him expelled from that island, Nicholas might well consider David de Salmeton a serious source of danger to Gelis and Jodi as well as to himself. But when Tobie asked Mistress Clémence, she shook her head.

'A gentleman of excessive good looks, charming although not very tall, and last heard of in royal favour in Cyprus? I have been given no instructions, nor have I seen such a person. But, of course, now I shall watch.'

She sounded remarkably placid. Gazing at her, Tobie was struck by enlightenment. He said, 'Wait a moment. Does this mean you are in *communication* with Nicholas? Have you known all along where he was?' He felt himself becoming indignant.

She had smiled. 'He is too astute for that, don't you think? No. I send my accounting through a third person, and any reply, if it is needed, returns in the same way. He knows at least they are safe.'

It reminded him of something Gelis had said, in reply to an incautious comment of his. 'No. He is not divining. He has not tried to divine since he left.' And had added curtly, when Tobie was silent, 'When he does, I can feel it.'

If you believed that, then now it made sense. Tobie said to the nurse, 'So he doesn't need to divine. You tell him everything.'

And Mistress Clémence, like Gelis, had treated him with impatience. 'And you are a doctor? I assure him, in not more than a sentence, of the health of his wife and his child. I say nothing more, nor does he ask. You do not heal a wound by tearing it open.'

Later, back at the Bank, Tobie had drunk soup for his supper and closeted himself, for a brief spell, with Gregorio. He had not given Clémence away, but satisfied himself that, whatever Nicholas had feared, the Vatachino were in abeyance, and David de Salmeton was no longer their man and had quite disappeared. He mentioned to Clémence that Nicholas was wasting his money, in case she wished to pass on the advice.

That had been in the middle of winter. From what he could gather, the position today was the same. The muscular groom was still here, and the nimbly watchful manservant, but their special skills had not been required. He had refrained from mentioning it to Clémence again. Only, discussing foreign trends with Gregorio quite recently, Tobie had asked the source of his news from the Germanies, which seemed suddenly to have become much more explicit. And Gregorio had explained that much of this sprang from the friendly offices of Julius, although the best reports might arrive unsolicited, from nameless merchants hoping one day to change masters. Gelis was an expert with these.

Well, thought Tobie, sitting now in Mistress Clémence's parlour, there would be no more reports for a while from Julius. And perhaps, unless his guess was quite wrong, none from any other guiltily anonymous source, surprisingly au fait with Prussian matters. He remarked, 'It is true, apparently, that Nicholas was paid to go to Tabriz. It can hardly have influenced him, with the wealth he already has. He has gone because of the woman.'

'Perhaps,' the nurse said. She was sewing. Since her under-maid Pasque had returned to their homeland in France, Clémence had performed most of the small tasks herself. She said, 'Have you ever spoken to M. Govaerts about the realisation of the investments in Scotland?'

Sometimes, Mistress Clémence seemed to know a great deal too much. Tobie said, 'No. Why?'

'It is probably not worth your while. But it involved, I am told, a number of tedious and convoluted transactions. I would not have mentioned it, except that the indications are that M. de Fleury has no money at all, apart from the sum set aside for his family's protection.'

'The letter said nothing of that,' Tobie said. He paused. 'I would need to speak to Kathi herself.' He paused again. The nurse knotted her thread and bit off the end. She had a fine set of teeth. Tobie said, 'There was something else in the letter.'

Mistress Clémence sat up. She said, 'If you wish to know where I stand, I am unwilling, as yet, to form a judgement. The lady of Berecrofts may be correct, and your friend must be left to repair his own character. In such cases, it is wise to appoint a sympathetic observer, and the Gräfin may prove to be such. Monseigneur's own intentions, of course, may be less responsible. What does the young lady suggest?'

Tobie was silent. Every line of Kathi's letter had been an implicit appeal to Gelis to take back her husband. What else she had written he was not as yet free to quote. Tobie said, 'She understands that Gelis must decide for herself. I understand that whatever remorse Nicholas may feel, it need not prevent him from going out and committing the same crimes again. I don't want to know whether he tried to kill Julius deliberately.'

'Yes. I comprehend. I think,' said Mistress Clémence, folding up her sewing and rising, 'that neither of us can know what to do until you have consulted with the Lady. I shall wait, and follow your direction.'

'You will?' Tobie said, with marked incredulity.

'Within limits,' Mistress Clémence agreed.

Chapter 14

That was in the third week in July. Before the next week had ended, couriers recently tumbled over the Alps were racing to Rome, to Florence, to Venice, relaying their news from the Burgundian frontier at Luxembourg. The war simmering ever since the fiasco at Trèves was about to break out between Duke Charles and the Emperor Frederick. And the precise trigger was a dispute between the two princes over Cologne. A Burgundian herald, arriving in Venice, petitioned the Doge and the Senate to permit the Duke to hire the services of the great condottiere Colleoni, a request which was refused. In the Ca' Niccolò, Gregorio and his partners called an internal meeting which lasted all day.

In Cologne, heart of the quarrel, lay the tenantless business of Julius. In Flanders, working the last of their official contract, lay the mercenary army of the Banco di Niccolò, as yet without new direction. They talked all day, and in the end, were reduced to silence by the unanswerable arguments of Gelis.

'I have practised with Julius in Cologne. I have worked with Diniz in Bruges, and seen how the army is managed. I have heard my husband's schemes and hopes for the company. Let me go to the Flemish Bank, and help them devise what to do for the soldiers and Julius. We may be separate concerns, but we all need to support each other now.'

They agreed, in the end. The orders were given that would transfer her household, her staff and her child north-west to Flanders, and turn her face from her husband, not towards him. When the meeting was over, she asked Tobie to come to her room.

'Will you come to Bruges? Or will you stay?'

She knew what she was asking. This time, he had not been idle in Venice: his uncle's printing-presses were almost ready, and so were the experiments, so long delayed, that he intended to publish. He thought that, on the whole, he would not mind leaving them for a while, to see

Moriz again, and Diniz and John. He had another reason as well, which he thought he shared with the lady of Beltrees, although he approached the subject with caution.

'The letter from Katelijne.'

'Yes?' He was the only one, apart from herself, who had read it through. Her tone indicated that he was not to presume on it.

Tobie said, 'Are you going to the Bosco del Montello before you leave Venice? She said the vicomte de Fleury was there. Adorne's son had seen him, and told Julius.'

'I haven't forgotten,' she said. 'But he is Nicholas's grandfather, not mine.'

He persevered, as carefully as he knew how. 'Jodi has no one else.'

'I hardly think,' Gelis said, 'that a speechless, paralysed old man could do anything other than terrify Jodi, or be terrified himself, for that matter, if someone saw fit to badger him about his dead daughter, poor man. It has occurred to you that the truth about Nicholas's birth may be very nasty indeed?' She looked at him, with an exasperation that was not wholly unkind. 'Unless you've decided, with Kathi and Anna, that we should all forgive him, and take steps to fabricate his birthright? Have *you* found it possible to overlook what Nicholas did?'

'No one could,' Tobie said. 'The theory is that a good woman might redeem him.'

'I am afraid,' Gelis said, 'that I don't know any such.' She waited. 'But Clémence thinks otherwise?'

'I haven't discussed it with her,' said Tobie. 'I speak as a doctor. I dislike the idea of an old man dying neglected because his grandson has gone. According to Kathi, Nicholas supported him.'

'So why should he have stopped? Arrangements are easy to make, and Nicholas is hardly in want.'

'I hear otherwise,' Tobie said. 'I think someone should make sure the money is there.'

'You hear otherwise? From whom?' Gelis said. When he didn't reply, her tone softened. 'Tobie, he may have lost his income, but somewhere, Nicholas must have salted away all his past profits. By now it will be ten times as much as I've given the Bank. Wherever he is, Nicholas is rich.'

'You may be right,' Tobie said. 'It doesn't matter. But you wouldn't mind if I went to see the old man and made sure? I would pay his dues myself. You have done more than enough.'

'I should mind very much,' Gelis said. 'If anyone goes, then I do. If anyone pays, then it is someone of Jodi's blood. If anyone hears the truth, then —'

She broke off, perhaps before the look on his face. Tobie said, 'I know the truth about his other son, and I don't remember anyone doubting my discretion. But if you don't want me to go, then I shan't.' He hadn't meant to insult her. He felt as she did about Nicholas: thinking about him revived all the nausea. Neither he nor Gelis, as yet, had attained even the limited tolerance of Kathi and Anna. Tobie felt responsible for the old man, that was all. He had even considered telling Gelis what he knew about the vicomte and his brother and Nicholas, but had decided against it. If Thibault de Fleury proved to be dying, or dead, there was no reason for her ever to know.

Something of his humane purpose must have come to her. He saw her swallow. Gelis said, 'I'm sorry. Go to Montello, of course, if you want. Write to Nicholas, if you wish, when you have been. Or go and join Nicholas.' Her eyes were bright, and her fists folded tight in her lap.

Tobie said, 'I thought I was part of your household. If you want me, I'm with you.' He considered her, sharing her trouble, as he had shared the long, dreary pilgrimage which had begun with the disaster at Trèves and had ended here in Venice. On that journey, he had not mentioned her husband to Gelis, for he knew he could not fully comprehend what she felt. For himself, all he would allow was that the focus of a consuming interest had gone; a source of fascination and study that had begun fifteen years ago, at an unsavoury turning point in his own life. Gelis had been a child then.

Her partnership with Nicholas, when it came, had been a physical one so intense that its reverberations were evident still, underscoring, undermining all they both did. Perhaps Nicholas would succeed in securing something to match it, but Tobie suspected that Gelis would not. With the loss of Nicholas, Gelis was left with an intellectual life, nothing else. And unlike Kathi, she was not made to support it . . . Kathi, to whom Tobie had been and was doctor, consultant, but also devoted companion and friend.

He had no similar bond with Gelis. He felt pity for her, and admiration and even occasionally lust. But he did not understand her, or she would not allow him the means. And he knew she had never tried to understand him. He simply applied, therefore, his general experience of humankind, and acted accordingly.

Tobie said, 'I still think someone should go to the monastery. It would only be a day's journey there, and another day back. Would you come with me?'

She frowned, but her hands had loosened a little. 'I don't know.'

'Tell me later,' he said. 'I expect Jodi is waiting for you just now.'

GELIS REACHED HER DECISION that night. Two days later, in the cool of the dawn, she and Tobias Beventini left Venice together, with two servants and four men-at-arms, and took the road that led north, towards the looming range of the Venetian Alps with, behind them, the peaks of the Dolomites. By the time the sun was high, its heat beating down on their straw hats and dust-covered cloaks, they had reached the ancient provincial capital of Treviso, with its frescoed houses, and its cathedral, and its brick church dedicated to San Niccolò. Here, as in every trading town, the Bank had clients and correspondents but today, by mutual consent, the Lady and the doctor avoided them. Instead, they passed the midday hours resting in the shady garden of a small tavern, with the waters of the little Sile running at its foot, and the scent of flowers mixed with the dung of the stables. They were given pork in jelly, and curds, and sipped wine, and let the time pass in silence. The heat dwindled. Tobie said, 'They tell me the road gets steeper from now on. The place is on a hill?'

'On one of a little group of low hills, covered with trees. Oak. The Bosco del Montello, owned of course by Venice: we are still in the Veneto. The Carthusians are supposed to pursue lives of silence and simplicity in the wilderness, and this was presumably the nearest that this lot could get. It's about as wild, I suppose, as the Cartusia outside Perth.'

'Perth?'

'St John's town of Perth in Scotland. The first King James built a Carthusian monastery there, prodded by his cousin Bishop Kennedy and his English Queen, who was a granddaughter of John of Gaunt. It still has the occasional Prior from Ghent, and organises some of its finances through the Carthusian convents in Bruges, much supported by the Adorne family. That is why Anselm Adorne's brother became a lay monk at Montello at the end of his life. And why Adorne makes gifts to the Cartusia in Scotland.'

'Does he?' said Tobie.

'Yes. His son Maarten served there. Now Maarten's a Carthusian monk at the Holy Cross monastery in Bruges. His grandfather died in the same place nine years ago, and his sister Margareta is a Carthusian nun. It's a very ascetic order,' Gelis said. 'They may not welcome visitors. Kathi said she had to wait here in Treviso.'

'We don't want to see the choir monks,' Tobie said. 'If he's paralysed, the vicomte must be living apart. In a hospice, perhaps.'

'They are not a hospital order.'

'Then how did he get there?' said Tobie.

'Money,' Gelis said. 'Presumably they were paid a lot of money. Perhaps he has his own servants and nurses. Did you know that . . .' She hesitated.

'What?' said Tobie.

His brusqueness seemed to reassure her: she glanced at him, and then resumed. 'Gregorio tells me that Tasse retired to live quite near here. The little maid who used to serve Marian de Charetty, my predecessor in the marital bed. Tasse is dead now, of course. As is Marian, and Primaflora, who followed her.'

'You sound as if you blame Nicholas,' Tobie said.

'Only for attracting bad luck,' Gelis said. 'He was in another country when each of them perished. I suppose we are only unfortunate, all of us, that we met him. Should we perhaps be riding on?'

SHE HAD BEEN RIGHT about the trees. They had only twelve miles to travel, and quite soon, as they left behind the vineyards and grazings, Tobie welcomed the fact that the fiercest heat was no longer continuous, but increasingly dissipated under a dappled green canopy. Soon, it became apparent that the road they had begun to traverse led not through random trees, but into the outlying groves of a forest. The men-at-arms, who were paid by the Bank and knew each other well, closed up watchfully, cursing the servants who were less accustomed to the saddle and fell behind. Gelis's man, chosen from the Bank's workshops instead of its stables, was especially culpable, straying from one side to the other and lingering behind trees like a man with the flux. Then he would spur on his horse, and scamper up and talk to the Lady. They saw him waving his arms. Once, he seemed to be holding his hands out for her to sniff. And another time, instead of catching up, he cried out for her to come over to where a blackened patch told that something had been burned.

Had there not been a good beaten path, they might even have lost their way with his antics, although after a while it was obvious where the monastery was, because of the numbers of people they met coming towards them, picking their way through the woods with baskets and bowls and loaves under their arms stamped with the initials of the Blessed Virgin and St Jerome. It was the day for alms, it would seem. One of the groups had a wheelbarrow, and another a sledge pulled behind them, although both were empty. They all stopped when they saw the horses, and the men would pull off their caps and hold them until the cavalcade had gone past.

Then they had to climb to the gates, where they dismounted and the porter asked them to wait. Gelis said suddenly, 'It was March, when Adorne was here.'

'What?' Tobie said. Now they were out of the trees, he could see that the monastery was surrounded by vineyards, climbing up the slope of the hill behind the church tower. He saw the end of a vegetable garden, and a bakehouse and a dairy.

'When we all left Venice three years ago. Kathi and Adorne and his son travelled home this way. Then four days later, John and Father Moriz and Julius and I left for the Tyrol the other way, reaching Trento by the river. You came with us as far as Padua.'

He remembered. He had been on his way to Pavia. Nicholas had just snatched his child and disappeared. It had been the second last time Tobie had parted from Nicholas. He said, 'Was that when it happened?' At least, nothing seemed to have happened. Jan Adorne presumably mentioned the old man when next he met Julius, which must have been in Rome that December. And Julius, in the throes of his new passion for Anna, had forgotten about it until now. Julius, although inquisitive, was selective in the matters that interested him. Julius had been as reasonable a friend as most men hoped to have, but all the same, Nicholas had shot him.

Then the porter broke into his thoughts, returning with an authoritative figure in white who gazed with disdain at Gelis, and, addressing himself to Tobie's dust-laden physician's gown, hood and cap, imparted, in Latin, a lofty dismissal.

Gelis said, 'Say how surprised we are, considering the hospitality he has just clearly proffered to the suffering and the needy. Ask how many came for alms today.'

Tobie asked, and relayed the answer. His Pavian Latin was better than the Procurator's. 'Five hundred. He finds it hard to believe that we are needy. They do not have travellers' quarters or a hospice. They are a silent order.'

'We know that, of course. We had hoped,' Gelis said, 'that the Prior would extend to us the same kindness he showed three years ago to our friend the Duke of Burgundy's eminent councillor, and benefactor of your order, my lord Anselm Adorne, Baron Cortachy. His brother was, we believe, a religious here.'

She had spoken directly, this time, to the Procurator, in the same French-Latin as his own. The Procurator looked from her to the doctor and back. Then he said, 'Exceptions were made. I am sorry.' The belligerence had faded a little.

'It is impossible even to admit a single physician?' Tobie said. 'Would you have turned away my late uncle Giammatteo Ferrari?'

He did not often invoke his famous late uncle, with whom he had not seen eye to eye. He was all the more surprised when Gelis broke in, disrupting his strategy. 'I am sure you would find Dr Tobias professionally helpful. But I myself wish to speak to the Prior. We request admission for three: Dr Tobias, myself and my colleague.'

Tobie gazed at her and then stared, as did the Procurator, at the sturdy, liveried form of her servant. The Procurator said, in a tone of finality, 'In that case, madame, I am afraid there is no question of entering.'

'To discuss certain matters of forestry,' Gelis serenely continued, 'of particular concern to ourselves, as officials of the Casa di Niccolò. And of even more concern to my companion, as representing the Lords and Commissioners of the Arsenal, reporting to the Council of Ten.'

There was a silence. The Procurator said, 'I have misunderstood. I am sorry. Perhaps the two gentlemen and the lady would be kind enough to come in?'

Waiting, wild-eyed, before Christ Crucified in a spartan reception-room, Tobie addressed Gelis under his breath on the subject of her cheerfully insouciant companion. 'He's the Bank's head carpenter! He doesn't come from the Arsenal!'

'He did. He used to examine their trees,' Gelis said. 'Montello is one of the Arsenal's principal forests. If this is mismanaged, Venice can't get the timber she needs for her ships. Sit and watch this.' Then the door opened, and the Prior of the monastery entered.

Tobie's heart bled for him before the interview had lasted five minutes. Tobie thought he knew Gelis. He had forgotten how much she had picked up from Nicholas. He had forgotten how alike she and Nicholas were, in many ways. With seductive calm and pitiless logic, the lady of Beltrees, partner in the Venetian Bank of Ca' Niccolò, detailed for the Prior, with the help of her timber adviser, all the transgressions of the monastery of the Blessed Virgin and St Jerome, situated in the Arsenal's forest of Bosco del Montello. *Charcoal-burners* admitted? Sheep and cattle permitted to pasture? An absence of ditching; a patent neglect of the requirements of thinning, trimming and sealing; the evidence of flooding caused by the unwise admission of mill-dams? And if, as would be freely admitted, much of this was the responsibility of the commune, what of the ravages of five hundred pilgrims, allowed to traverse the forest when coming for alms, and departing, if the eye were to be believed, with something of far greater value? How much prime ship's timber was carried off weekly in those barrows and sledges, to end up as firewood?

And then, the gambit that had worked so well round a hundred conference tables: How could the Prior be blamed, when his mind dwelled, as it should, on higher things? Perhaps a little help was what was required, rather than an adverse report to the Lords and Commissioners. What if a lumberman were employed, to patrol or even live in the forest? What if the alms were to be given outside, rather than inside the wood? What if . . . ? The timber expert, consulted, produced a few sensible, inexpensive ideas which the Prior, now supported by his senior religious, believed he might well recommend to the commune.

Surprisingly, wine was brought. Unsurprisingly, when Gelis, gracefully expressing her gratification, turned the conversation harmlessly to the pious work of the monastery, the Prior was relieved and happy to answer her questions.

Almost, Tobie had forgotten why they had come. It was, therefore, with something approaching a shiver that he heard Gelis say, 'And Lord Cortachy mentioned, I think, that an old friend of my husband's was here. It was my other reason for calling. I believe we owe a great deal to your care of M. le vicomte de Fleury?'

She was clever. She sat, pure as an angel, with her throat and hair veiled, and the silken fall of her hood caught at her breast with a reliquary brooch worth more than a few Montello oak trees. The Prior said, 'The name of my lord your husband is known to us, of course. We have often wondered whether there was some kinship.'

'A distant one only,' Gelis lied. 'But Lord Beltrees has always interested himself, of course, in the old gentleman's welfare. You may not even have been aware of the source of the payments. They continue satisfactorily?'

The Prior looked at his bursar, who coughed. The bursar said, 'We would not wish to complain.'

Tobie let out his breath. Gelis said, 'If it is inadequate, of course you must tell me. This is a personal matter, and has no bearing on our business arrangements.' Her voice was almost normal. Until he heard it, Tobie hadn't realised the strain that she, too, had borne until now. The old man was alive. He was here.

Then the Prior said, 'I am sure there is nothing that cannot be simply adjusted. But day and night help is expensive. His own servant, however devoted, is no longer young, and deserves relief.'

'Who could refuse that?' Gelis said. 'We shall talk of that soon, and in detail. But first, I should like to meet and thank the servant you speak of. And perhaps, on behalf of my husband, to look upon my lord the vicomte himself, however briefly?'

If they knew that her husband was no longer in Venice, no one mentioned it. The lumber expert, full of wine, was allowed to depart. Tobie followed Gelis and the Prior out of his quarters and across the immaculate domain to where, against the encircling walls, the cabins of the monastery's own little infirmary clung to the slope of the hill with its well and its plot of tilled ground, in which flowers and vegetables seemed to be growing together. There were juniper bushes, and some lavender, and a sturdy vine arbour for shade, with a few stools and a small table within, and a litter, with someone sleeping on it. The cicadas shrilled, and you could hear a hum as of bees: the prayers drifting up from the church. There was no sound from the cloisters.

A man in the robes of a lay brother rose and came forward, bowing, and waited. The Prior said, 'This is Brother Huon, to whose tender care M. le vicomte undoubtedly owes his life. Brother, the lady is Egidia, wife to my lord Niccolò de Fleury, a kinsman of the vicomte's, and his protector. You have heard of the Banco di Niccolò. And this is Master Tobias

Beventini da Grado, physician and nephew of your great hero of Pavia. I leave you together.'

He left. The monk looked from the lady to the doctor, his straw hat gripped in his hands in an attitude of uncertainty, even wariness. His tonsured scalp gleamed, smooth and rosy above a face browned by sun and withered by years, which yet had white lines of laughter radiating from the weak eyes, and a touch of stubbornness about the gentle mouth. Tobie said, 'One doctor meets another. I am glad.'

'Oh no!' the man said. 'I have no training. I have a small experience of remedies, that is all. The sick in the infirmary are cared for by a visiting physician.' He smiled and added, 'We have no one sick just now.' He was watching Gelis, whose gaze was resting on the arbour.

She said, 'Then that is the vicomte?'

'He is sleeping,' the monk answered quickly. He did not offer to take her across.

'You have been with him a long time?' said Tobie. 'Perhaps the lady might sit, while you tell us a little about him?'

'Her husband is a relative? Another relative?' the monk said. He hesitated, and then led the way past the arbour to where a low house stood on its own, its door open, with a bench set in the shade under the thatch, and some stools. Gelis sat, and Tobie followed her slowly, using his eyes.

The motionless form on the litter had not stirred. The man was lying on his back, with a thin coverlet drawn up to his chest, and his loosely clad arms resting on top of it. The hand Tobie could see was heavily veined, but its long fingers, though thin, were not wasted. The sick man's head, turned away, was concealed by a mane of combed, silvery hair, which merged into a full, curling beard. The hair, unusually for an ailing person, was glossy, and everything about him looked cared-for and clean.

Tobie sat down saying, smiling, 'You are to be congratulated,' and then realised what the monk had just said.

Brother Huon returned the smile. 'He is an easy patient. He was clean-shaven, but shaving is tiring. We stopped at the time of the seizure and then did not restart.' He turned to Gelis, who had suddenly spoken. 'Madame?'

Gelis repeated her question. 'He has had visits from other family members?'

'Recently, no. Since the old lady died, he has had fewer regular visitors. But three years ago, the Burgundian gentleman visited him. M. Anselm Adorne. I believed him to be a kinsman. Was he not?'

'Did he claim to be? I didn't know,' Gelis said. 'Did he manage to speak, then, with M. le vicomte?'

'He saw him, certainly,' said the monk. 'But it was not a good day, and M. Adorne had brought with him a young man, his son, who was impatient. In a sickroom, one must be considerate.' He smiled again. 'The old lady was helping me then. She soon turned them away.'

'An old lady? Here?' Gelis said. Even to Tobie, her voice sounded artificial.

'We have servants to clean,' said Brother Huon. 'Although Mistress Tasse was not a servant: she had long retired from her work before she came to settle in the Trevisana. Then she —' He broke off. 'But perhaps you know her? She left to nurse the child of the director of the Banco di Niccolò, and she was dead within the month, drowned in Venice before her charge was even born?'

Gelis frowned. Tobie said aside, 'You never knew her. She died when you and Nicholas were in Scotland. A good little soul, Tasse. I met her once in Geneva. She was still working for Jaak and Esota, just as she did when Nicholas was there as a boy. Jaak de Fleury, the vicomte's younger brother.'

Her eyes were fastened on his. Neither heard the sound that prompted Brother Huon to jump to his feet and look across at the litter. The monk said, 'He is awake. Let me go to him.' He crossed the grass and, bending over the recumbent figure, appeared to be addressing it. He did not immediately return.

Gelis spoke in a low voice. 'I didn't know you had met Thibault's brother. Why didn't you tell me? What else do you know about Thibault de Fleury?'

It was her right to hear. It was his own fault that he had tried to avoid this. Tobie said, 'Only what I've picked up from others. He must be eighty, or more. He married twice, once when he was young, and once thirty years later; so that he ended with a daughter, Adelina de Fleury, who was two years younger than Nicholas, his grandson and her nephew. The vicomte's second wife died soon after the birth, and Nicholas's mother cared for the two children until she died in turn, and they were both sent to the household of the vicomte's brother Jaak, since the vicomte by then was incapable. Jaak . . .' He paused. 'He ran the family business in Geneva. Rich. Violent. No children, and a half-crazy wife called Esota. The little girl, Adelina, was only five and was lucky to be sent off soon to a convent: she's been in and out of convents ever since, repudiating her family. Nicholas stayed until he was sent off to Bruges, to be apprenticed to Cornelis de Charetty, Marian's first husband. The old vicomte stayed on, helpless, in Fleury and Jaak de Fleury flourished in Geneva until —' He broke off.

'Until?'

'Until Nicholas grew old enough to take his revenge. He ruined Jaak's business, which incidentally impoverished the vicomte as well. In the riots that followed, Jaak's wife Esota was killed. And then Jaak himself died when he came to Bruges and tried to take over Marian's business.'

'Nicholas killed him?' Gelis said.

'He fought him. No, he didn't kill him,' Tobie said.

'You mean, not directly,' Gelis said. 'Nicholas rarely destroys anything directly.' She gazed at the arbour where the monk, silent now, was placing pillows behind the disabled man's head, and pouring him water. Gelis said, 'I suppose I know why you have suddenly decided to confess all this now. This is a man whom Nicholas ruined, and whose brother he virtually killed. If he has any recollection of that, he will not welcome us.'

Tobie said, 'This is also the man who made no provision for Nicholas while he was well, so that his keepers could do what they liked. If he has enough wit, as you say, then he might regret it enough to explain. We're here to discover who the father of Nicholas was. Nicholas was born in the vicomte's house at Fleury and lived there with his mother until he was seven. His mother claimed that Nicholas was the legitimate son of her husband, Simon de St Pol. Simon maintains that the child wasn't his, because he hadn't lain with his wife since she miscarried of a first son. She said she was innocent, but the St Pols did not believe her. But would the vicomte have allowed her to stay if the birth had been shameful?'

'He needed her,' Gelis said. 'To run the household, and rear his legitimate daughter. Or perhaps he was too ill to know.'

'Perhaps,' Tobie said. 'Have you ever worked out what Simon's age must have been at his marriage? He must have been fifteen or sixteen. Thirteen years younger than Sophie.'

'I know,' Gelis said, after a silence. 'You would say she had trapped him into marriage, except that she was well born and her family possibly richer than his. My guess is that Simon did what he usually does: took what he wanted. And when it led to a child, he was compelled by both families to marry. He would resent that.'

'So he might have lied to get out of the marriage?'

'He might,' Gelis said. 'But I don't think he did. Simon truly believes that his wife cheated. Just as Nicholas truly believes that he is Simon's son.'

Tobie looked at her. She had spoken with her usual composure, but had broken off at the end, as if her throat had stopped. Nicholas had always believed he was Simon's son: Tobie knew that. Gelis's exploitation of that fact had been one of the cruellest features of the bitter contest between Nicholas and herself. If, in the outcome, Nicholas had outraged them all, he had some excuse. But not enough.

Then the monk called Brother Huon came towards them, his gown brushing the grass, and said, 'He is ready to see you: please come. But perhaps you would have care not to tire him. His strength does not last long.'

'We shall be careful. I shall call you at the first hint of difficulty,' Tobie said.

The monk smiled. 'Have no fear. I do not repeat private conversations. I have told him who you are. He wishes to see you. But communication would be difficult without me.'

Private conversations! Tobie said, 'Forgive me. We have received reports of the vicomte's health and understanding . . . that were perhaps erroneous?'

A sound came from the litter. Brother Huon looked across with an affectionate smile which he then bent on Tobie. 'The reports were probably true at the time,' the monk said. 'He has had many episodes of paralysis, although not for some years. Before he came into our care, he was kept much under opiates, and because he was unable to speak, or to use his hands, it was thought that his intellect was also deficient. This was not so; and now that his limbs are free, we can converse.' The smile widened. 'You heard my lord laugh. Your remark amused him, although he will take you to task about your other assumptions.'

Gelis said, 'He heard what we were saying?'

'His hearing is excellent, my lady. When one power is lost, the others often become sharper. Pray come. He is waiting.'

Chapter 15

AT THE AGE OF eighty-one, towards the end of a life blighted by physical rigours and the misguided ministrations of others, Thibault, vicomte de Fleury, possessed the power still to surprise those who came, uninformed, to his bedside. Many things about him were remarkable, but the greatest of these, perhaps, was his beauty.

Lying propped on his pillows, the scent of flowers about him, he had closed his eyes against the chequered green light of his baldaquin, so that it was possible for a moment to study him. Gelis drew in her breath. But Tobie was looking at a likeness of the face of the dead Jaak de Fleury: the classical nose, the well-shaped lips, the sculptured cheek-bones and full-lidded eyes; the head and jaw mantled and softened, unlike Jaak's, by the spread of curling grey hair. Then the deep eyes slowly opened, and the intelligence within might have recalled that of the shrewd younger brother, but the tolerant humour belonged somewhere else. The eyes were grey, and when the lips smiled, the clothed cheeks betrayed two fleeting dimples.

Tobie dragged off his cap and said, glaring, *'He needed you.'*

The monk moved. The man in the litter lifted his head, his eyes sharp, holding Tobie's. Then he raised a finger, and looking at Huon, began to sign to him. Then he stopped, and turned his gaze back to Tobie. Tobie became very still.

The monk said, 'He speaks to you in French.'

'And?' said Tobie.

'My lord says, "My grandson needed the help of a cripple? The man who succeeded in ruining my brother?" ' The monk translated. The man on the pillow was smiling, but with his lips only.

Tobie said, 'You know what your brother was. Nicholas held nothing against you, because he was told you were ill. Perhaps you were. But why did you not tell him when you were better?' He heard himself with despair. This was not why he was here. Gelis would think he was mad. He said, 'Nicholas pays for you!'

The long fingers stirred and replied. He could not read the vicomte's face. The monk said, 'My lord says that his grandson merely continued what the demoiselle de Charetty began. He says that he was able, at least, to have the boy sent to Bruges when he discovered how he had been treated at Geneva.'

'But not to Fleury?' Tobie said.

'His illness forbade it.' The fingers had stilled, but the monk continued, his eyes on his master's face. 'He will allow me perhaps to say more. He was given to believe that his own end was near, or that, surviving, his powers of reasoning would fail. He would not have a boy saddled with that.'

'I understand that,' Tobie said. 'But when it proved to be untrue . . . Can he not imagine what it would have meant to Nicholas, to know as much?'

The fingers moved. 'But by then, Master Nicholas himself had performed those acts of destruction you mentioned. And the paralysis returned. What is the doctor's interest in Nicholas?' the fingers asked. But the eyes had moved to Gelis.

Gelis answered. 'He loves him.'

Tobie said, 'Once.'

'And you?' asked the fingers of the vicomte, his gaze steady on Gelis.

'Once,' she repeated as steadily. 'I have given Nicholas a young son, your great-grandson. If Nicholas is legitimate, you would have a legitimate heir.'

The lips smiled. 'I have no money.'

'You have a name,' Gelis said. 'Nicholas has none.'

'And you think I can help you? I cannot.'

Tobie said, 'My lord. Tell us what you know.'

The man on the pillows sighed a little and moved. Then he lifted his hands once again. The monk interpreted in the same even voice. 'I can tell you two things of my daughter. She bore a dead child before Nicholas. Between one birth and the next, I know of no indiscretion. And between one birth and the next, her husband Simon did not come near her.'

'Then how do you explain it?' said Tobie.

'I cannot,' the fingers said. 'And having no land and no name, the boy would always have had to make his own way. He seems to have done so.'

'But even a bastard,' said Tobie, 'may be introduced, these days, into noble society, can be educated to take his place with his peers.'

'Tell that to God,' the vicomte said. 'Or to the devil who sent me my illness; or the greater devil who —'

The monk's voice stopped, his anxious gaze on his master. The signing hands had interleaved and lay, not in repose but as a barrier over the heart; a pulse throbbed at his temple. With bitter reluctance, Tobie spoke as a doctor. 'I am sorry. We must stop. He should rest.' And realised as the vicomte's eyes turned impatiently on him that he had committed the witless sin: he had spoken as if the man were not there, listening and able.

Gelis, oddly, was wiser; or obeyed some sudden intuition denied to Tobie. As he watched with knitted brows, she moved close and sank by the litter, holding the sick man's eyes with her own. 'What disturbs you now, through the days, through the nights, will still disturb you after we have gone. If I were Nicholas, rich and charming and powerful, clever enough to win through to success despite every assault, every adversary, would you not allow me to deal with your devil? You might even find that your devil is dead.'

The fingers unlaced. 'Rich and charming and powerful?' they said. The monk's voice was flat, but the vicomte's face expressed mockery. 'But no longer lovable, because he kills rather too readily? Indirectly, you said.'

'Not his family,' Tobie said. The sick man's eyes moved up to his face. Tobie said, 'Jaak tried to kill Nicholas, and Nicholas only defended himself. He didn't mean Esota to die. The St Pols have been consistently murderous, but in my opinion he has never plotted to kill them. He can be goaded. But I have seen him go to any lengths, face any danger, to avoid harming those he believes to be kin.'

The vicomte's gaze returned to Gelis. 'Then,' the fingers said, 'my devil would be quite safe from you, would he not, if you were Nicholas?'

Gelis's eyes had grown very large. Tobie, watching her, was reminded abruptly of another sickbed, another time when he had stood and watched a duel like this, between a dying man and this obsessed woman, over Nicholas. Gelis said, 'Your devil was Simon's father, Jordan de Ribérac? Perhaps he came when you were ill. He denounced your daughter, and proclaimed her son as a bastard, and forbade you . . . ' She was reading his face. She said, 'He forbade you to rear Nicholas, or have him fittingly educated? But you need not have obeyed him. Or your lawyers could have refused?'

She was guessing. The vicomte lay, his hands disengaged, his lids heavy, and invited her by his stillness to continue. Tobie, leaning forward, laid his fingers on the arched wrist and the sick man looked up at him, fleetingly, with the shadowed traces of a half-smile. Gelis said slowly, 'He threatened not you, then, but Nicholas? And perhaps your two daughters and later, Marian de Charetty? Bring up this boy as an underling, or I will hurt you?'

The eyes assented.

'And in any case, unable to speak, unable to write, you could do nothing. And now? Does he still threaten you?'

The hands remained still. The monk said, 'The vicomte de Ribérac does not know of this partial recovery. It is one reason why we are here, and why the Prior does not easily admit visitors. Were we to communicate with my lord Thibault's family, both he and they might well suffer.'

Gelis said, 'Nicholas cannot suffer more than he has done already. It must be the same for Adelina. Can you hold a pen? Could you write to them? The Bank could try and trace Nicholas.'

The sick man looked up at the monk. Brother Huon said, 'My lord can write. It is slow. We have heard nothing of my lord's younger daughter since she left her last convent many years ago.'

'And where was that?' Tobie said.

The monk flushed. 'I say "we" from habit, but indeed, it was before my lord and I knew one another. The address was written down, but one came seeking it later, and my lord did not deny them the paper, since it was useless to us, and the demoiselle Adelina was no longer there.'

'Who took it?' Tobie said. 'Were you here by then?'

'I was, but it was my rest day. I do not know. The man was not the vicomte de Ribérac. My lord received the impression that he was a servant of the nobleman Anselm Adorne.'

Gelis rose and stood looking down. She said, 'So you do not know where your own daughter might be.'

The large eyes remained steady, then dropped. And the fingers stirred themselves this time to answer directly. 'Adelina desires, she has told me, to be the Bride of Christ in place of the daughter of her father. She is probably right.'

'She might be dead?' Gelis said. 'You would not even know? You have no other kinsfolk, and the girl has no other friends?'

The fingers did not trouble to answer, but the vicomte cast a glance at the monk. Brother Huon said, 'My lord's first wife had a younger sister who also became a religious, and whom the demoiselle Adelina revered. If still alive, she would be the same age as my lord, or a little younger. We know where she might be found.' He consulted the sick man with his eyes, and added, 'I have the direction in a coffer, if you will allow me to bring it.'

He hesitated and went. The vicomte's eyes followed him. Tobie said, 'You are fortunate to inspire such devotion. And I am sorry to have tired you. We wished to learn what we could for the child's sake, and because Nicholas, although he is all that Gelis has said, is oppressed by his situation, and can fall into error. Otherwise, you could be proud of him, and the child is without flaw.' He did not mention the boy's name. He prayed that the vicomte would not ask it. The vicomte asked nothing, but lay looking not at Tobie, but at Gelis.

She said, 'That is true. He has a fine nurse, from Chouzy. Nicholas took him to see where his mother your daughter was buried: she shares a vault with Marian de Charetty, and the priest is paid to care for the tombs. Nicholas is very like you, and so is our son. I am sorry I have no likeness to show you, or anything . . .' She stopped, but got no further, for the monk had come back, bearing a basket which he laid on the table and proceeded to empty, glancing at the vicomte between every phrase.

'The direction of the sister of the lady Josine, the first wife of my lord. A penner and paper, should my lord wish to write to his grandson. And the correspondence, my lord Thibault, that still awaits your attention.'

His tone was one of mock reprimand, and the vicomte smiled, lifting his hand for the bundle of papers. Tobie glanced at them, curious to know the nature of the old man's correspondents, and saw that the pages, in their differing inks, were filled, not with rambling reminiscences, but with cramped and closely written symbols, drawings, numbers, designs.

The monk said, 'My lord is a mathematician, and dabbles in music. Many write, and many come to compare theories. Cardinal Bessarion has sat with us here, and many great men from the Court of Ferrara, where we exchange monks with the Duke's great Certosa.' He smiled, the laughter lines radiating over his wrinkled cheeks and the vicomte smiled at him in return from where he lay. Brother Huon said, 'We have even had a visit from Father Ludovico da Bologna, the Patriarch of Antioch, whose family supply timber from Ferrara, of course, to the Arsenal. You would think, with his knowledge, that he would be ready to find faults with our forest, but he seems, so far, to have vouchsafed no complaints.'

'You should be glad,' Tobie said, his air serious. He was watching the vicomte, who had made a small sign.

'We are,' said the monk, without hurry. 'And now, in order that my lord may not weary you while he writes, perhaps the lady would enter our house with the doctor, and take a glass of wine, and gratify my poor ears with a discourse on the doctor's revered uncle, Giammatteo Ferrari da Grado, that great physician?'

Despite its subject, the discourse was pleasant enough, and the wine good. He and Gelis had no chance to confer, but he thought needed none. At the end, they found themselves once more out at the arbour, where a packet had been placed, sealed, on the table by the pillow on which the vicomte now lay back. It was thick: thick enough to contain a letter of several pages, and perhaps some enclosures. For the first time, now, Thibault de Fleury looked frail.

Tobie said, 'It has been too much. Take some wine. Attempt no more letters.'

'I do not intend to. It is done,' the vicomte said through his fingers. On the missive he had closed was a seal, and Nicholas's name, written in his grandfather's hand. The same hand lifted the missive and held it to Gelis, who took it. The fingers put a last question. 'You can find him?'

'I think so.' Her eyes were on the paper she held. Then with her other hand, she felt for the purse that hung at her girdle and, hardly requiring to search, drew from it a much shorter paper bearing no seal, but closely covered with swift, confident writing, of the kind used at the desks of the Curia. She said, 'It is not the same handwriting as yours, for he had himself specially taught. But it might tell you something.'

Tobie stared at her, and at the document, which the old man received and, unfolding, started to read. He made the sound which Tobie now knew for laughter and looked up, his eyes bright, at the girl. Tobie said, 'From Nicholas?' It was hardly creased. It was addressed to Gregorio and unsigned. The courier's mark showed that it had travelled through Danzig.

Gelis said, 'He sends anonymous reports, not to me. I hope you will not repeat the contents, which are serious. His choice of language is not.'

The fingers stirred. 'No. I know the end of that quotation, but hope that you do not.' He read it through to the end, and then again, and then folded it and returned it with care. 'I should like to keep it, but it is better with you. Perhaps one day —' The fingers stopped, and the monk looked at them both.

Gelis said, 'Nicholas is a long way away. Perhaps one day, he will come.'

His lids had closed. They took their leave, saying only what was commonplace, and walked down to the Prior's house with the monk. Brother Huon said, 'He bears it all with such patience. Is there anything more that can be done?'

'For his health, no,' Tobie said. 'Were he anywhere else in the world, he could have no better treatment: peace and beauty and loving attention, and the mental stimulation of his peers.'

'He misses music,' the monk said. 'The order enjoins silence, and is sparing in its use of liturgy. I sing to him, when I can, and when the wind blows from the south. And he reads his music, and imagines it. When you have passed years of paralysis, much of your world is in your mind.'

'I shall send you music,' Gelis said. 'I am going to see the Prior now, to make sure that you have all the help and comforts you need. And meanwhile, I want you to have this.' It was the reliquary brooch from her cloak. The monk protested but eventually took it, his face shining. Then they parted from him, and Gelis went to the Prior.

Tobie was drinking milk in the dairy when they sent to tell him the Lady was leaving. Breaking off his illicit talk, he emerged to take his own leave of the Prior, who was flushed, as Brother Huon had been, and accompanied them as far as the gate. There their escort was waiting, the better for bread and ale sent out to them by the monks. They set off to return to Treviso, riding in silence.

There was everything and nothing to say. The visit had failed to clear the doubts about Nicholas's birth, but had rather confirmed them: his father could not have been Simon de St Pol; his grandfather was not Jordan de Ribérac. Tobie had wondered, now and then, whether this was not the conclusion which Gelis had hoped for. Once, her sister had been married to Simon. If Nicholas had proved to be Simon's son, then his marriage to Gelis was illegal, and his own son had been born out of wedlock. Nicholas himself would not want that. It explained, perhaps, why he had dropped his early desperate campaign to force Simon to acknowledge him. It explained also, perhaps, why he had left Thibault alone.

Thibault de Fleury. Seeing, communicating with the living man whom they had expected to find a senile invalid; witnessing the stubborn remnants of a fine physique and uncommon gifts, Tobie had been moved as he knew Gelis had been affected by the death-bed of their priest and friend Godscalc. On that day five years ago, Godscalc had exacted a promise which Nicholas had surprisingly honoured, and which had kept him from Scotland for two years. Until the catastrophe at Trèves, no one had understood why. Now Tobie saw that already, Godscalc had read the other man's mind and, dying, agonised, had tried to protect Nicholas from himself, and Scotland from his machinations.

All that had to be remembered. Today, he and Gelis had experienced pity, but had learned nothing that should alter their opinion of what Nicholas had done, or become. Tobie had once had the confidence of the old maidservant called Tasse. He knew what had occurred in that sombre house in Geneva, whose owners did not survive. Equally, the viciousness of that gross bully Jordan de Ribérac had always explained, if not excused, some of Nicholas's behaviour, and the news of Jordan's earlier perfidy changed nothing now. De Ribérac was in exile in Madeira with his exquisite son Simon, and Henry, his brat of a grandson. Again, Nicholas had devastated all those who crossed him. And yet . . .

And yet, seated alone with Gelis at supper that night, Tobie saw that she had been weeping, and understood why. Like her, he did not want to forgive Nicholas yet again. Nicholas did not deserve it. At last he spoke.

'It distressed you. I'm sorry.'

She said, 'They have the same eyes. If the old man had been as fit as de Ribérac . . .'

'It might not have made very much difference. De Ribérac is a man of action, and Thibault is and was a dreamer, I think.'

Silence fell. Gelis said, 'I didn't know that Nicholas grew up in the midst of that sort of hatred. He was so brash, so clever, so —' She broke off.

'He received quite a lot of affection, too, and learned to inspire it. That has been the secret, if you like, of his survival, as well as the worst aspect of his plots. He cannot help making friends, whatever act of destruction he may be planning.'

'Friends of a sort,' Gelis said. 'He makes and loses them with equal indifference, it seems. It is reassuring, I suppose, how he has contrived that nothing affects him.'

Tobie was silent. However adroit he might be at dissembling, Nicholas had not been impervious to the loss of his early friends — Godscalc, Umar. Gelis knew that. And my God, he had not shown indifference on learning, as he believed, of the death of Gelis herself. Even now, remembering that night, Tobie shivered. You could condemn Nicholas with every justification but you could never claim, as Gelis was trying to do, that he was immune to hurt. Kathi and young Robin knew as much: it was that knowledge which had sent them to Poland. But, found, Nicholas had shown — or allowed to appear — no remorse, no compunction. He had left for the Black Sea with Anna, after an incident which brought Julius close to death. He might be protecting her. He might be advising the Bank — how extraordinary! — from a stricken conscience. He might be misleading them or — in remorseless pattern — himself. But Gelis had obtained and was keeping his notes.

Tobie said, 'Send him his grandfather's letter. It may cut the knot, free him from the past, let him devise a new life, wherever he is.'

'Perhaps Anna will convert him,' she said.

Later, when she had retired, Tobie sat for a long time under the single lamp, thinking of all he might have said to Thibault de Fleury, had there been no intermediary. Monks in silent orders were, of course, adept in the secret signs of the deaf. He knew a little himself: enough to tell how accurate Huon's interpretation had been; but he did not have the speed or the finesse for the great questions he longed to have answered. *Did you never love him? Why not?* He had not asked, either, about the source of the gift of divining.

Perhaps it was as well. The span remaining to Thibault de Fleury was short — shorter than he had let Huon think; and a life-long invalid deserved peace at the close. Today had been their first and last chance to learn something, and for his grandson, half a world distant, there was no chance at all.

Tobias Beventini heard again the sounds of Montello as they had accompanied his departure: the tessitura of leaves and the lowing of cattle and the syncopated drone of responses and prayer from the monastery. And remote behind these, the singing voice of one man lulling another to sleep. A melodious voice in its day, that of Huon; and pleasing to Thibault de Fleury, as he lay speechless under the vine leaves, never knowing the incomparable voice he had missed.

Chapter 16

'DO THAT *once more*,' said the Lady, 'and I shall have you thrashed. Why shall I have you thrashed?'

'Because I didn't come when you called,' said Nicholas miserably. He stood drooping, his prayer mat half rolled in his fists.

'What?' said Anna von Hanseyck.

'Khatun. Because, Khatun, I didn't come when you called,' said Nicholas hurriedly. He knew, without looking, that there was a gleam in her eye. It had been there ever since they had left the fondaco at Bielogrod and adopted their present guise of woman trader and Mameluke secretary. It was (Anna decreed) how they must now appear, up to their arrival in Caffa and all through their stay there. She was not in danger, being German, but he was. They had been three weeks on the road, and were at best three-quarters of the way to their destination.

Not unaccustomed to travelling with piquant, competent women, Nicholas had still found the journey surprising. It had begun, for him, with a sense of turmoil: the parting with Julius and the proximity of Anna and the black confusion which obscured the future. He had not been present, of course, at the leave-taking between Anna and Julius, but his own had been relatively easy: Julius, weak but no longer voiceless, had given him the tongue-lashing he deserved and had informed him that if he laid a finger on Anna he would kill him. He had then given him an amiable farewell, in the expectation of following them, once he could travel. Julius, the survivor, had survived.

The subsequent journey across Greater Poland had been eventful and strenuous enough, but the heat of July had been tempered by the green shade of the forests they passed through, and they had travelled in convoy, picking up motley bands of churchmen and smiths, dish-sellers and traders and horse-dealers passing from one hamlet or town to the next and, armed with letters from Straube, unloading their wagon of mattresses at those houses where Julius's agent was known. Once, led astray, they all had to camp in the open, with guards to keep off wild beasts and marauders. And once they had lodged very grandly indeed, in the Archbishop's palace at Dunajow, where Gregory of Sanok, professor of Italian literature and earliest patron in Poland of Filippo Buonaccorsi, sat surrounded by poets and scholars and exacted an intellectual fee for his hospitality.

Here, dressed as befitted her rank, Anna bestowed on the company all that store of wise charm which had smoothed their journey from Thorn, but had excused herself, with wicked modesty, from the cut and thrust of the debate. Nicholas, stranded, had hoped to do likewise: he had no wish to put up a performance for Anna or anyone else, and found the Archbishop's insistence all the more tiresome since he suspected its source. So far as he remembered, indeed, he kept to platitudes until halfway through the evening, when the wine presumably loosened his tongue. Next day, he seemed to remember a great deal of argument, much of it on his own part and pointed if not impolite; there had also been some lurid gossip and one or two very good jokes.

Meeting, ruefully, Anna's benign eye the following morning, he had temperately agreed to remain for a further night in the Archbishop's company, and because he stayed sober this time, kept a very clear recollection of the discussion and the course it had taken. They had placed in his hands — he had turned the pages of — an exquisite copy of the *De Republica*; and for the first time in his life, he had desired to be rich in order to own such a thing. But, of course, it was not for sale, and he had nowhere to keep it, even if it had been. They embraced him when he and Anna departed, accompanied by a small escort to take them on the next stage of their journey. He felt a little dazed, a little silent and, had he been honest, even more deeply confused.

Anna had left him alone until the first rest for the horses, when the party settled under the trees, and she came to spread her skirts at his side and eat melon. Her eyes smiled above her wet chin. 'So you have theories, but must be drunk to express them.'

'Drunk, mad or stupid,' Nicholas said. 'I thought I'd grown out of all that.'

'Of course,' Anna said, 'you may be above it. Or perhaps it's really the opposite: you missed it all when you were young, and didn't know how good you were. But now you do.'

'That's fine. So I'm happy,' said Nicholas. 'And I don't need to do it again.'

Anna completed her pacific munching and wiped her chin. 'You're not happy,' she said. 'Because you have a picture of yourself and your life that doesn't fit in with the world of ideas. You're afraid of religion and music because you think you'd have to give up horseplay and plotting.'

'Well, exactly. No contest,' said Nicholas reasonably. He stood, and leaned to help her to her feet. 'So what would you do if I retired to my cave with a begging-bowl? You wouldn't come to visit me.'

'That would depend,' Anna said, 'on how full the begging-bowl was.' But when he raised his eyebrows, she laughed. 'You don't understand? Never mind. I shall explain it all to you one day.'

She said no more after that, and they resumed riding very soon. Thinking about it, he recognised the truth in much of what she had said. However unregulated he might appear, he was not blind to the inconsistencies of his own character, or the circumstances which had created them. He did not, however, propose to offer himself for dissection, any more than he was anxious to offer his theories. It suited him that they rode in amicable silence from station to station of this journey, although she poured her energy, as he did, into all that was necessary for its success, and sustained without complaint the disappointments and hazards that did not fail to occur.

They were following in the footsteps of Ludovico da Bologna and his party, but so far had not overtaken them. The organisation of the expedition fell to Nicholas, but it owed much to Anna as well that a demanding company and its servants would arrive in good heart at the end of a stressful day's journey. It was not surprising, therefore, that she chose to spend the evenings of such days in well-earned seclusion, with only Brygidy her maid to be soothed and encouraged. Intentionally or not, it freed Nicholas to spend those leisure hours as he wished, carousing of course, with his fellow merchants in this tavern or that, but also straying to where his curiosity led him, from the booths of the Armenian artisans in Lemberg to the rocky fortifications of Kamenets.

He fell into conversation, too, with families taking the air and men playing at board games or arguing over their ale; and he compared what they said with the gossip he absorbed every day from his fellow travellers. Also, he stopped whenever he found someone at work in the mellow sunlight of evening, and sat beside them and talked. Often, weavers set up their looms in the open, as he remembered them in another place, mirrored — white cotton, black arms — in the water. The clack of the shuttle would draw him like rope to a capstan, although the sound appeared thin to his ears, accustomed to the lively retort of brick walls. The weavers, especially, talked.

It was not, however, because of what he learned that he changed his plans at Bielogrod, where the power of their safe conducts ended. Here, on the estuary of the Dniester, was the furthermost frontier of Greater Poland, which ran from gale-beaten Danzig to this, the balmy west shore of the Black Sea. And here they would receive the protection at last of the Papal and Imperial Legate, whose privileged company they would join, to wait for a ship to the land of the Crim Tartars.

Except that they arrived in Bielogrod to discover that the Papal and Imperial Legate was not there, and had not been there for a week. Directed by God to the harbour, Ludovico da Bologna had found an empty grain ship bound for Caffa, and left.

Setting aside the consequence to themselves, it was a bold move, as Anna remarked. The south coast of the Black Sea was wholly Turkish these days, and so of course was the Sultan's city of Constantinople at its south-western corner, a position it shared with the entire Turkish fleet. If the notorious Pontic storms didn't sink it, the Patriarch's ship would have to run the gamut of Turks and of pirates before it found a safe harbour in the Crimean Peninsula. The rashness of the voyage, indeed, was of a piece with the lunacy of the whole expedition, which, to Ludovico da Bologna, was no more than routine. He had been in Caffa before. Nicholas had not.

'So?' had said Anna, inviting suggestions.

'So,' had said Nicholas, 'we shan't get a ship, so we may as well set off round the coast. You can learn to charm Tartars. We'll hire a guard, or attach ourselves to a party of Genoese.'

'We won't,' she said. 'Or not until you have acquired a new history and a new name. Do you think I haven't heard what you've heard? I wish I had never let you come.'

'You couldn't have stopped me,' said Nicholas. He spoke gently enough, for he wanted to reassure her. It had always been obvious that, while he could expect to proceed unmolested to Tabriz, he could not pass through a Genoese colony as Nicholas de Fleury, former banker of Venice. Venice, it was now clear to everyone, was showering weapons, money and envoys at the feet of Uzum Hasan, the Turk's wiliest enemy. To favour a Venetian in these parts was tantamount to inviting the wrath of Sultan Mehmet of Turkey himself, and neither the Tartars nor the Genoese wanted that. Then, of course, there was the other complication which she might not know about, and which he had not hurried to tell her.

Hence Nicholas de Fleury was completing the journey to Caffa in the person of Nicomack ibn Abdallah of Cairo, downtrodden steward and secretary to the lady Anna, here to trade for her husband. He had made the transformation before. It was simple to dye his hair black, including the nascent beard he had left unshaven since Thorn. With his red cap and high-buttoned galabiyya over linen trousers and shirt he was the envy of Anna for coolness, as well as an object of curiosity and astonishment. But for him it was a familiar disguise: he had used it in Egypt and Africa, where the Arab tongue had become as familiar to him as his own. Black-haired Circassian slaves reared as Mamelukes had his height and build; he had met them. Some of them, trained as scholars, had Greek and

Latin as he did, and were conversant with Italian tongues. In Caffa, Anna would need an interpreter.

For the Turkish–Mongol languages they had hired a guide, Petru, to attend them. Of the servants who had come with them from Thorn they had retained none but Anna's maid Brygidy, who would have gone to considerable lengths, including her own, rather than betray any friend of her Lady. Nicholas, having left the inquisitive Jelita in Thorn, had only a hireling to shed: as a servant himself he could not replace him. Finally, they acquired local men for the packmules and wagon and purchased food and tents. Then they set off.

The experience this time was different. The difficult, swampy terrain and the lack of villages meant that seclusion was no longer possible. They shared their evening meal; their tents were close, for security. And during the day, instead of the voluble company they were used to, there was none but their grumbling, half-Tartar escort and the silent figures of Petru and Brygidy, one sullen, one grim.

That at least, could be repaired. Without being told, Anna invited the two to sit with her in the evening, and chatted to them both through the day. Nicholas made the escort his business, employing a ragbag of languages, but principally his talent for coarse visual jokes eked out with mime. They always ended by gambling, and he always lost. It reminded him of his first ship, the *San Niccolò*, but he dismissed the African trip from his mind. He did not propose to resurrect his first months with Gelis. He had a feeling that Anna was one day going to mention her.

About his own relations with Anna, he had made up his mind from his departure from Thorn, in a way that would have staggered some of his friends — his former friends — and aroused the derision of others. She was sympathetic, intelligent, beautiful, and he had half killed her husband. To a contrite man, despite the absence of the Patriarch, she would clearly be sacrosanct. To Nicholas, the happy predator, the juvenile libertine, she would obviously fall prey within hours.

All that and more, Nicholas recognised. Inescapably, she was desirable. By the edicts of a greater compulsion, however hungry, however desolate, he had vowed this time to deny himself.

It was a matter of management. Everything was. During this long, awkward journey he had seen displayed, without ostentation, all her grace, all her skills, all that had first drawn him to her, and more. He dealt with it. He dealt with her effect upon others. He had long known that she was also an excellent horsewoman and an accurate shot: the men of the escort ate better because of it, and had begun to admire her. It was to keep the admiration in its place that he suggested, when the third night approached, that he should sleep, as her servant, in the forepart of the small pavilion that Anna shared with her maid. After a moment's thought, Anna agreed. There would be a curtain between them. In any case, she had never been coy; her attitude to himself, or to Julius for that matter, was one of mild, faintly mocking affection: she was one of the most self-possessed women he had ever known.

He had not probed beneath the control. He had seen it slip, once, when she thought Julius dead and had screamed at him. She had taken time, after the shock, to soften what she had said, and now did him the courtesy of speaking freely of Julius; she had done so, with a touch of rueful tenderness, only today. Nicholas wondered again why they had no children, and this led his thoughts to Kathi's coming child and prompted him, in unwise and contrary mood, to speculate on where and how Robin sired it. In a gentlemanly way, he was sure. Not like his. Not like his with Gelis in Africa.

It was, perhaps, because he had let his guard down that he made his mistake, entering his tent in a hurry; sore with himself, dismayed by his lack of control. It was the time — he had forgotten — when Brygidy brought in the buckets for Anna's primitive shower. Water was scarce and he kept none for himself, being able to splash with the men in some stream where their nakedness would not offend. It was by accident therefore that he came in before the curtain was drawn, and saw Anna facing him as once he had dreamed. Or more divine than his dream: her dark-centred breasts and belly and thighs glistening in hazy sunlight; her wet black hair clinging like leaves. The badge between her thighs was night-black as well.

He looked there first, and then the shock hit him physically. It seized her as well: with shame and alarm that caused her to drop where she stood, kneeling in the wet tub, her head bowed, the cloak of hair screening her body. Then the maid came up, shouting, and ripped the screen closed.

He had been offered women — children — in some of the yurts they had passed, but had so far refused. There were no women where they were now. It was as well.

That evening, having absented himself from the meal, he asked Brygidy if her Lady would join him outside. The broad, middle-aged face, half-German, half-Polish, showed neither fright nor distaste: she had come with Straube's highest recommendation and had proved solidly loyal. Although far from frivolous, Brygidy had many good qualities: her fortitude in the face of men's stupidity reminded Nicholas of some aspects of Bel. Bel from Scotland, another forbidden subject. Then Anna came out.

The men, distant silhouettes round the fire, paid no attention: they had heard the scream, but believed it due to a snake. Petru had joined them. Brygidy seated herself some distance away. The air was heavy and feathered with insects; the soil coughed and creaked and breathed out the heat of the day.

Anna stood by his side. He got up and stood looking penitential. It was an attitude the other men were accustomed to, and they could not hear what was said. She remarked, 'What do you usually say when that happens?' Her light cloak and gown were the serviceable ones she kept for the evenings, but she had turned back her hood. Her expression, dimly revealed, was not so much resolute as resigned.

'It depends on what happens next,' Nicholas said, his voice tentative. He could not quite gauge her mood.

'But you rather assumed that I wouldn't put your eyes out,' Anna said. She sat down, pointing to the blanket before her. He knelt, then sat carefully back. She said, 'But it *was* careless, wasn't it? Or was it deliberate?'

He could feel his lips twitch. 'I got a bigger shock than you did, I think. No, it wasn't deliberate, but these things happen when travelling, Anna. I could go on apologising, or even rhapsodising if you like, except that it's best to forget it. I saw nothing. It didn't happen.'

She had unexpectedly flushed. But she did nothing but remark, 'Then it didn't happen. You are right.' She paused. 'Nicholas?'

Her cloak, sliding a little, had bared the neck of her gown. The flush still coloured her throat. He said, 'Tell me.'

The large eyes studied him. 'I think I shall tell you,' she said. 'With your sins fresh upon you, perhaps you will be kind enough to forgive mine. I brought you here with a lie.'

The men's voices murmured. Remotely, a horse neighed, and the croaking of frogs filled the distance like a flotilla of ducks, like the frogs in the wetlands below Mewe. Her body breathed under its cloak. Nicholas said, 'How was that?'

'Julius made up the story,' she said, 'that a client was dying, and his business needed our help. It wasn't true. The business in need of help is ours, Nicholas. I had to make this journey, or it would fail.'

He let her talk, bemused by her beauty, roused by her hardihood as Julius must have been from the day that he met her. The story was not unexpected. Establishing a separate business had not been easy for Julius. The company at Cologne did not possess the resources of Venice or Bruges, and all Anna's own money was sunk in investments. They had no liquid resources. They were living on loans: she had borrowed the gold to pay for her share of the *Fleury*. Julius had considered it safe; they had successfully extended their business, and had laid out money in ermines and sables which were to be brought south to Sinbaldo, their agent in Caffa, to be resold at dazzling profit. But Kazaks, outlaws, had waylaid and stolen the furs, and the consul at Caffa could only attempt to demand reparation if she or Julius appeared there in person.

'Reparation?' Nicholas had queried, speaking for the first time.

'Don't you remember the practice from Bruges? If one merchant fails to deliver, then the goods of his fellow nationals are impounded until the loss is made good.'

'So all the fur traders in Caffa are in prison?' Nicholas said. 'You are going to be popular. Or no, I see. I am.'

'You needn't concern yourself with it,' she said. 'Or you might think you owe it to Julius. If Julius had been here, he would have forced them to repay.'

There were circles under her eyes. He said, 'How did this happen, Anna? He is a lawyer. He should be able to run a business without incurring this sort of debt.'

'But he always had you to advise him,' she said. Her voice sounded tired. She said, 'We are even in your debt for your ship.'

He said, 'It isn't my ship, it's the Bank's. So why not tell me before? Because you thought I wouldn't come?'

'Because I didn't know if I could trust you,' she said. There was a gleam in her eye. He saw it.

'And now you can?' He sent his voice up just a trifle. 'And now you can, because I didn't leap over and ravish you?'

'Because of your expression,' she said. 'You looked *petrified*.'

'Surely not,' Nicholas said. He was prepared to say more — he expected to be required to say more — but she rose calmly then and excused herself, saying that he must be tired and that he should have time to decide what he wanted to do.

He knew what he wanted to do.

HIS HAIR DRIPPING, his mighty cassock soaked from the climb, Ludovico da Bologna stood in the heat outside the Genoese citadel gazing north: surveying the white, hazy curve of the great bay of Caffa, and the city which spread itself on its near slopes.

He was not interested in the view. He knew all about it. The first Bishop of Caffa had been a Franciscan monk. He himself had been here three times in nine years, and it was a week since he sailed into that harbour, wide and sound enough to shelter two hundred ships, lying calm in the lee of the mountains. What he was looking at, what he had come to look at, was a situation.

He had explained the situation now to five Heirs of St Peter and countless thickheaded rulers. Popes and merchants generally knew their geography: you couldn't rule a world business without it, and the Middle Sea (to date) was the hub of the world. You had to explain to some princes that the Middle Sea was joined by the Straits of Constantinople to the Black Sea, and that within the Black Sea, the Crimean Peninsula jutted south like a misshapen diamond, with the bight of Caffa below its east point. The Genoese had held Caffa and most of the Crimean seaports for centuries, hanging on to their fabulous trade and paying tribute to the heirs of Ghengis Khan, whose massed Mongol tribes claimed the steppes.

What created the situation, and kept altering it, was that the Mongol–Tartar overlordship was breaking up. The Golden Horde, once the first khanate of them all, still sat on the banks of the Volga and held its neighbours in thrall, while shaking the occasional fist over Caffa. But a separate horde, the horde of Crim Tartars had settled into the Black Sea Peninsula and, finding the pickings rich and the traders nervous but willing, had reached an accommodation which would make them all wealthy. The Peninsula was ruled from his inland stronghold by the Khan of the Tartars. The Genoese ports might have local officials, but were managed from Caffa by a committee of Genoese bankers and a Tartar Tudun, a Governor picked by themselves and the Khan. By paying their taxes, Christians bought tolerance in a Muslim community: uneasy bedfellows, held together by the golden cord of trade. And laid upon them and dreaded by all, the considering eye of the Sultan of Turkey, who leaned now and then from his palace in Constantinople to remind the Khan of the Crim Tartars that Allah was Lord over them both, and that security did not come cheap.

These were serious matters: their significance to the world was surely plain. But by the time Ludovico da Bologna had arrived so far in his account, the ruler's eyes would have flickered; his foot found occasion to tap; his throat subjected to clearing in order to break in and thank him. And the rest of the tale would be consigned to the ears of the princely advisers. All envoys suffered from lack of understanding, even those of the Pope. It gave rise, within the breed, to a strange and cynical friendship, even among those of wholly opposite camps. It gave rise also, of course, to venality.

Nicholas de Fleury had not arrived yet, but was on his way, so it seemed, dressed as a Mameluke. When Providence had found him a ship at Bielogrod, the Patriarch had considered it to be his duty to leave, not to wait. He had no positive proof that de Fleury was coming. If he had indeed set out with the woman, they possessed enough brains between them to manage. And so it had proved. The Patriarch held a coded message in his purse, telling him how they were coming, and asking his help to find them a house in the Christian quarter of Caffa. He had just arranged it with the Genoese consul, who knew about Straube's client with the missing consignment of furs. He'd had the same experience on one occasion himself. It was time the Muscovites were given a lesson.

There had been a time, too, when Ludovico da Bologna had despised the machinations of trade. Latterly he had been forced to recognise, with angry reluctance, that the growing exchange of commodities was a weapon he could not afford to neglect. Like it or not, trade was a network that bound peoples together. Even while rulers fought, their merchants were agreeing in corners. Whether from good motives or bad, from personal greed, from a distaste for war and a benevolent wish for general prosperity or (as sordid a reason as any) for the sheer pleasure of intellectual exercise, nations of different faiths helped one another in the name of a flourishing commerce. And so he had renewed his interest in Nicholas, for the boy, half his age, was significant in his own field, and able to create from thin air, were he asked, a business opportunity which would bring Archimandrites and cannibals round the same table. And now that de Fleury had come, the Patriarch did not think he would go back. Not with that woman there.

His thoughts had travelled so far when a rattling made itself heard and he turned to see some of the Sicilian mercenaries run from the fort to the stables. The consul emerged strolling behind, adjusting his sword while a page came with his cuirass and helm. 'Trouble?' said Father Ludovico.

Antoniotto della Gabella looked down his long, sun-bronzed nose. 'Nothing that a whipping won't cure. Some mannerless louts from the north are mobbing an incoming caravan. The gatehouse guard have it in hand. Tonight at the Bishop's?'

'Tonight at the Bishop's,' the Patriarch agreed, to his back. He unhitched his mule and, straddling it, gave it a kick. He thought he knew whose the caravan was, and even who the assailants might be. His crucifix bucked as he rode and, lifting his voice, he banged out psalms at the heretic skies until fragmented Allahs fell down, and the ruts of the road filled with peeled ululations.

Chapter 17

If there was a reward for good conduct, Nicholas received it then, on the last stretch of the journey to Caffa. There were several reasons. The pretence at wealth, for sure, had not been of Anna's choosing, and she was relieved at its end. Also, she was reassured, in a curious way, by his handling of the recent embarrassment. The easy rapport between them had returned. He had also taken care to put matters right with her servant Brygidy, going to find her the day after the mishap, as soon as they made camp.

He did not make a long speech, merely apologised for the fright he had given her, and assured her that there would be no repetition. She already realised, he thought, that it was accidental, and now said as much, briefly. He had caught her at work: kneeling beside a small stream with soap and a pile of Anna's fine linen. It was not, to be fair, a seemly place for a man, and he apologised a second time, later. Cornered, however, he would have had to confess to a startled fascination at his first glimpse of those thin embroidered chemises, reeking of horse, soiled exactly like his by the grime of travel and the all-pervasive soot from the cooking. Her undergarments were too fine for this trip, yet she had brought them, and worn them. Now he could imagine, as Julius could, the bridal lawns beneath the plain gowns. As to what would be revealed, drawing asunder the lawn, he had no need to imagine: he knew. But not, of course, as Julius did.

On their last night before Caffa, when it seemed they were safe, she asked him what he would have done if Turks had captured them, or someone who knew him of old.

They were in the forepart of her tent, under cover, for in public they maintained the fiction of harsh mistress and blundering dragoman. He had been striving, ever since Bielogrod, to improve his fluency in the tongue of the Tartars. Turkish coloured most of the languages round the Black Sea, including the Turcoman he had learned during and after his last visit here, which had been concerned with the south coast of the

Euxine. She knew about that. She also knew about his other disguise, when he and Tobie had met Sultan Mehmet during his war against Trebizond. 'But he wouldn't know me again,' Nicholas said. 'It was thirteen years ago. Tobie was a dumb camel doctor, and I was his assistant. And it was a different Grand Vizier.'

He waited, prepared to be angry with Julius, but Julius seemed to have kept some of that incident at least to himself. Anna only said, 'Dr Tobias? Why dumb?'

'Because he didn't know the language,' Nicholas said. 'We filled his mouth with raw liver and pretended his tongue was cut out. We had to talk to each other by sign. It wasn't funny.'

'I think it must have been,' Anna said, spluttering a little. Then she said, 'What? Is something wrong?'

'I don't know,' Nicholas said, a little blankly. He pulled himself together. 'No, of course there isn't. But perhaps we should rest. It will be a long day tomorrow.'

A month ago, she wouldn't have asked. Now she said, 'I shall go if you tell me what's wrong. What happened in Trebizond? Or has something happened now? Nicholas, are you divining?'

Nicholas stared at her without answering. He didn't need to divine. He hadn't divined since the fiasco at Thorn. It was partly because he was trying to forget, and partly because he knew that if bad news were to come, it would come to him direct, rather like this, but much worse. Eventually he shook his head and said, 'It was the pickled oysters, very likely.'

The dense blue eyes searched his. 'A premonition? What? Has something happened to Gelis? Or to Jodi? Or is Kathi suffering because of the child? You aren't divining, but perhaps you ought to be. Where is your pendulum?'

He schooled his breath, and his pulse. 'Nothing has happened to Gelis or Jodi. It was something remote: a chance echo, perhaps a mistake. Don't worry. I'm going to bed.'

She rose. 'I don't quite believe you. I'm going to bring you something to drink. And while we speak of it, I should like to apologise. I talked of Jodi in Thorn, and distressed you. I saw the burned letter.'

'It doesn't matter,' he said.

'It does,' Anna said. 'He wrote it for you, and it's gone.'

'It really wasn't a very good poem,' Nicholas said. 'But it hasn't gone.' And smiling a little, he repeated it.

At the end, she went to find the little wine they had left, and poured him some. Then she returned to her cushion and sat. 'You have a good memory. It is not a bad poem, for a child. Would you let me set it to music?'

He looked at her in profound astonishment. A little thought told him that she was not offering a personal service: composition could be no less alien to her than any other branch of the art: he had never seen a musical instrument in Julius's house. But the German states were full of ready-made folk tunes and glib Court composers: she would have her pick, he realised, of friends. Presumably she would send it by courier. He said, 'I don't know. You heard it. The beat is erratic, to say the least.'

'There is paper. Write it all out,' Anna said. 'Then sleep. Jodi will know you are thinking of him.'

She hesitated, then left with a smile. Bel would have patted his shoulder. Kathi would have stayed and insisted on helping him. Gelis . . . He could not imagine Gelis making a gesture of comfort or one — he tried not to remember the Play — that was not immediately cancelled. The sense of ancient desolation returned, and he had to concentrate to dispel it. He wondered, with harsh amusement, what Benecke would have made of him now — a grown man alone, wanting sympathy. He missed the masculine rivalry. He missed the cold in the sweet, sticky heat of this land. He missed the life he had nearly chosen, as Colà. But before he threw himself on his bed he did take his pen and write out the verses his small son had sent him, to be ready for Anna next morning. Then, against all expectations, he slept.

THEY REACHED CAFFA two hours after midday, when men of sense take to their beds in high summer, and even the din of the harbour is stilled. The Genoese wall with its towers encircled the high ground of the city, ending with a fort at the sea on each side. It was to be expected that the portal they approached should be manned at its upper windows, and that men in half-armour awaited them. Caffa was a fief of the Crim Tartar khanate, and a town as large and as rich as Seville. Outside its confines were ferocious hillmen, opportunist nomads and professional robbers. Far outside were the lands of the Turk. And crowded inside were the houses, warehouses and churches, the mosques and cathedrals, the markets, stables and orchards of close to a hundred thousand inhabitants of every colour and faith: Armenian and Tartar, Russian and Circassian and Georgian, Polish and Lithuanian, Moldavian and Gothian, Venetian and Genoese. The citadels, the arsenals and the prisons were Genoese.

Anna had sent word ahead of their coming: openly to the Protectors of the Bank of St George who represented Genoa, and to the Patriarch with more circumspection. Their arrival was therefore expected. The soldiers of the guardhouse were sluggish but civil, glancing at her letters and making cursory examination of their baggage, which included samples but no goods to sell. Then they were bidden to wait, while a detail was prepared to take them to the temporary shelter of the Franciscan monastery. They now required not only a house, but servants and protection, for they had turned off their escort that morning with a settlement lavish enough to earn Nicholas some strong-smelling, matted embraces: he had proved a very bad gambler. Petru had received his last payment too, and although never given to hilarity, had allowed his gloom (encouraged by Nicholas) to lighten a trifle. Wishing to find new employment, he rode into the city ahead of his former employers, who were now reduced to a party of eight: the German lady, her maid, her Mameluke, and the five soldiers of the guard who presently joined them, yawning and with their straps half undone. They rode through the vault of the gate, the cart rumbling, and out into the sunlight of Caffa.

They were out of sight of the fortification when they were attacked. The four soldiers who rode two on each side of the packmules and wagon did not even notice at first, and their leader, deep in charmed conversation with the beautiful Contessa, was almost as slow to observe the carts drawn across the narrow road down which they were pacing, between two high walls broken only by the frontage of an old wooden house just ahead. Then, as the leader shouted and turned to his fellows, they saw that the same thing had happened in their rear. Their way was cut off, and from before and behind, twenty men were running towards them, shouting and brandishing staves. And curiously, there was no one but themselves to see them, for the road was empty but for a single rider who had left just before them, and who now flung himself from his horse and rushed to the one silent house, where he could be seen hammering frantically on a door. The door opened, and closed quickly behind him. Petru was safe.

The soldiers were armed with short swords, and carried maces and whips. There were only five of them, but there was a full body of troops in the garrison. The leader raised a trumpet to summon them, and had it struck from his face by a stone. The Mameluke, far from helping, jumped from his horse and began to haul the ladies out of their saddles, resisting all efforts to stop him. He was a very big man. The Genoese leader, holding his face, yelled at the fellow: 'Get the ladies into that house for your lives! Leave the wagon! Let the bastards do what they like with your merchandise!'

'That sounds like sense,' said Anna in German. Her cloak and hat gone, she was in the grip of Nicholas, who was successfully propelling her towards her own wagon. She saw he had a grasp of Brygidy also. She heard him swearing, with some presence of mind, in the same language.

'It's you they want, not your spoons,' Nicholas said. 'It's a trap. The house belongs to the ambushers. Get into the wagon.'

'Me?' Anna said. She rose in the air and landed, hard, in the wagon. Brygidy also arrived, with a crash.

'You,' Nicholas said. He was lashing their horses and his own to the wagon. 'Listen to the men at the barriers. They're Russians.' He made a grab for his bow.

'Holy Mary!' said Anna piously, and disappeared under the canopy.

'And throw me a tinder-box,' Nicholas added.

Afterwards, there was disagreement about what next happened. The ambushers, bearded men in tunics and trousers, raced up and encircled their victims but at first did nothing more than demand that the soldiers disarm and hand over the woman. When the soldiers refused, surrounding the little convoy with drawn swords, the leader of the ambushers, stepping forward, asked in a reasonable voice if they wanted to die, as they were five against twenty, and they couldn't suppose their horses were immune to arrows? There followed some threats, which the soldiers appeared to understand, for one of them suddenly drew back his arm and threw a knife. There was a grating scream and a furious roar, followed by a squeal and a thud as the knife-thrower's horse staggered and fell with a spear in its throat. The leading soldier yelled to the others. 'That's enough. Get the women across to that house and barricade it. Don't let the Mameluke stop you. Where is he?'

No one replied, for just then the wooden house began to crackle and smoke at a place to one side of the door, where suddenly flames began to appear. A flare sailed through the sky, and another spot started to glow, then another. Shouting came from inside the house, and from outside, as the ambuscaders hurried towards it. Then the front barricade burst into flame and the smoke, rising into the shimmering sky, finally told the soldiers at the gate tower that something was wrong.

Bursting through the first barrier in their way, the men from the tower found themselves in a circle of fire within which a group of blistered, smoke-blackened Russians appeared to be trapped. They rounded them up, while the fire-drum hammered its warning. There was no sign of the German Contessa, or her servant, or her Mameluke. There was no sign, either, of her baggage-train. That, as it happened, had arrived already, seared and blackened, at the gates of the Franciscan monastery, where the Abbot, summoned at once, found a group of terrified animals and a lady in a still-smoking wagon whose driver, a bearded Egyptian, or perhaps Circassian, addressed him politely in French.

'Lord, receive the peerless Gräfin Onna von Hanseyck,' said the heathen humbly. 'Esteemed friend of the lord Ludovico, prince of the Faithful, who, scattering joy, gifts and alms, will generously condescend to join us, I believe, almost at once, may Allah treasure him for his zeal.'

'Oh, be quiet,' said the Lady. 'Father, may we come in?'

. . .

TO LUDOVICO DA BOLOGNA, later, she said, 'It was frightening at the time. Nicholas says that they wouldn't have harmed me, only used me to bargain with. They haven't much money, and they're afraid the Genoese will ruin them over this claim for compensation unless I agree to give it up and go home. They come from the Russian states that Moscow claims sovereignty over, but Moscow changes its mind every week about whom it supports — Venice and the Golden Horde, or Genoa and the Crim Tartars. So they felt compelled to act for themselves.'

'That is a fair assessment,' said the Patriarch kindly. 'But have no fear. They will be severely chastised for it.'

'Will they?' she said, rather pleased. They were sitting in a private room in the Abbot's guest-quarters. The Patriarch, in appearance vaguely unwashed but perfectly vigorous, had made no apology whatever for having abandoned them on their way here. She said, 'Nicholas believes it will adjust itself soon. Apparently the case is being affected by local politics.'

'You could say that,' the Patriarch said.

'What local politics?'

'What? Oh, the Tartar Governor for Caffa has died. The Tartars are divided over which of two men should replace him, and the Genoese are in two camps as well, being well bribed for their support by each party. You could say the Russians are caught in the middle.'

'And me. I want their money,' said Anna. She was smiling. 'I hope Nicholas can get it for me. Will you wait for him? I wish I knew where he went.'

'To beg off the Russians, I imagine,' the Patriarch said. 'Earn their gratitude. Get their complicity. He wouldn't want you to be there. You don't want to hear the names he'll be calling you.'

'In the cause of business,' said Anna rather blankly.

'Oh, yes. Mahir, King of the Monkeys. You know the Abbot thinks you are called Countess Onna?'

'It was a mistake,' Anna said. 'Wasn't it?' She watched the Patriarch preparing to laugh, and held her tongue. She was naturally patient, and had had practice, with Julius.

NICHOLAS ARRIVED a good deal after that, and expressed no surprise at finding Anna retired, and the nuncio of the Pope and the Emperor Frederick still sitting at ease in the guest-parlour, the remains of a frumenty frosting his gown. Instead, he threw his satchel into a corner, poured and drank off some wine and, holding the half-empty cup, walked backwards and forwards, sipping occasionally. He looked like an actor conducting a mental rehearsal.

'You are angry, I take it,' said the Patriarch. 'So sit down and tell me what you wish you had said. And make sure that door is closed. Mameluke stewards do not sit or drink in my presence. Nor do decent Christians, but you are never going to be that.'

Nicholas was angry, largely because it had been impossible to say what he had wanted to say. Since it was reasonable, indeed essential, that the Patriarch should know, Nicholas delivered a curt résumé. Guided by one of the monks, he had reported, on behalf of his mistress, at Constantine's Tower, where the Genoese consul was interviewing the would-be kidnappers. He had seen some of them dragged away.

'Well beaten, I imagine?' had said the Patriarch dryly.

'Naturally. But alive, so far as I could see. A former guide of ours, Petru, was among them.'

'A spy?'

'A sympathiser, at least, with the Russians. The soldiers had broken both his arms. Then I was questioned over the complaint about the furs, and the credentials of the Gräfin, and they brought in the agent, Sinbaldo di Manfredo, who had imported the furs, and finally hauled back the leader of the Russians . . .'

But he needed more wine while he considered that. The men who had tried to waylay Anna had not been a band of common thieves. He had the impression that they were not even permanent colleagues, although they lived in the same quarter. They were simply a group of small merchants and their servants; men who had contracted with a German–Polish company to buy a consignment of furs for them in Moscow. Then, when on their way to Caffa to deliver the goods, the pelts had been stolen and they were now being asked to refund their value.

The case had been stated fairly enough by Sinbaldo the agent and by himself, and had been endorsed by the prisoner, through his swollen mouth and broken teeth. His name was Dymitr, and he was Ruthenian, his family being that of the Wiśniowiecki, the lords of Cherry Village. Mishandling could not disguise his athleticism: the man was long-limbed and chestnut-bearded, with glowing black eyes spitting fire. At present, he looked the way the captain of the *San Matteo* had probably looked, when Paúeli had finished with him. The load of ermines and sables had gone the way of the 'Last Judgement,' with Tommaso sitting contrite in his pan. It remained to be seen whether Julius would have better luck than Adorne had had.

'Who was the leader? Dymitr? And who else was there, besides the agent?' the Patriarch asked.

The consul had been present, the sallow-faced man with the expensive clothes and superior manner: Antoniotto della Gabella. And another man, soft-voiced and lighter in colouring, who had said very little, but appeared to be Genoese too.

'Oberto Squarciafico,' the Patriarch said in a satisfied way. 'One of the representatives of the Bank of St George. Indeed, the treasurer. Well, well, my boy — and you walked free, with an apology? You were lucky. The penalty for fire-raising is death.'

Nicholas said, 'I think the feeling was that they were happy to take it out of the Russians, so long as I could get the Countess to forget her furs and turn round and go home.'

'*Forget* her furs?'

'There aren't any,' said Nicholas. 'So no one could impound them. And they haven't any money to speak of in Caffa. It'll have to be thrashed out by lawyers, and the compensation brought down from Moscow, which could take half the winter. Or, likelier, it won't come at all. The difficulty is that she does need the money.'

'So you want to wait and negotiate? Or wait and open up some new trade for her?'

'Both,' Nicholas said. 'It shouldn't upset your own plans. Tabriz is humming with envoys, they tell me. Finish your business here and go on without me. I'll come when I can.'

'With or without the Gräfin?' said the Patriarch, raising the hedge of his brows.

'Julius is coming for her,' Nicholas said irritably. 'When he is well.'

'It seems,' the Patriarch said, 'that you are about to have an interesting winter. May I make a suggestion? When this immediate business is over — when the consul is convinced that you are staying, and that an official complaint is being made, and compensation will be insisted on — you should take a little trip into the country. That is, since you have chosen to appear in the dress of a heretic, you might as well visit the chief of the heretics. I know him well. I shall give you a letter. You must ride to Baçi Saray, and climb to Qirq-yer, the mountain citadel of Mengli-Girey, the Khan of the Tartars.'

'You know him well,' Nicholas repeated.

'Yes. Like his father, he is a dangerous man, but a shrewd one. He sides with the Genoese since it suits him. He may continue to side with them if western merchants such as yourself offer prospects of lucrative trade. Or one day, he may change his mind about all his alliances. You are not a Franciscan friar, for which we all thank God, but you have some native shrewdness. I should be interested to have your views on the Khan.'

'You mean, spy on him?' Nicholas said.

Ludovico da Bologna favoured him with a pitying glare. 'Do I have to spell out what is happening? Do you think the fortunes of a pretty woman and her unfortunate husband count beside this? This is not about furs. This is about a balance of power between factions which shifts from week to week, and which, out of greed, out of fear, out of petulance, can determine at least the fate of the Latins in my Patriarchate, at worst the future sovereignty and beliefs of the West. I hope to go to Tabriz, but I cannot leave while these puppies are quarrelling. Resign yourself. Julius cannot come before summer. You are going to know the Peninsula well before you depart. You may as well make yourself useful. Unless, of course, you wish to take the lady back empty-handed, and spend the winter frozen in Thorn at the bedside of the stricken Julius.'

'That would seem a waste,' Nicholas said.

THUS HE CAME to spend the autumn in Caffa, and learned to know it as well as he knew Bruges or Nicosia or Venice, Cairo or Timbuktu. When he first came, in the summer, it had the look and smell of the rich emporia of Pera and Trebizond, with the stone stalls piled with scented exotica under the palms, the teeming streets with no two tongues or costumes the same, the silken awnings, the glittering churches, the dazzle of sails in the harbour. And outside, the wagons soft-piled with grapes swaying into the city, through air swimming with chaff and scored with the songs of the threshers. Later, when the violent ultramarine of the harbour had cooled to blue-grey, it reminded him unexpectedly of the estuary of Edinburgh, glimpsed through an arch from on high. Only here, the sounds were different from those of a Christian town: the invocations of the muezzin throbbed through the gull cries and babble, and the clack of the conventual sounding-boards interrupted the carpenter's mallet. Bells were not permitted in Caffa, where the mosques outnumbered the churches.

He did not leave the city at all for some time, being closeted obsequiously with the consul in pursuit of Anna's affairs, or attending Anna herself at the desks of her agent and lawyers. The German Contessa had her own house by then. Tartar and Circassian servants were common: every house had its Fatma. The identity of the Contessa's Mameluke steward had never been questioned, although Sinbaldo, knowing Straube, had to be told. He appeared to be impressed by the stratagem, but Nicholas, when he wished to send letters, preferred to use other carriers.

The Russians, heavily penalised, had been freed, and were allowed to drag their aching bodies back to their quarter, but forbidden to leave until the dispute was settled. Since then, by amazing coincidence, Nicholas had bumped into their leader, Dymitr, at the fish-market, and after a single tense moment, had abruptly made a remark which resulted, presently, in the two men leaving the market together.

Returning, Nicholas reported to Anna.

'Father Ludovico said you'd do that,' she said, viewing him. Although he had left his baskets in the care of the cook, an odour of fish clung to his clothes and would adhere, no doubt, to the plain plaster walls and timber ceilings of the house the Patriarch had borrowed for her, and for which she could not pay. She had also made him take off his slippers. His feet, muscular, clean and well-shaped, were not the offence they might have been in Cologne, for example. Men with bare feet were professionally used to tread grapes, or press caviare into the barrel. Nicholas said that for caviare, they got very small men, with dimpled toes.

He had been increasingly cheerful since they settled in Caffa. He was cheerful now, smiling at her above the black rim of beard and sporting a sashed tunic dripping with shellfish. He looked, in a terrible way, like the Patriarch. 'I've just spent an hour with the Russians. Petru included.'

She was still taken aback, despite the Patriarch's surmise. 'They might have killed you, or held you to ransom.' She paused. 'They didn't. They fed you with oysters. You promised to help them against me.'

'Of course,' Nicholas said. 'Even Petru remembered what a heartless mistress you were, although they understand I have to stay for the wages. It doesn't immediately help, because they don't have any money, and it may not come even after they've sent for it. But I get all the gossip. And anyone with a good intelligence service can make money in trade, if they're quick.'

'Can you make me rich by next week?' Anna said.

'No,' said Nicholas. 'But I still have some of the money Zeno gave me.' A ripple of joy crossed his face. 'D'you know Zeno auctioned off his own Venetian clerk to square his debts and free himself to go home? Martin. He's scrubbing latrines in the Armenian monastery. Zeno told him he'd get him a pension provided he swears he volunteered to be sold. They won't put up with Venetian envoys. Two others came through in June and had to hide in the church. It's a threat, see, to the deals that the Genoese and the Russians are possibly doing with the Golden Horde and the Crim Tartars and Poland. And Hungary. And Uzum Hasan.'

'You love this,' said Anna, astonished.

Below the trousers, his naked feet were crossed in a parody of coy submission. 'I'd forgotten what it was like. What are you writing? Something for me to copy?'

'Something for you to play. Music for Jodi.'

His feet returned flat to floor, and his palms to his knees. Then he said, 'I didn't know you made music. Who taught you? Your parents?'

'My parents died before I grew up,' Anna said. Then she said, 'Have I said something?'

Nicholas smiled at her. 'No. I misunderstood. I thought Julius had said that he met them.'

'He sometimes said that,' Anna said. 'Just as he liked to say that I was wealthy. I was, of course, once. If Julius cares too much about show, it is only because he himself was a foundling. The Church paid for his legal course at Bologna. He was better off, I think, than he knew. No one sent you to be educated, except as an apprentice. And look how far you have come.'

'Penniless to Caffa, disguised as a Mameluke servant. But see what company I can boast,' Nicholas said. He looked down at the paper she had given him: his son's verses with musical notes written above them. They sang themselves in his head, the words he had committed to memory, like a crime, in his room in Thorn. The tune was simple and charming and clever, and he couldn't speak.

Then he said, 'I'm sorry. It took me by surprise. I'm sentimental about Jodi. You may have noticed.'

She said, 'If you hadn't cared, I wouldn't have troubled. Do you want to talk about him?'

'No,' said Nicholas.

'But you can hear the tune? You know what it is?'

'Oh yes,' Nicholas said. 'It is perfect. It should be sung with a flute.'

'Or another voice,' Anna said.

'Yes,' he said. He got up slowly. 'May I have it? We could talk of it later?'

'Yes, of course,' Anna said.

HE KNEW, naturally, that he should have stayed. But music — his greatest skill, his deepest pleasure — was the last of the possessions which he had set out to jettison, and he had not faced that yet. It struck him that his record so far was not especially impressive. He had believed, quite some time ago, that he had reduced all his relationships to manageable ciphers, and then had found that Jodi escaped him. Now he had a chance to excise two weaknesses at the same time, through a child's terrible verse and a jingle.

So the diviner's will, at least, had it. The diviner's spirit, as before, contradicted. The verse, however childish, however broken, was still endearing, even enchanting. The music matched it exactly.

He hadn't known of this gift. His image of Anna had been incomplete; the burning image he had carried ever since he first saw her, and every step of the long journey here. He had never touched her, so far. He had not wooed her, except by being different from Julius. He had taken great care.

And now, this.

But when, later, she tapped on his door, he rose at once and opened it and said, 'Of course, the time has come for a performance. You have a flute?'

And Anna said, 'Is the voice not enough, or are you too grand?' Then, because this was hardly an occupation for a Saracen servant, she led him outside, to the kiosk under the fig trees. The house and small garden were empty: Brygidy had gone to church, and they would be unheard; or so she said. She had a dish of cherries, and her hair, loosely knotted, drifted in wisps at her ears above her usual plain, high-necked gown. She set the cherries down, placed him on a bench by the thin, woven wall and, seating herself, took the paper from his hand and studied it, smiling.

Her voice was so soft that he did not immediately realise that she was not speaking, but was singing the words of his son, to her music. It unfolded; he sat in silence, watching and listening. Feeling his attention, she crinkled her eyes and allowed her voice to expand. It was as smooth as syrup, and dark, and flowed from one register to the next without flaw. Primaflora had had a schooled voice like this, and a young woman called Phemie in Scotland. Kathi's voice, high and free, was a freak of nature as was his own, recently given some semblance of art by a man in Scotland who thought he loved them both, and was right to love Kathi.

Music and Willie Roger. Nicholas de Fleury had had ten months to notice that they were not precisely man-eating dragons. One could conjure with them, and live. At the end of this song, Nicholas said lightly, 'Now you have surprised me. Shall we try that together?' And watched her eyes, her full-lidded violet eyes, as, sharing the bench and the page, he and she repeated the little performance, at first muted, in unison, and then with her voice moving in harmony above and below, until they ended together. Then she looked at him, her colour high.

He said, 'Do I thank Kathi for this? You and I have never spoken of music. I didn't know you could sing.'

'But everyone knows of your voice,' she said. 'There was a famous motet someone made for you in Edinburgh. Lord Cortachy used to say that he wept.'

'It was probably tedious enough to deserve it,' Nicholas said. She had remained at his side, the paper loose in one hand. When he leaned to offer her fruit, she lifted twin cherries, and tilted her head to admire them. 'We spoke of my parents,' she said. 'But where did that voice come from? Or don't you know?'

'I don't know,' Nicholas said. 'My mother's side, at a guess. She died when I was quite young.'

Anna looked at him. 'Were you sad?'

'I thought the sun would never shine again.'

'You were an only child? My sisters died.'

Nicholas said, 'I wasn't brought up alone. I had an aunt two years younger than I was. Adelina. A red-headed spitfire.'

Anna laid down the stalks. 'She was in Geneva. Julius told me. When your mother died, Adelina went to Jaak de Fleury at the same time as you did? So you would comfort each other?'

'We might have, but they kept us apart. Didn't Julius hear about that?' Nicholas said.

'He doesn't speak about her. After all, he didn't come to Geneva until you and she had both gone. What happened, Nicholas?' Anna said. The plate of cherries lay between them. She leaned across it and laid her hand on his arm. 'What happened? Your great-uncle beat you. Did he beat the little girl, too?'

'I saw him beat her. I saw him kiss her,' Nicholas said. 'Then she went to a convent. She was too young to know what was happening.'

The hand on his arm was steady and cool. 'But you were not. Did he beat and kiss you?' Anna said.

Nicholas gave a grimace. 'He beat me. Better men have managed to do it as well, and I deserved some of it, I expect. I didn't like him, but not simply for that.'

'And the wife, Jaak's wife Esota? Julius didn't like either of them,' Anna said.

'They were both strange,' Nicholas said. 'I escaped and so did my little aunt. It's a common enough sort of childhood, and did me no lasting harm, although there were some things my uncle did later that I couldn't forgive him for. As for Adelina, I expect she went on to make a wise and good-hearted nun. Or perhaps she changed course and married, and is the matriarch of a brilliant, red-headed family. I wish I knew her. My wife — my first wife, Marian de Charetty — wanted to help her and was hurt, I know, to learn that she didn't want to be found. But I hope she's happy, wherever she is.'

'And rich,' Anna said glumly, and took her hand back in order to choose another couple of cherries. 'While here we are, starving in penury.' Her gentle mockery was for him, and herself.

His gaze had been on the cherries. She didn't spit the stones out, just removed them in a practical way from her lips and laid them down. He said abruptly, 'I haven't made music since Trèves. Did you know that?'

'It was a very small hurdle,' she said.

'Not to me. You have been very kind, and I want to repay you. Anna, I have found some good trading outlets for Julius, but they all need investment.'

'I know you have no money either,' she said. 'Unless, of course, you are volunteering to put yourself up for auction?'

'Goodness, I've already done that,' Nicholas said. 'Where do you think I go in the evenings? No. I, too, have a confession to make. I didn't come here because of you or the Patriarch, but because of some gold that was stolen from me in Africa. My shipmaster is said to be somewhere here. If I find him, I may find the gold. Or he may have lost it, or spent it, or never really had it at all.'

'But?' she said steadily.

'But if I find it, then it will be my investment in Julius's company. If it is suitable. If you will allow me,' Nicholas said.

She sat looking at him, her eyes bright. 'Because of Julius?' she said.

'I have a chance to begin again,' Nicholas said. 'It is not a bad thing, to forget the past. This way, we shall all have some hope of recovering. As you say, I like dealing. In fact, the only loser will be the Patriarch, who can always find use for some gold. But I expect I can help him in other ways.'

Her gaze was still fixed on his, but her skin was illumined with colour. She said, as if at random, 'I should have known you would have your own reasons for coming.' She held out her hand, and he took it. She said, 'Whether you find it or not, thank you for thinking of us, Nicholas.' She stopped, before adding as if compelled, 'I wish you'd told Julius.'

Continually, she surprised him. 'I thought you were rich,' Nicholas said. 'I thought I needed the gold for myself. But you changed my mind. Or I grew wiser.'

She moved her fingers but, when he freed them at once, simply used them to trace the solid width of his palm, compellingly, over and over. She said, 'I think you are wise. But don't place yourself in danger, trying to look for this man.'

'Oh, I expect he will find me,' Nicholas said. 'If he is alive. And meanwhile there is business to be arranged, and the Patriarch to keep satisfied. But don't lose heart. Somehow, the rent will be paid.'

She smiled, and rose when he did, her hand falling free. But before they moved from the kiosk, she slipped it up to his shoulder and touched her lips, faintly sticky with juice, to his cheek. 'From Julius,' she said.

'One of his better kisses,' Nicholas answered. It sounded placid, which, considering his quickening senses, was a feat in itself. He removed himself while he could.

Soon after that, he went to Ludovico da Bologna and advised him that he was prepared to make the journey to the citadel of the Khan of the Crim Tartars at Baçi Saray.

'Refused you, has she?' said the Patriarch, who had just returned from a trip to the north. 'Well, you'll find plenty of both sexes at Qirqyer. Do my business. Stay, if you're asked. I'll tell them to expect you.'

'Will you?' said Nicholas.

The Patriarch stared. 'You can pass for a Mameluke with wandering tribesmen and foreigners, but Mengli-Girey isn't going to be deceived. Unless, that is, you plan to do something your bedmates don't know about.'

He was a fiendish old man for whom, recently, Nicholas had begun to form a grudging respect. 'Had it done years ago,' Nicholas said unconvincingly. 'So what else do you want me to do? For you, anything.'

Chapter 18

ONCE, THEY BLINDED those who might betray the approach to a Tartar khan's fortress. Now, the Tartars who had accompanied him in relays throughout the strenuous journey south-west from Caffa merely blindfolded Nicholas as they began the long climb up the Mairam Dere ravine to the citadel of Qirq-yer, the Forty Fortifications.

The ride had taken the better part of a week, for their route lay through the range of weird limestone mountains, gnarled and battlemented, whose shelter fostered the apricots, the almonds, the vines of the fragrant south-eastern coast, and allowed the Genoese ships to lie calm in each harbour. Because, until he met the Khan, he was still the Contessa's Mameluke factor, Nicholas rode short-stirruped in his tunic and leggings with his prayer-mat behind, and passed easily enough with his Arab-Egyptian accent; the more so that for the last stretch he was given a camel of evil disposition, and mastered its tantrums with ease. Then they got to Baçi Saray, a pleasant, well-watered plain to which the khanate of the Crim Tartars had moved since making their base in the north forty years before.

The multitude of their beasts, sheep and horses, goats and oxen and camels, could pasture here. The tented wagons with the women and children of these descendants of the great Mongol hordes could plant their woven homes in these meadows, where the tomb of their last khan had been raised. The summer palace of the ruler was here. But his permanent home, their refuge in war, the forty acres of honeycombed rock which was the heartland of their tribe, was half an hour's steep climb from this place. Before they blindfolded Nicholas, his companions searched for and took his short sword and his knife, and even the scissors he used for his beard. They themselves were well armed. Weapons were forbidden to Tartars in Caffa, but once outside the town, it was different.

There was no escape therefore, by the time the climb levelled off, and the modest heat of the sun was cut off by a gateway and a wall, and what seemed like a line of irregular buildings, which gave off echoes and voices and the smells that Anna disliked and which Nicholas was not fastidious enough to find objectionable — the Tartar smells of horseflesh and goat and rancid fat and (he rather thought) cannabis seeds heating on stones. When, eventually, he was brought to enter a building and his bandage was removed, it was to find himself alone in a small, whitewashed room containing little more than the means of ablution and a change of dress, superior in fabric to his own. His own baggage was missing. He knew better than to complain, or to knock on the door when he found they had locked it, but sat down, with apparent patience, to wait. A strand of music entered his mind, and he annihilated it. He set himself to compile, from the recollection of his unfettered senses, a rutter of the ascent he had just made, and was dwelling, with interest, on the one smell he had found quite astonishing, when the door rattled and opened. The prince had sent for him.

Two centuries and more after Ghengis Khan and a hundred years after Kublai, the high-boned Mongol face, broad and gold-brown and seamed, with its almond eyes forever narrowed against the winds of the steppes, remained true to its blood, as did the fashions of hair and of dress: the long limp moustaches and beard, and the sashed robe over tunic, trousers and boots. In winter, the Khan's robe would have been lined with sables, and his conical hat trimmed with deep fur which would cover his ears. In autumn, the same dress was made of light-quilted damask, but the bulky squat outline was the same, here displayed as he sat in his hall of state.

It was a plain enough chamber, except that its walls were lined with decorative bricks and ceramics, and the bed-like throne it contained, with its footstool, was fenced with a gilded tracery of finely carved wood, and its base chased with gold leaf. Beside Mengli-Girey sat his favoured wife, while others sat to his left, on folding stools. Several richly dressed men stood on the other, the west side. The servants stood by the door, close to the bench on which rested skins of liquor, a covered ewer on a stand, and several cups. The floor was laid with hexagonal blue and white tiles, and the contents of his luggage lay in a neat pile upon it. It included, along with his personal possessions, two bales of Genoese velvet, and a small bag of silver. Ludovico da Bologna's letter, already opened, lay at the Tartar Khan's side. Nicholas walked a few paces, and sank on both knees.

'This is the man? He has no interpreter?' the Khan said.

'One claims he speaks Arabic,' someone observed. Lifting his head, Nicholas saw a heavily built man of about his own age wearing the turbaned helm of a professional soldier. His tone was one of contemptuous dislike, but his accent was Cairene: from that, and his size and his good looks, he was probably a genuine Circassian. If he had read the Patriarch's letter, then he had some education as well.

Nicholas said, 'Lord, I have Arabic, and some of your tongue.' The unknown man stared at him.

'Then we shall proceed. My lord Abdan Khan will help at need, I am sure. Your name is Niccolò, and you are from Venice, that female Pope among cities?'

There was no time to blink. If the quote was unexpected, so was the presence of the Circassian, if the Circassian was really Abdan Khan, the commander of the Gothian stronghold of Mánkup, that crowned another cliff-top like this, to the south. Yet, of course, Christian and Tartar were in alliance against their common predator, the Ottoman Turk. Nicholas kept his eyes on the Crim Khan. 'I founded a Bank, lord, which I have now given up. I have come to trade on behalf of a friend, and to assist the great Patriarch in his efforts for peace, which must assure all supplicants their station in Heaven.'

'The Great Patriarch has been here,' said Mengli-Girey. 'My father — O blessed and exalted is he! — my father received him.'

Nicholas knew that. They hadn't dared blindfold Father Ludovico, nor had they required him to kneel. All priests were thought to be lucky. The Genoese had been lucky for the khanate as well, managing their commerce and making them wealthy. When Mengli-Girey's father had died, the Genoese had enabled this shrewd man to succeed him, although he was not the eldest son, and two of his brothers had to be locked up with Genoese connivance. They were still in prison in Soldaia. In return, Mengli-Girey had reduced the amount of the Genoese tribute and would certainly (they believed) help them resist any onslaught by the Turks.

Nicholas said, 'You have the Patriarch's letter. He asks your help. And I, in my turn, have to offer you what aid is in my power.'

'You lead armies?' It was the Circassian, sneering.

Nicholas looked at him. 'I used to own one. It fought in Cyprus, as you probably know.'

'Against the Genoese. Against a Mameluke company.'

'It ended a war. The truth about the Mamelukes you probably know. And the Sultan Qayt Bey was able, as a result, to increase the sum of his tribute from Cyprus. Certainly, he has continued to favour my Bank, both when I was concerned with it, and since.'

The Circassian looked at the Khan. 'For what it is worth, this is the man, lord,' he said.

There was a silence. One of the women, who had been playing with her delicate hands, gave a pretty cough. The Khan's black eyes gleamed between their pursed lids. He said, 'We are sure it is. We beg him to rise and be seated, that we may learn what we have done to deserve such generosity. Only a colleague of the Great Patriarch would bring us coffers so delightfully filled. Unless you mean their contents for some other potentate?'

'No, indeed. All that is there was intended for you, lord,' Nicholas said. It was true of the velvet, at least. His eye rested, with some regret, on his excellent razor and a sash he had found rather useful. He supposed his weapons were already impounded.

'We receive them with gratitude. You will take some refreshment?' said the Khan. 'Later, you will be shown to your lodging. And in the days to come, we shall talk.'

There was a choice of rice wine, or the fermented liquors of millet, mare's milk, or honey. He took rice wine because he felt like it, and not because it would make very much difference. Drink, to a Tartar, was in its excess a measure of friendship as well as virility, although they would not (they said) drink themselves senseless like animals, but would achieve it like men, to the sound of the harp, or a boy singing, or a bard reciting a poem.

After the women had gone, the Khan left his seat of state and sat with the men, while stories were exchanged and jokes told. As the singers exhausted their repertoire or were dismissed, the Khan would call on one of the company for a song. Once, the choice fell upon a snub-nosed Tartar of middle years whose quick reactions Nicholas had already marked out. He looked as if he would be better pleased solving problems than sitting at drink. He was named as Karaï Mirza, and he sang, without overmuch tune, a ditty so long and so hilarious that he was clearly famous for it. Then, when they had finished hammering him on the shoulders, the Circassian suggested that Niccolò, the non-Venetian, should favour them with a song.

He had been considering, since it began, what to do. Fermented liquor was not unknown in the orthodox Muslim communities he was accustomed to, and he had heard some of the bawdier songs. Even so, he would not presume to follow Karaï Mirza, or spoil what he had done. Instead, therefore, he asked for a flute, and after playing absently for a moment or two, ventured upon something whose effect he could not predict: a song from a man to a woman which he had sung once in Cairo.

He had an exceptional voice: it was the Circassian's bad luck that he would not appear a fool for that reason, at least. It was his own good fortune that the tune he had chosen to sing coincided with the maudlin humour of his half-comatose audience. It coincided too with his own, for although he had a very hard head, he was less than sober by then. Indeed, when thickly pressed to continue, he was sufficiently out of himself to sing something quite out of place; something of a connotation so wounding, so terrifying, so destructive that for seven years he had not allowed himself to think of it, or of the place called Taghaza with which it was linked. Taghaza, where he had parted with the African scholar, the ex-slave and dear friend called Loppe, or Lopez, or Umar, who had shared that music with him before leaving to go to his death. Nicholas supposed, with blurred surprise, that he had Anna to thank for crossing this hurdle, too.

And he had crossed it, he believed. The music which might have been insupportable was not. Here, surrounded by Arab voices, Muslim practices, it seemed just and true, its meaning common to all. His hearers, clasping him in drunken embrace at the end, were moved by the nobility of the cadences and not by the words, for the liturgy of the Latin church was foreign to them. Or to all but one of them. Mengli-Girey, wet-eyed, took him by the hand, but he saw the Circassian staring.

In the end, uncertainly upright and fondly accompanied, he was introduced to the house he was to have, and dropped to his mattress as he was, waking to find the place attended by soft-footed servants, all at his personal disposal. Despite the tenderness in his skull, he was reasonably pleased. The Patriarch had said it would be simple. It was not. But at least he was here. All he had to do was leave as successfully, when his task was done. And since he did not intend to stay long, he reviewed his objectives and set out to achieve them. It took him two weeks.

The business for Anna was easiest. Julius had never been an innovator, and Anna, though wiser and subtler by far, lacked experience. Posing as her representative in Caffa, Nicholas had found little trouble in identifying the merchandise which would fit into a trade such as theirs, and the conditions required to make it profitable. Here, he found his counterpart in the Tartar secretary of the Khan: the monosyllabic, quizzical Karaï Mirza whose magical ability to emerge unimpaired from the most catastrophic night of heavy drinking impressed Nicholas hardly less than his grasp of the hard facts of trade. From the moment that his trials of initiation ceased, which was not at once, Nicholas was careful to cultivate the man. Then, when the time seemed right, he made his wants known.

The interview took place in one of the other buildings in that part of the citadel where the Khan held audiences, and where his palace and harem were situated, together with his kennels and mews and the offices of his scribes and chief secretary. Nicholas had never penetrated beyond the high walls which cut it off from the rest of the fortress, but he had climbed unimpeded to the roof of his lodging and had seen, as he was meant to see, the sheer plunge on each side; the impregnability of the eyrie of the Crim Tartar Horde. But of the garrison, the stables, the arsenal, the stores of food and of water, the accommodation for people and beasts, he knew nothing as yet. The answers lay beyond the high walls.

Hence, when his talk with Karaï Mirza, succinct, business-like, came to a halt, he expected the other man to say, as he did, 'I can see that the trade you propose will produce revenue, but to us, not to you. All your profit depends, it seems to me, on our willingness to reconsider our tax. But where, then, would be the advantage to us?'

'There are invisible taxes, and invisible payments,' Nicholas said. He sat cross-legged as the other man did, his skirts spread about him, a cup of *qumiz* in his hands. The mare's milk was fermented here, but the cup was Syrian-made, its lotus motifs from Cathay. He continued without haste. 'The Genoese contracted Michelozzi to work on their fortifications in the island of Chios. The Grand Duke of Moscow has bought the military engineer Fioravanti, they say, and the Italian who rebuilt the defences of Caffa no doubt contributed to these walls.'

'You are an engineer, an architect?' the Tartar said. His tone was polite.

'I have access to such,' Nicholas said. 'I know the worth of the mercenaries who were once in my employ, and their guns. I have had some success, myself, in the field of infiltration and battle strategy. On the other hand, the Khan's present dispositions may be more than adequate. I have no means of judging.'

The half-closed eyes twinkled. 'It is perhaps your skills in infiltration which have denied you the means,' said Karaï Mirza. 'As you will have noticed, one blindfolds a cheetah when hunting.'

'On the road, to be sure. But in the field, one must release and then trust him. Will the great Mengli-Girey allow me to survey his citadel?' Nicholas said.

'I shall ask,' the other man said. The meeting broke up, and he left. Very much later, he returned. 'The Khan understands your dislike of confinement. He invites you to hunt for a day or two with him. The deer season has opened, and he would also wish to try his new hawks. You have heard of them?'

Everyone had. Caffa sent fifty white falcons to Constantinople each year, as part of its other, Ottoman tribute. Occasionally, the Golden Horde got a sweetener, too. Running a trading colony in the Levant came expensive.

The hunt, as might be guessed, was both a test and a chance to display the Khan's riches and vigour. Five hundred men and eighty couples of greyhounds went with them, with wagons carrying food and bedding, tents and furnishings. The Khan, wearing his spired helm and cuirass, killed his animals *jirgeh*-style, with the beasts rounded up and driven towards him. He took a boar, though, himself, and another nearly took Nicholas. Abdan Khan, who was meant to be his partner, did nothing to save him. Since their initial encounter, the Circassian from Mánkup had been little seen, and seldom deigned to address the Khan's guest. In the hunting-ground, they were occasionally paired, but did not meet for the most part until the tents were raised in the evening, when the uproarious drinking and dancing began, and Abdan Khan would initiate some contest for Mengli-Girey's amusement.

Nicholas, prayerfully steering a course designed to earn him neither death nor contempt, refused some of the invitations tauntingly put in his way, and accepted others. He was becoming increasingly irritated. It was unfortunate, therefore, that on the last day, already ruffled if not otherwise damaged by the episode of the boar, Nicholas found himself rallied for his continued refusal to gamble.

The reason was simple enough: he could not afford to. The Khan had seized all he had, and the rest was in Caffa and sacrosanct. Lastly, he suspected that Abdan Khan could cheat as deftly as he could. Cairo was a great teacher.

'So what shall we do?' the big man exclaimed in mock despair. 'A contest for the best wrestler? But I don't suppose Niccolò the non-Venetian can wrestle?'

'Why not?' said Nicholas agreeably. It was, of course, an invitation to a duel. Tough though the Tartars might be, they were men of low height, and wrestling was a sport where reach could make a difference. Circassians were tall and good-looking and strong: it was why their men flourished in Egypt as Mamelukes, and their girls commanded such a punishing tariff as slaves. Abdan Khan would win all his bouts, and so, very likely, would Nicholas.

It did not take long: the amount of *buza* everyone had drunk saw to that. A space was cleared, and the contestants assembled, already stripped of all but their breeches. Then they opposed each other, two at a time. The man who ended dead or unconscious had lost. There were no other rules.

In a perverted way, it riled Nicholas to be fighting half-sober and therefore unfairly. Height and reach could be counteracted by endurance and skill, and the Crim Tartars had both of these. He did not underestimate them — the state of his body proved how right he was in that — but he faced his real opponent in the end, as he knew he would, regretting that the way should have been paved with disappointment and loss of face for those who had not been born Circassian. And the man's air of ineffable superiority was due to more than that, as he now knew. Abdan Khan was related to one sultan at least: his father had fled when Khushcadam had become ruler of Egypt, and Abdan had ended, a highly trained Mameluke, commanding the army of the ruler of Gothia, that strange, mixed community that survived in the Crimea at Mánkup.

It made no sense, this aggravation between them. Caffa and Gothia were in equal need of help against Turkey, as was the Crimean Horde.

They needed each other. That was why a highly trained commander like Abdan Khan was here, teaching his skills to the armies of Qirq-yer as well as Mánkup. This hostility made as much sense as the useless quarrel in Caffa over who the next Tartar governor ought to be. Facing the other man now, his hands spread, his bare feet planting themselves on worn grass, Nicholas decided to concentrate.

They had a manner of wrestling in Iceland which he had seen, and which he had had described to him exactly. It was not unlike the kind he had just experienced. Through the years, he had experimented with other styles, too, as anyone would, in a war camp with time to put off. He also knew a great deal about the principles of leverage, as imparted to him impatiently by a brilliant engineer. The engineer whom Abdan Khan might hope to have at his side, if he would bloody cease trying to kill his intermediary.

Except that, of course, if Nicholas sent for him, the same engineer would refuse.

He got thrown, then. It was extremely painful, and taught him to keep his mind on his work. It also made him nearly as angry as the Circassian was.

The Khan, observing the fall, was moved to question his adviser in the subsequent roar, which almost extinguished the din of the field-drums. 'Was this contest wise?'

'I have tried reasoned argument,' said Karaï Mirza. 'It is better that one man or the other is out of the way.' He spoke with regret, for he could see the good and the bad in most men, and did not like waste. The Khan said, 'Their hâkim, it is true, will not mind if this man dies. The imam will be angry.'

'It is my belief,' said Karaï Mirza, 'that the Patriarch also has gambled, and will abide by the result. We should have to pay compensation. He may even be counting on that.'

'The non-Venetian knows a great many holds,' said the Khan, with some interest. 'It is not Rustam against Puladvand, but it is well enough. Tell them to bring up more torches.'

The extra light, to Nicholas, was not an advantage. It aborted a sequence of moves for which darkness was preferable, and allowed his opponent a sight of the red and blue swellings, the raw and ripped patches of flesh on which he might profitably concentrate. And if the Circassian's eyes were truly sharp, he would notice the shape of one wrist, which was not as it should be. It had started to swell since their last harsh, twisting struggle and, sprained or snapped, was now useless. His chances, therefore, were not good — but they hadn't been good, either, on the raft, when he and Benecke had had their slight disagreement. Suddenly cheered, for no reason whatever, Nicholas decided he ought to fix this bastard, too. Ramming his right arm violently under Abdan's left shoulder so that he inadvertently turned, Nicholas thrust out his right leg and, meeting hard flesh and bone, drove Abdan's left leg so high that both his feet flailed and he crashed breathlessly to the ground with Nicholas fully on top. Then Nicholas took him by the throat.

He had, however, the use of only one hand. Abdan, half concussed, opened his eyes and, baring his teeth, gripped and wrung — not the hand at his throat, but the grotesque, swollen wrist of the other. Nicholas grunted. Despite himself, his throttling hand slackened, and, kicking, the Circassian wrenched himself free, rolled apart and sprang to his feet, scooping up something as he did so. When Nicholas rose, swearing fluently, Abdan was approaching him, a stone in either hand.

Nicholas viewed him. They had not, he was conscious, been following any laws of tradition or chivalry: Firdawsi would have been disappointed. But out-and-out hooliganism offered, refreshingly, a new form of licence. As Abdan Khan lifted his arm to throw, or to beat, Nicholas snatched a torch and calmly set fire to him. The Circassian bellowed, flailing and dropping the stones. The spectators screamed. Nicholas, drawing back his good hand, knocked Abdan Khan down and helpfully sat on him, smothering the incandescent breeches and flicking a motherly hand at his smouldering top-knot. Even bald, he was an extraordinarily handsome young man, and could have taught Benecke a thing or two about fighting. He opened his eyes and lay still.

Nicholas said, 'You didn't need the stones, you were winning. I don't know what this is all about, but I don't bear a grudge. Will you drink with me?'

'The winner!' said the Khan's voice at his side.

Nicholas got up. Abdan Khan, blinking, attempted to sit. The Khan said, 'Be at ease. You fought well, but the Frank here was more cunning. What does he wish for his prize?'

'The Khan's trust,' Nicholas said.

'An excellent answer,' said the Khan. 'But what of your conquest tonight? What do you demand of Abdan Khan?'

Dust and sweat plastered his body; his gashes stung, his wrist throbbed like the wrestling-drums. Nicholas said, 'A game of chess, when we have returned to the citadel. If, that is, the commander agrees.'

'He must agree,' the Khan said. 'He has lost.'

They returned to Qirq-yer the following day, Nicholas with his wrist in a sling, and the Circassian riding apart, but glancing at him now and then. Soon after they arrived, the man came to his door and was admitted. He carried a box and board in his hands, and his face, stiff with bruises, was unsmiling. From beneath the snowy turban, the perfect tunic and leggings, there emerged a faint smell of singeing. Nicholas said, 'Will you sit and drink with me first? It was good sport. Where did you learn?'

The other man hesitated, then setting down what he carried, took the stool and the cup he was given. He said, 'From my father. And in Cairo, under the Sultan Inal, a kinsman. The students wrestled.'

'In al-Azhar the Resplendent,' Nicholas said. 'I was there, briefly, in the time of the present honoured Sultan, Qayt Bey.'

'And went to the Greeks' church in Sinai, I heard. Your Arabic is good for a Frank, but strangely mixed: sometimes classical, sometimes Maghgribian.'

'I have been in Timbuktu,' Nicholas said. 'I bought gold. I studied with many wise men who died when war came. The Patriarch will confirm it. He sent me here to prove that I am not a spy. So say to me what you wish.'

'War came to Trebizond,' the man said. 'You were there too. Buying jewels. Studying, perhaps. They talk of you in Mánkup.'

'In Mánkup?' The cliff-fortress of the rulers of Gothia attracted many races, most of them Christian, and all of them practised in war, so that the Khan of the Crimean Tartars found them an asset, as he did the Genoese. Once, Mánkup, Gazaria, and the Crimea had been subject to Trebizond; had shared some of its luxuries, and its decadence. He had tasted candied fruits here which he had only come across once before.

'Naturally, in Mánkup,' the man said a little impatiently. 'Did you not know the last rulers of Trebizond? The Emperor David, who was killed with his sons. The daughters who were placed in harems — although the lady Anna, they say, has been freed. That was after you admitted the Turks, you and your army.'

Thirteen years before, the city he spoke of had fallen: the last outpost of great Byzantium had been ravaged by Turks. Nicholas had not been quite twenty-one. He said, speaking slowly, 'The Emperor betrayed his own people and surrendered. I shall tell you the whole tale if you like. But why are you angry? You are a Circassian. These were Greeks. You pay the same tribute today, but to Turkey.'

'My lord is part Greek,' the other man said. 'Did you not know that remnants of the house of the Comneni fled to the Crimea? The Emperor died, but men of his blood have lived on, and fought. I and others like me are doing what you failed to do. We are his army.'

No one came in. You could hear, if you listened, the soft voices of servants outside; pigeons cooing, a dog barking somewhere, his noise taken up soon by others. From beyond the Saray enclosure, there percolated, as ever, the impression of great companies in regular exercise, with faint drumbeats, and occasionally the sound of a horn. Passing swiftly through to the hunt, he had been given no chance to see anything beyond the extent of the domain and the scale of the walls that enclosed it. It did not look, now, as if he would see more.

Once, a boy of twenty, he thought he held the fate of Trebizond in his hands, and had taken his dilemma to the good priest Godscalc, now dead. He had risked his life and the lives of his friends for the Emperor, but the Emperor had surrendered, and dragged all his family into ignominy and death. With time, Nicholas had come to understand, if not to forgive. He had shown no grief in public when the Emperor lost his life. All but a small child had died or been sold off for pleasure. But now the lady Anna was free. And there were free men in Gothia.

Someone spoke. Abdan Khan said, 'Do I not speak the truth?' There was an unexpected note in his voice.

Nicholas looked up. 'Forgive me. I did not know. Explanations, I suppose, would be tedious. I am only sorry that, being here, and willing to help, I do not have your confidence.'

The other man said, 'What, then, is your account of what happened at Trebizond? Why do you insist that you are not Venetian, when the rulers of Trebizond died, but Venetians and their riches were borne by your own ships to safety?' And then, with a gesture of rebuttal: 'I do not wish to be appeased with *qumiz*. I want facts.'

THE COCKS WERE CROWING, and the late dawn of October was tinging the skies above the rocks of Qirq-yer when Karaï Mirza, the Khan's close adviser, called at the house of the Patriarch's emissary and, dismissing his escort, opened the door of the inner chamber himself.

Abdan Khan, dispatched yesterday to taste the fruits of defeat with his chessboard, was still in the room. He was not awake, nor yet in bed, having apparently fallen asleep on the floor while playing a stiff game of chess. The room reeked of liquor, and the chessboard, to a practised eye, announced a long, hard game between two well-matched opponents. Seeking further, the visitor observed that the other player was also present, and also asleep, although he at least had found his way to his mattress and freed himself of some of his clothes, including his cap. His skin was flushed, and his beard, densely black, had produced sparkling gold at its roots. The Circassian, sensitive no doubt to his looks, had not unwound his headgear, of which he held a tail in his grasp like a child. The turban had become skittishly tilted, and there was a bruise like a stain on his throat.

Karaï Mirza stood for a while, reflecting, then left. To the Khan he said, 'It is for you to declare, lord. But I would say, show this man Niccolò all that is reasonable.'

Chapter 19

In the days that followed, Nicholas de Fleury was shown everything and told everything that he needed to know. At first, it was a physical inventory — an examination of the stables and barracks, the forges and workshops and cook-houses, the places in which food and fodder and weapons, tents and wagons, fuel and utensils were stored and maintained, including the pastureland for the flocks and the ranges of extraordinary caverns within which, in case of attack, the families from the plains could be housed.

After that, he established himself in the secretary's office and familiarised himself with the chain of supply, its strengths and its weaknesses. And last of all, he discussed what he had learned in the context of war, and the shifting alliances of the Peninsula. The common enemy, you would say, was the Turk. But allegiances altered, and trade, which he knew about, was one of the determining factors. The defence of the Genoese colonies could depend on decisions taken many months before in Genoa and Milan, in reaction to other decisions arrived at in Venice or Naples or Rome, or in the money markets of Flanders. Confidence in evident allies, such as Uzum Hasan, could be shaken by Uzum's friendship with Venice, which supplied him with arms. Trade, throttled by Constantinople, required to pass from the Peninsula to the West via Poland, but Poland felt herself in danger from Muscovy and the two Tartar Hordes almost as much as she felt menaced by Turkey. All these things must be weighed. And if, having done so, one felt inclined to predict the future, there was still the matter of Venice, who, for the sake of her trade, might end her war with the Turk as easily as she was presently inciting the Golden Horde and the Persians to attack him.

By the time the talk had turned in this direction, Nicholas would be alone with the two mentors who were with him wherever he went, Abdan Khan and Karaï Mirza. With the latter, he now had a rapport built on mutual respect and a private repertoire of unrepeatable ballads. In Abdan Khan, he had been confronted by a professional soldier, jealous of his command and buttressed with prejudices. The change had begun with the wrestling bout, but was largely due to the evening that followed. Later, when they had played chess and got drunk together and discovered that they were well matched in both, Nicholas had watched Abdan fall into peaceful slumber and supposed that this was the first time in his own life that his blighted past had in some way come to serve him. That night, he had answered Abdan Khan's questions, and had described what had happened in Trebizond, even though he preferred not to remember it. It had hurt, and Abdan had noticed as much. Since then, in a guarded way, he had acted towards Nicholas as the vizier of a large country might act to the vizier of a smaller, and occasionally made soldier's jokes. He was not a witty young man, but he did not need to be, to be good at his job.

The Khan did not appear at these meetings: that was for later, when Nicholas had learned and imparted all that he could, and conclusions might be drawn. More and more, he recognised that he was in fact the Patriarch's emissary: that what he was doing was assessing, and enabling Mengli-Girey to assess, the variables in the future, and the best way to meet them. The Patriarch might preach religion, but it was the privilege of a trader to point out the material advantages of one course over another: something that the Bank of St George would understand, and Uzum Hasan, and Ivan in Moscow and Callimachus Experiens at the King's Court in Cracow. That was why the former owner of the Banco di Niccolò had been brought here. He understood it, but he also understood that it was probably useless. There was religion, and there was self-interest, and there was the unknown brigand who, bursting with energy, looked at the weather one morning, and decided that it was a really good day for a massacre.

Towards the end, he wrote his report. Sometimes, Karaï Mirza would stand beside him, requesting to know what he was saying; commenting, disagreeing politely, asking questions — which he answered, because that was why he was here. On the last day, when the interrogation at last slackened and halted, the stocky secretary spoke on a different subject. 'You suggest we support the proposed link between Gothia and Moscow, and we are inclined to agree. Is it still your intention, when you return, to act as agent for your friend in Cologne?'

Nicholas laid down his pen with delicacy, and looked up. 'I look forward, yes, to developing his trade in the Peninsula, once he has recovered his outlay in furs. At present, sadly, he has little to invest.'

'But if that were repaired?'

'The possibilities appear to me endless. It troubles me only to know which Tudun to apply to, in arranging my affairs. The Khan has agreed to name one Tartar governor, but the Genoese, I am told, now favour another.' He waited, his expression pellucid. If he were now to be trusted, he might as well discover how far.

Karaï Mirza answered with calm. 'The Genoese have lost confidence, it is true, in the first candidate, the last Tudun's brother. Many prefer his nephew, the son of the last Tudun's widow. The lady is rich.'

'And so?' Nicholas said.

'And so I cannot advise you at present. My Khan does not wish to force his opinion on the traders to whom he has given these fiefs. When he has reached a conclusion, you may hear it. He will wish to see you soon. But meanwhile, have you not written enough for today? Does your left hand still pain you, or did our care of it help? Abdan Khan knows of another shaman, he tells me, and could take you to him whenever you wish.'

'I am not sure —' Nicholas began.

'You should go with him,' the older man said. 'If not now, then certainly before you depart from Qirq-yer.' When he was being jocular, his cheeks became bossed, and his eyes were curved downwards like sickles. Now, he was not being jocular. Against all inclination, Nicholas conveyed his acceptance and thanks.

He would have to go, but not today; not until the last moment, when whatever transpired could not mar the effect of his visit. He remembered too well what had happened after the new-found camaraderie of the chess game. Then, observing the state of his wrist, Abdan Khan had insisted on having it attended to. There were physicians in the fortress of Qirq-yer, but the treatment was carried out in a yurt in the plain, beside a small fire of dung whose smoke rose through the peak of the conical roof of the tent. Like all its kind, it was fitted out as a home, with wall-carpets and matting, cushions and boxes, and ledges crowded with objects.

The man who studied his arm, sitting crosslegged beside him, was not old, despite his beard and his crumpled, long-skirted gown. The possessions around him were modest, but the prayer-beads in his sash were not cheap, and neither was the brooch that pinned the upturned brim of his high cap. He spoke very seldom, and then in a mixture of languages, but often hummed to himself. The most eloquent sound in the room was that of a little half-drum, which kept up a continuous tapping, loud and soft, slow or quick, according, you would say, to the physician's wishes and moods. Yet he never spoke, or even looked towards the boy who was playing.

Nicholas had heard of the shaman religion, practised long ago on the shores of the Black Sea and elsewhere. He recognised the soothing effect of the wordless voice and the drum, for it conjured a feeling he already knew, when he surrendered his conscious mind to the pendulum. Recognition brought a surge of annoyance, but he did not let it reach the hand in the shaman's possession, or his face, or the rest of his body.

Or so he thought, until the shaman's eyes lifted to his, and he said, 'Do not be afraid.'

'He will not hurt you,' said Abdan Khan.

'It is not pain that he fears,' the shaman had answered, and smiled. 'We are in the same trade.'

'What?' had said Abdan Khan.

And the weathered face, neither Tartar nor Georgian, had turned the smile on Nicholas. 'Ask us what the weather will be in December. When will the Khan die? What predator will sail into Caffa, and when?'

'You would not answer,' Abdan Khan said. But he was looking at Nicholas.

'Neither should I,' Nicholas said. He could hear the harshness in his own voice.

'A pity,' said the shaman blandly. 'There is no harm in throwing a crumb. I cast a shoulder-blade on the fire now and then, and announce which concubine will quicken by sunrise. I am rarely wrong.' But even as he mocked, his fingertips pressing and prodding, Nicholas felt the fires of the pain dying down. Through all that followed, there was nothing that was not bearable, and the physician fell into silence, but for the absent whistle and drone from his lips, like that of a groom with a horse. When the bandaging was complete, the hands withdrew while the drum gave a last, gentle flourish. Only then, when the tall Circassian bent and, producing his flask, poured drink for them all, did the physician lean back on his cushions and say, 'So, my lord Niccolò, divining makes you afraid. Let me see if I can explain it. What do you see in your cup?'

There was nothing in his cup but strong drink, which he had not yet tasted. The liquid swirled, and the small flames danced and flickered. Nicholas heard himself saying, 'I see an eagle. I have seen it before.'

Abdan Khan, his face intent, said, 'I see nothing. The eagle of the Byzantine Empire? Of Moscow? Of the Great Emperor of the West, or of Rome?'

'Not this eagle,' said the shaman. 'It is an eagle of the future, not the present. And it is not an emblem of empires, but of something quite simple: an act of humanity, perhaps.'

'Of the *future*?' Nicholas had said.

'You are relieved? Oh, yes. You have been afraid of the past: perhaps you should be. But the shadows you see, the broken messages that have almost found their way home, are not from the past, but the future.'

'I see,' he recalled saying. He remembered draining his cup without pause until the eagle had gone, and embarking with firmness on the business of thanks, and of payment. Only at the very last, following Abdan Khan from the tent, had he been impelled to fling round and confront the complacent bastard. 'I want no messages. How can I stop them?'

'By death,' the shaman had said. 'If you wish to deny them. For the poor-spirited, the grave is the ultimate refuge.'

He was silent, then tried again, full of childish rebellion. 'But surely there must be some other way. The interference must have a conduit. What led me to see the eagle this time?'

'How did you see it before?' Abdan Khan had stopped, and was listening.

'I don't remember. It was connected with death, and a child, and with snow. With riding on snow.'

'There are shamans in the north,' the physician said. 'They have their own goddess, a woman. She is called Slata Baba.' He smiled. 'I see I have given you something. It is nothing of practical use, my lord Abdan: I should tell you and your prince if it were. My patient has a gift which he cannot control, and which is too frail, in my view, to exploit. I shall tell the Khan myself, if you wish.'

And after that, they had left. It had been another test. But ever since, the wrist had mended as if by a miracle.

THE KHAN MET HIM ALONE, on the final day. Tomorrow morning, with Abdan Khan and an escort to guide them, Nicholas was to start on his way back to Caffa. He had left his servants to pack, not knowing which of his borrowed clothes and equipment to leave, and which to take for the journey. It was the last of three long discussions which had taken place since his report had been completed: one with the Khan and his mentors, one with the Khan and his inner council, and now this, where those things could be aired which no one else ought to hear.

Mengli-Girey came breathless to the table, his broad face and shoulders encased in chain mail and his weapons still rattling at his side: he had led the army exercises that morning, and his hard hands were black from using mace and javelin without gloves. He was a capable leader and knew how to keep his men happy. The Tartar nobles enjoyed the security he and his father had given them, but chafed at the price. Tribute to Turkey they understood, but they were lords of the Peninsula, and should not have to pander to a few thousand heretic foreigners. They were fortunate to have in Mengli-Girey a leader who understood strategy, and realised that gains were only accomplished through guile and forethought and, sometimes, a sacrifice.

He had long known, as Nicholas was aware, that it was wise not to aggravate his Muslim neighbour. A Turkish attack on the Crimea could not be stopped, except by a Venetian fleet, or a combined fleet such as the one which had set out and lost heart a few years ago. Genoese and Venetian rivalry might well prevent another from coming.

What might come, for sure, was a Christian overland army. A mercenary company from the West, with its own sappers and gunners, with the expertise and means to cast cannon, could confront and possibly outface a Turkish fleet, answer its bombardments and repel the landing parties which could starve out its citadels. But even if such a troop were available, it could not arrive before summer. And the prince who presently patronised it might not wish its release. The Banco di Niccolò had such a force, but Burgundy was currently its employer.

'Nevertheless,' Nicholas had ended, speaking again of these things to the Khan, 'you should make your necessity known, and I shall send my own messages to the West. Meanwhile, my great lord, you should welcome any help to keep the Turk otherwise occupied in the spring.'

'I read what you recommend,' the Khan said. 'Karaï Mirza agrees. Let the Turk attack Crete, or reply to a threat from Uzum Hasan, or from the Horde at Saray, or from Moscow. This the Patriarch has also said. I appreciate this, and I appreciate the alliances you and he are trying to make. If we survive, he and his church will have our favour. What you must tell him, however, is that we have little time to await these diversions. The Peninsula is a cauldron, presently simmering. If it explodes, this gossamer web of alliances may be swept wholly aside.'

'Then you need a competent Tudun in Caffa,' Nicholas said. 'And a Genoese consul who does not take bribes.'

The strong face turned. 'We are too late, I fear, for the latter,' Mengli-Girey said. 'As for the Tudun, the older candidate is a fool, and the younger a knave. There is only one man fit for the post. You have met him.'

'Karaï Mirza, of course,' Nicholas said. 'You will propose him?'

'When the time is right,' said the Khan. 'I shall send him to Caffa this winter to observe, and to be seen. He has orders to smooth the path of your business, where it may be beneficial to all of us. There is also the matter of your baggage. You left it here.'

'My lord, I hope it has not been inconvenient,' Nicholas said.

'No. But I have told my men to remove it. The coffer-mules will fetch it to you tomorrow, on your way to the shaman.'

'The shaman?' Nicholas said.

'I understand,' said the Khan, 'that there was an undertaking to visit a shaman on your way to the plain? Abdan Khan seemed quite sure.'

'Of course,' Nicholas said. 'It is my rule, as it is the rule of the Patriarch. Whatever we promise, we undertake.'

He emerged, thoughtfully, and crossed to his house. The coffer-mules had not yet arrived but the coffers were there, in his chamber. There were six, the same number that he had brought. At first glance, the contents appeared the same, except that the velvet had gone. In its place was a small bag of silver. Only if you knew his possessions would you recognise that the footwear, the dress, the linen were subtly superior, as were the razor, and the small knife kept concealed in its sheath. The only object which remained the same was his favourite sash, which was his favourite because of the hidden pockets and seams it contained. It lay on top, depressing the contents of the rest of the basket. 'The non-Venetian is disappointed?' said a Tartar voice gravely.

Karaï Mirza stood behind. 'Seriously so,' Nicholas said. 'The Great Khan has omitted a breeding mare and a fully manned galley. The velvet was meant as a gift.'

'The Khan misunderstood. He would still wish to pay, having regard to its extremely high quality. This receipt, for the Customs at Caffa, explains that no further taxes are due. You observe your sash on the top, for your convenience when travelling.'

'I observe it,' Nicholas said. 'Karaï Mirza, where shall we next meet? I hear Abdan Khan is to come with me part of the way.'

'We shall meet in Caffa one day,' said the secretary. 'Although I may pass you in the street, being haughty and of very short memory. Meanwhile, of course, there is to be a supper tonight. I have brought some of the *darasun* in advance, to ask your advice as to its quality. If I may take the liberty?'

Departure next day was quiet. There was no excitement and no guard of honour: he was a merchant whom the Khan had invited, and for whom the Khan had given a parting supper which had lasted most of the night. There had been some dancing and singing, a deal of hilarity and a vast amount of drinking: the silence this morning was one of languor. Nicholas had already spoken to the many he knew, and was able, now, to reward those who had served him. But when he joined his short cavalcade, and rode with Abdan Khan through the arched outer doors of the citadel, he was conscious of carrying away something more than material gifts. He had arrived, a merchant on business, as once he had arrived at the Westmann Isles, or the banks of the Joliba, or Cyprus, and was departing now, as then, with a purse full of scraps: gold and dust, disasters and wisdom.

Departing, to face what lay before him. He had tried through these weeks to forget it, but there was too much to remind him. From Karaï Mirza, who heard news from everywhere, he had learned of the death of Zacco's son, the infant ruler of Cyprus, leaving the kingdom to Venice. If Zacco had lived, Nicholas might have sent him his son.

Jodi. Gelis. And Anna. Now he was leaving his mountain, the remorseless clamp of his personal life was closing about him again. Well, if he could propose (in mare's milk) a strategy for the survival of Eastern Christianity, coupled with the name of the Khan of the Crimea, he could presumably control his own interests. When Abdan Khan, drawing rein, said something about the hermit he had promised to visit, Nicholas felt almost charitable. Whoever wished to cast the first shoulder-blade was welcome to do so, while bearing in mind all that Karaï Mirza had said. His unexploitable talent was fragile and so, this particular morning, was he. Nicholas dismounted, and looked about.

The knobbed limestone heights of Qirq-yer were riddled with caves. Cool and dry, impervious to wind and rain, private or neighbourly in situation and amenable to endless extension, the cave cities of the Crimea shared the qualities of the badger-run and the warren, providing store-houses and homes for generations of inhabitants or — perpetually available, perpetually in repair — a timely refuge for hundreds.

The solitary also esteemed them. As in the desert of Sinai, the early monks had settled here, between cliffs, high above the rest of the world. Nicholas had seen their empty cells, cut in the wooded walls of the ravine which concealed the precipitous path to the citadel. There was a Father Superior's house, built on a ledge; and a flight of neatly hewn steps led to the narrow façade of a monastery gouged out of the mountain, its hollow windows open to rain, its surface tinted with the faint, unblinking faces of saints, timelessly teased by the joggling green branches. He looked at Abdan Khan. 'Your shaman dwells here?'

For some reason, the Circassian was angry. He said, 'These burrows serve many purposes. Holy fools use them, and men whom the Khan does not wish to entertain in the citadel. They also make excellent prisons.'

He was not annoyed with Nicholas, he was annoyed with the Khan. Behind them, the coffer-mules patiently stood, bearing their six modest baskets, and the soldiers' horses jingled their harness. The men belonged to Abdan Khan and his army at Mánkup. Nicholas said, 'I know the lord Mengli-Girey. Honest men have nothing to fear from him.' It was reasonably true, if not of particular relevance. Then he heard a horse neigh somewhere near, to be answered immediately by one of the horses behind him. Among the smells of plants and plaster and earth, of unwashed men and their beasts there floated a scent that he had recognised, even when riding blindfolded. He added, 'And do I pass this test, if I tell you that you have summoned someone from Mánkup who knows me from Gaza or Cairo or, likeliest of all, from where that incense is blended and ground?'

'He wished to come,' said the Circassian curtly. 'Before this man arrived, the lord Khan had satisfied himself as to your good intentions. You bear the proof in your luggage.'

He did, in a way. But as had been pointed out, caves made very good prisons, and gifts could be recovered. He was carrying away a great many secrets.

He was presently carrying them, Abdan Khan at his side, up the long, stone staircase to the monastery. The baggage-train and its men had disappeared. The smell of incense grew stronger. Pausing by the crumbling shell of a bell tower, you could see again how wild the place was. The striated crags that bulged over his head were duplicated on the opposite side of the ravine, where they sprawled, irregular as a crouched animal, above the steep grassy slopes where goats grazed. Far below him, a solitary thorn tree stood in a perennial crimping of fine cotton twists: knotted prayers for good fortune. No one had built a church round it. A voice over his head rebuked his thoughts, or at least interrupted them. It spoke in Greek.

'Greetings, my lord Abdan Khan. Pray ascend. And yes, the man with you is M. de Fleury. He visited the tomb of St Catherine four years ago. He may even remember my name.'

'Of course, Friar Lorenzo,' said Nicholas.

The monk had not changed. Seated presently in a small, dank room with leprous frescoes, Nicholas studied the spare, familiar figure, attired in the tall hat and flowing black robes of the Greek Orthodox Church. The uncompromising eyes and decisive manner reminded him of Karaï Mirza. A comparison between Cretan and Tartar was not as ludicrous as it might seem. Friar Lorenzo was the treasurer and steward of the church and convent of St Catherine's, Mount Sinai, to which he had conducted Anselm Adorne and his niece Katelijne four years ago, when Nicholas . . . and some others . . . had been lodged there. Nicholas had been staying there for a purpose, and he and Adorne had fallen out. Adorne was Genoese. It had, perhaps, appeared unduly sinister. But if, as he hoped, the Khan was satisfied that he was not primarily a Genoa-hater, Nicholas must have been conducted here for another reason, of which Abdan Khan was unaware.

He was alert, therefore, for the implications of the manoeuvre when, laying aside the Candian wine and fresh cakes, the monk requested Abdan Khan's leave to borrow his Christian companion for a brief, seemly prayer before travel. The Circassian, lulled by wine, had agreed peacefully. His apprehension had been, Nicholas saw, that Mengli-Girey was not as well-intentioned as he appeared. It might still be so. But the conversation so far, though beginning with Gothia, had also touched on the Sultan Qayt Bey of Cairo, on the friendly relations between the Christian monastery and its Muslim neighbours, and, reassuringly, on the good reputation of Nicholas in both quarters. To anyone stationed in Mánkup, there was nothing unusual about this mutual support between faiths. There was a mosque inside the monastery of St Catherine's, built for the use of its Bedouin servants. There was an empty monastery here, where Christian friends of the Khan might come to practise their religion. Tolerance was a powerful weapon, as the Turks also knew.

Entering the chapel to which he was taken, Nicholas thought at first that he was mistaken, and he was here for the good of his soul. The candles guttered on the small marble altar with its woven cloth, newly unfolded, and sparkling with red and gold thread. There was a lectern with a painted Gospel laid on it, and clean cushions on the newly swept floor. Brother Lorenzo had brought his own necessities with him from wherever he had been summoned — Sinai or Cairo or Crete, or Cyprus, or Mánkup. He might even have come straight from Caffa. Ludovico da Bologna had spent time with Nicholas in the monastery at Mount Sinai, four years ago. He had brought Gelis there.

The monk said, 'They call Qirq-yer the fort of the Forty Fortifications, but I suspect they mean Martyrs. There were Christians here six hundred years ago. I am told you are destitute.'

'Complaints are for martyrs,' Nicholas said. 'I am quite content. Why are you here?'

'I travel, as do Latin monks and confessors,' Lorenzo said. 'The Patriarch of Antioch and I are both Christians, and concerned with halting the advance of the Ottoman Turks, to the extent of courting unorthodox allies — Uzum Hasan of Persia, the Sultan and jurists of Cairo, and even yourself.'

'Thank you,' Nicholas said.

'Not at all. It seemed to the Patriarch and myself that, given some financial security, you might usefully be employed in these parts, and that I could, in passing, strengthen your credentials with the Greek community, as some visiting teacher from Cairo might commend you to those of the Muslim faith. Also, I would like both you and the Patriarch to know what Abdan Khan cannot or will not tell you about the Gothian strength at Mánkup.'

'I should be interested in that,' Nicholas said. 'But am I worthy?'

'It is a failing of Abdan Khan's,' said the monk, 'that he resists advice. He is a first-class captain, who has grown up in awe of the heroes who trained him. Whereas you, I understand, have made your own mould. It is praiseworthy. The dangers are those of over-confidence, even of dogged entrenchment. You must work to avoid them. Now I shall give you some information which you will kindly pass to the Patriarch, and also ponder upon to the best of your ability.'

Nicholas inhaled sharply, and then let it go. All right, he wasn't a martyr. The monk gazed at him with a certain compassion, and then started to speak.

What he said was comprehensive, but of necessity brief: even if the Circassian had fallen asleep, the escort had not, and they had to reach their next station by nightfall. Having finished with Mánkup, Friar Lorenzo added his assessment of the wider campaigns against Turkey, as viewed from Cairo and Cyprus and Rhodes. When he ended, Nicholas found the grace to apologise, as well as to thank him.

The monk smiled, rising to his feet. 'You are human. Wrong turnings may be beneficial. Tampering with magic is not. The Patriarch will be relieved to hear that you refused to divine.'

Nicholas smiled, but not very widely. His restraint was noted, he saw. He was over-confident enough, he wished to say, to change his mind and divine if he pleased, and to hell with the unintrenched Patriarch.

They passed a network of caves on the way from the chapel. The monk, holding a lantern, showed him one. 'They run all through the hill. A man in trouble can live here a long time. The citadel knows when someone is present, but strangers would not notice the clues. There, if you look. The person who stayed here has gone, and someone will rub the mark out. One day, another will come. See. They can be made quite comfortable.' And moving past the discreet mark on the wall, he raised the lamp.

It depended, of course, on what you called comfort. The movable furnishings had presumably gone, but a broken bucket remained, and a stone hearth and cistern, and a platform of flags with some straw. The walls were full of irregular holes, cut for storage, and in places the rock had been smoothed to receive imaginative charcoal drawings of saints mortifying the wives of deceived men, or men copulating without difficulty with well-drawn but unusual partners. 'There is a well outside at the back,' continued Friar Lorenzo. 'And a fire gives light. There is plenty of fuel. And assuming the citadel approves, there will be a bag of meal from time to time, and some dried fish, perhaps. Their refugees rarely starve.'

'No,' Nicholas said. His attention was fixed on the back of the cavern where, taking shape in the brightening lamplight, there seemed to be — there were — some abandoned possessions, dumbly eloquent of the fugitive owner now gone. Fashioned from lambskin and straw, trimmed with feathers and velvet and ribbon, a row of hats clung to the wall, cocky as tarts at a hanging.

'Ochoa!' Nicholas said. He suffocated, and started again. '*Ochoa de Marchena* was here?'

Brother Lorenzo's gaze was quite placid. 'The shipmaster who was lost with your gold? Yes. He has escaped from the Knights of St John. He wishes to meet you. He can tell you where your gold is.'

He waited, with tolerance, until Nicholas had ceased to wheeze. 'The reward of virtue,' observed Brother Lorenzo. 'I brought some balm from the Mount. Give it, from me, to the friends whom I met there. And make wise use of your gold, when you find it.'

Chapter 20

For Nicholas de Fleury, the journey home passed like a dream: he hardly remembered parting with the Circassian. In Caffa, paying off the last of his escort, he burst into Anna's house and discovered that he had overtaken his own harbinger and that Brygidy, alarmed, was telling him that the Genoese Oberto Squarciafico was here, and M. de Fleury must revert, quickly, to his role as Mameluke servant.

He couldn't pretend, now, that he hadn't arrived, so he sent a servant, humbly, to tell his mistress that her servant Nicomack ibn Abdallah had returned from Qirq-yer. He still looked the part, but after weeks of autonomy, his manner required some adjusting.

He saw Squarciafico briefly, as the fiscal agent took his leave, and Anna called her steward for an exchange of courtesies. Nicholas answered questions politely: he had been amazed by the nature of the citadel; he had found the Khan gracious but prone to waste time on hunting and other pleasures, in which he had been compelled to take part; he had, in the end, been permitted to outline the Contessa's hopes and plans, but it was by no means clear whether the Khan felt able to help him — he had been told simply to wait.

All the time he was speaking, half his gaze was on Anna's brilliant face; on the violet eyes which had lit when she saw him but veiled when he spoke, and she had to believe that her business and her steward's appeal had not prospered. The Genoese, taking his leave, had been consoling, and she had accepted his sympathy prettily. Then, leaving, he remembered Nicholas and said, 'Come and see me tomorrow. The consul will have some questions about Mengli-Girey.'

Nicholas was sure that he would. Reports from Caffa reached the citadel of Qirq-yer in a stream: compared with the lack-lustre Genoese, the Khan's spies were infinitely superior. All the time he had stayed in the citadel, Nicholas had been assured, if indirectly, of the safety of

Anna, and the public movements, at least, of the Patriarch. He would have to go to Father Ludovico immediately and tell all that he had learned. He would have no trouble speaking tomorrow to the Bank and the consul, and was fully prepared for the tale he must tell Sinbaldo the agent. To all of them, the story would be the same. There was some hope for the Contessa's trade, but the Khan would not commit himself until the new Tudun was in place to advise. And neither Nicomack ibn Abdallah nor Nicholas de Fleury knew (or cared) who the new Tudun would be.

But before that, he had the real news to give Anna.

She was so beautiful. He had forgotten the glow behind the self-possession, the glorious eyes, the smile, the hair like a houri's, clinging unbound to her neck and her fine, narrow gown. He said, 'Are you glad to see me?'

He had come into her parlour just as he was, without even supervising the six baskets now being unstrapped outside. He had the bag of coins in his hat.

Anna said, 'I don't think so. What have you been riding? A camel?'

'It's a healthy smell,' Nicholas said. 'Was he bothering you? Has anyone been bothering you?'

'Apart from creditors?' she said whimsically. 'I wish I could say so, but it has been remarkably dull. No advance has been made with the Russians. The Genoese tend to call whenever they hear I've had letters, and they ask me how Julius is doing — to which the answer is well, Nicholas; he is walking again. They also want to know what I have been hearing from you, which I had to tell them was nothing: you really have been most extraordinarily lax. Were you truly dragooned into weeks of tedious hunting? And, I suppose, drinking. And dancing. And perhaps even distasteful exchanges with girls?'

Her voice was mocking, but the delicate glow was still there. He wondered what she would say if he admitted that, yes, there had been girls. It was part of the Khan's hospitality. And even had it not been, he could not have refused when the rice wine had gone round, and the men had thrown off their coats and begun dancing the thudding, menacing dances that dated back to the times of the Polovtsy. Then the drums would double their beat, and the Circassian girls would slip into the light of the fire, slender and pliant as vines with their long pigtails swaying and their faces averted. At first, they linked arms as they danced, but not later. Then, as in the Tyrol, you waited, whatever your state, until the Khan had locked his girl to himself. And after that, you were free to prove, in the firelight, that you were a man. A man sometimes in despair, for the sake of a pact he had made with himself.

Anna said, 'I daren't ask what you are dreaming about. Nicholas? I am sorry it didn't go well, but I am glad that you tried. And look, there are letters for you, personal letters come through Sinbaldo: news, perhaps of Gelis and Jodi. He will have his music quite soon.' She touched his hand. 'You look well. I missed you. Was it a great wrench to come back?'

'I needed the rest,' Nicholas said. 'Anyway, you couldn't have kept me away. And that's true, although you know how I lie. Don't you know how I lie? I was lying to Squarciafico just now. And you had better polish up your duplicity, because you are going to have to be very mendacious as well.'

Her face had become grave, and even a little frightened. She said, 'What have you done?'

He looked at her, arrested in the midst of euphoria. Then he put his calming hand over hers. 'Nothing,' he said. 'I haven't hurt, or planned to hurt, anyone.'

'But?' she said. The blood pulsed in her skin, intensifying the scent she always wore. He cleared his throat.

'But I lied when I said it wasn't successful. If the Khan gets the Tudun he wants, Julius can depend on trading in Caffa at a profit. I think the right Governor will come, provided the Genoese are handled with care, and provided that they don't think we are involved in a conspiracy. They must believe that you have been promised nothing, and have no stake in Tartar appointments. Hence you, too, must prevaricate: that is all.'

She said, 'But we do have a stake. You have a promise from the Khan's candidate. Who is he? Eminek, the old brother?'

'It's better you shouldn't know. We don't need to help him: he'll be promoted very efficiently by the Tartar community. And at worst,' Nicholas added, 'we shan't be in a debtors' prison. The Khan paid for the velvet.' And he placed the bag of coins in her hands.

It was heavy. She looked up, astonished. 'It was a gift! And worth less than this.'

'He decided to buy it. It should clear off all the immediate debts. And there is something else,' Nicholas said. 'But really, it should be done in a fur hat and boots. And with clapping.'

'I can clap,' Anna said. Her eyes were brilliant.

'No, you've got to stand and hold this,' Nicholas said, presenting her with the end of his sash. 'It's a reversal of genders. I spin and you reap.'

He began, languidly, to revolve. The sash, unravelling, drooped in her unready grasp until, with a snort of laughter, she clawed in the slack with both hands, and settled to draw at the pace of his turning. Evidently finding this slow, she began sedately to accelerate matters by pulling a little. Very soon, she was hauling with joyous ferocity while Nicholas obliged like a Polovtsian dancer, stamping, shouting and snapping his fingers over his head as he whirled. He was at the top of his spin, arms outstretched, when the sash flew to its end and they both crashed to the floor, yelping and breathless. The sash stood all over the room like a caterpillar.

'Twenty yards,' said Nicholas groggily. 'Twenty yards of silver coins, enough to see us through the winter. Are you glad I came back?' And grinned as she flung her arms round him and kissed him.

'I think we should do it again,' Anna said, sitting back. 'But I expect the servants would worry. Now what's all this about *money*? Show me.'

Snug in their long, narrow channels, the coins made no sound as they issued. He unpicked only a corner to show her. They were of silver, the same as the coins in the bag: Karaï Mirza had been thoughtful. 'I don't suppose,' Anna said, 'that we could be wholly improvident and invest them? If we really are allowed to establish our trade, we'd need something to start with.'

'As it happens,' Nicholas said, 'that has been taken care of as well. I didn't want to excite you too much at once. But, Anna . . . you remember my African gold? I think I might be going to find it.'

She blinked; then tilted her head, leaning back on her hands. 'Well, of course. I thought your boots seemed too heavy.' But she had turned pale.

'No,' he said. 'I'm sorry. After all the bad luck, it sounds mad, but it's true. Sit. I'll fold this out of the way. Then I'll tell you everything that happened at Qirq-yer.'

He made it brief, because it was mid-afternoon and the household would wonder, although it was natural enough that he should be giving her his accounting. Throughout, she sat very still. He left out the name of Karaï Mirza, but told her most of what he had done to earn that sash full of silver. He tried to explain. 'The Khan understands his people, understands the country, understands the enemy a hundred times better than I do. But I know what the western world, and not only the Genoese, can supply him with. And I can let it be known what he needs.'

They were sitting on separate chairs, and her face was in shadow. She said, 'And you did all this, for Ludovico da Bologna, and Julius.'

'And for you,' Nicholas said. Their eyes held.

At some point, she said, her voice low, 'And the man in the cave, Friar Lorenzo. He will not give you away? He knows who you are.'

'None of them will give me away,' Nicholas said. 'They trust the Patriarch.' Karaï Mirza's receipt had brought him unscathed through the portals of Caffa: they had not even turned out his baggage. Wearing the sash, he had been somewhat relieved.

Anna said, 'And your long-lost sea captain is to meet you in Soldaia, but the monk could not say when. That might be dangerous too. That might be a trap.'

'I trust Father Lorenzo,' Nicholas said. 'And Ochoa is already a fugitive from the Genoese and the Knights of St John. I don't think he would send me word simply to harm me.'

'But then why?' Anna said. 'Does he love you so much? Or does he love the gold, and cannot reach it without you?'

'That is very possible,' Nicholas said. He paused. 'I am sorry. I forget I am not alone. If something happens to me, you would be left on your own until Julius could come.'

'The Patriarch would be here till the spring,' Anna said. 'I managed my own life in Germany before I met Julius. Am I not allowed to be afraid for you as a dear friend?'

After a moment he turned his head, breaking their gaze. He had not answered. Anna sprang up and said, 'The letters. I have kept you from reading your letters. Here they are. Let me go and see to your room while you read them. It is probably a millet store now, or a place where they hang all the cheese.' He took the letters and looked after her as she walked steadily out: the black hair, the straight, lissom carriage; the Polovtsian drums. He picked up the first letter.

It was one of three from the same source, although you would have had to know the watermark and ink of the outer cover to identify them as coming from Venice. Since his first, anonymous notes to the Casa di Niccolò, a method of acknowledgement had been established, as was usual between a Bank and its informants. All the Bank's responses so far had been minimal. Sometimes, to his amusement, they had contained small sums of money, on the cautious tariff he himself had once set up with Gregorio. On occasion, there had been a brief added comment. Now, for the first time, there was business news.

In the first letter, it was no more than a word or two, without comment, on a deal in Murano upon which Nicholas had specialised knowledge. In the second, it was a matter of Flemish shipping, as pertained to an intricate project he had launched when in office. The third was different again: it noticed that the mercenary company of the Bank, under contract to Burgundy, was helping the Duke besiege the town of Neuss, outside Cologne.

That was all. He had thrown some scraps, from the East, to the Bank. The Bank had thanked him, but had not asked for more. Instead, someone was saying, quietly, *This is where they need advice, Gregorio, Julius, Diniz. This is how you can help us.* He wondered if she knew that he would recognise her handwriting, and remembered that, of course, she did.

There were only three letters more, and two of them were routine reports. The first said, *They are all well.* The second, *We depart at once from Bruges, with the doctor. There is talk of Ghent, and then Neuss.*

They did not know that he had been out of reach for so long. He would write, but the decisions would already be taken; the crisis at

Neuss, whatever it was, would be over. It might even mean that his army was free. His former army.

The November light was failing now; yellow lamps bloomed outside his window where the town rose on its slopes from the sea. His view was the garden, and the kiosk where Anna had touched him with cherry-stained lips. A passing kiss, like today's. He turned to the last packet of all.

The writing was unknown. The cover, buckled and soiled, seemed, surprisingly, to have followed a route not unlike that of all the others. Its fastening had broken. The inner wrapper bore the name of a courier at Treviso, and had carried a wax seal, now slit. He set it down.

No.

No, when he was here and alone. No, when Marian was gone, and even Tasse was dead. No, when he was doing what he was doing. No. No. No.

Then he opened it.

It began, *À monsieur mon petit-fils.*

And the signature, when he tumbled the pages, was *Thibault, vicomte de Fleury*.

IT WAS FULLY DARK when Anna came in, so that she thought at first that he had gone. Then she saw the chair by the window, and the crouched shadow in it. She hesitated, and then walked steadily forward in the dim light from the doorway. When she rested her hands on his shoulders, a tremor passed through him. She said, 'I read it. It was open. I was afraid it was urgent.' Then she said, 'Did you think the vicomte was dead?'

The question was gentle, reflective, compelling no immediate answer. Her fingers caressed, calming, reassuring, until he lifted his face from his hands. Then she moved, taking a seat a little away, where she could see him, if barely. He spoke.

'No. I knew where he was. I thought this was news of his death.'

He did not go on. She let time pass, then spoke again. 'Did you also know what he told you?'

Again, a silence. Again, he answered. 'It was what I was told. No one believed it. There is no proof.'

She said, 'But you fought at first to be recognised.'

'There was no point,' he said. 'And less, now. It would invalidate my marriage to Gelis. It would make Jodi a bastard.'

She held out her hand, but he did not take it, and she brought it gently back to her lap. She said, 'But none of that, surely, should matter? This is your grandfather, who seemed to care nothing for you. You have found each other.'

'He has found me,' Nicholas said. 'The rest does not follow.'

After a while, she said, 'You will be better alone. When you want it, your room is prepared.' All the letters lay at his side, as he had dropped them. The missive from Treviso rested uppermost, its pages aligned, its position secure on the pile. He had not torn it, or crushed it, or cast it away. He had not reduced it to ashes. Her face full of pity, Anna rose and left him with his trouble, closing the door.

He heard it close. After a while, he moved from his chair and, lighting the lamp, locked away the money he had brought from Qirq-yer, which was now so irrelevant. Presumably someone had unpacked and seen to his animals. Presumably some story had been told to explain his abnormal arrival: he was fatigued from the journey, or sick. That, at least, was not far from the truth. He did not know who the man was who had whirled like a lunatic in this room only hours ago. The same man whose grandfather had thought to write him a letter.

He read it again on his bed, the door locked this time, and the chamber lit. He knew it mostly by heart. *'Sois tolérant à l'égard des caprices d'un vieux . . .'* It was a long time since someone had *tutoyé*'d him in that brand of French. The handwriting, once elegant, was now cramped with age, or weakness, or pain. The intelligence was not cramped at all. The man he had always thought senile had a mind as clear as his own. Clearer, probably. That had been the shock, not what he had had to say. Or one of the shocks.

Gelis had been there.

It did not matter to him, really, that Gelis had been there, or that Anna, reading this letter (and hence Julius — and hence all the world), should know the excuse, the explanation to which his mother had clung, when a second child had followed a still-birth, during her husband's long absence.

> *Such a sweet child!* his grandfather had written of his daughter Sophie. *You would have adored her — I mean as a man: you did adore her, of course, as a child. Simon, a beautiful, lascivious boy, was sufficiently dazzled to get her with child. Her passion for him never died, but a forced marriage cured his at once: he stayed long enough to please his father, then left her. She never recovered, silly girl. The loss of the first child sent her crazy: she did not realise another was coming until it was born prematurely, during the festivities for St Nicholas' Day. There was no disguising what had happened, and no explaining it either. Well-disposed persons suggested that she had been ravished while out of her mind, and hence could not remember it. Considering my condition, this was deemed not unlikely: clearly, mindlessness ran in the family. Only later, based on hearsay and old women's tales, did a different theory*

emerge. You may know it. I did not feel it my place to mention it to the delightful lady your wife.

It was, of course, the story his mother had told: the explanation Nicholas had adhered to all these years until, an apprentice of eighteen at Sluys, he had come face to face with the same beautiful, lascivious boy, now an exquisite man. He had hoped for kindness from Simon, and Simon, cornered, had riposted, in the end, with cold steel.

Yet the theory was well-founded enough. When twins are conceived, it sometimes happens that one will miscarry quite soon, while the other will persist and survive. The infant boy who had died had been twin as well as brother to Nicholas. And his own puny birth, far from premature, had taken place at full term or beyond.

It was a good theory, had there been any proof. His grandfather thought so, as well. The vicomte mentioned it as if viewing the case from afar, as indeed he seemed to view his own illness and its consequence; and the actions of his brother; and of Nicholas in taking vengeance on Jaak. He referred to his second daughter, Adelina, only in the context of her half-sister Sophie's goodness in rearing her, and the kindness of the convent which had embraced her, a furious beauty, at eight. It was the solitary lapse Nicholas noticed, for Adelina had left Jaak de Fleury's home when she was six. But the vicomte Thibault, then helpless, would hardly register dates.

The oddity was that, in reading about them, Nicholas also found himself questioning how much it mattered, all these pains of the past. Of his own life of agony, Thibault had said remarkably little. He left it to be assumed that, unable to speak, slipping in and out of full consciousness, he had been unable to arrange or endorse or forbid what had happened to Nicholas. He said little of Simon, and nothing of Henry, who was supposed to be Simon's son, but was not. He mentioned Jordan de Ribérac, Simon's fat, malevolent father, not at all.

His reasons, Nicholas supposed, were to be found in the only words of advice that the letter contained.

Why feel bitter? Life is unfair. People are often unfair. You and I were born with certain advantages. One does not waste time, then, on resentment. As your wife and your doctor will tell you, I live in peace with a friend, and consider the ambiguities of the world, and make music. You and I did not meet, and I am sorry. But I am content. Should you not be, also?

Then had slipped from the pages the first and last gifts his grandfather had sent him. A sheet of music, minutely ciphered, of a sort he had never heard in his life. And a page of delicate gibberish: a puzzle.

Speechless, paralysed, discounted by his carers as senile, Thibault de Fleury had lain thinking, devising, conjecturing for half his days. And when the demons retreated, he had called up his talents and burnished them, and set them out to garnish his last years.

Nicholas put out the light, and lay looking up into darkness. It was too late, by now, for him to meet Thibault in life, whatever haste he might have made earlier. It was even possible that Thibault had not wanted a meeting. But Nicholas knew that when he came to untangle the puzzle, to track the music, phrase by phrase, with his voice, he would wish that he could imagine his grandfather there, his face critical, pained, full of exasperation for sure, but not without — perhaps not without some trace of approval.

But he could not imagine it, for he had not seen his grandfather's face. Gelis had.

Chapter 21

THESE DAYS, when Gelis van Borselen moved, the trading world noticed. By the end of July, it was known that she was leaving Venice for the Bank's house in Bruges, taking her child and the company physician, and an escort of exceptional strength. She crossed the Alps in fine weather, and made, at a leisurely pace, directly for Bruges, where she arrived at the end of September. It was, of course, a mark of the power of her Bank that safe conducts should be so readily procurable at a time of unease. It was interesting that, having invested heavily and operated successfully with the Venetian branch, the Lady should now, it appeared, be showing a similar interest in the Bruges–Antwerp company.

Meanwhile, of course, her estranged husband was moving through Europe as aide to the Patriarch of Antioch, which might bring in healthy new business, even though de Fleury had officially withdrawn from the Bank. There had been no scandal over his departure, other than the usual marital nonsense. His colleagues had been upset, it was clear, but there had been no hint of malpractice or fraud. He might even come back.

The merchant world approved of Gelis van Borselen.

THE BANK IN BRUGES was not quite so sure. Rooms were set aside for her in the Bank's great range of buildings in Spangnaerts Street — the apartments that Nicholas had used when he stayed. A party of honour was arranged to ride out and meet her. No one spoke very much. Ever since Nicholas left, having exhausted the Bank to further his private vendetta in Scotland, they had avoided talking of him, except to maintain the fiction which explained his departure, or to curse the death by neglect of some little project he had kept to himself. Then Gelis had pushed into the business, and had silenced them by proving her reliability as well as her management skills.

Which was good, the Venice branch seemed to think. Diniz, now controlling the Flemish side he had once managed for Nicholas, had been inclined to agree, until his wife and her sister had expressed their opinion. 'Of course Gelis is working from morning till night, amassing valuable friends, gaining credence. This is what she wanted, isn't it? Nicholas is out of the way, and she is proving that she is better than he was. Wait. She'll buy it all back — Venice, Bruges, Cologne, Scotland. Then she'll laugh at him.'

'Doesn't he deserve it?' Father Moriz had said. And they had been silent because, of course, the chaplain was right. At the same time, none of them felt free of unease over Gelis, and it was this mood which prevailed on the day they rode out to escort her into Bruges.

The encounter was formal but pleasant enough: the Flemish party was cheered to see Dr Tobie but amazed at the number of soldiers. What were they carrying that needed so much armed protection? Jogging into the city, Dr Tobie was quizzed by the chaplain, and returned a piercing pale stare, at odds with his bland, rosy face. 'What do you think is most worth protecting, of all that that idiot has left her? The guard is for Jodi.'

The priest, being astonished (*that idiot?*), allowed his eyebrows to rise. The child, he had to admit, had impressed him, trotting flushed and dimpled and fair between his nurse and his beautiful mother. So had the composure of the same mother, subtly increased in authority. Moriz remarked, 'Because he is the crown prince, do you mean? It seems to Diniz that the Lady is about to supplant him, and possibly Gregorio and Julius as well.'

'Then tell him that Gregorio doesn't feel threatened. He didn't want Gelis to leave. Or don't tell him. He'll find out soon enough for himself.'

He was probably right. It was equally possible that Gelis had never been deeply committed to Venice, except as a testing-ground. The business in Bruges, grown from the dyeworks of Marian de Charetty, had been the heart and fount of Nicholas's empire, indeed of his life. Gelis might well want to own it.

It remained interesting, however, that her first words had not been about Diniz's health, or that of his wife, or the company. Her first words, immediately echoed by Tobie, had been, 'Is Katelijne back, and how is she?'

KATELIJNE SERSANDERS, dame of Berecrofts, had been at home for two months, and was instantly told when Gelis arrived, first by her uncle (crisp and disapproving) and secondly by Robin her husband (apprehensive). She accepted the news without comment, sent no messages, and went about her usual business. A week later, Gelis herself was announced. Jodi was with her.

Kathi, treading across her own parlour, came to an abrupt, smiling halt. Then she transferred the smile, broadened, to Gelis. Gelis returned it. 'This is the lady Katelijne of Berecrofts. Bow to her, Jodi.'

Two solemn grey eyes; a velvet cap with a feather on top of a cushion of furzy brown hair; an absence of dimples. The bow was performed, and the child, straightening, retrieved his mother's hand at once. His eyes were enormous. He said, 'Where is the boy you were with?'

'Oh dear,' Gelis said. 'I read out part of your letter. Jodi, it hasn't come yet.'

'And it may not be a boy, although I hope that it is, for I have a very nice nurse waiting for him. As nice, perhaps, as Mistress Clémence. She makes gingerbread.'

'Jodi likes gingerbread,' Gelis said. 'I don't suppose . . . '

It could not be said that Jordan de Fleury was avid for gingerbread, but the nurse came, and Jodi departed, and Kathi was alone with her guest, who turned to her saying, 'I wanted you to see him. I wanted to see you. Is it so soon? A nurse already?'

Kathi explained, pouring wine. She was used to explaining. She was well; the birth was not due until the turn of the year; her uncle had insisted that she hire a capable lady who would look after her and the child and, knowing the history of his concern, even Robin would not gainsay him. And she was busy, of course: running her own home for Robin, and helping to supervise those neighbouring houses occupied by some of her uncle's young family. Since his wife Margriet had died, Adorne himself was often to be found at his house along the Verversdijk, by the Scots trading quarter, and less and less in his grand house, the Hôtel Jerusalem, in which Nicholas had celebrated his first wedding.

Even to Gelis, Kathi did not say much of her uncle, or the nature of their arrival from Poland. The Duke, receiving Adorne, had listened to his report, and accepted the good hunting-dogs and fine amber dispatched, with their goodwill, by the merchants of Danzig. For the rest, he was evidently absorbed in his present campaign, and oblivious to the blow that his recall had inflicted. Was it not true, after all, that Father Ludovico da Bologna would continue to represent the papal, Imperial and Burgundian interests at Tabriz? And did he not have the banker de Fleury to assist him?

The Duke did not know, of course, of anything to the detriment of de Fleury, and had forgotten that he was no longer a banker. Adorne had not enlightened him. But the reference had rankled as he rode grimly home from his audience, bearing the customary ducal donation of gold plate and refunded expenses. His fellow merchants had given him a banquet to mark what he had achieved, and to console him for what he had been forced to abandon. There were murmurs of a high civic appointment, of the kind his father had held. He was grateful, but the distaste remained. He already held a commission in Scotland. Men of exalted office in Bruges, or in Antwerp, or in Ghent were apt to find themselves caught between their burgher friends and the Duke, and not every townsman proved understanding. All through the feast, Tommaso Portinari had glared.

Adorne's niece did not expect to discuss any of that with Egidia van Borselen, who was not here, of a certainty, to talk about business, or Adorne. Gelis had taken trouble and spent time with Jodi: a glance at the child showed as much. But her overriding interest, for good or for evil, was to collect news of Nicholas. Whatever excuse she had given, that was why Gelis was here now in Bruges, composed, svelte and golden, sipping wine and asking after everyone's health. Kathi said, 'And what about you? The merchant community is riveted by news of your triumphs in Venice. Are you enjoying it all?'

'Am I here to oust Diniz? No,' Gelis said. 'Nicholas damaged the Bank. I aim to repair it, and leave.'

'They might believe it — eventually,' Kathi said. 'Nicholas might even believe it.'

'Do you think so?' Gelis said. 'Of course, Dr Tobie has stayed with me, but there might be other reasons for that.' The irises of her eyes were of an unvarying clear, pallid blue under the veiling and velvet. She said, 'Do you believe me?'

'I understand you feel responsible,' Kathi said. 'Nicholas feels even worse. He tried to cut free of you all and become the carefree lout people once took him for. Alichino, hooray. Then he went too far, managed to put an arrow through Julius, and sobered up sufficiently to offer to escort Anna to the Black Sea. I think he will stay in the Crimea, or Poland, or Germany. He loves intrigue, and attracts learned men. Good teachers will find him.'

Gelis said, 'I wondered. He shot Julius because he had been drinking?'

'It looked like that,' Kathi said. 'But he was upset as well: edgy and changeable. The way he looks when the pendulum has dragged him down.'

'*Had* he been divining?' Gelis said.

'I'm sure he had, although I don't know the reason. Perhaps Julius had been goading him recently, and he suddenly lost his head. Because Nicholas was so equable as a boy,' Kathi said, 'no one expects him to have a temper. But now, I suppose, he has a position in the world, and has learned to defend it by showing anger. Certainly he desperately regretted the shot. He collapsed when he saw what he had done. Thank God Julius didn't die.'

'I wish I had been there,' Gelis said.

'He hated me for seeing it,' Kathi said quickly. 'Anyway, you were doing something more useful. Tobie told me. You went to see Thibault de Fleury, and he wrote a letter. Nicholas will have it by now. He may even turn back and go to Montello?'

'He couldn't get there in time. And with his grandfather gone, he would have no motive for going,' Gelis said flatly. 'He doesn't want to prove that he is Simon's son, now. He wouldn't even want to trace Adelina, if he thought she had proof.'

'And you?' Kathi said. 'Would you prefer to discover the truth, even if no one ever knew what you found, even Nicholas?'

Gelis was silent. Then she said, 'I should like to have been able, one day, to go to Simon and his father and say, This man whose life you have made wretched from boyhood is Nicholas de St Pol of Kilmirren, your legitimate heir. But Nicholas would not want it. And I think they would kill him.'

'Probably,' Kathi said. 'But is he a St Pol? Tobie didn't think so, after what you both learned at Montello. So think of it the other way round. Prove that Nicholas is illegitimate, and you will solve all his problems, or some of them. *Did* you send Thibault music?'

Gelis bent her neck. 'Yes.' It sounded curt. Then she added, 'I had brought some from Scotland,' and this time there was no mistaking the note in her voice.

'The Play?' Kathi said. 'You gave him your copy of the music for the *Nativity Play*?' She meant the play Nicholas had devised and produced, the one true, magnificent thing he had done in all his time in Scotland, for which Willie Roger had written the music. There would be other copies. But this was the one, filthy, dog-eared, annotated, which Willie, weeping, had pressed into Gelis's hands at the end of that towering performance. And Gelis had kept it, ignorant of music as she was, divided from Nicholas as she was. And had given it now to the person whom Nicholas would most want to have it.

Kathi said, with satisfaction, 'Now I know why he married you!' and Gelis looked up in tears.

When Robin came home some hours later, his wife and Gelis van Borselen were still sitting talking together, this time on the same settle. Kathi looked reassuringly healthy and Gelis, rising swiftly, seemed less reserved than he had found her before, and almost happy to see him. Then Jodi came hurtling into the room, intent on finding and being reunited with his Robin, and had to be persuaded that Robin was not wholly his property and about to live in his house. In the end, Robin solved the dilemma by escorting Jodi and his mother in person back to the Bank. After all, they all lived in Spangnaerts Street. Then he returned.

'Well? What did you think?'

As once before, Kathi was painting a cradle, this time for herself. During the short time Robin had been gone, she had dragged it out, fetched her brushes and jars, and was now attempting to put on an apron. With some added string, it was just possible. 'You'll strangle him,' Robin added, patting her fondly. The Berecrofts under the apron punched in return.

'It's the other way round,' Kathi said in a grumbling voice. If Robin's son was to be born in the land of his fathers, they would have to leave for Scotland quite soon, and she hadn't got Gelis fully untangled as yet. She said, on that subject, 'She's dreadfully frightened, but she isn't trying to supplant Nicholas, just put right what he did. She agrees he needs time, and Anna can probably help him. Gelis was astonished to hear of the gold.'

'I'm sure she was,' Robin said, picking up a dry brush. 'I hope she thanked you for getting the truth out of Elzbiete.'

'She was glad I told Anna. Otherwise Nicholas might have changed his mind, and gone sailing the seas with Paúel Benecke. Don't do that!'

'Why not? In case my heir catapults out sneezing like Tobie?' Robin put down the brush. 'So what else?'

She knew why he was restless. It was a hard time for him, and he kept himself busy, as a rule. Her heart ached, but she went on evenly talking and painting. She spoke of Thibault de Fleury at Montello, adding the little that Tobie had not already described. For the sake of the old man, no one was announcing his partial recovery. But for Anna, they would never have found him. Anna, whose daughter Bonne might be marrying either a bastard or the son of a bastard. Anna had nothing to gain by introducing Nicholas to his grandfather. She had put her own interests last, in order to secure a little happiness, perhaps, for the two men.

Robin's mind was in the same quarter. 'And so what about this betrothal? The idea of reuniting the Bank by contracting Jodi to Bonne? Was Gelis alarmed, puzzled, pleased?'

'She was surprised,' Kathi said.

It would take too long to describe, even to Robin, the stillness with which Gelis had received that information, or the long moment of silence while she considered it. Then Gelis had said, 'I hadn't heard. Whose idea was it? What did Nicholas think?'

To which Kathi could only reply, however unwillingly, with the truth. 'It was Nicholas, I believe, who suggested it.'

'Really?' said Gelis.

'To combine the two inheritances, I suppose. The Bank was in pieces. Nicholas might have felt grateful to Julius, who had invited him to join his own company . . .'

'And then Nicholas shot him?' remarked Gelis, with not unreasonable scepticism.

'Anna hasn't withdrawn the idea of a union, that I know of. Of course, Jodi is young. No steps have been taken. Talks would have to take place. It was understood that your wishes would be fully consulted.'

'When?' Gelis had said. 'Now that Julius is on his sickbed, and Anna and Nicholas are in Caffa?' Her colour was suddenly flagrant.

'Send and forbid it,' Kathi had said. 'If that's what you want. Letters do get there eventually. And you can trust Nicholas, surely, in this. He would never commit Jodi to something as important as this unless you agreed. You know he wouldn't.'

'Do I?' said Gelis.

'Well, I do,' Kathi had said. 'What is it? You're not concerned about Anna? She's the sensible sister Nicholas ought to have had. And after what he did to Julius, Nicholas will treat her like the eleven thousand virgins all rolled into one. At least he still has the grace to be remorseful.'

But Gelis had not immediately replied.

'Well?' Robin was saying now, persevering. His hand oscillated in front of her eyes. Blinking, Kathi directed her gaze at him. 'What did Gelis think of the marriage proposal?'

'Oh. That it's ten years too early, of course. And privately, she must be afraid that it marks a rejection of Jodi. At any rate, she won't take steps until she hears from Nicholas. She doesn't want to write to him herself.'

'In case he burns it,' said Robin.

Kathi laid down her brush. 'Gelis didn't know about that. A lot of friends are honoured with poems by Jodi: Anna must have picked up one of these, and thought it would overwhelm Nicholas with nostalgia and lead to a reunion.'

'You told Gelis exactly what happened?'

'I told her that he couldn't bear to keep it, he missed Jodi so much. At least she would know, despite the marriage nonsense, that he wasn't uncaring.'

'You and Anna want Gelis to take Jodi and join him. It's too soon, Kathi.'

'I know that. Anyway, Gelis is determined to work for the Bank all this winter. Do you know what she is going to do?'

'Diniz told me. He was stiff with anxiety, and Govaerts and Moriz weren't much better. She's going to consult with them in Bruges, and then go and join the Duchess's household at Ghent. Gelis used to be maid of honour to Margaret of Burgundy. She can speak English. She can do what even Nicholas couldn't. She can stay where the financial decisions are being taken — for the war, for the future of the towns and the Burgundian states. And she can act as the voice of the Bank.'

'And the Bank's army,' Kathi said. 'You know she'll make her way to the war front. You know she'll deal with Astorre, and talk to John, and work out their contracts. You ought to be in the field. It's what Nicholas was training you for.'

In recent times, with mild horror, she occasionally heard herself giving voice to some feminine plea of this kind. It was unfair, for he couldn't give way. Robin was a conscientious young merchant, worthy successor to the business and lands of his family. However poor the country might be, fatherhood called him to Scotland and duty would chain him there: cheap fanfares of renunciation wouldn't help him at present.

The fact remained that the brief training for war under Nicholas had shown Robin to be ideally suited to the chivalrous arts. It had been one of the happiest times of his life. Even the military structure of Poland had entranced him. After this baby was born, she must release him for a little, to put some of his youth and talents at venture, so that he would return yet more skilled, yet more robust. He was Robin of Berecrofts, whom she was refining for Scotland because she, too, felt that she should have foreseen and stopped what her friend, her other friend, her mortifying other friend had accomplished. Anna would have forced Nicholas to stop.

Anna didn't have Robin. Anna only had Julius.

'I can't go to Neuss. I don't want to. What are you thinking of?' Robin said.

'That I'm tired of painting,' said Kathi with infinite pathos.

Chapter 22

By December, winter had fallen with unusual severity on the merchant city of Caffa, fraying the palm trees and congealing the seas to the north. Although daily awaited, no message arrived from the seamaster Ochoa de Marchena. The lost gold remained lost. After some weeks of deepening anxiety, Anna von Hanseyck cornered her elusive Circassian steward. 'You have been divining.'

He wondered how she had guessed, for his hands were unmarked and he worked only at night, when the toll it took would not be obvious. Now he did not deny it, but told her the truth. 'I didn't want to distress you or the Patriarch. I did think I ought to try, for Ochoa's sake. He is alive, but not near.'

Her voice, striving for calm, sounded strained. 'You will harm yourself with that pendulum more than you harm either of us. So now you have found him, can you stop?'

'For a bit. The occasional question won't kill me. He's on the other side of the Black Sea, probably waiting to sail when the weather clears.' He smiled. 'What will you do when you are rich again? Buy an estate and become a great lady, with Julius? Give up the business and raise children, and teach them to sing?'

'What will you do?' she said.

'What would you have me do?' He tried to speak to her with his eyes.

For a space, she made no reply. Then she said, 'Send for Gelis. That is what we have told you from the beginning. Send for Gelis and Jodi.' With whatever effort, her manner was normal, even admonitory. But her amazing eyes, scanning his, now held pain.

Enclosed in an alien place in one house with this remarkable woman, Nicholas had never thought it would be easy to keep the promise he had made to himself. He had not anticipated its effect upon her.

The mansion, in itself, was the best managed he had ever lived in: everything in it formed for comfort and striking in its simplicity. The staff, all of them good Christians chosen by Brygidy, had learned to treat

Nicholas, when alone, as their master, since it was impossible to maintain his pretended race at close quarters for so long. Yet in all that time, he had never touched Anna. So far.

He managed it partly by absence. Fortified now by the coins from Qirq-yer, he was free to explore at least some of the business openings he was seeking for Julius. It had helped to authenticate his reasons for remaining so long with the Khan. The threatened meeting with Squarciafico and the Genoese consul had not been unreservedly pleasant but Nicholas had convinced them, he thought, that he had been lustfully revelling in the stews of Qirq-yer, rather than interfering with the Tuduns of Caffa. He had taken the consul some fermented liquor, and gratified him, as they drank, with a number of tales of a breathtakingly physical character, some of them true. When he left, Squarciafico was sweating.

To Father Ludovico da Bologna, on the other hand, he told everything.

The Patriarch listened. At first, his comments were purely political. He turned to the personal later. 'Russia. The Tartar–Muscovite betrothal seems likely. Your pretty lady may well get her furs, but you would have to prepare the way first. Confess to Dymitr Wiśniowiecki that you are not a Circassian. He may betray you to the Genoese, but I rather think not. If he is sufficiently pleased, he will support the Khan's Tudun when he comes. The pretty lady in the meantime should know nothing. Joy is an uncertain emotion, always indiscreet and often short-lived.'

'I must remember,' Nicholas had said. 'Shall I tell her about the gold?'

'Oh yes, you wish me to congratulate you on your fiendish divining. You also remind me that the gold is your fee. Leave her in the belief that the shipmaster is where you have said. It is safer for her. Given the chance, the Genoese would claim both Ochoa de Marchena and his gold. Do you want me to tell you that I find your assistance quite useful?'

'It would worry me,' Nicholas said. 'I was coming anyway, for the gold.'

'That's what I thought,' the Patriarch said.

Hence Nicholas for several weeks had found an easy excuse to be absent, as Anna, too, was seldom at home, having occasion to visit Sinbaldo her agent, and cultivate those merchants and shippers she knew. Winter in the Crimea was normally sociable for, isolated by ice and by storms, the permanent groups within the colony took leisure to renew their communal bonds. The Christian lawyers and agents in Caffa were married members of a complex community, tracing their presence back for over three hundred years. The high officials were appointed, on the contrary, for a single short term, and seldom imported their families. As a result, the Caffa brothels were of exceptional quality, as were the courtesans who fulfilled the functions of wives. But to a man such as the Genoese consul, vanity required that he dazzle his guests with a truly blue-blooded hostess — no less than the gracious Contessa Anna von Hanseyck. Nor did Anna object. It led to introductions, and knowledge, and social credit which in due course she could transfer to Julius.

Once, escorting her home from the castle at night, her servants had led her past the quiet, discreet street of the baths, and their lantern had glanced on a face that she knew. Warm with wine and laughter and civilised company she had slid from her horse and, catching her veil, had called after him softly. But Nicholas turned on his heel, and had vanished before she could reach him.

The days passed. The Feast of St Nicholas came and went unremarked, for Mameluke servants did not celebrate such anniversaries. Nicholas was thirty-four years of age, and since the Feast of St Catherine, Kathi had been twenty-one. She was no longer in Bruges. Nicholas thought she and Robin had travelled to Scotland, but for some time was not perfectly sure, as he preferred to limit the hours of his divining.

He did not know if Kathi's baby was born. He did know that Julius was still alive, and in Thorn. He knew all the time that Gelis and Jodi were well, through Mistress Clémence. It was through Mistress Clémence that he finally learned that Gelis had gone to Ghent, and that Jodi was travelling with Kathi and Robin to Scotland. Tobie and the nurse were going with them.

It meant that Clémence was no longer with Gelis, and that his bodyguards, from what she hinted, had been split. He did not know whether or not to be afraid, but forced himself not to misuse the pendulum, for Gelis had learned to tell when he was tracing her, and he did not want her to be troubled. Gelis, or anyone else. These people were nothing to do with him, now. He must not shackle them. And he had other things to think of soon enough, from the moment that the Khan's secretary Karaï Mirza made his promised visit to Caffa.

Nicholas was playing argumentative chess with Dymitr in the Russian quarter when the man from Qirq-yer, heavily muffled, was ushered into the low-ceilinged room. There was a second man with him. Karaï Mirza threw off his cloak, and Nicholas leaped up, filled with unexpected pleasure at the sight of the broad Tartar face with its smiling cheekbones. They embraced, and Dymitr strode up to shake hands, while the stranger unfastened his great hooded cloak. Beneath it, he wore the robes and turban of an Islamic religious teacher, a jurist, an imam.

. . . *As some visiting teacher from Cairo might commend you to those of Muslim faith*.

Nicholas stood still while the Tartar, his smile deepening, introduced him. The man's name was Ibrahiim. He bowed to Dymitr his host, but addressed Nicholas in Arabic. 'Misra Niqula. The professors of al-Azhar know of you.'

Misra Niqula: Egyptian Niccolò. 'You come from Cairo?' Nicholas asked. The grave, bearded face of the imam was brown and not black, and wholly unlike that of the pedagogue best known to him, unless you counted a sense of stillness, of composure, of peace that had been Katib Musa's as well.

'He has come here to teach for the winter,' said Karaï Mirza, answering for the imam as they sat. 'You may visit him in any of the towns where his classes are held. As for me, my stay will be shorter, and we should not be seen together in public: I have imposed myself on our good friend Dymitr simply to tell you that I have great hopes of obtaining your furs, but success will largely depend on which Tudun will be chosen to rule in the Khan's name in Caffa. So tell me. What views have you heard expressed?'

Karaï Mirza was here to talk of the disputed appointment. His own possible candidature was not mentioned. None the less, in extracting the views of the household, his very competence threw into relief the weaknesses of the late Governor's brother and son. He was not only experienced, after all. He was of the inner council of Mengli-Girey himself.

The Russians, Nicholas could see, were won over. If Karaï Mirza were to be accepted as governor, Dymitr and his friends might expect a spring present from Moscow which would allow them to compensate Anna and escape the penalty for her loss. It was a bonus, naturally, for Nicholas too.

The visitors did not stay long. Before he left, the imam Ibrahiim took Nicholas to one side. 'I have a letter for you from Brother Lorenzo. Find me if you wish to reply. I have not read it.'

'I shall like to find you, if I may, in any case,' Nicholas said. 'And hear news of my friends.'

The imam closed the folds of his hood over his beard. 'I am busy,' he said. 'But of course, you may always attend one of my classes. Any Believer will tell you where to go.'

Nicholas caught Karaï Mirza's small Tartar grin as he left. Damn Karaï Mirza. Then he tore open the letter and retracted it all, for inside was a message from Ochoa.

He took it to Anna. As once before, he hurled himself into his house and had to be halted: the Lady was entertaining. The guests included one of the more self-important officials of the Uffizio della Compagna of Genoa: having got rid of them all with extraordinary speed, the Gräfin shed her fine, high-bred calm and, hearing Nicholas out, hugged him at the end of his recital as closely as she might have hugged Julius. 'You've heard from Ochoa! And he's bringing the gold in the spring!' And then, pulling away, 'Show me! Wait, we must have wine — Brygidy, bring us more wine. Now, show me.'

Only when he spread the page before her did her face cloud. 'It's gibberish! I can't read it! Cipher?'

'Of course you can read it,' said Nicholas. But although he was patient, she found the sheet of letters beyond her and instead turned, like a satisfied mother, to stroking the words of his transliteration. 'All your gold, in the spring. He has deceived the Knights of St John? And once he can move, he will send you word where it is?'

'In code,' Nicholas said. 'So you mustn't fall out with me, whatever I ask, before then.' Then he drew a breath, wishing he had put it some other way, or left the whole story till morning, for her lips had parted and her eyes had become very bright.

Anna said, 'But we shall never fall out. Our fortunes are bound together. Don't you feel it?'

What he felt he did not want to put into words, although there were many words for it. Nicholas presented her with one of his generous grins, only a little breathless, and said, 'Naturally. I'm joining your company, and am about to make you both exceedingly rich. I didn't tell you that Moscow is about to compensate you for the loss of your furs? Well, possibly. And only if the Khan thinks I am helping him. And not at all if the Genoese get to hear that I met his secretary at the Russians' tonight . . .'

The story took a little time in the telling, and allowed him to master himself, and presently to leave her in a civilised way, and take himself back to his room. Even then, he continued to think of her. The night was not over. Long and industrious practice had taught him some understanding of women's desires, and he was afraid for Anna as well as himself. It was not surprise that shook him, therefore, when he heard a sound at his door, and Anna's voice spoke his name. It sounded muffled. He rose, and let her in.

She had been on her way to bed. Her hair flowed over her bedgown, and his mind's eye saw below the hair, and the gown. Then he saw, as she stood looking at him, that her eyes were wet, and her face tracked with tears.

Nicholas walked away from her and turned. He said, 'I am sorry. You shouldn't be here.'

The door had closed. She stood before it, the tears running, and said, 'Are you never lonely? Are you never lonely because you are happy, and have no one to share it with?' And coming forward, she dropped on a seat and said, as if she could not help herself, 'Talk to me of Jodi. I wish Jodi were mine.'

The early childhood of her own daughter was over: Bonne's life in a convent was now separate from that of her mother; and there was no one to nurture. Nicholas knew how skilful Anna could be with the young. He remembered her sure understanding when dealing with Henry; with the unacknowledged son she did not know he possessed. He remembered her perception on other long-past occasions which had nothing to do with the young, such as a moment in Bruges when they had faced one another, and she had recognised his exhaustion, as not even Diniz had done. He said, almost at random, 'Who can own Jodi? We belong to ourselves. We possess no one. It is by being alone that we learn.'

'Who told you that?' Anna said. 'The Greeks, the Muslims, the humanists, the emissaries of the Pope? None of them is alone, as we are.'

'I am not alone,' Nicholas said; and standing aside, let her see the smoke feathering up from the brazier. The scent was different from hers. He said, 'I shall be asleep before you are in bed. Shall I give you some?'

She rose. For a long moment, they faced one another. Then she said, 'No, Nicholas,' and turned slowly, and left.

As soon as her footfalls had died, he raked out the pastilles and dismantled the embers until the brazier was black. The sickly smell faded. He stood at the open window until the cold made him shiver, and then closed it and turned back to bed. He had smothered the fire, for this one night at least.

THE SHOCK OF ISOLATION struck Gelis in Ghent that December, when she realised that the chain of communication between herself and Nicholas was now stretched too far. The smooth, informative messages from the Black Sea to Venice, to Bruges, could not be expected to seek her out where she was now, or where she was going. The informative messages which latterly had contained, here and there, a comment, an allusion, a fragment of gossip which were for her eyes alone, and which brought back, in a flood, all that once she and Nicholas had shared. And she had begun to reply in kind. She had begun, out of longing, to refashion the chain that once had linked them, but now it ended in nothing. She had lost Nicholas, and she had sent Jodi away. It had been necessary to keep the child safe, but she mourned the lost routines, the high, swooping voice, and the pattering step. For a year, she had been close to her son as never before, and had come to understand and to value him. Now he, too, had gone.

For a year, she had also been occupied in restoring the fortunes of the Bank, and now in something much greater, in planning the growth of the Bank within the duchy. But she had not realised until now how much she had come to rely on the motley collection of men and women who had been the friends, the family, the long-suffering partners of Nicholas, and who had been willing to lend to his wife some of the tolerance he had so wilfully forfeited.

Now she was alone, if anyone could be alone in Ghent, moving between the vast garden palace of Hof Ten Walle, the home of the Duchess and her step-daughter, and the grim walls of the Gravenkasteel, prison, law court and mint, where the high officers of state — Chancellor Hugonet among them — prosecuted their business while responding, with a calmness they may not have felt, to the continual importunities of the Duke, shouting from some distant frontier for men, for arms, for money, money and still more money.

In a month, wielding the power of her name and her Bank, Gelis van Borselen had extended some of her contracts and secured openings for others which Diniz from Bruges and his agents might not have perceived, or have risked. Other contracts she allowed to end, or did not pursue. The future of Burgundy depended on too many imponderables: on the rashness of the Duke and the skill of his enemies; on the power of the towns; on simple accidents of mortality which might reverse every plan. Weighing up the probabilities, in the past, Nicholas had discarded France in favour of the Empire or Burgundy. Now the Empire was in dispute with Burgundy, and from Ghent, she could not tell how the die was likely to fall. To study that — and to deal direct, for her Bank, with the Duke — she must go to the war-front at Neuss.

It was not a long journey: in summer it would take a good rider six days. She travelled just before Christmas, at a time when Ghent would be given over to festivities, and her safe conduct was signed by the Chancellor. Raffo, her best man-at-arms, had gone with Jodi, with whom he had formed a firm friendship; but she had another, Manoli, nearly as good, and a strong escort to protect her after she left Jooris, their agent at Antwerp, and took the Roman road south-east to Maastricht, and then, for safety, to Aix. She had written to that one-eyed veteran Captain Astorre, who was already encamped with the Bank's troop of mercenaries, besieging Neuss with the Duke, and had received a reply which indicated that she would be met. He did not say by whom.

It snowed. The countryside for miles around the west bank of the Rhine had been scavenged for food by the army: as her party approached, they found taverns closed, or unwelcoming. They had brought their own fodder and fortified themselves with food they had carried from Ghent. Shivering over some chill, smoking brazier, Gelis envisaged the scented warmth, the indolent peace of the Genoese colonies in the closed months when trade ceased, and intimate relationships formed. Nicholas, with his gift for attracting companions, would probably make his own arrangements in Caffa; would be surrounded by eclectic new friends. Thinking of it, from the sober perspective now forced upon her, Gelis recognised that, even when Nicholas was sought-after and rich, she had never seriously feared his casual liaisons, or even minded the strange intellectual attachments which he continually half admitted, then shed.

It was news of a lasting physical bond that, against all reason, she dreaded to hear.

But at least there was Anna beside him. Kathi had faith in Anna's powers to protect Nicholas; and she was probably right. Anna herself would be sacrosanct: after what had happened to Julius, that was certain. She was not jealous of Anna. Only, as the days passed and the pendulum did not find her, she wondered why.

CAPTAIN ASTORRE was not against women in camp: he regularly exceeded the Burgundian ration of thirty per company, and always found they made handy auxiliaries. He was accustomed, too, to women as negotiators: Muslims and Christians both made well-accredited use of their wives and their mothers; Uzum Hasan and the present Sultan of Turkey sent their old ladies all over the place. When Gelis van Borselen set off for Neuss, Astorre dispatched his most famous gunner to meet her. Astorre and his soldiers missed Nicholas, but if the fellow didn't choose to come back, then maybe he'd get his wife to talk sense to the Duke. Whatever Nicholas had done, Astorre didn't mind.

The engineer John le Grant did. He rode to intercept the wife of Nicholas without pleasure, knowing that she had suffered, as he had, over the wreck of their achievements in Scotland, but that she must be allotted some share of the blame. Once, when his hair was a brighter red and his Aberdonian tongue still round and raw, he would have begun by announcing as much. But now he was in middle years, with a great reputation behind him, and a desire not to be embroiled any more in the life of Nicholas de Fleury. He had had enough.

It reassured him, locating her tavern, to find that her entourage was well controlled and well armed, and that they had had the sense to bring food and conceal it. He thought, when shown into her chamber, that, long-limbed and fair as she was, she had the air of a pre-occupied man, of an upper seaman, you would say, preparing to tackle some puzzling duty. He saw that the rumours of what she had been doing in Venice must be true. Although they had met many times, from Scotland stretching back to Mount Sinai, his greeting was deliberately commonplace, and he plunged into business as soon as they were seated over the flask he had brought. 'We need to take some decisions. Do you want me to speak, or would you rather wait and talk to Astorre?'

'I want to talk. How is he?' she said.

John le Grant grunted. 'His joints ache. He's still the best in the profession.'

'You must both get offers,' she said. He had forgotten what she was like.

'We're both daft,' said John le Grant shortly. 'So what d'ye want to know first?'

To his relief, she took company statistics for granted. Astorre and his guns and a hundred lances had been lodged on the river-banks of the corn port of Neuss ever since the end of July, when Duke Charles hit on the idea of intimidating Cologne by surprising and capturing its small Roman neighbour. Except that on the knoll of Neuss or Novaesium was a stout little town, stuffed with food, stuffed with arms, which declined to fall, and had chosen, vindictively, to allow itself to be besieged. According to history, it had already survived thirteen sieges, and clearly aspired to a lucky fourteenth. Meanwhile, it was successfully occupying Duke Charles and the finest army he had ever assembled.

'Really?' had said Gelis when John used the phrase.

'I was exaggerating,' said John. 'Thirty bombards, fifty great serpentines, a hundred smaller pieces of ordnance, and twenty thousand Flemish, English, Italians and borderline Germans, all with their own whimsies, fancies, prejudices and silly ideas, led by Charles the Mange, who listens to nobody. And while his Castilian siege machine sinks, and the wheels come off his Italian castle, and the Neussois sally forth and kill hundreds, the Emperor Frederick and the French and the Austrians and the Swiss are making friends and arranging to dine off him.'

'He wants Cologne,' Gelis said. 'He wants to tidy his frontier with Germany. He wants to join his lands in the Low Countries with Burgundy. Meanwhile, he's accidentally opened so many fronts that he'll pay you to fight almost anywhere. You think I'm here to get you to protect Dijon and Fleury for Jordan. I'm not.'

He felt like being sardonic. 'Nicholas doesn't want his son to have Fleury?'

Gelis said, 'He couldn't afford it. We've traced his grandfather. Nicholas has no provable right to the vicomté of Fleury.'

'He could buy the land.'

'Nicholas has no money,' Gelis explained, in the same helpful, even solicitous manner. 'Tobie mentioned a rumour, and I investigated with Govaerts. When the business in Scotland closed down, the funds passed through various accounts on their way to the Bank's central ledgers. On the way, Nicholas arranged for them to sweep up all his own personal money and include it as part of the Bank's commercial surplus from Scotland. No one noticed.'

'No one *noticed*!'

'It wasn't difficult. Would you have questioned what the contents of the castle of Beltrees might be worth? Except that they weren't worth anything: the money that bought them was borrowed by Nicholas. But Govaerts didn't know that. The ledger showed a good sale, the equivalent money was there, and he accepted it. So what are the Duke's chances at Neuss?'

'Slim,' le Grant said, though not immediately. He stared at her, his mind on Nicholas's eccentric behaviour. 'You're saying that Nicholas made a camouflaged gift of his own private funds to the Bank, and didn't tell anyone? Why? What did Govaerts think, and the rest, when you told them?'

'Remorse, the theory goes. There wasn't so much: he had showered his own money as well as the Bank's into all those neat, faulty schemes that were meant to pull Scotland apart. He'll acquire another fortune, I'm sure, but he'll have to work for it. The next offer the army receives may be from the rulers of Tabriz or Caffa. Astorre might even accept.'

'He might, but I wouldn't,' said le Grant. 'And these days, I'm part of the deal.' He added bluntly, 'So you're not here about Fleury. You're here to make sure that we shan't sign our next contract with Nicholas?'

'I knew you wouldn't,' Gelis said. 'Nicholas knows it as well, I'm quite sure. No. I wondered if he had pretended to ask you. He would mean it to tell us something.'

'What?'

She looked at him with momentary surprise. 'About the course of events where he is. Trouble in the Crimea affects Russia and Poland, which affects Julius and Cologne and, in the long run, might damage Diniz in Bruges. He has been sending warnings ever since he went east.'

John le Grant set down his cup. 'You've been in touch with him? You trust what he says?' Then, with increasing incredulity, 'Is this why you've been learning the business? You've managed to forget how Nicholas fooled us? You'd like us to invite Nicholas back to head a new combined Bank with his wife!'

Annoyingly, she didn't look defensive; just tired. She said, 'I thought I'd just told you. I knew you wouldn't tolerate him for a minute. Neither would Diniz or Moriz or Tobie. Neither would Gregorio. He can't come back.'

John le Grant listened. Then he said what he had held back until now. 'And you? It wouldn't have happened but for you.'

'I know that,' she said.

He didn't know Gelis well. His world was a masculine one: he had been struck in Alexandria and in Iceland by the exuberant intelligence and sweetness of Kathi, but knew Gelis only through other men's eyes, and by her sharp-witted performance at events where application and analysis were required. Had he stopped to think, he might have deduced that Kathi was an asexual being with a very feminine form of intuition, while Gelis was a ravishing woman with a mathematical brain.

He had now stopped to think. He said, slowly, 'You don't expect

Nicholas back. You expect to go to him?' Until then, he had thought the marriage already part sundered.

She smiled. Her eyes were still tired. She said, 'It isn't as easy as that. And I have work I want to do first. About your expiring contract, for a start. I need to know what you and Astorre want to do about that after Neuss. What do you think? Leave Fleury out of it.'

They talked then, as master gunner to agent, and reached certain conclusions; after which John le Grant went to bed, and rose next morning to escort Gelis van Borselen to Neuss, in what his friend Father Moriz would have referred to as a measuring frame of mind.

He did not know, because she had not told him, of the other measure Nicholas had taken, which she had just learned from Tobie. When giving up all his reserves, Nicholas had kept something back: the wages of two men to protect herself and Jodi.

She had spoken since to Manoli, the man in her employment. He knew no more than Tobie had told her, which Tobie had learned in turn from Clémence. Manoli was to guard her with his life, but against whom had not been explained. Gelis believed what Tobie had written. Nicholas was afraid of the corpulent vicomte de Ribérac, even when he was safely banished to a Portuguese island. And he was determined, too, to leave no loophole for David de Salmeton.

She had not spoken of it to John, for it made her seem less than self-sufficient. It also implied a relationship between Nicholas and herself which did not exist. He had always been over-anxious about Jodi.

At Neuss, Captain Astorre seemed more concerned, at first, to learn about the military training of Jodi than to decide where his next contract ought to be served. The house in which he received Gelis was one of several good timber erections not unlike those which Nicholas and Jodi had occupied, she had heard, in the Burgundian camp outside Hesdin. The muddy lands around the low hill of Neuss, however, were to contain the Duke's person as well as his armies. The besiegers lived in a vast phantom city of hundreds of tents and fine houses, fortified by walls, ditches and drawbridge, and furnished with baths and drinkhouses, shops and forges and taverns, barbers and brewhouses and cart-makers, joiners, cutlers and drapers, priests and apothecaries. Musicians sang every morning outside the Duke's prefabricated mansion of elegant carpentry-work, while the state visitors to the duchy were received in luxurious silken pavilions, stocked with magnificent chests and gold plate. The envoys of Naples, Hungary and the Palatinate had already undergone the experience, while the Venetian ambassador, dazzled, had asked leave to have a painting of it all done in oils.

'Then we had King Christian of Denmark,' said Astorre, who liked boasting about extravagant masters. 'They got him on a barque on the Rhine, and the Duke received him in his good tunic. A hundred thousand florins' worth of real pearls. Remember, he wore it at Trèves.' Astorre never had qualms about mentioning Trèves, which Gelis found soothing.

She said, as she might not have said to anyone else, 'Did he talk about Scotland?' The Queen of Scotland was King Christian's daughter.

'There was some nonsense about Scotland and Russia. But mainly, it was all about the King's visit to Rome. The Holy Father wants us to stop besieging Neuss and go to fight Ottoman Turkey instead. As if we could.'

Gelis decided not to pursue Scotland and Russia. She remarked, 'It's what Ludovico da Bologna was always demanding.'

'Well, that's his job. We did fight in Cyprus and Trebizond. But Charles'd be mad to send his army off now: the Emperor and the Swiss would step in and march all over his territory. Then, of course, the English army is coming.' The sewn eye in the grizzled face confronted her as well as the open one. 'If they're still coming. They're supposed to invade France with our help this summer.'

'They're still coming,' said Gelis. 'So you're not tempted to take the company east?'

'Why, does Nicholas want me to?' said Astorre, astonished. 'We'd earn more money here.'

'I don't know what Nicholas wants,' Gelis said. 'You and John must decide. And if you stay in the West, you ought to think where you most want to be. The Duke will be fighting on three fronts at least, by my reckoning.'

'I fancy the French,' Astorre said. 'I've always fancied the French. And the Duke wouldn't be breathing over my shoulder.'

'He would, if your contract is with him,' Gelis said. 'Not if it's with the Bank. You could choose. When you're ready, we'll talk about it.'

She spoke distinctly, because of the copious echoes, both within the wooden building and outside, where the alleys were belaboured by the cries of the fish- and vegetable-sellers, the rumbling of carts and the clang of the armourers over the groundswell of wrangling voices of soldiers and their women, and the squeals of their infants. Beyond that, distantly, was the roar of a crowd at a wrestling match, and the whoops from the jeu de paume court, backed by the ever-present thresh and grind of the wind- and watermills which ringed the whole camp. And behind those, if you listened, the skittish pops and occasional bangs which represented the war: a warning, a sally, a counter-attack. There was a burial ground here, but no sound came from that.

'. . . twenty thousand marks,' Astorre was saying.

'I'm sorry?' said Gelis.

'The peace between England and Scotland. Didn't you hear before you left Ghent? King James has undertaken to marry his son to King Edward's young filly Cecilia. That's the dowry. Scotland gets all that money, so that England can choose to invade France without Scotsmen attacking her borders. That Nicholas,' Astorre said. 'He was a fool, closing his business in Scotland. Look at them. Rich.'

She could not speak.

Later, alone with John le Grant, she found a way of asking his opinion on the matter. He gazed at her appraisingly. 'Rich is hardly the word for it. The King's a spendthrift, and the money is coming in stages. His son is just one year old, for God's sake. The currency is still in a mess, and the merchants may like the peace but the Borderers don't — they'd rather be raiding the English under young brother Albany. It'll take more than one infant marriage to repair the damage Nicholas did.'

'But it's something,' she said. And then, because it was in her mind, she added, 'We have an infant marriage afoot. Concerning Jodi. Nicholas wants Jodi to marry Anna von Hanseyck's young daughter.'

The white-fringed eyes opened wide. 'The deil!' said John le Grant. It sounded blank.

She said, 'It makes sense for the future. Julius has asked Nicholas to join his part of the company.'

'I dare say,' John le Grant said. 'Nicholas can't afford, from what you say, to be choosy. But I wouldna throw your fortune into Julius's lap until you've made a few enquiries. Ask Moriz.'

The German priest Moriz from Augsburg was also the Bank's specialist in the mining and casting of metals. 'I have,' Gelis said. 'I've also worked with Julius in Cologne. His credit is good. With the von Hanseyck connection, he could raise loans to start again anywhere.'

'As you say,' John agreed. 'The Graf was well known and respected, although he didna leave as much, Moriz says, as you'd think. I believe Anna herself has no kin.'

Gelis was faintly amused. 'She doesn't need them. Doors open wherever she goes. The von Hanseycks are connected to everybody, whereas no one knows who Nicholas is. In terms of degree, it isn't a bad marriage for Jodi. I was weighing it rather in terms of free choice. Childhood unions are common with princes, but merchants can usually wait.'

The engineer watched her in silence. Then he said, 'Have you met the lassie? Bonne?'

She had, of course. She had lived in Cologne during the days of Julius's earliest courtship, and the child had been eight. She said, 'Recently, no. If you know where she is, Anna would be glad to hear she is well.'

'I dare say,' said John. 'I'm a wee tate thrang just at present to call on her. Syne you should get back to the Duchess and Bruges. Tell Diniz you all guessed quite right, and the old man is keen to fight France, and not averse to signing up with the Bank, and that I'll stay and load his balls till his old gun gives up and he drops.' He sounded cross. He continued, 'Tell me something. Why did ye put Nicholas through all that ye did?'

The old accusation. His eyes were a steady, raw blue; his lined skin, russet-brown, held the vague freckled marling of summer. His hair, dulled from its original red, was still at once belligerent and disarming. Even as she drew breath, she remembered how long Nicholas had known him, and how tired she was of avoiding that particular question. She looked him in the eyes and said, 'I was afraid of him. Can you understand that?'

'Yes. Did he know?'

She stared at him, conveying perhaps more than she meant, for he enlarged, uncharacteristically, on the question. 'You learn about fear, in the army. You teach by challenging.'

She considered Nicholas, the eternal apprentice, thus elevated to the status of teacher. She shook her head. Untenable. No.

'Have you never watched your son with his da?' asked le Grant.

She had watched him. *This is what a horse likes to eat. This is how a ship sails. Why don't you sing this with me?*

John le Grant was speaking again, irritability in his manner. 'What right have I to talk? I've seen Nicholas de Fleury deaf and blind to the world for the sake of some toy he was making, and I was the fool who encouraged him. If you failed to notice your share in what became of him, I failed to see mine. But that doesna mean he should come back. Among us, we've made him a wrecker.'

She said, 'Kathi thinks he must teach himself now. He has Anna.'

'He has you and Kathi as well,' John le Grant said. 'Tell him the news. Answer his messages. A woman can do what a man can't.'

'Keep his place warm, until the rest of you make up your minds? No, thank you,' said Gelis.

But, of course, it was what she was doing.

She stayed for three days, during which time she had an audience with the Duke, and Astorre took her round the battle positions. Afterwards, John remonstrated with his captain. 'Yon was dangerous. She could have been killed.'

'She wanted it. She's a pretty woman. She'll tell Nicholas, and he'll maybe be tempted.'

'She'll tell the Duchess and Hugonet, more to the point, and maybe shame them into raising more money. You were talking to her about Cyprus.'

'About Zacco's son being dead,' said Captain Astorre, his beard jutting. 'I didn't tell her about David de Salmeton. Mind you, I think Nicholas ought to know.'

'Then tell him,' John le Grant said. 'If you know where he is.' The old man and he scowled at each other and parted in perfect understanding. Riding back to his guns, John le Grant found himself thinking of Gelis in quite a different way from before. He wondered where she was now, stoically commuting, like the factor she had become; methodically tracing the routes between Neuss and Brussels and Bruges, Ghent and Antwerp.

In all the world, only her entourage could have revealed that her destination that day was quite different. Gelis van Borselen, semi-detached lady of Beltrees, was on her way to seek out her possible daughter-in-law, the young encloistered Fräulein called Bonne.

Only her entourage could have told, or a man far away in the East, sitting alone, and at last, hesitatingly, lifting a pendulum.

THE CONVENT, when she reached it, was not welcoming, but perseverance obtained her an interview with the Abbess. That firm-chinned lady, cantilevered in voile, refused to send for the Fräulein von Hanseyck until convinced, by the depth of her purse, that the eminent lady was as superior as she claimed to be. They were allowed fifteen minutes.

At the age of eight, Bonne had possessed handsome blue eyes and thick hair, but little else that was attractive. Time had improved her. Entering the room in her cap and plain gown, she made her greeting and sat with a mixture of demureness and grace at once reminiscent of Anna. There was a suggestion of feminine roundness that had not been there before, as well as a firmer mould to the face. Scanning the full lips, the large downcast eyes, the rippling dark hair with its stray glints of chestnut, Gelis was smitten with longing for a young person quite different: for the fresh-faced dimpled boy, not yet six, whom she had sent north to Scotland for safety. She said, smiling, 'I had to come and see my son's bride.'

The large eyes opened on hers, and turned to the Abbess. The Abbess said, 'This, Bonne, is the lady of Beltrees from the Banco di Niccolò. I was not informed that you were to marry her son.'

'It is too soon to be sure,' said the girl. 'Although, naturally, I should be pleased and honoured were it to be arranged. Is Jordan with you, my lady?'

Gelis gazed at her. 'You knew of it? No. I sent him to Scotland, since I must travel so much for the Bank. He is not as old as you are, as perhaps you know.'

'But he can ride a horse?' the girl said. 'Or if not, of course I could teach him.'

'You like riding?' Gelis said. 'Where did you learn?'

'The Graf my father had many hundreds of horses. Falcons also, and hounds. I can shoot with a crossbow. I have ridden since I was a baby.'

'At your grandparents', of course,' Gelis said. 'Where was that? Do you go there still, or are they both dead?'

The girl lowered her eyes, her brow clouded. The Abbess said, 'They are in heaven. We pray for them, but the very house has gone now. Bonne has none but the Graf's noble relatives left.'

'And her mother in Caffa,' Gelis said. 'If I were the Gräfin, I don't think I could have borne to leave such a dear maid behind me.'

'But you sent your son to Scotland?' said the girl. 'I am sure that you love him as much — even more, if your marriage has ended. I am fortunate. I have stepfather Julius.'

'We pray for him, too,' said the Abbess. 'He has suffered. The wound, we are assured, was an accident.'

Beneath two pairs of eyes, Gelis felt herself stiffening. She said, 'I am quite sure that it was. And you like your stepfather, Bonne?'

The girl smiled. 'My mother likes him. That is what matters, is it not?'

'Bonne!' exclaimed the Abbess quite sharply. She rose. 'The girl has work to finish. You will excuse her, I'm sure. Her lady mother will be happy to hear that her daughter is in good health, as you see, and a credit to her professors. We look forward to the day when the Gräfin returns. Do we not?'

The daughter of Anna von Hanseyck performed a neat curtsey, briskly sweeping her toe. 'The day my mother comes home will be the happiest, I think, of my life.' She lifted her lashes to Gelis. 'Except, of course, for the day when I wed my young husband. That will be happier still.'

'How many good things,' said Gelis, 'there are to look forward to. And you have Jordan's father to meet. That must be arranged. You will surprise one another.'

'He surprised my stepfather Julius,' said Bonne.

Shaken, Gelis departed. If you were to call the encounter a joust, the inmates of the convent had undoubtedly carried the day. It was only when reviewing it later that she began, with some admiration, to laugh. But by then she had written to Scotland: a cheerful message for Jodi; a direction for Clémence his nurse; and an urgent commission for Dr Tobias. And more important than any of these, a deceptive letter of friendly reassurance to Kathi, whose son, surely, was about to be born.

Chapter 23

In December that year, the Emperor Frederick, outraged by Cologne and encouraged by Louis of France, declared war on Duke Charles, and prepared his armies to march. His intention, after safeguarding his frontiers, was to filch Luxembourg and the Low Countries from Burgundy; France was to have Picardy, Artois and Burgundy itself. He was quite optimistic.

Julius of Bologna, recuperating with resolution in Poland, read the signs and received with beating heart the tender letters that found their way, all through that winter, from his lovely, his remarkable wife. He did not necessarily broadcast her news. He did not mention anything whatsoever about gold. But as time went on, he cheerfully reaffirmed to all his clients, his colleagues (and his creditors) his decision to set out for Caffa by spring.

And as winter ended, Anna von Hanseyck in Caffa was found by her Mameluke steward to be weeping over a letter from Bonne.

It should have been a day of light-hearted reunion, for Nicholas had been absent from Caffa for some time, on an unplanned fishing expedition led by Dymitr Wiśniowiecki and his friends from the Russian community. Anna, the least possessive of women, had hastened him on his way. Temporary stewards were easily found. And she recognised, none better, the frustration Nicholas had begun to experience, with every business avenue long since explored, and his leisure occupations confined to those places where it was safe for a man in Mameluke guise to appear. Which meant, in practical terms, the Russian or Muslim quarters, the Franciscan monastery, or the house which she shared.

She had resolved, in her calm way, to provide a form of companionship with music, with poetry, with books, which he might find undemanding and familiar; and was pleased when she was able to tempt him to sing, or take the lute or the viol, or talk. In his turn, although she — so much in demand — could have filled her days with her own new-found friends, Nicholas set aside time to introduce her to a side of Caffa she might otherwise have missed: encounters with men and women and children who were not Genoese or Polish or German, and who held to different customs. She always tried to do as he wished, although sometimes, smiling, she had to confess that the Patriarch had already accompanied her to this salutary convocation or that. And Nicholas would then laugh unabashed, and remark that if she would only do as she was told they would make her, between them, the first lady Patriarch in Christendom.

She understood, she thought, what occasioned these explorations. She understood the insatiable curiosity which penetrated far beyond everyday life. She understood the hunger to share it. But after her first visit to the Caffa medrese when, crosslegged in muffling robes, she listened in silence to the teachings of a man she did not know, in a language in which she was not expert, she refused, gently, to accede to Nicholas's infatuation with the imam they called Ibrahiim. But when he challenged her, next, to visit the Greeks in their enclave, she did so as willingly, if only once, because later, he would talk to her. She thought that he needed to talk.

She was not sorry, however, when the fishing expedition was mooted, although she was amazed (although not quite as transfixed as Nicholas) when the Patriarch of Antioch elected to join it. There was some sense in the casual exodus. The dispute over the next Tartar Governor of Caffa was becoming daily more serious and, having done what they could, outsiders should now stand aside. As for the gold, nothing could happen until Ochoa's ship came in the spring. And if by any chance, said Nicholas smiling, Ochoa managed to sail under the ice into Caffa, he knew he could depend upon Anna to act for them both.

She had returned the smile with a freedom never seen by her noble Hanseyck kinsmen, who thought it ill-bred to show any emotion, far less happiness. Now, she took pleasure in observing her moods reflected in Nicholas's pensive grey eyes. This winter, she had set herself to know him, and every day taught her more of the cast of his mind, at once bright and dark, and never simple. The eloquent voice of the imam, the harmonious chant of the Koran readers, had meant little to her compared with the physical profile of Nicholas listening: the heavy, black-bearded heel of his jaw; the substantial cheek; the thin, contradictory nose with its quaintly fastidious nostril; the rounded lips sheltering one another; the stark, unwavering gaze. She remembered the same open gaze resting on her. But then the lips had parted a little, as he drew breath.

When, leaving the medrese, he had talked to her of what they had heard, she had at first fallen silent, rather than confess that it was not the teaching that had absorbed her, but his interest in the imam, connected as it must be with his past in West Africa, and Umar, the jurist and friend who had died there. Yet when, at length, she asked him frankly about it, he had not mentioned Timbuktu in his answer, although he hesitated a moment, as if examining the question in his own mind. 'Why should I concern myself with Muslim philosophy? Do you never wonder why you choose one course of action in place of another? My divining seems to tell me that however much I strive, the future cannot be altered. And I don't wish to believe that.'

And 'Why not?' she had said. 'If it is true, it relieves us of great responsibilities. But do we not always follow our desires, whatever punishment threatens in this world or the next?'

'Not always,' he said. 'Surely, one learns from one's errors. One learns, whether from fear or from conscience, that there are other people in the world who deserve to live out their lives, whatever their failings.'

'Such as the people of Scotland?' she had dared to say, softly. And when he bent his head, she had added, 'And do you need an imam, Nicholas, to tell you how to make peace with yourself? To remind you what part of your boyhood your mistakes, your agonising, your conscience all spring from? Nicholas, how did your mother die?'

He had risen, and she had thought for a moment that he might reply. But he had said only, 'Not today. But the next time you ask, I shall tell you.' Then, a few days after that, he had left.

For Nicholas himself, the expedition that took him from Caffa was a strange adventure: an interregnum quite different from the hearty, drunken escapades with Paúel Benecke, although he was not always sober, and often quite as close to risking his life. It had more in common with Iceland, but with no shuddering springs, and with Ludovico da Bologna in place of Katla and Hekla. Kathi and Robin were also missing, having business of a more adult and permanent nature to prosecute, a long way away.

It was the climate, of course, which reminded him. The unusual winter, bringing stinging rain and wet snow even to the palmy shores of the Crim, had frozen the steppes of the north and iced its rivers, so that, in place of mud-swaddled oxen, canopied sledges skimmed over the whiteness, swallowing space as if it were smoke. He had seen them burst through the sunlight of morning in a dazzle of spume; men and sledges and horses encrusted with sparkling frost; beards and manes sheathed and flashing like mirrors.

He had heard tales of the fishing here since he was an apprentice in Bruges: seamen's accounts of the mythical four-hundredweight sturgeon of the River Yaik, forging up from the Caspian to breed; and of the beluga eighteen feet long, white as veal, sweet as marrow, that could hardly be carried by thirty strong men from the Dnieper. In the spring, men would launch boats to spear them, and to gather in carp and pike, bream and chub as they swarmed to their nets. In winter, as now, the fishing was done from holes hewn in the ice by men who travelled in caravans of powerful sledges, with the great frozen rivers their highway.

The tales of these were cautionary too: of unskilled steering which could overturn horse and sledge on clear ice; of the fights between rival fishermen, and the chance attacks from war-bands of Tartars, come to unearth the salt and caviare buried under the snow, and — timber-starved — to burst apart the boxes, the barrels, the temporary shacks and take them away to make houses and wagons.

With Dymitr Wiśniowiecki there was not much fear of that, although the sledges carried weapons, as well as twenty men and their servants, food and drink and utensils, fuel and stoves, and their fishing and hunting equipment, with their spare horses and dogs running beside. To a man of Dymitr's race, the frozen marshes and steppes to the north were familiar ground, and his practices were already half Tartar. His had not been the inept party which, travelling from Moscow, had lost Anna her furs — although, like his fellow merchants, he was the poorer for it.

No one troubled to speak of that; there was no time. Already, exploring the country, Nicholas had found his way to some of its rivers, and to the channel which led from the sterile Black Sea to the vast stretch of the Sea of Azov, Palus Maeotis: so rich in fish that both Venice and Genoa had chosen to command it from its northernmost point, where the walled double city of Tana lay on the banks of the Don. But Nicholas knew it only from the soft time of the year, when the Genoese ships crowded the havens, ready to enter and cross the Black Sea with their cargoes of fish and honey and furs, and the traffic in slaves was at its height. The traffic which, of course, Ochoa de Marchena was engaged in.

No ships moved now, but there was life on the steppes: elk and deer and high-leaping wild sheep to be shot, and fat birds to fall to their falcons, and later shrivel and brown on the spit. They ate as they travelled, as Tartars did, until they came to the fish: then they gorged as they worked on mighty salmon, cooked in the gloss of near-life, with the curd thick as cream between the pink flakes of flesh. And of course they wrestled, and roared out their ballads, and flung themselves into violent, joint-wrenching dances, howling over the wheeze of the pipes (they had learned a dirty song about bagpipes) and the twang of someone's chipped, eight-stringed lute. And naturally, they drank. But it reminded Nicholas of that other country in the north because among the badinage, the talk was not without purpose: it was concerned with the land and its bounty, and the ways of the people who lived on the land. And at night, round the crackling blue fire in the makeshift shelters they found or created, they would fall silent and listen to the ruminative, rumbling voice of the elderly priest from Bologna, who passed the days enthroned like Perun on his sledge, chewing meat and bellowing orders, but brought to the lit circle at night stories such as even they had never heard, for he had been further than any of them and seen, it seemed, all that there was to see.

And even though the servants crowded in, and the chance might seem irresistible, Ludovico da Bologna said nothing at all of either the Latin church or the Orthodox one they belonged to; only rattled off, at bedtime, the routine benediction you would expect from any master at the close of the day. But if a man asked to see him apart, he would take him off silently, and he would bind a wound, testily, or set a leg if he had to, striking the man if he yelled without cause. After they had been away for ten days, someone asked him about Roman practices. He replied in three sentences, but showed no anxiety to continue, although he would consider a question if asked. Some days after that, Nicholas sought him out.

'So this is how you do it?'

'What?' The Patriarch, in the process of going to bed, wore two robes over two pairs of quilted trousers and boots made of horse-hide lined with bear fur. His blanket, which was also his cloak, was a vast and noisome collage of black sheepskins, which he was currently binding himself into with rope. He showed no interest in Nicholas. He had shown intense interest in the account Nicholas had given him of Mengli-Girey and Abdan Khan and Brother Lorenzo. He was responsible, very likely, for the appearance of the imam Ibrahiim in the Crimea. He showed no curiosity whatever about Nicholas's spiritual condition, which, of course, suited Nicholas very well.

Nicholas said, 'So this is how you go fishing.'

'It depends,' the Patriarch said, 'upon whether I'm after sturgeon or anchovies. I hear you've found a taste for profound theological issues since you started travelling from Poland. If your divining scares you so much, why not stop it?'

'Anna has been to see you?' Nicholas said. Extreme irritation filled him once more. His hands were in gloves, and far too cold to show weals. He didn't know how the old man could have noticed.

The Patriarch's bulbous features creased. 'I told her you weren't even an anchovy. Anyway, what advice could I give you that Cardinal Bessarion didn't?'

His voice was prosaic, delivering a truth with no trace of false modesty. If he knew of that grave, private meeting in France three summers before, he knew that Nicholas had already heard, at first hand, the finest Christian teaching from the dying Bessarion, the Greek who had devoted his life to reconciling the Latin and Orthodox churches. It had not, of course, saved him from any of his blunders. Nicholas said, 'I'm sure Anna will think of something. I hear you meet quite a lot.'

'She worries,' said Father Ludovico. 'I told her to start praying for Caffa, not you. The Genoese are pressing the Khan to refuse to keep Eminek as Tudun. They say Eminek holds secret talks with the Turks.'

'He probably does,' Nicholas said.

The Patriarch sat down on his mat. 'Dear Lord, of course they all do, Mengli-Girey included. They're not fools: they need to sound out the enemy, otherwise they'll never know when to change sides. Fortunately, Turkey isn't much interested in the Crimea: the Sultan's just sent his stepmother to Venice to ask for a truce, which of course — if he gets it — will let him rest and regroup so that he can attack the Venetians in Crete in the summer.'

'You think so?' Nicholas said.

'Venice expects it. They've diverted to Crete all the artillery they promised Uzum. But that is next summer. The present issue is whether Mengli-Girey will now succeed in appointing your clever friend Karaï, or whether he'll be forced to agree to the idiot Sertak. Have they been giving you trouble?'

'The Genoese? Squarciafico brought me in twice for questioning, but Anna invites him to rich German suppers and he goes away mollified. So what are your plans?'

'The same,' the Patriarch said. 'You and I can't do more than we have. We're leaving for Persia as soon as the weather allows. The end of next month, if we're lucky. That is, you are still coming, with the lady Contessa?'

'Oh yes,' Nicholas said with conviction. He supposed he was coming. It was part of his self-imposed task, to provide mercantile outlets for Anna and Julius and he was aware that, with gold to spend, Anna was planning to accompany him. Also, his conscience told him, inconveniently, that he owed something to both Uzum Hasan and the Patriarch. He added aloud, 'Anna should have her furs soon. Sinbaldo will look after the business while she is away, and Julius, if he arrives. Unless Julius wants to follow us to Tabriz.'

'He'd be too late. Uzum Hasan may not be at Tabriz,' the Patriarch said. 'One of his sons staged a revolt in the south, and Uzum marched his troops down to Shiraz. He's spending the winter at Qom surrounded by desperate Venetian envoys, waiting to find out whether he's going to make war on his sons or the Turk. I want to know, too, so you and the lady can expect a long trip to wherever they are if you want to do business. Unless, of course, you'd rather go back to the West. What about this man Ochoa and your gold?'

'Leave Ochoa to me,' Nicholas said. 'I am not tempted to go back, and I am not tempted to send for my family. Perhaps you can convince Anna of that, since I can't.'

'Oh, I believe you,' the Patriarch said. 'But your army might join you now of their own accord. I hear they share Julius's forgiving nature. And the war over Cologne appears extraordinarily confused.'

Nicholas stood up. 'Have you sent for them?'

'I thought of it, but without a letter from you, they wouldn't move. I still think you should invite them to Persia. You'd enjoy playing patron again. Would you put the candle out as you go? And take that with you. You really shouldn't leave it lying about.'

'Nikita!' someone bawled from outside. Dymitr, anxious to gamble.

Nicholas looked from the priest, indistinguishable from the sheepskin that wrapped him, to the object to which he referred. He said, 'Where did you get it?'

'In your tent,' said the old ruffian blandly. 'If Dymitr had seen it, he would have started to wonder.'

Staring at him, Nicholas swore under his breath. Then, snuffing the candle, he rammed the object under his cloak and left the shelter. Behind him, Father Ludovico pronounced a small benediction from his sheepskin. Nicholas crossed to his tent, then joined the others in the big wattle cabin for a night of gaming and drinking and trials of strength. When at length he was free to retire, he sat for a while alone in the light of his candle before he rose to take something out of his purse, and to pick up and bring back the article that Ludovico da Bologna had borrowed.

Unrolled, it revealed itself to be a broad-brimmed straw hat, swathed in ribbons and attached to a streamer of chiffon. He held it on his knee with one hand, while he took the cord of his pendulum in the other. It began to circle almost at once.

He left the camp at first light the next day, to the baffled displeasure of Wiśniowiecki, and a complacent silence on the part of the Patriarch. Then, with four strongly armed men and spare horses, Nicholas de Fleury set off on the long sledge ride back to the Peninsula. And this time, gliding over the sparkling wastes, he was seized with a mindless and untrammelled pleasure, born of the joys of the present and the promise of what lay ahead. To the alarm of his companions, he sang.

IN WINTER, no one ever approached Soldaia unseen: the waterlogged valleys behind were impassable, and the precipitous routes by the coast were too few. As for the sea, nothing moved in the bay or the river-mouth without being watched from the fortress. Nicomack ibn Abdallah was therefore observed, as he approached the town walls, having long since sent back first his sledge, then his escort. There was, however, no reason to spurn a Mameluke steward from Caffa, properly arrived before curfew, and the gate-keepers allowed him to enter, with his single horse and his saddlebag. These days, Caffa and Soldaia were both licensed Genoese towns, with only a day's ride between them in summer. They had a long enough history. The uncle of Marco Polo had had a house here.

Nicholas had been in Soldaia before. He had even climbed the landward slope to the separate city, the vast sea-cliff domain, encircled by towers and walls, which contained the Genoese garrison and their servants. But this time, he had come on purely family business: being invited to visit his cousin, who lived with his Egyptian wife in the leafy quarter of the Muslim slave-traders. He had no cousin, but it was still a clever device: Genoese merchants made half their profit from slaves, and the consul seldom troubled this district. It was why Ochoa had chosen it, and described it accurately in the message he sent.

Ochoa was not yet here. There was no trace in this simple white house, with its luxurious furnishings, of the Spanish pirate whom Nicholas had hired long ago to help him buy African gold, and who later had been waylaid by the Knights of St John and captured with all his precious cargo. The Knights, friends of Genoa, had forced Ochoa de Marchena to work for them in Rhodes, until he escaped. Venturing into Soldaia now, he risked recapture and hanging.

'Yet, for Messer Niccolò of Bruges, he would do it,' explained the unknown Circassian cousin, a handsome, well-nourished man in his forties. Reclining at ease on the floor, he waved Nicholas to another pile of deep cushions. 'I am to hear as soon as he comes, upon which he desired me to call you from Caffa. But you say you suspect he is coming already?' He accepted a cup from his wife, a dark-eyed nymph veiled like Salome, who came, stooping, to offer another to Nicholas. He smiled at her, answering.

'I thought it best to come early in case. Since I had cause to visit the Khan, the Treasurer and his friends interest themselves in my movements.'

The girl, who had half risen, stopped, but composed herself when the Circassian spoke to her soothingly. After she had slipped from the room, he turned to Nicholas. 'That strutting cock of a Squarciafico!'

Nicholas gazed at his cup. 'It is an old family, as you know. They have administered Chios and Caffa as long as the Genoese ruled there.'

'And think every native their whore! A Squarciafico calls with his friend on a Tartar and, drawing aside the man's wife, he pulls out her breast for his companion to finger. Then, when her husband has gone, he sits himself down and bids the wife search his underlinen for lice, which, kneeling, she does, with all the respect she has been taught. It has happened. My wife knows of such a case.'

'Franks bring wealth,' Nicholas said.

'So do the Circassian Mamelukes in Egypt,' his host said. 'And competent rule for a time. Then comes insolence, and its fellow, revolt, and next, a new master is welcomed, because he offers wealth with respect. For a time.'

'Your imam does not preach revolt,' Nicholas said. 'In the medreses of Soldaia or Caffa.'

'The scholar Ibrahiim? He says the same of your friend, the Frankish priest, the Pope's envoy. He says he asks men to look for the truth, and what is best for their country as well as their souls. Otherwise you would not be here. Everyone with friends in the Maghgrib knows Ochoa, but we do not all do as he asks.'

'I am beholden,' said Nicholas.

Word came in two days. No shipmaster came to the house. Instead Nicholas, mildly resistant, was given into the hands of a servant and, blindfolded at night, was pulled up and down steep muddy alleys and finally thrust through a low doorway and left.

The atmosphere, warmly rank, was familiar and, when you thought of it, not so surprising: Ochoa de Marchena spent a long time at sea. Nicholas said aloud, 'Well, have you got two for me? Or do we have to make do with each other?' And the next moment his eyes had been freed and, embraced by his shipmaster, he was being led into an empty room in the best seafront brothel in Soldaia.

Nicholas had been almost twenty-four years of age when he had hired a Spanish pirate at Lagos in Portugal, and placed him in charge of the *Ghost*, one of the little fleet of two ships with which he had sailed down the west coast of Africa. With Gelis. With Bel. With Diniz. With the priest Godscalc, now dead, whose dream had been to reach Ethiopia, but who had not been equipped with the brutal qualities of a Ludovico da Bologna.

In ten years, Ochoa had hardly altered at all. The pock-marked face, toothless, elastic as wax, was pleated into the same patterns of joyous enthusiasm; the black eyes snapped; the voice swooped; the hands, relieving Nicholas of his outer clothing, probed the new-crusted scars and the plentiful corrugations of the old ones. 'And they said you were a banker, my dear!'

'The girls find it exciting,' said Nicholas. He viewed the captain. 'What about you?'

Ochoa cast a glance at his clothing. 'The wool cap, the sheepskin, the boots? The merest expediency, in crossing from Bielogrod. Let me once get to my boxes, and you will soon see the old Ochoa.'

'I am pleased enough to see the new one,' Nicholas said.

He let the interview set its own pace, putting ten years of experience into the handling of it. To an ebullient free spirit like Ochoa, subservience to the Knights of St John had been embarrassing. He had, Nicholas deduced, made several unsuccessful attempts to escape before at last winning his present precarious freedom. Plied with rich food and wine, paid for by Nicholas, he found his greatest satisfaction at first in relating the successes of the past years: the conquests he had made for the Knights, but also the happy occasions on which he had totally misled that worthy Christian foundation, to their detriment. No one mentioned gold.

Some time later, further fortified, the captain had progressed to boasting of his recent adventure with the Sicilian mercenaries on the Dniester, when King Stephen had achieved a great victory over the Turks, with the consequence to Mánkup which Señor Niccolò would of course know.

Nicholas was waiting, with patience, to hear of his gold. Instead, he found himself learning of an upheaval in Mánkup, the mountain fortress of Isáac of Gothia, in whom the shadow of the empire of Trebizond persisted still. But Stephen, King of Moldavia, was building his own empire on the west coast of the Black Sea and, friend of Poland and arch-enemy of the Turks, was suspicious of Isaac.

'Of course, the lovely prince Isáac was exchanging sweet messages with the Turks — who is not? — but King Stephen, a nervous man, apparently thought that he was about to surrender. Such a hot-head! At any rate, he sent Isáac's brother Aleksandre to Mánkup with my friends, the three hundred Sicilians (one of them was my cousin). Aleksandre obligingly murdered his brother and will now rule as prince in his place. Gothia is secure from the Turks. Are you pleased?'

'Not especially. What happened to Abdan Khan?'

'Isáac's Circassian general? He survived. They need him. The mountain Mamelukes were all trained in Cairo, and share the Sultan's hatred of Turkey. Anyway, you should be pleased. Your Ochoa is here, because his friends helped him to cross the Peninsula. And now you will hear what I have done for you.'

They had been speaking before in Italian. Now, for safety, Ochoa turned mostly to Spanish. It was the story Nicholas had already received, in gist, through Brother Lorenzo. At the end, Nicholas stared at him thoughtfully. 'Of course, you should never have allowed yourself to be captured by the Knights in the first place. All you had to do was sail home with my gold. Slovenly seamanship . . .'

Ochoa jumped to his feet, his bared gums a short seam in their gusset. 'I told you! The storm!'

'And then all those years working for them before you actually managed to escape and make the effort to find me. But since you did, I owe you something,' Nicholas said. 'Even though you would have walked off with the extra had you been able to. How did you persuade the Knights that they had everything?'

'I am very persuasive,' said Ochoa. 'And so how much do you owe me?'

'Your wages, I suppose. As for the gold, I have to get it yet,' Nicholas said. 'And as you tell me yourself, nothing can be done until the seas open. The trouble is, I have to travel south with the Patriarch next month.'

'And the pretty woman?' said the shipmaster. 'I hear about the pretty woman. But surely you will go and get the gold first? You know I cannot do it.' He brightened suddenly. 'Perhaps the pretty woman could get it. She and I, while you go south.'

'Her name is the Gräfin von Hanseyck,' Nicholas said. 'And she is someone else's pretty woman. Do I take it, then, that you are going to stay here until spring?'

'Why, it is kind of you to suggest it,' said Ochoa. 'It is a little expensive, but there might be somewhere cheaper nearby, and it would be worth the outlay to you, I am sure. I could ask my cousin, but then he would insist on sharing the gold, which would only spoil him.'

He could never keep a straight face with Ochoa. 'But it wouldn't spoil you?' Nicholas said. 'What will you do with your share? When I have decided, that is, what it will be.'

The toothless face expressed exaggerated surprise. 'But what you and Paúeli decided. A third each, and the use of the *Peter*.'

'Wait a moment,' Nicholas said. 'Paúeli? Paúel Benecke? I made no arrangement with him. I wasted a whole bloody winter trying to get him to say where you were, and the bastard sailed off without telling me. I'd never have known, except that his daughter wanted to spite him, and told someone.' He stopped and drew breath. 'You've been talking to Benecke?'

'We communicate,' said the Spaniard coldly. 'Yes, he sails the vulgar Baltic, where a real seaman prefers the great Middle Sea, but there are rivers between. Messages pass. I am Catalan; I do not always sail galleys; I know the Western Ocean as your friend Crackbene does; as you do. We all know that the Portuguese hold on the gold trade has weakened. With the *Peter* there is nothing we could not do, given the gold to finance the voyage.'

'To Africa,' Nicholas said.

'You are slow,' Ochoa said. 'The love nest with the pretty woman has made you slow. I tell you, keep to your plan. Go back to Caffa tomorrow. But excuse yourself from your trip to the south. Collect the gold. And then put it to use. What better way is there to spend the rest of your life than at sea, in a venture with seamen?'

'I see,' Nicholas said. He fell into silence. Ochoa drank, occasionally missing his mouth with the flask. Muffled, from behind the closed door came the somersaulting notes of a guitar, and high voices giggling, and the occasional hoarse shout.

Nicholas said, 'There is a month to decide. I have to go back to Caffa, but I shall pay for your keep in Soldaia, or wherever you think you will be safe. If and when I go for the gold, I shall tell you.'

'My dear, of course,' said Ochoa de Marchena. 'For if anything were to go wrong, our friend Paúeli would be very distressed. Now let us consider the details.'

They considered the details. It did not take long, and it was Ochoa's idea to celebrate the occasion by calling upon the house's resources.

'Girls. Or boys. Or both together, if you wish. Come. Unless you have been mating with elk, you must have a mighty hunger to satisfy. Consider the young Tartar wenches — so modest, so lissom! They have this delightful practice: a gentleman sits, and they kneel, and then —'

'I can imagine. What must it be like with two or three? Here. Purchase what you want, and there is my purse for your keep. I must go,' Nicholas said. 'I suppose I have to find my own way back to the trading-quarter? Why all the precautions?'

'I did not know,' said Ochoa simply, 'whether the Niccolò that Benecke told me of would be the same crazy young señor that I knew. But as soon as I saw your bruises, I knew that it was.'

TWO DAYS LATER, after long absence, Nicholas set open the door of his parlour in Caffa to find Anna alone and in tears, cradling a frayed, loving note from her daughter. A moment later and, somehow, she was fast in his arms.

Chapter 24

OCHOA HAD BEEN RIGHT: it had been a long time since Nicholas had touched a woman of his own kind. Closing his arms about Anna had been an instinctive gesture of comfort. But then what had been distant was transformed into light, yielding substance, scented and warm, and all his senses awoke with a shiver. For a moment, they held each other unmoving; he felt her hands spread at his shoulder and waist and, looking down at her profile, saw the tears below the closed eyes. Then her brow creased, and she loosed herself from his embrace, but instead sought his right hand and clasped it tightly.

She said, 'I have been so afraid. Come and sit by me.' And kept his hand as they sat close together, his free arm laid in a sheltering way along the wood of the settle behind her. She said, 'You didn't come home. The Patriarch said you left by yourself. I was afraid they had killed you.'

'The bears?' Nicholas said. Her lips were quivering.

She made an attempt at a smile. 'Worse than that. Nicholas, have you not heard? Did you not see the change at the gates?'

It was safe to say that he had observed the change at the gates. The guard had not wished to let him through, and he had been stopped several times in the streets. There were soldiers everywhere. By now, he also had a good idea of the reason, but he let her tell him. He had been fishing, and she had steered the business alone through an upheaval that might well have wrecked it.

For, it seemed, the Khan Mengli-Girey had not persuaded the Genoese to appoint the Tudun he wanted. Politely, he had agreed to discard the possibly traitorous Eminek. He had even agreed, a very special concession, to ride down from his snowy mountain to Caffa and attend the installation of Eminek's successor. The outrage occurred when it was discovered: the Khan proposed that the successor should be his secretary, the noble Karaï Mirza.

'Of course, the Genoese had been bribed to appoint the widow's son Sertak, and they forced the Khan in the end to agree. But it was ugly, Nicholas, for a while, and they are still suspicious of anyone who has had to do with the Khan or, of course, with Karaï Mirza. They questioned Sinbaldo, and came here to talk about the business. I thought I had persuaded them to leave us alone when —' She stopped.

'What?' Nicholas said. 'The Genoese are your friends. They won't harm you. And I can look after myself. What frightened you?'

Her face was pale, looking up at him. 'The furs came,' Anna said.

'All the furs that you and Julius were owed? But that is wonderful!' Nicholas said.

'More than we were owed. An ox-cart full. Ermines, martens, sables, everything. A surplus more than we could ever pay for if it wasn't a gift. If it wasn't a bribe from the Khan, made possible by his friendship with Moscow and Mánkup.'

'A bribe to do what?' Nicholas said. He rose quickly. 'Look, I'm going to give you some wine. It's all right. They can't prove we did anything.'

'They think we did,' Anna said. 'They think the Khan gave us silver to buy support for Karaï Mirza, and that the furs are our reward. I told them they were wrong. So did the Patriarch, when he came back.'

'Well, that ought to convince them,' said Nicholas. 'At least it can be proved that you had nothing to do with it. If they have to blame someone, it'll be me. Do you know why the Khan agreed to give up so easily? After all, he is the lord of the Crim Horde.'

Anna put down the cup he had given her. Colour had returned to her cheeks. She said, 'Mengli-Girey's worst enemies are two older brothers who wanted to rule in his place. The Genoese threatened to release them from prison, unless the Khan appointed the Tudun they wanted. Nicholas, where have you been?'

He smiled. 'Fishing,' he said. 'And just as well, perhaps, although it left you to bear all the brunt of this nonsense. Fishing, and visiting Soldaia. Can you guess why?'

Her eyes flamed. 'Nicholas!' And then, as her eye fell on the pendulum that he held in his hand: 'The gold is here! You divined it! That is why you came back?'

He sat down, and touched his cup to hers. 'Because of the gold. It isn't here yet, but I did see Ochoa, and have paid him something, at least. Now we have to wait until ships can sail.'

'And then it will come here, or to Soldaia? Where is it coming from?'

'I don't know. Neither does Ochoa. That is why he couldn't trace it without me. I have to divine when it is coming.'

'But why? Who has it, if not Ochoa? Is it safe?'

'He assures me it is. The Knights were hounding him: he had to lay a false trail. But it is coming. For you and for Julius. For us all.'

'For us all? Does Ochoa approve of your plans for it?' Anna asked.

Nicholas refilled her cup. 'He doesn't know. He wants me to invest in a new expedition to Africa with himself and Paúel Benecke.'

'But you won't?' Anna said. 'Shall I tell you why I was weeping when you came in? Why especially I was weeping, after all the anxiety?'

He said, 'I saw it was a letter from Bonne. You would have told me if it were bad news. So you are homesick, and wish to go back?'

'Not when Julius is coming,' she said. 'But yes, I was homesick and yes, I miss my little daughter, as you must lie awake, missing Jodi. Do you know that Gelis went to see Bonne?'

'Gelis?' he said.

'She was at Neuss, not far away. She was so kind, Bonne said. She spoke of Jodi . . . Nicholas, send for your wife. She needs you. You must long for her, and your son. And I know what it is like, to dress for no one, to smile for no one, never to touch, or to caress. You may pay for your pleasure, but it cannot be the same. And I do not have even that.'

'What are you asking?' Nicholas said.

She was weeping again. She said, 'To let me sit like this, with my head on your shoulder.'

But it was not enough, for after a while she spoke again, her voice blurred, her hand like a stranger's, guiding his. 'Nicholas, help me.'

HE DID NOT see her next morning, being much occupied with the business that had accumulated in his absence, and with reacquainting himself with the city and its gossip. As soon as he returned, Anna asked him to receive her.

It was formally done, and she stood in front of him in his office as a client might have done, rather than a mistress. She was again very pale. She said, 'I thought you might have left for another house. I am grateful that you have stayed. I wished to make you my apologies, and to tell you that I now know, if I ever doubted it, what a staunch friend Julius has. I shall be eternally ashamed that I asked, and I shall be eternally grateful that you walked out of the room.'

There was a long pause. Then Nicholas said, 'Any other man would have remained. But I shot Julius.'

Their eyes held. Anna said, 'Then do you still want to work for him? With me? We should keep together, for safety.'

'Of course. It never happened. And if we are careful, all will be well. Leave it to me,' Nicholas said.

. . .

HE THOUGHT at the time that he could control it all. He thought so up to the moment next day when he was taking stock in Sinbaldo's fur warehouse and the Patriarch's secretary trotted up, fell off his mule and, forgetting all prudence, cried 'Signor Niccolò! Signor Niccolò! Come quickly!' Then he added his news.

Ochoa had been captured.

No one had heard Brother Orazio's words. Pulled into the warehouse, he recounted his story, shaken by whooping fur-induced coughs. Listening, surrounded by deep, lustrous pelts, Nicholas suddenly discovered a seething hatred of fur, especially sleek fur in exotic colours: smoke and silver and black, cream and tortoiseshell, orange and butter.

Ochoa had been surprised in his lodging and taken. He was in the Genoese fortress at Soldaia, accused of piracy and theft. The Patriarch was on his way there already to provide Christian solace.

Nicholas spoke to Sinbaldo. He took Orazio back to the house, merely to collect a packbag and horses, and leave a message for Anna. Anna was already there, barring his way, ordering the grooms to forbid him the stables. 'You are not to go. They will kill you. They are suspicious already.'

Her Genoese gossips had told her. She was ashen. All she felt showed itself, in essence, as anger. It would serve no purpose to show her his own.

'Do you think I would leave him?' Nicholas said. 'And really, you underrate my ingenuity.'

'You are not going. You are not going. Nicholas, I forbid you to go. I know Ochoa once was a friend. I know how you feel about Africa, and all who remind you of it. But he has had his life, and made little of it, and you are at the threshold of yours. Nicholas, leave it to the Patriarch. He will do what he can.'

'He doesn't seem over-confident,' Nicholas said. 'He has sent Brother Orazio for me.'

'Then he is a fool, or he doesn't realise the risks you would run.' Her frowning eyes, scanning his face, opened suddenly. 'Or perhaps the Patriarch knows of the gold?'

Despite himself, Nicholas smiled. 'Father Ludovico, plotting to appropriate funds for the Church? No. I think your first guess was right. He doesn't know they suspect me of anything. He simply knows that Ochoa has served me, and thinks I should help him in trouble. I think so, too.'

The frowning eyes returned to his face. 'They may imprison you, also. They may find out who you are.'

'Then I shall have to explain myself,' he said. 'And you mustn't try to extract me. This doesn't involve you or the Patriarch. I shall swear that I deceived you both, too.' He paused. 'Anna, I know you don't want me to go. But you really can't stop me.'

They looked at one another. Her eyes softened. She said, 'Then I shan't try. He is part of your past. You must love him.'

'With that stupid, toothless face and those hats? I don't care if he hangs from the ribbons,' Nicholas said. 'But I'd rather he didn't buy a reprieve by telling them all about me and our gold.'

He smiled at her again. He felt sick.

On the way to Soldaia he hardly spoke, although Brother Orazio rode anxiously at his side, glancing at him now and then. When they arrived at the gates, it did not greatly astonish Nicholas to find that all the other travellers from Caffa were received through the portals before him, or that Brother Orazio was invited to pass through on his own. The monk, unexpectedly stubborn, stood objecting in the vernacular of Ferrara, until Nicholas, with a small, fierce signal, made him desist.

Once he was alone, there came a time when Nicholas objected as well, if in a somewhat token way, since he had no weapons, and was one man against a special detachment from the Genoese garrison. Presently the soldiers, becoming tired of the argument, simply wrestled him to the ground and kicked him until his voice stopped.

IN THE MONASTERY of Montello, a nobleman died. Because he had lived there for a long time, the funeral mass was carried out in every particular as he had wanted, even to the inclusion of that type of impassioned liturgy which the Abbot personally despised. No relatives were present, or indeed invited; but afterwards the vicomte's possessions were gathered and laid in four chests by Brother Huon, whose silent grief, in defiance of the Divine Purpose, drew a rebuke from the Abbot. Brother Huon did penance, and in due course, the chests were sent off.

FURTHER WEST, Gelis van Borselen spent the early months of the year commuting between Ghent and the west bank of the Rhine, with frequent visits to Bruges. For a space, her private concerns became almost manageable, as most of her thoughts and all her skills were required by the Bank: to commend its resources and its fighting force to Duke Charles through the Duchess, while steering a far-sighted course over loans, as distinct from the flamboyantly short-sighted course that, sooner or later, was going to ruin Tommaso Portinari.

No one could deny that the money was needed. The town of Neuss was still holding out, while the evil combination of the Swiss Federation and its allies was continually engaging Burgundian forces elsewhere, to irritating cries of *Berne and St Vincent!* Worse than that, the largest German army for centuries was marching through rain, wind, snow and hail down the right bank of the Rhine towards Linz, after which it proposed to enforce an entry of the True Defender into the capital of the diocese, Cologne.

Also, the Duke of Burgundy had promised to supply six thousand men to help his brother-in-law the monarch of England reconquer France in the summer, his reward being the return of the Somme towns and a few other substantial concessions. Captain Astorre had looked forward to being reserved for this purpose, until it was brought home to him (and to England) that the invasion of France appeared temporarily to have slipped the Duke's mind.

During that winter, Gelis grew accustomed to the tirades of Astorre and le Grant against the Duke and his shortcomings, and sometimes even joined the debate: the arguments, surprisingly enjoyable, relieved their feelings and added another dimension to her education. Since December, her letters to Mistress Clémence in Scotland had begun to include promptings about finding a proper governor for Jodi: one who, in the absence of his father, could also instruct him in arms. Gelis believed, but did not say, that military proficiency would be of advantage to any man working with Clémence. The exception being, of course, Dr Tobias.

Gelis had written to Tobie on certain other matters, and he had replied. She had also spoken, when in Bruges, to Father Moriz on those same other matters. She had even gone out of her way, sojourning in Neuss and in Ghent, to question merchant barons and wealthy mercenaries who, for one reason or another, had been employed in the past by German princes. At times, she felt that this was none of her business. At other times, she would have agreed that there are certain apprehensions no amount of distraction can shift, and that action, even deluded action, may ease them.

She received a letter from Nicholas.

It was the first direct communication between them for over a year, and it had been several months on its way. It reached her in Neuss, plainly sealed, but she knew the handwriting as well as her own. She laid it on her lap and sat for a long time, looking at it, before she pared it open slowly and carefully, as if it might bleed. Inside were two pages, covered on both sides with lines, widely spaced, in the same writing. From beginning to end, it was in code.

So, nothing personal. Not, in that case, a signal that he was pining for company, or about to break the unwritten covenant and return. Not a message to Jodi. A matter of business. A business communication so intriguing, it seemed, that he had not used the company code, but a variant personally known to them both. And he had presumably sent her the message for the simple reason that she could decipher it.

Or so she thought at first. After she had written it all out in clear, and paused in staggered deference to its contents, she understood that Nicholas had other understandable motives: that as before, he was passing information to her because she represented the Bank, and could act on it to the Bank's benefit. In this instance, there was nothing at present to act on: the company was being informed of an enterprise, and warned to stand by for news, that was all. As she had anticipated, there were no greetings to her or to Jodi; no mention of Anna or Julius, nothing of Caffa or his new life. It might have been addressed to Diniz, Moriz or Govaerts, John or Gregorio, had they been able to decipher the code. Her instructions were to tell John and Moriz, but no one else until she heard further. He thought that might take until April.

April. April, and spring.

After a while, she did what he had once done and, taking a candle, touched the flame to the papers. Upholding the rectangle of light, she looked for the last time at the completed work: at her writing alternating with his: writer speaking to writer. It was not accidental. It was why, unusually, he had spaced out his lines. She imagined him preparing to write, head in hand, and pausing as the trivial idea occurred. She felt she recognised the ultimate obstinacy, the vulnerability even, which had led him to sink his quill in the ink, and proceed with it. And there was something else to be noticed. Belatedly, with an immense burst of surprise, she grasped that Nicholas had sent this letter to her direct: that he had returned to his hated medium at last, in order to trace her.

The burning pages blackened and dropped. Gelis crushed them with a sure hand, and put the ashes away, keeping nothing. Then she went to find John le Grant, walking scrupulously, like a prisoner taking the air.

IN CYPRUS, the treasurer of the monastery of St Catherine's, Mount Sinai, newly returned from the Crimea, visited his fellow monks in the Karpass and then travelled south, in order to sail to the Syrian coast. On his way, he made certain calls, although with difficulty, since the Venetians, who now controlled Cyprus, preferred the Latin church to the Greek; and the Queen's uncle Marco Corner owned the largest sugar concession outside that of the Knights of St John. They were, of course, a capable family. Another Marco Corner had once been in prison in Tabriz.

As a result of his travels, Brother Lorenzo sent two letters, one by fast boat to Alexandria and the other to the director of what was still called the Banco di Niccolò in Venice who would, he understood, pass on the unfortunate news in private to Bruges. He also compiled a report, which he hoped to deliver in person, advising the Sultan at Cairo of the condition of the Arab and Muslim population of the Crimea, with particular reference to the Mamelukes. Then he returned to his abbot.

IN SCOTLAND, the boy called Jordan de Fleury attained his sixth birthday in the absence of his father, whom he had not seen for fourteen months, and his mother, whom he had not seen for three.

Although occasionally querulous, Jodi was not gravely disturbed by their defection, having at his side the formidable person of Mistress Clémence his nurse, who had been with him since birth, and the reassuringly irritable attentions of Dr Tobias his physician, who tended to be wherever Mistress Clémence was. It further added to his sense of security that he was living in exactly the same house in the Canongate, Edinburgh, once owned by his father, with the difference that it was now part of the Berecrofts assembly of lodgings and offices. Best of all, his friend Robin, who once used to live next door, now occupied the same building with Katelijne his wife, who had grown very fat and who, Jodi had repeatedly been told, was expecting a baby.

Jodi kept out of her way. In his view, when the baby saw how fat the lady was, it would leave. He had been afraid that Robin would leave. The biggest gift he was to have for his birthday, arranged by his mother and Robin, was a regular master-at-arms to give him lessons. Master Cuthbert would not, of course, be with him all the time, as he taught other people. The baby, however, was bound to be impressed.

THE CARE DEVOTED to the upbringing of the de Fleury child did not escape the notice of the merchants of Edinburgh, none of whom knew the reason for its father's departure, despite intensive questioning of the Berecrofts family, including Kathi Sersanders and her brother. No one had been quite blate enough to quiz Anselm Adorne himself, the lass's uncle, when he made a brief visit to Scotland, seeing to his lands and his duties as Conservator of the Scots Privileges in Bruges. And whether a body spoke out with his questions or not, he never got any answers, devil take it. Even Will Roger, the King's own musician, got his neb near nippit off by the puggie-faced doctor with the bald heid. Nicholas de Fleury was establishing a new business with some papal nuncio east of the Baltic. No one could say when he'd be back.

Not even Will Roger, who loved Nicholas and did his best to spoil his son, knew that he was not coming back. And of those who did know, only perhaps Dr Tobias recognised that in the rearing of Jodi, they were collectively compensating for a ridiculous feeling of guilt, and for the vacuum left in their lives by his father.

The exception to all this remained Adorne. His sickening visit to Poland had, it seemed, given him no reason to like Nicholas any better, or to condone what he had done. He would not comment on what had happened to Julius. He was kind to Jodi, as he would be to any child, but no more. On his single Scottish foray, he had been absent much of the time at the Priory of Haddington, where he had business with the Prioress, a doughty exporter, and reacquainted himself with the noble inhabitants, nuns and lay persons. He had also spent some time travelling to Perth, where his nephew Sersanders had established a corner as merchant and agent. Then he returned to Bruges, a quieter, happier man, despite being wrenched away before his niece's delivery. When December ended, and Kathi's baby had still not been born, Anselm Adorne took the unwise if natural step of dispatching to Scotland his own distinguished physician, Dr Andreas.

Katelijne Sersanders, nine months pregnant, sat breathing heavily while being told of her uncle's solicitous gesture, and then sent for Dr Tobias and Mistress Clémence to attend her at once. When they did so, she closed the door, resumed her lodgement on a greatly quelled cushion and said, 'All right. Dr Andreas is coming. What are you going to tell him?'

'That we don't need another doctor,' Tobie snapped. Mistress Clémence cast her eyes upwards.

'He knows that,' said Kathi patiently. 'My uncle doesn't, but Andreas does. I'll tell you why he is coming. Because he's an astrologer. Because he's inquisitive. Because, even, he's got wind of what you and I and Gelis are doing, and would like to know more. In which case, do you think we should tell him?'

'No,' said Tobie.

'Um,' said the nurse. Tobie looked at her, astonished.

'I thought it might be Um,' said Kathi, with a kind of fond irritation. 'Suppose you both go off and discuss it? It's time you reached some sort of decision. But don't take too long, or you'll have to explain to more than one of us.' The door closed, and Kathi took up her sewing and dropped it, casting about for a while before she discovered it on her lap.

In Mistress Clémence's parlour, Tobie took one or two turns while Clémence stood, in her composed way, and watched him. Tobie came to a halt. 'Those letters from Gelis are private. You and I know what's in them, and Kathi. But it isn't Andreas's affair. I don't think we should tell him.'

'Probably not,' Mistress Clémence remarked. Within the closely pinned linen, her plain face was remarkably placid.

'Then what else,' Tobie said, 'are we supposed to be talking about?' He had reddened.

'We don't seem to be talking about anything,' Clémence said, in the same friendly way. 'Unless I give you a hint. Dr Andreas has a close friend in France. Her home is in Blois, near Coulanges, and he visits her regularly.'

Mistress Clémence came from Coulanges. 'He knows your family? You never said.' Tobie, frowning, dragged off his cap. The lateral puffs of faded hair stood in disarray. Mistress Clémence, looking at them, stirred as if moved to delve in her apron. She desisted.

Unexpectedly, Tobie laughed. He said, 'Your comb has Jodi's name on it. You mean that there is gossip, and Andreas will have heard it, or may spread it? Gossip about you and me?'

'And Master Nicholas,' Clémence said. 'We are all bound together. Certainly, there are some things Dr Andreas had better not know, but there are others he must.'

'But we are talking about you and me,' Tobie said. When narrowly trained, his gaze, of a very pale blue, appeared shrewish in its intensity. Three feet separated them. Of the two, she was a little the taller and, surprisingly, very much younger.

She said, 'I suppose so. The case history by now is quite extensive. It may be time for a diagnosis.'

Her self-command, added to a touch of amusement, steadied him. He took out his handkerchief, waited, and sneezed into it neatly. Then he put it away. 'Very well. First, the facts of the case. The patient is forty-four years of age, of a choleric disposition, with a rude past and a record of transient commerce.'

'None of it promising,' Clémence said thoughtfully. She brightened a little. 'He has shown himself, in recent times, capable of a certain constancy. But perhaps appearances are misleading?'

'In this case, no,' Tobie said. 'But with age, there is observable a certain timidity, a fear of change, a fear of causing disappointment, and inviting it. Every man wishes to act the child for part of his life. But —'

'Many of them do, for all of it,' said Clémence de Coulanges. 'For myself, I am fond of children, but prefer to spend my leisure with adults. No child has ever been as important to me as a grown man or woman could be.'

He scanned her face: the straight Gallic nose, the sallow skin, the black, shining studs of her eyes. The air of calm domination, which might equally stem from a fierce independence. 'You do not give that impression,' he said. 'Of being interested in adults. In men.'

'Then it is not surprising,' she said, 'if, without the facts, you have reached a wrong diagnosis. I have had lovers. But none since we met.'

She was smiling: a half-teasing, remembering smile he had caught on her face now and then, but had not understood. He felt a great, a staggering amazement. He felt an idiot. He said, 'I wanted . . . I wondered . . . But there was Jodi, and Gelis. I didn't know how to tell her.'

Clémence laughed aloud. 'Gelis guessed long before you did. And what do you suppose Kathi has sent us to do?'

And then he, too, was catching his breath in something like laughter as, his robe and her apron confused, he set the tilt of her head with one hand, and used the other to trace, like a gratified father, the contours of brow, temple and cheek. 'Why,' he said, 'to find out, at last, what colour of hair my wife has.'

But he still had not found out when he kissed her; and after that, did not care.

LATER, WHEN THE HOUSEHOLD had been told and the celebrations were over, Katelijne set aside her weariness and asked Tobie to stay.

Opening the door of her room, he had no qualms about his reception, for she had already expressed her delight. As Clémence had hinted, the news of their betrothal had astonished nobody, any more than the fact that a reputable Italian physician was to marry a French-speaking Burgundian who worked for her living. Clémence might be without parents or dowry, but she was an educated member of a seigneurial family. And since her appointment by Gelis six years ago, she had kept her employer's household in order as discreetly as she had seen to the rearing of Jodi.

Soon, of course, that would end, although Clémence did not wish to marry immediately. But in another year, Nicholas's son would be seven, and ready to move into a masculine world. Already, embarrassed, Tobie realised that Gelis had planned for it. A maidservant, a tutor, a master-at-arms would replace the loving nursery of the past. Or would not replace it, for he and Clémence would be near at hand. While there was a Flemish company, he wanted to serve it. He had already told Kathi so.

They knew each other very well, the bald doctor and Adorne's young Flemish niece who had shared a journey to Egypt five years ago. Watching him cross to her now, Kathi flung wide her arms in a renewed fit of delight. 'Will you be annoyed if I say that this is right for you, as Robin is for me? I am so glad for you.' Then she sat back, memory jarred.

He said, 'What?' He was her doctor.

'Nicholas said that in Poland. Great minds.'

'He was so glad? About Robin?'

'About me. About nothing. It was only important because for six words at least, he stopped acting.' She paused. 'He sent me some balm. Balm from Sinai, to keep for the christening. One anonymous seal; one signature, Nicholas. I gave a little to Haddington.' Her smile became pursed.

'Kathi?' he said. 'What is it? The reports about Anna? Is it so bad that Gelis can find out nothing about her from Germany? She married into high station, and if her origins were obscure, then she and her husband may have decided to leave them so. We know she did marry the Graf, and he never denied that Bonne was his child. She fell in love with Julius and made up a tale to impress him, but what of it? If she wasn't wealthy, he was. She has all the Graf's friends. And there is no doubt that it is a good marriage.'

'No. I know,' Kathi said. 'And I know, I think, how Gelis feels. Nicholas has tried to make some amends, and it's tempting to throw him a lifeline. Gelis wants to believe Anna can help him. His bastardy isn't important, but you all want to attach him to some sort of substitute family. That was really why you went to Montello, after Anna told us about Thibault de Fleury.'

She stopped.

'So were we wrong?' Tobie said. He thought that no one but Kathi, in all the discomfort and anguish of an over-long pregnancy, would be addressing herself to the emotional problems of a contrary bastard with a penchant for numbers.

'No, you were right; but there were repercussions. While we were spying on Anna, she was experiencing them. Thibault sent a message to Caffa, to Nicholas. Anna has written to tell me what happened.'

'Oh,' said Tobie. His mind performed a lightning review, partnered heavily by his stomach. He said, 'It sounds as if we shouldn't have gone to Montello. I thought it was harmless.'

'Of course you had to go,' Kathi said. 'And Anna thought it was harmless, or she wouldn't have told me in the first place. That's why she's upset about Nicholas. She doesn't even say what his grandfather wrote. She just says it was all a mistake, and she wants Gelis to come. She sounds frightened.'

'Of Nicholas?' Tobie said. *Damn the man*. Damn the man and his immature appetites. One should settle down some time.

Kathi looked at him. 'You expect Nicholas to live like a monk? But no, not afraid of him, but for him. Whatever the letter said, Nicholas took it badly. Anna says he locked himself into his room.'

'With a bottle,' said Tobie uneasily.

'She says she broke into his chamber, it worried her so. His brazier was reeking with drugs.'

They looked at one another. Tobie swore, and forgot to apologise.

Kathi said, 'From all you say of the vicomte, I'm sure there was nothing unkind in his letter. It was just the fact that it had arrived, and too late.'

'So should we tell Gelis?' Tobie said. He didn't suggest Gelis should join Anna and Julius and Nicholas and whatever Nicholas was burning on his brazier. He agreed, on the whole, that Nicholas should be expected to reconstitute himself without help. It didn't rule out temporary help, unless it resigned.

'No,' said Kathi. 'But I think we should tell Gelis not to try to investigate any more. No matter who Anna is, she is good for Nicholas, and we shouldn't discredit her. And equally, Gelis should break off the search for this nun Thibault mentioned. The best news for Nicholas would be final proof that he was born outside marriage. It is virtually proved. We should leave it.'

'I agree,' Tobie said. He spoke slowly, for he was not sure if he meant it.

She said suddenly, 'But still, I don't like it. Why isn't the Patriarch helping? Why should Anna have to deal with all this alone?'

Damn the man indeed. Tobie said carelessly, 'No, I don't like it either, but Anna's better at this than the Patriarch. She can manage Nicholas. And it won't be for long. Julius will be there in the spring. He and Anna will leave, and Nicholas will settle down and become Khan of Caffa. He might even discover his gold. No one mentions the gold?'

'Don't cheer me up,' Kathi said.

'All right, I won't,' Tobie said. 'When are you planning to give birth? June's a nice month.'

Dr Andreas of Vesalia, arriving in the same month of January, hired some horses at Leith and, chatting all the way, as was his wont, presented himself at the Berecrofts house, once the Banco di Niccolò, in the Canongate. By then, he was not surprised to find the door at the stairhead wide open, and the inner rooms packed with the rosy faces and thick, fancy headgear of merchants, accompanied by their chirruping wives. Among the many faces he knew was that of the man of the house, Robin of Berecrofts, his fair hair dark with sweat, his eyes brilliant. He called Dr Andreas's name, and lifted over a cup.

'Your heir is born?' Dr Andreas cried. Across the room, he glimpsed the scarlet face, matching his robe, of his fellow physician Tobias. Tobie waved. From the insouciant nature of the wave, Dr Andreas deduced that the mother was well, and that the child was born, separated, bathed, swaddled and fed, and probably at least a day old. Following the father out of the room, Dr Andreas treated himself to an impolite sigh. Horoscopes required to be exact, and wine-clouded memories seldom yielded the desirable details. But he was an ex–royal physician, a (reasonably) responsible doctor of Bruges, who had long performed services for the family of Anselm Adorne, and he had a very warm spot indeed for the young niece, Adorne's pleasingly quick-witted Kathi.

Dr Andreas stepped into the maternal chamber and viewed with interest the large, expensive draped bed, rosily illuminated by the flames from an even more expensive stone hearth installed by the previous owner, whose recipe for fertility, as it happened, had been presented to his wife in this very same room, in unfortunate circumstances.

Within the bed, staring eye to eye with a baby, was the diminutive form of Katelijne Sersanders, her hair brushed neatly over her temporary bosom and her forearms supporting the child. Below its clothes, the infant's legs hung like short tallow candles, and the back of its cranium resembled a bun. The girl's expression was thoughtful.

Robin said, 'Here is Dr Andreas.' His wife's eyes turned, and she smiled. A six-year-old boy turned as well and, jumping down from the bed-step, ran to Robin while shouting to Dr Andreas, whom he knew. Robin swung him up in his arms.

'It didn't come!' screamed Jodi de Fleury, red with pleasure. 'The boy she was expecting didn't come! Look! They sent a girl-baby instead!'

'Jodi,' said Robin.

'Well, he's right,' Kathi said. 'You can't deny that he hasn't got it just right. But all the same . . .' Reversing her hands, she turned the morsel in a satisfied way to face outwards. 'All the same, I don't think it's a bad try for beginners. What do you think, Dr Andreas?'

Its legs, pigeon-toed, still hung like short tallow candles. Its face resembled a fig. 'Delightful,' he said. 'Truly delightful.'

'Oh, I shouldn't go as far as that,' Kathi said; and she and her husband hooted with laughter while the six-year-old kicked to be put down.

A nurse arrived, and Dr Andreas laid forth his gifts and retreated. The door closed on the parents. Behind it, although it was hard to be certain, they seemed to be arguing over the pitch of the child's cry at birth.

Later, Dr Tobie worked his way to his side. 'Childish, were they? It's just relief. Adorne lost a son. Those two wouldn't admit it, but it was a girl they both hoped for. It's to be called after Adorne's wife. Must you do them a horoscope?'

'Why not?' the astrologer asked.

'I don't know,' Tobie said. 'But they seem to have had bad luck enough, all of them. I'd like Fate to forget them for a while. I'd like that little maid Margaret of Berecrofts to lay her own mark on the future.'

'As she will. As we all do,' Andreas said.

Chapter 25

PRISONERS IN THE Genoese citadel of Soldaia were normally kept in the Governor's castle, a group of lofty, rectangular buildings, segregated by walls, that cut the sky at the upper edge of the vast, sprawling arena — a second town — which accommodated the garrison. The crag upon which all this was built plummeted sheer to the sea on the Governor's side, and on the other descended towards town and river in a series of precipitous humps and steep channels.

The view from the keep was dramatic. Provided you were unbruised and unbound and fully in your right senses, you could survey the entire sweep of the dark, sandy bay with its crowded jetties, and the civilian town lying inland, and the low ranges of hills, with strange schisty outcrops further off. Between houses and hills lay a broad, fertile expanse, currently covered with slush, but yielding in summer wheat and grapes and grazing aplenty. A paradise in summer, was the Crimea — and even in winter, in a normal year.

To Nicholas de Fleury, who was not having a normal year, the view was not visible, although he knew that it was there: that if he stood in the free air on the battlements he would see the whole garrison town laid out sloping before him, with its barracks and workshops and market, its churches and mosque, its cisterns and storehouses and armoury, and the circuit of its great striding walls with their massive towers, one for each Governor whose pleasure and duty it was, in the year of his office, to build one. One such bulwark, not far from the great drawbridge entrance, bore the arms of Prosper Adorno, Doge of the city of Genoa. Kinsman, naturally, of Anselm Adorne. There was no escape from one's friends.

At that point, lying on a hard pallet with his limbs aching and his eyes stuck shut with blood, Nicholas remembered what he was here for, and laughed.

'Ah. Misra Niqula,' remarked someone in the smooth, mellifluous

Arabic of the schools. 'Allah has been pleased to wake thee at last. Give thanks to the Lord, and Mohammed His Prophet.'

Imam Ibrahiim. Nicholas opened his eyes.

The room was small, but it was not precisely a cell. It was furnished. The imam, seated bearded and grave on his cushions, was indeed the man he had first met at the Russians' in the company of Karaï Mirza. The man who had brought him a missive from Brother Lorenzo, and to whom he had listened many times since; once, with Anna. There was, however, a guard, standing inside the door.

The imam continued, this time using passable Italian. 'I am glad, of course, that you came, for I have only Maghgribian Spanish, and cannot always comprehend Señor Ochoa. But it was stupid of you not to explain, and they were quite within their rights to beat you. Wash yourself. It is nearly the hour for prayer. Then I shall take you to the Governor, who wishes to interrogate the prisoner. You will interpret.'

'I am ashamed, lord. I value your advice,' Nicholas said. There was a place to wash; he found a decent tunic from his pack, and he was given a prayer-mat. His pack, of course, had been searched. Pressing his brow to the ground made his head and eyes throb, but he had done this a thousand times, and no one could fault his performance. His mind, now working again, told him that he was witnessing some form of collusion between the imam and Ludovico da Bologna. In his disguise as a Mameluke, Nicholas had no claim on the time of a Latin Patriarch. The imam, on the other hand, was already holding classes in the medrese, and had every excuse to call on the faithful in the little mosque that served the garrison servants. His Spanish, limited though it was, would ensure that he was sought out. And from there, it was a simple step to suggest Donna Anna's Mameluke steward, who spoke such excellent Catalan from his days of North African trading, and could even translate into the everyday language of Genoa.

It was a pity that no one had had time to tell him before he arrived. It was even more of a pity that no one had informed the guard at the gates, who seemed to have been carrying out quite contrary orders. It seemed to Nicholas that Anna had been right; that the Genoese, made increasingly suspicious by his visit to Qirq-yer, his familiarity with the Russians and the arrival of the furs, had issued orders to arrest him if he returned to Soldaia. And that someone else, or even two people, had belatedly convinced the commander that his credentials were better than they seemed, and that he held some sort of brief as an interpreter. Which meant he would gain access to Ochoa. Which meant, with any luck, that he could help Ochoa to escape. He had to.

The imam said, 'Such devotion deserves its rewards but I think, my son, that the Governor awaits us.' And Nicholas rose creakily from his knees and followed him out of the room.

Ochoa, when he limped into the commander's office, looked the way Nicholas felt, with a suffused eye and a lot of rags here and there with dried blood on them. He was not wearing one of his hats, but a common seaman's woollen cap, jammed on, nevertheless, with panache. His lips were pursed, stretching his rubbery skin into chasms and awnings between the short bones of his face. At sight of Nicholas, his gums made a hole.

Nicholas muttered. The imam, hearing him, replied sharply in Arabic. The Governor, a youngish man in a smart feathered hat and engraved cuirass, said, 'What? You will kindly speak Genoese in this room.'

The imam bowed. 'Lord, excuse us. The man Nicomack was complaining that the size of his fee had not been discussed. I have told him that it is sufficient for him, a Mameluke servant, to do his utmost to please you. I have said that, if he interprets with skill, I am sure your lordship will be liberal.'

'And if he does not, he will suffer for it,' said the Governor. He looked at Nicholas. 'I want you to question this dog. Ask him whether he is not Ochoa de Marchena, former seamaster and pirate, escaped from lifetime service to the Knights Hospitaller of St John at Rhodes. Ask, if he denies it, what is his business in Soldaia, and why was he hiding. Ask who helped him come to Soldaia. Ask the name of his master.'

There was a pause.

'*Well?*' said the Governor.

'Lord. I am sorry, lord. But I cannot remember so many questions,' said Nicholas piteously; and jumped as the Governor brought his stick down with a crack.

'Why am I surrounded by idiots? An interpreter who is a fool, and a criminal who cannot understand simple Italian. How did the Knights communicate with you?' demanded the Commander.

Ochoa de Marchena, who spoke seven languages, gazed at him helplessly. Nicholas, ranging himself hurriedly on the side of authority, translated the question into Catalan and repeated it loudly in faithful copy of the commander's bullying tone. It contained a little addendum in the same language. 'You stupid bastard, how did they trace you? How do you suppose we can get you out?'

Ochoa glared at him. The volley of Catalan, when it came, nearly overturned his own vocabulary. Nicholas turned to the Governor. 'There is a Spanish Langue, and Spanish sailors on Rhodes. He asks how many tongues the Governor has.'

'He asks for a flogging,' said the Governor. 'Put the questions.'

What followed represented, in its macabre way, the funniest piece of theatre for which Nicholas had ever invented a script, with Ochoa de Marchena, of the scowling, toothless face and ferocious invention, as his unreliable partner. The Governor, slightly pink, put the questions.

Nicholas, having no need to translate them, put a number of questions of his own in convoluted Spanish to Ochoa, adding, as the fancy took him, some convenient insults. Ochoa replied with equally unseemly comments about Nicholas, about the Governor, and about the individual soldiers of the garrison who had incurred his displeasure. He dispensed, at intervals, nuggets of information about the routine of the garrison and the exact disposition of his cell. He expressed the opinion that Nicholas would have made a mess of lifting Moses out of his basket, and might as well go back to his pretty woman and leave Ochoa to escape on his own, which he could in the blink of an eye if someone would slip him a knife. Nicholas said irritably that he didn't have a knife, and Ochoa was to do nothing at all until he heard from him.

To the Governor, who was understandably keen to take some share in this torrent of Spanish, Nicholas reported that the man said he was not Ochoa de Marchena but a man who took orders for parrots; that he had just crossed the Straits of Kerch on a camel, but the camel had died, and so had his parrots, and he had been forced to conceal himself from his creditors. As soon as spring came, he would travel back to Seville and return with a fresh batch of birds.

'And if he has no money, how does he pay for this travel?' asked the Governor.

'He awaits friends,' Nicholas explained, at the end of a tirade. He hoped Ochoa was listening. 'He has two friends arriving soon in Soldaia. They will vouch for him, and they bring money, he says. He says he has committed no crime, but would be prepared to give you or your family a free parrot, when he returns.'

'Is this true?' the Governor said.

The imam said nothing. Ochoa said (in Catalan), 'Is the poor man expected to believe this? Could you not have invented something more likely? Parrots! My darling Nicholas, I would sell you a slave, but a parrot?'

'You'd sell me your mother, and she would be a parrot,' said Nicholas. And switching to Genoese: 'Lord, it seems to be true. Ask this man anything about parrots, and he will tell you. What do they eat, when do they lay, how do you teach them to speak. His mother and his mother's mother kept parrots. Ask anything.'

'Bastard!' said Ochoa. 'My life hangs in the balance, and I am to talk about parrots?'

'What does he say?' said the Governor.

'Alas!' Nicholas said. 'He mourns his dead birds, his camel. He says the Genoese may as well take his life. He wishes to leave his hats to his friends. They will be here in two weeks. The friends. If I may use my lord's paper, I shall write down their names.'

Ochoa peered. 'You have spelled that one wrongly,' he said. For once, he looked impressed.

Nicholas glared at him and handed the names of the prisoner's friends to the Governor. They were, so far as he could remember, those of two of the highest commanders in the Order of St John.

The Governor said, 'A man who takes orders for parrots? How can he know people such as these?'

'Did I say he only sells parrots, lord?' Nicholas said. 'He sells parrots. He travels. He spies for the Knights. I suppose they will not be happy to learn that he is here, a condemned prisoner.'

'He is lying,' said the Governor.

'It is possible, my lord,' Nicholas said. 'In two weeks, one will know.'

He looked at Ochoa. The Governor, silent, was thinking. Ochoa's lips, drawing back, revealed the smile he didn't have. It reached to his ears. Then with the greatest delicacy, he spat. 'That's a promise,' he said. 'Get me out. Get yourself out. And then we're going off together. You and me and Paúli — no one would touch us.'

'No one would want to,' said Nicholas with distaste, and watched the guards, summoned, come forward and propel Ochoa, with a blow, to the door. His voice, imitating a parrot, faded into the distance, syncopated by the cuffs of his handlers.

The imam said, 'I am expected at the mosque. Will there be further interrogations? Do you wish this man to remain?'

They required Nicomack ibn Abdallah to remain. He was given a pallet, and found, to his embarrassment, that the jurist was to share the small chamber. Between then and nightfall, the hilarity of the episode faded. Once he and imam Ibrahiim were alone, Nicholas apologised. 'You incurred danger, lending yourself to this scheme, and Ochoa and I acted like children.'

'It is his nature, you can see that. It is perhaps why you are drawn to him. He behaved thus when you first met?'

'Wilful, crazy, respectful of no one. He deserved to be caught by the Genoese.'

'Well, you have bought him two weeks: the Governor will do nothing until these problematical great gentlemen arrive. Do they exist?'

'Oh, yes. But so far as I know, they are in Rhodes,' Nicholas said, 'and have no intention of coming to the Crimea. I shall have got him out before then. With all that information, I can hardly fail. But you must leave first.'

'Perhaps. You are not afraid for yourself?' the imam said. 'For you, as for Señor Ochoa, this is sport?'

'I suppose it is,' Nicholas said. He saw the imam was already in bed, and put his own candle out. Darkness fell.

'You are not, then, afraid of death?' continued the musical voice, in its courtly Arabic. 'But only of discussing it. Yet it is a worthy thing, to contemplate one's end with tranquillity; without recoil, and equally without pusillanimous eagerness. It is less meritorious to be unable to accept the dying of others. In that case, it is our own loss we dread, or we mourn.'

'We may be so selfish,' Nicholas said. 'But may we not also mourn the loss to others — to friends, family, even the world, of someone cut off at the height of his powers?'

'We may feel sorrow, of course,' said the imam. 'But there are many such, and we cannot spend our lives in impassioned grief for them all. Your St Bernard allowed human grief, but preached Christian forbearance. The Stoics respected their consolers. And even the anguish of personal loss is relieved by the passage of time. If it does not diminish, if it still cannot be spoken about, then it has not been confronted, it has not been given the exorcism through pain that is its due. And that, my son, is an insult to the person who has perished. *You are in paradise,* you say to the loved one. *You are in paradise, but how dare you leave me!*'

'And when children die?' Nicholas said.

'Ah, the unfulfilled lives! The young, gone to the other world in their blond childhood! How much ink, how much agony has been lavished on these! Why do you ask me, a Muslim, when you have heard the philosophers; when you have read the urging of Cicero, who wrote that destiny is unavoidable, and often cruel, but that it is the task of human beings to conquer?'

He paused. 'Niqula, you ask me questions to which you already know all the possible answers. You are not untaught. You have heard these matters debated many times, in many countries, in many voices. You have read. You have listened to some of the wisest men of the age. Yet you clutch your ills to your heart; you will not submit to the light of reason what is troubling you. No man can hope to find purpose until he is at peace with his past.'

'I see,' said Nicholas, 'that I owe something to Ludovico da Bologna.'

'Not, certainly, his courage,' the imam said.

Nicholas fell silent. Presently, in the darkness, he allowed himself a wry rebuttal. 'I am talking to you.'

The imam's voice held no levity. 'As you talked, I am told, to the Cardinal Bessarion. How angry you will be when I, too, meet my death,' said imam Ibrahiim. 'But it will excuse you from thinking. Until your excellent intelligence awakes once again, and you are driven again to seek advice, and again find yourself prevented, by your delicate sensibilities, from taking it. I am wasting my breath,' said the imam.

The silence that followed was long. Then Nicholas said, 'You are probably right.'

And this time, the imam forbore to reply; perhaps because he distinguished in a man, in the darkness, what an angry doctor had once glimpsed in a boy.

OBERTO SQUARCIAFICO, the consul's Treasurer, arrived the following day. The disturbance of it echoed from the great vaulted fort of the gate through all the sloping ways of the fortress, interrupting the blows of the armourer, the roar of the market, the staccato commands from the exercise ground. There were twenty armed men trotting uphill behind him.

Afterwards, it was seen to be no coincidence that the renegade Mameluke steward was in the garrison mosque, cynically inviting Allah to preserve his black soul while the Governor's murderous Spanish prisoner staged his escape, as if the presence of the lord Squarciafico in the citadel would provide a distraction. But, of course, the soldiers of the citadel of Soldaia were far from fools, and the alarm was raised even while the man was skulking in the crowd, incompetently disguised in the tattered high-buttoned tunic and trousers of a Muslim servant, with a felt cap over his hair and a scarf wrapped about his miserable mouth. The renegade, called to the steps of the mosque by the uproar, was therefore able to witness the pirate Ochoa de Marchena start from the grasp of his captors and set off between the buildings, fast as a monkey, until the whole hill-top had been alerted to the chase, and there was no way out for him but the ladders which led to the heights of the buttress nearest to him.

One would never know what was in the lunatic's head: whether he thought he could climb to the outward wall and descend somehow into the chasm beyond. At any rate, he was not given the chance, for he had not reached the second storey when someone with a ready-strung bow aimed and shot the little brute clean through the eye. He hung for a while, and then dropped.

Nicholas saw it. So, crowding behind him, did his fellow worshippers from the mosque, and the imam. Nicholas said, without looking round at any one person, *'Get back, and leave.'* Then he walked down the steps.

So great was the blow, he hardly knew what he was doing. Because of him Ochoa was dead: the happy insouciant scoundrel who had trusted him with his life. Nicholas could not imagine why, after all the hilarious, meticulous planning, the captain should have made this inept dash, but he scented treachery somewhere. The Genoese, among others, wanted rid of Ochoa. Nicholas should have foreseen it. He knew Ochoa. He knew that, had it been possible to purloin the gold for himself, Ochoa would have done it — but that was not the point. Nicholas should have protected him. He should have done something.

There was nothing he could have done.

Nicholas did not, at the time, give much thought to himself. The imam and the Papal Nuncio between them had apparently passed him off as Ochoa's interpreter, and this had been accepted. He might be questioned about Ochoa's escape, but he could hardly be blamed for it, or so he thought. He was conscious, at the back of his mind, that a danger of another kind might be hovering, but he could not bring himself to dwell on it. Despite recent lectures, he was beginning to wonder if anything mattered.

He was prepared, therefore, to be met by soldiers as soon as he set foot on the ground, and to be hustled up the long incline into the keep, with inquisitive faces around him. He was less prepared, entering the Governor's room, to find himself in the crippling grasp of two guards who, thrusting him forward, cast him headlong at the feet of the Governor, with Oberto Squarciafico at his side.

There was no doubt which held the higher authority. Regardless of his wayward hair, his indolent gaze and his slender build, the Bank of St George's fiscal agent Squarciafico belonged to the family of empire-builders and lechers who, along with the Adorno, administered the Genoese rule on the island of Chios. Twenty years ago, a namesake had voted to increase the taxes on Chios. Over a century ago, the galley of Meliaduc Adorno had helped capture the island for Genoa, just as Genoa had captured Famagusta, and a Contarini's ships had been sent to take Caffa. The tower from which Ochoa had fallen had borne the name of Adorno. Every country, every race took what it could. Only, some ruled better than others.

Nicholas fell to his knees, as a frightened Mameluke interpreter should. He mumbled something.

'What?' said Squarciafico with contempt.

'The man says,' offered the Governor, 'that he understands his services are no longer required, and he will therefore be content with a small fee.'

'Indeed,' said his superior slowly. He lifted his eyes to the guard. 'In that case, we should show equal magnanimity. Give this person a seat.'

The soldier he addressed, looking taken aback, lifted a stool and placed it at the Saracen's dishevelled shoulder. Nicholas scrambled up and sat, his neck bent. Despite his indifference, his nape pricked.

'And perhaps, before leaving, he will take some refreshment?' the musical voice continued reflectively. 'Wine, we understand, is not allowed. But a sweetmeat? I am told they are delicious.'

Now, not only his nape pricked but everything about Nicholas insisted on danger. He said, 'Lord,' and lifted his head.

Before him was a salver in the hands of a servant. And upon the salver was an open box of exactly the delicacy which the Genoese had described. A variety of pale-coloured sweetmeats: candied fruits, to be quite precise. A luxury which a Mameluke steward would rarely be offered, unless by a doting mistress, or a client initiating a bribe.

Nicholas said, 'My lord, it is too much. I am quite content to take my fee.'

'But we are pleased with you,' Squarciafico said. 'We should take offence if you do not allow us to show it. Let me see you eat a handful. Now.'

Nicholas sat very still. 'My lord, my religion does not allow.'

'I was afraid of that,' said Squarciafico cheerfully. 'So, see, I have asked your imam to come and reassure you. Master Ibrahiim, there is no rule against sweetmeats?'

They had indeed sent for the jurist. He stood, his face grave, and looked at them all, his gaze falling last upon Nicholas. He said, 'I know of no reason why these may not be eaten, if your servant desires. I do not know his medical condition.'

'Surely,' said Squarciafico, with gentle amusement, 'there is no medical condition that precludes eating candied fruits? For the last time, my man. Take and eat, if you please.'

'I cannot,' said Nicholas.

'Then shall we make you?' said the Genoese sweetly. And stepping forward, he seized Nicholas suddenly by the hair and, scooping a handful of fruits, dragged his head back and made to force his lips open.

Nicholas twisted aside. Against his thrust arm, the whole box tilted and fell, scattering sugar over the floor. Two of the soldiers wrenched him back and dragged his hands behind his back while Squarciafico, lifting his palm, delivered a blow to the side of his face. A third soldier, his eyes on the glistening delicacies, stepped forward as if he would collect them.

Squarciafico laughed. 'Lift them up if you like. But don't lick your fingers after, and above all, my friends, don't think to eat them. Or you will suffer what our friend here and his dead accomplice came to inflict on someone else.'

He turned to the Governor. 'Why do you think the man de Marchena contrived to be captured and brought here in the first place? Why should this man trouble to come and interpret for him? They both wished to enter the citadel. They wished to find their way to the prisons. These sweetmeats, these singular Trapezuntine, Gothian sweetmeats, were to be offered to the two brothers of Mengli-Girey. Had they been eaten, the

Khan of Qirq-yer could flout us all as he pleased, for his older brothers, his rivals would be dead and could no longer oust him. They would be dead, because these fruits are poisoned. And this man would not eat, for he knew it.'

And that, at least, was true, Nicholas thought. He had known, because he had seen them before, these pretty sweets, which he might so easily have obtained, but had not, from Abdan Khan, the Circassian general. *Will this food harm me?* He had not needed the pendulum, this time, to warn him.

Someone had been very clever and yet, surprisingly, not clever enough. He felt not sick but suddenly mortally tired. He did not even listen to what Squarciafico was saying. He thought, gratefully, that at least the imam was safe. When they took him from the room, he expected that they would kill him immediately. Then the clamour of voices rose behind him, and someone shouted angrily, and he was stopped, and held where he stood at the top of the stairs. But by then he knew what had happened, for he had heard Anna's voice.

Chapter 26

ANNA WAS THERE when they brought him back to the Governor's room, in her anger more commanding than he had ever seen her before. And Squarciafico, standing before her, exhibited below his overt annoyance a shadow of something else which might have been discomfiture.

She glanced at Nicholas once, an assessing glance such as any mistress would bestow on her property, and then returned her gaze to Squarciafico and the Governor standing before her.

'Do I hear aright? I permit my servant to come and help you with some pitiful difficulty over a prisoner; the prisoner escapes, and rather than admit to ineptitude, you attempt to implicate an unfortunate Muslim? Offending, of course, the whole race on which you will depend to agree to your choice of Tudun?'

'We have explained,' said Squarciafico. 'The poisoned sweetmeats . . .'

'You have explained. Your explanation is ludicrous. Was or was not this man searched when he arrived at Soldaia? No such sweetmeats were found. Was his pack not searched for a second time, here in the citadel? I am told that it was, and again, no sweetmeats were found.'

'Then why,' said Squarciafico swiftly, 'did he refuse to eat them?'

She could not answer that. She turned to Nicholas. Her eyes were storm-dark and anguished.

Nicholas said, 'Because, lord, I had seen such sweetmeats before, on a voyage to Alexandria. They originated in Trebizond, from where the formula seems to have travelled to Gothia. A boy died after stealing and eating them.'

'A fabrication,' said Squarciafico.

'There were witnesses,' Nicholas said. 'Of high degree — two of them Genoese, of the family of Adorno. If my lord will allow, my lady could send for their statements.'

'And on that occasion,' Squarciafico said, 'who was attempting to poison whom?'

'I am a Mameluke,' Nicholas said. 'There was trouble at that time between the Venetians and the Mamelukes on Cyprus. I should not malign them, but there is a connection between the Corner family and Trebizond.'

Everyone knew what that was. He saw Anna's face alter. The Treasurer said, 'And the fact that the Spanish prisoner was wearing your clothes, and bore in his possession a note written by you, detailing the plans for his escape?'

'The note is not mine. As for the clothes, I discarded them, lord, as soon as I arrived in the citadel. I never saw them again. I had no opportunity to pass them to de Marchena. I did not know him. I cannot tell why he believed I would help him, except that he would seize any chance to escape. In humility, lord,' said Nicholas, his eyes on the floor, 'I fear I am being made scapegoat for a killing which the Knights of St John will take badly, since it deprives them of one of the best seamen of his day. The man need not have been shot.'

There was a silence.

'Well?' said Anna.

Squarciafico stirred. 'Madonna, I am sorry. We have given you and this man a hearing, but these are serious matters. It is not clear, even now, who is at fault.'

'It is clear to me,' Anna said. 'It will be clear to the papal nuncio, under whose protection I travelled to Caffa. This man has served me loyally and well. He went to Qirq-yer at my desire, not his own. The negotiations he has undertaken on behalf of my company will bring prosperity to Caffa and to the Genoese both here and at home. He has no acquaintance with the dead prisoner, and no interest in him beyond that of the service he was asked to perform for which, I understand, he has not even been paid. Is he now to die because of a rumour?'

'The accusation is serious,' Squarciafico said again. 'We cannot ignore it, madonna.'

'Nor can you put him to death without trial,' Anna said. 'He has offered you witnesses. I have told you that your suspicions are baseless. Surrender him back to my keeping, and I will stand surety for him. Otherwise, I shall surely complain to a higher authority.'

They stood facing one another, the aristocratic Genoese and the fine-featured German Contessa. She had dressed for the journey as if attending a feast, in a high-waisted gown more ornate than any she normally wore, and her finest girdle and brooch. The loop of her headdress contrasted with the white of her brow, and its veil softened the jewels with which it was sewn. They were, Nicholas knew, all she had. They were to have paid for her return from Caffa if all else had failed. But he had saved her from that.

Squarciafico did not look at the jewels. He spoke instead, his eyes fixed on hers. 'Contessa, it is not within my powers to release a possible spy. He cannot continue to live in this colony. He must stand trial, or leave.'

There was a little silence. 'Or leave? But we are not leaving till spring,' Anna said.

'Madonna, I should ask no lady to travel in winter. But a man, a Circassian Mameluke accustomed to hardship, would surely survive. I trust to have the pleasure of your company for many weeks still to come,' said Squarciafico. 'But unless he wishes to submit to a trial whose outcome I cannot predict, your man must leave now.'

Nicholas lifted his head. For the first time since the beginning, Anna's eyes rested on his. Nicholas said, 'I would wish to continue serving my lady. But if there is no choice, I will leave.'

'Then I agree,' Anna said; and bit her lip. She did not look round as he was turned from the room, and he did not see her leave, for by then he was locked in a cell. When, finally, he had begun to lose confidence, the door was opened, his pack was thrust in his arms, and he was marched under guard from the fortress. He thought, striding down past the mosque, that he saw the imam's face, but he made no effort to stop. Nor did he pause as he passed the bulwark of Prosper Adorno, the blood already washed from its walls.

His escort changed at the drawbridge, and when he was turned out through the portals of Soldaia he was surprised to recover his horse. His Genoese safe conduct, of course, was now lacking. He could not enter Soldaia or Caffa, Gurzuf or Alupka, Alushta or Simiez. He could not sail through the ice. He could not go home. He was, however, alive. Anna had saved him. He had not saved Ochoa.

There were a few things he could do, most of them dependent on other people's initiatives. It had not taken long, indeed, to work out what all the possibilities were. In the aftermath of all that had happened, Nicholas found in himself a chilly resistance to more fruitless planning. There was a hospice most Latins stayed at, halfway between Soldaia and Caffa, which possessed a separate building for servants. By the time he got there he was cold, wet, and prepared to be fully uncooperative, even when one of the possibilities became a reality, and he was met by a groom that he knew. With the groom was another horse, and a saddlebag containing all the garments necessary to an Italian gentleman, including a razor. There was also a safe conduct, permitting Signor Paolo of Simiez to visit his cousins in Caffa.

It was not a wise plan, at this stage, to give way to his instincts.

Nicholas accepted the bounty provided and descended next day upon Caffa in new guise, or in one which passed muster, at least, with the unsuspecting guards at the portals. Then he made his way, as directed, to the Franciscan monastery, where he was joined in due course by Ludovico da Bologna and the extraordinary woman who had just rescued him from a cruelly planned death.

The Patriarch, viewing him, issued a bark. 'The puppy, restored! So, how are you proposing to thank us?'

'By converting from the Muslim religion,' Nicholas said. It was automatic. All his essence was concentrated on the still person of Anna, standing in the doorway, her smiling face running with tears.

She said, 'What a transformation. I could almost marry you myself.'

'Almost?' Nicholas said. Her eyes looked feverish.

'If she didn't happen to be married already,' said the Patriarch shortly. 'I didn't know your friend was a fool. How did that happen?'

'Someone helped him escape in my name. They wanted to kill him.'

'A Genoese scheme?' said the Patriarch.

'Obviously,' Nicholas said. 'It got rid of Ochoa, and gave them an excuse to get rid of me, whom they suspected. They didn't expect Anna to race to my defence with such brio. I am sorry. I should be overwhelming you both with my gratitude. I can't believe he is dead.'

'It pains us, too,' said Anna gently. 'It was not your fault. You nearly lost your own life in attempting to rescue him. You've taken all the risks since we came — to obtain the goodwill of the Khan, and all the profit that brought. Now the Patriarch has arranged for you to hide here for the weeks that are left. Julius will come. And when we leave for Persia, we leave together.'

The Patriarch grunted. He knew, of course, as much as Brother Lorenzo about the gold and Ochoa. 'Financial security' had been the term Lorenzo had used. The Patriarch also knew that Anna and even Julius would expect, armed with gold, to descend upon Persia with Nicholas. Anna would have been frank about that. Now she said, hesitating, 'Unless our plans ought to change. Ochoa is dead. It may not seem fitting to collect the gold and then leave, as if nothing had happened.'

'There is no one else to receive it,' said Nicholas. 'It is mine, and I want to use it as I have said.'

He did not want to talk, and she respected it. Another woman who had done what she had would have longed to have her ingenuity praised; would have wished to relive, phase by phase, the threatening events of the day and their resolution. Anna left him alone, moving quietly about the guest-quarters they had been given. Presently the Patriarch went out, without waiting to share the supper dishes that a lay brother brought to their parlour. Even there, joining Nicholas, Anna asked his leave to sit down, as if he were her patient and she was his doctor.

Then Nicholas, pulling himself together, said, 'Of course we must talk. I didn't intend to go into retreat. Ochoa was scarcely a soul-mate, but I felt responsible for him; and it left me a good deal to think about.'

'And reach certain conclusions?' Anna asked.

She was dressed in the same gown she had worn to outface Squarciafico in the citadel. Only tonight, being private, she had set aside the stiff, jewelled headdress and allowed her hair to flow over her breast, while the heavy swathes at either temple were drawn back and united within a jewelled clasp. She had removed, too, the voile that had covered her throat and softened the neck of her gown. Now he could see the small pearls with which the neckline was sewn; and her breathing.

It was quiet. The candles flickered on the cloth, the dishes, the wooden trenchers, the good pewter cups filled with Chios wine. Nicholas felt both disembodied and its opposite — his head appeared light, but his senses were disrupted by the change in his dress: the thin lawn of the shirt; the velvet case of the doublet, wide at shoulder, narrow at waist; the libidinous freedom of untrammelled limbs, naked from ankle to thigh save for close-fitting hose. The contours of his face seemed to him untrammelled too; the play of muscle no longer stiffened with hair. Quite suddenly he began to feel, not a stranger, but his own person again.

Anna was watching him. She added, 'Do the bruises hurt?'

He had forgotten his beating. He and Ochoa had both received a blow to the eye. Ochoa's was cured.

Nicholas said, 'Nothing hurts, when the alternative would have been death. Yes, I have reached some conclusions. Perhaps I should tell you tomorrow.'

'Because I shall dislike them?' she said. 'Tell me tonight. And put down your knife. You are not eating.'

'Very well,' Nicholas said. He put down the knife and looked up. 'I can't stay on here. The Franciscans are being too generous. I can dress as a monk or a groom and escape detection, I suppose, for a while. But if I'm found out, they will pay for it, and so will the Patriarch. I shall need a day or two to prepare, but after that I shall start making my own way to the south. When spring comes, I shall be part of the way to Tabriz, and you and Julius will join me.'

Her eyes were black in the uncertain light. She said, 'You would take such care for the monks? I am not surprised.' Then she said, steadily, 'So you will give up the gold? Without you, no one can trace it.'

'Yes, they can,' Nicholas said. 'You can. I have the name of the ship it is coming by, and the name of the captain, and the password which will identify the lawful recipient. Ochoa wished me to have sole control, through use of the pendulum. I asked him to give me these facts to pass on to my heirs, who could not divine. He agreed. You and Julius are my heirs.'

Now all her face appeared shadowed. 'Along with you. I do not want the gold if you are not there to share it. I don't want you to travel alone, when you could remain here, safe with us until it comes. Nicholas, no. Stay with us here. Watch for the ship. Use your pendulum. Discover the gold in any way that you want, or let it go. But don't disappear into the Crimea alone.' And when he was obdurate: 'Decide in the morning,' Anna said. 'You are tired, and mourning your friend. Make no decisions tonight.'

He was tired. He agreed, with a half-smile. 'I see you are depending on the persuasive powers of the Patriarch.'

'Or of mine,' Anna said. She rose, lifting the flask ready to refill his cup, but stood instead, the metal gripped with both hands. She said, 'If you go, this may be our last night in the same rooms, alone.'

'You will have other company,' Nicholas said. He sat very still.

'But no one who owes me what you do,' she said. 'What value, Nicholas, do you set on your life? Is its redemption worth a kiss?'

Nicholas rose, but did not move from his place. He said, 'What would Julius find seemly?'

'I do not know,' Anna said. Within the boneless clasp of her hands the flask tilted then languorously slipped; as she made a slight movement to catch it, the scented liquid pooled and fell from its lip, infiltrating the damask weave of her gown, dropping in luminous gouts among the small jewels and dyeing the warp and weft of the textile so that the pattern sprang into life, its leafy boughs, its blossom and tendrils enclosing her body. Ceres, goddess of harvests.

She dropped the flask in a daze and, plucking at the sodden gown, began to open it. Then, finding his eyes on her, she stopped.

Nicholas said, 'Your maid will do that. Where is your room?'

In the warmer light, mellower than that of the tent, he saw again the fine modulations, the finished exactitude of the skin which clothed the rounded flesh of her breasts. Compared with that ethereal tailoring, his own dress scraped as if woven from husks. She took him by the sleeve and began to draw him erratically with her. She opened a door.

The bedchamber inside was empty. Nicholas said, 'Anna.'

She shut the door. She said, 'Julius cannot give me a child.'

'Then neither can I,' Nicholas said.

'You will not give me a child, even after today? Then lie still,' Anna said. 'And I will take one.'

She tried to trap his wrists when he turned, and when he still pulled away, she dragged his doublet free of its clasps and tore the cambric. She clung to him as he moved, step by step across the tiled floor of the room, and leaned her weight on his shoulder as he took a seat at the writing desk, fending her off with one hand, which she seized. When he stretched out the other, she cried, 'What are you doing?'

'Writing,' he said. 'Giving you the secret of the gold. If I don't survive, it is yours.'

She did not speak. As he wrote quickly, awkwardly on the shifting paper — the name of the ship, the other information he wanted her to have — she settled low at his side, sheathing his arm with both her own, her brow resting against him. Finishing, he saw, looking down, that her eyes were closed. He moved the paper gently towards her. 'Anna.'

She opened her eyes. They looked sightless. She said, 'You didn't kill Julius. What do you owe him?'

'This,' Nicholas said. 'And afterwards, you would hate yourself, and then me.'

Then she lifted her head. 'If Julius were dead, would you love me?'

He laid the paper close to her hand, and rose before she could hold him. He said, 'Is this love?'

'I don't know,' Anna said. 'I have never experienced it.'

He had been going to leave, but he paused. Then, as if he had again changed his mind, he turned and walked from the room, drawing the door to its close all in silence, so that the single clap as it shut bit the air.

He had said that he would stay for some days. But when they knocked on his door the following morning, they discovered that he had gone.

Ludovico da Bologna, when Anna found him, was philosophical. 'Such altruism! Rubbish. A man of restless disposition, that is all. I should hardly have offered protection if I could not provide it. However. He has left me a note. I gather he believes he can amuse himself in the interior until the seas open again. He plans to join me on the way to Tabriz.'

Anna said, 'He has a Genoese pass.'

'He thinks it safer, it seems, to avoid Genoese seaports.' The priest, who was eating, glanced up at her. 'As soon as ships can sail, I must go. When is your husband arriving in Caffa?'

This morning, her face was frowning, and white. 'In June. I wish it were earlier. And what do we do if we still cannot leave because we have to wait for this wretched gold? It belongs to Nicholas,' said Anna fretfully. 'He should have stayed.'

'I am glad,' said Ludovico da Bologna, 'to see that you have joined the ranks of those who have learned to view the rogue in his true colours. Of course he should have stayed. Since he has not, I suppose your husband will decide what is best for his business. I shall be returning to the West, as is obvious, through Caffa. If you are still here, you may have my protection on your own journey homewards. The person of a papal nuncio, as you will have noticed, is sacrosanct.'

She could not tell whether he was serious. She supposed that he was, and thanked him. She felt a faint scorn, in the midst of her torment, that a man of God should be so little aware of human desires, and human fallibility.

NICHOLAS HAD GONE from Caffa when the letter from Brother Huon arrived at the Franciscans'. By that time, which was the third week in March, even the Patriarch had departed; but the German Contessa still held court in the town, and was pleased to take charge of the message, promising that Signor Niccolò would receive it as soon as he returned from his business in Persia. Then she presented the dazzled Brother with a little silver for the good of his house. He thought she looked sad.

At about the same date, late in March, a letter from the Abbot of the monastery of Montello found its way, along with four boxes, to the residence of Egidia van Borselen at Spangnaerts Street, Bruges. Having taken delivery, Gelis sat for a long time alone in her room with the letter, which informed her, with regret, of the death of the noble vicomte Thibault de Fleury. The brethren (it continued) would pray for his soul, and Brother Huon and the monastery remained the grateful beneficiaries of the family's generosity. The boxes, which contained all the vicomte's belongings, had been sent to her upon instructions conveyed by the vicomte in the last days of his life. He had died at peace in the Lord.

She wondered if he had. Then she laid hands on the chests, and unpacked them.

It took a long time. When at last it was done, Gelis van Borselen called her servants and had them replace and put into store the worldly possessions, superb in quality but no longer new, of the late Burgundian nobleman. Along with the doublets and cloaks, the gloves, the boots, the fine shirts and the jewels, the magnificent old-fashioned saddle and the silver harness stamped with his crest, she placed cartons of papers, neatly packaged and labelled in Brother Huon's precise script, and containing the cream of his master's correspondence over the years of his partial recovery — all of it scholarly, and relating, as she now knew to expect, to matters musical, mathematical, and philosophical. There was the battered script of a play. There were no family documents.

Except, that is, for the most recent packet of all, which was addressed in her husband's handwriting to *Monseigneur le vicomte de Fleury*, and which she set aside, and reopened when her servants had left her.

The letter from Nicholas to his grandfather had arrived in time to be read. He had written it the day after receiving the message it answered, and had sent it by post: by a chain of couriers who, changing riders and horses, had taken it across Europe, in winter, in half the time necessary for a man on his own. She could not imagine what it had cost, or how he had paid for it.

Enclosed with his letter, Nicholas had sent to Montello a tract of music in two different inks, and a sheet containing a delicate puzzle which was clearly not of his authorship. This miracle of penmanship, circular in design, had nothing in common with the coded snippets that Nicholas sent her, dealing with practical matters. This was a work of art, elegant, poetic, mischievous even, for it contained words and phrases and fragments of verse which contributed by their shape to the picture, even though the whole made no sense. Then she turned the sheet over, and saw that Nicholas, setting his mind to follow his grandfather's, had drawn and sent him the resolution, in identical form. The translation began at the heart, as the smallest writing had done, and unfurled to the outermost edges. Beyond that, there was a space, and then a sheaf of words which were not in translation at all, but in the form of the original puzzle, which Nicholas had taken and used to add something of his own.

She thought at first that it was beyond her. The complexity of the puzzle far exceeded anything she had ever attempted before, or anything she had ever seen Nicholas do. And yet he had broken the code, and at a speed that had enabled him to send the letter off the following day. She sat thinking of that: of the locked room like this one in Caffa; of the silence, like this; and of the intensity of his concentration, hour after hour, until he won through to the solution. Until he did what his grandfather desired of him, and showed that their minds were alike.

It was simpler for her, for she had his translation of the main text before her, and it was only a case of finding the key. Even so, it was many hours before she knew what Nicholas had added, in that many-layered code, to his grandfather's puzzle. And by then, she knew the words of the puzzle itself almost by heart.

The kernel of it had come ready-made, and there was little that was personal in it: words of solace, words of beauty, words of counsel culled from all the quarters, all the ages of the world. There was wit and irony, and some grains of rough humour: the spices of Thibault's own mind that flavoured it all. Over and above that, the short addendum that bound it together was simply one of good sense and friendship.

We might have liked one another. There is no place for regrets. But it is not a bad thing to face life with a flower at the ear, as a dancer does, and this is my flourish for you. If you can read it.

She missed his other comment at first because it was attached to a classical quote, and itself in Latin. The excerpt, elegiac and simple, spoke of the poet's grief over the death, by her own hand, of a dearly loved daughter. Thibault's had added three sentences. *What is harder than that to forgive? Harder even than hatred? Tell me if you know.*

A long time later she began to translate, bit by bit, the reply which Nicholas had added; simple in content; ornamental only in its execution.

> *I shall keep your work for my son, who will pass it to his: yours is an evergreen flourish.*
>
> *I have no daughter; I can make no comparisons; I cannot forgive.*
>
> *We shall never know how our own lives, yours and mine, might have touched. But now my love has looked on your face, and in meeting her, you have met me, or part of the core of me that does not seem to alter. The rest is a bruised thing which passes from person to person, and which never seems whole. But perhaps time will cure that.*
>
> *May your journey, when it comes, be a swift one, with happiness waiting, and friends.*

It had reached Thibault, that letter, in the last days of his life. And deciphering the words of his grandson, the vicomte had given the order which had consigned all his possessions to Gelis . . . including that private note added by Nicholas, that steadfast declaration in cipher for which no translation was sent.

An exchange of messages between Nicholas and the grandfather he had never met, so he had told her, save as a child brought to a darkened sickroom, to kiss the motionless hand of a man whose face he could not see.

Complex minds; complex hearts.

Encoded messages.

Encoded love.

Then Gelis, mistress of self-control, put down her pen and broke into desperate tears, tears for herself, and for Nicholas, and for the chain which, unknown to her, had always been there.

Part III

POLOVTSIAN DANCES

Chapter 27

BEING ENTIRELY SURE of the powers of Providence, and reasonably sure of those of Nicholas de Fleury, the papal envoy to the ruler of Persia was unsurprised, after a stormy crossing of the Black Sea, to discover de Fleury waiting for him on the south shore, at a Christian house in the seaport of Fasso (Phasis, the ancients had called it). Sent for, he turned up at the religious establishment upon which the Patriarch had bestowed his temporary patronage. He was wearing a thick cloak against the searing chill winds, and below that, a quilted pourpoint and doublet instead of the dress of a Mameluke steward. Otherwise he seemed much as before, if less good-humoured. 'How shouldn't we meet? I left messages all round the coast. But the seamen said this was the port that you'd make for.'

He had a small amount of money, it seemed. Some of it was Signor Zeno's; some was a portion from Qirq-yer. And, escaping south, he had obtained a commission from the new prince at Mánkup, before setting sail with some Greeks from Cembalo. He said, 'You didn't bring the Gräfin?'

'She wouldn't come,' the Patriarch answered. He noted that, despite all that had happened, de Fleury was still bent on enlarging the extraordinary commercial empire he was creating for the man he had shot. The Patriarch added, 'I warned her she'd be better travelling with me than waiting about for her husband. I reminded her you couldn't set foot in Caffa again as a Mameluke.'

'She's an obstinate woman,' said de Fleury.

'So was Carlotta of Cyprus,' said the Patriarch. 'But she's bested: given up all hope of Cyprus and gone crawling bankrupt to Rome. What is this one lingering for, apart from her man? Did you tell her to wait for your gold?'

'Of course not,' said de Fleury. 'If she does, it's her own idea entirely. In the end, it's to help Julius's business. They may both think it worth while.'

'You don't want the stuff?' the Patriarch enquired.

'Only as an investment,' the other man said; and dismissed the subject. Within three days, they set off.

De Fleury had bought himself a serving-lad; the Patriarch had one already, as well as Brother Orazio, a guide, and two cheap Armenians to handle the horses and baggage. The Patriarch had covered this ground before, but routes changed, and so did local governors and the bribes they expected. Without gifts, no provincial governor or village headman would offer hospitality or even safe passage.

De Fleury, as anticipated, was an asset, as might be expected. He lost his temper quite often; but then so did the Patriarch. He also took charge of the valuables. Franciscans were known to carry no money. In Father Ludovico's case, a spectacular representation of unsavoury poverty had been enough, in the past, to inhibit casual robbers, while the minor monasteries and Christian villages in the various small states which lay between the Black Sea and Persia could be depended on for a little salt fish and dried fruit, and even some bread. They knew him, in any case, from previous visits.

Despite the detours entailed, Father Ludovico visited a great many of these in the course of his journey, doubling the length of the odyssey which began, by boat and camel and horse, by the broad, ice-rimmed reaches of the Phasis and proceeded as week followed week between afforested mountains, through snow and then mud. This he did out of conscience and not to favour his belly, as de Fleury liked to profess.

Historically, a hundred villages in this area had once lain under the spiritual administration of Antioch, and he thought of it still as his parish. Sixty years ago, Franciscan missions had brought the Gospel, with loving care, to the infidels, and tended the flame of the Roman church among the Latin colonists in alien lands. Now (as de Fleury had commented), the primary task of an apostolic mission was not conversion, but diplomacy. The Patriarch of Antioch was known to most courts by now. (Even the Assassins were given a welcome, if they wanted Christian aid for a good enough cause.)

And Nicholas de Fleury was known in these parts as well, if not initially by so grand a name. It was fourteen years since that first meeting in Florence between the former Bruges apprentice, not yet de Fleury, and the Franciscan friar, not yet a Patriarch, who was leading to Europe the envoys of Georgia and Armenia and Trebizond to beg help against the Ottoman Turk. The backing of the Medici had brought de Fleury to Trebizond, and established his connections with Georgia and Persia. Since then, the channels of communication between the Banco di Niccolò and Uzum Hasan had remained open, and de Fleury's potential, as a supplier of men, of arms, of new openings for trade was still perceived as worth exploring, whatever his new business arrangements might be. His was the secular side of the Apostolic Legate's mission to incite the ruler of Persia to war.

Nevertheless, on the road, it paid to escape attention. Mingrelian marauders and the many impatient toll-keepers and customs officials in the rough region between the Black Sea and Persia had, fortunately, never heard of the Bishop of Rome and, viewing the Patriarch's modest retinue and shabby appearance, received little presents of biscuit with no more than an outburst of routine resentment. When it came to the lofty timber citadels of provincial governors, the Patriarch found a clean gown, had his brasses rubbed up, and brought himself and his lordly sponsors forcefully to the memory of the magnate in question. This produced a roof, a pallet and a better class of food, which in turn had to be paid for by the superior presents which de Fleury was currently carrying and which, occasionally, he made some pretence of having lost. He was an ingenious fellow, but required to learn respect for authority.

This, Father Ludovico did his best to instil as they made their way from Kutaisi to Gori, from Tiflis to the mountains of Ayrarat (which they did not trouble to scale, in order to bring down a plank of the Ark), and south towards Tabriz. Accustomed to solitary travel with the silent Orazio, the Patriarch enjoyed his wrangles with his younger companion, which strictly excluded all matters of serious content. De Fleury was useful. He hunted and brought in fresh meat. He knew how to make horsehair foot-mats for the snow. Although strange to this part of the country, he had experienced the interior as far south as Erzerum, and was unalarmed by confrontations with stave-carrying bullies with shaved heads and trailing moustaches. He sensed when to call the bluff of petty tax collectors come to demand everything they possessed down to the clothes off their backs. Equally, and as important, he sensed when to give in.

To sustain them, they savoured the legendary tales, picked up every few days, of their predecessor the Venetian envoy who had passed the same way the previous summer. After a week spent in hiding in Caffa, Ambrogio Contarini, bearer of the most reviled name in the colony, had been bled dry of money and dignity from the moment he crossed the Black Sea (at an enhanced price of one hundred ducats) till the time he arrived in Tabriz and found no one there.

Humble interpreters, tears in their eyes, described how the Venetian thought that Bendian, lord of Mingrelia, was mad, because he sent him a pig's head, and received him sitting under a tree. He seemingly considered the Georgians equally crazed, although the castellan of Kutaisi had invited him to a good supper of turnip and bread, properly served on a skin on the ground. (And while there might have been grease on the skin, it was a lie to suggest that it was thick enough to boil up a cauldron of cabbages.) Next, it was the King of Georgia's fault that the Venetian had to wait hungry all night in the open, and after being received, had to beg for guides and safe conducts (for which he was not at all willing to pay), while the royal clerks naturally examined his possessions and took what was due to the King. Then, at the halt after that, he would hardly believe that it was customary to pay his guide and his host all over again, and objected when he had to buy his own food. As for drink (the interpreters said), the offence was the opposite: when hospitably invited to carouse at no cost to himself, the contemptible Venetian would always refuse.

'Why?' de Fleury had asked when told that. 'It sounds as if he'd have been happier drunk.'

'Not everyone is happier drunk,' said the Patriarch. 'I heard in Caffa that Signor Ambrogio has a weak stomach and never indulged, even in hiding. I salute him.'

'You're not travelling with him,' de Fleury said. 'Is he weak mentally, too?'

'He is used to what he considers to be civilised practices,' the Patriarch said, 'and thinks himself slighted when others fail to observe them. The lords he meets are, of course, aware of this, and take pleasure in treating him as a caravan. We are known. Our behaviour is different and so, therefore, is their attitude to us.' He used the plural, as a concession. The King of Georgia had cause to remember how Trebizond fell, and the ship that the man John le Grant had sailed to Batum with the Empress Helen aboard. The Empress Helen whose predecessor had been sister to the princes of Gothia.

'You mean you put the fear of God into them,' de Fleury said.

'Naturally,' the Patriarch answered. The mud was stiffening under the sun, and turning to grass. There was a resinous scent in the air. Spring had come, with summer burning behind.

AT FIRST SIGHT the dust haze was pink, dulling to violet; its mass against the blue of the sky was like that of a blanket cloud at sunset. Then, as it neared, there sparkled within it the motes which enlarged into helmet and chain mail and harness, while an apparent flurry of wind thickened into the sound of a murmurous trampling, overlaid by a shrilling like birdsong. Nearer yet, and the cloud yielded a swaying grove of thirty thousand caparisoned camels, and the same number of horses and mules, behind which trembled the hoops of six thousand carriages, frail as spectral silk flowers in the gloom. Positioned close to the servants and children, the women trotted in veils tall as stove-pipes, reins gathered high, finger-whips flicking, precious cradles fixed in the pommels before them. Then came the cattle, the sheep, the goats, the hunting dogs and the falcons and the supercilious leopards chained in their carts. The noise was furious, the stench was vile, the dust was half a day deep, which brought with it the approaching Court and army of Uzum Hasan, prince of Persia, ruler of Cappadocia, Armenia, Kurdistan and Mesopotamia, and sole power in the Levant capable of opposing the ambitions of Ottoman Turkey.

The place was two days' journey south of Tabriz, the date was the second last day of May, and the papal, Burgundian and Imperial Legate was about to fulfil his mission at last.

THEY WERE RECEIVED the following morning since, after all, they were long expected. Efficiently attired from his own husbanded resources and a tailor of imagination in Tabriz, Nicholas de Fleury followed the Patriarch and Brother Orazio in silence as they were led through the lanes of a tented camp thirty miles in circumference, which would remain as long as the grazing allowed. Already the bazaars had been set up with their trestles of food, and the merchants, the armourers, the apothecaries were arranging their goods. The sun, not yet high, had yet to ripen the smells. The noise was already overwhelming.

The Patriarch said, 'You are comparing this with the merchant caravans of the Sahel, or the Tartar yurts, or the military encampments you have known in Cyprus or the Somme? Will Neuss be like this?'

He disliked having his thoughts read. Nicholas said, 'Neuss? That will be over by now.' He thought it must be, for the last time he had tried to find her, Gelis had been in Bruges. After that, he had stopped divining for a while, in order not to frighten her any more. He didn't know why he thought she was frightened, since she must know by now how well protected she was.

He was sorry, in a way, that this journey was over. It was easy to avoid major decisions when travelling demanded so many of the other kind. Now he would have to work, establishing trading connections which could be operated from the Baltic and Poland, assuming he stayed there, or Julius did. And if conditions — which he had yet to discover — precluded that, he could still make suggestions on behalf of the Bank, even though he no longer represented it. Some day, if a long war stretched ahead, Gelis or Diniz or Gregorio would be able to offer weapons and men to replace the cannon and trained gunners that Venice had dispatched, but then diverted to Crete.

He could have done with knowing more about this family rebellion and the course it was likely to take. It had begun, they said, with a Kurdish rumour to the effect that Uzum Hasan had died. He was in his seventies now and, given the existence of sons of all ages by four different mothers (one of them Kurdish), there was liable to be the same sort of murderous falling-out that had been prompted in Caffa, for example, by the old Tudun's widow and her bribes on behalf of her son.

They managed things better in the West. Philip of Burgundy had possessed just as many sons, but without having married their mothers, and had brought them up to be strong and confident allies with no need to usurp him. The merchant empires of Medici and Strozzi depended on the loyalty of fond, hard-working, highly trained offspring. Further back, of course, western kings had behaved as Uzum's sons and the brethren of Gothia were doing, and simply got rid of their rivals. Certainly, it could prevent civil war and save time and expense and distress: look at Scotland and the struggle between James and his brothers. Yet a sufficient supply of sons and daughters was necessary — daughters for useful alliances, and sons (speaking of course without bias), outside marriage as well as within it, to ensure the survival of somebody competent. Principalities organised their successions in the way that their people condoned and their religion allowed and experience had shown to be best at the time. The secret was to know when to change.

Someone should tell Jordan de Ribérac.

They were nearly at the central pavilion. He already knew that there were few people here he would recognise. He had never met Uzum Hasan, although he had had trade dealings for a long time with his officials, and owed a long-standing debt to his late mother. His other friend of fourteen years, Uzum's principal envoy Hadji Mehmet, had already returned to the West, but his reports to his master of Nicholas also spanned fourteen years. If the Banco di Niccolò had not always supported Uzum Hasan, its reasons would be understood. In any case, that was past history. Nicholas was being taken round Tartar and Turcoman princes in order to make mercantile offers which would increase their dependence on the West. It happened to suit him, and so he conformed. He was also attached to the Patriarch's angelic skirts because — as the Patriarch had gone to the trouble of finding out — he had an army which, although no longer his, was still loyal to him. Nevertheless, although Nicholas de Fleury might be acceptable to Uzum Hasan, and the Patriarch of Antioch could almost be termed his familiar, none of this would necessarily be reflected in public. For their initial audience (they were reminded), diplomacy demanded a certain formality. Later, there would be room for something more personal.

'Isn't that a slight?' Nicholas had enquired innocently after the source of this news had departed.

The Patriarch had merely grunted. A cool reception was nothing, if it was strategically necessary. It would have been more of a slight had the Patriarch appeared in full battered feather as triple nuncio of the Pope, the Holy Roman Emperor and Charles, Duke of Burgundy, which in the absence of Adorne, he was entitled to do. He was not, however, a fool. In the presence of two Venetian envoys and a Russian ambassador, it was best to forget the Pope (at present offended by Venice) and the Emperor Frederick (at present at war with the Duke). The Patriarch felt it sufficient to present himself simply as legate of Charles, Duke of Burgundy, who, in return for the dukedom of Guelders, had promised ten thousand soldiers to combat the Turk. When they were available. If they were needed.

'And am I slighted too?' Nicholas had persisted, to receive the full glare beneath poisonous eyebrows.

'Slighted? You do not exist. You are part of my train. You produce the gifts. You fraternise with the underlings.'

'Which ones?' Nicholas had asked.

'Holy God! Which side paid you to come here? The Venetians! The Venetians! I can't do it, but you can. And the Russians. Marco Rosso, envoy of Duke Ivan of Moscow. A bustling rat masquerading as beaver. Barbaro lived in the Rosso family house all those years he was fishing from Tana. I'm talking of the Venetian consul Josaphat Barbaro. If you didn't meet him in Venice, you probably came across him in Cyprus. You'll get on with him. He knows the Crimea like the back of his mistress, speaks the language, and was picked by the Signoria to bring all that arsenal over to Uzum two years ago. Then Zacco died, and Barbaro was made to stay over in Cyprus till the uproar subsided and the summer campaign collapsed, and then they took all the arms and the presents and sent them to Crete instead of on to Uzum. It says a lot for his character that he came to Court none the less, and Uzum has kept him since April last year. I think there are times when they are both sick of Venice.'

'I shall get on with him,' Nicholas said. He spoke politely. 'And the other Venetian? A newcomer?' He ran through his mind all the names he had heard.

'I'll leave you to find out for yourself,' the Patriarch said. 'Just be nice to him.'

THE BURGUNDIAN TRIBUTE of cloth of gold, crimson velvet and violet, which Nicholas had carried sewn into his bedroll all the way from Fasso, was adequate in its splendour, although outmatched by the hangings of Uzum Hasan's travelling pavilion of scarlet felt within which, neatened up for the occasion, the Italian Franciscan Ludovico de Severi da Bologna, Patriarch of Antioch, presented, with an inclination of the head, his Latin letters of credence and then proceeded, on a nod from the throne, to deliver the greetings and prayers of his lord.

The Duke of Burgundy, so far as Nicholas could gather, had been remarkably vague in his exhortations and remarkably prolix in his expression of them. The Patriarch, whose native ripeness of language had affronted half Europe, discovered, droning, fifteen tedious ways of appealing to the Lord Uzum Hasan to attack his brother the Turk. The interpreter's voice obediently followed, and the lord Uzum Hasan listened with grace but no visible interest. Tall as his nickname suggested, the old man sat erect on his cushions with one hand on the jewels of his scimitar, the other teasing the chin of his hound. Within the worked golden headgear of ceremony, the prince's features were dish-shaped and gamboge: the willowy moustaches and beard drooped among the blue pebbled chains of raw turquoises. His nobles, coated with chased and ribbed metal, provided the vast red pavilion with a motionless lining of ruby.

Among them, the ambassadors, glimmering uneasily, identified themselves to Nicholas's large and disengaged eye. Short Marco Rosso, the Venetian rat turned Muscovite beaver: a man in his thirties, with a black Russian moustache and spade beard above a long buttoned coat in pale damask. Josaphat Barbaro, whom he was expected to like, in the red hat and robe of a well-bred Venetian; his narrow face lined with the marks of thirty-five years in the Levant; his eyes, brown as topazes, moving between the Patriarch and the passive bulk of Nicholas, his anonymous henchman. And the third man, also the spokesman of Venice, whom Nicholas had never seen before, but whom he felt instantly that he knew: knew the pale, fretful face and broad nose and the shaving scar on the neck under the fashionable bulk of the hairline, displayed by the very tall hat.

At first, it didn't seem possible. The man in question had passed south the previous summer, and would surely have gone before now. But when the Patriarch's lecture had ended, and the prince had replied with the necessary courtesies and a promise to consider the matter, the first person to file out beside Nicholas was the barbered envoy. 'Do I gather that you speak the Venetian tongue?' said the gentleman.

'I do my best,' Nicholas said. 'I have the honour of addressing a nobleman of that Republic?'

'Indeed,' said the gentleman, halting and raising his large, lidded eyes. 'My name is Ambrogio Contarini, son of Messer Benedetto, and ambassador of the Illustrious Signoria to the magnificent lord Uzum Hasan. And you are the Franciscan friar's secretary? Or the Patriarch, are we invited to call him? Although I thought the title now held by another.'

'I am honoured,' said Nicholas. 'His secretary, no. Some men profess to think writing important, yet what is it but chicken marks on a skin? I care for his camels. He lets me carry his pyx. He sometimes allows me to sing the responses. Orpheus the Thracian Wizard, they call me.'

The face below him turned pink. 'Or Nicholas de Fleury of Beltrees, formerly of the Banco di Niccolò,' said a chiding voice from behind. 'Ambrogio, he is joking with you. This is a merchant companion of the Patriarch, and one who knows that Father Ludovico is too diplomatic, perhaps, to insist upon his full ecclesiastical title today. My name is Josaphat Barbaro, Messer Niccolò. You may not remember me. But we three strangers would be honoured if you and the Patriarch would join us in our pavilion. We are permitted wine.'

'Even the lord Uzum Hasan is permitted wine,' said Ambrogio Contarini, surveying Nicholas narrowly. 'Too much of it, some of us think.'

'Is it possible?' Nicholas said, a little thickly. But before he could amuse himself further, the Patriarch strode swirling over, executed a volley of greetings and benisons, and swept him away. 'Have you no sense?'

'The situation didn't call for any,' said Nicholas. 'He's an ass.'

'He's Venetian,' the Patriarch said. 'A Venetian ass isn't the same as a Flemish one. Its ears are bigger. And don't add what I am sure you are longing to add.'

'I shouldn't dare,' Nicholas said. The Patriarch was, of course, right. He had been a fool. He had been a fool because he did not want to think about what he was doing.

He tried to put matters right, as was only fair, on the trek back to Tabriz, which was made in the company of the entire royal migration. Ambassador Contarini still didn't know what to make of an ex-banker who (it was true) carried a pyx on a double-humped camel; but the small Veneto-Russian was amenable and Ambassador Barbaro, who chose to ride with him, turned out to be agreeably informative. It appeared that the Persian ruler's rebellious son had fled with his family to the Turks after giving up Shiraz, which was still a frontier town and vital because of its armourers, even though the caravans no longer poured up from the Gulf with their jewels and their spice and their indigo.

In the days when Marco Polo rode through, the Tabriz fondacos had been full of the merchants and consuls of Venice and Genoa. Now, fine though it was — M. de Fleury had seen it — the place was largely a staging post for Caspian silk going through to Aleppo in Syria, just as Caffa had become an entrepôt for slaves and grain and preserved fish and furs instead of an emporium for the mighty caravans crossing from Astrakhan. The way to Cathay was blocked; the spice route through the Black Sea had become throttled by Turks; but traders regrouped and forced their way through somewhere else: they always did. When they found a way to circumnavigate Africa, that would be a different challenge again.

At that point, the pleasant voice paused, but not necessarily to invite speech. Nicholas nevertheless accepted the invitation. 'Yes, I remember your excellency,' he said. 'Four years ago, at the time of our meetings in

Venice, when my Bank decided not to invest in the Levant. And then later in Cyprus, when the King died.' He looked round, and met Barbaro's eyes.

The Venetian said, 'Zacco held you in high regard. We were not enemies, either, he and I, although he made me his whipping-horse often enough. It was the Captain-General, Mocenigo, none of us had patience with. Cruel and unnecessary destruction.'

'Smyrna burned to the ground, and two hundred and fifteen Turkish heads pronged on the yards of his ship,' Nicholas said. 'And he hanged the ringleaders of the rising in Cyprus. Who killed Zacco?'

He spoke through his scarf, as the other did: the dust and the noise lashed against them.

Barbaro said, 'A Venetian, of course. I don't know which. It was not I. I was at his funeral Mass. I was present when his son was baptised. They were fools. They could have ruled through him. You could have helped us all, once. The other, the artistic young man, was too vain. David de Salmeton. You had him thrown out.'

'You have spoken to Hadji Mehmet,' Nicholas said.

'We travelled from Venice together. He is discreet. And so am I,' observed Josaphat Barbaro, coughing into his veil. 'Indeed, in this climate, who wants to be talkative?'

Tabriz was under garrison, as it had been when they had passed through: as in Bruges, as in most towns these days, the hardworking inhabitants were not necessarily about to take arms and rush to extract their revered ruler from whatever silly mess he had got himself into elsewhere. Uzum Hasan did not try to compel them, but left a round thousand soldiers to make sure that his son didn't rush in and capture Tabriz while he was gone.

In other respects, the city was not much like Bruges. Set in its high, mountain-girt plain, deep in snow through the winter, seared by sun through all the long summer, Tabriz had no need of walls; owned no windmills. Its irrigation was underground, from the little two-forked river, the Adschy Tchai, which emptied itself far away into the long barren sump of a salt lake, home of wild duck and flamingos and arid, sulphurous fish. But water Tabriz possessed, and therefore gardens, and the population of merchants, administrators, artisans which required this array of glittering edifices, twenty miles in circumference: the domes, the minarets, the silken awnings and carved, gilded wood; the porcelain tiles that glowed in the high, clear sunlight of early summer.

Then when the sun sank, as now, when the Shah came to enter his city, the lamps bloomed within, tinselling the chain mail and helms of his soldiers lining the streets; illuminating the white tulip-heads of his kneeling people, rousing the dim gold of archways and doors as the echoes were roused by flute and bagpipe and drum, and the thud of horses' feet, and the unctuous padding of camels. Ahead, the Blue Mosque stood aflame like a ship, bright as St Sophia, whose thousand lamps could be seen twenty miles off at sea. There was a smell of dung and spiced meat, flowers and horses, sweat and urine and bath-oils. There were wandering whiffs of something that made the Patriarch's ready lip curl. 'Luxury, debauchery and defilement.'

'I hope so,' said Nicholas automatically.

This time, as guests of the Shah, they were not compelled to lodge in the austere recesses of the Armenian church of St Mary's, but were led towards the Palace itself, to those quarters overlooking the Meidan set apart for visiting envoys. Since their first encounter with Uzum Hasan, they had not yet been called for a second audience. It was understandable. The son's revolt was an increasing embarrassment, and any consequent reversal of policy would be best announced in the full theatre of state. As for the Shah's private discussions, secrecy could be better guaranteed behind walls than in tents. After the recent charade, Nicholas was looking forward to watching Uzum Hasan and the Patriarch together.

The procession ended. Porters carried the Patriarch's meagre boxes through night-scented gardens and set open the doors of the spacious chamber which, it appeared, Nicholas and the Patriarch were to share. As he was not unaccustomed to doing, Nicholas directed the unpacking for both of them, with the admiring help of Brother Orazio, who later departed. They were offered food. They were not offered, but received, a double guard at their doors. They were finally alone, and the Patriarch was saying his prayers, when harsh voices erupted outside and Nicholas, who had been standing motionless at the window, his fingers pinching the cord at his throat, turned his head. Then the doors opened, and a visitor was announced.

The Patriarch broke off and rose. Nicholas moved. Their eyes met, and Nicholas laid hands on his cloak. But it was not an olive-skinned royal clerk, come in robe and slippers and turban to take them at last to his master. This was a clean-shaven, muscular man in rich clothes, in rich *western* clothes, who strode in and stood surveying them both with an athletic zest that still recalled his years as a soldier.

'Well, Nicholas,' the newcomer remarked. 'And you thought you'd contrived to get rid of me. So where is she? What have you done with my wife, you young goat?'

Julius.

Chapter 28

'JULIUS.'

Trained to dissemble — caught, indeed, in the act of sustaining one of the most difficult deceptions of his life — Nicholas brought out the name with a flatness he could not prevent, his brain having no surplus capacity. Then the flood of calculation was over, and he was able to register the bonhomie on Julius's face, and the cheerfulness in his voice, and produce words of his own that sounded normal.

'Julius, you bastard! I thought you were going to Caffa? Anna isn't here: she decided to wait for you. Come in and sit. Are you better?'

And as Julius, entering fully, eased himself grinning down to the cushions, Nicholas added, 'I don't seem to have made a very good job of getting rid of you. You look well enough for another ten years, if you give up competition archery.' And Julius, agreeing amiably, hit him a reasonably painful blow in return. After which, Nicholas opened the wine, and kept pouring.

Julius did in fact look little different. Perhaps the high cheek-bones were sharper, the handsome body less mobile, but the oblique stare was the same, if a little more lingering. He was rested, for he had been here for several days. He'd come to Tabriz the day after Nicholas left, but decided to wait for him. My God, Nicholas was well in with the prince: he should see where Julius was staying, in the stinking *canosta*. But of course, Nicholas had the benefit of his spiritual friend: how was Father Ludovico?

Father Ludovico, who had after all given Julius's wife his protection all through Julius's absence, and helped her establish in Caffa, opined that it was late, he was tired, and they would no doubt encounter one another next day. He then returned to his prie-dieu while Julius, half rising, sat down again beside Nicholas in a temporary fashion, refilled his cup in an absent manner and said, 'All right, I'm going, but tell me. You're about to get hold of the gold, and Anna says you'll invest it with us? I won't say I'm not pleased — business hasn't done as well as I'd hoped — but you did owe me something, you murdering brat. I was only hoping it would come in time for Anna to join us. But I suppose she's better staying in Caffa. I'd rather get the gold home overland than trust it to the Middle Sea and all those bloody bandits.'

'Such as the Knights of St John,' Nicholas said. 'You heard Ochoa died?' He emptied and filled his own cup, to keep level.

'He was always going to die. Like Benecke,' Julius said. 'You should be glad Anna made you see sense and go east with her. She's all right? She's a good business-woman. You'll have noticed.'

'I'm surprised she let you come to Tabriz on your own,' Nicholas said. 'What are you supposed to be doing? Supervising my deals with Uzum Hasan?'

'Have you made any? Anna reckons,' Julius said, 'that he's going to need weapons if he's going to face an attack from this son. And he won't get them from Venice: not for a family quarrel, and when Venice needs them herself. Whereas I can get them with a much better margin from the Tyrol and Germany, unless Venice stops the delivery.'

'They won't,' Nicholas said. The Patriarch, his eyes glaring, was praying louder.

'Why not?' asked Julius. He gave an intent grin, and got up.

'Because they don't want Uzum to give way before a Turkish army with his own son helping to lead it. It's what Caterino Zeno was afraid of. That's why I was bribed to come and sell non-Venetian arms to Uzum against the wishes of Venetian arms merchants. You don't need to do any deals with Uzum Hasan: you just leave that to me.'

Julius's face looked, for a moment, the way Nicholas had felt half an hour before. Julius said, 'So when are you seeing him?'

'I'll tell you,' said Nicholas.

He accompanied Julius to the door, exchanging scraps of news mixed with banter: of Anna's conquests in Caffa, and Nicholas's ridiculous life as a Mameluke. Julius, straying on to the subject of the lunacy of Duke Charles at Neuss, thought to add, with a display of his fine upper teeth, 'Of course, if they'd listened to Gelis and Astorre, the siege would have ended before it began. You know she's practically enrolled as a mercenary? They may knight her in the field: you'll get her helmet and spurs if she's killed. But the boy is all right. Jordan? Jodi? She sent him to Scotland with Kathi.'

They were actually standing within the half-open doors. Gauzy insects blundered over their shoulders, lured by the Patriarch's lamp. Outside, the scent of roses and jasmine mingled with the other, libidinous odours so reviled by the Patriarch, and somewhere, a beguiling trickle of water was exchanging notes with a nimbly played harp. Nicholas became aware that he hadn't yet spoken. 'And Kathi?' he enquired. It sounded quite cordial, as he intended.

'Oh, she's produced. I heard just as I left. To that poor little sod Robin of Berecrofts. Between them, they've managed a daughter. They're calling it Margaret.'

Nicholas heard him; but from his desert, his morass, his sea of moral squalor, found himself this time rendered irreparably dumb. Julius, oblivious, took his leave and was met and guided out of the grounds, walking erratically. He had drunk quite a lot. They had both drunk quite a lot. It was like old times. Nicholas stood for a while, and then went in and joined the Patriarch, who had finished praying and was preparing for bed.

The Patriarch looked up, leered, and then gave a nod towards the now-vacant cushion. 'Does everyone know he's a *koekoek*?'

In the Netherlands, it meant 'willing cuckold.' 'He isn't,' Nicholas said.

'Isn't a cuckold, or doesn't know it?' the Patriarch asked.

'You decide.' Nicholas was half stripped already.

The Patriarch gazed at him with a kind of contentment. 'You'd like me to be soft. I expect you confided in Godscalc. Nearly unmanned you, didn't he, Julius, talking of your lady wife and your little son and Katelijne Sersanders?'

'But you've braced me again,' Nicholas said. He went out, got rid of the wine, and came back.

The chamber was dark, but the Patriarch's voice continued to flow, sonorously, as if nothing had happened. 'You want someone soft because you can't stand isolation. You've got the brains, but you haven't the guts, to make a good friar.'

'If you say so,' Nicholas said, from his bed, carefully.

'Oh, I say so, and correctly, or how else have I made you spitting angry? A youth finds a priest or a doctor and dribbles out all that ails him. A thinking man keeps his own counsel, listens to teachers, and applies what he learns to himself. In private. With due humility, with unrelenting honesty, and in private. So don't try to piss your woes over me.'

Nicholas closed his eyes, anchored his breathing, and spoke succinctly into the darkness. 'And how are you going to stop me? The night is young, and I've got them all written out, with spaces ready for guidance and blessings. I can remember them even with the light out.'

There was a rumbling sound from the other pallet. 'A good effort,' the Patriarch said. 'We'll toughen you yet. You might even be able to stand up to what's lying ahead of you.'

There was a silence. 'I thought you didn't know, or want to know, anything about my affairs,' Nicholas said. He had straightened his neck from the pillow.

'Oh, I don't,' said the Patriarch cheerfully. 'But I shall tell you something of note. The Shah's advisers will not invite Master Julius to their negotiations; only you, who are known from past dealings. You will be able to speak for your unfortunate victim, and with better success, I am sure. You may redeem yourself yet.'

'Julius won't like it,' Nicholas said. He dropped back his head with an unequivocal thump, and hoped the Patriarch heard it. It made his skull ache.

HE SAW QUITE A BIT of Julius in the six days that followed, and gleaned all the news of the city from without the airy heights of the Palace of Hesht Behesht, the Eight Heavens. He was aware that Julius, catching sight of glimmering walls and ribbed domes and towering cedarwood doors worked with mother of pearl and silver and gold, considered Nicholas to be overprivileged. Nevertheless the lawyer was kind enough, as his elder and tutor, to share his superior acquaintance with the city, hurrying Nicholas through the shadowy maze of bazaars to investigate the retail price for ginger and indigo; paying aggressive calls on the weavers of silk carpets and embarking on inquisitions in the billowing heat around the kilns where thin tiles were sawn into their intricate shapes, and glazed, and fired, and laid face down on the faintly lined, age-old cartoons to receive their backing of plaster. Tabrizi tiles clothed the great mosque at Bursa. Tabrizi ceramists had become masters in Cairo, in Damascus. Astonished, Julius inspected, from the outside, the vast red-brick bulk of the citadel. He even got into the hospital, and examined the herb garden and pharmacy which he reported, with mystification, to be as good as that of the Knights of St John.

Nicholas obliged him by letting him do it, and experienced thankfulness mixed with contrition when, attending the great marketplace of the Meidan, Julius did not have to be deterred from leaping into the stadium with the wrestlers, or taking the place of the men tussling with wolves, but watched from the side, not far from the gallery used by Uzum Hasan's younger sons, too small as yet for rebellion. His daughters, his two unmarried Christian daughters, were absent with their Christian mother at Kharput. No other Venetian envoy was about to observe her in bed with her husband.

It was obvious, then, that Julius was not quite the man that had been. He declared as much, without words, by inviting Nicholas to the bathhouse he favoured, so that the other man might admire, along with his trim, well-preserved body, the ragged scar, scarlet and angry, that marred it. But Julius, sleek with massage and bath-oils, seemed actually to hold no grudge over that, and if, strolling home pink and scented, he took care to leave a certain space between himself and his dimpled companion, it was only because of the other young men who walked, hand in hand, in that district.

He had asked, several times, whether or not Nicholas had yet had his audience, and Nicholas had assured him that he hadn't. It was not strictly true. In fact it was not at all true. Within that short time, Nicholas had been summoned twice to secret enclave in the Palace: once to see a chamberlain he knew well at second hand, and the second time to answer to the Persian ruler himself.

That meeting had not taken place among the gold cushions and flowering carpets of the divine royal kiosk with its twining rivulet of sweet running water. Uzum Hasan received this alien merchant beneath the dome of a carved timber room, sheltered by awnings and set apart under a spread of ancient elms. His chief minister and a clerk were also present, but no singers or dancers accompanied them, or the liquid voices of poets, intoning the love-crazed nightingale's songs of Hafiz. Only somewhere, disembodied by distance, a man's voice seemed to be singing, perhaps in melancholy, perhaps lulling another to sleep.

Nicholas de Fleury lowered his eyes and performed, without haste, the sequence of obeisances which brought him kneeling at length before this old man, leader and warrior, whom even Zacco had esteemed. A man whose oldest son wished to kill him. Nicholas uttered the conventional greeting, *'Salam aleikom,'* and received the tart rejoinder due to Franks: 'Peace be with those who follow the right path.' He lifted his head.

As he knew already, the face he saw was not that of the cast of magnificent Cyrus, Darius, Xerxes or Alexander who conquered the world. Their civilisations had been followed by six hundred years of Arab rule, and then another two hundred of Mongol devastation by Genghis Khan and his successors. This was the lord of a Turcoman state who had managed to conquer and hold the western part of a great land mass which the West regarded as Persia, and you could see his inheritance in the slight Mongolian cast of the lids, the Eastern tinge in the skin round the broken-veined cheeks.

But he had conquered. And he had built on what he had conquered. So the lord Hasan, nicknamed Uzum for his height as Timur had been nicknamed Tamurlane for his limp, looked at him and said, 'Rise. Sit. I am told you have a proposition to place before us.'

He had: a well-constructed one to do with the purchase of gall nuts, insect dye, lapis and silks. He described, when requested, his present status as that of experienced dealer, working especially for the business of Julius of Bologna and his offices in Germany, Poland and Caffa. He agreed that he had access to mercenaries, bombardiers and artillery, of the sort Messer Josaphat had been prevented from bringing to Persia. He indicated, in a manner so oblique that only an Arab mind could have followed it, that it would be undesirable to undertake such an expensive commission without knowing how soon the goods would be wanted, and for what; and what certainty there might be of full payment. Or, in other words, whom are you going to fight? And will you have lost before my army could reach you?

'And do you not think you already know the answer, Messer Niccolò?' the prince asked. 'You do not lack confidence, surely, in what we can do?' The clerk, on a sign, had risen and gone.

'I fear only,' said Nicholas, 'that your victories will be so great and so immediate that you will have no use for men or guns by the time they arrive. Further, by crushing the Turk, you will re-open the trading-routes, which would increase my purchases here a hundredfold. I speak, for example, of alum. All that depends on, and will be shaped by the events of coming months.'

'You are very cautious, for a merchant,' said Uzum Hasan. 'Perhaps we may allay some of your fears. About payment, for instance.'

Boxes had appeared: precious boxes of silver and ivory which the clerk, returned, laid before Nicholas and then started to open. They all contained jewels. Dully glowing, piled without order, these were not the personal jewels of a shah, but the tributes of state: the ambassadorial gifts which poured into the Persian treasury from all those princes Arab and Oriental whose merchandise travelled these lands. Nicholas knew enough about gems to judge their weight and their quality: he had valued rubies in Trebizond, although none quite like these, round and solid as chestnuts. There were strings of balas stones here, of thirty carats, of eighty or even a hundred. There were emeralds, and pink and black pearls. There were also other objects, far more ancient: pendants and brooches, fillets and necklaces the like of which he had seen before only in papal collections, or in the villas of the Medici.

Uzum Hasan said, 'Take one box. I trust you. And should you find Persia a desert on your return, then at least you can pay the costs of your army.'

No one spoke. The gems glowed in the sun. 'My lord,' Nicholas said. 'I cannot take them. It would require an army to secure their safe passage. And even then, having arrived, I could not promise to find or send the men that you need, who may be committed elsewhere.'

The faintly Mongoloid eyes rested on him. Uzum Hasan said slowly, 'I think perhaps you are wise. I do not see, then, any way in which we may serve one another?'

'It is not impossible,' Nicholas said. 'My lord makes his needs known. The princes of the West contribute the payment, and my company is commissioned to fulfil your wants. Send your envoys to the Pope and the Emperor. Send them to Ivan of Muscovy. Depend on the good offices of the Patriarch of Antioch, who can pass between every faction. We have worked together before. We are friendly with Cairo, and have helped protect Cyprus against the Ottomans.'

'We have heard,' the Shah said. 'We shall consider. We shall speak again.' And he was dismissed.

The Patriarch, duly apprised, had seemed resigned, and not entirely displeased. 'At least you weren't fool enough to snatch at the treasure: that would have done for you and your Julius for good. As for the rest, what did you expect? He doesn't know yet what front to fight on. His instinct is to wipe out the threat from his son, but he may have to leave that to face an outright attack by the Sultan. Meanwhile, envoys are a nuisance. He'll get rid of us.'

'All of us?' Nicholas said.

'He's tried to dismiss Contarini three times. Rosso wants to go anyway. He'll keep Barbaro: he's a good, able man who knows the language and has lived for years in the region. He's taken Zeno's place as a drinking companion to the prince.'

'I can see Contarini wouldn't do. And you and I?' Nicholas asked.

'He's got most of what he wants from both of us, as we have from him. There's nothing much we can do, unless you want to stay another full year and make a living out of it. I'd prefer to go back to Caffa and home.'

'I'll speak to Julius,' Nicholas said.

HE SPOKE TO JULIUS that Wednesday, just after it had been announced that the illustrious lord Uzum Hasan was leaving Tabriz, and would give an audience the following day to his guests the ambassadors. In the ensuing atmosphere of abandon, permission had been given for Nicholas to admit his colleague to the wonders of the prince's menagerie, and they spoke, standing under trees in a stinking hot courtyard, watching an elephant nervously rehearsing how to go down on one knee and bow its head. Its mahout, from India but not Indian, was addressing it irritably. There was a Circassian Mameluke army under the rule of the Sultan of Herat. Julius was complaining.

'Contarini says they're going to send all of us home. I can't believe it. All this distance, and nothing even discussed!'

'Well . . .' Nicholas said; and confessed.

Julius took his duplicity rather well; listening all through the reports, as accurate as Nicholas could make them, of his two business meetings at the Palace, and interrupting only to put pertinent questions. At the end, he made the expected scathing strictures, but his chief reaction, clearly, was one of relief. 'I had to swear to keep quiet,' Nicholas said. 'There are spies. Talk about arms at the moment is unwise. He's promised one final meeting outside Tabriz if we want it.'

'When?' Julius asked. They were standing in front of a cage with a lion, and another with a silk-bodied beast with black stripes who reminded Nicholas, for no reason at all, of the vicomte Jordan de Ribérac. The beast opened its lips, revealing fangs shaped like just-swallowed doges. *More. More. Something to take the taste away.*

'Keep walking,' Nicholas said. 'My guess is that he's leaving tomorrow: the place is in a ferment. The rumour is that he'll shed us up north, after letting us see the real strength of his army. After that, the Patriarch goes on to Caffa, and those who want to, go with him and home.'

'And you?' Julius said. They passed an ounce. It was lying flat, waiting for snow.

Nicholas said, 'I've thought about it, but I don't want to stay here. What do you feel? Could you do with me in the Crimea, or even somewhere like Trebizond, if you don't mind punitive Turkish taxes? Look, there's an ostrich.'

Julius had seen it already. 'Christ, do you remember when you rode one in Bruges? You were a mad devil, Nicholas. And Trebizond isn't a bad idea. We could both go there from here, unless you'd rather make straight for Caffa and see to the gold. Anna should have it by now. She said you'd given her the password.'

They were looking up at a giraffe. A Seraph, they had called it in Egypt. Nicholas thought of a kite, and Kathi, and John le Grant crying with laughter. He thought of what it felt like, believing Gelis was dead. He said, 'I did, but I cheated. I gave Anna half the password, that's all. I didn't want to worry her, or upset her, but the Genoese had their suspicions of Ochoa. They're never out of the house. If she had got the gold, they would have found it.'

Julius's face slowly inflated and reddened, becoming a picture of luminous outrage. 'You did *what*! You lied to Anna? You left her stranded in Caffa without money!' The Seraph waded aside, revealing the sun.

'She has plenty. The furs. The silver. Enough for all summer. I told you.'

'And if you had been killed on this trip, what would have become of the gold? Ochoa *died* for it!'

'I know he did. So would you rather the Genoese got it? I promise you, that was the alternative. The only way to be sure was to arrange a password to be delivered by me. I have to be there.'

'Then you should have stayed!' Julius said loudly. The elephant skidded, and the mahout looked daggers, or perhaps knouts, at them both.

'Well, of course, but I didn't know you were coming to Tabriz!' Nicholas retorted in high irritation. 'And much bloody thanks I get for trying to fix up your trade with Uzum Hasan! I was told you'd be in Caffa, panting to warm up your marriage-bed.'

'Well, I'll wager you didn't get there anyway, you young bastard,' said Julius. 'I expect that's what this is all about, eh? She wouldn't lie down on her back, so you thought you'd just make her wait for the gold?'

He was so confident. He was so unforgivably confident. Nicholas said, 'And what makes you think *I* don't lie down on *my* back? Any port in a long, tedious winter. She was reasonably good. But come the spring, a man wants a change. She'll be quite happy to —' He caught Julius's arm as it moved and held it, hard. 'Prove me wrong.'

The arm resisted his violently, and then began to relax. Julius said, 'I don't need to. I know the way your silly mind works. If you hadn't shot me, you might have tried it. But you didn't.'

He didn't want a vote of confidence. He suddenly wanted to upset Julius as badly as he had been upset. He said deliberately, 'I didn't say I did try it. I said that she did.'

Julius pulled himself away. He said, 'I won't hear this. I won't have Anna made the victim of one of your games. I tell you I know, as if God had told me, that Anna would never be unfaithful with you.'

Genuine, unmistakable certainty rang in his voice. So did fury. So did distress. Julius stood, breathing fast, and fixing Nicholas with his gaze. There was a long pause. Then Nicholas stirred and said, 'Well, who would have believed it? Julius jumping through hoops over a joke. I'll dream up a better one next time. Calm down, and think about all that fine gold instead.'

'You God-damned —' Julius was still shaking with anger.

'I know,' said Nicholas penitently. 'I didn't know you'd turned serious in your old age. What do you want to see next?' People were still looking at them.

'Nothing,' said Julius. He pulled himself together. 'All right. If you've stopped playing the fool, you might as well tell me the other half of the password. If you mean us to have it. If you aren't planning to keep all the gold for yourself.'

'Of course I am. That's why I didn't stay with it in Caffa,' said Nicholas, exasperation and relief in his voice. 'You can have the entire password with pleasure. The point is, you silly sod, that I have to be there to say it. I told you. So we'll go to Caffa together. We'll collect the gold. You can have it for your business. Everything will be ineffably glorious provided you keep your head, lower your voice, and walk out of this yard before the keepers let loose all the animals. *Now!*'

They got out; and outwardly, at least, the wilful little dispute seemed to have ended. Nicholas supposed that he had been sure that it would. He tried, for the hundredth time, to stop thinking of Anna in Caffa; and experienced a bruised ache of pity for Julius's absolute faith in her chastity. Then he returned to his apartment, and the cheerful indifference of the Patriarch.

Chapter 29

FOR THEIR CEREMONIAL (and final) appearance before the lord Uzum Hasan in Tabriz, his guests had been endowed with garments of Persian provenance to replace their travelworn dress. Stepping out the following morning, escorted by beautiful youths and observed by deferential persons of birth — the turbaned nobles in satins and silks, the diminutive women with their skin swelling white within the open Persian bodices — Nicholas had looked forward to witnessing the Patriarch of Antioch emerge before him; to see him tramp up the marble steps of the Palace of the Eight Heavens with his overgrown tonsure enfolded in fine gauzy muslin, his stained cassock overlaid with lascivious silks, and his horny feet in embroidered gold sandals.

It was not to be. Attended humbly by Brother Orazio, Father Ludovico took his place in the small cortège wearing a marginally fancier version of his usual caped hood and cassock, with his crucifix clanking in front and an ancient Gospel held in both hands. The two Venetian envoys and Rosso were however in Persian attire, and so were Julius and Nicholas, behind them. It pleased Nicholas to note, in his present state of rebellious nausea, that Julius found the long tunic and trousers encumbering, and had not discovered the knack of knotting his head-linen under one ear. It was fine, seven-ducat stuff, and generally looked best (although Nicholas didn't suggest it) when worn with one earring. He himself had chosen a simple one of plain gold.

This time, Julius couldn't complain of discrimination. Musicians escorted them into the heart of the domain, where Nicholas himself had never yet penetrated, so that they glimpsed, bowered in green, the outlying buildings — the summer kiosks, the stables, the workshops, the library. The cupolas of the pavilions and the baths; the immense one-storey complex of the harem. The high decorated walls of a garden and, between marble arcades, the pink and white volutes of birds, swans and flamingos, mirrored in water. Then they began to pass through the different courtyards, so that they were plunged from heat to coolness, darkness to light. The morning sun stippled soaring towers of basket-weave brick, and glowed on surfaces where brick and faience were mingled together, paste-red and lustrous turquoise and ultramarine, forming geometric patterns, or flowers, or sacred words sprawling upwards in ecstasy, their shape cut by angels in spectacles. Some walls were set wholly with tiles and shone as if a gondola, passing, had rinsed them.

The vaults they walked under were tiled, or worked in faceted stucco such as they had in Granada, although Nicholas had seen only replicas, far from Spain, and ill-kept and dusty at that. Fashioned like honeycombs, they cascaded over his head in stone and plaster and wood. Carved stucco and tiles lined the anterooms and chambers and passages which led, ultimately, to the great central hall, its dadoes enamelled and gilded; its round silk carpet perfectly fitted to its circular floor and, high above, a painted ceiling so fresh that it glistened.

It showed Persian victories. It pictured, in gold and silver and blue, the splendour of subservient Ottoman embassies (their outcome enscripted); the magnificence of the prince's hunting expeditions and the wonders of his menagerie. There was a water-horse.

Nicholas gazed up at it, forgetting Uzum Hasan on his canopied dais. The Palace of the Eight Heavens: *Hesht Behesht*. The Muslim cosmos allowed for seven superimposed heavens: above these was only God on his throne. *Allah-u Akbar*. He said, half aloud, 'Who painted that?'

Josaphat Barbaro murmured. 'They claim someone from the court atelier at Herat — even Bihzad himself. I don't believe it. If you can paint a beautiful miniature, you can do the same on a wall. Tamerlane used Tabrizi artists in Samarkand.'

The Venetian knew a lot about Persia. He was the only one of them to be invited to stay: they knew that for certain by now. Contarini, threatening to indulge in a last, foolish protest, had been sternly advised to refrain — with patience by Barbaro, and with grating scorn by the envoy of Duke Charles of Burgundy, still gripping his Gospel. Now, majestic in his stiff robe of state and plumed cap with its diadem band, the prince Uzum Hasan confirmed the edict. They were to return to their virtuous masters, and affirm to them that he was about to go to war with the Ottoman. Letters would be prepared. The Shah added the appropriate felicities, commending each man, and sending his greetings through them to the exalted, respected, honoured and esteemed princes of Christendom, upholders of the religion of the sons of baptism (may their end be blissful), who might wish to join him. Finally, he expressed the hope that — in his unavoidable absence — their excellencies would do him the honour of indulging themselves at his table.

They were dismissed. His eye had lingered on Nicholas's earring. He wore two himself, each with a large pendant pearl.

In one of the pavilions, a further array of light silken gowns had been prepared, two for each of them. The Patriarch, as was his custom, took all he was given. Then they entered the gardens to sup.

Under any other circumstances, the Eighth Heaven would have borne out its name. Paradise, to a Persian, was a garden. Enclosed, the piercing green of washed leaves, the unwavering fountains amid the pools and channels of water shut out the shaly waterless desert of rubble and sand, grey and dun with its grey and dun villages; the densely ordered massed flowers with their heady scent stopped the senses: shock set its foot on the throat and then released it, to admit desire.

Not to Nicholas. The 'ud played; slender girls danced barefoot under the fruit trees and between the tall cypresses; dark-eyed pages stood, stirring the air with long-stemmed peacock fans. The sunlight moved through pierced marble screens and damascened the carpets on which the silver dishes were set and the goblets of wine, replenished over and over. Dim through the silks of the awnings the banks of blossom — pale narcissus, languid jonquils and lilies — swayed and lay still like indolent houris scarved in anemones. Nicholas picked up his bowl, which was inscribed with a legend in Kufic: *Deliberation before Action Protects against Regret*. His lip twitched.

'Mine is even more succinct,' said Josaphat Barbaro at his side. '*He who talks a lot, spills a lot*. I see you admiring the irrigation. They bring in *qanat* builders from Yazd who alone, they say, have the courage to crawl under the soil and stone to lead the pipes where they should go. You must have hoped, being knowledgeable about such things, that the prince would ask you to stay. He might have done, for he likes you. But I have had the advantage of living at Court through the winter.'

'The boon companion,' Nicholas said. Beyond the Patriarch on his other side, Julius was displaying all the gloomy discomfort of a civilised man compelled to eat on the ground with his shins crossed. Or the cramps might derive from his wound.

Barbaro wiped mutton grease from his fingers and watched a fresh procession of platters approach. They contained fantasies moulded from sugar, with sweet confections arranged all around them. The Venetian remarked, choosing one, 'You refer to the Book of Government, the primer of Sultans. Myself, I would make it required reading for every ambassador who comes to this country, believing the prince does not dream what the secret duties of an ambassador are: how we are expected to report on every idiosyncrasy of the land that we visit, down to the ability of the prince to hold his drink. But the boon companion is different. He is assumed to be of the prince's own race.'

'Does the Book say so?' Nicholas said. He drew on his memory.

'The common society of nobles leads to an assumption of arrogance, and tends to diminish the majesty of a king. A king cannot reign who

has not found boon companions with whom he can enjoy absolute freedom and intimacy. Those who are accepted for companionship should occupy no public office. Men of position require to hold the King in perpetual fear, whereas boon companions should be familiar, so that the King may say to them a thousand things, serious and frivolous, which would not befit the ears of his nobles. The boon companion must be well bred and accomplished, with an ample fund of astonishing anecdotes. He must be a pleasant partner for backgammon and chess; a musician perhaps; certainly a good conversationalist. But as to everything to do with the country and its cultivation, warfare, journeys and honours, the King should consult with his ministers, for that business is theirs.'

He paused and smiled. 'Does it not describe Caterino Zeno? Does it not describe you?'

'Does it not describe Mocenigo's ten Turkish concubines?' said the Patriarch sourly on his other side.

Barbaro laughed. 'You think western rulers should be above boon companions.'

'I do not think,' Nicholas said, 'that the Patriarch has given particular thought to their chosen position, but I can tell you that he is much against confidants. Every man should solve his own problems.'

'I should imagine,' remarked Josaphat Barbaro gently, 'that such advice is measured against the quality of the man, and the pressure upon him. I should give help where it is needed.'

His eyes had moved elsewhere. The Patriarch's followed them. The Patriarch snorted. 'And much good has it done the abstemious Ambrogio Contarini, whatever help you thought you were giving him. The man's a dangerous idiot.'

'It is a great house with many members,' Barbaro said. 'They cannot all be gifted with wisdom. There were two Barbaros and six Contarinis among the dead when Constantinople fell, and this man's excellent brother was my *sopracomito* on Cyprus and will follow me, I hope, in Albania.'

'We shall protect your friend if we can,' Nicholas said. 'But you know that I no longer represent my Bank, or have any connection with Venice.'

'Then you should do well in Caffa,' Barbaro said. 'You should stay there. They need men of sense.' There was grey in the brown strands of his hair, but he had the firm, flexible voice of a man much accustomed to debate and conversation and, it turned out, the exercise of lenient mimicry. And for an aristocrat from a Venetian palazzo (if not quite Contarini's Ca' Doro), he could produce a campfire laugh of the dimension of a Tartar attack. An ambassador as shrewd and observant as any, and a boon companion as well, to those who felt unable to rule their own lives.

It was afternoon when they left the garden, their servants bearing their gifts, and filed again through the Palace to take formal leave of the prince. He received them this time in a light coat that showed mail armour beneath, and his trousers were thrust into boots. Outside, the streets were full of drovers and carts, but the main army had gone. Within the hour, the prince had left Tabriz as well.

It was not a final separation. Two days later, the ambassadors followed, travelling north, and for nearly three weeks kept company with their host and his army, living in tents, and lingering in one place or another, so long as the grazing allowed. Occasionally he would receive them in the field, and presents of food sometimes arrived from his cooks. Nicholas had a last, business-like meeting at which Julius was present, and was given, in private, a small casket whose contents, drawn from a larger, he recognised. Contarini, Rosso and the Patriarch received personal gifts and formal ones to present to their masters, including pairs of magnificent swords. Josaphat Barbaro, who was not leaving, contrived to see Nicholas alone.

'I told you. You are in favour. You could come back one day.' He had seen the casket of jewels.

Nicholas said, 'I wish you were coming. So what secret reports have you confided to Messer Ambrogio, that being the duty of an ambassador? Or would you prefer not to tell me? They say we have moved out of Tabriz because of plague.'

The other man smiled. 'There is plague, and it is spreading. But of course the prince left to make war.'

'And then stopped,' Nicholas said.

'And then, certainly, slowed. My guess is that he has had news, and is waiting for more. His couriers are the fastest in the world.'

His couriers rode racing dromedaries. 'Crete?' Nicholas said. 'The Sultan has launched his attack against Crete, and so, for the moment, Uzum Hasan is free to do as he wants?'

Barbaro's brown gaze was direct. 'The Turkish fleet left Constantinople last month. They carried an army, but where they went is not known. Crete is likely. It is rich, and Venetian, and acts as an arsenal for her ships in the Levant. I am telling you this because, whatever has happened, it will be known in Venice long before Ambrogio gets there. And yes, if Turkey is busy elsewhere, the prince can march to deal with his son. I am waiting to see what occurs. Then I, too, shall leave.'

'I am sorry,' Nicholas said. With the part of his mind that was not numb, he wished he could convey the fact that he distrusted Venice, and yet regretted the decline in its glory for the sake of men such as this: the adventurers, the pioneers, the inquisitive merchants. All through his journey in Persia, Josaphat Barbaro had observed and filed what he saw, from the black oil of the Caspian, which could be lit but not drunk, to the smallest detail of the places and people he had encountered.

He had done the same in the years spent as Venetian consul in Tana. From his own perspective of one solitary winter in disguise, Nicholas had worn several nights through with the Venetian, recreating that strange Crimean society, half icy, half tropical; discussing, conjecturing; sharing knowledge. Thirty-seven years ago, Tana had been a Venetian colony, and Barbaro had befriended the Tartars who came there. They suffered, he said, from sore mouths caused, they claimed, by lack of salt. But Barbaro had seen mouths like that among seamen, and it was not caused by an absence of salt.

Then, Nicholas had said nothing of Ochoa, as he said nothing, up to that point, about gold. Barbaro's tales were not about achievements or money. One of the best had to do with his mortifying endeavour (for a bet) to dig for Carpathian gold in a burial mound, hacking through frozen sub-soil with crews of sceptical labourers, to uncover no more than you would on a rubbish heap. It was in the wake of that lugubrious story that Barbaro suddenly said, 'But you know, of course, that there is treasure in Cyprus. Or was.'

He could be silent, or pretend. Instead, Nicholas said, 'I know of Zacco's will, which referred to it. It may well have gone by now. I do not have it.'

Barbaro said, 'The story ran that it was yours.'

'It was put there by a man called Ochoa, with Zacco's collusion. Zacco did not like the Knights of St John.'

'They were claiming it? I do not like them myself,' Barbaro said. 'I hope the right person receives it, and that the recipient does not prove to be the small, scented person I once mentioned.'

'David de Salmeton? He could not return,' Nicholas said. 'Your Venetians would kill him.'

'We Venetians like money,' Barbaro said. 'Which reminds me. I have brought my own dice, much better loaded than yours. What shall we play, and what shall we play for?'

He had a store of good bawdy songs, from the long winter nights in the fishing-grounds, and knew all the verses of some of those the Russians sang. The bagpipe ditty had become an unspoken favourite, launched upon at a certain stage of the night when Contarini was not within hearing, and reaching its last two lines, and refrain, with a shout:

. . . De cop de cotel
Fu sa muse perchie . . .

Cibalala du riaus du riaus
Cibalala durie.

Their parting, when it came, was brisk and friendly, as befitted men who were not boon companions.

On that, the final day with the prince, his guests were treated to a ceremonial parade of his army, viewed from a pavilion raised on a bluff. Contarini, anxiously calculating, counted ten thousand foot and twenty-five thousand cavalry passing below them. Rosso and Barbaro said nothing. Nicholas stared at them unseeing, blinded by the dazzle on helmets and cuirasses, the brilliant harness; the housings on horses and camels; the intricate work on the round silken shields. The tall standards crowded like hollyhocks and the sun flashed from raised swords. The prince was marching upon his son, or upon the Turk: no one was quite certain which. Or if they were, they did not say.

On Wednesday, the twenty-eighth day of June, the envoys left Uzum Hasan for the last time. Two Persian legates went with them. For some — the Patriarch, Rosso — it was the end of one of several such visits, and carried no significance beyond what was obvious: the prince, in age, was striving after twenty-two years to hold his throne against enemies from within and from without, and might not long survive. For Contarini, in tears, it was a blessed release from a horrid assignment, marred by the parting from his dear friend Messer Josaphat. For Julius, it represented a business coup now complete, which he immediately set aside, in order to dwell on the treasure that waited in Caffa.

For Nicholas, it was the laying to rest of a myth that had pursued him all his life. He had met the son of Sara Khatun for long enough to show that there was a career for him here, if only when Barbaro concluded his mission and left. In the event, Nicholas did not think that he would return so far south after Caffa. He had not rejected the Levant. It seemed to him that his future might well lie there, on one side of the Black Sea or the other. But not at Spaan or Shiraz or Tabriz. There was a tide running here which Venice might have changed once, but no longer would. And he could not dam it back, any more than could the Patriarch.

For both of them, the ride back towards Caffa covered much the same ground as before, but this time they travelled in the heat and the dust of high summer, and the cavalcade was very much bigger, for the routes of the Venetian and Russian envoys passed through Caffa as well.

It did not preserve them from trouble. The formidable personality of the Patriarch might wring hospitality, once again, from the scattered Christian communities, but the two envoys of Uzum Hasan turned out to be untravelled novices; they carried no weight once the Georgian frontier was crossed, and precious little before it. With sobering frequency, they lost horses, money and weapons to troops of soldiers, official and unofficial, or to the population of some village which took against them, or to the keepers of river crossings. Women were often the worst. In Mingrelia, King Bendian had just died, and it was safest to sleep in the forests.

Julius rode beside Nicholas, sometimes silent, sometimes passing time in irritable interrogation; Julius, who once enjoyed campaigning, now preferred comfort. He was quick, however, to lend his authority at moments of danger, and showed himself invaluable on occasions such as the woodland feast of bleeding beef and rivers of wine offered by the monarch of Georgia, where Julius held his own (as did Nicholas) in a testing debauch which continued all night. The Venetian ambassador excused himself almost before it began, and his pious entourage followed him.

The rest of the time, Julius showed a tendency to return, in a roundabout manner, to the topic of Anna, although in terms nothing like the abrasive ones of their quarrel at Tabriz. Even so, circumvention was difficult, even sickening. Unlike that of Barbaro, Julius's conversation had always been personal, the hidden motives piercing the surface like rocks. When Julius riled him, travelling north, Nicholas frequently broke into song, forcing Julius to join him. He couldn't sing, but some of the others could, and it stopped some of the questions. But not all.

'What exactly did you promise the Khan to make him send for your furs? Anna said you *saved* her from the Russians.' (Spoken with Rosso within earshot.)

'What concessions should we extract from this new Tudun Karaï Mirza? If he ate off skins, Anna must have found him amusing.'

Then: 'Who is this imam Ibrahiim you made Anna listen to: some black friend of Umar's? What happened to Brother Lorenzo? How much gold exactly do you think there will be?'

And, as it finally occurred to him one day: 'How do you propose to get into Caffa, considering that the Genoese threw you out?'

He could give Julius the answer to that one at least. If Contarini could get in, then he could. There was still a Venetian consul who would hide them until he could construct a new identity.

At some such point, tiring of the inquisition, Nicholas would ride off to the two Persian envoys, with whom he was attempting to make friends. They were both scared, and therefore defensive. One of them, on his way to Moscow with Rosso, he would never see again. Or so he prayed. The other was going to the Duke of Burgundy, and would meet at least someone Nicholas knew.

He had been waiting for Julius to mention Gelis and he did, the day before they were due to arrive on the shores of the Black Sea at last. It was four weeks to the day since they had left Barbaro and Uzum Hasan, and had plunged into a world of isolated monasteries and unfriendly alien towns. In Fasso, there would be shipping, and news.

There would also be Genoese. Coming south, Contarini's small party had escaped notice by merging with the twilight Latin community: Venetians who had turned Muslim and Genoese who had made local marriages. He and Rosso proposed to perform the last stage of the journey with their companions by boat, and make for Contarini's last lodging, at the house of a Circassian called Marta. The Patriarch, Julius and Nicholas, unobtrusive in western dress, set off to the same destination with their guides and servants by horse. It was hotter, but offered some escape, it was said, from the gnats. Sheltering under a lone tree at noon, chewing crusts and spooning down millet paste in a vortex of feathery insects, the travellers were inclined to doubt this. Julius, whose growing cheerfulness nothing could shake, tended a choking smudge fire, and rallied Nicholas when they were alone. 'Don't complain. At least you're not in the boat getting swamp fever. I don't want you sick yet. Not until you're made us all rich at Caffa.'

For a day he had talked of nothing but Caffa, questioning Nicholas again and again about details. He asked how Anna looked when Nicholas had seen her last: how she wore her hair, what gowns she had had made. It was as if the scene in Tabriz had never taken place, obliterated by the present prospect of joy. Caffa was there, within reach, a short journey over the sea, and all Julius's hopes and desires leaped towards it. He smiled, and said, 'You sneer at my singing, but now you know what Anna can do. She said she'd made some music for Jodi.'

Nicholas had already stopped trying to eat. He said, 'It was charming. I remember.' He started to rise.

Julius put a hand on his arm. 'No. I want to say this. You know Gelis visited Bonne, and talked about Jodi and marriage? If she is happy, and you still agree, it would make the best of all we are doing. The Patriarch thinks so as well. And as for old Thibault, it doesn't matter.'

'Thibault?' Nicholas said. He ceased to move.

'Gelis went to see him in Montello, didn't she? After Anna and Kathi suggested it. Anna wrote that you were upset, and I'm sorry. But I thought you wouldn't mind knowing the truth.'

'Do I know the truth?' Nicholas said.

Another man would have looked embarrassed: Julius displayed impatience. 'Well, you don't seem to be legitimate; not unless the tale of twins can be proved. And the old man held out no hope of that, from what I hear. Who would have thought he was shamming, the devil?'

The gnats sang and buzzed round his head, high as reeds: like an organ, like bagpipes inflating, or deflating. (*De cop de cotel/Fu sa muse perchie.*)

'I don't think he was. Pretending,' Nicholas said.

'He let all that happen to you?'

'He was ill, then. When he could, he tried to do something. He didn't wish harm to me, or Adelina. I pity him. Fate was more cruel to him than to us.'

'Fate was better to you than Adelina,' Julius said. 'Wherever she is, she suffered three years of hell.'

'One,' Nicholas said. 'She went to a convent.' The gnats wailed. He looked up.

'You were told she went to a convent,' Julius said. 'I found out later. She went to a house Jaak had outside Geneva. He used to spend the night there.'

'Until she was eight,' Nicholas said very slowly. His grandfather's letter had said so. He added, 'I didn't know.' That emerged slowly, too. The black oil of Baku: turgid; choking; inflammable.

'Why should you?' Julius said. 'You were a boy. You knew nothing of that.'

He was waiting. Nicholas knew it; knew why; knew what he ought to say, but could not. He drew together all his forces, and spoke. 'I don't look back. All those people are dead, and those who are alive don't deserve blame, or are not worth troubling over. You have a happy life now. So have I, near enough.'

'I wonder if Adelina has,' Julius said. 'Gelis is trying to find her.' He rose, and stretched, and stood smiling. 'But what's that to us? Are you going to sit there all day? We are going to Caffa!'

Cibalala du riaus du riaus
Cibalala durie.

IN FASSO, there was shipping, and news. The hibernation, the isolation, the incubation was over; the odyssey which had started in March was ending now, in the last days of July, its adventurers alive, unharmed, ready to take their place again in the busy highways washed by the sea.

Their guide discovered the Circassian's house, but no one within it to greet them. Inside, they found familiar baggage. Contarini and Rosso had arrived, so it seemed, and gone out. Julius, too eager to wait, strode off to find them. The Patriarch, who was expected elsewhere, decided to linger. Brother Orazio and the servants went off, leaving Nicholas and Father Ludovico together. The Patriarch said, 'Are you not eager, also, for news?'

'No,' said Nicholas.

'Because you fear for your friends? The lord Uzum Hasan, if the Turkish fleet has passed down the coast and its armies are invading his country? Or Brother Lorenzo and his fellows on Crete, where the monks of Mount Sinai have a monastery? Or does everything seem uninteresting to you but the pleasures of returning to Caffa?'

'You do not want to hear my troubles,' Nicholas said.

'I don't ask to hear your troubles, you fool,' the Patriarch said. 'I ask about your hopes.'

'They are the same thing,' Nicholas said.

Soon after that, they heard the sound of running footsteps, and calling. The Venetian ambassador would never run, although they heard his shrill voice in the clamour; Rosso's grating tones also. But it was Julius who burst in through the door and stood gasping against it, his high-boned face smeared with tears, and mucus, and sweat. And it was Julius who uttered the news.

'We can't join Anna in Caffa. There is no Caffa. There hasn't been for seven weeks. The Turkish fleet wasn't going to Crete; it was coming to the Crimea. It landed its guns, and its armies, and mastered it all. The Peninsula is a graveyard; every foreigner killed or enslaved; every town, every fortress demolished. And none of us was there.'

The Patriarch's hand closed on his crucifix. He said, 'Do you think we could have stopped it? Is there any news of your wife?'

Nicholas shut his eyes.

Julius said, 'How could there be? At best, she'll be in some — some Turkish hothouse.' He choked.

'Perhaps not,' Nicholas said. He did not entirely believe what he was saying. Women generally received the fate Julius feared. He understood all Julius felt about Anna mainly because he felt it himself, about some stubborn Russians who would not heed advice, and a great Cairene teacher who, whatever threatened, would not abandon his flock. He said, 'You might find her.'

Julius had become very still. He said, 'Then I am going to Caffa.'

'You can't,' said Rosso. It was contemptuous.

'I can. I will,' Julius said. He had quietened; looking at no one; preoccupied with his thoughts.

There was a space. The Patriarch looked at Nicholas, saying nothing.

Nicholas said, 'Then I go with you. For if Anna has escaped, I know where to find her.'

Chapter 30

PLUNGED INTO ITS OWN summer wars, the West did not hear of the shocking events in the Levant until the end of the season. When Venice relayed the warning that something nasty was brewing in retaliation for the Turkish defeat in Moldavia, Caffa had already fallen. No one knew it. The Black Sea, now a Turkish lake, let nothing leak out in summer but anchovies. And even if it had, nothing would have been done about it. Among the Christian nations that summer there were few issues as important — how could there be? — as the King of England's invasion of France. The better-known pirates, in particular, were flocking to Gascony.

Gelis, now a military veteran, found a macabre enjoyment in sharing with John le Grant the army's screaming exasperation with Charles of Burgundy: his addiction to Neuss and his escalating conflicts with the Swiss which continued even when the Emperor marched into Cologne in March, and young Duke René of Lorraine decided to change sides in May. That said, it all increased the Bank's profit and kept Gelis occupied. Unlike others she could name, she and Diniz in Bruges kept strict control of the Bank's response to its increasing opportunities. It was firmly in Burgundian favour, but not over-extended. The damage done by Nicholas was almost repaired.

She tried not to think of him, or of the letter he had promised to send about an enterprise of which she had heard nothing more. As far as she knew, Nicholas was still in Caffa with Anna and now, presumably, Julius. From Julius and Anna, returning, the Bank could no doubt expect some news; but not before the end of the summer. Then, of course, there would arise this proposed betrothal between Jodi and Bonne.

She still could not understand it. Nor, she knew, could John. He talked of Nicholas now and then, usually when reminded by some unfortunate event on the battlefield. She had not realised, until then, how much fighting the two men had seen together, dovetailing their skills: setting traps for the Turks at Trebizond; mining, tunnelling, designing, casting cannon. Guns required numeracy; so did navigation, and hydraulics, and toys. She heard about their mechanical elephant, and the carnival at Florence where they met. Nicholas had come hunting for the engineer who had almost saved Constantinople, and John had been with him, more or less, ever since.

'And come to regret it,' Gelis said; and he had nodded.

'He's a wrecker. I told you. And an innocent at the same time, what's worse.'

'An *innocent*!' Gelis had said; and he had looked at her, russet brows raised.

'You didn't see him at Trebizond. Not just in retrieving that silly wee bitch from Doria, but plunging into hopeless dilemmas. Which to rescue; which to kill; which to betray. Good and bad, right and wrong; duty; loyalty. In the Tyrol as well. And in Cyprus.' He broke off and said, 'I bubbled, myself, at Famagusta. You don't know a man until you know what makes him greet. An innocent. No grasp of reality.'

'He saved your life,' she said. Astorre had said that.

'Oh, aye. As Julius saved his. We made a good team.'

It was only later that she discovered that the *silly wee bitch* was Catherine de Charetty, the younger sister in Bruges who was going to marry her own second cousin. It was very much later that she found out what le Grant had meant about Famagusta. It had nothing to do with her sister, who had died there, but she was charitable enough to suppose that Nicholas had been affected by that as well.

She had not seen Nicholas in Trebizond, but she had watched him in Africa, where a simple voyage for profit had also turned into a trial of character and a testing-place for beliefs. She understood, for the first time, what John le Grant might mean by innocent; and, not for the first time, how alike he and Nicholas were. She had begun to realise, ever since Edinburgh, that these men and women were Nicholas's family, as much as she or Jodi or Marian de Charetty could ever be or have been. And she realised that the act by which he had divorced himself from them was wholly hapless.

Nicholas had ruined his own life for nothing; because of a simple refusal to school his own talents, and a level of undiluted physical energy that made him excessively hard to control. Only Kathi, sometimes, had been able to manage that. And of course she herself had a key, but had vowed not to apply it. Passion was not enough, as her sister would have discovered. The question was . . . The question increasingly was, whether it was better than nothing.

As April approached, it seemed to Gelis that she had been separated from her son for long enough. She wrote to Scotland, asking with affection after the infant Margaret of Berecrofts, and enquiring what her parents' plans might be for the summer. She also wrote to Clémence de

Coulanges, in the friendly, easier terms that befitted her altered relationship with the future wife of Dr Tobie, and asked for her news, and her advice.

At that time, it seemed to Gelis that Jodi was safer in Scotland than within reach of the cannons of France. She had a journey to make, and a letter to wait for. Then she would go to Scotland.

IN ROME, packed with the Easter pilgrims of a jubilee year, the name of Nicholas de Fleury had begun to irritate Anselm Adorne's eldest son, a lawyer in clerical orders in the household of Cardinal Hugonet. Jan Adorne, who was thirty, had known de Fleury from boyhood and already despised him as a jumped-up apprentice, even before the present ceaseless reports of de Fleury's doings in Poland, linked as they were to the dismissal of Jan's own father. First, prominent at every Roman reception, there appeared a Persian mission led by Caterino Zeno the Venetian diplomat, who had advanced de Fleury money, it seemed, to help take his own father's place. Then came further tales of de Fleury's friendship with the Queen of Poland and the traitor Buonaccorsi, related by his father's friend Cardinal Barbo, the papal legate to Poland.

The saga even continued in Naples, where Jan Adorne found himself on both papal and Burgundian affairs, since his master was brother to Hugonet, the Duke of Burgundy's Chancellor. The Duke wanted soldiers, and had sent the Grand Bastard his brother to pick up a mercenary army under the nose of the Pope. It would be awkward, of course, since the army was intended to fight the Holy Roman Emperor, not the Turk. The Duke trusted his brother to explain that Burgundy was already opposing the Turk by sending to the court of Uzum Hasan the worthy Patriarch Ludovico da Bologna, and the excellent Nicholas de Fleury the banker, whose former partners in Bruges and at Neuss were so ably assisting the Duke. The Duke trusted that if, as a consequence, Uzum Hasan were to march on the Turk, due honour would be paid to these two intrepid men.

Jan's noble Genoese blood boiled. Someone said (at the reception that followed), 'Any such honour was deserved, of course, by your father. The Mission should have been his. I cannot understand why Lord Cortachy was recalled.'

'Venetian jealousy,' Jan Adorne said. He could only have said it to someone else of Genoese extraction. This was Prosper Schiaffino de Camulio de' Medici, once the peppery Milanese envoy to France, whose Camogli ancestors had exercised their fishing skills close to Tana, and who knew all about Venetian jealousy. Jan turned fully, and gave the man a smile. Beside Camulio, he now saw, was a courtier of quite another kind: a man whose beauty of feature and hair quite overcame his lack of height, and whose lustrous eyes, dwelling on Jan, caused Jan's smile to widen quite naturally.

'Ah, Venice!' the stranger said, casting a glance, half affectionate, half comical at his companion Camulio. 'At least in Scotland you will be free of her.'

Jan Adorne, changing his smile, turned his gaze back to the Genoese. 'I should have congratulated you! They have extended your remit! Papal notary, collector for the Apostolic Camera and nuncio of the Pope in England, Ireland *and* Scotland! My father will be ravished!' He kept his smile in place. His father, no admirer of Pope Sixtus, was not likely to be entranced by the appearance in Scotland of Camulio, a middle-aged protégé of the Pope's nephew.

'And so will the Pope's dear Giuliano,' observed the beautiful stranger gravely from behind. 'But not enough, I fear, to send Prosper so far from his side. Fortunately for me, it seems that I may act for him as his business adviser. I hope to be in Scotland by June. I may even be fortunate enough to meet your dear father pursuing his duties. Or your cousins, Sersanders and Katelijne. Or even the wife and son of poor Nicholas de Fleury who, I hear, is pursuing some dreary task in the Levant.'

Jan gazed at him, reddening. 'I am sorry . . . ?'

'My dear Jan, why should you remember your visit to Cairo, exalted as you now are in the heart of the Christian world? My name is David de Salmeton, formerly of the Vatachino. David de Salmeton, adviser to the Collector for the Apostolic Camera in Scotland, our mutual friend Prosper. Is it not delightful? Would Nicholas not be enchanted, if he knew?'

That night, Jan Adorne wrote to his father.

I'm sure you remember de Salmeton. I can tell you at least he is rich: I have seen the palazzo he lives in, and he spends, they say, like a prince. Do I remember that Kathi didn't like him? She'd better change her mind now that she's married a Berecrofts. A man with the ear of the Curia can make or break a merchant firm like her husband's.

That letter went off in April and reached Anselm Adorne in June, at the height of the solemn Masses, the rich processions, the extravagant banquets staged at Neuss by the Duke and the Emperor (without Nicholas de Fleury), to celebrate the end of the war and the siege. Adorne attended them without joy. Time, lives, and a hundred thousand florins of Burgundian money had been squandered on fruitless campaigns which had lapsed only because France had entered the field once again, and England was demanding attention.

Anselm Adorne read his son's letter in his tent, and sent for his chamberlain, for here was something he could deal with which was personal to his own family. God knew, he had little time for de Fleury, but he knew more than Jan about the nature of David de Salmeton. De Fleury was not, of course, within reach of M. de Salmeton's displeasure, but his family were, and Kathi, who had helped foil him in Cairo. Anselm Adorne wrote to her in Scotland immediately, and also to his nephew Sersanders. Lastly, he sent word to de Fleury's wife, supposing she still held that name, suggesting a meeting in Ghent.

IN PEACE AND WAR, Anselm Adorne, Baron Cortachy, was a frequent and favoured visitor to both the palace and castle in Ghent. His sister had married Daniel Sersanders, a political firebrand, but born of a great local family. His daughter had served the Duchess of Burgundy's English mother in London. He was a friend of Louis de Gruuthuse who was a member of the permanent Council. With generations of fiscal skills behind him, Adorne was one of the advisers upon whom the Duchess Margaret relied when she was forced to raise money, yet again, for the ducal wars. The calls Anselm Adorne made to the Duchess's court were rarely social ones: they were to guide and warn the Duchess and Chancellor Hugonet in their dealings with those independent and rough-spoken communities within Flemish Burgundy which the Duke so blithely regarded as his vassals.

Technically, no doubt, they were. Technically, they had no right to revolt as Liège and Ghent itself had done in the past. As a boy, Adorne himself had been forced to flee with his family during another upset in his own Bruges. Merchants, diplomats, farmers of taxes incurred duties both to the burghers whom they represented, and to the Duke whom they also served. A clever man, trusted by both sides, could often keep both sides out of trouble. But not always. And sometimes wealth and high office did not seem worth the strain.

On this particular warm day in June, Adorne rode first to the castle, where the Chancellor awaited him. Although different in nature, the two men had long formed a useful alliance which had produced, among other things, Jan's present post with Cardinal Philibert, the Chancellor's brother. The Chancellor knew the gossip of Rome. He also knew Gelis van Borselen, who was in Ghent these days almost as often as Adorne, and who seemed to be proving herself to be as useful to Burgundy as her husband had been at Trèves.

The Chancellor had listened, in the interstices of a more urgent discussion, to the gist of Jan's message. He said, 'Camulio is a plotter; you know that. He will spy for anyone, but mostly for Genoa and Milan. With what he knows, he makes an excellent collector of taxes. But even he cannot travel everywhere. Your David de Salmeton will be expected to exert local pressure. You say he is a dealer?'

'He was an agent of the firm of Vatachino. They asked him to leave, I was told, after some error of judgement in Cyprus which lost them all their property on the island. He has not been heard of from then until now.' He was merely reporting. He did not expect Hugonet to possess information, but knew that he could rely on him now to make enquiries. Since the Vatachino had called in its agents and withered, there had been no comparable power in that field. One wondered if the infiltration of Gelis van Borselen had contributed to that failure. The other theory, of course, held that the Vatachino had only been created to vanquish Nicholas de Fleury in business. De Fleury had gone, and so had his strongest competitors; except for this man, for whom the contest, it seemed, had become personal.

When, presently, Adorne repaired to the small house he still kept in Ghent, he found Gelis van Borselen already waiting, with the engineer John le Grant standing beside her. Their expressions puzzled him. Then comprehension broke, and he said quickly, 'I have no news, good or bad, from the Levant; only a warning about David de Salmeton. You remember him?'

Their response this time was all he expected, and more. 'What? What about him?' the engineer said.

The woman who cared for the house entered and poured them some wine. He smiled at her. It was not the family mansion in which Anselm and Katelijne had been born: that had long since been sold. This small property still belonged to the Sersanders family: Adorne maintained it, and his nephew and niece used it when in Ghent. Kathi's household would require, he thought, amused, to remain small. He raised his glass, and drank, and spoke when the woman was gone.

'De Salmeton is going to Scotland. He has an advisory post with the Papal Collector. His dislike of your husband could affect your son and my niece, and I suggest it is worth exercising a little caution. Kathi intended coming to Flanders this autumn. I have told her instead to come right away, and bring your son and her husband and child. The man may have reformed. But until we know more, I feel our families will be safer in Bruges for a little while. I had no time to ask your permission. I hope you agree.'

'How did you hear?' the man said. The woman was gazing at him.

'You do agree?' Adorne asked her, troubled.

'Yes! Of course, yes!' Gelis said. She loosened her hands. 'Of course, thank you. But how did you hear?'

He told them, while the three glasses of wine lay untouched. Once only, the woman interrupted. 'David de Salmeton had money?'

'He was rich, according to Jan.'

'He would be,' said the engineer flatly. 'My lord, you've got your niece there to think of, but our wee lad is sore threatened, too. What boat did ye send with your letter?'

Our wee lad. It was not, perhaps, surprising. The marriage was broken, and this was a kind man, with a streak of genius about him, like the other one. Adorne said, 'Not even the Banco di Niccolò, I promise you, could have provided anything faster. I mean no offence, but the post of Conservator of Scots Privileges has its uses. And I have asked Sersanders's partner to bring them back personally.'

'I'm sorry. We're anxious,' said le Grant.

'You came here especially to tell me,' said Gelis van Borselen. She was desperately pale. She said, 'I cannot quite understand how such a man comes to be attached to a papal official.'

It was what Adorne had sought to find out from Hugonet. Now he said, 'He has been accused of nothing. Nothing has been proved against him but some maladroit behaviour in Cyprus. And even if it had, Prospero de Camulio has asked for him, and for this Pope, that is enough.' He waited. Then he said, 'You have worked with de Salmeton. You have seen what he did with the Vatachino. Is he clever? Is he dangerous? Or is he vindictive only where it is safe, at some petty court?'

The woman answered. 'He is clever. He is dangerous. And in Scotland, he has found just such another petty court.'

LATER, IN THE GARDEN of the tavern where they did not share beds, Gelis raged to herself and to John, who sat, saying little. Her furious anxiety, beginning with Jodi, dwelt on all the possible victims: Kathi and her husband and baby; Bel of Cuthilgurdy; the Berecrofts family themselves. Then her voice changed. 'Robin's family don't know de Salmeton. They may not believe he's a danger. They may not let Kathi go.'

At which John had stared at her in genuine derision and said, 'You think they could stop Katelijne Sersanders if she wanted to leave? Dinna fret. She'll tell them all she knows, and they'll be the first to send them to safety. They're a tough old crew, the merchants of Berecrofts. If de Salmeton wants a trade war, he'll get one.'

'If the warning comes in time,' Gelis said.

Neither of them had so far discussed de Salmeton's affluence and, in his stubborn soul, John was glad to kick the subject aside. Two months ago, he had been present in Neuss when, returned blanched and stiff from a long absence, Gelis had found and opened the promised missive from Nicholas. Except that it had not been from Nicholas: the message was not in his writing, nor in code, and had arrived by no recondite path of the mind. It had come redirected from Bruges, and before that from Venice. *Inform John and Moriz that the enterprise sadly is void. They should not speak of it.*

Nicholas had had to send the first message direct: if he died, the information was important. Now it was no longer important, and he hadn't troubled to write.

For Gelis, that was the blight; not the contents of the message, about which it was possible to be philosophic: endeavours did fail. Yet John had been surprised to notice how soon she recovered. It was as if her feelings were no longer engaged, or were differently focused, or as if she were armed by some unimaginable talisman. He wondered if she would have shown as much fear if Nicholas were in danger, not Jodi. Then he thought, ashamed, that she probably would, because he himself would. You didn't need to be someone's husband or wife to admire them, and be concerned for them, and desire to know they were safe. He wished he had the detachment of Nicholas; and then remembered, uncomfortably, the tales he had resurrected for Gelis which made the opposite point. A man who did not care for his fellows would have resented and shed them. Only an idiot would shower them with helpful statistics. He forced himself to remember, belatedly, just what Nicholas had done in Scotland, and to Julius, and why he deserved all that had happened to him.

He looked at Gelis and said shortly, 'It's all right. We'll hear from him soon.'

IN EDINBURGH, where the month opened less warmly, Katelijne Sersanders, lady of Berecrofts, had no premonition of her uncle's warning racing towards her, being satisfactorily immersed in a promising young household. Her greatest problem had lain in the handling of Jodi, Nicholas's small son and her husband Robin's disciple and critic. Her own care, above all, had been to refrain from replacing Gelis: to preserve, against all her inclinations, a demeanour towards Gelis's son which was friendly, but not over-close: that of a sensible aunt. Her greatest triumph, had she been asked to name it, lay in the fact that Jodi had grown to be decently tolerant of his five-month-old co-habitant Margaret, who after all was only a girl, and not allowed to go hunting.

It compensated for the professional friction between Jodi's new master-at-arms and Raffo, his bodyguard. A brawny, middle-aged mercenary with spectacular scars, Raffo had been one of the two men engaged to look after Gelis and Jodi. Jodi was proud to be the pupil of Captain Cuthbert, but Raffo, eighteen months at his side, was his friend. This, since his parents were missing, and Clémence and Tobie were in the absent-minded stage of betrothal, appeared to Kathi to be extremely convenient. A boy needed someone to teach him how to kill things, and Clémence had reached her limit in that direction, now she had Tobie.

In any case, Kathi had Bel. In a city of stout-hearted, strong-willed old women, Bel of Cuthilgurdy had had more than most to do with Nicholas and his estranged Scottish family, and had shared his voyage to Africa with Gelis. Although her home was in the west, close to the Beltrees of Nicholas and the Kilmirren castle of the vicomte de Ribérac, Bel shared an Edinburgh house with her neighbour the vicomte, and since his absence in Portugal, often stayed there. Jodi grew accustomed to climbing the steep hill of the Canongate, passing through and up to the High Street of Edinburgh, and then being hoisted by Raffo to chap at the door of his wee Aunty Bel.

Today, to begin with, it was entirely as usual: he was welcomed in, his bonnet taken off, and his striped hose and new belt admired, while Raffo went off down the stairs, where the giggling always started, sooner or later. Then Jodi was given a biscuit and, seated beside his wee aunt (his *old* wee aunt), was asked to say what Margaret was doing these days (teething); when he had last heard from his clever mother (yesterday); and whether he had made any more drawings to keep for his father, who was away selling cloth to men with slanty eyes and flat faces.

Jodi, who preferred to believe that his father was away fighting Turks with slanty swords and hooked noses, described his latest drawing, which showed himself on a horse hunting foxes, but without the leading-rein and Captain Cuthbert riding beside him. Drawing the fox had given him some trouble, as he had only been once, and they hadn't caught any. He could improve on it next time. Or he could ask Master Cochrane to help him.

It was just at this point that someone else chapped on the street door and unusual things started to happen, such as Aunty Bel's serving-woman going to open it and then giving a cry, while the sound of trampling and jingling came from the outer room, as if a band of jousters had come in by mistake. Then, suddenly, Aunty Bel's room was full of men. The door in front was flung back by the jousters, and the one at the back was thrown open by Raffo, who leaped through it, drawing his sword.

It had happened before. It had happened in Trèves. Jodi's lip trembled, and he opened his mouth. Then he squeaked, having the breath knocked out of him by Aunty Bel's stout little arms clipping him fast to her side. '*Now then!*' said Aunty Bel. 'The first loon to take ane step forrit will get a ball in the tripes. Hand me that gun.'

Round-eyed, Jodi saw that there *was* a gun, propped up at the back of a cabinet. There was a wooden box by it. Raffo fetched them both. He said hoarsely, 'Let me.'

'No, no,' said Aunty Bel. 'I'm to load, you're to split the first one that tries to stop me. You could light the match, mind.'

Jodi loved Aunty Bel. He thought Raffo was the bravest man he had ever met, except for his father and, perhaps, Robin. He was amazed and alarmed when the leader of the men in the doorway just laughed. He wore spurs, and had proper armour under his tunic, but he was too small to be a real soldier, and his hair, when he pushed back his chain hood, was black and waving and scented — like a lassie's, Captain Cuthbert would have said. And it was silly to laugh.

The man said, 'And when we have killed your henchman, what happens? Do you think you will have loaded the hackbut by then? Put the gun down, Mistress Bel. It isn't Lagos. We're not here to harm you. I only wish a word with the boy.'

'Oh, aye?' said Aunty Bel. You could see she knew what to do with a hackbut. She had taken some powder from a flask in the box, and was pouring it into the muzzle. She lifted a ball from a leather bag and gave it to Jodi to hold. It was heavy. The men in the doorway started to move, but the leader put out his hand. He was still smiling. Aunty Bel said, 'And if that's all, why the soldiers? Afraid the wee man will hit ye? I seem to remember, you fall down easy. Come another day. On your lane.'

'So you do remember me?' said the leader. 'If for a somewhat unflattering reason. Under the circumstances, it is brave of you to refer to it. And the little boy's mother, of course, was also present. Poor Gelis. The child has a look of her. I shall tell him tales of his mother. And his father, of course. How is Nicholas, wherever he is?'

'Able to look after his own, even at a distance,' said Aunty Bel. She held out her hand for the slow match.

'I can see that,' said the jouster. He had big dark eyes, and a dent in his chin, and the kind of teeth Mistress Clémence wanted to see Jodi have next. Jodi wished that Mistress Clémence was here, although he was glad to have Raffo behind him. The jouster said, 'But does he have a writ that runs in the Curia? You may not know my latest appointment. Fate — and the good Prosper Camulio — have made me a Pustule Collector. You might say that I have come to collect your small charge.'

He seemed to think he had made a joke. He was probably not a Pustule Collector. Aunty Bel gave a grunt. 'And you might say that the charge failed to go off,' she said, in a steady way, going on with priming the gun.

It annoyed the jouster. He stopped making jokes. He said, 'Take that thing from her and get rid of the man.'

Aunty Bel stopped what she was doing. Raffo stepped forward. Several jousters started to run in as if they meant to hurt him and then slowed down, looking over their shoulders. One of them stumbled and fell. Others bumped into each other and went sideways.

'Mercy me!' said a loud voice. 'What have we done, Mistress Bel? Come to mend the roof like we said, and here, we've jiggled your guests, and spoiled all their lovely new tunics.' And sure enough, the loaded sacks now being carried into the room were dribbling powder all over the jousters.

There were far more workmen than jousters, and the leader, who had big shoulders and black brows and a squashed face like a wrestler, was a much stronger-looking man than the Pustule Collector. Indeed, whatever a pustule might be, the newcomer didn't seem to be afraid of him. He swung his load down, stood before him, and smiled. Jodi recognised him. He was a friend of Aunt Kathi's brother Sersanders. He said, 'Hello, Jodi!' And then, turning back to the Pustule, 'Hello, David.'

'Well, Andro. I thought we were on the same side.'

'We only came through the same door,' the roof-mender said. 'And now you're going out by it.' He took a look behind him. 'And fast. She's finished priming it.'

Jodi gazed at his wee aunt. She had indeed finished preparing the hackbut. She had settled it. She was aiming it. A spiral of smoke rose from the match. She was staring at the roof-mender, and the roof-mender was looking back with a certain expression. It was the look Mistress Clémence put on, without speaking, when she wanted Jodi to bow or say thank you. Aunty Bel didn't bow or say thank you. She just tightened her mouth, and set the match to the touch hole.

The leading jouster gave a cry of annoyance and ran forward, knocking the hackbut aside. It exploded. Raffo pulled Jodi back and jumped at the Pustule Collector, so that their swords clacked and screamed. The roof-mender swung his bag at the Collector, hitting him on the shoulder. As he staggered, Aunty Bel pushed him hard, and he fell. There was a rumbling noise high above, and everyone opened their mouths and looked up as a hole appeared in the ceiling, and bits of wood and showers of grit and sections of plaster, big as tally-boards, began to fall down on them. Jodi sat down. The roof-mender sat down as well, as one of the biggest bits hit him. Aunty Bel, her headgear bent and full of pockets of plaster, cried out and jumped up to go to him. The Pustule Collector, his face and lips and eyelashes white, jerked up his sword and brought it whistling down on her head. But Raffo was there first.

Jodi shrieked. The roof-mender got up. Through the whirling fog, you could see that the other men had stopped fighting. His Aunty Bel stood where she was, covered in powder, with one hand gripping her chair. On the floor was someone else covered in powder, except that it was all turning red. Jodi's Raffo. And above him the man whose big sword had hit him, the Pustule Collector called David. There was red all over his sword, but it was getting salty-looking with white. He said, 'You all saw him attack me. Give me the boy.'

Jodi stared up at him from the rubble. The wall hurt his elbows and bottom. The roof-mender stood with Raffo's sword in his fist and said, 'I've done this once, and I can do it again. You're not leaving this house alive.'

'Yes, he is,' said Aunty Bel. 'He's right. He has a protected position, and it'll be his word against ours. Forbye, it's my fault. I was putting off time. I knew that Raffo'd send a lassie to fetch you. I had no right to let it get so far.' She was trembling.

'That was my mistake, not yours,' said the roofman. 'Leave me to deal with it, and take the boy to young Robin's and stay there. There's a lot that needs doing.'

After that, Jodi didn't see what happened, for he and his wee aunty helped each other down the back stairs, and brushed off some of the powder, and left by the back door with two big men of the roof-mender's to guard them. Except, of course, that he was not a roof-mender, but Uncle Sersanders' friend Master Wodman, using that as an excuse to get in.

Before he got taken out of the room, Jodi scrambled up and went over to Raffo, but someone had put a cloth over him, and he didn't look as if he were coming just yet. Jodi spoke his name, for he was supposed not to leave him, but turned away when his wee aunty called.

Chapter 31

GELIS VAN BORSELEN abandoned the Bank, her army and the Duke and Duchess of Burgundy that June in order to haunt the river and barge-ports of Bruges, awaiting the shipping from Scotland. The Duke raised camp at Neuss without catching her attention, and marched south to Luxembourg, ready to invade young Duke René's Lorraine without her pained protestations joining those of John and Astorre. She failed to join the queue seeking speech with Chancellor Hugonet when it was announced that a meeting of the Estates of Flanders and Brabant would take place in Bruges in July, to be addressed by the Duke.

She did take heed, not being deaf, dumb or blind, when, at the instigation of his brother-in-law (absent in Luxembourg), the King of England (thirty-one and running to fat) arrived in Calais with fifteen thousand mounted archers, fifteen hundred lances, the flower of English nobility (including, reluctantly, the King's brother Richard) and the Scottish Lord Boyd, parent of Thomas. The plan, to re-occupy France with the help of Burgundy, seemed somewhat weakened by the Duke of Burgundy's absence on the way to Lorraine, and even more by the fact that the King of France was now attacking the territory of Burgundy, putting Dijon in peril.

Gelis did notice that. Putting up in a house near the Town Hall at Damme and riding back and forth to the sea-wharves at Sluys, she still kept enough sense to have word sent to her daily from Bruges. She had never really expected to discover an inheritance at Fleury for Jodi, but she would like to see it stay Burgundian. Nicholas had sold his wares cheerfully to every ruler in turn, but had virtually decided, she knew, that the Bank's future lay with that of the Duke of Burgundy. It was what she was trying to consolidate, with the respectable backing of Diniz and Moriz and Govaerts. Well, they now had to manage without her.

Sixteen years ago, on this canal bank at Damme, although she did not know it, there had occurred the fateful meeting with a wooden-legged daemon which had brought Nicholas and her sister together, and had led to his first marriage, and to his acquisition of the Bank. Seven years ago, and burned into her memory, was her own arrival from a sojourn in Scotland, and the silent Nicholas awaiting her, his grey eyes dark; and the look on his face when he saw her. And then the avowal. And then their marriage.

In meeting her, you have met me, or part of the core of me that does not seem to alter. He was not here, seven years later, but he had written that to his grandfather. And he had left her his son to guard.

In July, on the anniversary of her wedding, a ship from Leith sailed into Sluys. The master, who brought ashore the first boat, was the Bank's own man, Michael Crackbene. And on board were Dr Tobie and Clémence, and Kathi and Robin, and a six-month-old child with a tooth, and a tall boy with grey eyes who hung back for a moment on landing, and then put his head down and ran to her arms. They were both crying, she and Jodi. She tried to send it to Nicholas: tears and joy; he is safe, *are you safe?*

And then, as she began to free herself to kiss Kathi, and admire the baby, and give her first embrace to Clémence de Coulanges, who was going to marry the month after next, Jodi said, 'The man killed Raffo. Aunty Bel tried to shoot him, and Master Wodman knocked him down with a bag. Maman, maman; Raffo's dead.'

Gelis looked up in horror. Behind the friends closing about her, she now saw there was a man whom she recognised: a broken-nosed, burly man with coarse black hair and a watchful expression. *I have asked Sersanders's partner to bring them back*. Adorne's new business associate in Scotland was Wodman. Andro Wodman who, before retiring to Scotland, had served the French King and Jordan de St Pol, vicomte de Ribérac, that massive cruel man filled with venom for Nicholas.

Gelis opened her mouth, and Kathi said quickly, 'We'll tell you later. It was bad. It's all right now.'

THEY SPENT THE NIGHT with her at Damme, and Adorne sent an escort for Kathi next morning. The shock of the story they had to tell her remained. Gelis had never appreciated Nicholas's lenience towards David de Salmeton, and she had been proved right: forgiveness makes a bitter pill. Adorne had been right to bring his family back to where he could guard them. She wished Bel had come. It sickened her that the episode had cost Raffo his life: that Jodi's friend had had to die, and under his eyes. And even Kathi's bracing pronouncements had not reassured her about Wodman's new role as escort on the ship.

'Crackbene and Robin were with us,' Kathi had said. 'He did save

Jodi in Edinburgh. I've seen him, too, in other places where he could have harmed Nicholas, but didn't. Of course, Nicholas treats him with caution, but Wodman left his post in France to come back to Scotland. Bel knows nothing against him. My brother trusts him; my uncle says he has a good business head and learned a lot from those years when de Ribérac was France's leading adviser. If David de Salmeton settles to do business in Scotland, Wodman should be on our side. He'll be one of his rivals.'

'Should be?' Gelis had said. She was beginning to know Kathi, and her instinct to console and encourage.

'I know. We'll watch him,' said Kathi. 'My brother Anselm will watch him. No one will go back to Scotland until it's safe.' She paused. She said, 'We could do with Nicholas to advise us. You said he divined where you were?'

Gelis had told them about the encoded message. As he had asked, she had not revealed its contents. Gelis said, 'I can't divine. It would take three months to get a letter to Caffa.'

'All the same. If Nicholas has taken to using his pendulum, he may have sensed Jodi's danger by now. Intense feeling travels,' said Kathi. 'He may come back.'

'He can't,' said Gelis. 'Your uncle would quite properly charge him with fraud. And David de Salmeton would kill him.'

SHE SPENT THE WEEKS that followed in Spangnaerts Street, secure with Jodi in the Charetty-Niccolò house. Andro Wodman went home. Crackbene stayed, and took part in a company discussion on the future use of its ships: Biscay had become the favourite target for pirates, in the lawful lawlessness sanctioned by the French and Breton and Burgundian wars. Picking up his wine and his salt, Crackbene had met a few old Hanse friends, he said, in compromising circumstances. He had come across the *Peter von Danzig* the previous summer.

Gelis had been the first to speak. 'With Paúel Benecke still in command?'

Crackbene had allowed himself a twitch of the lips. He was a mercenary of the sea: a grim, heavy-limbed man of Scandinavian fairness, who had settled with no single master until he met Nicholas; and not even then until they had half killed one another. He was the only one of them whose trade had taken him regularly back to Scotland since the Bank itself had withdrawn. He had a woman and children at Coldingham.

He said, 'The crew were sailing the ship. Benecke was sober, now and then. He was expecting M. de Fleury to join him.'

'What!' It was Dr Tobie.

'Along with Ochoa de Marchena. I thought you knew. Ochoa de Marchena and the African gold, split three ways. Ochoa was having it sent on to Caffa, and M. de Fleury and he were to meet there. Benecke expected them to bring it to Danzig.'

His square face was bland. So far as it went, it was probably perfectly true. All these professionals knew one another. Gelis quite believed that Benecke and Ochoa had dreamed of a fine new career with the congenial help of Nicholas and his gold. They might even have tried to persuade him. Two winters ago, they might have succeeded. But not now, when he was safely established in Caffa, with Anna and Julius beside him. Crackbene must know that as well as she did. In any case . . .

'You don't believe it?' said Crackbene.

'Benecke's an idiot,' the priest Moriz said. 'Of course, you have reported correctly. You do not, however, know all the facts. Mistress Gelis, may I state them?'

She nodded. There was no harm in it now. Moriz and John, who was not here, already knew, and Diniz, Govaerts and Tobie might as well learn.

The priest said, 'I speak of the two messages sent Mistress Gelis by or for Nicholas. One was to say that the African gold was not on its way to the Crimea, as Ochoa told Benecke, but was still buried in Cyprus. The other, dated in January this year, indicated that the gold in Cyprus was gone, and that there was no prospect of its recovery.'

'It was on its way to Ochoa,' Diniz said. He was flushed. He knew Cyprus well. He had been there during the siege, with Gelis's sister.

'Surely not,' Moriz said. 'Or we should have heard by now from Julius, at least. Such paeans of triumph! More, the message would not have closed the matter so firmly. John and the lady and I were to say nothing.'

Tobie said, 'But Ochoa told Benecke it was coming. Maybe he thought that it was. But now his plans must have changed. I wonder if he met Nicholas at all.'

'He was afraid of the Knights of St John. Benecke wouldn't let him aboard without gold. My guess,' Crackbene said, 'is that the little bastard would run to Caffa and pretend it was coming, so that someone would hide him. Let me sail to La Rochelle this autumn. I'll find out what's going on.'

It was agreed. Gelis could see on all their faces the mixed feelings that the story had brought, for she had felt them herself. A little fortune had gone; one which, again, Nicholas had not proposed to keep for himself, but which he had planned to extract for the Bank.

He had been forestalled. By whom had not been discussed. Nicholas had wanted the subject closed, she guessed, to save them all from further danger. Their lives mattered more than the gold. But David de Salmeton's connection with Cyprus was known to Diniz, and above all to Tobie and Crackbene, who both had reason to loathe him. As the meeting drew to a close, Gelis found herself silently praying that de Salmeton would stay in Scotland, and that these men, whom she liked, would be held by events safe in Flanders.

Her prayers were answered. From Anselm Adorne to the youngest fisherman on the quays, no one could afford to leave Bruges in the second week in July, during that acutely uncomfortable time when the Duke called before him the representatives of the people of Flanders and reviled them as traitors and misers who had starved him of money for Neuss, and were permitting France to ravage Artois and Picardy.

He was given a hearing. But his demand for an army, to be raised in two weeks on pain of punishment, met with a polite but steadfast refusal. It could not be done. In any case, it was against the Duke's own best interests. Flanders had already sent thousands to Neuss, and more had been raised to defend their own coasts. It was not their concern to mend fences outside their own country: the Duke's father had never expected it. The Duke's father had understood that he would get no more money from Flanders if its commerce failed, through all its merchants and weavers being haled off for soldiers.

The firmness belonged to the burgh delegates. The politeness and moderation came from Adorne, party to both sides, attempting to mediate in an impossible situation. When the Duke lost his temper, the Estates did not retaliate, but neither did they give way. The Duke of Burgundy marched from the assembly and took horse for Calais, where he rode through the camp of the new-landed English invasion force to meet and quarrel with King Edward his brother-in-law, who had expected to be welcomed by the flower of Brittany, the cream of the disaffected nobles of France and, of course, the forces of Burgundy, whose joint venture this was supposed to be.

Predictably, the King of England expressed his astonishment that the entire Burgundian army should be absent pillaging in Lorraine, on the assumption (he would not say pretext) that it would protect Edward's rear until the joyous day of his anointment in Rheims. Predictably, the King of England went on to voice his surprise that a few Swiss and the little Duke of Lorraine should so concern (he did not say frighten) his brother-in-law. The Duke replied. He spoke very good English.

The shockwaves of the encounter travelled east, to where Anselm Adorne sat in Kathi's small house in Spangnaerts Street, rubbing his cheek over and over. 'The Duke is mad. He was ready to sacrifice us, to send fishermen marching to Ath, so long as he could stay in Lorraine.

Did he think England would ever accept that? How can the King of England risk a campaign without the full force of Burgundy? It will come to nothing. We have been forced to anger the Duke, and endanger his relations with Flanders, all for nothing.'

'He will trust you,' Kathi had said, touching his shoulder. 'He and the Duchess know what they owe to you.'

'Perhaps,' Adorne had answered. 'But it is going to cost everyone dear to mend this.'

His prediction was correct. As August opened, Edward of England stood on English soil at Calais in France, and formally declared war on King Louis. The herald by whom the challenge was sent returned with one hundred marks, thirty ells of red velvet, and a smile. The day after his dispute with Duke Charles, Edward of England quietly opened negotiations of quite a different nature with France. The declaration of war was withdrawn. Louis offered a truce, and Edward accepted it, along with an annual pension of fifty thousand florins for life, a deal for reciprocal free trade, a royal marriage, and a compensation of seventy-five thousand florins against war expenses.

To Duke Charles, thrashing the road from Valenciennes to Péronne in white fury, Edward had no inclination to apologise. Five days later, the new trust between France and England was sealed upon a bridge spanning the Somme, with the opposing armies lining the banks. Crossing each from his own armoured side, the Kings of England and France met and embraced in the centre, through the holes of a security grille. It was the end of the English invasion of France.

Diniz, accompanied by Father Moriz, left to attend the Duchess in Ghent, and follow Chancellor Hugonet to the meetings which would conclude, undoubtedly, with a painful peace treaty between Duke Charles and France. Gelis had made a half-hearted offer to go, but Tobie had restrained her. Jodi needed her.

In this, the last month before their marriage, Tobie and Clémence had lent her the kind of support she had seen Kathi attract, since Kathi, in turn, had made everyone's troubles her affair, while Gelis had been wrapped up in one thing only.

Nicholas was still central to her every waking thought, but her child came next, and Bruges was safer for him than anywhere. Gelis no longer travelled to Ghent, or to Brussels, or to Veere, where she usually did business with her Borselen cousins. Now, she saw Paul van Borselen only when he visited Catherine de Charetty in Spangnaerts Street. Catherine, the *silly wee bitch* whom Nicholas had rescued from Trebizond, now a pretty fiancée, driving Paul to distraction because she would not marry without her stepfather's sanction.

Catherine had written to Nicholas at Caffa, and Paul had added a line recommending himself, endorsed by Robin. Paul should not be blamed (he said) for the shortcomings of the rest of his family. The approach did not mean in any sense a rapprochement between Nicholas and his step-daughters: rather it indicated that, taught by experience, Catherine was intent on making sure that this time, her marriage was legal. Neither of the Charetty sisters spoke much of Nicholas, and it was hard to know what they thought. Tilde, the elder, was pregnant again after four years, and feeling poorly: Catherine, with Clémence's advice, helped to keep little Marian amused.

They would all miss Clémence, although the house she and Tobie would live in was not far away. Jodi would visit them. Father Moriz would continue his education. Chivalric training, interrupted by Raffo's death, would resume. For some reason, Jodi had taken against Manoli, Raffo's partner, with whom he had got on perfectly well before Scotland. Kathi's husband had offered to help, to Jodi's joy. But Robin, sooner or later, would be taking his family back to Scotland. The only question was, when?

Whenever news from Scotland came, touching on David de Salmeton, Gelis depended on Tobie to glean it. By the middle of August, they knew that the adviser to the Apostolic Collector had not returned to Rome, but had rented a warehouse at Leith and bought himself a house in the Canongate of Edinburgh, from which he was soliciting orders. His terms were low, and had already attracted royal attention. One of his specific aims, it would appear, was to undercut the business of Archie of Berecrofts, and that of Anselm Sersanders in Edinburgh and Perth.

Such at least was the opinion of the Scottish merchants in Bruges. From the letters her brother sent Kathi, this appeared to be true. It was also apparent that so far, de Salmeton had caused no other disturbances, and had made no attempt to harass Bel of Cuthilgurdy. In any case, Sersanders wrote, Bel was being well looked after by Andro, his partner.

This appeared a doubtful blessing. Gelis waited, with hard-tried patience, for Kathi to bring her next letter. When two weeks passed and she did not, Gelis collected Jodi and walked round to see what had happened. Robin answered the door and asked her in, displaying a mixture of embarrassment and high spirits, which were soon explained. She went to see Kathi, but didn't stay long. On the way home Jodi, who had learned a lot in a year, looked up at his mother severely. 'Why are you smiling?'

'Because I've just had some news. News about Aunty Kathi.'

'She's going to have another baby next year. I know. Why are you smiling?' said Jodi. Then, before she could answer, he said, 'Wee Aunty Bel doesn't have babies. She can load a hackbut and shoot it.'

'So can I,' said Gelis unwisely.

Jodi said, 'But you could have babies if you wanted to.'

It was a busy street. People smiled. Gelis said, 'Well, I don't want to. I have you. I don't need any more.'

'You can't have any more. Papa has gone away and you can't make them without him. I hope he doesn't come back,' Jodi said. He wasn't crying, but his face was quite red. 'I don't want to see him.'

'Well, I'm sure he wants to see you,' Gelis said. 'Don't you think he misses your poems? He hasn't even seen your new horse. Let's go to the stables and see him. You might ride with Ser Tommaso's children tomorrow.'

That evening, after Jodi was sleeping, Gelis asked Tobie to sit with her in her chamber. The cushioned seats, the light hangings, the tables, all of which had been her choice, looked mellow in the long summer twilight. Outside the open windows, swallows shrilled, and by leaning out, one could look down on Spangnaerts Street, quiet now, the dust of its cobbles printed with the marks of the day's bootprints and hoof-marks and wheels, either climbing upwards on the way to the Square, or bumping down to the working canal. The canal itself was out of sight: the bridge, the stacked kegs and moored barges concealed by the turns of the narrow street, dark as a canyon between its double row of tall houses. At night, you might hear the ducks quacking. At the top of the street, modest in shadow, the White Bear of Brugge presided from its high niche, listening perhaps to the faint laughter and music which floated from the Society's windows around it.

Gelis gave Tobie wine, and he pulled off his cap, so that the weak pink light glowed on his scalp and his short, kittenish mouth and curled nostrils. He did not look like the army surgeon of the Duke of Urbino, accustomed to wielding his saw and mallet and knife in the great bloody tents that followed the cannon. He said, prosaically, 'So what is wrong? Jodi? If it is about Jodi, you would be better with Clémence.'

But he listened, and at the end said, 'No. You were right. This is not about Jodi, it is about Nicholas.'

'It is about them both,' Gelis said. 'As he grows, Jodi will deserve some explanation. I don't wish him to turn against Nicholas. But Nicholas doesn't write, except about business.' It was true. *Part of the core of me*. It was untrue.

'Because he has decided on a clean break from all except business. I happen to think he is right. Are you asking whether you should take Jodi and go to him?'

'Without being invited?' Gelis said.

Tobie looked at her. 'Are you thinking of yourself, or of him? If you have convinced yourself that he wants you or needs you, then go. I suppose you can afford an armed troop to protect you. But don't take Jodi with you. After all that has happened, that child needs to step into a home, not a trial marriage.'

She said, 'I couldn't leave Jodi.'

'Anna wanted you to go,' Tobie said. 'Anna was desperate for you to go, after we had been to Montello.'

'It was Anna who sent us to Montello,' Gelis said.

'She wanted to help Nicholas, and us. We might have proved his legitimacy. She didn't know the outcome would oppress him.'

'She gave him Jodi's poem,' Gelis said. 'She's good for him, but she isn't as perceptive as Kathi. If he can't come back, and if it's not certain whether I could, or would, or should join him, it would be kinder to let him forget. She should allow him time to make his own choice, and send to tell me himself. She is simply causing hurt, otherwise.'

There was a silence. Her heart beat. Tobie said, 'I want to say something. Since Julius left, you must have exchanged messages with his company. Friczo Straube in Thorn. The agents in Augsburg and Cologne. When you were with him, they did well. What is the state of his business now?'

She was silent.

Tobie said, 'You don't want to say it, because Julius proved himself a good manager both here and in Venice. But we know Anna brought him no money. Perhaps she burdened him with considerable debts. And the company obviously hasn't recovered, although he has been too proud or too vain to tell us. Anna must have had great hopes of the African gold when Kathi told her about it. And Julius thought it important enough to abandon his office to juniors and join her in Caffa. It was a rash thing to do, unless he was fairly sure that Nicholas would use the gold to help him.'

Gelis drew a deep breath. She kept her voice steady, because it was so important and she was so glad it was in the open.

'Everyone thought it was coming to Caffa last autumn,' she said. 'But it didn't. Nicholas knew, as late as last November, that it was still buried in Cyprus. By January it had gone, but it couldn't have reached the Crimea through the winter. If Ochoa dug it up, everyone would have to wait until the spring.'

'Ochoa didn't dig it up,' Tobie said. 'A Hanse ship is just in, with some Genoese merchants. They all rushed to their quarter as if reporting the plague, but I heard some waterfront gossip. Everyone knows Ochoa de Marchena. They said the Genoese captured him during the winter, and he was killed trying to escape. There was no mention of gold. And that was in February.'

'Poor, silly Ochoa,' Gelis said. 'So David de Salmeton has it, unless Ochoa left it to others to bring for him.'

'But then, Nicholas would have told you,' Tobie said. 'There's something else I want to say. Do you remember the nun you wrote me about? The one we heard of from Thibault de Fleury? His late-born little daughter was fond of her.'

She remembered. The nun was called Ysabeau, and was sister to Josine, the vicomte's first wife. She had sent to the address Brother Huon had given her, and then to two other convents. The last one had been a Cistercian foundation in Scotland. She said, 'We decided not to investigate further.'

'Then you don't want to hear what I found?' Tobie said. 'I was going to keep quiet. But now I'm not sure if I should.'

'You mean I might not have to annul my marriage, because it was never legal in the first place?' said Gelis with irony. She clasped her hands hard together.

'No,' said Tobie. 'No. It has nothing to do with Nicholas's birth. I hoped this Ysabeau might know something about that, but she only remembered the scandal. Eccles is a very small priory, and the Sister suffers from deafness, but she did tell me something. She remembered Thibault's daughter Adelina. Blue eyes and red hair: wilful, pretty, intelligent. Walked out on her family with just enough to pay her way into a convent, but was transferred from one to another because of the trouble she gave. Finally parted company with religious life at nineteen, when she disappeared for a month and turned up with a baby, a daughter.'

'A daughter?' Gelis said.

It had become dark while they were speaking. The swallows flashed past the window, silhouetted in the moonlight; their shadows flickered inside the room, slashing across the white bed, the unlit brazier, the grim, ghostly features of Tobie. She rose to lift a candle and light it. A daughter. A daughter. Her fingers shook.

'Fourteen years ago,' Tobie said. 'So it wasn't Bonne. And Anna is black-haired, and German. She introduced herself to Julius in Cologne, and Julius adored her on sight. You were there. Then she committed the Graf's business to Julius, and that brought her in touch with the Bank. Nicholas liked her as well. We all did. Kathi thinks she is the sister that Nicholas needs. And that is what matters, even if she is not the person she says she is: even if Moriz can find no trace even to prove she is German. Shall we go on talking?'

She turned and sat down. 'There is more?' According to Kathi, Nicholas had been devastated, afterwards, by what he had caused to happen to Julius. She had been sure, she was still sure, that whomsoever he took to his bed, it would not be Anna.

Tobie got up, walked to the window, and sneezed. He took out his kerchief and sneezed several times more, blew his nose and then, without asking permission, took the spill and lit all the remaining candles. Then he shuttered the windows, refilled their glasses, and sat and looked at her.

He said, 'It's something about Adelina, Thibault's daughter. Clémence knows this, but no one else; not even Nicholas. I learned it years ago in Geneva, from Tasse, the little woman who lived near Montello.'

He stopped. Gelis said, 'Drink. Don't tell me, if you don't want to.'

'No. I must.' But he drank. Then he resumed. 'Little Tasse. She was a serving-maid in the house of Jaak de Fleury, the brother of Thibault. She worked there all her life. She remembered Nicholas; you could see that she loved him. She was fond of Julius. She knew Adelina. Even after Adelina had gone, she heard the rumours and she spoke to people who had met her as she moved from one place to another.' He paused. 'Tasse didn't speak of a baby. What she heard was quite different, and she believed it. She said that because of her childhood, Adelina could never have children.'

'Her *childhood*?' Gelis said.

'I think,' Tobie said, 'that that is all you need to know. But if that rumour is true, then the theory that Adelina had an illegitimate baby is wrong. Whereas Anna did have a child: the Graf's daughter Bonne.'

It was hot now. Her eyes stung in the candlelight. Tobie had emptied his glass and was refilling it. Once, she had heard, his drinking had nearly wrecked him, but his discovery of Nicholas had changed that. He had discharged himself from that patient, but was still, out of duty, prescribing for the last of his ailments. It was not likely to drive him to drink: Clémence would see to that. He was making free with it now, because he wanted Gelis to tell him something.

Gelis said, 'I don't know what it all means. I don't want to know, unless it is going to harm Nicholas. Is it?'

'I don't know,' Tobie said. 'I don't even know whether to try to tell him. That's why I wondered whether you seriously intended to join him.'

'No,' she said. She had already begun to reach that conclusion. This time, it was firm.

'Then will you write? Or shall I?'

'It might fall into the wrong hands,' Gelis said. 'I suppose I could put it in code.' Her thoughts turned. She said, 'Would Nicholas have known the nun you met? Ysabeau, Josine's sister?'

'Josine died before he was born,' Tobie said. 'The nun told me that. He never knew his grandmother, or had anything to do with her sister, although Adelina did. He never knew, apparently, that his mother Sophie was a twin. She had a sister.'

'But that is — Nicholas has an aunt?' Gelis exclaimed. 'Where? Can we find her?' And reading his face, she answered herself, 'No.'

'No,' Tobie said. 'The twin was born dead. No witness for the antecedents of Nicholas. If you want to write to Nicholas, I've told you all I know.'

Again, the invitation. Again, she refused it. She had begun by worrying over Jodi: about his fatherless future; about the dangers from de Salmeton and Wodman. Now she had another perspective.

She could not explain, but she could affirm, at least. 'I love him, you see,' she said to Tobie. 'You ought to know that.'

'Do you think I don't?' the doctor said.

The words remained, long after he had gone; after she had lost the chance of asking him what they meant.

And soon, it hardly mattered.

IT WAS ROBIN OF BERECROFTS who came to the Bank the next day and, avoiding the bureau, had himself shown to her quarters. She saw his face, and sent Jodi away. 'Kathi?' she said.

His face relaxed, and then tightened. 'No! Bless you, but no. Gelis — you know of yesterday's ship, that brought some Genoese merchants from Poland? Tobie told you?'

'They brought news,' she said. She pushed aside the notes on her desk. They were already encoded.

'Bad news,' he said. 'Bad for Genoa; worse for us; worst for you.'

'Then it's Nicholas,' Gelis said. Quite slowly, everything came to a halt.

'It isn't certain,' he said. 'Gelis, it may be all right. But Caffa has fallen. The Turkish army landed at the beginning of June and overran Caffa and Soldaia and Gothia: took the whole Crimean Peninsula, and captured or killed every foreigner whom they could reach. No one knows who escaped, but some did. Nicholas would have Julius with him. Anna is clever. If Ludovico da Bologna is also still there, they would have a better chance of survival than most. We don't know yet, that's all.' He was kneeling beside her, his warm hands around hers.

Gelis gazed at him. *The beginning of June.* Three months ago. No wonder she had had no further messages. No wonder Nicholas had not sensed de Salmeton's attempt to seize Jodi; had not apparently followed the move from Scotland to Bruges, or anything that had happened since. He was dead.

Then she thought: I would know.

She said, 'Can I go and find out?'

Robin's face was full of pity and pain. He said, 'The Crimea is full of Ottoman soldiers. No one can get in. The news came through Moldavia. Of course, there will be formal representations: Genoa and the Pope will send diplomats, especially if the Patriarch is still there.' He stopped and said, 'I wanted to go, but they made me see that it would be useless. It's over. We killed him. We killed him by turning him out.'

She could not see his face now. He had come to comfort her, but instead, she felt his tears fall on her hands. She said, 'He's alive. Robin, I know.'

He looked up then, with a guarded hope that she, too, had briefly felt. They talked, and when in the end she sent him away, he was half convinced that Nicholas might indeed be alive. She was sure of it. It had given her comfort, too, until she remembered who might be with him.

She must tell Tobie and the rest. She sat for a long time, without weeping, before she rose and picked up the notes from her desk to tear them into small pieces. There was no point, now, in completing them. Now, no warnings could pass, either way.

Chapter 32

THAT AUGUST, Nicholas de Fleury was alive simply because he had not yet got himself back into Caffa.

A boat had to be found to take him, with Julius. And once found, it had to be bought, since no one would lease or charter a vessel which would certainly never return. It was, astonishingly, Ludovico da Bologna who bade Orazio open the rat-trap of his purse and help buy it, and his acquaintances from the Greek Christian community who found local fishermen who would crew it, provided that they sailed it one way, and thereafter kept the boat itself as their fee. They would land two crazy Franks on the coast, but they weren't going to wait for them.

Rosso, the Muscovite envoy, paid no attention, being deep in his own dogged plans to leave the Black Sea and find another safe route north to Moscow. Contarini, having begged to go with him, gasped with horror when told his itinerary and took to his bed, overcome by what he feared was the plague, but which might have been simply a bad attack of the flux.

Ludovico da Bologna, having hitherto kept the party safely together by his bullying, now made a number of simple, efficient plans, and departed from Fasso before anybody. To the Venetian envoy's accusing shrieks, he had merely stated that it was time for each of them to care for his own safety. With him, he carried Uzum Hasan's envoy, loaded with presents for Charles of Burgundy, in recognition of the Duke's unremitting attention to the struggle against the Turk in the Levant.

The Patriarch was travelling home by way of Moscow, as was Rosso. Only, unlike Rosso, Ludovico da Bologna was taking a route twice as dangerous, for which there were no guides, and which would have been impossible for anyone without prior knowledge. The Patriarch was travelling by boat and by horse up the eastern coast of the Black Sea, where the cliffs grudgingly gave way now and then to the shore, and the small mixed communities harboured Christians from the Patriarch's strange, far-flung parish. It would bring him, in the end, to the river which would launch him towards Moscow. It would also bring him to the Straits of Kerch, the doorway to the Sea of Azov, and the one safe crossing which fleeing refugees from the Crimea might use. That summer, the eastern shore of the Black Sea was where penniless bands of Genoese and Venetians would be in need of succour.

'He might find Anna!' Julius had said; but Nicholas thought it unlikely. The Genoese who were Anna's patrons would have been the first to be captured or killed. She was not a part of the working community of Caffa, which, given a chance, would know where to go. In any case, from what he heard, not many had been given a chance. The same was true, of course, of the Russians; and of the imam Ibrahiim who, to some Turks, represented the Sultan Qayt Bey more than he represented Allah.

The voyage, when it came, was one of the worst Nicholas ever remembered. The Black Sea, over five hundred miles from east to west, made its own storms, even in August, and was known as a graveyard of vessels. They worked the ship, stripped to their dark Turkish breeches, and the rest of the time slept exhausted in corners; he and Julius hardly spoke. On the first day, when the enormity of what had happened smote them in Fasso, Julius had looked up at Nicholas eventually and said, 'The gold. I suppose this is the end of the gold. If it came, the Turks have it. And the furs.'

And Nicholas had said, 'You have lost the furs, certainly. As for the gold, it may have turned back, if the carrier saw what had happened in time.' And then, as Julius's sceptical gaze darkened, Nicholas had said, 'No. I suppose it has gone.'

'But you still think you can find Anna?'

He had been plain, offering facts rather than hopes. 'I have Circassian friends in Soldaia. If they are still there, they may know what has happened. If she's alive, if she hasn't been caught, she'll have gone to the hills where I found Father Lorenzo. The Greeks would know of it, and the Franciscans, if they got out. It's a chance.' He thought Julius looked sick. It was the way he felt himself. He felt so ill sometimes, it made him afraid.

They landed quietly by night at Soldaia, the heights above them darkening the stars, which winked instead through the ragged holes in the crenellated walls that still crowned them. Below the mount, everything was wrecked. The slave-traders' quarter was a mess of buckled rubbish, where porcelain crackled under the feet, and scarf-ends fluttered, and the broken neck of the pipe which once linked the hill springs with the citadel was jammed with the buzzing carcass of a dog, its stench at one with the sweet smell of decay that hung everywhere. The house of Nicholas's Circassian cousin did not exist, except as a heap of black stone and burnt wood. Of all the Genoese towns, Soldaia had withstood the

Turks longest. After all the rest had surrendered, Soldaia had fought on for a month, and had been punished for it.

All the same, the town was not empty. Specks of light glinted in other quarters, among what had been the massed houses of the port, now sparsely occupied by reliable citizens, or new settlers perhaps. The artisan districts appeared as an irregular stain, lightless and silent, where wooden workshops once stood. Here and there, voices thinly echoed, either in pairs, or in faint bursts of sociable dispute, or raucous singing. He guessed there was some sort of a garrison, although there must be little to guard and nowhere to house them: the citadel showed a sprinkling of lights, but was mostly in darkness. It was only a few weeks since the conquest. The flies, leaving the dog, fussed about him.

There was no point in risking both their lives. In the shell of this quarter, Julius was safe. Nicholas left him there, and went on his errand.

For a big man, he moved very quietly, as a Danziger pirate had once observed, and his shabby robe and dark cap discouraged notice. Slipping through broken spaces and along shadowed walls, he made his way down to the seafront, and found the one establishment which, although damaged, could be counted on to have survived the invasion. The music and laughter within were enough to cover his movements, although it was some time before he managed to attract the attention of the particular girl he was hoping for. His transaction with her took place in the dark and was quick, but less expensive than usual, since all he wanted was information and she happened to remember and like Ochoa de Marchena. 'The devil!' she said, her voice fond. 'That soft mouth he had, and what he could do with it!'

After that, instead of returning to Julius, he made his way, sinuous as a cat, through the hacked piles of carved stone and painted plaster, the wrack of gilt wood and cracked marble, until he came to the lower reaches of the vast, irregular crag upon which the citadel had been built. Then he began, in silence, to climb.

Julius was asleep when he found him again, and would have cried out, if Nicholas had not sealed his mouth with his palm. His peace offering was a napkin of food and a bottle of exceptional wine. 'The Turks didn't want it,' Nicholas said. 'I've bought two mules for us. We get out of town now, and they bring them to a rendezvous tomorrow. Come on. We can't talk here. We'll eat once we're safe.'

'Tell me now,' Julius said. 'She's dead, isn't she?'

'I'm sorry. I should have told you at once. She did get out, Julius. The Turks found the house empty. She apparently didn't go north, so they think she went inland and south.'

'To the caves?'

'To the caves,' Nicholas said. 'At least, that is where we are going.'

'And what about the imam?' Julius said. Nicholas hadn't thought he would remember.

'Oh, he died,' Nicholas said.

They spent the rest of the night out of sight of the town, in a vineyard. Someone had stripped all the grapes with rough hands, breaking the vines which had filled the wagons, just a year ago, with their tender, sun-glowing loads. There was no reason to speak of it. By then, Nicholas had told as much as he wanted of what he had discovered.

The fleet had been quite irresistible. Under Gedik Ahmed Pasha, the Grand Vizier, nearly five hundred warships and transports had sailed to attack the Crimea, with artillery capable of breaking through the stone walls of Caffa, new and old, with their twenty-six towers, and sealing off Soldaia to the point of starvation. Even before the towns surrendered, hundreds had died.

The Poles, the Russians, the Georgians, the Wallachians had been the first to be sold as slaves or imprisoned, all their wealth being seized. Next had come the selection of young men and girls for the Sultan, three thousand in all. Finally, there had come a demand for an accounting from all those remaining — Italians, Armenians, Greeks and Jews, with torture for those who tried to conceal what they had. Then, after the mulcting, the Grand Vizier had let it be known that all Italians were required to pack their remaining goods, and board Turkish transports for Constantinople. The fate of the Genoese consul was not known, but Oberto Squarciafico had been among those compelled to sail for Turkey, having backed the wrong candidate without lasting benefit from the widow's two thousand ducats.

Eminek, the chosen Tudun, stayed in Caffa in triumph, as Tartar Governor under the Ottomans. The brothers of the Khan Mengli-Girey had been freed, the elder to rule in his place. The Khan himself had been taken to Constantinople by command of the Sultan: his fate, and that of his wise adviser Karaï Mirza, had not yet been heard. No one knew what had happened to Sinbaldo di Manfredo, Straube's agent, or to the Circassian, or to Dymitr Wiśniowiecki and his Russians. Probably no one would ever know. It was believed — but he did not tell Julius — that some Genoese had escaped across the Straits of Kerch to Kabardia. The Patriarch's faith had been justified.

He had wondered, for a while, whether Anna might have fled to Mánkup, until he learned that mountain Gothia, with its thirty thousand families, its fifteen thousand fighting men and three hundred Sicilians under the usurping, militant brother Aleksandre, prince of Theodoro, had been under siege by the Turkish troops of Ahmed Pasha ever since the coastal towns gave in, and was still holding out. None of his friends could be there, whereas they might be in the caves he had told Julius about. Julius would try to go there in any case, so he might as well take him. If the Turks were there already, it couldn't be helped.

Lying beside Julius, cocooned in cloth, with the gnats whining about them, Nicholas allowed his mind, for the first time, to dwell upon death.

It is a worthy thing, to contemplate one's end with tranquillity; without recoil, and equally without pusillanimous eagerness.

How angry you will be when I, too, meet my death. But it will excuse you from thinking.

The imam had prepared him for his own end. Yet he had not known, he had not had an inkling of how he would die.

Tonight, Nicholas had climbed to the citadel of Soldaia and, stepping silently through the breached walls, had walked from one familiar place to the next in the desolate grounds. There were windows lit within the jagged outline of the former Governor's buildings on the ridge, and in the Little Eye, the four-man watchtower on the high peak beyond it. There were lights, also, in the old Venetian customs building which the Genoese had turned into a guardroom. The Venetians, too, had been thrown out of Soldaia in their day; and had complained about it. There was no one else around. There was no reason why there should be.

The Turkish guns had smashed through the perimeter, but the garrison buildings within were intact. Nicholas moved in their shadows, easing his foot now and then from some object or other dropped during the pillaging. There were no stalls in the marketplace. Even the grass under his feet was new, replacing what had been eaten, along with the dogs, and the cats, and the rats. He knew what it was like. He saw the vast, rectangular roof of the sunken cistern, dry now, whose care was committed afresh to each new Governor, as he arrived, bright and confident, on the first day of March every year.

Nicholas remembered the man — Cristoforo? — who had interviewed him: youngish, easily angered; and wondered if he had laid the foundations of his statutory tower before the Turkish cannon were trained on it. Most of the tall, three-walled bulwarks were shattered, their bracing-timbers awry in the starlight. They were made of juniper wood, which hardened with age. He knew the groves it had been cut from, and the quarry where the dull yellow stone had been hewn. He walked to the tower where Ochoa had died, but couldn't see whether the plaque was still there, unread, bearing the name of Adorne.

They had smashed the Armenian church. The mosque looked whole, but he knew it was not, and could not bring himself to go in, and look again at the mihrab, and the painted Genoese coats of arms. He turned downhill and back, past the empty warehouses and food stores, until he reached the Christian church.

The girl at the brothel, telling him about it, had said that the Governor had been quite right to do what he did. The attackers, angered by the long resistance, had broken loose from their officers and had swept killing, burning, pillaging through the town. It had been wise to leave the broken castle and take cover; to allow the Turkish soldiery to indulge in their passions below, and to wait until Gedik Ahmed Pasha or someone with sufficient authority brought an official troop up the hill to meet the Governor, and receive his formal surrender.

'And?' Nicholas had said.

'And so the Governor marshalled all his men, many hundreds of them, in the church of St Mary's. Without arms, to show they offered no resistance. They expected, of course, to be taken to Constantinople. They did not expect to be freed.'

He had asked, then, about the imam Ibrahiim, and the girl had pulled a face. 'The Governor would not let him join them in the church. He was an infidel, like the Turk, and the Turk would deal with him, they said. If he chose to serve the wrong sultan, it was not the Governor's fault.'

And so Gedik Ahmed Pasha's men had climbed to the citadel, and had found the imam Ibrahiim praying in the mosque, and had killed him, but not before attempting to extract from him, by torture, anything he might have to say about Cairo. Later, his pupils took him to Caffa for burial.

And the Governor and his garrison?

The Governor was here, where Nicholas also was standing, high above the sea on a hot August night, with the flies and the cicadas buzzing. Here by these blackened buildings where, despite the hot summer sun, the stink of burning, the stench of carnage persisted. The Turks had sealed the windows and doors of the church, and set fire to it, killing the hundreds within it. Their remains were still there.

May we not also mourn the loss to others?

We may feel sorrow, of course. But even the anguish of personal loss is relieved by the passage of time. If it does not diminish, then it has not been confronted.

The imam had counselled him before death. His friend Umar had not. Umar had left, saying nothing, to go to face a terrible end. Perhaps he believed Nicholas self-sufficient, requiring no admonitions, no comfort. Gelis had thought so.

Or perhaps, all the time they were together, Umar had been conveying something, and he had not understood. The imam had said the same. *I am wasting my breath.* His own friends had given up, too.

As the imam said, it deserved thought. There would never be a better time for it.

BAÇI SARAY WAS EMPTY. The broad plain was dust, which once held the summer pavilions of the Khan, surrounded by the wagons, the herds, the strange cylindrical tents of his people. The shaman had gone. Cure thyself.

There had been fighting in the ravine. Before the Turks came, Mengli-Girey had sent his people away, and had ridden to join the forces in Caffa with fifteen hundred loyal men. Since then, the mountain fortress must have seemed to offer refuge to those few Genoese who escaped, or who found themselves outside the walls of their city at the time of its investment. But Ahmed Pasha, of course, had forestalled them. The bodies they passed, as they rode up the crooked, overhung path between precipices, had been stripped down to the boots: you could only tell their race because of their colouring, and the absence of beards, and the length of their hair. Occasionally, when the dress had been so hacked it was not worth removing, you could tell from that, too.

Some time ago, Julius had stopped speaking. There had been no women's corpses, so far. Nicholas had thought of reassuring him: the caves were not easy to find, and their labyrinthine depths offered infinite perils from ambush. A small troop of Turks, unwilling to linger for nothing, might well not trouble to stay. Certainly, there was none remaining here now.

On the other hand, before they went, they might have had hardihood enough to explore. They might have found what they were looking for, including Anna. Or they might have found her too late. It was three months since the Turks entered Caffa, and there was no longer a beneficent Khan to send a bag of meal or some dried fish from the fortress. That Khan was in Constantinople, and his brother ruled, with his new Tudun, in Caffa.

The monastery of the Dormition had been looted, and the odour of incense had been replaced by other, stale smells signifying contempt. The chalky saints, staring imperviously down through the trees, appeared unimpressed. So far, they had met no one alive. As the path grew narrow and steeper, they dismounted and led their horses quietly. They were both soaked with sweat, and sleeplessness, rarely of consequence to Nicholas, seemed to be clogging his limbs, already stiff from their night on the ground. He felt disembodied, and its reverse. He felt the way he had done at his last meeting with Anna, when the wine had spread through the warp and weft of her dress, and stained her skin underneath, as with cherries. *You will not give me a child? Then lie still, and I will take one.*

If Julius were dead, would you love me?

Dear Christ.

The boulder crashed upon them at the next bend. It came from high on the rock-face above them, tearing its way through the trees and knocking them both off their feet. Nicholas lay, hearing one of the horses screaming, and was for a moment unable to stir. Then he heard Julius cursing, and found that the broken branch that had pinned him was movable. Nicholas was scrambling up, and Julius was half on his feet with his sword out, when the second boulder arrived, followed by the thud of bodies descending, and an angular implosion of clubs, distorted like light-beams through trees. Nicholas regarded them, hollow-eyed, from his fresco, and was not entirely sorry when one of them put him to sleep.

When he awoke, someone was apologising in Russian. The relief was so great that, despite a crashing headache, he laughed. 'Dymitr, you *bastard*!'

The cave was dim, as he remembered. The row of cocky hats, of course, was no longer there: he had abstracted them himself, and the owner would no longer need them. He saw, hanging above him instead, the broad, thick-skinned faces of the men he had played chess with, and bought furs from, and in whose presence he had first been introduced to the Cairene justiciar Ibrahiim. Dymitr Wiśniowiecki said, 'We are sorry. There have been many brigands, as well as Turks. But how were we to know, you fool, that you would come back?'

He could not see beyond the circle of faces. He began, 'My merchant friend Julius —' and was interrupted by lascivious groans.

'Ah! We know now why you both came. Look! The love birds! Is it not beautiful?'

They leaned back to afford him a view, and he raised himself on one elbow.

It was, he supposed, beautiful. Julius, stripped to the waist, was lying on the other side of the cave on a pallet. Although the cloth round his diaphragm was stained with red, his eyes were open. They were open, and soft, and gazing up into the eyes of his wife, the Gräfin Anna von Hanseyck, who knelt at his side. She looked up and over to Nicholas. 'God is good,' she said simply. 'He has brought you both safely back to me.' Her voice shook a little, as might be expected.

'See. She is alive,' Julius said. And after a moment, smiling, 'You are as stunned as I was! Have you nothing to say?'

His head throbbed. 'No. Yes,' Nicholas said. His weighted lids, descending, concentrated his gaze on the place where it had last rested in Caffa: where her gown opened, or was pulled fully open. In Anna's white face, thin with privation, a flush rose. Nicholas added blearily, 'God is good.'

'You're half awake, man,' Julius said. 'Well, you'd better get yourself some rest. We're getting out of the Crimea. We're going back to the Baltic. We're going as far as Moscow with Dymitr here.'

'You're hurt?' Nicholas said.

'Some billy-goat shot me last year, and another banged me on the wound. It's nothing,' Julius said. 'They've got horses coming. They say we can travel by the end of the week.'

It was not a good idea. Nicholas spoke to Dymitr. 'No. We'll reduce your chances.'

As he expected, Julius's irritated disclaimer clashed with Dymitr's. The Russian said, 'It will make little difference.'

'Then let us split into two parties,' Nicholas said. He said it with difficulty, because his teeth wanted to chatter. He wished someone would light a fire.

Again, Dymitr's voice spoke in tandem with that of Julius. There was a long way to travel. They would go together.

'But —' Nicholas said, and got no further. He heard a movement, and understood that Julius had got himself up, and was bending over him.

'What?' Dymitr was saying. Nicholas looked up at him soulfully.

'He's got marsh-fever,' said Julius irritably. 'We'll have to wait for him.'

But in the end, they left separately after all, because the symptoms Nicholas developed were not entirely those of marsh-fever, but appeared to have quite a lot in common with the complaint of the Magnifico Messer Ambrogio Contarini, which might or might not have been the flux. The main body of the Russians left with Anna and Julius, the latter carefully strapped on his horse, and issuing worried and angry directions to Dymitr who remained, with three other bold souls, to care for Nicholas.

Half a day later Nicholas, who did have marsh-fever but did not have the flux, left in the same direction but by a different route, in a wagon drawn by two camels, with the four Russians riding grinning beside him. 'Although why you cannot tell the poor man that you are being seduced by his wife, I do not know,' Dymitr said. 'If she offers herself to you, take her! If you want to marry her, tell your friend! Or are you a man with tastes you have not told us? Did you create these interesting drawings on the walls?'

But fortunately Nicholas, shaking and sweating, was excused from answering. Indeed, having forced himself to make the necessary arrangements, he saw very little of his departure from the Crimea, from the land of the Genoese and the Tartars, where three hundred and fifty years of Italian trading had ended, because of a mother's blind championship of her son.

He saw something of the journey, for marsh-fever has its own clock, and between bouts he was sane for a while. He knew when Dymitr told him that Julius and his friends had been overtaken, although, asleep in some humble monastery, they did not know it. When the deep snow came, he survived in his wagon, wrapped in furs like the rest, and he was well enough to ride his own horse when the forests parted, and he saw for the first time the carpet of snow-capped wooden cabins, the glimpse of grey river-ice, the slivers of yellow-grey walls enclosing the modest mound of stouter buildings that represented the Kremlin, the princely domain of the ruler of Moscow.

He had known he would not find, here, the tall painted gables of Danzig, or the barbaric glitter of the Tartar and Turcoman tribes; the broken colonnades of Alexandria, or the secret gardens and bright domes of Cairo. The soaring churches and palaces of Rome, Venice, Florence seemed no more here than the dream-cities that swam in the air above the glaciers of Iceland.

For a moment, thinking of Iceland, he was brushed by a sensation he had also felt there, and was at a loss to account for it. There was nothing white and gold here: the snow was shadowed blue, and trampled into sepia. He had seen no eagles as yet. A vision of a woman entered his mind, but she was not Gelis, or Kathi, or Anna, although her hair was densely black. She was far more powerful than any of these. Like Violante, perhaps. Then the fevered shadows cleared from his mind, for they were entering the first of the portals, and Dymitr was receiving a welcome. A moment later, the whole train was passing through, and on to the greatest of the fortified monasteries where hospitality was dispensed.

They were in Muscovy. He had escaped from the Crimea with his life. He had won, at the very least, a breathing space in which to resolve what to do. From here, he could go anywhere.

He was weak, and apprehensive, and at the same time, mysteriously happy — even before he entered a room and the person within addressed him not in Russian or Italian or Latin, but in Bolognese French.

'Well, to God's praise and reverence, you are here! And what are we going to do with you now?' said Ludovico da Bologna. 'Warm of head, tender of heart and eager to commend yourself, I am sure, to the other foreigners in Moscow, such as the Grand Duchess Sophia herself, whom Rome knew as Zoe, ward of Cardinal Bessarion. I hear she was once mistaken for the Gräfin Anna in Rome. Did you ever meet her?'

'I heard that story,' Nicholas said. Julius had told him. It involved that young rascal Nerio.

'Quite,' the Patriarch said. 'She has brought her friends. Moscow contains so many familiar faces that you will feel you are living in Florence, or Bologna, or among the lady's Greek-Florentine kinsmen in the Morea. They tell me you have had the plague and are better again. How convenient.'

'As you say. And this is your lodging?' said Nicholas, looking about.

'Not exactly. This is my prison,' said the Patriarch affably. 'And yours also, now.'

. . .

As ever, news from the four quarters of the world travelled at its own private pace, so that where it passed, like some ancient comet, men were left struggling to adjust to its retarded burden. Astrologers were brought in, not only to predict events that still lay in the future, but to surmise the effects of events which had already occurred. Fleets and envoys were diverted. Consignments of arms and placatory gifts were recycled.

After it was known that Caffa had fallen, the Curia waited a month to discover the fate of the Patriarch of Antioch, and learned it so soon only because the tidings came from Tabriz before Caffa was conquered. First to bring the news from Rome was the Bastard Anthony, the Duke of Burgundy's famous half-brother, who carried it, with his new-gathered mercenary army, to Lorraine, where the Duke was currently fighting. It reached Bruges, brought by John le Grant, in September.

It was the month in which Clémence de Coulanges and Tobias Beventini of Grado celebrated their marriage, at Anselm Adorne's invitation, in the private Bruges church where, fifteen years previously, Nicholas the apprentice had married his employer.

Margriet, his dear wife, was no longer there to welcome his guests to the Hôtel Jerusalem, but the ensuing banquet was dextrously controlled by his chamberlain, and Adorne, calm and elegant, was supported by his well-mannered family. Some of his guests had come from Scotland, among them his nephew Sersanders, and a bright-eyed noblewoman from the Priory at Haddington who was referred to as Mistress Phemie. Dr Andreas was also present, with Robin's father, Archie of Berecrofts.

Not all, of course, had come solely to see Tobie married. This was the season when Anselm Adorne took up his appointment as burgomaster of Bruges, an office he would hold for a year. Merchants from the foreign community — Tommaso Portinari, Stephen Angus, Jehan Metteneye — were here for his sake, as well as their connection with the Bank to which Tobie was physician. The Bank itself was here in its entirety: lacking only Captain Astorre, who was disbelievingly attacking Lorraine; John le Grant, who had not yet arrived; and Gregorio, who was in Venice. And, of course, Nicholas de Fleury and Julius, who were probably dead.

During the entertainment which followed the feasting, Katelijne (who liked weddings) said to Gelis (who did not), 'Look at Tobie and Clémence. Not at all in awe of one another, but neither harms the other's true dignity. I think it is a marriage made in heaven. Your doing.'

'Jodi's,' Gelis said. 'But I agree.' She had been bleak, like this, for a long while.

Kathi, who had reached that comfortable post-nausea condition of pregnancy where all problems seemed small, said, 'How would Nicholas feel about it, if he knew?'

Gelis said, 'Thankful, I imagine, to lose two of his nurses at once. If he were alive, and had achieved an independent existence, that is.'

Kathi had taken a great deal of trouble, recently, to analyse Gelis. 'More than that, surely,' she said, giving it thought. 'They may not fully understand him, but Nicholas understands them very well. I'm only afraid that they'll breed. Clémence would give day to nothing but medical prodigies.'

She gazed down the table at the bride, making an effort, as had they all, to conceal her astonishment. Clémence, divested of her coif of professional linen, was revealed to be a straight-backed young woman, Gallic in feature, white of throat, whose black hair fell lustrous and low from a fine net of pearls, and whose silk gown, with its trailing sleeves and discreet neckline, revealed a trim, athletic body of excellent promise. War had prevented the family of de Montcourt of Chouzy from travelling to Bruges, but their eccentric kinswoman did not require their endorsement. Tobie had known what he was doing.

As had Robin of Berecrofts. With more than a little contentment, Kathi watched her husband and his father talking animatedly together, their fresh-skinned faces, so alike, mirroring their absorption. Although his soul might be elsewhere, Robin had turned himself into a useful manager of the Berecrofts business in Bruges, and was capable of making still greater improvements. But he was his father's heir, and by next summer, they would have to return to Scotland, to the orbit of David de Salmeton — if only because David de Salmeton was emerging as a competitor.

Where Nicholas de Fleury, and the Vatachino, once the man's own employer, had withdrawn, there remained a niche in Scottish trade, and in the retiring rooms of the King, for an amiable and entertaining man of good looks, whose shrewd advice promised delightful returns. Naturally, de Salmeton's increasing influence had caused some dissatisfaction among other merchants, but the man had papal connections, and had conducted himself with disarming modesty, even to attempting to mediate in the jealous scenes between the King and his brother. It was not true, of course that Albany, driven by rage, had actually attempted to poison King James: that was simply a Milanese rumour.

In many ways, Katelijne Sersanders wanted to go back to Scotland; the more so that her uncle had virtually abandoned both his visits there and his office: as burgomaster of Bruges he could scarcely attend as he should to the duties of the Conservator of Scots Privileges in Bruges. She wanted to go back for other reasons. She missed Willie Roger, and the group of mad musicians and artists who had helped Nicholas create his Play. She missed her friends at Haddington. She missed the princesses for whom once she cared: Margaret, too strong-willed for her own good and Mary, torn from her beloved first husband but reconciled, in her mild, shallow way, to producing heirs for her next. She missed the small foreign Queen, with half the sensuality of her husband's two sisters and twice their intelligence, resentfully enduring her pregnancies, and obstinately closing her heart to her husband, because no one had taught her that, whether or not the marital bed suits your taste, it is best to be generous. And if you are fortunate, loving kindness will be your reward.

Kathi was still afraid of David de Salmeton, but he had been careful not to repeat his ill-conceived assault of the summer. Bel wrote regularly. And if Sersanders were to be believed, Andro Wodman continued to prove himself an assiduous watchdog, and a solid partner in business. Although, of course, it was hard for anyone to outbid David de Salmeton if he possessed — as he might possess — all the vanished store of African gold.

The evening ended. Clémence, having been married from Adorne's house, remained there with her husband for the night, and Robin and his father took Kathi home to where Cristen, a nurse of Clémence's training, looked after her sleeping daughter. It reminded Kathi yet again of the infinite care bestowed by Clémence on her charges, and how well she had managed the parting with Gelis's son, even to reconciling him with his protector, Manoli. She hoped that, tonight, Clémence would be repaid with joy.

But it was Tobie's ecstatic cries which caused Anselm Adorne to smile from the quiet of his chamber, although he ceased being aware of them presently, having other concerns of his own.

Chapter 33

THE BARON CORTACHY, owner of the Hôtel Jerusalem, was late in rising next morning, and hardly prepared when John le Grant came to the door, accompanied by the wife of Nicholas, Gelis. Receiving them, Anselm Adorne found that it was not an untimely descent to explain le Grant's tardy arrival. They had news.

The young woman, Gelis van Borselen, was alight with it. 'Nicholas was not in Caffa when it was taken. Nor was Julius. They were both with the Patriarch in Tabriz.'

'He reached Tabriz,' Adorne said. Then, realising that he had been ungracious: 'But that is good news, of course. Tobie will be delighted. He and his wife are still sleeping.' And, after further thought, 'And the Gräfin? Was she safe in Tabriz as well?'

It appeared that she was not. It troubled Adorne to think of that lovely young woman in Turkish hands. His visitors agreed. Then they asked after Tobie, and he invited them to stay until the doctor appeared. It led, of course, to an excruciatingly noisy reunion, but very soon they had all left for Spangnaerts Street, where he himself was to join them, in turn. Adorne sat alone for the time being, thinking. If de Fleury was with Uzum Hasan, then presumably he would stay there. Adorne was sorry for his clever wife.

JOHN LE GRANT remained in Bruges, since it was necessary at the end of the season to review the army's plans for the future. Or so he told himself. He was as thankful as anyone to know that Nicholas was safe. In his moral, Aberdonian way, he was more devastated even than Gelis when the next news arrived, in November.

It was old. It was based on a letter in Latin, written from a monastery to the south of the Black Sea, and sent off in August. It reported that, ignorant of the disaster in the Crimea, the Patriarch of Antioch had arrived at a seaport called Fasso, intending to make his way home.

Finding his intended route blocked, Father Ludovico had left to return through the Duchy of Moscow. His two companions, by name Nicholas and Julius, had elected, against all advice, to re-enter Caffa in search of a Christian lady. It was an unreasonable hope, since the poor lady, if not sent to her account in the fighting, would have been exposed by this time to the lusts of unspeakable savages elsewhere. And the two nobly intentioned persons, if caught, would be allotted no mercy.

Had he not known Gelis better by now, John le Grant would have been surprised by her calm, or wondered if she doubted the news, which carried (if you knew Julius and Nicholas) the ring of absolute, crazed authenticity. Both Diniz and Moriz showed sharp distress, but nothing to compare with that of Tobie, who exploded, uttering impossible threats and proposing impossible expeditions, until Gelis herself brought him to order. 'You sound like young Robin, forgetting he has a coming child to think of next year, just as you have a wife. There is nothing we can do. It is winter. This happened in August. It is over. Even if it is not over, it will be spring before we have any more news; summer or later before we see any survivors. What we need to do now is consider what can be done to help Julius's business. There is Bonne.'

They talked. Watching Gelis, painfully white, sitting at the Bank's table shuffling papers, le Grant knew she had simply expelled from her mind, for the moment, all the other implications of the news. Perhaps she was fortified still by the conviction that she would know if Nicholas died. Perhaps she was right. Or perhaps, with the passing of time, the link had weakened or vanished, if it ever existed. He had recognised some time ago that, although a difficult woman, she had what he considered an unfeminine brain, and a dry humour, without coquetry, which he liked. He liked a great deal about her.

Their strategy, which they would follow all winter, was easily settled. Father Moriz would visit Cologne, taking Govaerts, and offering temporary management of Julius's business until he and his wife should return. Govaerts would remain until that time in Germany, with Moriz supervising from Bruges, and assuring himself of the wellbeing of Bonne.

On the future of the army, John had already brought back the recommendations of Astorre, modified by his own advice. Pestered by Swiss attacks on Savoy, and driven from pride and greed to try to conquer Lorraine, the Duke was mad enough to fight all through the winter.

The opposition was rough but unreliable. It included Sigismond of the Tyrol, who might be discounted. It also included the goodwill of France, who would undertake to support them but wouldn't, any more than they had supported the Emperor. And the Duke had a big enough army, with English archers, and Campobasso and his band of trained mercenaries. They could do without Astorre.

But, unusually, they were well off for money — the Low Countries, prompted discreetly by Anselm Adorne, had voted the Duke a hundred thousand thalers a year for three years, in passionate gratitude for his decision not to invade France, or to continue to engage with the Emperor. John (and Astorre) thought that Duke Charles was probably crazy, but that, if there was money to be had through the winter, Astorre's company might as well share in it.

'You mean you would stay with Astorre?' Father Moriz had said. 'What about the central army? The Bastard Anthony? Aren't you expected to serve with the main artillery alongside Lalaing and the rest?'

And John had said, 'I would, if the Duke didn't command it. Anything good they designed, he would wreck.'

'Then,' Gelis had said, 'should you and Astorre trust your company to the Duke's wars? Or should you not look about for a better commander?'

'We could,' John had said. 'But Burgundy is the patron of the Bank, and I thought that all branches of the Bank should contribute to its welfare. If that is still the Bank's policy.'

And Diniz had exchanged looks with the others and had said, 'It is. It is what Nicholas planned.' And it was, of course, while the unimaginable wealth of the old Duke seemed inexhaustible, and the duchy was closer than ever before to becoming the Kingdom of Greater Burgundy: potentially as mighty as the Empire and France. Nicholas had formed his plans, at the time, for sound, commercial reasons; but anyone was free to alter them now. Except that it seemed that Diniz and Gelis would not; and neither, as it happened, would John. And the duchy of Burgundy encompassed both Fleury and Flanders.

John le Grant left before Christmas, because he was needed, and because his reluctance to abandon Bruges was tempered by the domesticated air of the city in winter, its trade in recession, its harbours empty save for fishing-vessels and great ships idling out the weeks until spring. Busy offices gave place to bovine homes. Tilde de Charetty was brought to bed of her second daughter, baptised Lucia. Catherine de Charetty, her face glossy with unexplained tears, agreed at last to arrange her marriage to Wolfaert van Borselen's son. Kathi Sersanders grew round, and her husband became uncharacteristically short-tempered. Arnaud Adorne, second youngest son of Lord Cortachy, got with child the nice girl he was courting, and a hasty marriage was arranged for the first week in January. John decided to leave.

He spent the last evening with Gelis. Part of it had to do, as was usual, with figures and calculations, but eventually the papers were put away, and the wine brought, a fortified red one from Portugal which had reached her through the sinful Arnaud Adorne and a man called Thomas

Perrot. Gelis and he sat together by lamplight in her parlour which was imbued with no memories, for Nicholas had never lived here with his wife and his once-loved son Jodi, now nearly seven.

Jodi and the sandy-haired engineer had, in these last weeks, attained a mild degree of affinity, based on a mutual liking for mechanical toys and model ships. Because John had a meticulous sense of fairness, it had not gone beyond that. Neither had his own extended stay in Spangnaerts Street attracted any particular attention inside the building or out of it, at least until the day when Crackbene had put in from La Rochelle, and unloaded his wine, and brought the Bank his report.

As authorised, Mick Crackbene had sailed round the French coast past Brittany and, as expected, had met there the *Peter*, once of that very place, with Paúel Benecke in command. Benecke had been drunk. He had tried to race Crackbene's ship into port.

'And?' Father Moriz had said at that point, with impatience. Father Moriz was not tolerant of self-indulgence.

'And the *Peter* sank,' Crackbene had explained with simplicity.

There had been a silence. Some years ago, a Vatachino ship called the *Fortado* had suffered a similar fate, having incurred the displeasure of Nicholas. Tobie had said, 'You sank her?'

'A vessel with a beam of forty feet, a length of a hundred and seventy, and three hundred crewmen? I suppose I could have done,' said Mick Crackbene, pausing to reflect, 'but I didn't. She wrecked herself on the rocks. A treacherous coast.'

'I remember,' Diniz had said, with irony. 'But Paúel Benecke managed to survive?'

'All of them did. He's a good seaman. He'll get another boat soon.'

'Will he? How?'

'He has plans,' Crackbene had said casually. 'He thought he might not go back to Danzig. Woman trouble. Hanse trouble too, I expect. He knows Ochoa is dead and the gold lost, so there is nothing to wait for. He thought he might go to Seville, build a caravel, and offer himself for a bit of trading down the coast. Down the African coast. Down where the Portuguese used to have a monopoly.'

'Trading in gold?' Diniz had said. And then, 'How would he raise the money to build his own ship?'

'He didn't tell me in so many words,' Mick Crackbene had said. 'But I think he mentioned insurance.'

This deserved, and received, some slow applause, during which John found himself exchanging a long look with Gelis. When he turned, he had found Crackbene's eyes on them both. After that, Crackbene had watched him a lot.

Now, sitting studying Gelis on the last evening before he went back to war, the engineer spoke in his own language, bluntly. 'You're certain sure Nicholas is still alive. But you canna sense that he's divining?'

She didn't avoid the question, or the subject. 'I think he's alive. He may not be able to divine. He needs quiet, and a pendulum.'

'Could he divine where David de Salmeton is?' John said.

'He would want to,' Gelis said. 'He could do nothing about it. I can't understand, as it is, why de Salmeton hasn't come after us: you, myself, Jodi, Kathi, Tobie, Crackbene. Even to taunt us.'

He had thought about that himself. He said, 'It wouldna give him as much satisfaction without Nicholas here, or at least knowing about it. I think de Salmeton'll stay where he is, waiting for Nicholas to make a move in the spring, or be found. Then, if we don't warn Nicholas of his threats, de Salmeton will. He wants to lure Nicholas home.'

'I wondered,' said Gelis. After a while she said, 'If he could, he would come. I was thinking of it when Crackbene was here. Nicholas would come, but whatever he did about de Salmeton, he couldn't stay. And rather than go back, now that so much has changed, he might be tempted by Benecke. He might choose to go on to Africa, and make a life for himself, sailing and trading. Slaves. Gold. Exploring the coast. The spices of India, maybe, one of these days. Fighting off the Spanish, the English, the Portuguese. Perhaps fighting off Jordan de Ribérac, and Simon his son, and even young Henry, his grandson. That was what Mick Crackbene was thinking, too.'

'It's possible,' le Grant said. Mention of de Ribérac reminded him just how much he disliked that fat nobleman and his spoiled grandson Henry. John le Grant had personally fought against the grandfather at Trèves, and had nearly found himself killed while trying to teach the boy gunnery. He could understand Nicholas being tempted to retaliate. But not, surely, on Benecke's ship. He said, 'I wouldna say Crackbene dotes on the notion of Nicholas drinking his way round to India in another man's ship. And for sure, he doesna love David de Salmeton. He took time to mention to Benecke that Ochoa's precious puckle of gold had been lifted by David from Cyprus.'

She was sitting upright. 'He did? So that Benecke . . .'

'So that, if David de Salmeton is sailing anywhere, he would be well advised,' John said, 'to look out for pirates.'

It was daft, of course. She examined him, and then smiled and said, 'They'll never meet, will they? But it makes me feel better, imagining it.' She seemed to hesitate. She said, 'Will you be back? In the spring?'

'It might be difficult,' he said. 'But all the others are here.'

'I know. I am lucky,' she said.

. . .

JULIUS, DESCENDING upon Moscow at last, found himself in a ducal city of low wooden cots and squat Russians. His resentment was hardly dispelled by the helpful welcome he received from Dymitr Wiśniowiecki, from whom he learned, to his further irritation, that Nicholas had already arrived. Nevertheless, by the time he and Anna had been installed in their inferior lodging, with stables, in the old merchant quarter of Kitay-Gorod, his spirits had lifted.

'They're in prison!' he had exclaimed, shutting the door on the Russians and joining the exquisite bundle of furs that was Anna, huddled before the smoking, newly lit stove. Happily convulsed, he sank his arm round her. 'Nicholas and the Patriarch. Representatives of the heinous Roman church, from which Orthodox believers must be protected. The Metropolitan took one look at them and stuck them into quarantine in the Troitsa.'

In Rome, the Cardinal Bessarion had trained the future Grand Duchess Zoe-Sophia in the Latin mode of worship, to which it was hoped she would convert her untutored husband, leading to a union of the Greek and Latin churches. Much, unfortunately, had depended on her personal charms, but there seemed no reason for total despair: she had two daughters already, and might be about to carry a son.

'Upon which Ivan will convert out of gratitude, and the Patriarch and Nicholas will be freed? Poor things,' Anna said. 'I think we might try to release them before then.'

'I'll go and see them,' said Julius vaguely. He felt better about being stranded in Moscow. The prospects were not as bad as they looked. There were a lot of merchants about, some from Poland and Germany. There was an engineer from Bologna he knew, and a goldsmith, and an elderly compatriot of the Grand Duchess's from the Morea whom Nicholas would certainly recognise. Julius looked forward to telling him when he saw him.

Anna's cheek settled into the curve of his shoulder. He cast an oblique glance, to note how her furs opened. Even to have his arm round her felt strange. They had been apart for more than a year, and had been travelling ever since his knock at the caves. Finding one another again, they had been silent in their relief. Later, although never alone, they had fallen into talk as they always did, exchanging news, making tentative plans. He had not rebuked her, nor questioned her over anything she had done, and she had not interrogated him. He didn't believe — he never had believed — what Nicholas had baited him with in the Tabriz menagerie. He supposed that neither he nor Anna had spent the separation in quite the way the other expected, but so far as congress with Nicholas was concerned, he trusted her, as he had said, as if he had God's assurance.

When he found how the furs unfastened, and she didn't object, he went on to determine how everything else opened as well, and they ended up on the straw by the stove which was quite warm by then, although not as inflamed as they were: at one point, he thought he was dying. It had never been quite like this, since the night they decided to marry. She fought him, devoured him, denied him until he was out of his mind with desire; then forced a climax that lasted so long he almost fainted. Then later, it began all over again.

He performed well, for he had much to make up for, but that night he was unable to match his magnificent wife. He was not ashamed. He couldn't remember when he had ever been so exhausted with pleasure. And all his doubts were set to rest.

Two days later, he made the thirty-mile ride to the walled town of the lavra of the Holy Trinity and St Sergius, the largest and richest of Moscow's defensive circle of fortified monasteries. Permission had not been easy to get: he was accompanied by a compulsory armed escort and Dymitr, who had insinuated himself as his interpreter. Anna had been forbidden to come: except for the Grand Duchess herself, women were not allowed at the Troitsa unless for rare festivals. The place for well-bred consorts in Muscovy was at home in the terems, where they spent their days sewing, spinning, and embroidering without soiling their hands.

They said that the Grand Duchess was in the course of changing all that. They said she was in the course of changing the habits of Ivan Vasilievich her husband, who paid grovelling tribute to the Tartars, and sprawled in drunken slumber at table, and lounged in sloth on his throne while others fought to preserve his realm. Zoe-Sophia, daughter of Imperial Byzantium, would not approve of that. Julius thought that she and Anna would get on well together.

It entertained him that Nicholas proved to think so as well, being already deep, when he found him, in plans for founding a business in Russia that would take the place of the promising Caffa emporium now lost. It was not hard to locate him, as one armed escort gave way to another, and Julius, with Dymitr beside him, was led over a frozen stream, through a portico and into a vast enclosed territory where diverse snow-burdened buildings of wood, brick and stone threw back the muffled *ting tang* of metal on metal, and the lowing of animals, and the cries of the labouring servants and workmen in their sheepskin caps and hide jackets. The monks themselves, in their tall hats and shawled robes, were either low-voiced or silent, and tramped the clogged wooden paths alone, or in clusters, bent like black barrel staves against the white of the snow. The cathedral, high against the grey sky, exuded incense, and the thrum and pipe of industrious chanting, such as you would hear in a rope-walk, or a finishing-shed, or on a good working vessel at sea. Musical instruments were not allowed in the lavra.

Privacy was not allowed, either, to visitors. A pair of bearded monks, hands tucked in sleeves, attended the vaulted stone chambers in which were incarcerated the two suspect Friazines: the Latin priest Ludovico da Bologna, so-called Patriarch of Antioch, and his large Frankish companion from Bruges. The invigilation did not, however, appear to be too severe: the sound of animated and agreeable conversation emerged as Julius and Dymitr crossed the threshold. The monks were ejaculating and smiling, and the Patriarch and Nicholas were arguing with one another in Russian, which Julius did not understand. Father Ludovico, his lips moving rapidly, was seated with a spare cassock over his knees, darning a hole in the skirt, and Nicholas, watching him, was replying. He appeared, as Dymitr had reported, fully recovered, and broke off immediately to jump up and give Julius a welcome. 'I heard you got here. And Anna? She's well?'

'Yes, you dog,' said Julius with meaningful malice; and was delighted to see Nicholas pull one of his faces. *That* for the Tabriz menagerie.

'Well, I hope you're hungry,' Nicholas said. 'Brother Gubka and Brother Ostafi have arranged a feast for us. In the inner room. Here.'

As prisons went, it was not unacceptable, and as guests, they received meat and wine. Also, in his disingenuous way Nicholas had arrived at a system of communication which satisfied the rules of the lavra while preserving some discretion. Among themselves, they spoke Russian. When Julius entered the conversation, Nicholas replied to him in Flemish, and translated both sides of the dialogue into Russian. If he missed a few items in the translation, Dymitr gave no appearance of noticing and the monks couldn't tell.

Later, reporting to Anna, Julius recalled all he could of the talk. 'It was mostly about setting up business. He's been busy, and has found some good trading contacts in the monastery itself. To develop it properly, we'd need to visit the Hanse halls at Novgorod to set up an agent, but that's only eight days away, so long as we travel in winter, by sledge. Once that is done, the best time to leave Russia altogether is in January or February, when the snow is still firm. Then we can catch the March ships at Danzig.' Until he spoke to Nicholas he had assumed that they would have to wait until the spring.

Anna said, 'Would they let him go to Novgorod with us?'

'He thinks so,' said Julius. He had waited, while she thought. She was a good planner. But when she spoke, it was about something different.

'Did you tell him about the letter from Brother Huon?'

The letter had come to Caffa in March, too late to catch Nicholas, already expelled and on his way south to Tabriz. She had opened it. She had wanted very much to break the news to Nicholas herself, but had left Julius to do it.

He had not minded: he was deeply curious to know what Nicholas thought of Thibault de Fleury. In effect, the news of his death seemed to move him hardly at all. He read the letter, which Julius had handed to him with his condolences, and then folded and put it away. Julius, disappointed, had probed. 'He says he's sending the vicomte's boxes to Gelis.'

'So I saw. She visited him. How did you find out where he was?'

He had been surprised, for Anna, surely, had been explicit. 'You know. Jan Adorne visited the monastery with his father. He heard the vicomte was there. He told me about it at Rome.'

'You didn't ever see him, then?'

Julius had stared at him. 'My God, no! Don't you think I would have told you if I had! We all thought the old fellow was senile. I didn't think you would thank me for news of him. It was Anna who thought you should know.'

'Then I have to thank you both,' Nicholas had said. 'And I do thank you. If you hadn't told me, he would have died and I should never have known.'

'But you didn't learn any more about anything? About your childhood?'

'No,' Nicholas had said. 'And I'm glad. I'd rather leave it alone. I want to work with you, and forget it.'

Repeating this, Julius caught Anna in a small grimace. 'I don't think he truly meant that,' she said. 'I wish I had been there. That news must have been sad for him. I told you what happened when his grandfather's letter arrived. I saw his face then.'

'Well, I saw his face this time. There was nothing on it,' said Julius. It annoyed him when she tried to imply that she knew Nicholas better than he did. Then she chuckled, drawing him close.

'These days, I think you are in a dream, Julius. I wonder why? And tell me, did you give him our other news? About our visit from his elegant, aged, youth-loving friend Nicholai Giorgio de' Acciajuoli, the Greek whose leg he broke at Damme?'

'Yes, I told him,' had said Julius, still a little ruffled. 'But he knew. His lordship had already threatened to call on him.'

'Oh,' said Anna. She sighed. 'I have to say, I am not fond of Moscow. It is inconvenient to have so little freedom. But if we all go to Novgorod, it will be better.' Her head turned in the crook of his arm, and she laughed up at him with those inviting, sparkling eyes. He kissed them, as a beginning.

'It is considered proper,' said the Patriarch of Antioch, 'to mourn for a grandfather. I am sorry to see you indifferent.'

He spoke in French. Julius and Dymitr had gone, but the Russian monks were still there at the small table, quietly conversing. Nicholas was standing by the narrow, mica-filled window, red in the sunset. He did not reply.

'On the other hand, you have eaten little,' the Patriarch said. 'A mark of refined sensibilities or common belly-ache.' And as Nicholas still did not answer: 'Do I seem to you brainless? Or pukingly sentimental? Or an obnoxious maker of tyrannical demands?'

'All of these,' Nicholas said. But he turned. The monks had stopped speaking, which was not surprising, as the Patriarch's voice had increased to a shout.

'Very well,' said Ludovico da Bologna. 'Come here. Drop on your knees. Bend that stiff neck and fold those murderous hands and be quiet and listen. My friends' — looking to the table and switching to calm, resonant Russian — 'my brethren in Christ, this young man has lost a revered grandfather, excellent, noble, well loved, and would have us utter prayers for his soul. Will you join me?'

They came forward and knelt, and the ruddy light touched their crowns and their hands, its blessing impartial, while Latin and Greek sent Thibault de Fleury on his way.

Chapter 34

SINCE NO MAN is a God, the dark days between November and December witnessed a mild diminution of Julius's ardour, which of course Anna understood and forgave. At the same time, she began to find Moscow tiresome. In the Crimea, her own mistress, planning, intriguing, negotiating her way to success, she had found every day stimulating — or, at least, until Nicholas left. Now, the planning and negotiating were appropriated by Julius, whose growing enthusiasm for founding a Russian-based business had first surprised her, and then caused her to remonstrate. 'We have to go back. You are making promises we can't really fulfil.' And, of course, he agreed. But all the same, as the date approached for their journey to Novgorod, he seemed to be interviewing more merchants, and visiting Nicholas in the Troitsa more often. While she was debarred.

She was not, of course, wholly confined. Her face and head covered, her feet booted, fur-lined cloak folded tightly about her, she stood on the bridges and walked on the ice of Moscow's two encircling rivers where the markets were held and the wind was less searing. The bright-coloured bustling peasants brought Bruges and Poland to mind, but here, they showed their wares differently. When you bought meat in Bruges, you did not look to find it mustered to await you, as here, on the frozen waterways, where the beasts stood motionless on the snow in their hundreds, skinned and frozen and stiff as humble clay offerings. From hares to chickens, from pyramids of butter to eggs, everything in the market was frozen, and sold by the axe, whose crack and thud resounded back from the walls, followed like cannon shot by glittering fragments. In Moscow, the meat on your table had been killed three months before. Walking about, she made useful acquaintances. Men who had vegetables to sell, or honey in summer. Unemployed men who would do anything.

The market only lasted until just after noon, for daylight began to vanish soon after, and the custom was to repair to the taverns and stay there. It infuriated the western merchants, some of whom she knew from

Thorn and Germany, and whom she entertained with Julius now and then. They were avid for news of their escape and curious, she could tell, to know how it had left Julius and herself financially. The answer was, destitute. The Russians had paid the cost of their journey to Moscow, using money, they said, from a fortunate late sale of furs. It was likelier to have been looted. But they themselves had had nothing until the other day, on one of Julius's visits to the Troitsa, when Nicholas had slipped a packet into his hands.

He had unwrapped it at home. Inside were six jewels, of such a size and such a quality that they would pay for their house, their food and their journey home or, alternatively, the deposit necessary for any new business venture. Julius had been flushed. 'He got them from Uzum Hasan, and meant to keep them to live on. But he wanted us to have them. He thinks that, if we stay, we could be rich.'

Examining them, she had caught her breath, despite herself. 'He is so generous,' Anna said. 'He strips himself, for our sake. But Julius, we must go back. I have Bonne.'

He had agreed. But the sale of just one of the gems had paid for a better house, and her furs, and good servants. So, escorted, she was enabled to pay visits to the small merchant quarter, where wives were not common, and to improve her acquaintance with the Italians whom Julius had already met. One of them was a fellow graduate from Bologna, here with his son and a pupil to create a cathedral for the Grand Duchess. Anna called on the architect, at his invitation, in the rectangular house he had been given close to the far from rectangular pile of the Grand Duke's antiquated timber castle-palace. Her host, a powerful black-haired man in his forties, was there with his son. And with him was another visitor from the West: the elderly Florentine called Acciajuoli, whose intermittent dealings with Nicholas had so often been related to her, with mirth, by her husband.

After the rough ways of the Muscovites, the amused eyes and smooth manners of the old gentleman were undoubtedly pleasing. Tall and slender and bearded, his wooden leg skilfully hidden by impeccable velvets, he spoke with all the gentle authority of a member of a great Italian family, a kinsman by marriage of the Medici, and a nobleman of the Morea, that part of Byzantine Greece once ruled by the Grand Duchess's family. The fall of Constantinople had ended all that, and nearly ended the life of his brothers, who traded there. Travelling Europe to raise ransom money, he had come from Scotland to Bruges, and to Nicholas.

'Claes,' he said, ruminatively, when she reminded him. 'He used to be an apprentice called Claes. And now he is in prison again. Should I find it surprising?'

She had enjoyed his company, despite the insistent presence of Andrea, the architect's son, a good-looking young man of modest attributes, who nodded and smiled at Signor Acciajuoli's every word. After the meal, his father sent him off on an errand, and Anna did not stay long after that. It was not her purpose to further Julius's awakening interest in the market for engineering supplies. She wanted, as soon as possible, to go home.

Having watched her departure, her host turned back to his other guest with a small shrug. The Florentine Acciajuoli smiled from his chair. 'You need not have sent Andrea away. I am not about to seduce him, and I am perfectly capable of indicating as much. By the same token, Maestro Fioravanti, you are not about to kiss the shoe of the Gräfin?'

'What makes you think that?' said the engineer. Fioravanti was not a name he had used often since graduating in mathematics at the University of Bologna. He had been city engineer there in the mid-fifties, when the lady Anna's husband had become secretary to Cardinal Bessarion. He remembered receiving a bonus of fifty florins from Bessarion for his skill in shifting a tower from one place to another (shifting towers was his speciality). His trade name these days was Aristotele, but Julius still called him Rudolfo. He had been glad to see Julius married and apparently prosperous: as a wild young lawyer in Bologna, he had spent his first earnings like water, and nearly ended up in jail like this other man. Claes. Nicholas de Fleury. Sharing a cell with the Patriarch, another well-remembered compatriot. Moscow was a Bologna commune.

The sly old Florentine was smiling at him. Fioravanti explained himself. 'I sound ungracious. I cannot tell you the reason. The lady is beautiful, but Julius was always easily flattered.'

'He looks happy enough,' the lame man said. 'But you wanted to meet my other friend, Nicholas. At least, he wants to meet you. I suspect he wishes to help Julius found an empire.'

'For him to manage, while Julius goes home? Or the other way round?' Fioravanti asked. He pulled forward a settle with ease. He had never been tall, but he had always had powerful muscles. He couldn't do his job otherwise, even though he was no longer juggling obelisks in Rome.

The old gentleman said, 'Neither, I fancy. What Nicholas de Fleury would like, I rather think, is to consolidate with Julius a permanent Muscovite partnership: a new Banco Niccolò-Giulio based in Great Novgorod. The Gräfin and her husband are taking him there very soon: Julius of course is becoming enthused.' He paused. 'No doubt you have views. As you have indicated, you know his nature.'

'Julius is decorative,' said Fioravanti, after some thought. 'He carries out well what others initiate. He does not have the vision, I would say, to sustain a great business for a long time alone.'

'On the other hand,' the old gentleman said, 'de Fleury has an original mind and has been concerned with many innovative projects, I am told. He would understand your requirements, and anything that benefited your great work would please the Grand Duchess, of course.' He paused. 'Father Ludovico is not insensible of the niceties.'

They looked at one another. Fioravanti said, 'Then I am inclined to hold to my opinion. I should like to talk to de Fleury. Can you arrange it?'

'Give me a few days.' Smiling, his visitor rose, collecting his stick, and managing the false leg with adroitness. 'I shall come with you. And bring Andrea. Nicholas is very good with young men. Quite unlike me. Bracing. Robust. Unless you have pretty maids, you need never be apprehensive about Nicholas.'

THE MEETING WAS DELAYED, because of the Troitsa's preoccupation with the Feast of the chief saint of Russia. Nicholas became one year older, and was able, from a discreet vantage point, to take his first look at the ducal procession entering the cathedral. Ushered by the Metropolitan Philip and the Archimandrite in a dazzle of ecclesiastical vestments trod the tall, jewelled form, aged thirty-five, grimly sober, of Ivan III Vasilievich, by the grace of God, Grand Duke of Muscovy; the bent figure of his mother Maria; his two brothers Andrew and Boris; the sullen child of his first marriage, Ivan; and — painted, crimped, studded with Byzantine metals and swinging with Byzantine pendicles — the short-necked, globular person of Zoe-Sophia, his Duchess.

Long ago, weeping with laughter, Julius had described the cruel joke involving Anselm Adorne's son and the youth Nerio in Venice, and later in Rome, when the same Jan had confused the pneumatic Zoe with Anna. At least the exquisite Nerio, by-blow of a princess of Trebizond, had been advised not to come with his Florentine benefactor: Nicholai de' Acciajuoli limped alone in the Grand Duchess's procession. Watching, Nicholas saw him glance towards the deep, shadowed porch where he and the Patriarch stood. A moment later, the Grand Duchess glanced over also. In the inflated pink visage, the magnificent eyes with their well-drawn outlines were unexpectedly sharp. On an impulse, Nicholas drew from his memory and performed the obeisance he had last given to David Comnenos of Trebizond, whose race at root was the same as her own. She inclined her head in reply.

The next day, Nicholai de' Acciajuoli was ushered into the Patriarch's room at the Troitsa, bringing with him a solid, black, olive-skinned engineer from Bologna with a hoarse voice, and spatulate fingers, and nostrils smeared like John le Grant's from the engineer's habit of pinching his nose when in doubt. It made Nicholas feel better, if not much. The news that Acciajuoli was in Moscow had staggered him. He had never been cowed by this man, but however spaced their rare meetings, he always felt apprehension. Nicholai de'Acciajuoli had never done him any harm, to his knowledge, except as much as an idle, mischievous man might do, who thought himself to have exceptional powers. He had frightened Gelis, as well.

At the moment, however, there seemed nothing ominous in his greeting. He made a mild joke about enclosed orders, and the Patriarch replied with affable coarseness. They had no guard and no audience: a member of the Grand Duchess's circle could dispense with such things. Then Fioravanti was introduced, and the talk suddenly moved from the general to the particular, simply because Nicholas was intensely interested in the plans to rebuild the Kremlin cathedral, and to know what had caused the walls to fall down in the first place. He was in the middle of an argument about hoists when someone laid a hand on his shoulder, and he realised that the Patriarch and their Florentine visitor had been excluded from the conversation for the last hour, and were now making their presence felt again. They did not appear unduly disturbed, having spent the interval, so it seemed, in tolerably uncontentious conversation of their own. It had never occurred to Nicholas that they would have anything in common.

Soon after, the visitors left, without having done more than affirm a desire, in due course, for other meetings. In his strange, suspended mode of existence, Nicholas was conscious of elation. The world was opening again. He had found someone whom he could work with, and who wanted, he thought, to work with him. And there was plenty of time. Even if everything ceased over Christmas, which was celebrated here on the seventh day of January, weeks of winter still lay ahead in which to collect the information he needed.

The Grand Duchess, having found a barbaric country, was intent first on imposing upon it an appearance at least of the magnificence of the courts of her forefathers. The second Byzantium, the third Rome must have splendid buildings, opulent dress and gold plate, formal ceremony. Only after that could come the roads and bridges, the fortifications, the arms. For anyone who wished to be an importer, a factor, or a ducal adviser, it required careful planning.

It was not a handicap, on the whole, to be in the Troitsa. Fioravanti visited several times more before Christmas, by grand-ducal permission, and proved a mine of information about outlying lands, for his grand design for the Uspensky had taken him to study churches in Novgorod, in Suzdal, in Vladimir. He also acted as courier between the prisoners and Julius, who did not qualify for frequent access, and had to suffer the Brothers Ostafi and Gubka when he did. It did not disturb him too much: his eyes glowing, he was already anticipating deep and profitable negotiations in Novgorod. He brushed aside Anna's misgivings: every ruler allowed dispensations at Christmas, and the Patriarch and his companion had surely expiated their crimes, if it was a crime to represent the Latin faith instead of another, and to bring the sins of Venice to mind.

When the Christmas festival ended, without the reappearance of either Father Ludovico or Nicholas, Julius made enquiries and returned, full of amused exasperation, to Anna. 'They're holding them for debt.'

Sometimes, she didn't see the humour of things. 'So tell me,' she said in a cool voice, and sat on the chair, not the settle.

Julius was enjoying himself too much to care. He threw himself on the settle. 'After the Patriarch left us at Fasso, he travelled round the Black Sea and lost all his possessions to robbers on the coast of Abkhazia. That's one story. His servants say that they were managing to beat off the thieves, when the Patriarch went insane, stopped the fight and handed the robbers not only his purse, but all the costly gifts meant for Duke Charles of Burgundy. That is, he claimed they weren't robbers at all, but starving Latins fleeing from Caffa. Uzum Hasan's envoy returned home in disgust, and the Patriarch proceeded to Moscow, living on loans. He can't repay what he borrowed.'

'But Nicholas could,' Anna said. She stared at him, her brows lined. 'The jewels! Why did Nicholas give us the jewels? You must take the rest back.'

Julius laughed. 'He gave us the jewels because he didn't want Father Ludovico to waste them. They're going to finance the new business: you know that. Anyway, Acciajuoli says Father Ludovico doesn't want to get out. It suits him to wait, collecting news of what's happening in the south and keeping a Latin presence in Moscow. If Zoe wants her Italian craftsmen, she's going to have to let them have their own chaplains. And if there's a Latin community, it's the Patriarch's job to supervise it.' He reflected, smiling. 'He's a crafty old devil.'

'No doubt,' Anna said. Her colour had become extraordinarily high. She added, 'He has no right to keep Nicholas prisoner. Take the jewels back. I want Nicholas with us at Novgorod. If he isn't with us, I am not going.'

It was the worst quarrel — the only quarrel — that Julius had ever had with his beautiful wife. It was brief, and her voice was never once raised. At the end of it, he rode off with the jewels, and a day later returned, tight-lipped, and threw them before her. 'Nicholas sent them back, with a note. They are for the business. The Grand Duke won't release him or the Patriarch, whether they pay their debts or not. We are to go to Novgorod, and set up an office, and report back. He will help all he can. He may be free by then.'

'No,' she said.

'Then I'll go without you,' said Julius. 'And you can waste time in Moscow by yourself.'

Then she had turned. 'Does money matter more than I do?'

He shook his head. 'Anna, of course not. But what can you do, what can I do in Moscow? Nicholas is under restraint. They won't let him out. Where is the harm in using the time to some purpose?'

She said, 'If we're going home, we have to start while it's winter.' She broke off. She said, 'We're not going home, are we? Because Nicholas can't travel, and you won't abandon him, the snows will melt before we could leave.'

'I was trying to tell you,' said Julius. 'We might as well go to Novgorod. And report back to Nicholas. And hope he is free soon after that. Then we can go. You will see Bonne by autumn.'

She came to him then, not wild, but sweetly tender and sad, and he and she made their peace. Thinking about it all later, Julius had to admit to being perplexed by her variable moods. Unless, of course — he sat up with shock — unless, of course, she was with child. His child. A son. An heir. A real dynastic marriage. He remained for a while in a state of half-serious, pleased contemplation; and felt a little ashamed, because he did not care much for Bonne.

Very soon after that, as he had hoped, he and Anna joined the fleet of sledges that called at their door and were on their way, in convoy, to Novgorod. They would be back in Moscow, he hoped, in a month.

A week later, the elderly Florentine from the Morea called on the Patriarch of Antioch in his apartment in the Troitsa monastery, and told him that he and his companion were free.

'The Archimandrite has given his permission?' Father Ludovico exclaimed. 'The Grand Duke is agreeable? The soldiers of the garrison have been informed? What a pity that they could not all have done so seven days ago, when the party was leaving for Novgorod.'

'One could, I suppose, overtake them?' Nicholai de' Acciajuoli said. 'If that were Signor Niccolò's preference. But our eminent friend from Bologna has serious plans to discuss with him, and the Grand Duchess herself has desired him to remain in Moscow. What am I to tell her?'

'That I am honoured, of course, and shall remain,' Nicholas said. 'What more could a man want than this?'

HE DID NOT MEAN IT, of course. But he was conscious, as he spoke, that behind the irony lay the deeper irony that once, when his exile began, he had thought to persuade himself that, indeed, he had all he desired. He wondered where Paúel Benecke was now, if indeed he were alive, and had not met a fate like Ochoa's. He tried not to think of Ochoa or Anna, for it meant opening a vent to the wretchedness that underlay all he did, and if that were to be broached, he could not continue.

He had no news from the West, from his previous life. Now that he could use his pendulum again he was doing so, sparingly. He knew that Gelis and Jodi were both in the Low Countries, and he had touched Kathi, once. She was safe. The stab of relief made his heart ache, for he had no right to feel it. He had forfeited the right to feel it for Gelis and Jodi as well, yet nothing but death could change that. He had not known, until recently, that love could exist in such different forms.

He filled his days. Living now close to the castle, he saw much less of the Patriarch, having taken up residence in the house and workshop of Fioravanti, with whom a strange unofficial partnership had grown. Blessed with an early grasp of mechanical principles, Nicholas had benefited from years of working with John le Grant and, later, Moriz the priest: his fascination with the subject went back to Donatello's experiments with perspective. So he was drawn to something he recognised as a radical advance on what he already knew, and spent the dark days, and the days of lengthening spring deep in discussion over plans and designs at tables littered with instruments; and in sheds filled with gritty samples of brick, and fragments of plaster, and buckets of evil-smelling mixtures of mortar. The cathedral of the Uspensky was to be Muscovy's triumphant proclamation to the West: Russian in style, but incorporating the best the world had to offer in materials and design. The princes of Muscovy would be crowned there.

During all this time, Nicholas continued to strengthen the connections he had already established, on behalf of Julius's business, with the small trading community, both inside Moscow and outside it. Already, for the building of the cathedral, elaborate plans had to be laid to ensure that the materials, the masons, the labourers, the scaffolding experts were commissioned and brought into Moscow during those periods when travel was possible. Couriers passed between Nicholas and Julius, rapt in building his business at Novgorod, and entranced at this new dimension. Anna never wrote; but at least she did not abandon her spouse and go home.

Lastly, for fastidious adviser in all this, Fioravanti had obtained the services of the one resident who had both Greek and Florentine blood; who had business links with the West and the Levant and who was also close to the work's greatest patron. Nicholai Giorgio de' Acciajuoli, having politely sacrificed several weeks of his leisure to act as escort and interpreter during grand-ducal audiences, finally agreed to move into the architect's household.

He seemed to find it amusing. As an individual, he proved, as

Nicholas had always suspected, to be a superior bastard whose superiority was perfectly justified. After a period of wary adjustment, Nicholas suddenly learned how to deal with him. Fioravanti was a brilliant visionary, but the Greek with the wooden leg provided the rapier tongue, the cynicism, the wit that gave spice to their lives together. Nicholas fed Julius in Novgorod with work, and prayed that he wouldn't come home. For one thing, Acciajuoli would eat him alive.

In March, Rudolfo's son left, bearing two white gerfalcons for the Duke of Milan, who was fond of Fioravanti, and would also have building work to be done in the future. Acciajuoli, learning of the proposed trip, had been encouraging. 'But of course, Nicholas, you will be returning as well? The proud husband and father, so long deprived? Even if they won't allow you in Bruges (and so I hear, although I cannot imagine why), you might be reunited with your family in Cracow? In Danzig? In Lübeck?'

Nicholas considered this willingly. 'I thought of it,' he said. They were standing on the site of the cathedral, now being cleared of the errors of Messrs Miskin and Krivtsov and the persevering masons of Pskov.

'That is a good sign,' said the Florentine. His long-nosed face was blue in the wind, and his beard almost white. Below the costly black fox of his hat, he looked like an ikon, or a figure by Rublev from one of the pulverised frescoes shovelled up over there; an eye and two fingers admonishing from an old barrow.

'A good sign that I was thinking?' Nicholas said. 'But then, I thought how much cheaper it would be if they paid their own expenses to come all the way here. And the advantages. Egidia could manage the house, Marfa the Mayoress, and the boy would keep us all merry. He must be seven; old enough to be taught to watch out for your leg.' He smiled generously.

'You have decided,' Acciajuoli said, 'to be tiresome. Very well. I merely wondered, now that we know what we do, whether you had elected to spend your future in Russia.'

Now that we know what we do. Nicholas had thought of spending his future in Caffa, or with Uzum Hasan. Uzum Hasan had not spent the winter preparing to go to war with the Turk. He had marched north, as a show of strength against those rulers who might have aided his rebel son; then he had returned to his base. Barbaro was still with him, but only because his routes home were all closed. For the foreseeable future, the ruler of Persia would be battling against his own family, not the Turk.

And the Crimea, of course, was quite closed, although there was some news he had heard with mixed feelings. Oberto Squarciafico, carried to Constantinople with the Genoese he had betrayed, had been instantly executed by the Turks. The ousted Khan Mengli-Girey, on the other hand, had been shown clemency by the Sultan and freed, ready to return one day as Khan of the Crimea.

Nicholas did not find it hard to believe. He was prepared to hear that even Karaï Mirza had been spared. For, of course, the Turks had not invaded Caffa uninvited, after the widow's son had been imposed as Tudun. Enraged by Genoese interference, the well-born supporters of the two deposed candidates had combined to invite the Ottoman Sultan to intervene. Which he had done, to effect. The channels between Qirq-yer and Constantinople had always been open, as Nicholas had known.

So, plot within plot, thread within thread, the Crimean conspiracy had played itself out, with the wisest and coolest heads winning. Nothing had quite been as it appeared; he had known that. But Squarciafico, thank God, had lost, with the widow's ducats spilled from his satchel, and the widow herself could cause no more dissent, or her son. Nicholas wondered whether the same, one day, would come to be said of Zoe-Sophia, this formidable Duchess who some time, for sure, would have sons, and who would eye the young, shambling Ivan her step-son, so much their inferior. Some mothers, some timid mothers failed to fight for their sons, and gave up. Some gave up, it might even be, because they glimpsed the harm it might cause. But Nicholas would put nothing past Zoe.

Now he turned to Acciajuoli and said, 'Why? Do you think I should stay?'

And the man had said, without his customary irony, 'It depends, does it not, on your reasons? It happens, sometimes, that a country and a man come together at the right moment: that the man's imagination is gripped, and he sees not what is before him, but what could be there. Might this happen to you?' The large, dark eyes held his own, as if the question were of consummate importance.

It came to Nicholas, strangely, that to Acciajuoli, it was: that this was why the Greek from Florence was here; that to receive this answer was his only reason for coming to Muscovy. And then he saw beyond that, to the significance of the question itself, which he had never considered. For Nicholas had no interest in the future of Muscovy, any more than he had felt for the Crimea and Persia; any more indeed than he had felt for Bruges and for Venice, except in so far as they affected his experiments with the Bank. Any more than he had felt for Scotland, when he had used that, also, for his own purposes.

He said, 'Muscovy is not my country. I have no country.'

The other man's gaze remained shrewd. He said, 'I believe that. But the saviour of a nation is not always one of its own. Sometimes the Messiah comes from outside. You are a clever man, and a powerful one — for an apprentice.' His lip curled.

Nicholas said calmly, 'I was not bred to lead.'

'You were not bred to follow,' Acciajuoli said. 'You study others. You know how to infect them with enthusiasm; how to rally them in adversity. You plan, you organise, you communicate. In what you do undertake, your confidence, one notices, is enviably absolute. What do you lack?'

Neither of them was smiling, now. 'Arrogance,' Nicholas said.

'No,' said the other man. Deep in thought, he had ceased to shiver. 'Ambition, perhaps. And not, I think, because you are afraid to launch a great undertaking, and fail. You are not ambitious because you were born to be content.' He fell silent. He said, 'If none of us had interfered, you would be content still, would you not? Managing her business for Marian de Charetty; growing old peacefully with your children in Bruges.'

'My children?' Nicholas said.

'You have step-daughters,' said the other man. He made a sudden, irascible movement, not without an echo of pain, as if the empty socket in his thigh had rebelled against his standing so long in the cold. He said, 'Then, if you are not the principal, consider that you may be the forerunner. In which case, you are right to safeguard your line. And you are wrong in treating the world as your cabbage patch: sowing, exploiting and moving on. It is time you set to planting for life.'

'My children?' Nicholas repeated, as if he had not heard.

'A figure of speech,' Acciajuoli said.

MUCH LATER, Julius came back. He brought Anna to Fioravanti's house, where his host and Pietro his pupil plied them both with Chiot wine, while Julius poured out in aromatic detail the tally of his triumphs since winter. It was the money from Uzum Hasan's jewels that had established the business, taking the place of poor Ochoa's lost gold. Julius was solvent. He had appointed an agent in Novgorod. He was prepared to spend a few weeks in Moscow in order to establish another, with Nicholas's concurrence and help. Then they could all go home.

'Well, you can,' Nicholas said, when his congratulations had been given and his own news briefly recounted. 'You can go home whenever you like. But I'm under contract to the Grand Duchess to stay. And ask Rudolfo exactly what that means. Acceptance or prison.'

Julius stared at him. He looked remarkably well: hard and bright-eyed and vigorous and wholly recovered. Anna, smiling, sipping, watching Nicholas, hardly spoke. She was not discourteous, and her manner to Julius was unchanged, but it was possible to guess that the bloom of marriage had dimmed. It was even possible to guess that Julius had not noticed it.

Now he said, a little blankly, 'You don't know what you're saying. I didn't come to stay here for ever. I didn't even mean to come here in the first place.'

Anna spoke, her voice quiet. 'He's trying to say, Nicholas, that of course we can go home when we wish, but that you must go home too. Forget what brought you here. Forget why you thought you couldn't go back. If you don't go back, you may regret it for the rest of your life.'

Nicholas felt very cold. He saw Fioravanti's frown of concern, and the interested look on the face of Pietro. Julius had flushed.

He had used the pendulum within the last week, and everyone he cared for was living. Julius could not have possessed later, and worse news than Nicholas had. Nevertheless, he felt rigid with dread. He said, 'Why should I go back?'

Anna said, 'Can you trust your pendulum, Nicholas? Have you sensed nothing? Did you feel nothing last summer, when you were with Uzum Hasan? David de Salmeton travelled to Edinburgh and tried to seize your son Jodi, killing his bodyguard and attacking the old dame he was visiting. They got Jodi away, and sent him to Gelis in Flanders, but de Salmeton has set up business in Scotland, and so has another man you will know — Andro Wodman, who was there when Jodi was attacked. Wodman has gone into partnership with Anselm Sersanders. And de Salmeton is in favour with everybody, trading abroad, befriended at Court. He is staying in Scotland, he has said, until summer. Then he will cross to Bruges, and seek payment, at leisure, for all the damage done to him in the past. Gelis. Jodi. Kathi. Tobie. Everyone.'

'How do you know?' Nicholas said. His voice sounded dry. He could not be there by the summer. He could not be there at all.

Julius said, 'The Bruges office has been trying to find you. As soon as they knew where we were, they sent couriers. I got a message at Novgorod. I have another for you.' He handed over a letter.

It was in Gelis's writing. Nicholas didn't open it. He said simply, 'Rudolfo?'

But the architect slowly shook his dark head, his face sympathetic. 'The Grand Duchess won't let you go.'

Anna's face was pallid and puzzled. Even Julius looked shocked. Nicholas said, 'I can't come. Julius, you'll have to go. Please go. Please help them.'

'Of course you can go!' Anna said sharply. 'Isn't it worth it? Isn't it worth at least trying, even if Zoe's men were to kill you? Don't you owe Gelis that much at least?' She stared at him, the bones of her face stark through the flesh. (*If Julius were dead, would you love me?*) 'You can escape! Surely you can escape, with our help! Nicholas, what are you thinking of?'

Of Gelis. Of Jodi. Of Kathi. He said, 'You might be killed as well. No. Go. Go and help them.'

Then Anna rose to her feet and said, 'I do not think I wish to share a room with a self-seeking coward. Goodbye.'

The door closed. After a moment Julius also rose, murmured something apologetic and followed her.

The architect said, 'What will happen?' He glanced at Pietro, who looked surprised, and then left.

'They won't go,' Nicholas said. He had put the letter away. His jammed hands rattled into each other, and his heart was in torque to a windlass.

'You believe so?' said the other man doubtfully.

'I know so,' said Nicholas. Which, of course, was the case. Which left David de Salmeton in Bruges. Which left all those he loved unprotected. Or unprotected by him. Or unprotected by him, except in a way they would never know.

And now, he felt he had too much to bear.

Chapter 35

In Bruges, as elsewhere, the months of silence passed, bringing apprehension but not yet the pain that the months of revelation would inflict. The only reports that reached Spangnaerts Street without fail had to do with the achievements in Scotland of the former Vatachino agent David de Salmeton.

De Salmeton was remaining in Edinburgh. He was deepening and expanding his Scottish involvement: riding north with King James to quell risings; encouraging the King to favour Italian merchants; and guiding Prosper de Camulio to better relations with the English King and the Pope. In trade, he was competing directly and astutely with the Berecrofts family, and with Kathi's brother Sersanders, and his efficient, undesirable partner Andro Wodman. Since the previous year, de Salmeton had attempted no further assaults. The menace, dressed in mockery, lay in that remorseless stream of small notifications, for this deal or that, which burst upon the desks of half the merchants in Bruges every time a Scots cargo came in. *I am here. I am waiting.*

Waiting for Nicholas.

News came, of course, from Astorre and John le Grant with the Duke. Winter had not stopped Charles of Burgundy from his impassioned attempt to consolidate and safeguard his south-eastern frontiers and, with Savoy as his ally, to punish the Swiss, and to crush young René of Lorraine (*With the aid of God and St George, I go to liberate the subjects of Burgundy*). Ambassadors, floundering after his train, found themselves placed on a col three thousand feet up, deep in the snow, in order to witness a parade of the Burgundian army, much as their brethren in Persia, in broiling sunshine, had once watched a review of the army of Uzum Hasan with its hundreds of tents, its silver, its gems, its state robes, its carpets. Of the two, the Duke had bigger guns, but no camels.

On Ash Wednesday, the Duke accepted the honourable surrender of Grandson, the significant little mountainside fortress at the west end of

Lake Neuchâtel; but thought it necessary, to the distaste of the foreign ambassadors, to hang or drown four hundred of the defenders. Three days later, faced with twenty thousand of the Swiss confederation and its allies, the Burgundian army took flight, and the Swiss re-entered Grandson, reverently to clip the thickets of dead from the trees. The Duke and his ageing half-brother the Grand Bastard Anthony escaped with their lives, as did most of the army. Among the thousand slain was Jean de Lalaing.

Overrunning the Burgundian camp, the Swiss soldier boys broke into Paradise. All the riches of Burgundy had been brought to the field by its Duke and lay now abandoned, to the tune of hundreds of millions of marks, together with artillery, handguns, thousands of axes, crossbows, lances, horses and tents. There were more than six hundred precious banners and standards, many with the Duke's device *Je l'ay emprins*; I have dared.

In their counting-houses and their clubs, the merchants of Flanders heard the news with muted scorn and bilious fury. Diniz Vasquez, describing it to his family and partners, still found it hard to believe. 'Astorre says they lost everything. The Duke's clothes, his jewels, his manuscripts, his tapestries, the gold from his chapel. The rabble had it cleaned out before their officers could collect it, and as a result, the whole of the Confederation has turned into a vast underground amateur market, with twenty-thousand-ducat jewels changing hands for three francs. They also got two thousand Burgundian whores, but they knew the value of those.'

'So is the Duke retiring?' said Gelis. Now, with Moriz and Govaerts away, she and Tobie were the only ones left he could talk to.

'You don't mean it,' said Diniz. 'After a slight reversal like that? It only happened because of a misunderstanding. No. He's off to Lausanne, to muster an international army and do some real damage. I wish we could get Astorre and John out.'

'So do I,' Gelis said. 'But the good commanders are all that is holding Burgundy together.' She let the subject drop, for these days she did not talk very much.

It was much the same, that winter, with Katelijne Sersanders. Stoically, she ministered to the morning sickness of her cousin's child bride, both before and after the wedding; and as the weather improved, Agnes reciprocated, in a gingerly fashion, by coming to gaze at the encouraging sight of Katelijne tramping about, looking virtually normal, after presenting her husband with a second child. Aware, herself, of the necessity of producing a son for Arnaud and Anselm his father, Agnes was shocked by Kathi's apparent insouciance. If her own first-born was a daughter, she would die. But Kathi didn't even seem to think it mattered: she had greeted the appearance of a son exactly as she had welcomed Margaret. Incomprehensibly, her husband Robin had behaved no differently either. You would think that sons and daughters were the same.

Had she been a little older, Agnes might have detected, beneath a layer of anxiety, a certain well-concealed satisfaction in both parents. In truth, Kathi was properly sensible of the need for heirs for the family business, and Robin was not blind enough to think this unimportant, although personally he preferred little maids. They disagreed, amiably, about the child's name (*wait till it's ripe, and then boil it through twelve Ave Marias*) before agreeing, amiably, on a compromise. Kathi had an idea that Tilde was planning already to marry it to her new daughter Lucia, which would give the Berecrofts family a nice interest in Madeira, and that of the Vasquez a nice interest in Scotland. She pondered, in between worrying, over the amazing predictability of merchant marriages, and then thought of Bonne and Jodi and went back to worrying.

As the intransigent months gave way to spring, outside news began at last to trickle in. In Venice (Gregorio wrote), Doge Mocenigo had died, worn out by his ten Turkish concubines rather more than by his exploits at sea. The Sultan of Turkey had recovered from his sickness of gout, the Queen of maladies, and the Turkish armies were moving westwards again: the governor of Albania, Francesco Contarini, had been killed in the fighting. There was plague in Rome. Despite or because of it, the Pope had imposed a punitive crusading tax on tentless Burgundy, and Jan Adorne, defiant in celibacy, had found himself unable to leave for the coming birth of his brother's offspring in Bruges.

Her uncle, Kathi noted, was not stricken. As burgomaster of the councillors of Bruges, Anselm Adorne had little time these days for anything but the management of the city, and perpetual journeys abroad as its representative. After entirely friendly exchanges between Scotland and Flanders, he had given up his post as Conservator of Scots Privileges in Bruges, opportunely for James of Scotland, who was to make political capital out of it. On the list of appointments routinely reviewed on the King's attainment of his majority appeared the name of Anselm Adorne, divested of his Conservatorship 'partly on the grounds that he was an alien.'

Brought this news by her husband, Kathi had been rendered thoughtful. 'Do I detect the hand of David de Salmeton somewhere in this?'

'I don't know,' Robin had said. Firmly happy, confident in his marriage and in his work, he carried still, as she did, a cache of painful misgivings. He jogged the baby, who hung over his shoulder, and added a casual question. 'Your uncle didn't tell you who the next Conservator is to be?'

For once, she misread him. 'No, but I expect we shall hear. Not you, or Archie, or Sersanders, because you're all connected with Adorne. A Scot with good connections abroad. John Bonkle? Too naïve. Thom Swift? Not too young, but possible. Same with Haliburton. John Napier? Too important to travel so much. Andrew Crawford, or perhaps even Richard?'

'I meant, the new man's been chosen,' said Robin. 'That's him puked. Will I put him down now?'

'It depends who you're talking about,' said Kathi, taking the child. 'So who is the next Conservator?'

'Andro Wodman,' Robin said.

Kathi put the child down. It turned red. 'Andro . . . ? He doesn't qualify as a Scot!'

'He does,' Robin said. 'Family from Aberdeen. Brother an abbot. Fine connections with Flanders and France.'

'Friend of de Ribérac and his son, who want rid of Nicholas. Robin!'

'They're in Portugal,' Robin said. 'And that's over. Wodman has worked for Bel, too. And your brother thinks enough of him to have suggested him. Your uncle agreed.'

His son screamed. Kathi, sitting down, felt like doing the same, but restrained herself, because Robin looked so harassed as well.

Then, next day, it was swept from her mind by Dr Tobie, banging on her door on his way to a patient, and throwing himself into a seat in her parlour, his box and his man left outside.

'News at last. By Russian trader from Moscow to Novgorod; German dealer from Novgorod to Reval; amber official from Reval to Lübeck; fish merchant from Lübeck to Antwerp . . .'

'Tobie?' Kathi said. She said it quite politely, and he laughed and gave up.

'Nicholas is safe, and out of the Crimea. Some Russian fur traders got him to Moscow in December. It seems he'll have to stay for a while, but he could travel anywhere he likes after that.'

'Except the Crimea,' Kathi said. She let herself down at his feet. 'Was he alone?' She looked up.

'Ludovico da Bologna was already in Moscow. They're together.'

'Thank God,' said Kathi, 'for quite large blessings, if doubtless in rather poor Latin. You haven't told me about Julius and Anna.'

'They're in Moscow as well,' the doctor said. 'But not in the same place. Nicholas and the Patriarch, I am told, are in prison.'

Kathi stared at him. Her whole face, gradually warming, felt suffused. She said, 'Whom else have you told? Have you told Gelis?'

'The first,' Tobie said.

'And how did she take it?'

'The same way as you,' Tobie said. 'Sensible questions, and big, silly tears. So, show me the children. According to Clémence, they are still surprisingly normal.'

. . .

AFTER THAT, Kathi waited for Gelis to come. It would not be, she knew, for several days; they were not young, impetuous girls, although, Heaven knew, they were not old. Their occasional meetings, of which Robin was not necessarily aware, did not even mean they were confidantes, never mind bosom friends. She did not know how to describe the rapprochement between them, except to say that they were two sides of the triangle, and that the third side was Nicholas. And jealousy did not enter into it. If Gelis was envious of Kathi, it would be because she was properly married, with a loving husband and children. And Kathi could not be jealous of Nicholas's wife, for what she had, Kathi did not have, or want to have.

Kathi knew, as did Tobie, the story of the boxes from Montello. With gentle hands, she had helped Gelis finally turn out the contents, and had studied the pages of harmony. There was no doubt, now, where Nicholas's gift of music had come from. A coded message, it seemed, had also passed between Thibault and his grandson, but was now in Gelis's keeping. Gelis referred to it, smiling, but did not offer to produce it, and Kathi was careful not to ask. It had brought happiness in some way, she could see, and she was thankful.

They spoke of Moscow, and Wodman, and David de Salmeton. Gelis used measured tones, even when speaking of the exquisite, sardonic man who had cheated her, and brought about the refined torture Nicholas had suffered in Cairo and, more than once, his near-death. She said, 'You realise that if we know where Nicholas is, so does David. Now his threats against us will reach Moscow.'

Kathi said, 'If we can see through his motives, so can Nicholas. We are guarded. We know who the enemy is. Nicholas would gain nothing by coming.'

'I have told him,' Gelis said. 'I have written to Moscow, telling Nicholas not to come back.'

She fell silent, and Kathi said nothing, for she thought, given the courage, that she would have done the same. Then Gelis said, still looking down, 'Father Moriz ought to be here very soon. By now he should have spoken to Bonne. Since he went back to Germany, I think he has begun to feel, too, that he would like to know more about her and her mother. So does Tobie, I think.'

'The truth can hurt,' Kathi said. 'Worse than death, for some people.'

'I know,' Gelis said. She gave a half-laugh and exclaimed, in a shaken voice, 'Father Ludovico!'

'Never underestimate the Church,' Kathi said.

. . .

A TENSE SPRING evolved into an overstrained summer, during which no news of moment reached Bruges from Russia except for the concerted wails of displaced Genoese on their way home to their relatives. Robin, exiled from Scotland, tried to concentrate on building his business, but was visibly restless. The same was true of Gelis, hitherto single-minded in her devotion to the wellbeing of the Bank. It was as if, having explored every possibility and set in train every project she could think of, she had found herself sated, or had reached the margins of her interest and perhaps of her considerable ability. Certainly, she had accomplished what she had set out to do. With some small help from Nicholas himself, the Bank stood where it was before he had plundered it.

It was true also that, although she possessed friends, Gelis was more solitary than once she had been. Jodi, aged between seven and eight, divided his time between his various tutors, and had found playmates among the polyglot children of the Bruges merchant community, as his father had done, in the moments he could spare from the dyeyard. But Jodi, sturdy though he was, was not impressed by the impertinent wildness of the common apprentices, and would never, in years to come, find himself haled before Anselm Adorne, or beaten and locked in the Steen, although he would not connect his distaste with incidents which had occurred once in Trèves, and in Scotland. He liked jokes, and singing, and stories, and had a taste for drawing, caught from his early childhood in Scotland: if mislaid, he was often to be found in some kindly workshop, tied into a smock smeared with paint. He still visited Mistress Clémence in her new house from time to time, but was never made to accompany her when she went to see his wee younger aunt's second baby, which Mistress Clémence helped with now and then, even though the baby had a very good nurse of its own. Jodi didn't like boy babies at all, but found Margaret innocuous enough; and his Robin always had time for him.

Gelis also missed John le Grant and, against her will, felt concerned for his safety. Now, in the high season of fighting, the great, coagulating mass of the Duke's troops, with their quarrelling Burgundians and Picards and Lombards, their companies of trained English archers, their packs of loot-seeking Italian mercenaries, seemed to move from blunder to blunder, and with them trundled the hapless foreign envoys, the court, and the Duke's entourage. The low point of the campaign came in June, when — having made a pact of perpetual peace with the Emperor and his son — the Duke resolved, against all advice, to risk his whole Swiss campaign in an attack to free Morat, a Savoy fief occupied by a strong army from Berne.

It failed. In the ensuing battle with the rescuing armies of the Confederation and Lorraine, hampered by torrents of rain and a witless intelligence service, the Burgundian army endured defeat followed by carnage in which the Duke's soldiers had their throats cut in their tents, or were drowned in the lake; noble commanders and condottieri were cut down; and the Spanish ambassador received two sabre cuts on the head. The Duke and the Grand Bastard escaped, and so, it was later learned, did the greater part of Captain Astorre's company, including his master gunner.

Gelis was not present at Salins when the Estates of Upper Burgundy, harangued by the Duke, agreed to pay to defend their own frontiers provided that the Duke should no longer risk his person in battle, and that he should make peace whenever the chance should occur. She was in Ghent, later in the same month, when the Estates of Flanders not only rejected all the demands of the Chancellor Hugonet, but proposed to withdraw their grants to the army, on the grounds that the army no longer existed.

This was optimistic. Whatever happened, Duke Charles was determined to master Lorraine, and make of its capital, Nancy, the seat of all the Burgundian states. The King of France, who had spared himself the effort of fighting, pityingly watched the Duke doing it for him, and mentioned that he thought the poor man was mad. The Milanese, his allies, agreed. A Milanese, carrying messages, called in to Bruges and was entertained by the burgomaster of councillors in the Hôtel Jerusalem, where, for the period, Anselm Adorne had again made his home.

Adorne, although polite, made a distracted host, as his son's wife had been brought to bed of a child, and the health of both was giving Dr Andreas concern. Even when his Italian visitor had gone, it was a day before matters settled, and Adorne felt free to ask Gelis van Borselen to call on him.

She came, full of concern for young Agnes, and genuinely thankful, he saw, that the child at least was well. It was a daughter. Adorne did not make much of the fact, and neither did his guest. Of all his vast family, every son was childless but one, and that son had nothing but girls. And now Arnaud, too. Anselm Adorne had once, to his bitter shame, betrayed how much he yearned for a son who might carry his name, and his wife, striving to please him, had died of it.

This young wife of Arnaud's would have the best nursing his nuns could provide, and the infant as well. He had already thought he might invite Phemie from Scotland. Kathi would enjoy her company, and being only of the tertiary order in her priory, she could mix with his friends. He had fallen into some kind of waking reflection when he realised that de Fleury's wife was still sitting quietly beside him, smiling a little. She said, 'You are tired. You had a message for me?'

She was relieving him, courteously, of the need to prolong her visit. In the last eighteen months, he had revised his opinion of Gelis van

Borselen. Adorne said, 'I am not so tired that I cannot enjoy entertaining a handsome young woman. I have news of your husband. See: take this glass and let us drink a salute to the child. And then hear what our Milanese friend had to say.'

It was interesting enough. The man had been at court with the Duke of Milan when a young man, Andrea Fioravanti, had arrived from Russia with a gift from his father. Recounting the gossip of Moscow, the youth had mentioned the group of Italians and Germans who had escaped from the Crimea. Two of them were in Moscow: Niccolò de Fleury, and a Latin prelate called Ludovico da Bologna. Two, a merchant called Julius and his wife, had travelled north to the trading centre of Novgorod, where they were building a business. It was the man Julius who had entrusted a message to Andrea. Not simply a message, but a warning of danger.

'I have a letter for you,' said Anselm Adorne. 'Julius wrote it for you, but he also gave its message to Andrea, in case the letter did not survive. He has heard about David de Salmeton's attempt on your son in Scotland. He wants you to know that he and his wife intend to bring Nicholas back with them to protect you.'

The young woman's eyes, of a very pale blue, were quite steady. She said, 'But Nicholas knows he couldn't come home. So does Julius.'

'I imagine,' said Adorne dryly, 'that he would guess the embargo might be lifted, in time of exceptional need.'

She appeared to consider this. 'You are saying that he might be allowed to return to protect us, provided that it didn't last long, and he left when we were safe?'

He was a little disturbed, but did not show it. 'That would seem to me fair.'

Gelis van Borselen said, 'Thank you. I agree. But in fact, I have written telling Nicholas not to come. We can defend ourselves from de Salmeton. Nicholas would give up his livelihood and waste months of his life to no purpose.'

He studied her. 'You have not thought of joining him, by any chance?'

'I thought of it,' she replied. 'But communications being what they are, we should probably cross one another on the journey.'

There was a silence. Adorne said, 'You were affected, as were we all, by his brutal dealings in Scotland?'

'I am not excusing him,' Gelis said. 'He has tried to make recompense, to a degree. Many of us believe, now, that he is ashamed of it. I do not know, though, whether or not he would do it again.'

'His colleagues feel as you do?' Adorne said. He had wondered. Nicholas was a disarming young man, hard to forget. His partners had all worked closely with him. As time elapsed, a movement towards clemency might well gather.

'I don't know,' Gelis said. 'But even if they do, they would not agree, unless you did, to permit him to work again in the West. I think it is better if he does not come home meantime.'

'I think you are right,' Adorne said. 'And if he comes, he should know that he cannot stay.'

He watched her leave, presently. He could not guess the pitch of anxiety to which he had brought her. Julius meant to bring Nicholas from Moscow. Whether or not he received, or agreed with her letter, now Nicholas had to decide whether to come, or to be branded a coward. And if Milan and Bruges thought that Nicholas might be coming, Scotland would know. Nicholas might be coming, and it was time — so David de Salmeton would be deciding — it was time for all the adversaries in this war to assemble in Bruges. So that, whether Nicholas did come or not, she would have to face his enemies for him, this autumn.

It was then, arriving home, that she saw that the yard, busy with porters and wagons, displayed also the small, extra activity connected with visitors. A horse she did not recognise was being led away, and boxes carried indoors. At the same moment, at her back, she heard the voices of Diniz and Tobie. Diniz said, 'I was going to find you. Father Moriz is back. We should have a meeting.'

THERE WERE NO OTHER WOMEN in the room where they gathered, for Father Moriz did not wish to report, as yet, to Kathi or Clémence, or even to Tilde and Catherine de Charetty, the step-daughters of Nicholas. So Gelis found herself with three men whom, however, she trusted: Diniz Vasquez, the young Scots-Portuguese director of what had been the house of Charetty-Niccolò, and Dr Tobias, its physician, who had gone with her to Montello. And beside her, the formidable little chaplain from Augsburg who had spent a winter with John and Nicholas in the Tyrol and had been with them in Scotland and Iceland, and who had just returned from re-establishing Julius's business in Cologne — and from making some enquiries.

He made his statement quite simply, relegating the details of Julius's affairs to a future discussion, with the assurance that all should now be well. Fluent in several languages, the priest retained, as ever, his uncompromising German accent. If anything, it was thicker than Gelis remembered it. 'That is,' Father Moriz was saying, 'the records were well kept in the early days, and are now being returned to that state. The confusion between, which has occupied me, related to the estate of Graf Wenzel von Hanseyck, and its integration into the Bank's affairs.' He was looking at Gelis.

She said, 'I was in Cologne when they met, Julius and the Gräfin. He was bewitched.'

'Yes. Well, so were the accounts,' said the priest dryly. 'I have pursued the anomalies as best I could. I have spoken, perforce, to many of the Graf's noble kinsfolk, and have felt entitled to press, rather more than polite usage allows, for information about the Count's business and marriage. I have even spoken to relatives of the Graf's late first wife.'

'And?' said Tobie. His dress, since his marriage to Clémence, showed a startling absence of stains, and round his neck hung the cord of a pair of spectacles.

Father Moriz looked round at them all, and delivered his answer. 'The distortions cannot be laid at the Graf's door. When he died, his affairs were in order, and he left property of reasonable value, which Anna inherited, with some provision for Bonne. The confusions started thereafter. The money she was supposed to invest in the business, and in the ship, came from unsecured loans. She was married to the Graf, but there is no evidence for anything she has ever said of her life before that. More, there seems a strong probability, some say a certainty, that the child Bonne is not the Graf's daughter. I have found people to swear that she already had a young child when the two met. She has never used the name she called herself then, and I have not been able to trace it in Augsburg or anywhere else.'

'An adventuress?' Diniz said. He had flushed. Tilde had always rallied him on his admiration for Anna.

'We rather suspected it,' Gelis said, glancing at Tobie. 'Maybe Julius did, too. But if she wanted someone to keep her, she was generous in the way that she paid for it. She could be wise. She was gifted. She was beautiful. Kathi found her a friend. So did I. So, we thought, did Nicholas. She was always thoughtful with Nicholas.'

'You might almost say,' Moriz said, 'that it was Nicholas she was interested in, and that marrying Julius was only a means to an end. Julius did not pursue her, although he thought he did. Anna was already enquiring about Nicholas from everyone she met, and had placed herself in Cologne before Julius encountered her at all. When Nicholas went to Poland, she followed. When he went on to Caffa she followed, too.'

'She wanted the gold,' Gelis said.

'I expect that played a part,' Moriz said, his voice softening a little. 'I expect Julius wanted it too, for his business. But now, of course, that has gone.'

'But,' said Diniz, 'why should she be interested in Nicholas? She married Julius. Nicholas had a wife and a family.' He broke off. He said, 'I thought she was fond of him. I saw them together, like Gelis did. I thought she was fond of Nicholas, like sister and brother.'

'You might not be wrong,' the priest said. 'Human nature being what it is. But there is something more there than simple congruity. I went to see Bonne.'

The tall, demure girl in the convent, whose submissive manner had proved to cloak something that might have been hatred. Gelis said, 'She didn't talk?'

'More, I think, than she did when you saw her,' said the priest. 'She is tired of being immured, and whatever her mother has promised her, it will not hold her in subjection much longer. She would not give her away, but on the other hand there is genuinely little she can remember of her earliest childhood, beyond being with Anna, and then in the house of the Graf. I did learn one thing, by trickery.'

'You?' said Tobie, pallidly sardonic.

'A matter of birth dates and arithmetic. Bonne is two years older than we have been led to believe.'

'In order to claim the paternity of the Graf?' It was Diniz who spoke. Gelis could not have found breath for a question. She heard Tobie shift, and made the slightest of gestures to reassure him. She did not look at him. She didn't want to see his expression. She could feel Father Moriz watching them both.

Father Moriz said, 'I assume so. Tobie: when you went to see the vicomte de Fleury, and later to Eccles, what did you learn about the vicomte's late-born little daughter Adelina?'

Now Gelis caught Tobie's gaze. He said slowly, 'That she was brought up in convents. That she cut herself off from the family.'

'That she had red hair?' the priest said.

'Yes,' said Tobie. He did not move. Neither did Gelis.

The priest said, 'For although Bonne told me little, I found a nun who knew, by accident, more than she did. She remembered Bonne's mother, she said, as a young girl in a convent in Burgundy. The strange thing was that her name then was different. And that her hair had not been black, but bright red.'

'Dear Christ,' Tobie said. He said it quite slowly, and his eyes, equally slowly, came to rest on the priest's face as if his despair and his knowledge could somehow pass unspoken between them.

But of course, it could not. So Father Moriz had to say, gently, 'I see that you know more of this girl, this red-headed girl of whom the vicomte was speaking. She would be, then — Diniz will correct me — the pretty child-aunt of Nicholas, two years his junior, who was reared in the same home by his mother, and shared his first years in the house of Jaak de Fleury? Then if you know more, I think you must tell us.'

'No,' said Gelis. She saw that Diniz, too, had become very pale.

'I agree,' Diniz said. 'I don't want to hear.'

'I commend you both,' the priest said. 'You are both concerned for the reputation and privacy of Nicholas. I am sure Tobie respects those as well. But I also fear that it will serve Nicholas better, in the end, if this particular seal of his childhood is broken. Am I right?'

Tobie did not answer, or observe any of the niceties. He sat, his neck bent, his hands spread on the unstained stretch of robe at his knees, and considered. When he spoke, it was in a slow measured voice, without passion. 'Jaak de Fleury was a man who abused children. Adelina was five. He kept her for a year in his house, and another two years, unknown to anyone else at the time, in a secret house outside Geneva. During that time he not only taught her to behave like a lover, he taught her to love him. Then the affair was discovered, and Adelina was separated from Jaak without explanation. She never saw him again.'

It was Father Moriz who asked, in a quieter voice than Gelis had ever heard him use before: 'And Nicholas?'

It was from Tasse, of course, that Tobie had all this knowledge: the knowledge he had withheld from Gelis herself on the only other occasion this had been mentioned. Tobie said, 'Jaak only liked girl children. He beat Nicholas and starved him, and threatened him, but Nicholas didn't mind, for he understood that he deserved most of it. And anyway, he had consolation.'

And now she knew. The loving, easy-going ways of the boy-apprentice in Bruges, taking his joy where he found it, and giving it, too. She said, 'Esota.'

'Jaak's wife,' said Tobie. 'As crazed as her husband, but different. The love she gave Nicholas was the same as his mother's, but with carnal happiness added, or a version of it which he accepted unquestioningly as he accepted the love of his mother, who had abandoned him and the unfeeling world at the same time. Esota was quite deranged by the time that I met her, but she must have been a feather bed of warmth to him in that cold household. Later, of course, he would grow to understand what had happened, but he must always have remembered how it was, then. I can't imagine how he felt, the day they told him she was dead, and because of something he had done.' He stopped and said, with an unexpected change of tone that was almost petulant, 'Now I shall have to tell Kathi.' And, a moment later, 'And she will ask me, yet again, how I could have left him.'

'No, she won't,' Gelis said curtly. 'This time, it was done for a reason.' For a moment she struggled. Then she said, 'But such a childhood — would it not unite a boy and girl who suffered through it together? Would they not want to find one another?'

'They were five and seven,' Father Moriz said quietly. 'Neither would realise what was happening at the time. But to the girl, it must have seemed that she was always the rejected one. Her mother died, and she was reared by her own grown-up half-sister Sophie who, however kind-hearted she was, must always have loved her little son Nicholas better. Then Sophie died, and Nicholas went straight to the arms of Esota, who was also Adelina's rival for Jaak. Of course, there is an affinity there: the affinity of blood, and experience. But there is also, I fear, the possibility of something much worse. After all, Adelina and Jaak were niece and uncle. She had learned, I think, to love Jaak's attentions. I believe she may try to force the same unnatural bond upon Nicholas. Fortunately Nicholas is a generation away from the taint.'

No one spoke. Gelis's spurt of anger over Tobie's deceit had already faded. He had been protecting Nicholas. And he had not discouraged the theories that Kathi and she herself had begun to entertain about the wise, considerate woman who was to be a sister to Nicholas. And now the whole tragedy was truly in the open.

Gelis said to Father Moriz, 'So you think — so we all think — that Thibault's daughter Adelina is Anna von Hanseyck.'

'It seems very likely,' said Father Moriz. His face, full of pity, told how accurately he had noted the new waves of dread that engulfed her.

'And I have told Nicholas not to come home,' Gelis said. 'Because of David de Salmeton, I have locked these two together in Moscow, as they were in Geneva.'

Chapter 36

IF COWARDICE COULD reveal itself, as had been shown, in a man's reluctance to exert himself for his own wife and family, then Nicholas maintained his dubious reputation in the following weeks, and did nothing that could be misinterpreted as courageous.

By exerting extraordinary caution, he succeeded in preserving his skin in a wild and dangerous land, where the frozen hardships of winter gave way to the creaking ice and scouring torrents of spring, and the breathless profusion of summer brought with it other ravening dangers, human and feral.

He achieved it largely by staying indoors with Fioravanti. When Julius, increasingly impatient with his self-limiting business, called to summon him to a race, or a bear-fight, or a fowling foray, Nicholas was always deep in consultation with a metal-founder, or required at a briefing for masons, or was expected to be in attendance on the Grand Duchess at the castle. He knew Julius was weary of Russia. He knew that on one of these hunting expeditions he would find himself tied to his horse, being conveyed, with the utmost good humour, in the direction of Bruges. He stayed indoors.

His engagements were not exclusively spurious. Because of his knowledge of Russian, he had appeared with Fioravanti before the boyar Duma and before the Grand Prince himself, assisting the Italian to explain his work and his theories as the cathedral progressed. Sometimes the interrogations strayed into other areas: Muscovites were eager to know about western construction and artillery. The questions varied with the experience of the boyar: recently, as the power of Moscow extended, princes from outside the city had come to join the representatives of the old, untitled Muscovite families; the Duma spoke with mixed voices. It was also apparent that, when roused, the Grand Prince harboured imperial ambitions: to place Novgorod the Great wholly under his suzerainty; to absorb the buffer regions that lay between him and the

Tartars; to free himself, one day, from the Golden Horde itself, and throw down the small, shaming, tribute-collecting office of the Tartars at his castle doors.

In all of this, he was liable to find himself nudged, Nicholas could see, by the former papal ward, his portly young wife, aged nineteen. Since the elaborate obeisance that had drawn her eye, Nicholas had found himself many times in her presence. She was always heavily attended by her women, and her bulk was always encased in great parallelograms of stiff jewel-sewn silk, with the pendicles of Byzantium dangling at each round, painted cheek. She dressed as her Imperial forefathers had done; she spoke Greek, not Italian; and she adhered to the Orthodox faith, not the Latin she had been sent to encourage. Her shining obesity and the coats of bright colour that disfigured her fine-grained young skin were also part of her Greek and Russian heritage, and in themselves the mark of beauty and authority. No one had quite understood as much in Cardinal Bessarion's palace in Rome, where, as he had heard, the catamite Nerio had smiled, and Jan Adorne had been tricked into bursts of crude laughter.

No one laughed here at the Grand Duchess Zoe-Sophia. Replying to her questions, you observed the etiquette of Constantinople, and bowed yourself out in the same manner. Sophia was not interested in gunpowder or weaponry, but she was interested in trade, and Julius's company was already buying for her. She was also avid for craftsmen. Under Bessarion, she had probably had her fill of learned lecturers: she had no plans to begin an academy. But it was Bessarion's enthusiasm for Fioravanti, whose very nickname was that of the Cardinal's hero, which had inspired the invitation that brought the mason-engineer here to Moscow. Now she wanted others, but found it hard to attract them. There was as much money and a better reputation to be had in the comfort of Mantua or Buda as there was in this country — unless, of course, you drew double wages as a spy. Some of the earlier incomers had tried that, and been found out. Now both Sophia and her husband were wary.

Nicholas was not, now, short of money himself. He had some jewels left, adroitly hidden, but since joining the architect, he had increasingly been offered payments for his work: where the building was concerned, expense was no object. And though Julius was now back and holding the reins of his own business, Nicholas had drawn some personal profit for the deals he had made, and continued to do so. Because living was cheap, and there were so few outlets for money, wealth soon accumulated. Fioravanti had used some of his capital to turn his workshop into a training school. Instead of being paid, many of the young men who came to work on his site or at the drawing boards offered him fees for the schooling he gave them. Half the work he did was experimental. He drew plans. He used new tools — a compass, a level. A special kiln had been built to make the hard, prime-quality bricks he required: the walls of white Kama sandstone were to be filled with brick and cement instead of gravel and sand, and he had taught the masons new ways to cut stone. This building, on the brow of the hill, was to brush the sky; was to be higher and lighter than anything Muscovy had previously known. The Dormition. The Assumption. The Uspenskii Sobor. The caves at Qirq-yer had possessed a Church of the Assumption as well.

When he and Nicholas talked, it was generally about the cathedral, but it might as easily be about road-making or bridges or dams. Often, he would draw Nicholas to speak of John le Grant and his cannon, and they would discuss, yet again, the problems of countering heavy artillery, and how to break the impasse of costly, time-wasting sieges where neither side had the ability to prevail. After these sessions, the wall-boards would be black with impassioned drawings. Nicholas lived, from day to day, in an agony of uncertainty and apprehension, but his work concealed his feelings and preserved them from crumbling, like Rudolfo's strictly mortared new walls.

As the weeks went by, there were cracks in the rampart of silence. He knew, before the winter was over, that Mánkup in Gothia had fallen; that the fratricidal prince Aleksandre had been executed and his wife and daughters sent to harems. It moved him more to hear, later, that Abdan Khan the commander had escaped, leading his Circassians east of Kerch to the valley of the Kuban, and safety. They said that his pregnant wife had given birth on the vessel that took them, and that he now had a son, Kesa. The name, picked in pride and defiance, was neither Cairene nor Gothian, but Cherkess.

He knew his own son was alive, but only because of the pendulum. He carried with him Gelis's letter, brought by Julius and therefore read by him. It added little to what Julius had already told him: that the danger from David de Salmeton was known, and would be dealt with, and that he was not to come back. And so he was not coming back.

He did not, of course, cut himself off from all connection with Julius or Anna: he simply entertained them in his house, and discouraged appeals to his better nature by filling the room with other people. Fioravanti generally had some business to talk over if Julius was present, and Nicholai de' Acciajuoli never absented himself from a social occasion on any level, whether to shine at it or deride it. Impatience overcame Julius once, to the extent that he upbraided Nicholas in public for neglecting his family and overstaying in Russia, when company business required them both elsewhere.

To that, Nicholas merely answered, 'Then go back yourself. I'll come when I can.' And, when pushed: 'Then expel me as your partner, and keep the loan you were given as my forfeit.' He thought, then, that Julius was within a fraction of going, but Anna restrained him.

The next time they came, Julius was called away suddenly, and left Anna behind, promising to return to escort her home. Fioravanti was absent, but there were three eminent boyars in the room, an Italian goldsmith, and a few of the absent architect's more promising trainees, who sat as close to Anna as possible, and gazed at her, awed. She smiled and spoke to them all, but spent more time, as was right, with the boyars, interrupting herself on occasion to spar with Acciajuoli, who liked to inject a light irony into the unrisen dough of boyar discourse, increasingly thickened by drink.

Watching the pretty woman and the elderly gentleman, so socially adept, Nicholas saw, yet again, how they took pleasure in their exchange. Both were solemn; only by the tone of their voices could you tell they were bantering. Anna's face was illumined. Nicholas remembered the times when he, too, had been free to talk to her like that, and the sound of her laughter. He could not risk that now. With Julius here, God knew how it would end.

In fact, of course, Julius was not there. The light waned, the youths reluctantly left, and still he had not returned. The princes one by one fell asleep, and their servants came, as was the custom, to carry them home. One roused on leaving, and broke into song, and then vomited. Acciajuoli said, 'I shall escort the Gräfin to her home. Her husband has been delayed.'

Anna smiled. She had bought silks in Novgorod, and her slender skirts moved upon one another, layer on layer, as she changed her position. Her sleeves lay at rest on Rudolfo's priceless tiled floor. She said, 'Are you afraid to leave Nicholas and myself together? Julius will come. He had enough confidence, you will remember, to confide me to Nicholas in the Crimea.'

'As her servant,' Nicholas said. 'Which, of course, I still am. Monsignore, go home. If no one comes, I shall escort her myself.'

A less skilful man might have thought it polite to insist. Acciajuoli smiled, kissed the lady's hand, and, escorted by Nicholas, limped to the door, where his servant was waiting. The door closed. Nicholas turned.

Except for Anna, the room was quite empty. The planed timber walls breathed their resin, and the precious objects of Fioravanti's collection, a little disarranged by the company, defined the declining light in slow-swimming glimmers of silver and marble and bronze. The air sank through the window: the acrid, earth-smells of Moscow, as distinct as the fruit, musk and incense of Trebizond; the fish, clay, and camel manure of Timbuktu. The sweat, flowers and bath-oils of Tabriz; the rotting fish of the Faroes. The hot, peppery, ammoniac stinks of the dyeyards in

Nicosia and Bruges. The scent of love in Bruges; the one he would remember, when all the others had gone.

He knew, as he moved into the room, how that memory had been induced. She had risen from Julius's bed to come here. Julius's dutiful bed.

There was a handsome table in front of the window, with his own cup still standing upon it. He collected the wine and sat down gently behind it, on the flattened tapestry on the sill. The air blew on his cheek. She had chosen to remain where she was, in the shadows, framed by the embroidery of Rudolfo's best chair. When she spoke, it was not easy to hear her, although he did. She said, 'I can't go home without you. That is why I have kept Julius in Russia. He wants to go back.'

He didn't know what to say. Finally, he said, 'I'm glad you told me, for I think there is a misunderstanding. There is nothing here for you, Anna. You have been my good friend, but that is all.'

'You would feel bound to lie,' she said.

'I'm not lying,' he said. 'And I don't understand, really. It was you who wanted Gelis to come.'

'Because I was afraid this would happen. I can't live without you. I've tried. Come with me, Nicholas.'

'Where?' He tried to sound patient, and kindly, and sensible. He tried to sound as if never, in any conceivable way, could he desire her.

'Anywhere. You wouldn't be breaking my marriage to Julius. Whatever you do, I'm leaving him.'

'But that's nonsense,' Nicholas said. 'You've persuaded yourself that something exists, and it doesn't. Go home. Forget me.' And as she did not answer, he felt he must go further. He said curtly, 'I'm afraid I told Julius what happened between us in Caffa. I'm sorry, but I owed it to him.'

'He told me. He didn't believe you,' Anna said.

She was unusually beautiful. Even as her fingers ran down the clasps of her gown, even as he prepared to forestall her, he felt the small lurch of the heart he always experienced when he saw her or heard her cool voice. But he could not let it go on. He said, 'Stop, Anna.' She had already pulled the gown down from her shoulder. The dying light, forsaking the statues, the flasks and the ewers, slipped past him to pool on the bare skin of her throat, then her breasts as she stood. He set his hand to the bell on the table and said, 'I am sorry. I am going to ring. Rudolfo's steward will come.'

'He will be too late,' Anna said. Something gleamed in her hand, against her fair skin. A knife.

Nicholas said, 'What good will that do?' He had risen, so that the air flowed unchecked through the window, although the table still stood between them. Anyone, glancing in as they passed, would be able to see her with her gown pulled down about her, and her chemise wrenched asunder below.

She did not care. She said, 'Will you come with me now? Take me somewhere and love me. Julius would not try to hold me after that.' The knife gleamed.

'No,' he said. There were people outside. He could hear distant voices.

'Then I have nothing left to live for,' said Anna blankly, and lifted her arm. Her eyes, supplicating, enormous, held his. Then she stretched her long, slender throat and looked up at the fruitless sprig, the lethal sliver she held poised above her.

'You won't do it,' said Nicholas. He had not moved. His voice was perfectly even.

She glanced at him, once. Then her eyes closed, and her hand swept down, hard.

He had not believed she would do it. Perhaps because of that, she did. Her breath escaped with the swing of her arm. As the point of the knife entered her body she gave a small, surprised sound, like a residual grunt; but as the blade went on its way, slicing and sucking, she drew a great breath and screamed, loudly enough for the bustle outside the window to falter, and for a murmur of voices to break out somewhere inside the house. After that, she only whimpered, letting the knife fall to the ground and clasping her hands vaguely over the wound. She took one or two uncertain steps and pitched forward, striking the edge of the table at which he still stood as if frozen.

He saw the blood, thick as good tournesol, welling over her skin, soaking into the edges of chemise and gown, flowing down to her lap. He could not see where it came from, but it was very like the first gush from the crossbow wound he had given Julius; her face and throat were untouched and lovely as ever. She sank down before him with her eyes fixed on his, as in prayer; unclasping one of her hands, she stretched out her glistening palm for a moment. Then it fell, and she slid to lie on the tiles, her cheek turned sideways under the loosened dark strands of her hair, her amazing violet eyes at last closed.

Then the commotion outside spilled closer, into the house, with voices somewhere among it that he knew. He still had not moved when the door crashed open and men poured in, one of them limping. The first to enter, the first to see Nicholas at the window was Julius. He said harshly, 'What have you done? Where is she?'

'There,' Nicholas said. A yellow light appeared somewhere and brightened: a lamp in the hand of Fioravanti, with Acciajuoli at his shoulder. The room's small treasures gleamed once again, and the fair skin of a woman, lying in her half-naked blood on the floor.

Julius knelt. When he rose, he held Anna's knife in his hand, and his pallor was as extreme as on the day when this had occurred to him also. He said to Nicholas, 'You tried to rape her, and stabbed her when she resisted you.'

'No,' said Nicholas. 'Look after her, and I will tell you what happened.'

'Look after her! She is dead,' Julius said.

'No. Let someone look at her. It was an accident.'

'An accident!' Julius said. 'You and she are alone in a room, and she is undressed and stabbed with her own knife. That is murder, you diabolical little savage. She was my wife. And now you pay for it.'

His sword came out so fast that Nicholas almost took the blade in his shoulder. He swerved, and when the blade sang again he abandoned the window at last and flung through the room, overturning chairs in his wake as Julius attempted to follow him. Then the brief, furious explosion was over: men had thrown themselves on Julius and relieved him of his sword while Acciajuoli, taking Nicholas by the shoulder, pressed him into a chair and put a cup of wine into his hand. He accepted it in a daze, half rising again as the Gräfin Anna von Hanseyck was tenderly lifted and carried away. He could hear Julius shouting, and see tears of shock in his eyes. Now it was over, he had begun to feel sick himself. He had not thought she would do it. He had challenged her to do it.

The voice of Fioravanti said, 'You wish to go to your wife, Signor Julius. But before you are freed, notice that, as a matter of law, the man you have just attacked was unarmed, and you cannot be permitted to execute him. In any case, you have not heard what he has to say. And, really, it cannot have occurred as you describe. Your wife's murderer would surely have one spot of blood on his clothes or his hands, and Niccolò has none. He did not move from the window — I would swear to that, I saw him from outside — and he could not have reached to stab her over the table. It must therefore, as he says, have been an accident.'

'Then,' said Julius, 'I am waiting to hear, with interest, what sort of accident it could have been. Perhaps she disrobed and murdered herself?'

'Later,' Nicholas said. 'I'll tell you what happened later.' He felt extraordinarily tired; as if he had endured a long day's campaigning, and the end was not yet in sight. He began to experience anxiety, in case his attention faltered. His gaze sank to his cup.

Nicholai de' Acciajuoli said, 'Are you feeling unwell? Perhaps you would be better in solitude until this whole affair can be examined by the authorities. I fear that our friend Julius will not let it lapse.'

'Anna?' asked Nicholas, with brevity. He did feel unwell. The room rocked and the face of Julius, lowering at him, was blurred.

'She is not dead. She will do. Come,' said the Greek sympathetically. 'Leave the explanations to others.'

'The wine,' said Nicholas crossly.

They were the last words he uttered that evening; and the last fragment he remembered, apart from Acciajuoli's cursory chuckle.

'So you find yourself back at the Troitsa. My dear Nicholas, you would make Ahasuerus feel depressed,' remarked Ludovico da Bologna.

Nicholas flung up his hands and sat down again in his cell. He had had two days in which to establish exactly where he was, although no one would tell him why. Food was brought by one of the brethren. He had caught sight, once, of Brother Gubka, who had then glided quickly away.

The Patriarch, in one of his tidier manifestations, was expressing modified derision. He looked well fed, and someone had cleaned up his crucifix. Rumour said that in the weeks since their original release, he had spent quite as much time in the monastery as he had in the foreign merchant quarter of Moscow. Nicholas had only met him on the rare occasions when he called on Rudolfo, when he seemed more interested in investigating his larder than the state of his soul. But with the Patriarch, as he now knew, appearances could be misleading. The Patriarch said, 'In case you don't know, the lady is not seriously hurt, merely in a state of discomfort.'

The permanent millstone operating between his breastbone and his stomach slipped several times, and began experimenting with different rhythms. 'So you know what happened,' Nicholas said.

'I imagine everyone but Julius knows what happened,' the Patriarch said. 'He says you raped her, and she says she can't remember.'

'So he is insisting on justice,' Nicholas said.

'Well, he was,' the Patriarch said, glancing about. 'But of course, they've gone, now.'

'Gone,' repeated Nicholas. He said, with an effort, 'If you're looking for food, there isn't any.'

'They're bringing food. I was looking for platters. Yes, gone back home. Left Moscow yesterday. Moscow hasn't time for petty disputes among Franks.'

Yesterday. They would go to Novgorod first. 'Who decided? Who sent them?' said Nicholas.

'It was left to the Latin community. They appointed their own judge. The Duke supplied the men to enforce the decision. They won't be allowed to stay in Novgorod,' the Patriarch said. The door opened and his thick face assumed an expression of expectancy.

The meal that entered was better than any Nicholas had been offered so far. The serving monk laid it down and retreated. 'And me?' Nicholas said. 'Why was I not sent off with them?'

'The Adjudicator,' said the Patriarch, helping himself, 'did not consider it wise. The dispute between you would only have caused trouble by erupting elsewhere. Hence you will be held until it is known that Julius has passed out of the ducal domains, and possibly even after.'

'How long?' Nicholas said. He looked, with disbelief, at what the Patriarch was doing with the food. The Patriarch laid it all down and surveyed him.

'As long as is necessary. Are you brain-soft? You couldn't all stay. You couldn't slaughter one another en route, so one party had to leave ahead of the other. And of the two, you are the one the Grand Duchess is paying to work for her.'

'I want to leave now,' Nicholas said.

'You can't,' the Patriarch said. He opened his mouth and filled it with something.

'Then I want to see the Adjudicator,' Nicholas said.

He waited. The Patriarch munched. The Patriarch swallowed, and picked up a small bird, and stretched his lips open again. Nicholas said, 'You are the Adjudicator.'

'Of course,' the Patriarch said.

EVEN IF IT DROVE HIM to the edge of his sanity, the violence with which Nicholas resisted this decree at least released part of the pent-up energy which had made the preceding weeks so tormenting. Now the torment was of a different kind. It was some consolation to discover, as he importuned everyone within sight, that he was not alone. Although they could not know his reasons, Nicholai de' Acciajuoli was not unwilling to intercede for him with the Grand Duchess, and Fioravanti, against his own preference and interest, was ready also to petition that Nicholas should be allowed to go home. It surprised him, finally, to discover that the Adjudicator's embargo had not been born of indifference or mischief. Father Ludovico had recommended to the Duke that Nicholas should be released after a week. The Duke had refused, and the Patriarch had not tried to insist.

In the past, when inconvenienced by Ludovico da Bologna, Nicholas had expected to manipulate his way out of the difficulty, and had generally found the process enjoyable even if, surprisingly, he did not always win. He realised, by now, that he had never understood Father Ludovico nor expected to understand him. It was not until this long exile that he had begun to learn, largely through other men's eyes, what impelled this gross caricature of a priest in his burst sandals to inflict his criticisms and trumpet his impossible demands in the faces of scared monks and Imperial rulers alike. Josaphat Barbaro, speaking of him in Persia, had said, 'One meets him everywhere, does one not, as one might expect to see the ubiquitous God? But what one meets is not God, but one's own conscience.'

He was not a man, therefore, to whom one took one's petty concerns. What lay between Anna and Nicholas was a matter only for the two of them, and for Julius. The Patriarch already knew, very likely, about the danger from David de Salmeton. If he thought Nicholas despicable for not going home before this, he had never troubled to mention it.

He had never mentioned, either, the obvious fact that Nicholas was once more seeking reassurance through his pendulum. It frightened him that he had felt nothing last summer, when de Salmeton's attack on Jodi had been made. And yet, another time, months ago, here in the Troitsa, he had stood in the cathedral and experienced a sense of loss so vivid that his heart thudded, as if he were swimming against a great tide of death. But no one dear to him had died, that he knew of, and when the visitation of grief had occurred, there had been no one else in the church, except the lanky person of the youth Andrea Fioravanti, about to leave on a well-prepared trip to Milan. The boy had shown no previous interest in the ikons, but had presumably been told by his father to study them. A decent enough lad; he had talked about gerfalcons all the way home.

Now, the cathedral in the Kremlin was beginning to rise. Tied by his invisible leash, Nicholas lived again with Fioravanti and helped him to build. He saw it in his mind's eye as one day Fioravanti would see it in reality: stepping through the prodigious hooded door and standing in unimaginable space, between the tall painted pillars, and enclosed on three sides by the figured walls soaring up to the sky, and on the fourth by the heavenly plates of the golden iconastasis. One day, a son of Ivan would be crowned Grand Prince in this place, and would father another Ivan, perhaps, in his turn. Above, there were to be five golden domes.

In theory, he could have escaped: concealed himself in a cart with money sewn in his dress and horses waiting outside the walls. In practice, he had to account for himself every night. And whoever helped him or overlooked his brief absence would suffer. He didn't know what was happening in Bruges, but here at least he could show that he did not fail friends. And the loyalty bred loyalty, in its turn.

Julius was long away, but not yet in Bruges when the slight commotion occurred at the Kremlin gates, and a troop of the Grand Duke's guard cantered out of the castle and, surrounding a group of disreputable incomers, brought them to lodge in the fortified quarters of the Andronikov monastery. In the castle, a meeting of the Duma was called. The following day, the newcomers were transferred, under redoubled guard, to the Troitsa, and Nicholai de' Acciajuoli gave himself the pleasure of calling at the house of Rudolfo Fioravanti, to take wine with Nicholas and tell him about the arrivals.

'Travellers,' the Greek explained, holding the goblet in delicate fingers and indolently crossing his good ankle over the other, both finely slippered below the magnificent double-cut gown. A jewel as big as a horse-brass flattened the folds of his florid, face-shadowing hat. Since the unexplained little *crime passionel*, the room had been rearranged, and the table-top leather replaced, although still avidly scanned by the several ladies who came with their husbands these days in the hope of encountering Nicholas. The tiles had been simple to wash.

'Refugees,' the Greek now continued. 'Or so the leader insisted on delineating himself and his companions. Certainly, they had not the appearance of men one would invite into one's house, being attired in ripped, filthy clothes and tattered old lambskin jackets and caps, thick with grease, so that the merchants who allowed them protection held their noses and begged them to keep their distance, they said, all the way from Riazan in Moscow. And what a tally of woe! Sick in Fasso; immured in a cowshed in Tiflis; struggling to winter in Derbent, half drowned while being rowed up the Caspian; threatened and cheated and robbed by the Tartars at Astrakhan; starved in the wilderness; chilled and soaked on the Volga and the Don; and now penniless here, owing Tartar and Russian merchants and the ambassador himself for all the money loaned them, at interest, on the journey.'

'The ambassador?' Nicholas said.

'Marco Rosso, the Grand Duke's envoy to Uzum Hasan. He brought this wretched man and his party from Derbent. But for his explanations, they would never have been allowed into Moscow. It is still not quite certain, it seems, whether they are who they claim to be.'

His voice was solemn. Knowing his nature, there was no need to believe all that he said. Nicholas believed most of it, because he had begun to realise, with a faint glow of shameful satisfaction, who the ragged refugee must surely be.

'Contarini,' he said.

The Greek looked at him, affecting surprise. 'Of course, you and the gentleman were at Tabriz together. Had you been at the gates, you might have identified him for the porters! The Magnificent Ambassador Ambrogio Contarini, of the Illustrious Signory of Venice. I understand the poor gentleman has a very weak head for drink.'

'I fear so,' said Nicholas.

'In which case, he is about to find the Grand Duke's banquets somewhat demanding. He is also a Venetian, of that Republic which has outraged the Grand Duke (he has now decided) by treating behind his back with the Golden Horde. He will not be well received.'

'I am sorry for him,' Nicholas said.

'And lastly, Signor Contarini owes a number of Russian subjects a great deal of money which he is unable to pay. None of them is likely to allow him to leave until Venice has been informed, and has sent to settle his debts. He may be here for some time.'

'I feel for him,' Nicholas said. He said it carefully, for he sensed something in the air. Fioravanti, who had been smiling broadly, looked at them both.

'Indeed. The Duke, of course, has been most pressing in his desire to retain your services, but there is now a question of accommodation to be considered. Signor Contarini's present rooms are not to his liking, and Signor Rosso, in the expectation of future satisfactory repayment, with interest, has suggested that he should be offered apartments somewhere more pleasant. There is, of course, a great scarcity of such places.'

Fioravanti lost his smile. 'No,' he said.

'You don't even know Signor Contarini!' said the Greek, mildly chiding.

'I've heard you just now. I know you. No!' said Fioravanti. 'In any case, I haven't the room.'

'But you would have, if Niccolò left,' Acciajuoli said.

There was a short silence. Nicholas said, 'How have you come so far without having your throat cut? Rudolfo, I didn't know this was happening, and I have to tell you that you would never finish the rest of the cathedral if Contarini comes to stay here. Say no. They'll find somewhere else.'

'There *is* nowhere else,' said the Greek. 'And much as you may enjoy being selfless, *I* have to tell *you* that this is your one chance of leaving Moscow forthwith. It permits the Duke to remain loftily impartial and you to depart without allotting blame for small matters like stabbings. It is a pity, I agree, for Rudolfo.'

'I am glad you agree,' said Rudolfo.

'But it will not last long. As soon as Niccolò has gone, someone will discover that your work has degenerated through overcrowding. Contarini will be asked to leave.'

'You promise?' said Fioravanti.

'I am a Greek from Florence,' said Acciajuoli. 'At this court, I have only to ask.'

'Really,' said Nicholas sourly. But his heart was suddenly high.

Chapter 37

After that, the end of Nicholas de Fleury's stay in Moscow came with extreme suddenness. There was time for several feasts, mindless with drink, with Dymitr Wiśniowiecki and his Russians; with Fioravanti and the entire working group from the cathedral; with the merchants he had worked with on Julius's behalf. He had an audience with the Grand Duchess, although not her husband, and was given, to his embarrassed astonishment, a cloak lined with ermine and a thousand squirrel skins, packed in a bag. He was also to have a guide, and a safe conduct which would procure him another at each stage of his journey. He failed to see Rosso, who had left to travel north with the Duke, but he went to renew his acquaintance with Ambrogio Contarini, for whom he was vacating his rooms.

The accommodation and stabling the Venetian occupied was certainly uninviting, although after the hardships he had endured, you might think that things could be worse. Hardships were not, however, much referred to by the ambassador, who preferred to remember graciously the delightful court of Uzum Hasan, and to express particular interest in the speed with which Messer Niccolò and his companions had made their way north to Moscow, with all the Crimea held in enemy hands. He must be as resourceful as his dear friends Josaphat Barbaro and Marco Rosso. Nicholas replied politely that the ambassador himself had proved at least as resourceful. In its way this was true, although he suspected that most of the resources had been provided by the two servants and elderly Father Stefano, his chaplain, who sat, yellow of skin, in exhausted silence. With a Barbaro, there might have been some profit in exchanging information. With Contarini, it was not worth the risk. Nicholas produced a reassuring account of Rudolfo Fioravanti's temper and living arrangements, and left. It was only as he stepped from the doorway that the name of the Patriarch of Antioch was mentioned, with distaste.

'That dreadful man! You know, of course, that he stole the Duke of

Burgundy's presents from the very arms of the Persian ambassador, and handed them over to thieves?'

'Thieves?' Nicholas said. 'Were they not —'

'Thieves,' said Signor Contarini, standing at the door in his cheap doublet and coat. 'Wherever they claimed to have run from. I had the story from Uzum Hasan's own ambassador, and made sure that Marco Rosso knew it as well. He little knew, our Patriarchal friend, that we should both survive to denounce him.'

'Surely not,' Nicholas said. 'You will find, I think, that his action was prompted by charity.'

'The Grand Duke did not think so,' said Contarini. 'As soon as Rosso informed him, he had the fellow taken from Moscow, and put back in the Troitsa monastery. What did you say?'

'I just mentioned,' Nicholas said, 'that we both know it quite well.'

'THEY'RE BOTH FOOLS,' said Father Ludovico, 'but Rosso's a rascal. Fortunately, there are some wise heads in the Duma still. They will play the Greek card, but keep the Latin one handy in case they need it. I'll go when I choose.'

'Not yet, then?' Nicholas said. He had brought enough delicacies for a week. They stood stacked all round the cell.

'Not with you, no. Not for a while. I want to hear from Uzum Hasan and see what happens in the Crimea. They're all too busy in the West to need me. I'll probably stay for the winter.' He looked just the same. He looked, if you really studied him, like a man in his sixties who had travelled further and lived rougher than perhaps any other now living, and who one day would find he was tired.

Nicholas said, 'Explain to me why you do it.'

'That took a long time to come,' the Patriarch said. His eyes gleamed.

'I'm a very slow learner,' Nicholas said. 'Are you truly fired by a mission to keep alive the Christian war against infidels by reminding the rulers of the world of their duties? Do you dream of converting the Uzum Hasans to Christianity, and the Grand Dukes to the Roman faith? Do you find you can persuade Burgundy or the Emperor or the Pope to investigate the prospects for a Crusade if you can also promise them information in return? Or are you angry that all the crusaders, all the missionaries of the past have seeded Europe, Africa, Asia with hearty Christian colonies which have now withered to frightened, isolated groups who have none to comfort them, none to regulate and renew their pastors unless some individual can beg, borrow or steal the money, the safe conducts, the time to maintain their lifeline?'

The old man had folded his arms, his sandals stuck out before him.

He said, 'You still think life is like a diagram for a cathedral. A cathedral is a box created from numbers, whose function is to keep the rain off your head, but also provide a temporary carapace for all the limp, wilful, wandering, helpless souls that don't operate by numbers at all, although they may occasionally refer to them. My reasons for doing something today are not what they were a year ago. They are not what they were, very likely, last week.'

'But you know what you want,' Nicholas said.

'Oh yes. You have listed, in your methodical way, most of the problems that exercise the True Church. They are tackled, not in order of their importance, but as opportunity offers. They may be mended by the decrees of theologians, or by fleets and armies sent by princes and popes. Or they may be patched, as I patch my cassock, when I have a little time and some thread.'

'So you are not, in the long run, the delegate of the Duke, or the Emperor, or the Pope,' Nicholas said. 'You are your own master.'

'God is my Master,' the Patriarch said. 'It makes for simplicity. I commend it. For that is your trouble, isn't it? An apprentice to too many masters, and never stopping to consider which one to choose. Still, all this experience is worth something. You have something to offer, now, when you go back. You're not going to be Alexander the Great — no, you started too low and too late for that.'

'But Bucephalus,' Nicholas said.

'The horse? Well, there's something to be said for a horse, if it has the right rider,' the Patriarch said. 'And if you lose one leg, you've still got three others. It's going to be dangerous.'

'It always was,' Nicholas said.

'Well, you're right there,' said the Patriarch. 'You only had to look out of the window, and trouble always came to you. Do you want a blessing?'

'Can you say one?' said Nicholas, surprised.

'Usually,' said the Patriarch. 'But I might as well get in some practice.'

THE GREEK JOINED HIM at the last moment. Nicholas de Fleury was actually riding out of Moscow for the last time, with his interpreter and his servant and four spare horses and a small string of packmules when someone called from behind, and Acciajuoli came riding up beside him, with a train as neat as his own, but with a wagon in place of the packmules. The old man said, 'Unless you have any objection?' He was wearing plainer headgear than usual, compensated for by the splendour of his cloak, which was collared and turned back with ermine.

'You've had an audience, too,' Nicholas said. 'But why? You didn't expect to be leaving?'

'I suddenly realised,' Acciajuoli said, 'that I was about to experience another winter in Moscow, and all the pretty boys had grown up. You are not going to travel through Novgorod?'

'It wouldn't be much use for Florence,' Nicholas said. 'No. I'm on the road for Viazma and Smolensk. Informed advice from the stables. And after that, the fastest way to Bruges. Will some of that suit you?'

'Perhaps all of it,' said the Greek. 'I shouldn't mind meeting your wife once again. I have always enjoyed meeting your wives.'

Stupidly, Nicholas saw in this nothing suspicious. His thoughts were occupied with the town he had just left, and the people in it; and after that, with the terminus of his journey. He had never set his mind, methodically, to thinking about Nicholai de' Acciajuoli, from the moment seventeen years before when that capricious, one-legged nobleman had appeared on the wharfside at Damme, fatally, at the same moment as Simon de St Pol and Gelis's sister.

It did not occur to Nicholas, then, that by wives, the Greek meant also lovers, and that among these had been Violante, the mother of the catamite Nerio. Violante, of the exotic family which had produced the first of those crystallised sweets which had failed to cause his death in Cairo, but might have done so in Soldaia had he not recognised them. Because of Acciajuoli, he had been bewitched by those secrets of trade that had sent him to Trebizond, and later kept him in Cyprus, where Acciajuoli's brother had tried to get rid of both him and young Diniz. Cyprus, where Nicholas had first met David de Salmeton.

The first day's ride out of Moscow was a long one, and open ground and uninterrupted sunshine were soon left behind them as they entered the forests, bumping their way along wide, uneven tracks, across log bridges and causeways and into occasional clearings where the charcoal-burners and beekeepers lived; and where you would find sometimes the huddled timber shacks of a village, the cabins made up of whole peeled trunks outside and shaved wood within. Better far, in cruel frost and searching sun, than sweating brick, the Muscovites said. And Fioravanti, if pushed, would sometimes agree with them.

Nicholas had no desire for much conversation, but the Greek was a tactful companion, discoursing agreeably on innocuous topics spiced with occasional scandal, and insisting on paying the casual expenses of the journey, from the roubles for tolls to the *den'gi* he tossed to the boy who brought sour milk from a cottage. He was, it was apparent, of considerable wealth, and did not mind displaying it.

He did not mind, either, admitting to the infirmities of age, although he took his rest in the wagon, after refreshment, with a sighing deprecation, and did not do more than shift in the saddle occasionally when his leg started to pain him. It did not augur well for the speed of the journey;

but for the moment Nicholas set the problem aside and suggested that they stop short of their chosen destination, and sleep in the open, rather than on infested straw in the village. They were debating this still when the wheel came off the wagon, and the question was resolved. Nicholas, man of utility, dismounted and settled to mend it, while Acciajuoli rode ahead with his servants to discover the village and send back whatever materials the repairs might require. He left the guide, since he was familiar, he said, with the way, and Nicholas kept the servant he had hired for the journey.

It was as well, for the servant was willing to strip to his shirt-sleeves like himself, whereas the guide, resting upon his recommendation from the castle, let it be known that his function was to interpret and to guide, not to strain his back levering up other men's cheap broken wagons. He announced, after a while, a call of nature and disappeared, displaying thereby a wholly unusual delicacy, which should in itself have been sufficient warning to Nicholas. As it was, faced with a chance to undertake a strenuous piece of simple engineering involving no moral decisions, Nicholas was contentedly whistling, gasping, and issuing comradely orders to his man when he became aware that the man was not replying. He turned, and the glare of a descending sword dazzled his eyes. The wielder was the guide.

The steel hissed as it swept down, angled to cut through his neck. Nicholas hurled himself to one side, taking the chop on his arm with a thud he could hear. The violence of the blow and his victim's unexpected movement made the man stagger, and Nicholas, still rolling aside, kicked his legs from under him while completing the movement to draw his own sword. His left arm was numb. Behind, on the grass, lay the dead, bloody figure of his servant. The guide got to his knees, sword in both hands, eyes open and glistening. He was used to assassination rather than fighting, but he knew enough to get back from a wounded man and play him until blood-loss made him weak. Nicholas watched his eyes, guessed where the next blow would come; parried it; made a slash of his own which was rebuffed and, feinting, kicked the man again, but this time in the groin. The guide gave a whistling grunt but held on to his sword, his face yellow, scrabbling to back out of range. Both men stumbled to their feet. Nicholas glanced at his horse. The other man's eyes followed, and he grinned queasily, shifting to block the way. He held his sword with two hands, Nicholas with one.

Nicholas threw his sword away. It arched into the air, drawing his attacker's attention. Then the man screamed and fell, with Nicholas's flying dagger sunk in his chest. Nicholas strode over and crouched.

It was over, or nearly so. The would-be assassin had no more than a few moments of life: enough to sneer up into his employer's face and say,

'You thought you'd escape if he dressed up as you. But they'll all be dead by now. And you won't get far with that arm.'

Nicholas clamped him by the elbow, but the man had gone. He recovered his knife and rose slowly. His own blood, swamping his sleeve, had left a random, sprinkled trail on the body, like a parting benison from a censer. For a moment, Nicholas stood. *You thought you'd escape if he dressed up as you*. He had suspected nothing. He had never set his mind, methodically, to thinking about Nicholai de' Acciajuoli.

There was cloth in his saddlebag. He twisted it round his arm and knotted it with his teeth to stop the blood pumping. Then he gathered the reins, threw himself into the saddle, and set off, the horse tossing its head. He had demonstrated at Thorn that he knew how to shoot and control his horse with his body at the same time. Now, he might be unable to shoot, but if he had to, he could both ride and fight with one hand. He prayed that he would have to. Well paid, and well provided with weapons, the villagers ahead would have been lying in wait. Or perhaps it would have been a band of pseudo-robbers who pounced on the party that was known to be riding from Moscow today, with one of the castle's own guides. He wondered if the Grand Duchess had anything to do with that, and thought not. Acciajuoli had been one of Sophia's men.

He did not, of course, have a guide. The forest roads were in themselves unmistakable, but quite often divided, or were joined by lesser tracks. Twice, he had to rein in at a junction and scan the ground for recent hoof-marks and new-settled dust. The rest of the time he rode headlong, heedless of noise and of the blinding, battering pain in his arm. Then came the intersection of paths where his way was identified for him by a riderless horse, prancing towards him.

Prancing was, indeed, the only way to describe its astonishing gait. First it would break into a canter, then pause, shaking its mane and bowing to kick its hooves scything behind it. Then, whinnying, it would rear, before crashing down and resuming its erratic progress towards him. The trees of the forest threw back its squeals. Then, as Nicholas raced towards it, he heard the other high, searing, menacing sound, and saw what the approaching beast was bringing with it. Round its head, stuck to its flanks, streaming in loops and whorls all about it, was a death-cloud of bees.

He knew then what had happened, for it was not unknown among Russian villages. If you wish to discourage intruders, set the bees on them. He knew what it looked like. He had seen a beekeeper rouse a hive, rapping with the palms of his hands on the sides to induce it to swarm. There might be forty thousand bees in each hive; the number of hives would, of course, vary.

Now, he plunged into the forest, sweeping back to the road once the maddened animal and its cargo had passed. As he rode, he tied his reins and emptied his saddlebags, binding a scarf round his face and pulling his hooded cloak round him with hands thrust into gloves. The rest he tried to drape as an improvised horse-cloth. Before he had finished, the air was filling with bees. Instead of the occasional flick of orange or white from a butterfly's wings, or a crane-fly's spidery rattle and click, or the probing black and yellow cylinder of a wasp, there were single black bodies everywhere, of bees, once concentrated and now dispersed, distrait, uncertain of purpose. They did not attack him. A crashing in the forest told that another horse had been less fortunate.

Acciajuoli had had four servants with him, and there had been ten horses in all. That accounted for two of them. The bees swung about him, still singly, and as the road turned and the light of early evening descended from a circular opening in the trees, Nicholas saw that he had come as far as Acciajuoli had come, to a stretch of trampled earth, with a stream, a small planting of kitchen vegetables, a byre, a pile of manure, and a haphazard group of battered timber houses whose doors stood open, and from which issued no sound. In fact, as he slowed, there was nothing at all to be heard in the clearing but the hiss of the distant leaves, and the trickle of water, and the sharp crochets and diminishing minims of solitary bees, interrupted now and then by the snarl of an attacking cluster.

The victims were presumably the escaping horses, for there was nothing left here worth attacking. That had already been done. Nicholas, dismounting, led his horse forward to where lay the dark bodies of four lifeless Russians in leather tunics and breeches, and two horses, both dead. One had fallen and broken its neck. The other had been killed, presumably to prevent its rider from escaping. The rest, crazed, had patently fled like the one he had seen. They would soon be caught. Horses were valuable. The men, their faces blotched and swollen, had been stung half to death. Those who had looked like surviving had been killed. All the packs had been emptied.

He had seen everything but the one man he sought. Then he heard a sound.

Least able to control a rearing horse, Nicholai de' Acciajuoli had lost his grip as soon as the maddened animal reared and, falling, had brought the beast down on himself. The horse had died. Its rider, less fortunate, had merely remained, trapped under its weight, with his head and torso and arms exposed to the venom that had felled him.

His hands were free. Although he might be numb from the waist down, the Greek had been able to drag about him his priceless, soiled ermine cloak, gift of the Grand Duchess Sophia, and turn his face into the ground. Racing to him, Nicholas thought that, left for dead, he might have a chance. Then he saw the blood on the cloak and the grey cast of the distorted face that turned slowly towards him. 'Ah, Niccolò,' said the Greek. 'Do not trouble. I am dead.'

'Not while I am here,' Nicholas said, kneeling. He had worked with a good doctor in the field: his fingers explored as he spoke. 'You knew this would happen?'

'I thought it possible,' the Greek said. His voice was thin, but his deep gaze was steady and clear.

'And you arranged for the wagon to break, to leave me behind? Why?'

'A whim,' the Greek said. His whitened lips in his grizzled beard moved a little. 'I am old. My life is my own. If we are given a few moments together, I might say more to you. I have a drug that would help in my purse. Sadly, that is under the horse.'

'Is there a difficulty?' Nicholas said. He spoke lightly, for by then he knew what he was dealing with. He also knew that Acciajuoli was an expert in opiates. On the day Anna was stabbed, the Greek had provided him with the respite he needed. He owed him something for that.

The horse presented another problem of leverage, but not so simple when single-handed in every sense and still losing blood. Nicholas stopped twice to let his eyes clear, but eventually it was done; the horse was raised, and the man pulled clear and laid on his cloak in the shade. Then Nicholas turned back his mantle.

Acciajuoli had been right. By itself, the weight of the horse might not have mattered: one leg was broken, but the other, which had taken the brunt, was intact, being fashioned of wood. His life was ending not because of the horse, but from the depth of the single stab wound in his body, evidently inflicted in haste. Perhaps, seeing his face, someone had realised that he was not the man they expected. Perhaps, afraid, their ambushers had made good their escape, assured that he could not live long.

He lay with his eyes closed while Nicholas did what he could. His horse, tied and covered, drooped nearby. The bees dispersed and were replaced by bluebottles, in buzzing indigo quilts. The purse was glazed with blood and squashed flat, but the kidskin packet with its powder was still intact inside. Nicholas brought water and, kneeling, spoke, causing the heavy patrician lids to make the effort to lift. 'I have what you asked for.'

He obeyed the directions he was given, having neither the insolence nor the inhumanity to question them. The first dose would bring relief for a short while; the second would kill. After that, the Greek said, Nicholas was to pull what he could into the houses and set them on fire, so that none would know that Nicholas himself had escaped. He asked, as the pain started to dull, about Nicholas's own useless arm, and Nicholas told him, making him frown. 'There, too! But poor men will do anything, given money.'

They had half an hour together, perhaps, as evening drew towards night, and the sky above them turned through all the pale, silky colours to opal. The Greek lay, a saddle for pillow, with his hair loose and the ermine drawn over his body, and Nicholas sat at his side, propped by the vast base of a tree. With proper bandaging and a sling, his own bleeding had stopped. He knew he must take what rest he could, for he could not stay here once it was over. His safety depended on his being thought to be dead. At the moment, it did not seem greatly to matter, in face of the service the other man had taken upon himself to perform. He had asked why. 'We are not related?'

The Greek's amusement had shown in his eyes. 'With what private misgiving you say it! No, Niccolò. We may be so, of course, in the future, but my present concern is merely to preserve for the world those boyish talents you have displayed so profusely since we first met. Eighteen, were you not? So uncouth!'

'I am sorry,' Nicholas said, also briefly amused.

'Oh, that is of course no longer so, or you would not be attracting this attention. It is as well that I heard a rumour of ambush. Now it is over, you will find that you make a quick journey. Ghosts travel fast.' He fell silent, breathing quickly, but holding Nicholas still with his large, soft, cynical eye.

Nicholas said, 'There is no need to talk.'

'Perhaps not,' the Greek said. 'But I should like to spend my last moments in some form of civilised employment. You know, of course, who your enemies are?'

A lifetime of habit dies hard. 'I thought they were in Bruges,' Nicholas said.

'Even yet!' the Greek said. 'Even yet, you will not break silence. I suppose I commend you. Nevertheless it is true, I take it, that the woman Anna offered herself to you in Moscow, and you refused? And that David de Salmeton has threatened you?'

Nicholas said, 'He is working with Camulio. Another alum-dealer, like you and your brother. And myself, of course, under your tuition. The bottom, you will have noticed, has dropped out of the alum market.'

'It has served its purpose,' the Greek said. 'It sent Zoe to Muscovy and you to the Levant. I am glad you at least perceived that you were being educated. A failed Crusade and your future all dependent on a man's acquaintance with Phocoean holly. I am only sorry that the greater prospect seems also to have failed. I cannot see Moscow and Persia crushing the Sultan between them.'

'That is what you hoped?' Nicholas said.

'That has been the hope of everyone still alive from Imperial Trebizond and Byzantium, and poetic visionaries such as Aeneas Sylvius, and earthworm visionaries such as our mutual friend Father Ludovico.' He broke off, but resumed again almost immediately. 'You learned something during your sojourn in Moscow, but did not lose your soul to military or domestic engineering?'

'Part of it, perhaps.'

'But you will not fill your life with cathedrals, any more than you will fill it with spectacles for the theatre or the blind. Russia may be too big for a man such as you, but these are too small. You must look for something that fits.' His whining whisper modulated between impatience and scorn.

'I shall do. I have friends who will help me. Rest,' Nicholas said. He felt sick with the tragedy of it, and the strangeness of the other man's intensity, underlined by its total detachment. Dying, Nicholai de' Acciajuoli lay self-sufficient as a figure in bronze, and invited neither pity nor comfort. A mechanical courier, formed to deliver its message, and unstoppable.

'You have friends, of course. Several men: you know their deficiencies. Two young women. I sometimes wonder if you know their strengths. I permit myself a crude question. You have no appetite for the Sersanders child, Katelijne?'

'It is a crude question,' Nicholas said.

'So hers is a name not to be trifled with. She represents something to you that perhaps you are only now coming to realise. You may come to realise, too, that it does not matter that she is married with children. Your masculine friends are so situated, and you do not shun them. For fleshly pleasures, of course, there is your wife.'

Nicholas was silent. The characteristic chuckle, now distorted, mildly mocked his forbearance before, wilfully, continuing. 'But, of course, she is clever as well, in a different way. I remember a discussion in Florence.'

'You told her I was not to remarry: that posterity was already served. She told me. I found it offensive,' said Nicholas suddenly. 'I felt that she and I and our family were nothing; that you were presuming to look beyond us.' He stopped abruptly. *Any strolling astrologer can frighten you,* Gelis had said.

'And when you are using your pendulum, are you not looking beyond?' the Greek said. 'It takes a strong man to do so, and to face what you see. Your life is important, but you will not live for ever.'

'I was not thinking of myself,' Nicholas said.

'I understand. You are concerned for the next generation. But all six children have been born who are to take care of your line in the future. Your role is that of father to Jordan, and protector, teacher, tutor and adviser to him and to the sons of other men. If you fail, there is always Dr Andreas. If you fear for your wife once you have gone, my lovely Nerio will see that she comes to no harm.'

The thought was grotesque, even when couched in irony. Nicholas held back a reply, and then saw, with growing dismay, that there were actually tears in the Greek's eyes. He spoke then in a different voice. 'Would your shade not be jealous?'

'I, jealous?' said the Greek, and his beard moved in a small, startled smile while a tear, dislodged, fell on his cheek. 'Would Nerio tell me everything, as he does, if I were? When Nerio watched you bedding Violante his mother, and later described all he had seen, I was not jealous, and yet I had cause. Not because the boy is my catamite, but because I got him on Violante myself. Nerio is my son.'

Of course. Of course. Of course.

'She did not say. I didn't know,' Nicholas said. He gave a sudden wide smile, impelled by an emotion he did not understand, and said, 'So your line, also, is established. It seems right.' To himself, he wondered, a little breathless, if Caterino Zeno knew the identity of his wife's lover; then realised that, of course, he had done. Zeno's marriage was one of convenience.

Even wet, the darkened eyes kept all their mockery. 'Fortunately,' said the Greek, 'Nerio has a charm which appeals to both sexes, and which will serve him well, even in age. Yes, my line, too, is established. I may leave when I choose.'

'And your master will commend you?' Nicholas said.

'You think I have a master?' the Greek said. 'Let us say rather that I prefer order in life, and do not lose time where I see a chance to establish it.'

'One who sees the beauty in roads and bridges and buildings,' Nicholas said.

'One who conceives the structure that will endow others with freedom, yes: that is true. But I am also human,' said Nicholai de' Acciajuoli. 'I lost my leg at Constantinople, for which I blame the Knights of St John. I like to think that one day, someone will even the score. Meanwhile, all that I have with me is yours, to take you safely home, except only my leg. I should like you to take that to Nerio.'

'I shall try,' Nicholas said.

'You will succeed,' said the Greek. 'It may better encourage you to know that it is filled from hip to toe with gold coins. If my other resources prove inadequate, I give you leave to dip into a knee joint. Only do not give the remainder to Violante. If she wishes gold, she must earn it from Zeno.' He waited and said, smiling still, 'You *are* going to Bruges?'

'I have this matter to deal with,' Nicholas said. 'I shall not, I suspect, be allowed to stay long.'

'My dear Niccolò,' the dying man said. 'Provided you live, it is your choice, not theirs. You are not, I hope, an apprentice to anyone, now.'

A little after that, he asked for the second half of the potion, and Nicholas brought it, and lifted his shoulders to allow him to drink. He tried to say, once again, what he felt, but the Greek shook his head.

'It was time. This is one death you do not have on your conscience.' He paused, patently searching for the fitting benediction which, eventually, he found. 'Violante spoke highly of you, in general, as a lover. She always held you had the advantage of Zeno.'

'But not of you,' Nicholas said. His voice conveyed what he felt: unwilling admiration mixed with regret.

'There, of course,' said the Greek, 'there could be no comparison.' He drank, and was smiling still as his lids fell.

Part IV

REPRISE

Chapter 38

A GHOST TRAVELS fast. A ghost with three legs travels faster.

Throughout the civilised world known to Europe, the autumn stasis set in, troubled only by small local disturbances, for the most part irritable and inconclusive: it promised to be a hard winter, and fighting men preferred to spend such months at home.

The ghost flitted, and those who inhabited its former homes in Venice, Flanders and Scotland waited, as they had done for three years, in fretful suspense, not knowing what to hope for, or what to fear. Then autumn began to move into winter, and the catchment area, the network, the web awaiting Nicholas de Fleury stirred into life, animated by a signal from Scotland.

Since the attempt upon Jodi in Edinburgh, his wee Aunty Bel had spent a great deal of time in the city, divided between her usual house and the office and home of the Berecrofts family. There, she and Archie of Berecrofts shared news from the Low Countries about Kathi, married to his son and heir Robin; and kept a combined, judicious eye on the commercial depredations of their mutual enemy, David de Salmeton.

Of the man himself, she had seen nothing at close quarters since the day of the bodyguard Raffo's death. He had lied his way out of that, and had since left them alone, being disinclined, Archie said, to risk the new business success he was working so hard to achieve. It was, therefore, all the more astonishing when David de Salmeton in person arrived one day at the grand Berecrofts house in the Canongate, had himself received in the parlour where Bel (how did he know?) was visiting Archie, and asked his host's permission to convey some sorrowful news.

Left to himself, Archie would have denied the man entrance. It had been Bel, better acquainted with de Salmeton, who had counselled otherwise and who, hearing him now, sat herself down with some care. Sorrowful news. Being only human, she thought first of her son; of Claude and the children. Then, ashamed, she drove her logical mind to assess the areas of much greater risk which were also of import to Archie, chief among them being Kathi and Robin. Kathi and Robin, dear God, and the babies.

David de Salmeton said, 'I speak, of course, of Nicholas de Fleury, who, you will have heard, is dead in Russia. His widow and son have yet to hear. Fortunately, there is a Scottish emissary leaving for Flanders. I hope to sail with him and enlighten the poor lady myself. A widow and a fatherless child. Is it not sad?'

'How d'ye know?' Archie had said. Robin's father, the most courteous of men, had no time for miniature beauties with waving black hair and large eyes, who killed people.

'Oh, everyone knows,' said David de Salmeton. 'And is it so surprising? The poor man had little to live for. But I digress. Time is short. I merely called, in case you had a word for the widow? Or young Kathi? It seemed to me that she and Nicholas were particularly close.'

'We shall send our own messages,' Archie said, 'when we know the truth.'

Shortly after that, the visitor bowed himself out. Archie swore.

'Oh, all of that,' said Bel of Cuthilgurdy. 'But do ye believe him?'

Archie pursed his lips. 'It's true that the King's sending his uncle to Burgundy. Half-uncle. James, Earl of Buchan. Hearty James. He's supposed to be advising Duke Charles to make peace with the Duke of the Tyrol. Him that's married to the King's aunt.'

'Eleanor,' Bel supplied helpfully. 'Our King James is sending his uncle to mediate between Duke Charles and the Tyrol, while Duke Charles is busy invading Lorraine? It doesna sound like very intelligent planning.'

'No,' said Archie. 'But that isn't why de Salmeton came, is it? He just wanted us to know that Nicholas de Fleury is dead, and de Salmeton is off to harass his son and his widow.' He paused. 'I'll need to go.'

'No, you don't,' Jodi's Aunty Bel said. 'They're well protected. We'll send word. There's a shipmaster I know. And forbye, there's a man who'll do more good nor you would.'

'Who?' Archie said.

'Ah,' said Bel. 'That'd be telling.'

There was a moment's silence. 'You don't believe this,' Archie said. 'You don't believe it, do you?'

Bel heaved herself upright. 'I don't want to believe it,' she said. 'You could say that, right enough. And I don't trust that little popinjay, that's another thing. But most of all, I must say, when Nicholas de Fleury manages to get himself killed, I think you'd ken by the bang, not the squeak.'

THE SAME RUMOUR reached Bruges, and was duly noted, if not necessarily believed, in the counting-houses, the mansions, the kitchens, the council-rooms and the cellars once haunted by Nicholas de Fleury. He had been gone for three years, and the commerce of Bruges was no longer affected by his absence, any more than the Banco di Niccolò, which had so successfully reconstituted itself.

In the Charetty-Niccolò bureau in Spangnaerts Street, Gelis van Borselen heard the rumours and, with Diniz's permission, called a meeting of all his chief partners, as once she had done in Venice. When it was over, she went to see Kathi.

Robin was out, and the babies were absent. Kathi said, 'If you've come to talk about Nicholas, I have to say I don't believe what they're saying.' Since Rankin's birth, she had become very slight.

Gelis said, 'You don't need to. He isn't dead. But if David de Salmeton thinks he is, then he might abandon Scotland this winter, and come and amuse himself instead with the rest of us. There is a Scottish embassy coming soon. He could join it.'

'The King is sending his uncle. I heard. I know Hearty James,' Kathi said. 'He quite likes Nicholas, too. In any case, we are safe. The Hôtel Jerusalem is a fortress. But what about you?'

Gelis said, 'I've just talked it over with everyone. I'm taking Jodi and joining the Duchess's tour. They don't need me in Bruges: trade has gone to sleep, and so has the war, until both sides can drum up soldiers and money. The Duchess is raising funds in the coast towns and Holland, and that is van Borselen country. My own kinsmen will be manning the escort, and when we come back, it will be to the Gravenkasteel or the palace in Ghent. And these, you will agree, are secure.'

This was true. It was why the Duke's wife and his one valuable daughter spent most of their lives there in the palace, or the castle so close to it. And Gelis would have her own noble relatives with her, as she said. Louis de Gruuthuse, of the council in Ghent, was married to one of her cousins. Another, Wolfaert van Borselen, seigneur of Veere, had been husband to Hearty James's sister, a princess of Scotland. Wolfaert's daughter, aged seven, was betrothed to the Duke of Burgundy's nephew. Wolfaert's bastard son was betrothed to Catherine de Charetty.

Kathi said, 'A Scottish embassy will have access to the Duchess.'

'Briefly, of course,' Gelis said. 'But they haven't come yet, and even in Ghent, they won't stay in the Hof Ten Walle or the castle. And by then, perhaps, it will be known that Nicholas isn't dead, and de Salmeton may stay away till he comes. He does want an audience.'

'You are sure,' Kathi said. Her clear, hazel eyes were hard to avoid. 'You always said you would know about Nicholas.'

'I am sure,' Gelis said. 'It's more than that. He wants me to know. He is divining, over and over.'

The forbidding gaze widened, then distanced itself. 'Ah,' said Kathi, and sank into thought.

Gelis sat silent. Once, she had never known when Nicholas set his pendulum swinging to find her. Then, the void between them had been empty. Time had filled it. Time had so inflamed, so compacted the spaces between them that each time he sought her, she knew it. And so he had stopped.

Until now. Until every hour, every day there came the minuscule jolt; the frisson that ran through her limbs, and buried itself in her body. *I am here. I am here. I am here.*

Kathi said. 'He is outrunning the news of his death. He must be coming. He wants it known to everyone that he is coming.'

And, of course, she was right. So long as Nicholas was thought to be on his way, in a grotesque fashion, their danger was lessened. David de Salmeton hated them all, but he wished Nicholas to witness what he did to them. And yet —

Gelis said, 'Unfortunately, not everyone shares our faith in the pendulum. Tobie, for one. He has gone to join Captain Astorre on campaign, convinced that Nicholas is dead.' She stopped, her hand to her lips. Then she added, 'Clémence let him go. She says he's weary with not knowing what to hope for.'

'I know,' Kathi said, her eyes bright, her smile wry. And looking at her, Gelis felt pain, and disbelief, and fright and compassion all at once.

'Not Robin? Not *Robin*?' she said.

'Who else?' Kathi answered. 'He's a man. He has to prove it. Now he has heirs. And like Tobie, he doesn't want any more hope.'

'But he leaves you—'

'Well protected. He didn't know, when he left, about James's embassy. It seemed too late in the season for David de Salmeton to trouble to come. He is better away,' Kathi said. 'He and Tobie will look after one another, and John. If there are no more troops to be got, the fighting will have to stop, anyway.'

'I should stay,' Gelis said.

'No. Go to the Duchess. You have Manoli. Take Clémence: apart from Jodi, it would be good for you both. And if you do meet Hearty James, suggest just whom he might send to the Tyrol. I doubt,' said Kathi, 'if David would go, but it does me good just to think of our Eleanor and that little peacock expecting to charm her.'

They parted presently on the same bracing note, after Gelis had stolen into the children's room to smile at Margaret and the baby. At least, Kathi had these. Meanwhile it was a fact, not referred to by either, that Kathi's young lover had gone, while the father of Gelis's son was alive and perhaps, at last, on his way home.

. . .

Disregarding the untimely cold of that autumn, the Duke of Burgundy's English wife dragged her great entourage of ladies, noblemen, soldiers, officials and servants across the fast-congealing northern reaches of the Low Countries to raise an army for her husband's conquest of Lorraine. As November descended, with its short days and long bitter nights, the Duchess traversed river ferries and sailed over gulfs, pausing to harangue the townspeople of Malines, Geertruidenberg, Dordrecht and Rotterdam, and passing magisterial nights in Leiden and Delft, Gouda and 's-Gravenhage.

Throughout it all, Gelis felt exhausted, but safe. She was well accustomed by now to the Duchess, whose marriage, as long as her own, had proved fruitless and made no pretence of being close. It had been created for reasons of state, to link the English King's sister to Burgundy; and Margaret of York, intelligent, well-read, energetic, had more than fulfilled her part of the bargain. The Duke's daughter had been loved, these eight years, as her own.

As for her van Borselen relatives, Gelis gritted her teeth and was polite. At least she knew they would strain every nerve to protect her. A few years ago, Jodi had nearly died on a visit to Veere, and Robin had been slighted. On this journey, she and Jodi were in the care of Wolfaert himself and his household, always at hand, always grimly dutiful to excess. It was fortunate that Clémence was here, briskly prepared for the moments when Jodi grew tired of exhibiting his straight back and desirable horsemanship, and simply wanted to sleep, or complain, or play games. He was not quite a page, yet.

At night, they slept in one room, the three of them and their young serving staff, but no one ever stayed awake for long, except Gelis van Borselen, lying straight under her coverlet, her hair brushed to her waist, her eyes closed, her hands crossed on the shift at her thighs. So she awaited the moment when Nicholas, too, would find privacy and, pushing aside his dish and his cup, would reach into his purse, and take something out — what? A pebble? A ring? — and, allowing it to drop from its cord, would address his unspoken question. Where is she now? Here? Or there? Then would come the pang, and her heart would start to thud.

Once, she had strung a pebble herself and tried to use it, but nothing had happened. Pretending a casual interest, she had engaged Dr Andreas in conversation, but to no avail. Physicians who carelessly predict the demise of rulers form a dislike, thereafter, of astrological questions. So she could not tell where Nicholas was: if he were locked by the winter in Russia, or travelling home. She did not know if he was alone. It was her guess, because of the messages, that no one was with him: that he was racing towards her, perhaps on this very route. He knew about David de Salmeton, but had not been deterred by her letter — perhaps because he knew more of the danger than she did. She had been wise to bring Jodi here, into the paramount security surrounding the Duchess. And although she would not admit it, she had been driven to come for another reason, for Nicholas knew where she was, and she was travelling towards him.

Lying there, her heart hammering still, she allowed herself at last to wonder what he was like now, this calm, clever, far-travelled man, still young, who had fathered her son, but had not claimed his rights as a husband in all the eight years of their marriage. As for what had happened in Scotland, she had recently re-assessed that, in the light of all she now knew about him. She would not condemn him again, until she had spoken to him. If she were to be given that chance.

That night, they had been entertained at the castle at 's-Gravenhage. Descending the steps in the candlelit morning, Gelis saw the white of frost through the door and heard the icy clarity of the sounds from the stables, as the wagons for the Duchess's ladies were brought out and harnessed: it was becoming too cold to ride. Yesterday, the sea had crawled sluggish and grey to its shore. The weather was closing in, and soon, they must make back for Ghent. She and Nicholas were not going to meet on this journey.

Jodi came hopping towards her, along with Manoli in his dazzling cuirass and Clémence in the furred, hooded cloak which was just rich enough for a physician's wife without appropriating the rank of a noblewoman. Clémence, the correct, the discreet; who knew all that Tobie knew, but did not speak unless asked.

But now, she had news. 'Have you heard? A courier has come from the Duke. It is confirmed at last. His daughter Marie is to marry the son of the Emperor. Official rejoicing is ordered.' Her dark eyes added what her voice did not say. Official rejoicing might well have to be ordered: not every town would produce it spontaneously. The marriage was to take place which had been on the table at Trèves, in return for the royal standing Charles craved. The Emperor, escaping from that, had simply waited for time. And now Frederick was to marry his son into Burgundy, and no sceptre or crown need change hands, for Burgundy needed the Emperor's help.

Then she said, 'Also, there are other arrivals, I am told; among them a man, travelling west, who heard of your presence and has asked to be permitted to see you.'

Gelis stood without speaking. She heard Clémence say, 'It may not be whom you expect. Let me take Jodi away. He can come back when we leave.'

She let him go. It could be anyone. Since she became a banker, and wealthy, unknown relatives and forgotten acquaintances had become eager to meet her. Then she saw, making his way between the chattering groups, the piles of luggage, the hurrying servants, a man whose cloak was lined and turned back with ermine and whose face was shadowed by glorious sables. She caught the sober intensity of his gaze as he saw her; saw his fine-gloved hand lifted in tentative greeting; glimpsed, even, that someone followed behind him.

The man advanced. As he drew nearer, Gelis observed that he was less than tall, and that his eyes were not unusually open and grey, or his cheeks furrowed with dimples. Indeed, the face beneath the fur hat was classically handsome, its cheek-bones distinctively high, its nose Roman.

The man coming towards her was Julius. And the slender figure pressing towards her, and taking her tenderly in her arms — the girl with the pure face, the dark hair, the subtle, unmistakable scent was the Gräfin Anna von Hanseyck, his wife.

If there was anything Gelis had learned in the years of her torment with Nicholas, it was how to disguise her feelings. She returned Anna's embrace cheek to cheek, and stretched to give her free hand to the lawyer. 'Julius! We were so distressed. I am so thankful to see you.' They had once thought him dead. Towards Julius, her relief and pleasure were genuine. She saw by the flush on his grave face that he recognised it.

He had enfolded her hand when Anna suddenly drew in her breath and pulled away from them both, her hand to her side.

Gelis said, 'Anna? Is something wrong?'

Julius, his arm round his wife, his face dark, began to say something, but Anna herself interrupted. She straightened, shaking her head. She was white. 'It is nothing. You will hear of it later. My dear, we have news to break to you first.' She glanced up at Julius.

Gelis said, 'Let me send for some wine. And don't think you have to break news about Nicholas. We know they say he is dead, but he isn't.'

'I am sorry,' said Anna. It sounded helpless. She looked again at her husband.

'She will have to hear the truth,' Julius said. The hall had emptied: the cavalcade outside was forming.

Manoli, his face stolid, appeared in front of her with one of the ducal grooms. 'Demoiselle. The Duchess is preparing to leave.'

'What truth?' Gelis said.

Anna said, 'You must go if the Duchess is waiting. Nicholas died in a fire, leaving Moscow. His body was found. We left before him, but have been travelling slowly, for my sake. The news reached us at Bremen.'

'Then it is wrong,' Gelis said. 'I know, because he has been divining. He was alive at least up to last night.'

'I wish that were so,' Anna said. 'But go. You are with the Duchess, and all the seats are required for her ladies.'

'I am sure the Duchess would make an exception,' Julius said. He spoke to the groom, who looked surprised, hesitated, and then bowed and went off.

Gelis said, 'I shall try to help, but I must stay with the Duchess. I can see that Anna needs care. Let her rest, and once we are in Ghent, you can tell me everything.'

Anna said, 'We must talk before then. If only, if only you had been with us . . . I can't say more, not when you have just been bereaved. But the Duchess will free you. And did I see Mistress Clémence? Is Jodi here?'

There *was* something wrong, it was clear: her face was drawn, the blue eyes heavy and shadowed. Before Gelis could speak, the groom returned swiftly. There was a seat on the last wagon, if the Gräfin would allow him to take her there. They parted in haste. Only Julius called, 'So we shall see you in Ghent?'

And Gelis waved, walking away.

There were advantages in being a van Borselen. Such was the disposition of the cortège that there was no question, that morning, of communication between the vehicles of the van and the tail. And at the very first stop, the power of the governors of Holland produced a speedy, small carriage which could convey the lovely invalid Gräfin direct to her destination, while her solicitous husband might ride at her side. He thanked the Duchess for her kindness, but there was no opportunity for Gelis to speak to him. It pained her to exclude him in such a way, and to deny herself all the questions she wanted to ask. But his loyalty had to be to Anna, and Gelis did not want to put it to the test.

That night, preparing for bed, Clémence slipped on her bedgown and, finding Gelis in a quiet part of the chamber, drew up a seat close beside her and set to combing her own soft, dark hair ready for plaiting. She spread a lock over her palm and gazed at it. 'That is natural. What did you think of the Gräfin's?'

'That it was cleverly treated, considering the time she has been travelling. Or did I deceive myself? Did I think I saw dye because I was looking for it?'

'No. You saw it,' said Clémence. 'I wonder if your husband saw it when they travelled together. She must have had to improvise dyes. And, of course, he is an expert in those.'

It had never struck her. He was, of course. In Egypt, he had dyed his own thick brown hair and bright beard. Gelis said, 'They still insist that Nicholas is dead.'

'They believe it,' Tobie's wife said. Her eyes followed her fingers, working down the long strands. 'I sat beside the Gräfin on the journey. She was reluctant to talk, but Master Julius insisted that she tell me how she came by her affliction. I was to convey it, if I thought fit, to you.' She lifted her eyes.

'She blamed Nicholas?' Gelis said. She understood Clémence now.

'It was a wound from a knife. The Gräfin presented it, to begin with, as an accident, but her husband, riding beside us, contradicted her in a childish way, exclaiming that your husband had tried to seduce her, and she had been injured when trying to defend herself.'

'Really?' said Gelis.

'Indeed. In a public place, with strangers listening. The Gräfin tried to say it was nonsense, but some of those around her were deeply impressed. Others toyed with the theory that she had turned the knife on herself out of shame. Forgive me.'

'Why? Do you believe it?' said Gelis.

'There are intemperate men,' Clémence said. She completed a plait and pinned it up. 'Your husband may be one. But his remorse over the wounding of Master Julius would more than deter him from seducing his wife. The story was an invention.' She paused. 'As you say, they are quite convinced that your husband is dead. They say that his cavalcade, leaving Moscow, was set upon by a party of brigands close to a hamlet. All were killed, and an accident set the timber houses on fire, so that the bodies were hardly identifiable. They knew him by his dress.'

Gelis said, 'You are saying that, believing Nicholas dead, Anna will now turn her hand against me. And that my instinct that he is alive may be wrong?'

Clémence de Coulanges finished pinning the second plait and rose gently. She said, 'Your husband is a man unlike others. Mine is less extraordinary, perhaps. But if I can tell you, as I can, that Tobias is at this moment alive, although not necessarily well, or comfortably quartered, or happy, then I am certain that you can do as much for your Nicholas. If you say so, then he lives.'

She was smiling. She held out her arm, as she had done so often to Jodi, and Gelis got up, and crossed it with her own, bringing her close, temple to temple, so that she rested, eyes closed, against the clean hair and the scrubbed, scentless skin.

THE COLD, at the same time, had begun to descend upon the besieging army of the Duke of Burgundy in Lorraine. Nothing momentous was happening, unless you counted the irritating frequency of enemy forays: well-organised bands from little garrison towns which fell upon the Duke's foraging parties, killing them to a man; which shadowed outlying patrols and cut their throats while they slept; which infiltrated, on one fearful occasion, the fringes of the Duke's siege camp before Nancy, and captured a large number of horses. The Duke's comments on that had not been pleasant.

Nothing positive was happening, because both sides had run out of soldiers and money. The Duke, possessed of all the Moselle valley from Dieulouard to Thionville, with a lifeline to Metz and his arsenal and treasury stationed at Luxembourg, still had too few men to take Nancy. Duke René, aged twenty-six, and adhering obstinately to his land to the south, had likewise too few men to dislodge him. René (or L'Enfant, as the Duke chose to call him) had provisioned Nancy for two months and gone off to beg help from Alsace and the Swiss. Duke Charles, ignoring all advice to withdraw and re-form over the winter, was awaiting what troops his Duchess and others might send.

Captain Astorre and his hundred lances, with the unexpected bonus of Dr Tobias and the polite young lad Berecrofts, took his share of the drills and the foraging, organised games, conferred with other captains and greatly enjoyed, of an evening, relating to Tobie and Robin all the tales that Thomas and John had stopped listening to. The new, good quarters made out of boarding, replacing the huts lost at Grandson, resounded to Astorre's opinions of the Duke, and his mercenary band of four hundred Italian lances, led by the famous Niccolò de Montfort, Count of Campobasso (real name Gambatesta), already flung out of Naples for supporting the old man, King René, and now, in the view of Captain Astorre, responsible for losing the Duke's Nancy in the first place, by advancing so slowly that it had to surrender to young René the grandson. The Count of Campobasso, Astorre said, was surreptitiously back in Angevin pay, mark his words. He was then reminded of the days when he himself had fought in Naples, on the opposite side, and the trouble he had had with that damned mercenary Piccinino.

The boy, Robin, would always ask then for more information, while John would be sitting morosely in a corner, filing down something that had fallen short of perfection, and Thomas snored, and the doctor got up, like as not, and went to tramp round the camp. Astorre hoped he wouldn't find himself run through by a pack of deserters. Cold and boredom led to that. The English, especially, had never encountered this kind of warfare and didn't like it at all. And there were some units who didn't get their provisions in, the way he did, and keep the men in good heart. Once they wearied, then you got the diseases. He ought to be glad Dr Tobie was here, even if it was years since he had been on campaign. But he had had his moments, by God, in the past. Captain Astorre thought he must remember, one night, to talk about Cyprus.

John le Grant, watching Tobie, could have told that he didn't wish to talk about Cyprus, or Albania, or Volterra. The boy Robin had come mostly because he was nineteen, and courageous, and wanted to be able to say, one day, that he had fought with an army. Tobie had come for other reasons, and finding himself back in the field, was remembering why he had left it.

John had accompanied Tobie when he received his first audience with the Duke, in the great, gilded wooden pavilion lined with tapestry which had been erected in the grounds of the old Commanderie of the Knights of St John, a mile or two from the ramparts of Nancy. It was the same pavilion and the same site occupied by the Duke in October, when he had entered Nancy in triumph but left it so poorly defended that René had taken it back again. The Duke, short and burly, pious and wilful, had not impressed a man who had been military surgeon to Urbino. Tobie had got on better with Matteo, the Duke's Portuguese doctor. Tobie had a new wife, and in John's opinion, was an ass to be here. And of course, if Nicholas were alive, he wouldn't be.

They had talked of Nicholas one night, he and Tobie. It was a subject he normally avoided, but recent conversations with Gelis had made him reconsider a number of things. At the end, Tobie had said, 'You used to call him a wrecker. You've mellowed.'

'That's because I'm alive and he's dead,' John remarked. 'Resurrect him, and I'll toughen again.'

A week later, Tobie rode across the crusted mud to his smithy to find him. 'Are you still interested in news of Nicholas?' An icicle dripped down his neck, and he looked up. 'Christ, I thought this place would be warm.'

'So did someone else. The fuel supply's gone, and I've just come from rewrapping the guns for the third time. So what about Nicholas?'

'A letter from Clémence,' said Tobie, shaking it in his gloved hand. 'They think he's alive. And Julius and Anna have come back to Flanders.'

'What!' said John. It came out sharply, and he saw Tobie's reaction.

'Ah,' said Tobie. 'Then we have something to talk about this evening. And I think we should include Robin.'

He didn't need to be told, then, what it was about. He had warned Gelis himself about trusting money to Anna and Julius. He had thought there was something fishy about the girl Bonne. He had not guessed what Tobie was to tell him that night about Anna, before the meagre fire in their cabin, with Robin pouring their ale. Or what he was to find out, infuriatingly, about that scented snake David de Salmeton.

It was not all new to Robin. Robin, he had already discovered, had observed a lot about Nicholas in Poland: enough to temper the hero-worship, but not to dispel it. You could see in him now, as he moved about, listening, the mixture of involuntary thankfulness and horror that he supposed he felt in himself. It impelled John to speak, out of contrariness, at the end of the recital. 'We still canna be sure about Nicholas. There was a rumour that he was dead. Gelis is now convinced that he isn't. There's no proof either way. Except that some envoy's priest begging money from Venice has spread a tale that he's met him coming from Moscow.'

'Don't you find that suggestive?' Tobie said. 'The priest knew him from Moscow, and Nicholas let himself be seen. If Nicholas thought Gelis was in danger, he would want it to be known as fast as possible that he was on his way. Shamming dead might have been his only way of escaping from Moscow.'

The boy said, 'But he may think he has nothing to face but David de Salmeton. This other thing may be far more dangerous. If Anna is Adelina, she's married Julius by trickery. She has deceived M. de Fleury all through their time together in Poland, in Caffa, in Moscow—'

'But never once managed to harm him,' Tobie said. 'Again, doesn't that suggest something to you?'

'That she only wanted to plague him?' said John slowly. 'That business with the knife. Julius apparently claims Nicholas was trying to seduce her, but mightn't it have been the other way round? Or maybe she genuinely fell in love, and he rejected her?'

'There were some accidents when they were together in Poland,' Robin said. He spoke without much expression.

'But then they stopped,' Tobie said. 'Nothing happened to Nicholas after that.'

'Because of the gold,' the boy suddenly said. His face, faceted by the fire, seemed composed of triangles. 'Kathi told her, before she went to Caffa, about Ochoa and the gold. She would want to wait till it came.'

Tobie was staring at him. He said, 'And it took a long time to come, didn't it? She must have been waiting still when Nicholas left her at Caffa. She nearly lost her life over that, when Caffa fell. But she also, surely, lost her hopes of the gold. Yet still, nothing happened to Nicholas in Moscow.'

'Julius was with them,' Robin said. 'And he and Anna stayed for the winter in Novgorod.'

'And Nicholas was always either in prison, it seems, or somewhere under the eye of the Patriarch. He got the news that David de Salmeton was in Scotland, but he obeyed Gelis and stayed where he was. He doesn't seem to have made any effort to leave until the scandal over the knife, when Julius and Anna were asked to go home, and he seems to have followed them.'

'Did he have any choice?' John said. 'He was probably asked politely to get out, as well.'

'But he seems to be coming *home*,' Tobie said. 'In spite of Gelis, in spite of Adorne's embargo and the kind of reception he could expect to get from the rest of us.'

John said, 'Perhaps he was attracted to Anna. Perhaps he was pursuing her. Perhaps that's why he shot Julius in the first place.'

'You didn't see him afterwards,' Robin said. Tobie looked at him.

'And of course,' Tobie said, still watching him, 'Nicholas would have made sure that Julius didn't survive the next time, if that had been so. In Tabriz, or travelling through occupied Caffa, it would have been easy to get rid of him, and then divorce Gelis and marry Anna. But he didn't. He kept in touch, indirectly, all the time, with Clémence and Gelis. He didn't push through his annulment.'

There was a silence. John broke it abruptly. 'I think you are saying—Are you saying that Nicholas knows who Anna is?' He saw Robin's face change.

Tobie said, 'That is what I am saying.' His expression was grim.

Contemplating him, the engineer felt something close to nausea. He thought of all it explained, and became aware that he was cursing continuously, under his breath. He pulled himself together and found an objection, but not because he had any real doubts. 'But if that is so, why didn't he confront her, denounce her?'

'Because Adelina is family, and he doesn't do that to family,' Tobie said. 'He kept her with him. He drew her east, as far from Gelis and Jodi as he could. The only time he left her, she was on leash in Caffa, waiting for the gold that never came, or stranded in Novgorod, while Julius founded his empire. But then she was sent home, and he followed, obviously, as soon as he could.'

'I must go back,' Robin said. The bleakness in his voice said it all.

Tobie looked at him. 'I thought the same, to begin with, but we're too far away. It doesn't matter. Clémence knows all that I do, and she and Gelis will be safe in the palace in Ghent, while Kathi can depend on Adorne. Robin, he won't let anything happen to her, or the babies.'

'Does Adorne know? Can he be told?' Robin said.

'About Anna? He's a magistrate: he doesn't like Nicholas; he might resist the truth without proof. But I think,' Tobie said, 'that you can depend on Kathi to find some plausible cause of alarm. And Gelis would have told them, now, at the Bank.'

Diniz and Father Moriz were the only partners now left in Spangnaerts Street. But, of course, it was a vast house, manned with employees and servants; bustling with the traffic of business. John said, 'The way to deal with it all is through Julius. Someone has to get hold of Julius, and persuade him . . .'

'. . . Persuade him that his wife's a scheming bitch who has lied to him from the start, and is still lying? Who only married him to get within reach of Nicholas? Oh, that'll be simple,' Tobie said. 'Meanwhile, let's stay and do something difficult, such as remaining alive while the Duke makes up his mind what to do.'

He drained his beaker and handed it out for a refill. Then he sneezed in an explosion of ale. He said, 'What are you worrying about? Young René won't raise the forces he wants. The two months will expire. The garrison in Nancy will surrender. The war will be over by Christmas.'

'Will you take a wager?' said John.

'Don't let's push it too far,' Tobie said.

Chapter 39

OVER THE LATTER part of November, as the cold war continued in Nancy, so events hung in chilly abeyance in Flanders, where the Duchess, at the end of her troop-raising duties, had returned thankfully to the voluminous hearths of the Hof Ten Walle in Ghent, in company with the lady Gelis van Borselen, her son and the wife of her doctor. The Duchess's step-daughter, who was the same age as Robin, had formed a liking for Jodi.

The lawyer Julius of Bologna called at the palace, but was informed, with great courtesy, that the Duchess could not spare the lady Gelis van Borselen at present. He left his address, from which Gelis learned that he and Anna were occupying a small gabled house leased from a cloth-weaving client, and situated close to the Ghent home, at present deserted, of Anselm Adorne and the Sersanders family.

Gelis presently sent Julius a note, in which she expressed her dismay at the account she had received of Anna's injury. She felt there must be some mistake, and was disinclined to discuss it until she heard the story from Nicholas, whom she still firmly believed to be alive. She hoped Julius would excuse her meantime.

She received a small note in return, signed by Anna, saying simply that she quite understood, and Gelis was to think no more about them. The handwriting was shaky, and Gelis was again reduced to discomfort.

In fact, her claim to be busy was not exaggerated. Warded by the familiar rigours of winter, the Duchess's court felt entitled to bend its thoughts towards the pleasures of Christmas. It began to dwell, in addition, upon the festive implications of the forthcoming marriage of the richest heiress in the world, the Duke's daughter. The Emperor Frederick's protonotary, arriving from Nancy and Metz, had already brought Marie jewels and a letter from her future bridegroom. In return, Marie had dispatched to the teen-aged Maximilian a diamond, her portrait, and her own personal note of acceptance. This entailed little effort, as she had done much the same for seven previous suitors, one of them being a former young Duke of Lorraine. Then the ceremonial planning began, and the dress fittings, and the recruitment of musicians and poets and painters, for which it would have been so convenient to have the assistance of the lady Gelis's ingenious husband, Nicholas de Fleury.

M. de Fleury was, and sadly remained, beyond call. But his lady was, of course, staying in Ghent, and at hand to advise on every difficulty. Gelis did not object to hard work, having anxieties of her own to subdue. But her isolation irked her at times, and she was pleased to be asked to the Hôtel de Ville banquet, at which the town of Ghent were to honour the future bride and her stepmother the Duchess. It would be in public. All of them would be stringently protected. And David de Salmeton hadn't come yet.

A MAN WHO HAS HELD the highest office in Bruges exerts a good deal of influence. He can ensure, for example, that an obscurely dressed traveller presenting himself at one of the portals of Ghent is discreetly challenged, surrounded, and swept directly to Bruges under an unobtrusive but competent escort. Once there, the man would be taken straight to the Lord Cortachy at the Hôtel Jerusalem.

None of the womenfolk of Anselm Adorne had attempted to alter this mandate. Quiet, aristocratic Phemie, that rare friend from Scotland, kept her thoughts to herself, and saw to the smooth running of the household and the care of the children. Katelijne Sersanders filled her days and often her nights with accurately executed projects, and found herself unable to eat. Rankin objected.

The men, of course, were the first to know when the trap was activated. Since the birth of Arnaud's weak child, Dr Andreas had remained in the house, with the man Bel had sent. It was the physician who came to find her. 'He is coming. Your uncle wishes you to be there, but no others.'

She had not dared propose it. She had forgotten how shrewd a man her uncle was. Adorne was a magistrate, and had spent half his life administering justice. He also believed that, because of this man, he himself had been recalled from Poland. Seated in a tall wooden chair, not far from the desk of her uncle, Kathi Sersanders jumped as the door opened, and wished Robin were here, and then was thankful that he was not.

The room was high-ceilinged and grand, but the man who came in was in harmony with it, both in his height and his carriage, and even his looks, once he had deliberately divested himself of all the muffling clothes and stood before his captor and judge. Nicholas de Fleury of Beltrees, at the end of a journey from Russia to Flanders, and a recent one, imposed upon him, from Ghent. He made two formal bows: one to Anselm Adorne, one to herself. But, entering, he had already cast a glance round the room, and she had caught the single, bright spark as he found her. To her fevered imagination, it conveyed something explosive and foreign — Elzbiete's clarion summons in Danzig: *Katarzynka!* Then it had gone.

'My lord,' he said to Adorne. He had been given no chance to remove the dirt of the journey. The familiar dimples were grooves, the eye-sockets trenches, and there was a sharp, thin line between his brows. He looked pre-occupied, rather than angry or nervous.

Adorne surveyed him, his fastidious hands on his desk, his heavy robe severe over his doublet, his embroidered cap set on the greying fair hair. He said, 'What! No recriminations?'

'Your captain gave me your message,' his prisoner said. 'My wife and child are safe in the palace at Ghent; the man de Salmeton has not arrived yet; and you wished to interrogate me.'

'Yet I am told you tried to resist,' Adorne said.

'You would probably have done so yourself. No free man enjoys coercion, my lord.'

'No man of sense courts it, unless for a reason. I wish to know, first, what your intentions are.'

'The same as your own, I am sure. To make sure that David de Salmeton, when he arrives, is rendered harmless. Then I leave, without engaging in business.'

'Leave for where?' Adorne said. After thirty miles on the road, any other man would have been invited to sit, but Nicholas de Fleury was not. He appeared not to notice, standing on the other side of the desk with the air, Kathi thought, of a courteous younger commander come to confer with an elder of equal intelligence. It was the first marked change Kathi noticed in him.

Nicholas de Fleury said, 'I shall tell you when I know, and see that it meets with your approval. I am not attempting to change the agreement we have already reached.'

'We shall see,' Adorne said. 'But meanwhile, you have not been entirely frank, have you? You brushed aside your persistence at Ghent, but you had another reason, had you not, for wishing to enter? A somewhat discreditable dispute, I am told, with your former friend Julius.'

Still the other man did not move. He said, 'Certainly, I was hoping to find out where Julius was. There has been a misunderstanding. It is personal, and affects a lady's honour. I propose to deal with it myself.'

Adorne's face reflected a weary distaste. 'The story runs that you injured the lady in Russia, and that her husband challenged you, and will revive the challenge as soon as he learns you are alive. It is your affair, as you say, but it also defiles all who deal with you. I wish you to conclude the matter quietly. My niece claims she can help, knowing the lady better than most. I may say I have tried to dissuade Katelijne.'

Nicholas turned. Kathi rose to her feet as he faced her. This time, what passed between them was not the single splinter of joy between friends. It was a flicker somewhere in his mind that began in what had been a deliberate vacuum and passed through growing devastation to full, mortal comprehension. Kathi saw the light leave his eyes as he realised, first, what she might know; and then what his prevarication just now must have betrayed to her. His gaze rested on hers, grey and unseeing; then he returned it to Anselm Adorne.

'The quarrel is mine: I shall settle it. The issue for you, surely, is the handling of David de Salmeton. He will first try to kill me and mine, but Kathi and Robin are also in danger.' Here, warned perhaps by the atmosphere, he interrupted himself. 'What? Something is wrong?'

'It depends,' said Anselm Adorne, 'on what reliance you place on your army. Katelijne's husband has joined it, feeling bound in conscience to fight for Duke Charles. He is in your Captain Astorre's camp at Nancy. And Tobias your doctor is with him.'

The magistrate's flick of the lash. The practised face of the grown man, repelling it. Nicholas said, 'Astorre is good company round a camp fire. They may not have much to do, Tobie and Robin, but they will enjoy it.'

'I am less certain than you,' Adorne said, 'that the army of Duke Charles will be idle. And if the fighting continues we must hope, must we not, that your band is well equipped and well led and well funded, and that this family does not suffer, yet again, because of you.' He stopped, and started again. 'Nevertheless, as you say, some plans must be made, and it will be convenient if you are here to make them. A room has been prepared, and you will remain with me until we hear of de Salmeton's arrival.'

There was a pensive silence. Nicholas de Fleury said, 'I follow your reasoning. But the Bank in Spangnaerts Street may expect me.'

Adorne's eyebrows rose. 'Perhaps they would welcome you: I do not know. My stipulation is that you do not rejoin your former business. They will be told where you are. If they wish, Master Diniz or Father Moriz may visit you. But I do not wish it generally known that you are in Bruges.'

'I see,' the other said. 'And what about the new Conservator, Andro Wodman? Is he to help with the planning?'

'He is staying here. It would appear sensible. Do you have some objection?' Adorne said. 'He preserved your son from de Salmeton in Scotland.'

'But he let de Salmeton go. Wodman used to serve Jordan de Ribérac, who has also threatened my son.'

'Wodman used to be an Archer in the service of France,' Adorne said. 'He is no longer with France or de Ribérac. He has joined my nephew as a dealer and merchant in Scotland, and I have found his conduct impeccable.'

'I don't trust him either,' said Kathi. She had not said as much outright before. She had tried to reassure Gelis, even while she felt that Gelis shared the same doubts. She had hoped to avoid this open difference with her uncle, but she knew too much about Jordan, vicomte de Ribérac, whose hatred had haunted Nicholas all his life. Reared in Scotland, established in high mercantile circles in France, de Ribérac had always been ruthless to the apprentice born of his son's wife.

Wodman had served the King of France and the vicomte de Ribérac. He might still be serving both.

Anselm Adorne said, 'I am sorry to hear that, Katelijne. I should be even more sorry to hear you mention your misgivings outside this room.'

'She is your niece. She could be right,' Nicholas said. He was still standing.

Afterwards, Kathi thought that it was his very obstinacy, underlining Adorne's own, that brought her uncle to his decision. He said, 'Very well. Suppose we put it to the test. I shall ask Andro to join us.'

'How will that help?' Kathi said. But Nicholas did not intervene, and her uncle had already rung for a servant.

While they waited, Adorne addressed his captive, his manner collected. 'I suppose, although you are neither free nor condemned, you are still permitted to sit. Or do you propose to stand there until nightfall?'

'Whatever pleases you,' Nicholas said. But he walked and sat down in the seat at one end of Adorne's desk, not far from Kathi. Then Wodman came in.

He was an ugly man, thick-necked, with black hair and coarse features. The powerful frame, however, was that of a professional archer, and the eyes which assessed the situation were astute. He said, 'Mistress. My lord?' But his gaze had already clashed with that of Nicholas.

Adorne waved him to a seat. 'You know de Fleury. He is here because of the threat from David de Salmeton. Tell us what you expect.'

'Something spiteful,' Wodman said. He sat with military precision, and continued to quiz, in silence, the travel-stained, impervious figure of Nicholas de Fleury.

'So you know de Salmeton well?' Kathi asked.

Wodman glanced at his predecessor. 'Tell her,' Adorne said. 'She will not believe me.'

'And M. de Fleury?' said Wodman.

'Tell him all you told me.'

'Perhaps I can guess,' Nicholas said. His voice was even. 'You do know de Salmeton well, because at one time you were a Scottish Archer in France. Then you committed a murder, and left.'

'David was an Archer at the same time,' Wodman said. 'I killed someone, and he and I left together. Twelve years ago, it all happened. David joined the merchant company of the Vatachino. I joined Jordan de Ribérac in his business. He always looked after good men of the Guard.'

'I'm sure he did,' Nicholas said. He spoke reflectively. Some of what Wodman said could be true, Kathi perceived. Before he became fat, or acquired a title, Jordan de St Pol had been a fine soldier, commanding a company of the Scottish Guard for the present King's father in France. Wodman had also served in the Guard. But —

Kathi said, 'But all the Scottish Archers were Scots.'

Her uncle smiled. He said, 'Andro is from Aberdeen. His brother is Abbot of Jedburgh.'

'And David de Salmeton is from Aberdeen also,' Wodman said. 'Salmeton is the French version of Simpson. David Simpson is his real name.'

Kathi stared at Nicholas, who had made a sound close to one of amusement. The fragrant, gazelle-eyed exotic of Cyprus and Cairo was an Aberdonian; a man like John le Grant. She could imagine John on receiving the news. *Davie Simpson! The loon, the wee cunt!* She said, quickly and clearly, 'Gelis didn't know that.'

'I know,' Nicholas said. During the passionate warfare between them, Gelis had secretly worked for the Vatachino, her husband's fiercest rival in business. She had disliked, and now loathed David de Salmeton, but had known nothing of his origins, Kathi could swear.

Nicholas was speaking again, this time to Wodman. 'But telling us about David de Salmeton is not quite enough, perhaps, to encourage us to fall into your arms? Have you no other secrets?'

Adorne smiled. Kathi, observing it, was overcome with something closer to despair than apprehension. She thought of Clémence, tamer of wilful children. But she was her uncle's niece, not his nurse, and whatever was coming, she could not protect Nicholas from it.

Wodman said, 'What about the biggest trade secret of all? You always wanted to know who your competitor was. You always wondered who owned the Vatachino.'

Nicholas sat very still. He had seen Adorne's smile. Now he could analyse it. Several times in the past Adorne had invested with the Vatachino: in Iceland, in Africa. Then they had been the greatest opponents of the Banco di Niccolò, aiming at the same markets, cheating their way to success. Kathi's uncle, unaware of their methods, had not been distressed on the occasions when the Vatachino had won. Then Gelis had joined them. Everything about the Vatachino was anathema to Nicholas de Fleury.

Wodman said, 'It isn't Anselm, in spite of that smile. The man was clever. You wouldn't suspect him. To hear him, the Vatachino were ruining his business. Except for David, his own agents didn't know who he was, and certainly Gelis did not. Can you guess?'

'I don't need to,' Nicholas said. 'You are going to tell me. And, of course, prove it.'

'Have you not had enough clues?' Wodman said. 'Did no one ever tell you what Vatachino represents in Italian? It means Walter. A good Breton name, like St Pol. As good as Simon, or Jordan.'

'I see,' Nicholas said. There was a long space. Then he said, 'Always good to men of the Guard. So you mentioned.'

Kathi said, 'Say it. Who was the owner?' But she knew.

Her uncle still smiled. Wodman glanced at him, grinning, but said nothing. Nicholas said, 'It seems that the man behind the Vatachino is Jordan de Ribérac. My—' He bit off the word, but Kathi knew what it was to have been. Jordan de Ribérac, his own unproved grandfather.

'That is so,' Wodman said. A prosaic man, he did not linger over the implications, but ploughed on heartily with the matter in hand. 'I have proof. Nothing you can use against the old man; I'm not David. But it means that de Ribérac could never deceive you again.'

'David de Salmeton turned against him?' Nicholas said. He had returned to the tone of a man calmly engaged in debate.

'David strayed, and was dismissed in short order. Now he wants to return and take over the business. Once he has killed the vicomte, that is.' Wodman grinned again. 'I thought you would be interested.'

'And now we trust you?' Kathi said. She cleared her throat.

The Conservator turned his smile on Adorne once more. 'You can trust me to help get rid of David. I don't work for de Ribérac now. Sometimes I think he's the world's greatest bastard. But he was a good captain once, and at least he is what he is, with no pretence about it.'

'Perhaps we should leave them to kill one another,' Nicholas said. 'Or no, the vicomte has been exiled to his Portuguese island. We shall have to do it ourselves after all. You didn't manage to catch him in Scotland?'

'He has a great many powerful friends. I scared him, though,' Wodman said. 'The old woman would tell you.'

Kathi reflected. The old woman? Bel. Bel, who had been with Jodi that day in Edinburgh when Raffo was killed. She saw Nicholas make the deduction, and glance at the other man.

'So you agree?' Adorne said. 'We need protection, and Andro can help us. I think he has proved his credentials.'

'I can go back to Russia,' Nicholas said.

'In due course,' Adorne said. 'I am sure you wish to stay now and see this man dealt with. Meanwhile, we should let Andro return to his desk. At least you can see, I am sure, that he had a genuine care for your Jordan.'

'I realise that. How shall I thank you?' Nicholas said. Kathi could not read the look in his eyes.

Wodman returned it unsmiling. 'By making mincemeat of David de Salmeton,' he said. 'If you get to him first.'

He left. She had no chance even to say to her uncle: *You already knew about Jordan de Ribérac.* For, of course, Wodman had told him beforehand. Today's trenchant exposé had not been wholly for Wodman's benefit, or for hers. There were some things that Adorne did not forgive.

THEY LOCKED HIM into his room. Nicholas discovered it as soon as the supper tray had been laid on his table, and the unsmiling servant had withdrawn. He was waiting, a billet by his hand, when the man returned later, but this time the door swung ostentatiously open and there was an armed man standing in attendance outside. The tray was removed and the door locked again. The window was barred and at an interesting height from the courtyard, which also held armed men. If David de Salmeton arrived, they were all going to be heroically safe.

It became fully dark, and extraordinarily cold. He had already noticed that there were no kindling materials in the room, although the bed was well provided with blankets, and there was the civilised equivalent of the *toleta* plank, to which no doubt he could make his way by the light of the moon. The room had been used as a prison before.

All the same . . .

He had made his preparations and was about to bang on the door and shout his complaint when he heard footsteps approaching and saw the rim of light under the door. When it opened, there were no armed men behind, only the small, athletic figure of Katelijne Sersanders, bearing a candle. She said, 'Knock me down if you must, but I came to tell you not to be silly. You can't possibly manage this on your own.'

He sat down.

She said, 'Don't. Don't. It does all depend on you, but you must keep your head. There isn't time for anything else.' She added shakily, 'I'll go out and come back in again, if you like.'

He lifted his face, his lips pressed together, until he could speak. Then he looked at her. 'No,' he said. He let his liquid breath drain away.

Kathi said, 'Ask about the children.'

'How are the children?'

She set down the candle, drew up a stool and sat down. He remained on the bed, back to the wall, but had allowed his braced arms to bend round his knees. She said, 'Margaret will have her second birthday in January. Perpetual health and divine grace, except when she is teething.'

'Dulle Griet,' he said. It meant furious Margaret. It was the name of a cannon. It meant he was recovering.

'So Jodi often remarks. He likes her,' Kathi said. 'Rankin, on the other hand, is a boy, and therefore a rival. Jodi remembers you very well: Gelis tells him about you. There is a parcel of drawings you will have to appraise. Other things, too. Some boxes came from Montello. She has been waiting for you to come.'

'How remarkable,' Nicholas said, 'that a simple query about your family should shift so quickly to mine. You are happy about the children. I can see that you are.'

'I find them rather nice. Like Robin,' Kathi said. 'And I let Robin go because he'd never forgive me for refusing, when we are both old and fat, but he is still three years younger than I am. You know Tobie is married to Clémence?'

He straightened, leaving the wall. '*Na baba*. You aren't serious?'

'Hooks marrying the Cods? Of course I'm serious: they're perfect for one another. He brushes his teeth every day, and she's working out what makes him sneeze. Jodi has his own minder and tutor, but still sees Clémence a lot, and she's been a godsend to Gelis. Aren't you cold?'

'I am warmed by your alchemy,' Nicholas said. '*The Book of Amazing Retorts*. I have blankets. We could sit like addorsed birds and share them.'

'We could light the brazier,' Kathi said. 'There's one in that corner.' And, as they dragged it out and set the candle solicitously to it: 'So did you turn to drugs,' Kathi said, 'when you found out what Anna was like?' She sat down again on her stool. Her hands trembled.

Nicholas remained standing. He mouthed, 'Mary, Mother of God,' like a fish out of water.

'If you're all right, we have to talk about it soon. She said it was because of your grandfather. She spent a lot of time suggesting how we could help you. I thought she was the perfect companion: the friend you needed to guide you. She kept asking us to send Gelis, and Jodi. Did you take drugs? Was that why?'

Nicholas sat. The brazier flickered. He said, 'No, I didn't. I wasn't in an especially hilarious mood. But mainly, I was trying to frighten her a little.' He broke off, his eyes resting on Kathi. He said, 'You have nothing to blame yourself for. It was my choice to go with her. I admired her, I even wanted her, but I did nothing about it. I didn't realise that she was missing Julius, and desperate for a lover. Then, when I disappointed her, she turned the knife on herself. That was all.'

He heard her sigh. She said, 'Nicholas. You must know who she is.'

His heart disengaged, idled, and resumed beating slowly in axeblows. *Whoever is unsupported by the Mystery of Love shall not achieve the grace of salvation. Whoever shall cast love aside shall lose everything.* He said, 'There is nothing to talk about.'

'Yes, there is,' Kathi said. 'You kept your word to yourself and your family. You didn't betray her. We found out for ourselves. But she is relentless. Even Julius is at risk, never mind your own family. Once he knows you are alive, he will try to fight you. And she will let him.'

He looked at her, his lips shut. She said, 'Everyone knows at least a little, barring my uncle. If you want to blame someone, blame me. Also Gelis and Tobie and John. Within the company, the secret is out. It needn't become public; it's enough that my uncle knows that David de Salmeton is coming, and his precautions will serve against both. But you must realise that there is no need to escape. You are not alone any longer. We are here.'

'You are mistaken,' he said.

And, her eyes full of pity, Kathi said, 'No. We have proof.' And told him everything.

At the end, she did not touch him, as Anna had done, so that he took his own time to lift his head from his hands and look up at her. Her face looked pinched.

He said, 'You do know everything, don't you?'

'Tobie is a doctor,' she said. 'As I tell it, the story sounds bald, but he spoke of it all with compassion. He understood Esota. He understood Jaak and the girl. He made us all see how it happened.' She paused. She said, 'She is beautiful, and has so many gifts. You must, many times, have felt close to her.'

'She knew who I was,' Nicholas said. 'She begged me to give her a child.'

'But—' Kathi began. She sounded stricken.

'I know,' Nicholas said. 'It was meant to sicken me, later.'

It was late. The brazier glowed. Despite the warmth, he felt stiff, and his arm ached. He remembered, abruptly, what else had happened today. He said, 'The news about Jordan de Ribérac. Does anyone else have to be told?'

Her face was hollow: she looked as tired as he felt. She said, 'About the Vatachino connection? My uncle and Wodman won't make it public, I'm sure. Someone ought to tell Diniz in confidence, and perhaps the rest of the Bank. Who else is there? Ah! You don't want Gelis to know?'

He said, 'She will have to know. I should like to have the chance to tell her.'

'That should be easy enough,' Kathi said. 'She's shut up in Ghent. She won't hear anything there. And Jordan de Ribérac must be the least of her troubles.' Her eyes scanned him, in the way Tobie's did, and her voice became sober and quiet. 'Don't leave us,' she said. 'Between us, we shall see this finished, as it should be, without shame.'

'It is too late for that,' Nicholas said. 'But yes, I shall stay. I have seldom found my private life the subject of a company project before.'

The words made her check as she rose, and he was sorry, but found it impossible to add anything normal. She bade him good night, her eyes clear, and went out, leaving him the candle, and the brazier, and the half-open door.

He shut it, and went to lie on his bed.

THE COLD DEEPENED.

In the Hof Ten Walle at Ghent, the lady Gelis van Borselen was seated on the floor with her son, companionably mourning a broken mechanical toy, when Clémence entered. Drawn to her feet by her expression, Gelis joined her. 'News of Tobie?'

'There is always news of Tobie,' Clémence said, which was indeed true. 'This is news of your husband. Good news. Come and sit. Now. Your instinct was right, as we knew it would be. He is alive. He is well. He is in Bruges.'

It was all there was to know, and it was only a whisper, not to be repeated; not to be told even to Jodi for safety's sake. But hugging her resistant son later, Gelis returned to the whisper over and over. He is alive. He is well. He is in Bruges. And soon, please God, they would face one another again, and say what should have been said long ago.

IN THE DUKE'S CAMP at Nancy, all incoming news paid its debt to distance and snow, and the fate of Nicholas was still an unresolved question. Tobie, penning his regular letters to Ghent, had said a great deal about discomfort and boredom, but less about the Duke's increasing irascibility; the temper that had killed a man, against all the chivalric code, for carrying news to the besieged inside Nancy, so that Duke René, to save face with his allies, hanged one hundred and twenty Burgundian prisoners in retaliation.

Robin, reared on dreams of chivalry, possessed of that rare brand of selfless rectitude to which Nicholas owed his life, had been revolted. Astorre, his experienced antennae trained rather on the activities of the Count of Campobasso, that well-known renegade, merely pointed out that Nancy still had provisions for two weeks, and no doubt would end it all after that.

He still appeared to think that he would be home for Christmas. It annoyed him extremely to learn that the King of Portugal was on his way, in the flesh, to ask his cousin Duke Charles to finish the war. You got the same kind of thing all the time from the Pope and the Emperor and the King of Hungary, but they didn't trouble to come in person and tie the camp into knots.

The garrison in Nancy, feeling its dried meat and sour milk, if not its oats, made a sudden sally, set fire to a whole row of tents and seized some guns and provisions. The Duke was furious, and Astorre was not best pleased himself. A mercenary deserved a tight, well-led army. He tried to think of one.

IN BRUGES, the fortress of the Hôtel Jerusalem was penetrated, after some lengthy preliminaries, by the director and chaplain of the Hof Charetty-Niccolò in Spangnaerts Street, and Diniz and Father Moriz laid eyes, for the first time for three years, on the discredited patron they had sent into exile.

Nicholas, liberated for the occasion into the luxury of Adorne's empty parlour, greeted them mildly, in the way of a visitor renewing a passing acquaintance. Disconcerted at first, Father Moriz began, without comment, to respond in the same way. Diniz, highly uncomfortable, answered questions about Catherine and Tilde and extracted, painlessly, their stepfather's scribbled endorsement of Catherine's marriage. Then Nicholas asked after the daughter of Diniz and Tilde.

'Daughters,' Diniz said, his face lighting. 'Marian and Lucia.'

'Lucia?' Nicholas said. His voice had warmed. 'For your mother.' And after a moment, 'How proud she would have been.'

It seemed to Diniz that he could be natural at last. He said impulsively, 'I shall tell my daughter. When she is old enough, I shall tell her how her grandmother died, and what you did, you and Julius.'

'You must do as you please,' Nicholas said. 'And Julius now? He must be anxious to know if his business survives.'

'We correspond,' Moriz said. 'That is, he has written to us. He has proposed several times to come to Bruges, but never at a time when Diniz or myself can be present.'

'That seems wise,' Nicholas said. 'Now, what can I tell you that would be helpful?'

They talked about business. It was as effective as any discussion they had had in the past — more so, because of the maturity now so evident in Nicholas. It might have lasted longer had it not inevitably strayed towards the personal. The subject of Gelis and her informed assistance in Venice, Bruges and Ghent was mentioned only once (by Father Moriz) and dropped immediately. Diniz, speaking of business intelligence, had been moved to blurt out, 'We got your messages after you left. And the money. Why give us your money?'

'I am afraid,' Nicholas said, 'I have no idea what you mean.'

But their dismissal came when Diniz remembered his grandfather, Jordan de Ribérac. He sat, his dark eyes full of anger and shame, and said, 'How could he do it! He set out to ruin the Bank, and me, and you, and was too base to admit it. He even let Gelis join him.' He broke off and said, 'I always thought Adorne might be behind the Vatachino.'

'He didn't know until Wodman told him,' Nicholas said. He rose from the chair. 'So that is sufficient? I was glad to hear all your news. But we ought, perhaps, to avoid becoming too close as yet.'

Returning home, Moriz had halted Diniz in the midst of a tirade. 'What did you expect? He let us down, we sent him away, and he has come back without leave. He is bound to be cautious. Also, by chance, we know far too much — all the most personal details of his childhood; all about Anna. She is still his family, and we have the power to destroy her.'

'But he needs us,' said Diniz.

'He knows that,' said Father Moriz. 'Today, he set the tone for all our future meetings. The next one is the one that will matter.'

BEHIND HIM, Anselm Adorne had re-entered his parlour, and chosen to invite Nicholas to remain and take wine with him. Then he asked to be told about Caffa.

It was, of course, to be expected. The loss of the Crimea was the worst blow that the Genoese Republic could have sustained, isolating their precious island of Chios, in which much of Adorne's fortune must be wrapped up. His cancelled mission to Tabriz had had a personal importance as well as a public one. Replying, therefore, Nicholas took infinite pains to describe and then analyse the situation as he had found it, and then, continuing, to develop his assessment of the strengths and weaknesses of Uzum Hasan and, so far as he could judge, the Ottoman Empire. Lastly, he spoke of the Tartars and Muscovy.

It took a long time. Occasionally, Adorne would interrupt with a question, and often he himself paused, in case he had misjudged what was wanted. But he was allowed to continue, and by the time he had concluded, two wine-flasks had been emptied and Anselm Adorne, a little flushed, was scrutinising him from his chair. He said, 'I used to be reckoned to have a hard head for liquor.'

Nicholas relaxed. He said, 'One has practice, among Slavs.'

Adorne said, 'You know that what you have presented is a perfect report. The dispatch an ambassador is expected to supply at the end of his mission.' His gaze, despite what he had drunk, was still excoriating.

Nicholas said, 'Ludovico da Bologna will bring the Pope something like it, and the Pope will probably disregard it. No one has ever understood or even believed what Father Ludovico has told them. Rulers give feasts with nobles dressed up as Persians and Turks, dancing and miming to laughter. Ambassadors from Georgia and Mingrelia are reviled as impostors because of their bald heads and strange clothes. Only Venice — and it is to her credit — only Venice, with all her far-travelled envoys, knows that this is what these peoples are like, and these their customs. Venice made Ludovico a priest, even though they had to lie about it to Pius. He is a hero.'

There was a silence. Then Adorne said, 'Ask him if he will give me his report.'

'He will,' Nicholas said. 'He was your representative. He did what he did because there was no chance that a Genoese would succeed. You would have been killed. You will get his report. You will also have mine. I have written it out for you to give to the Duke.'

'Present it yourself,' Adorne said. His gaze remained penetrating.

'It would prejudice my trade, if I return. I would rather you betrayed Uzum Hasan's secrets,' Nicholas said. 'Unless you object.'

'You imagine you can bribe your way back?' Adorne had said then, abruptly.

'I think it unlikely,' Nicholas had said. It was no more than the truth, and made him feel uncommonly gloomy.

He remembered presently finding his way to his room, and his bed. When he next wakened, it was because someone wished to take him elsewhere, to a larger room without bars, where the door was neither guarded nor locked. In the long journey home, he had taken one step, perhaps.

It did not mean that he was in free communication with anyone. He saw Kathi, usually in the children's room, where he had been introduced to the rowdy vigour of Margaret and the chubby sweetness of Rankin. They spoke of nothing personal, but she made no objection to fulfilling some unusual requests to do with paint, and small wood and metal objects, and springs. He renewed his acquaintance with Phemie, but never stayed with her long. The same applied to Dr Andreas, who sought his company more than he appreciated, once Nicholas had learned all he wished to know, which was the whereabouts of his young and lissom friend Nerio.

Since Nicholas was not allowed to go out, Nerio came to the Hôtel Jerusalem, on a day when Adorne was absent. He looked at first sight the same: the beautiful boy who, dressed as a girl, had shamed Adorne's son in Venice, and then in Rome, and who had spied on Nicholas and Violante his mother in Cyprus. The exile from Trebizond who had become a guest, with his compatriots, at the Burgundian court.

In the light from the window in Nicholas's room, it could be seen that time had passed. Nerio was twenty-four now, his skin coarsened beneath the light paint, his eyes anxious under the languor. He came in, none the less, like a courtesan, and, clasping his hand, stretched to kiss Nicholas lasciviously on the cheek. 'My dear! No more a banker! A scarred and beautiful giant, bruised by Fate, striding relentlessly onwards!'

He drew away, with his triangular smile, and then glanced down, for Nicholas still held his hand. 'I am sorry,' Nicholas said.

'Why?' said the boy. But the paint stood out on his cheeks.

Nicholas said, 'Your father is dead.'

It was like breaking the news to a girl, you might say, except that Nicholas had seen bearded men sit weeping like this, mewing in the extremity of their distress as the story unfolded. He had kept a flask of something strong for the time when it ended, but the boy crouched on his seat and did not touch it. Nicholas sat not far away, and said nothing until the sobs died, and Nerio lifted his head from his fingers. Nerio said, 'He would be here but for you.'

'I didn't ask him. I didn't know,' Nicholas said.

The immense, drowning eyes were full of anger. 'Why you, and not me?'

'Both of us,' Nicholas said. 'Whatever he believed was to happen, you have a role. He told me.'

'But without him,' Nerio said.

'Would you have him live on in pain?' Nicholas paused. 'I told you that he had left all the gold he had hidden for you.'

The lead-heavy wood had cost him something to bring across Europe, but Nerio lifted it in both hands and flung it from one side of the room to the other. A joint gave, and a few coins spun and settled. 'Do you think that I care?' Nerio said.

But when Nicholas pressed the cup again in his hands and, leaving him, went to empty the gold into the box he had prepared for it, Nerio did not protest; and he lifted the treasure when, as he left, Nicholas gave it him.

It seemed that that would be all. But at the last moment Nerio had thrust back, and taking up that sophisticated, elegant leg had carried it off, graceful as Hermes, in the curve of his arm.

IN A SMALL HOUSE in Ghent, Julius of Bologna had become reconciled with his wife after a period of unusual friction. With Nicholas dead, and Gelis for the moment inaccessible, Julius was inclined to see little point in remaining in Ghent, spending money, when he should be taking command of his business elsewhere. He had wanted to move immediately to Bruges, and then to Cologne, but Anna persuaded him to wait for a little. She still had hopes of talking to Gelis. The future of Bonne was at stake.

He agreed, against his will. He assumed he might at least visit

Spangnaerts Street, but she broke into uncharacteristic tears at the prospect, and he did not speak of it again. He did not tell her that he had tried to arrange a visit regardless, but had learned that both the Bank's officers would be away. He wrote to them instead: questions about the present state of the German business; a long account of the trade openings he had created in Caffa (before it fell), Poland and Muscovy. He mentioned Nicholas once, in connection with Tabriz, and once more to ask about a tale that Ambrogio Contarini's chaplain had seen him alive. He had not so far received an answer.

After two weeks of it, Anna's firmness of attitude, not for the first time, began to vex him. He knew a fair number of people in Ghent, but she seemed unwilling to entertain them, although she had little else to do. He began to wonder whether the separate couch, the abstraction, the uncertain moods were all truly due to the effects of her injury. He wondered if, in some unthinkable way, she missed Nicholas. And one day, rashly, he asked her.

Afterwards, he went out into the cold of the garden, and sat and retched. She had not troubled to give him a direct answer. She had simply narrated, movement by movement, the process by which Nicholas had raped her; and then, sinew-cracking and soft, tickling and searing, hot and cold, and finally, unremittingly, brutally agonising, her sensations while he did it, and her longing to die, at the end. He had not even been a man, Anna said. He had not completed the rape. His enjoyment came from the violence.

That night, Julius wept in her embrace, and the following morning, he had not wanted to leave her.

He had only determined under duress to visit his usual tavern and only by chance had fallen into talk with a pair of dyers from Bruges who were able to tell him (now, when he had something more important to think about) that Diniz and the German were at home in the Charetty-Niccolò house. More than that, one of them said. Would you believe it, young Claes was supposed to be back? Not that the Bank would admit it. It made you wonder —

It was as far as he got, since his companion pushed his head into his dish, and shortly after, they left. But it was enough. Kneeling beside his lovely, delicate wife, Julius said, 'Now you won't prevent me from going to Bruges. Now I am going to kill him.'

This time, she did not try to stop him.

Julius was already beating the frozen road out of town when the herald of James, Earl of Buchan, appeared in Ghent to announce the long-awaited arrival of his master, Scotland's envoy for peace between the Duke of Burgundy and Sigismond, Duke of the Tyrol.

The town was ready. A cavalcade of honour was assembled, and issued in due course to bring the prince to his lodging. It was understood that the Earl's visit would be a brief one, but the town was gratified to learn that my lord of Buchan would be pleased, as evidence of his delight in the forthcoming illustrious marriage, to attend the town's banquet to the Ladies of Burgundy.

He was assured that his brother-in-law Wolfaert van Borselen would be there, with all his van Borselen relatives. And the magistrates (they said) would consider themselves privileged if the Earl were to bring his full Scottish entourage, which included, as it happened, that adroit fellow, his merchant friend David de Salmeton.

Julius left without hearing the news. Clémence brought it to Gelis van Borselen. Anselm Adorne heard it from his own sources and, summoning Nicholas de Fleury, informed him that he could now leave for Ghent. The purpose for which he had travelled to Flanders was about to be served. David de Salmeton was here, and the mischief must be halted before it could begin.

Chapter 40

BITTEN BY FROST, preserved in illusory ice, the phantom Kingdom of Burgundy, the dream of its Duke, the land that was to stretch from Champagne to the Middle Sea, lay white as alum the following morning, as it was to remain for five weeks.

On the battlefield outside Nancy, it had started to snow.

In Ghent, the magistrates responsible for the Hôtel de Ville banquet woke to darkness and fog. Lamps glowed from horn windows all day, and the lanterns which lined the grand route from the Gravenkasteel to the Town Hall were no more than ghosts, barely illuminating the ice of the little Leie, and the stiffened hangings and wreaths of the tall, painted houses beyond, and the motionless helms of the town guard, set like street pumps before them. By the time the Duchess's cavalcade trotted through, even the bells and the cheering were muffled and the street tableaux, to the relief of the players, were cancelled. Everything congealed.

Gelis was warm, for all her senses told her that Nicholas was near.

From the beginning, his movements had been a matter of strategy: closely concealed, or misleadingly whispered abroad. She knew she must not try to communicate. It had disconcerted her, at first, to find that he and Clémence had re-opened a channel between them, of the same nature as the quiet, oblique lifeline that had sustained her at the start of his absence. A mechanical frog made its appearance, almost identical to John le Grant's defunct toy, except that this one croaked. She could not tell Jodi who had sent it. She could only watch the joy on his face. Then there came short, coded messages which might have come from anyone, except for the complexity of the cipher, and an identification — a word, a phrase which was wholly his. Everything about them was cerebral. Encoded messages, no more.

She prayed for his safety, she who never prayed. When news came that de Salmeton was coming, she could not breathe for fear. Naturally, the messages immediately stopped. Their practical purpose was finished. One thing only mattered: that all those who knew he was back should believe that today, the day of the banquet, Nicholas was still in Bruges.

She knew that she was going to meet David de Salmeton today, the one day that she must leave the castle. She could have feigned illness. She preferred to have it all over. Behind her, at least, Jodi was locked and guarded and safe.

She had dressed for her enemy. No one could vie with the Imperial fiancée and her stepmother, in their mantles of sable and ermine, their surcoats of glistening silver and gold over deep mingled velvets; their sleeves heavy with jewels. The dames of honour might wear what they chose, and someone had sent Gelis a thousand squirrel skins. Weightless, sinuous, downy, four hundred of them lined the saffron silk cloak she had had made for them, and edged its quilted hood embroidered with pearls. Voile and jewels hid her hair, and a belt of gold worked with jewels clasped the severe, high-waisted gown with its triangular neckline turned back with fur.

Clémence, keeping her company, waited with her on the cleared paving before the Hôtel de Ville as the eminent van of the procession mounted its steps, was welcomed, and receded into the depths of the building. Then the long line of the lesser guests was permitted to wind its way up the stairs. They entered a gallery, hung with banners. They were relieved of their cloaks. Then they were passing through the double doors of the Salon d'Honneur, its beams wreathed, its walls lined with escutcheons, its tableware rattling with the piercing stridency of a fanfare as they were ushered diligently to their seats. The fanfare redoubled, and the Ladies of Burgundy appeared from the side of the dais and, escorted by the high officials of the town, were led to their seats under the great canopy of state.

The long board for the demoiselles of honour was set to one side, as were the other tables for ladies. But standing there, making her reverence with the rest, Gelis van Borselen was silently occupied in putting a name to the men on and close to the dais: men hatted, square-shouldered and round as the beads on an abacus; their faces florid or pale; their doublets stuffed and quilted and pleated, their coats glittering; their shoulders furred with wide collars weighty as pillory boards.

Wolfaert van Borselen and Louis de Gruuthuse, Earl of Winchester, her relations. The Lieutenant General of the Low Countries. Chancellor Hugonet. The High Steward of Flanders. The Bailiff. The hosts of the town, the procurators, the judges. And below the gold and scarlet banner of his royal nephew, James Stewart of Auchterhouse, Earl of Buchan, with whom, according to Kathi, Nicholas had shared a memorable incident in Scotland involving a ladder, a looking-glass and a parrot. James Stewart's half-sister had once been married to Wolfaert van Borselen, and had been Countess of Buchan herself. Gelis knew James. But royal memories were not always long, and she should have been pleased when, under cover of the welcoming speech, he glanced across at her table, found her, and gave a slight, smiling bow. But that was because he had been nudged by his neighbour, David de Salmeton.

She had known what to expect. She was capable of observing all the courtesies: applauding the edible surprises and the inedible entertainments; conversing over and under the music and tasting, if not swallowing, some of the dishes that arrived and departed: the joints of beef and shoulders of mutton, the geese and pigeons and partridges, the calves' foot jellies and swans. The expensive frosted confections, and the fruit. There were lemons and oranges. And wine. And hippocras. And all the time David de Salmeton smiled at her with his deep-fringed dark eyes, rolling a sprig of parsley between his manicured nails, slowly biting a pear, and smoothing his dimpled chin and quirked lips with a kerchief of lace. And she could believe, now, that he was rich. The lapels of his overgown were of exotic brown lambskin, and the little purse at his belt displayed a pattern of rubies and pearls.

Towards the end, my lady the Duchess condescended to partner her step-daughter in a promenade dance, of the kind where musicians play, and well-born ladies exhibit their grace and their skill, when the tables are cleared, by visiting the four quarters of the room, two by two, in a swaying sinuous column. Gelis, leaning, pacing, curtseying with Clémence's precise hand in her own, was touched to see that no one found cause to ridicule the two fateful figures leading the dance: the young girl in her wreath of jewelled flowers glancing up lovingly at the towering English princess beside her, made taller still by the wedding coronet with its jewelled white roses on her pale, pleated hair. The Duchess was thirty, a year younger than Gelis. Ghent had always loved England; sometimes too well. In this town had been born John of Gaunt, whose blood ran in the royal houses of Portugal, England and Scotland; as well as in the veins of Duke Charles and his Duchess. Margaret of York had borne no children to her husband in the separate lives that they led, but had served the Duke and Burgundy, and had cherished his child as her own since Marie was eleven.

The dance ended, to hearty applause. Tumblers rushed in. The Duchess signalled to her ladies that she wished to retire, but one lady did not follow her. Gelis van Borselen, lifting her skirts to sweep from the room, was stopped on the threshold by the man who had passed his time watching her. David de Salmeton bathed her in one of his glorious smiles. 'Don't go. She won't miss you. I'm not about to create a scene here, my dear Gelis, I give you my word. But it would please me to talk. And unless you listen, you will never know, will you, what I am going to do?'

There were other people in the service rooms and the gallery. Soon, the great exodus would begin, and pages and porters and grooms, private house-servants and stewards would see to the cloaks and the mounts of their masters and mistresses. The Duchess and the guests of honour, who had arrived on caparisoned horseback, were to return on chairs of state within wagons. A chain of others would follow, conveying her attendants back to the Castle of Ten Walle through the deep cold and fog, between the glimmering lamps. Gelis saw that Clémence had left the Duchess and was standing, hands peacefully folded, watching her.

The man standing beside Gelis said, 'Your guard dog? Then perhaps you may feel you can risk a few words. I have to congratulate you on your looks and, of course, on your business acumen. One could have anticipated that the Vatachino would fail, but it took genius to usurp your own husband's company. They will miss you when you have gone.'

'I am going somewhere?' Gelis said. Below the perfect damask, the sturdy contours of his shoulders and arms were owed to muscle, not padding, and the wrists that turned the delicate fingers were supple and hard. He might look effeminate, but he had the flat back and poise of a swordsman.

'Of course,' said David de Salmeton. 'Your future is arranged. Best of all, your husband can share it, due to this mystifying ability, inherent in animals and simpletons, I am told, to trace a person by instinct.'

Gelis gazed at him. She said, 'Do you have much luck in general, with your planning? You told Bel: you know as well as I do that my husband is dead. I don't wear black, because our marriage was over. I hadn't seen him for years. Report says he was killed outside Moscow, escaping after some spectacular crime involving rape. Who is going to trace me by instinct?'

'He is with Adorne in Bruges,' said David de Salmeton, sighing. 'And your struggle to protect him would fill him with joy, no doubt, if he knew of it. Poor Anselm Adorne. What a pity the Scots squashed his appointment.'

'What a pity Andro Wodman got it instead,' Gelis said, giving up gracefully.

'Yes,' he admitted. 'That was unexpected. I thought of complaining. I thought of describing how he tried to kill me in Edinburgh. But for that, I should never have had to strike that poor man in self-defence.'

'It was not how I heard it,' said Gelis. 'So why not give up before you are killed in self-defence too?'

'My dear! Is that a threat?' said David de Salmeton. His lashes were wonderful. He said, 'You're going to say it's a promise.' He sounded mellow with pure delight.

'I'm going to say that mercenaries make good assassins. You are going to Nancy eventually?'

'Eventually,' de Salmeton said. 'I have my little tasks to perform here. But then, certainly, I must pay a visit to dear John, and dear Tobie, and dear Kathi's child husband. With so many pleasant duties in store, the order of execution hardly matters.'

'Why?' Gelis said. She could hear heightened voices and the scraping of chairs. The Duchess had gone back into the Salon. She said, 'What do you want, that you don't have? Nicholas had every excuse to call for your death, but he freed you. You have gold. Perhaps you have more gold than you should have. Is that why you want Nicholas out of the way?'

'What on earth do you mean?' said David de Salmeton. His brows, perfectly trimmed, rose in astonishment. 'I have money, yes, and position. But how does that compare with the pleasure of reducing an inferior to his proper state of humility?'

Gelis gazed at him. 'I don't know,' she said. 'You mean the way you were thrown out of Cyprus? I heard about that. Really, more people ought to hear about that. I'm sure it would give them incomparable pleasure.'

Clémence was touching her arm. Her cloak appeared. The noise had now regulated itself into the unmistakable ritual of closing speeches and farewells. Since she could not re-enter, she might as well wait until the Duchess emerged.

She turned. David de Salmeton's dark eyes were still examining her. He said, 'What a foolish woman you are. You have just killed your husband.' Then he left.

She stood shaking. Clémence said, 'What a very small man. But not malnourished. He could hold his own, I would imagine, against a person of his own height. Against a taller, he would lack the reach.'

The perfect nurse. Nevertheless . . . 'There is always the stab in the back,' Gelis said.

'That is true,' Clémence conceded. 'But that gentleman does not wish merely to kill. He wishes to mortify his chief victim. He wishes your husband to watch what is going to happen to you. So he will plan to trap him or ambush him first. Or, of course, bring him wherever he wishes by deceiving the pendulum.'

He had done that once before, by using her wedding ring. Tonight, he had not taken her wedding ring, or anything else belonging to her. He had other plans.

Well, she was a van Borselen. One did not hide, like a beast in a thicket. One gambled, and threw. Straight-backed, Gelis, lady of Fleury, left the safe purlieus of the Ghent Hôtel de Ville, and walked down the steps.

. . .

With darkness, the fog outside seemed to have thickened. It swirled, grey and curdling round the clusters of lamps, the arrays of four-pound candles with their dim, tinkling bells, the rimed garlands, the group of long whitened trumpets, gripped in numb hands. The sensible Ghenters were indoors, but the guilds stood in their ranks, with their emblems staunchly upheld, and the burgesses and their wives shivered shoulder to shoulder. Bells clanged as if muffled with cloth, and unseen fireworks pattered like used raindrops, discarded from shivering trees. The Ladies of Burgundy emerged to fanfares and cheering, and were handed into the velvet-draped wagon with its silver harness, its gold fringes and sculptures. The two horses stood to the whip and, stirring, dragged it into motion. The outriders paced at their side. One by one, the other carts followed.

Squirrel skins cushioned the cold. The ladies of honour, jolting together in the freezing air of the third wagon, envied the best-wrapped of their number, and did not know that she would have exchanged her dress, down to the skin, rather than be where she was. The head of the procession turned west past Sint Niklaaskerk, crackled over the bridge and moved north along the banks of the Leie. The rest followed.

Nothing happened. The Duchess and her step-daughter clung with one hand and waved with the other as their vehicle of state rumbled and slid over the half-frozen silt that coated the cobbles. They reached the fork where one river became two, enclosing the fish-market, and beyond that, the invisible bulk of the castle. Now, the number of spectators had dwindled, as had the noise, although the bells, the trumpets, the cries still hung behind them, wrapping the tail of the cavalcade. The van moved away from the slow, mist-filled Lieve and, passing between the blurred lights of mansions and warehouses, made its way west at last to the glare in the fog which was the fine castellated entrance to the Hof Ten Walle, the Duchess's palace.

In the courtyard, the household was waiting to welcome their mistress. Once the first wagon was emptied, the steps were put in place for the others. The man Manoli, Jodi's personal bodyguard, was the first to rush forward to these.

Clémence, descending, spoke first. 'Master Jordan?'

'He's safe. He's asleep. No one tried to harm him. But what about you?'

'Nothing happened,' Clémence said. 'I am concerned.' She was joined by her driver and three of the outriders, all with swords and mail tunics.

'Where is the Lady?' Manoli said. Behind, the third wagon rumbled over the stones, then the fourth. After that there was a space.

'In the last, as we agreed.' Clémence shook back her hood, revealing a frown of anxiety above Gelis's squirrel-skin mantle of yellow silk. 'Come. We must make sure.'

She had sensible shoes, as a precaution, below her fine gown, and was as agile as anyone, clutching her skirts and racing with Manoli and the rest through the fog to the entrance to the palace and beyond. Halfway down the road, they began to hear the shouts of men in dispute, and then came upon the cause of the trouble, a vehicle stuck on the road and holding up all the others behind it. One of the horses, breaking free, had added to the confusion. The wisest travellers had kept to their wagons; others had left them to indulge their curiosity, or even to set out for the palace on foot. The ladies of the last wagon, invited to leave, had all jumped down with a will, exclaiming over the cold, and pleased at the prospect of riding home pillionwise, with an arm round the warm waist of a soldier.

It was not an easy task, in the fog, to question and count them. All the same, it only took moments to discover that Gelis van Borselen was missing. And a little later, that one of the outriders had gone.

SEATED IN THE LAST WAGON, wearing Clémence's good velvet cloak, Gelis had not been surprised at the halt. This was the only occasion on which she would ever be within reach of de Salmeton's men. Deceived by the cloak, they would attack, discover their mistake, and be captured, she hoped, in their turn. After that, they would be encouraged to mention who paid them.

She did her best to remain in her wagon. When the hanging was pulled quickly back and a handsome outrider courteously invited the ladies to descend, she settled back in the gloom, and prepared to remain where she was. The voices receded, to join themselves to the other sounds of commotion ahead. The fog made her cough. A man, swinging up into the vehicle, gripped her arm and placed a palm over her mouth. A second, arriving as quietly, took both her wrists and lashed them together, while the first replaced his hand with a ball of cloth and a scarf.

'Apologies, my dear,' one of them said. 'Please don't kick. My friend here has a very bad temper.'

She had agreed it all beforehand. *If anything happens, exercise restraint. Do not invite retaliation; you won't be hurt until the bastard has the right audience.* But of course, being a van Borselen, she hurled aside all restraint: she sank her head in a groin, ground her joined knuckles into an eye, and scraped her buckled headdress across someone's face from ear to lip. Which was foolish for, panting, they simply slapped her unconscious; and kept her so.

. . .

SHE AWOKE SEVERAL HOURS LATER in the hold of a boat. This took a while to establish, as her head thudded, her body ached, and the darkness about her was total. She also discerned that the boat was not moving. Although welcome, this deduction was of limited use: Ghent was a major port, possessed of three rivers and a canal leading to Damme. Not all were frozen, and their banks were lined with moored boats. This one smelled of mildewed grain and cooked sausage; a watchman's fire, somewhere, had softened the worst of the cold.

Before wasting effort on her surroundings, she had established that she was leashed: her hands were shackled together and attached to a chain which rose to a wall-staple. She had further confirmed that her clothing was undisturbed: she had not been undressed or molested or used. The advantage — the only advantage — of eight years of celibacy was the austere witness it supplied to that fact.

Last of all, came the realisation that she was not alone.

Captors gloated; murderers would be brandishing lights. She tried to tell herself that only another prisoner would be lying still in the dark, far across the deck of what must be the hold of a barge, hardly stirring, barely audible except for the stifled sound of his breathing. If it was not David de Salmeton or one of his henchmen, it must be a captive like herself.

Her head cleared then, and she knew. Her body, which had been chilled, began to fill with slow waves of warmth, drowning any sense of amazement, or consternation, or dread. She knew who it was. She had begun to speak his name when a bolt crashed overhead, a lantern waved from the hatch, and an armed man slid down the ladder, to be joined by another. They crossed first to her, grinning, to hang one lantern above her, then took and hung the other above the man whose breathing she had heard, who did not resist when they kicked him and left, but lay bare-headed where he was chained, in his ruined outrider's dress, his bruised face transfigured, his grey eyes resting only on her.

Nicholas.

She said, 'I solved your grandfather's code.'

'I know. I felt it,' he said. He spoke like a boy.

The two men had left, and could be heard talking above. They sounded deferential. Someone new began to descend. Gelis did not even look up. She filled her eyes and heart with the sight of him: the low, calm brow and wide bones of his face, the stubborn hair, topiary-trimmed (by Adorne's barber?) to cling to his throat; the length and bulk of his body, part hunting-cat and part bear. They had torn off his boots and cuirass and greaves, leaving him in a soiled jacket and hose. He had drawn up a knee, and was supporting his weight on one hip and his elbow. His wrists were shackled like hers, with a little slack, and his broad, craftsman's hands were clasped lightly before him. She wondered, with a deep, lunatic pang of pure love, how he had managed to put the croak into the frog.

Gelis looked up at his face, and said, 'I would walk over, now.'

The third visitor stepped down into the light and stood, looking down at them both. 'We must arrange it,' the newcomer said.

It was not David de Salmeton; the man who had threatened her, who wanted Nicholas dead, and who bore a grudge against all who had slighted him. This was Julius's wife, Anna von Hanseyck.

Chapter 41

FOR NICHOLAS, the materialisation of Anna von Hanseyck should have been fearful. He had expected de Salmeton, and a long, teasing exchange involving physical discomfort, probably imposed by David himself, artistically supported by henchmen. De Salmeton would, however, have been gallant to Gelis, and might even have spared her, at the end.

Anna was different. She, too, would enjoy playing her fish before killing it, but she would make sure that Gelis would suffer as well. Also, she was who she was. Dealing with Anna would be far, far more difficult and delicate than dealing with a good-looking man whose hatred for Nicholas was rooted in envy. Nicholas should have been appalled, had he not possessed a boon which outweighed all these hazards.

He was with Gelis again. She was not going to die: he would see to that. But even so, he had her avowal: he could see in her face the same smothered radiance that suffused him. Whatever came to them both, they were together. *I would walk over now,* she had said.

But now, he must not look at Gelis; he must act. Nicholas sat up as best he could and, exhibiting incoherent amazement, exclaimed, *'Anna!'* The name rang round the hold, and the cloaked woman standing alone on the decking before him smiled with pleasure and spoke.

'Would you have preferred David de Salmeton? I am sorry. He has gone, I am told. Some unexpected change in his plans.'

Gone? He could not ask where. This was not about David de Salmeton. He frowned at the mocking, shadowy face, and spoke sharply. 'They were *your* men? But why?' The chain clanked with his changing position and he gave it a short, angry tug, confronting her with his bound hands. 'What's this, Anna? Another performance? Is Julius coming to run me through, this time? And what is Gelis here for?'

He glanced at Gelis when mentioning her name. She was pale, but watching him with composure. He was reminded that she was now a woman of business. In three years, she must have learned to recognise and deal with the critical opening moments of a negotiation. She had also worked with him before, on certain projects in Scotland. It might be enough. Anna and he had never performed together as part of a team. She would always either be her own mistress, or yours.

Julius's wife looked round for a box, pulled one forward, and sat on it. Beneath the cloak, she was wearing an exceptionally beautiful gown; as fine as the robe of occasion Gelis wore, and the cap confining her hair was decorated with jewels. Her smile, a little pitying, had widened.

She said, 'We have surprised one another. I didn't expect you in Ghent. Julius has gone off to Bruges to challenge you to a fight to the death. I'm sorry, Nicholas, I'm afraid I had to tell him what you did to me.'

'I didn't do anything,' Nicholas said. 'I'm sorry if you thought that an insult, but it isn't Gelis's fault. May she go?'

'You haven't been listening,' said Anna. 'I said that I thought you and Julius were in Bruges. It was Gelis I wanted. I didn't know you would come rushing to trap David de Salmeton with a singularly feeble plan for a decoy. But now I have you both.'

Gelis said, 'Why do you want both of us?'

'Wouldn't you like to die together?' said Anna.

'Die?' said Gelis. She sounded disbelieving, but not entirely unfriendly, as a well-brought-up young woman would, on finding another in the grip of sick fantasies. Gelis said, 'Is it because I didn't come to Caffa, with Jodi? You felt we all expected too much of you, alone in the Crimea with Nicholas. And it was his fault that Julius was hurt and couldn't be there.' She paused and said, 'I can see that. I'm sorry.'

Anna's eyes were on Nicholas. 'And you? Can you imagine why I should want you both dead?'

'I don't think you do,' Nicholas said. 'Wouldn't it make life rather dull?'

Anna laughed. Her cloak, already unhooked, slipped from her shoulders, and she let it fall. She said, 'When I heard they had captured you both, I thought I'd dress for you. I even washed out my hair.' And she raised her hands and unpinned and drew off her cap.

The hair that fell to her shoulders was not black. The strands that coiled, damp still, over her breast and her back were of a colour that even a dyer's apprentice would find hard to compose, although a jeweller might. Her hair was not red. Blood was red. This was the vermilion of a cardinal's tassels, seen through an eyeglass of amber.

Within this cascade of fire, Anna's eyes had remained fixed and distended on his. 'Well?'

Well, indeed. The opening gambit was over, and she had forced the real game to begin. Look at me. I have fooled you. I have won.

Gelis could have told her. There is more to a contest than that.

Nicholas released his breath, slowly and soundlessly. He wished that Gelis were not here and then cancelled the wish, for to have her here was the ultimate privilege. In any case, she seemed to have sensed what he wanted. Since she could not leave, she had sunk back from the light and was crouching motionless on the dusty floor, watching.

Nicholas said, 'I knew, Adelina.'

She must have heard him. She continued as if he had not spoken. She said, 'Shall I tell you who I am, Nicholas? I am not Anna von Hanseyck. My name is not even Anna. The woman you kissed, the woman you stared at so lasciviously in the tent — how foolish you looked! — is your own blood-relation. I am Adelina, the child who grew up with you. I am the child you allowed your great-uncle to take to his bed. I am the child who was left with no family, while you married and married again, taking your pleasure, wringing money out of all your women, using and discarding your mistresses. I am Adelina de Fleury, your grandfather's daughter.'

'I know,' he said again.

Her smile, full of triumph, gave way to a flicker of impatience. 'You can't know. Shall I say it again? I am—'

'Adelina de Fleury. *I know*,' Nicholas said. 'I have always known, ever since I set eyes on you in Bruges. Ever since you persuaded Julius to marry you, just for this day.'

Anna faced him. Behind her, Gelis was rigid with tension but did not pretend to surprise. He was a company project; he had no secrets now. Water lapped. The lanterns stirred, and muffled footsteps above told where the two henchmen were waiting. A stifled bell clanged, once, in the fog.

Anna said, 'You don't like being deceived by a woman. You can't even admit it.' Within the blazing hair, her face was austere. She added scathingly, 'You couldn't have known.'

Again, he wished he and she were alone; that this did not have to take place before Gelis.

As it was: 'Why not?' Nicholas said quietly. 'Because I didn't denounce you? Because I didn't tell anyone what Moriz found out about your finances? Because I didn't show I knew that you were coming to Caffa only in the hope of getting my gold? Do you think I didn't want Gelis, or my son? Why do you think I never sent for them, except that I knew you only wanted to kill them?'

He had supposed Gelis to have realised that, but he must have been wrong, for she gasped. Anna heard it, and swung round. '*You* knew nothing of this?'

At Anna's back, Nicholas made the faintest of movements. Gelis said, 'Some of us had begun to suspect, Adelina, but not because Nicholas told us. Until today, he has never mentioned your name.'

'Because until today, he didn't know,' Anna said. 'Now he is cringing, I trust, at the thought of what passed between us. How sad! To die branded as a lecherous rascal! To leave me rich as I should have been rich!' She blazed at him, still resolutely triumphant.

Nicholas waited. The echoes died. He schooled his voice to the same level tone. 'I was eight when we parted. Too young to understand, or to help, but not too young to remember. Your eyes were the same then, as now. I have never seen their like anywhere else. The colour; and the misery of the *putoduli*.'

Gelis looked down.

Adelina de Fleury said in a low voice, 'You wanted me. You can't deny it. But for Julius, you would have been in my bed. You took me everywhere. I was the chosen person to whom you prated about your feelings, your beliefs. You didn't know who I was; or how I despised you.' She had risen.

And again, he repeated his affirmation. 'I knew,' Nicholas said. 'I thought I could teach you that life held more than resentment, or money, or revenge. I thought I might leave you with a flourishing business and we might part, with nothing said. But that was all. I spoke of friendship, but did you hear me speak of love? Did you hear me mention the name of my wife or my son, or anything or anyone close to me? I try to forgive you, for at times, I have been no better than you have. I do understand. I ache for the waste and the misery in your life, but nothing would have brought me to confide in you.'

'You are lying,' Anna said, with sudden high fury. He understood all that she felt. Gelis, too, would understand, for he had once done this to her. In Trèves three years before, she had supposed herself to have won their long contest, only to find that he held all her secrets. In Trèves, he had spared Gelis that knowledge, until compelled to admit it by Jordan de Ribérac. Here, he was using the same device against Adelina with deliberate cruelty. He wanted, as he had never wanted with Gelis, to deprive this woman of her planned victory. He also wished to win time, in order to find a way to survive. He had laid plans. But in a fog like this, no plans were secure.

And still it was working, for even yet, with both of them in her power, Anna could not bear to continue until she had wrung a retraction from Nicholas. She repeated, fiercely, 'You are lying. You didn't know. You wanted Bonne to marry your son.'

For a moment, his gaze passed the woman before him, and rested on Gelis. He saw she was smiling, and happiness, yet again, overwhelmed the misery and the pain. Nicholas said, 'Because I had to make sure, in the short term, that Jodi and Gelis would live. Gelis is wealthy. Anything I had she would also inherit. She is still my wife.'

He had let his eyes speak, and Anna had seen it. She turned, and then whirled again back to Nicholas. She cried, 'You did know. You both knew.'

And now he wished he had not chosen to tell her. In a moment, she would let herself think of all that had happened between them, and realise finally how he had deceived her. In a moment, she would return to her purpose, and there would be no more time to win.

Anna stood, watching him; trying to imagine, he supposed, what precise degree of punishment he deserved of her, now. And Gelis. Oh God, he had to save Gelis. Anna said, 'You think you know yourself, Nicholas de Fleury. You think you know the harm you can do, and have done. You know nothing.'

He had thought she would call for her men. He had not dreamed that a few words could so infect him with dread. And to make matters worse, Gelis suddenly chose to address Adelina harshly.

'So what do you mean to do? What about Julius? If you harm either of us, the whole of Flanders would hound you!' She kept her eyes on Anna, who turned to her slowly.

Anna said, 'People drown in these waters, especially in fog. You will be found in the silt, close to where you strayed from your wagon. Julius will not especially mourn you. He expected to discover Nicholas in Bruges, and to challenge and kill him in defence of my honour. As it is, he will come back to find Nicholas dead. Another drowning, or caught in some drunken brawl. There will be nothing to show how it happened. Are you not sorry?' she said, looking at Nicholas. 'Are you not sorry you did not think more of me?'

She was standing close to him.

'I am only sorry,' Nicholas said, 'that I had to make believe that I wanted you. Did you think, that day unclothed in the tent, that the sight of you was alluring? With your ageing body and badly dyed hair, that smeared even your under-linen? You may have been well enough as a child,' Anna's nephew observed, 'but I didn't want my great-uncle's leavings.'

Her arm rose and swept down. He rocked with the blow, like the practised wrestler he was, and counter-attacked well enough, using his own momentum and Anna's precarious balance to kick her feet from under her, locking her with his knee and trapping her as she fell. His hands circled once, looping a length of chain round her throat. Then he pulled himself back to the wall like a swimmer saving another, and stopped, breathing fast. He had enough strength for that, but less than he wished.

Anna lay in his arms, looking up at him, with her breath throttled shut. He tightened his hands under her chin, until her back arched. 'Drop the knife,' Nicholas said. She made a guttural sound, and her arms fell back, her hands opening. Something bright glinted among the twists of delicate silk and dropped aside to the deck. He freed a heel and kicked it sideways, before immobilising her whole lower body again. Her scent, released by the pressure, filled the air. Footsteps sounded above. The hatch opened, and one of the henchmen looked down.

'I have your mistress,' Nicholas said. 'Do as I say, and I'll double your money. Don't, and I'll kill her.' His voice continued, unemotionally issuing instructions. The two men ran down the stairs, unbuckling their belts, and threw down their swords. Anna's face had become suffused, and her body began to grow lax.

Nicholas said, 'One of you unshackle that lady.'

One of the men crossed to Gelis. Gripping Anna, Nicholas watched him intently. It was possible to guess from his manner that this was not a common hireling, content to be purchased. Anna had the kind of beauty that quickly found slaves, and slaves would not let her die. In his present mood, Nicholas would not place himself in quite the same category. As Gelis was freed, Nicholas deliberately tightened his garrotting grip to render Anna unconscious. Then Gelis said, *'Nicholas!'* and he saw, looking down, that his fingers for once had obeyed his emotions instead of his brain. Anna's eyes were shut, her colour altered, her whole body frighteningly limp.

Nicholas loosened his hands. Beneath them, Anna's throat worked, drawing in air like a scream. Her eyes opened, wide and alert. Her hands, darting upwards, clawed at his skin and the chain, while she hurled her body aside, kicking and thrusting. He closed his arm round her neck, but her hands were both free, and a few raucous snatches of air allowed her enough strength to use them before he could again press her into submission. It gave her bodyguards just time enough. While he fought her, the two men flung themselves on him, and dragged their mistress free.

Gelis cast a single calculating glance at Nicholas, and plunged to the foot of the steps. She had swept up one of the scabbards when it was wrenched out of her hand, and she was pinioned by the arms. The second soldier snatched up the other, and unsheathed his sword with a whine, looking at Anna. Adelina de Fleury leaned gasping against the bulwark of the barge, one hand to her throat. Her hair, incandescent in the lamplight, mantled her torn and soiled gown, and there was a great, swollen ridge at her neck, where her skin was as fair as John le Grant's, with a suggestion of freckles. Nicholas sat untidily where he had been chained, panting and dizzy, but capable of thinking, at least. He trusted no one would notice that the knife was no longer where he had kicked it.

One of the two men lifted his sword. 'Now we kill them, Gräfin?'

He had been right. Slaves, not hirelings. The van Borselen name would make no difference here.

Adelina said, 'Now we kill them. But with cunning, my friend. The woman drowns. The man is beaten to death by footpads. Let him watch the woman die, first.'

Gelis said, 'Just now, he had the chance to strangle you, and didn't.'

'You distracted him,' Anna said. 'That is all. How sad your little son is going to be. But Bonne will comfort him, and I shall be an excellent guardian, having care for all his great inheritance, those precious shares in the Bank; perhaps even the Fleury estates, restored, one of these days. What a pity my father could not have lived to see how his scheme failed. He did not destroy me after all.'

Gelis, held fast, could not have spoken, but Nicholas did. 'It was not his fault,' he said. 'It was terrible, but it was not the fault of Thibault de Fleury, or of anyone else. There is no reason to do such harm. You will have to be on your guard for the rest of your life. You will weary.'

'I shall revel in it,' Anna said.

There was a water tank, in another compartment of the hold. They harnessed Gelis again to her staple while the two men went off to fetch it. Anna walked with them, holding the lantern. There were buckets to fill it with. Reduced to one source of light, the prisoners could just see one another.

Nicholas said, 'The Duke's bath. Julius and I floated in it from Sluys. A good astrologer should have stopped us.'

'I don't think,' Gelis said in a murmur, 'that you ought to give in to nostalgia. You do have a plan?'

'I did,' he said. 'For different weather. No *galoppini*.' He kept his voice soft, but could not prevent it from lightening. This was how, once, they had talked.

'Life is full of surprises,' Gelis said. 'You *have* got the knife?'

'Sitting on it,' he said.

'Painful,' said Gelis. 'They'll have to unshackle me to push my head under. I'll try what I can.'

'Gelis,' he said. His voice was not light, now.

The clanging got nearer, and the redoubled light.

'Thibault relayed your message,' she said. 'It is true for me, too. I am only sorry for . . .' But she could not speak his name.

'But Jodi is quite secure,' Nicholas said. He had lifted his voice, directing it at Anna, who had entered again. Behind her, with a sonorous clangour, the water magazine was approaching. Nicholas said, 'By tomorrow, everyone who matters will know who Anna is, and how unsuitable such a match will be. I have appointed other guardians. There is no possibility that Bonne and Jordan could ever marry.'

'No one would believe you,' Anna said.

'Oh yes,' Nicholas said. 'There is proof. I had hoped to deal with this privately, but if we both die, Father Moriz will publish the truth. Julius will learn it as well.'

'Julius!' Anna exclaimed. She laughed.

'Do you think he would stay married to you?' Nicholas said. 'If you let us go, you can return east with Julius and live out your life, respected and wealthy in Poland. If you do this, you lose everything.'

'Don't you think it is worth it?' she said. 'I want to watch your face as she dies. I want to tell you something that none of your friends knows, and then I want to watch you die, sobbing.'

They were filling the tank. The fog curled down from the hatch, and the icy air, and pools formed on the deck. It would not take long. They only needed enough to cover her head, when they held her face down. Anna sat. The men climbed up and down. Gelis watched the water, not Nicholas. She looked very tired, and as stiff as if she also had been kicked. Nicholas found Anna's gaze on them both, and looked down. Then the water was sufficiently deep, and Anna's men went to Gelis and unshackled her wrists, and she rose in their grasp, and looked at Nicholas.

Anna said, 'Would you like to say goodbye? A farewell kiss? Look, I think he is moist-eyed already. But first, perhaps we should take away the knife he is sitting on.'

Before she ended, Nicholas had twisted and kicked. As he hoped, Gelis threw herself forward, but the man at her right arm held fast, while the other leaped before her, intending to catch the knife as it flew. It meant that her left arm was free.

It would have offered nothing to graceful, feminine Anna. But this was Gelis, to whom a man's world was not simply hunting or ledgerwork, and who had fought on a ship off the African coast. Who had always fought, damn her.

She had seen, watching Nicholas, that there was nothing to catch. The kick had been a feint. The next moment, he sent the real knife skimming towards her, and Gelis lunged once again. Since both men were going to get it before she did, there was not much point, she evidently saw, in competing. She plunged for the nearest scabbard instead, heaved out its sword and banged the owner hard on the back so that he screamed and staggered forward. She put her foot out as he passed.

Before her husband's fascinated gaze, the man stumbled, flailed, and floundered up to the rim of the tank. There was a clang and a splash, and Nicholas laughed. Gelis frowned, and her remaining opponent looked round, which was unwise, for it allowed Gelis to knock the sword from his hand and slash at him with the point of her own. He gasped and fell. Anna screamed at him. The eyes of Nicholas were on Gelis who, stooping, collected the rod that unlocked the shackles, and started to back. In a whirl of red hair, Anna followed, the fallen man's sword held low in both hands, like a spear. It quivered. Her eyes were not on Gelis, but below her, to where Nicholas half knelt, still chained.

He said impatiently, 'Well, use your head.'

'I am!' said Gelis indignantly. Anna made a stroke at her and she countered, sobered. The staple and Nicholas were just behind her. The man she had knocked down was stirring, and an ominous splashing could be heard from the tank. Anna drove forward again, this time towards Nicholas. Gelis knocked the blade aside, and it fell. Nicholas said, 'Sweetheart, *date stones*.'

Without the endearment, it was a very old code between them. He saw Gelis stop, and glimpsed the curve of her cheek as she smiled. Then she ducked, and as Anna came forward again, Gelis picked up first one bucket, then another, and threw them, hard.

The pails were of leather, and heavy. They smashed into both lanterns, plunging them all into a darkness full of blundering figures. A person with whose shape he was intimately acquainted fell into his arms and sadly, out of them again, attended by a clatter of metal. His shackles fell off. He caught and kissed the nearest bare part of his rescuer and heard her breathlessly laugh. Then he and Gelis were fighting their way side by side in the dark to the steps. Fighting with fists and shoulders and elbows, for there was no place in this darkness for swords. He heard Gelis use, viciously, a word of Astorre's, and was swamped again with pain and with love.

They had the stairs at their back, when Nicholas heard the thud of many feet up above, and the barge sluggishly tilted. About him, the grasping hands slackened. Nicholas realised that the wounded man had fallen back, and that the other had stopped, apprehensive. Then came the rush of scent and the slither of silk and he sensed, since he could not see, that Anna had found a weapon, and was going to use it. Nicholas took his wife by the hand and pulled her, fast, up the steps, throwing up the hatch lid at the top. He did not know whom he was going to meet. It might be David de Salmeton.

He stepped out first; then drew Gelis up after him. Her hand was sinewy, and sweaty, and what he could only describe as protective. He wondered if she would think he was shaking from fear. Around them was freezing air, and darkness, and fog, and a circle of brands, glimmering in the grasp of a shadowy troop of armed men. There was nothing to show whose they were.

The hatch creaked, and another figure stepped into the thick, swimming light. Her hair gleamed red and gold, and her face was that of a ghost. 'Help me,' said Adelina de Fleury. 'This is my attacker, who has followed me all the way from Russia. And his wife, as perverted as he is. Help me, whoever you are.'

A man stepped forward. 'Me, I'm called Andro Wodman,' he said. 'Gentleman, and Conservator of Scots Privileges in Bruges. And this is the private militia of my lord Louis de Gruuthuse, Governor of Holland, whose wife, you may recollect, is a van Borselen. Our orders are to let your men go, and to take you to my lord's house in Ghent, where you may stay in a safe place until you are called to answer for what you have done. Pray to come forward. It is not our purpose to harm you.'

'What!' said the woman. She said a great deal more, but no one replied. Nicholas drew Gelis back as Adelina de Fleury was led respectfully past, and did not move when she struggled to face and revile him. When he did not reply, she fell silent, and allowed herself to be taken onwards again. Her footsteps descended, and faded. Only then did he heave a long, shaking sigh, and look at Wodman.

'The *galoppini*,' he said. 'You took your bloody time.'

'You obviously managed,' Wodman said. 'What are you whining for this time?'

THE MANSION OF Louis de Gruuthuse in Ghent was nothing near the size of his palace in Bruges, but it possessed secure rooms, and the kind of household which could both serve and guard anyone kept there. By the time the Scots Conservator and his two companions arrived there, Adelina de Fleury was not to be seen, and only Marguerite van Borselen was waiting, in her bedrobe, to bring them out of the fog and into the warmth of her chamber. There was steaming wine ready to pour.

'The young woman is safe, and being looked after. So sad! She seems very wild in her talk, but most persuasive: Louis says she is quite insane, and I am not to go near her, nor should you. And I should think not; look at you; this is what she has done to you both? And Nicholas? You are safely back?'

'I am safely back,' he said. 'But would not have remained so, except for Gelis. You have a very . . . *combative* cousin.'

'So was her sister,' said the lady of Gruuthuse. 'I always said, they needed a man to keep them in order. It does not do to cling together like shellfish; but nor does it do to stay apart for too long.'

'I must remember,' said Nicholas. Gelis looked at him, but he was gazing down at the cup in his hand. Under the blanket he had been given, he had stopped shivering, and the better light, while revealing the contusions, also showed her, for the first time in three years, the face she knew so well, and the changes in it. Then he looked up and smiled, and she felt the colour rise in her cheeks and her throat.

Nicholas cleared his own throat. He looked at Wodman and said, 'You say that the Gräfin's husband is coming?'

'Father Moriz will bring Julius tomorrow. Today,' Wodman corrected himself, looking at the dark windows. 'He will have been told what has happened. But of course, he will have to see for himself. As for our original anxiety, Buchan has gone, taking de Salmeton with him, and will presumably stay in the Tyrol until spring. All the threatened danger has gone. You and your family are safe.'

Nicholas said, 'I am glad you came when you did.' His eyes kept returning to Gelis, who was still flushing. He had forgotten what fine skin she had.

Her cousin Marguerite said, 'And now you are both going back to the palace? Come: I shall find you better clothes. You must be longing, Nicholas, to see your son again.'

'He will be asleep,' Gelis said. She glanced at Nicholas, and away.

'Then perhaps you would rather stay here? We have rooms enough!' She was being both tactful and kind. Before they were married, Gelis had admitted him to her room at the Hôtel Gruuthuse in Bruges. He rather thought Marguerite knew it. Marguerite said, 'Consider it while I bring you something comfortable to wear. Meester Wodman will help me.'

She disappeared with the Conservator, who appeared familiar with the house. Gelis said, 'He is staying here. I don't know if I want to be so close to Anna again.' She was sitting, her eyes on the fire.

Nicholas said, 'My luggage is at the Sersanders' house. Kathi gave me the key.'

'Who else is there?' Gelis said. She was looking at him again.

'No one. That is, there is a housekeeper who lives there. She will make whatever arrangements are wanted.'

'That sounds very suitable,' Gelis said. When told, Marguerite seemed to think so as well; Wodman grunted. It was not pleasant, issuing again into the cold, but the journey was short, and their escort delivered them to Anselm Adorne's house in good order. Nicholas had a key. He opened the door, and she entered a modest tiled hall, warmed by a stove, with three doors leading off, and a narrow staircase which rose to a second floor and then stopped. There was no sign of life.

Nicholas said, 'The housekeeper's room is beyond that door. There are two sleeping chambers upstairs. I put my coffers in one.'

'You thought you were going to face David de Salmeton's men,' Gelis said. 'You must have wondered whether you would come back here alive.'

Nicholas sat on the stairs. 'Not with my infallible plan. If they weren't misled by Clémence, they would try to take you. But I would be guarding your wagon, with Wodman somewhere close at hand to track me, and bring the militia.'

'But he got lost in the fog. And they captured you, as well as me. And it wasn't David, it was Anna.' Gelis leaned on the ornamental stair-post and looked down at him. She rested her chin on her arm. 'I thought you were clever.'

'Thank you,' he said.

She lifted her chin from her arm. 'That's not what I meant. How did they capture you?'

He said, 'They slapped you, and I offered myself as a professional mediator.'

'Just as I thought,' Gelis said. 'What happened to chivalry? Pretz and Paratge? Grant victory to this worthy knight, for whom await two rewards: heaven and the recognition of noble women?'

'It was too foggy. Noble women would never have noticed me.'

'You may be right,' Gelis said. He was gazing at his clasped hands, one knee up, his ravished sleeve against the stair-wall. She took a firmer grip of the banister. 'And even if they had, would they have deigned to proceed? You are still married.'

He looked up slowly. She could not read his eyes. He said, 'How do you know?'

'That you didn't annul it? You told Anna so. That you married in the first place? I seem to remember it. The *abboccamento*. The *impalmamento*. The *ductio*, even. I am sorry for what happened next.'

'You thought I deserved it,' he said. 'And then I seem to have proved that I did. We are back where we began. It is night. There is a bed. We may part; we may stay together. You must choose.'

'Nicholas?' Gelis said. He looked up. '*I* must choose? You care so little, you will let me break the marriage or not, as I want?'

'I care so much,' he said, 'that I can't in fairness speak for myself. How can I? You stand to lose far more than I do. You've found a fitting career at the Bank, but I couldn't join you. Once I've put away David de Salmeton, I should have to leave.'

'For Russia?' she said. 'You've launched a fine business there, so they tell me.'

'For Julius,' Nicholas said. 'Not necessarily for Russia. I came to realise, in the end, that I was treating Russia as I did Scotland. I was working for my own benefit, not for theirs. And if I couldn't do better, it would be wrong to go back.'

'You could do better. You could help them,' she said.

'No,' he said. 'It needs someone else.'

He had never spoken like that in her hearing before. She did not know what to do. She drew breath and went on, as evenly as she could.

'Poland, then? Or the Black Sea? Or Persia? Or Africa? I hear that Benecke is waiting for you to join him. I even hear talk of Jordan de Ribérac sending ships to the gold coasts from Portugal.'

She didn't know why she even mentioned him: Nicholas wasn't going to talk about Jordan de Ribérac. As it was, the strain in her manner drew his attention. 'You wouldn't enjoy sailing with Benecke,' Nicholas said. 'He drinks, and gambles, and is seduced into subversive activities, and takes pretty women to bed without considering what it would do to them, or their lives. I don't know where I shall go. You would have to help me choose that, as well.' He broke off, the tortured levity evaporating from his voice, and made a small gesture which she recognised, disconcerted, as one of helplessness. 'It's too uncertain. You don't know me. How can you decide?'

She moved thoughtfully then, sliding her hands from the polished wood, turning from the post to the stairs where he sat.

He stood.

Gelis said, 'I'm not sure.' She could not say why she was not sure. Or she could, but she was afraid. Her voice sounded steady. She held his gaze, her own eyes open and clear, so that he might know he could trust the channel between them, and that it was not unfriendly. His face, which had been drained of expression, slowly changed, and he looked at her differently, with understanding and patience, as if she had been Jodi. Her eyes filled.

He said, 'Of course. There are two rooms. Sleep tonight, Gelis. We can talk in the morning.' A dimple trembled, in an unattended way; oddly forlorn.

She hesitated, one hand fingering the cloak at her breast. He stepped down to where she stood and taking her fingers, set them formally to his lips. Then he released her and walked into the hall, where he looked up, with both smiling dimples, deep as coins.

'Good night, Monna Donnina.'

'Good night, Nicholas,' Gelis said.

They had not touched, except for that moment. He had kissed her on the boat, swiftly, as they confronted danger together. *Sweetheart,* he had said to her there. But not here, where a lifelong decision required to be taken without arousing those fires; for fires burn out, unless they are fairly tended, and fuel by itself is not enough.

She left him.

HE WAS VERY TIRED, and his bruises ached beneath the torn clothes he had not yet had a chance to change for the others, above. He listened to her weary footsteps climbing the stairs, followed by a small pause. Then a door shut. From the sound, he knew that it was not that of the room he had taken.

He turned aside, and ranged through the hall and into the little parlour of the Sersanders house now owned by Adorne. There was nothing in it that spoke to him of Kathi, to whom he owed the key, and the loving gift of this night. A gift which, however empty its outcome, would perform one office at least: it would close, one way or another, the wound he had borne for the last eight years of his life.

The room was small, but he dared not sit, for fear of falling asleep. He thought, and sighed and smiled at the thought, that Adorne would have to purchase a larger house for Kathi's expanding family. He felt no misgivings about Robin; only thankfulness that the quicksilver mind had found a wise young protector and shield.

He thought of Anna, and of what lay ahead, and wondered, suddenly, whether he could go on. He was not alone. Whatever they thought of him personally, Diniz, Moriz, Tobie and the rest seemed united in their resolve to help deal with Anna. But he alone was of the same blood as Anna; and must bear the onus of what was to happen to her, and to Julius, arriving tomorrow.

But of course, there was no alternative. Only the poor in spirit were permitted that kind of choice, as a sop.

He left the lamp in the hall and, stumbling a little, climbed the stairs to the top, where a half-consumed candle was set. There had been two. She had carried the other into her room.

He turned to his own room, where the open door showed him a lamp dutifully tended, and his cold bed already prepared. He realised only then that the other door was ajar.

He stood, frightened. Within, a low, golden light flickered over the carpet, and a chest with some silver stuff on it, although he could not immediately connect it with Gelis. He could see the platform of the bed, and the end-posts, with the cloth gathered back. He took three halting steps to the doorway, and stopped.

At first, he could see only darkness. Then he distinguished the white of the pillow, and the blur of her fair hair, loose upon it. Her breasts were curved and bare where the old, soft sheet crossed them, and below, the linen rested on the firm, breathing shapes of her body. Her eyes were deep in shadow, and open.

He walked over, and stepped up, and knelt; and she lifted her arms, touching his face tenderly with her palms, before she pressed him down to the crook of her shoulder. He smelled her scent, a girl's scent from long ago, breathing from a skin sleek and smooth as a girl's. His body remembered it first. She said softly, 'I am sure. Forgive me, as I forgive you for much less.'

He lay without speaking, and her fingertips passed and repassed through his hair. Then he raised his head, drawing away to rest on one elbow to view her, but also to let her see him as he was: defenceless; his guard melted away in the torrent of relief. But the relief was adult, not childish; and when he spoke, the words were both adult and formal.

'I have carried your hurts along with my own, and I think you have done the same with mine. We are both to blame, and we have both suffered for it.' Then he bowed his head and said, 'Is it ended?'

She had lifted herself a little to meet him. She laid her arms round his shoulders, and her head against his. 'Yes, it is ended. If you want it to end. If you want me.'

He said, 'I think . . . there is not much doubt of that.' He could hear his own breathing, and hers.

But she was not ready yet. Her hands slid down, and she held him by the upper arms, facing her, while her eyes examined his face. 'Why did you say I don't know you? God knows, once it was true, but surely not now. And surely, you know me now, too.'

He said, 'We are not the same as we were.'

'We shouldn't deserve each other if we were,' Gelis said. 'It's not given to many people to choose again after eight years.' She paused and said, 'I want no one else. I never will.'

He hesitated. 'But you weren't sure?' he said at last.

She flushed. The colour spread from her cheeks to her throat and below, where the sheet had fallen away. She said, 'I was sure of my feelings. But what if I am not the right person for you? Perhaps there is someone better.'

He rose to his feet, looking down at her. Her hands dropped from his arms and she sank back on the pillows, a smile fixed on her lips. She had exceptional courage. He had always known that.

Nicholas bent, and taking the sheet by the edge, turned it slowly back to the foot of the bed. Gelis said nothing and neither did he, as the light followed his hand, and his eyes travelled, too, over the veined breasts and delicate rib-arch and curved belly and thighs. He pulled the sheet free of the slender shin bones and narrow feet and let it drop.

She lay trembling and, looking down at her, he knew that he had come to the end of a long road. He said, 'There is no one better. I have what I want. Sweetheart, do I have leave?'

And then the smile was a real one, and her relief and her tears were the same as his own as she joined him on the step and said, 'Stop shaking. Yes, of course. Let me help you.'

His clothes, fortunately, were in tatters, and easily shed, and the sheet was already turned back. She stepped up, and then leaned out and brought him beside her.

It was eight years ago, and he was walking the streets, drunk with happiness, exploding with lust, on his way to bed the fierce lover who was now truly his bride. *Don't let go all at once,* she had cried to him then.

He must have said the words aloud, for Gelis repeated them now, in his arms, and then revoked them in the same breath.

'Let go now. Let go, Nicholas. You are home.'

He could not sing, with his labouring breath, but he remembered the song of that night, and whispered the words before thought and reason both fled.

Crions, chantons . . .

Bien vienne.

Chapter 42

JULIUS OF BOLOGNA arrived, thrashing a lathered horse, late the following day, attended by Diniz Vasquez and a hard-riding escort from the Hof Charetty-Niccolò, Bruges.

Julius had ridden to Bruges to find Nicholas gone. Worse, they had taken him aside, in the familiar house where he had worked for Marian de Charetty, and told him a tale about Anna, his wife. He had received the so-called revelation with an ashen horror which escalated into paroxysms of angry disbelief, and had now borne that incredulous fury all the way back to Ghent. Reaching the Gruuthuse mansion, he demanded his wife be set free, and obscenely derided the claim that she did not want to see him. Removed, with apologetic restraint, by Diniz's men, Julius had next demanded to be taken to Nicholas de Fleury.

It had been inevitable. Wodman had agreed — had indeed, told Diniz where to go. The hammering on the front door of the Sersanders house should not have been unexpected, unless to a dreaming man in the arms of his lover, claimed by sleep after a night which had begun at the dark edge of day, and had moved from term to term in different conditions of happiness, the greatest happiness being that there were so many as yet untried.

Nicholas had risen, at one point, to descend and speak to Adorne's housekeeper. He had returned, a little flushed, with beer and bread and some fruit. He had sent a message to the Hof Ten Walle, to satisfy Clémence that Jodi's mother would soon be returning, and his father, as well. She would know, of course, from Wodman and Marguerite van Borselen what had happened. She would not know what had happened today.

Then the banging came to the door.

Someone woke him with a snowfall of kisses. He ignored the banging, in the modest surge of reviving ideas.

'No,' said Gelis. 'No. No. It will be Julius.'

They were clothed, just, by the time the door to the bedchamber crashed open. It hardly mattered, even though Gelis sat, and he stood by the window. Nicholas could imagine how it all looked; the strewn chamber; their ruffled hair and enlarged eyes and flushed skin. Love, *that irrational passion that diminishes a man's responsibility for his actions,* as the laws of Venice maintained. And quite rightly, too.

Anna. Nicholas looked at Julius, shouting, and remembered what it had been like, eight years ago, when Gelis, young and maddened, had cheated him. This was different. But whatever happened, Julius's life was being sundered today.

Julius was crying: that was the first shocking thing: far worse than seeing the half-unsheathed sword he was trying to draw, hindered by Diniz and one of his soldiers. It was evident that he no longer wished to challenge Nicholas to a duel, but simply to kill him. It was not even a furious regenesis, Nicholas thought, of the husbandly outrage in Moscow. Julius now looked possessed: a man who would not believe, could not believe what he had been told of his wife, and who could only expunge what had happened by violence. It hardly mattered, now, whom he killed. At the moment, he wished to annihilate Nicholas.

On the face of it, there was reason enough. Had Diniz and Gelis not known what they did, they might have been convinced by Julius's incoherent accusations as he stood, pinned by the arms before Nicholas, cursing him with a vocabulary never before applied to him by the good-natured, exasperated tutor, bear-leader, practical joker of their joint youth. Nicholas bore it; bore being addressed as offal, traitor and pervert; bore being castigated as a lecher who tried to excuse himself by blaming his victims.

Nicholas said nothing. It was Gelis who sprang to his side, and interrupted the flow. 'Julius. It is true. I was there. She tried to kill us.'

'So you say,' Julius said. 'So, of course, all the van Borselens will say, and Louis de Gruuthuse.'

'You should thank him,' Gelis said. 'Because of him, Anna was allowed to stay in his house, instead of in public custody. Julius, she committed these crimes. You didn't know. You are not to blame. But don't blame Nicholas either. He was her principal victim.'

'Anna. You called her Anna,' Julius said. 'So that at least isn't true. The lie that she isn't the Gräfin.'

He had stopped struggling, and Diniz had slackened his grasp. Nicholas wondered why Diniz had come, and not Father Moriz. Beside him, Gelis drew closer, and he felt the touch of her hand. Nicholas enfolded it with his own, astonished, thankful, stupidly conscious that he had brought Julius close to death, and now had what Julius had not. But this had to be done. Nicholas said, 'She married the Graf. But her real name is Adelina de Fleury.'

'No,' Julius said. He was shivering. He continued to shiver and exclaim while Nicholas spoke, as gently as he knew how, piling fact upon fact, calling upon Gelis and Diniz for corroboration. At length, Nicholas managed to speak uninterrupted. He said, 'Defend her if you will. She is your wife; she is lovely. But she is wicked. She wanted me dead. She persuaded the Genoese to stage the death of Ochoa, when she believed she had the secret of the gold, and she wanted to silence him. When you were both expelled from Moscow, she made the plan that went wrong, and killed de' Acciajuoli instead of me. Last night, she deliberately trapped Gelis, and would have disposed of us both, but for Wodman. She sent you out of the way, to leave her free to do it. But eventually, of course, she meant to kill you as well.'

Julius tore himself free, but not to attack. Instead, he dropped into a seat as if he could no longer stand. 'It isn't true,' he said. 'Or if she did try to hurt you, it was because you seduced her.' But his voice no longer rang with conviction.

'And Gelis?' Nicholas said. 'Why do you suppose Anna should so dislike her, in that case?' He paused, choosing his words. 'Anna's ambition led her to marry you, but she always wanted more than she had. If we did not exist, Gelis and Jodi and I, she would be heiress to everything that we had amongst us. If Jodi survived, she could control his fortune she thought, by wedding him to Bonne. She was greedy. But most of all, she wanted to revenge herself against me, and those I might be fond of. You were the victim.'

The slanting eyes frowned. 'But if Anna is who you say she is, they couldn't marry. Bonne and Jodi would be related.'

'So I agreed to the marriage,' Nicholas said. 'I knew it couldn't take place. I knew who she was.'

Beside him, he felt Gelis move. Diniz, his dark face drawn, took a breath. Nicholas looked only at Julius, whom he knew so very well. Julius said, 'You *knew*?'

'Could you have forgotten those eyes, once you had seen them? I was sure, but it was not hard to collect other proofs. All the small lies. Why would a woman so dark require to protect her skin from the sun? Why was so little known of her past? Then others searched, and found the facts we have told you.'

'You knew, and didn't tell me?' Julius said. It sounded, on the surface, disbelieving and hard. Beneath was something that in another man would have verged on the piteous.

'Would you have thanked me? Would you have believed me?'

'No,' Julius said.

'No. And I needed you to believe in the gold, because that was the only reason she protracted my life. The mythical gold, brought by Ochoa.'

'Mythical?' Diniz intervened. He looked dazed.

Nicholas said, 'Oh, it existed. But it never left Cyprus, until David de Salmeton dug it up. Ochoa's messages told me that. But Anna couldn't read codes, and it was easy to persuade her that the gold was coming, and once I used my password, she could have it. Then Caffa fell, and the excuse had gone, and I had to look for other ways to escape her. It may not feel like it, but you are lucky, Julius.'

'It doesn't feel like it,' he said. 'She wouldn't see me.' It was a cry.

'Because she is guilty. They will keep her guarded in private just now. But when the courts are free, and they have sorted what advantages to draw from it, she will suffer, Julius,' Nicholas said. 'If you condone what she did, you will suffer as well.'

Leather creaked; the brazier whispered. Julius said, 'What are you going to do?' There was no fight in him now.

'About Anna? I won't bear witness against her, if that's what you're asking,' Nicholas said. 'I'm afraid that there is enough evidence, in any case, without me.'

'So what are you going to do?' Julius repeated. He looked ghastly.

'Go away,' Nicholas said. 'Once I have found David de Salmeton and dealt with him. He will be in the Tyrol, they say, until the spring. He can't do any harm there.'

'I beg your pardon,' Diniz said. The formality grated, even though Nicholas had imposed it himself. Diniz said, 'De Salmeton isn't in the Tyrol. The Duke summoned the Earl of Buchan to Nancy. Hearty James expects to spend the winter in camp, and to try to negotiate with the Tyrol from there. He has de Salmeton with him.'

Nicholas stood still. The fate of Anna left his mind, as, slowly, the hand of Gelis also slipped from his clasp. David de Salmeton was in Nancy with Robin; with Tobie; with John. No wonder the elegant Master Simpson had left Ghent with such alacrity. He could return to find Nicholas, once he had disposed of those he ranked as Nicholas's friends. Robin, and Tobie, and John.

Nicholas was aware that Julius was watching him. He had no time to nurse Julius now. He said, 'Why the change of plan? Why should the Duke entertain a Scottish envoy in Nancy?'

'Because Buchan is royal,' Diniz said. 'And there is another guest, too. The King of Portugal is due at the end of the month. The Duke's cousin. That's why I'm here. I've been summoned to Nancy to interpret.'

Diniz was half Portuguese. The uncle of Diniz had been secretary to the Duke's Portuguese mother. The hated grandfather of Diniz, Jordan de Ribérac, was currently living under Portuguese dominion, unaware that David de Salmeton, whom he had dismissed, was embarked on a campaign of destruction.

Nicholas said, 'If the King of Portugal is going to Nancy, might he take your grandfather with him?'

'It is possible,' Diniz said. He shut his lips. Diniz would not care if Jordan de Ribérac died. Perhaps no one would. But, oh God, de Ribérac was not the only possible victim, in that war camp at Nancy, facing David de Salmeton. They were none of them fools, these former companions and friends of Nicholas de Fleury; but de Salmeton was vain, and vindictive, and clever. And in war, accidents occurred very easily.

Nicholas saw that Gelis was studying him. Her eyes, immense with fatigue, were empty of appeal, but not of love. Her hand had left his, freeing him. She understood; he did not need to explain; but, nevertheless, his eyes sought her forgiveness.

One night. They had had only one night. He could not even hope to see Jodi. After three years, he could not return to Jodi and leave him on the same day.

Nicholas turned to Diniz. 'When are you leaving?'

'Today,' the other man said. He was not a child any more. He was thirty, and watching Nicholas with curiosity now, aware of the complexities of what was happening.

'Will you take me with you?' Nicholas said. Julius stiffened. Nicholas looked at him.

Julius said, 'What about Anna?'

'What about her?' Nicholas said. 'She will be brought to justice. She will be better off if I am not there.'

'If she is who you say, she's your family,' Julius said. 'She married me because of you. Everything happened because of you. And now you are leaving me with this mess?' The petulant, self-centred Julius of old, beginning to return through the anger and anguish.

Nicholas said, 'I expect to come back. No one has said you need stay.'

'Where would I go? To Moscow? To Caffa? To face Anna's noble kinsmen in Cologne?'

'You could come to Nancy,' Nicholas said. 'Astorre would welcome it. It would give you someone to fight, apart from Anna, and me, and yourself.'

'I went to Bruges to challenge you,' Julius said. He rose slowly. Some of his colour had returned.

'So perhaps we should be seen to have a match,' Nicholas said. 'Decently supervised. On the way to Nancy, if you like. The fault was Anna's, not mine, but I wouldn't have you lose face for it in public. Will you come?'

Julius agreed.

Diniz took Julius off to his lodging. There was not much time, if they were to leave the same day. Then, and only then did Nicholas shut the door and turn back to where Gelis stood.

There was no recrimination in her face: only sadness. 'You are good with Julius,' she said.

'I know him. Can you forgive me?' he said.

'I know you, too. I told you,' she said. 'A sensible woman would say, These are grown men, down there with the Duke. They can defend themselves against David de Salmeton. He will come back. You can deal with him in the spring.'

He said, 'You haven't married a sensible man. I should have had to join Astorre anyway, sooner or later. Robin and Tobie are with him because of me. And now de Salmeton is there because of me, and because of—' He broke off, too late.

'Because of Jordan de Ribérac?' Gelis said.

He lost his breath. Then he said, 'What do you know?'

Her smile was one-sided, and wry. 'What Tilde told me. That when I was working against you, I was working for Diniz's grandfather. I didn't know. I never knew who the head of the Vatachino was. That doesn't excuse it.'

'I have done worse,' he said. He had come close, and was looking down at her, painfully. 'I wanted to tell you myself, at the right time.'

'This is the right time,' Gelis said.

'I know,' he said. 'I know, I know.' His eyes were blurred, for the sake of all the words that had reduced themselves to the five she had spoken. He said blankly, 'I have to go.'

She had tied her robe in haste. He untied it, and drew the soft pads of his fingers slowly over her skin, down and down. He said, in sudden anguish, 'Perhaps last night was wrong. It was wrong. I should have been patient.'

She took his hand where it rested. 'Is that what your fingertips tell you? Would you rather have waited? Would you rather have something to remember, or nothing? Then no more do I. If this is all there is,' Gelis said, 'I shall thank God for it.'

His fingers were travelling again: shivering now, they spread and smoothed back her robe, and then parted his own. He drew a long, steadying breath. 'It *is* a leave-taking,' he said. 'And therefore reposeful, and a little grave, and sparing of all undue exertion until . . . For as long as might be.'

'Desire with self-control,' Gelis said. 'As the classicists say.' Her tight-squeezed lashes were soaked.

His hands, circling, stroking, were bringing her inside his robe. He had to lengthen his breathing to speak. 'It should be easy,' he said, with soft bitterness. 'It should be easy. We have had eight years to learn.'

. . .

In these, the last days of the campaign at Nancy, it was Captain Astorre's crowning joy to find his lads collected about him again.

They were not precisely lads, except in relation to himself and elderly Thomas, his henchman. Captain Astorre was fifty-eight years old; and the oldest of them, his prized gunner John, was ten years younger than that. You could even say that the youngest, Robin, was not really his, although he had trained him for a spell on the Somme. But in the months he'd been here, the fellow had won a place in Astorre's esteem, that was true. Deft, hard-working, steady under attack, he had a nice way about him. A nice *deferential* way, unlike that of his old sparring partner, Dr Tobie. By God, before a certain battle in Italy, Tobias Beventini had never risked so much as a sore toe in battle. He'd made up for it since. Astorre had fought under Skanderbeg in Albania alongside Tobie.

Tobie and Robin had arrived in the cold of November. Next had come freezing December and trouble, of the kind you got when a war was petering out, and snow was threatening, and men were desperate to leave. But soon, the trouble had shrunk to its proper size, for one day the captain had been in the cookhouse, complaining, when Robin had burst through the door, bringing slush and snow and a freezing draught that nearly put out the fire in the oven. Then Robin had said, 'It's M. de Fleury.' And by God, young Claes had followed him in, with Diniz, the lad who directed the Bruges business with Gelis van Borselen, and last, had come the Widow's notary, Julius.

He still thought of them like that, even though Marian de Charetty was dead, and young Claes, who had married her, was now a broad-shouldered man in a mantle as big as a bear, who pulled off his fur cap and stared at him.

'You've got smaller,' said Claes.

'To fit my wages,' snapped Captain Astorre.

Then they had hammered each other on the back, and he had greeted the others.

The best of it was at night, when he had heard or deduced all their news (Claes had returned to his wife; the German Gräfin had proved the menace they took her for) and he was able to sit them down before a fire and a modified feast, and tell them about his war. It was, of course, due to end in a week or two. (Thomas had grunted.) The besieged Lorrainers in Nancy had now started to starve: the two months were up; their supplies were finished; and L'Enfant René had not returned with an army to save them, despite pawning the silver and scrounging a loan from Strasbourg and obtaining thousands of francs from the King of France on the quiet. The Swiss Confederation had authorised the young man to enroll mercenaries, but mercenaries had to be paid. No one would come. Nancy would have to surrender. (Thomas had grunted again.)

'You sound sorry,' said Claes.

'Well. The Swiss are great fighters,' had said Astorre. 'Their skirmishing, you might say, is a treat. But what with the weather and one thing and another, I suppose you would have to call a good formal battle a luxury. We've had some trouble getting powder from Luxembourg, and our food's a bit low. I'm glad you brought what you did. Mind you, I've seen better ducks.'

'Complaint noted,' Claes said. 'What about your own men?' He did all the speaking, Astorre noticed. Diniz was always quiet before Nicholas, and the lawyer sat looking upset. Tobie and John had said very little after the first shock of the trio's arrival. Then Claes said, 'You haven't mentioned David de Salmeton.'

'Little turd,' Astorre said. 'John and Tobie saw him: I was away the day he came through. They'll tell you what happened.'

'Came through?' Claes said.

It was Tobie who answered. 'Hearty James was only here for a day. Then he went off with an escort to Innsbruck, David de Salmeton with him. They've gone for the winter.'

'Good riddance,' said Astorre.

'How?' said Claes.

It had been the doctor again, who chose to answer. 'International string-pulling. Duchess Eleanor of the Tyrol is Scottish, royal, and a sister of the first wife of Wolfaert van Borselen. Wolfaert is a cousin by marriage of Gruuthuse. Anselm Adorne sheltered the Duchess's niece when she was exiled from Scotland, and one of the Duchess's friends is a Scots lady called Bel of Cuthilgurdy, who seems to have Andro Wodman at her service. David de Salmeton makes threats: prosecution is not entirely possible: steps are therefore taken to send him where he can do no harm — for the moment, at least.'

'Eleanor will feed him to the dogs,' Claes said. He sounded shaken. He laughed. 'I needn't have come back from Russia.'

'Of course you should,' Astorre said, glaring at him. 'Where should you be but here, like a man?'

Thomas, who once had the pleasure of bear-leading a girl half over Europe for Claes, allowed himself a snort at that. 'Or in someone else's bed like a man,' remarked Thomas.

Which was all very true, Astorre granted.

IN FALLING SNOW, intelligence freezes. Burgundy, shivering in its camp before Nancy, did not know that the cantons were slowly opening their borders; that from Lucerne and Zurich, Berne and Soleure and the depths of the Oberland, ten thousand soldiers for René were being brought to assemble in Basle, a week's march away; that several thousand more were beginning to collect in Alsace. In the Burgundian camp, they only knew that success appeared certain, for the town they were besieging was dying. In Nancy, all the horses and dogs, all the cats and the vermin would soon be finished; the breaches made by the Burgundian guns were growing larger; and the garrison's powder was practically done. There was no fuel for heat. The warmth came from the flames of their cannon-smashed houses, burning unquenched in a landscape of ice.

They did not surrender. Waiting, in the snow and the cold, the besiegers also started to suffer. Cut off from fuel and food, the weakening army, depleted since Grandson and Morat, depleted further by desertions, began to grow sullen and sick. While the Duke stormed about camp, taking the flat of his sword to grumblers, Tobie tramped from tent to tent with his box. In unoccupied moments, Nicholas and Diniz went with him. They had done this before, in Famagusta.

By then, Nicholas had achieved a footing for himself in the company, in appearance much the same as before, although perhaps more subdued, as befitted a man who had turned his back on them, and had now returned on a whim. His treatment by his own former partners was different, displaying a caution modified, no doubt, by the knowledge he wished they did not possess. They had the sense, at least, to keep their distance, even if Diniz had shown signs, since Ghent, of forgetting to do so. On his side, he made no advances. He could have turned round and gone home: David de Salmeton was threatening nobody. He did not.

Hardship and proximity sometimes brought about lapses. Checking the armoury with John, stiff-fingered, their breath congealing on their unshaven jaws, Nicholas had commented, once, on the clever disposition of tools. For a moment, John had continued, without speaking. Then, 'Your wife's idea,' he had said, glancing round. 'She's a remarkable woman.'

'I know,' Nicholas said. And while the other man faced him still, his nose red, his cheeks blue, Nicholas continued, 'And you made a bloody awful job of that frog. I had to put in two new bolts and a lever.'

John grunted, and returned to his work. He had not mentioned Adelina. No one had, since he had made his first, brief report, to save Julius from having to do so.

Julius and he rarely spoke, and the others were careful. In fact, the situation was a little better now than it seemed. Against his expectations, Julius had kept him to his word about a fight on the journey from Ghent. It had taken place, but with poles instead of swords; and although they were both shaken and stiff the following day, nothing serious happened. Julius had won.

That night, alone with Nicholas in the dark, Julius had suddenly spoken. 'Was Anna a whore? Did she sleep with others? Did she sleep with you?'

Nicholas had claimed as much, he recalled, in Tabriz. He had been angry with himself, as much as with Julius. Nicholas said, 'I have never lain with her. I have never touched her. I told you a lie.'

'But she asked you,' Julius said.

It would do no good, this time, to prevaricate. 'Yes, she did,' Nicholas said. 'It was part of the punishment, that was all. On the day she chose to destroy me, I was to be told who she was, and be appalled by what we had done together. Not that she was unwilling to get rid of me earlier, if chance offered.'

The other pallet had creaked. Julius spoke, with a kind of dull horror. 'If she was Adelina . . .'

'You know what happened to her as a child. And to me. It helped her, when she grew up, to blame me. She hoped to remind me of it all. Jaak and Esota. Adelina and me.' He did not enjoy speaking of it. He had never spoken of it before. It was true, so far as it went. But what had consumed Adelina as Anna, and what might have consumed him had he let it, was not a manufactured attraction. Between them, something had called. That was where the tragedy lay.

After that, Julius had been silent, and in the days that followed, had not raised the subject again. But although he was remote, he was no longer an enemy. He was a man wrestling with anger and doubts, who had a new future to find.

Nicholas accordingly left him alone. But Robin sometimes rode at his side during the short daylight hours, dark with buffeting snow and crowded with difficult work: the incessant scouting and foraging; the short, fierce clashes with outlying marauders; the daily detail assigned to road-clearing and barricades, and to the securing and rationing of food and ice-melted water. The forgework on horseshoes and armour. The repairs to the freezing, splitting fabric of the camp and its furnishings, and the task to which all the rest appertained: the slow, sparing firing of cannon at Nancy's crumbling walls so that the Lorrainer marksmen were reduced, and quiet and sleep were impossible. And meanwhile, the besiegers had to be seen to: to be kept in health, to be heartened and exercised.

In a month, Robin had somehow absorbed the sense of all that, and could be seen to be what he was, which was not a merchant nor even a squire, but a man to whom a battlefield was a natural place to be: a place of orderly management, with corresponding opportunity for the quick-witted, and excitement, and perhaps glory. He was good with other men. With Nicholas, he spoke only of war, gleaning from him all he could tell of foreign countries and weapons and tactics. He said, once, stopping himself apologetically, 'I'm sorry. You must be sick of it, sir. But I can't believe that I'm here, and with you.'

'And when it is over?' Nicholas had said.

And Kathi's husband had said immediately, 'What will you do? Surely they will let you stay now? You could take this army anywhere.'

With Tobie and Diniz, who were not enchanted with war, there was a hardening of perception as the snow thickened and the degree of privation increased. By then, Nicholas had had his ducal audience in the Commanderie, and had visited the Bastard Anthony and his brother and the other captains — de Bièvres, Lannoy and de Chimay, Jacques Galeotto and Josse de Lalaing. Diniz Vasquez had been in garrison once in North Africa with the Grand Bastard and Baudouin, and Simon de Lalaing and his son.

Because of his Portuguese blood, Diniz saw more of the Duke than the rest, and he had come to act as alternating conduit and buffer between Tobie and his Burgundian counterpart, the doctor from the Duke's mother country of Portugal. Matteo Lope came from the frontier stronghold of Guarda, and was not unfamiliar with the Vasquez plantations on Madeira. Nicholas, making time to accompany the physicians; warding their chain of supplies; executing, without being asked, the worst and most squalid of tasks, was an unexpected, poignant reminder of the same man among the starving in Cyprus, succouring the dying behind the walls of a besieged city, instead of before them.

It caused Diniz, returning soaked from one such round, to burst out, as he had not done for years, against the horror and waste of siege warfare. It led Nicholas, unthinking, to set aside his own rules and try to explain the work of Fioravanti, so that John, engrossed, plunged into the talk. For a moment, the air was full, in the old way, with ideas and objections and counter-objections until Nicholas suddenly excused himself, and left.

Tobie had followed him out into the smothering snow, and across to the stables, where he had begun to talk to the horse-master. He showed no sign of particular stress; opening his stance as he spoke to include Tobie. Leaving, he walked down the lines, and Tobie walked with him. Tobie said, 'You must be used to this cold.'

'Cold with discipline, yes,' Nicholas said. 'Unregulated cold is more troublesome. I wanted to make rapturous noises about Clémence. She risked her life for Gelis in Ghent. You know how she cared for her and for Jodi, and kept me informed. I want you to separate so that I can marry her.'

'From what I hear,' Tobie said, 'you are already devastatingly accommodated, although you don't seem to appreciate it. What are you doing here? David de Salmeton has gone.' They had come to the end of the building, and he stopped. A horse blew on his shoulder.

Nicholas said, 'The King of Portugal has still to come.' His eyes rested on Tobie's face.

'And you think he will bring Jordan de Ribérac,' Tobie said. On the other man's face, lightly bearded, was the ghost of the scar given by the vicomte de Ribérac to Claes vander Poele, born to the wife of his son and repudiated. Tobie said, 'If he comes, will you kill him? He led the Vatachino. Kathi told us what Wodman said to you about that.'

Nicholas said, 'That isn't why I am here. Did you really think that it was?'

'I don't know,' Tobie said. He hesitated, and then made up his mind. 'Did Gelis tell you what . . . what Thibault de Fleury said of de Ribérac?' Carefully, he had said neither *your grandfather*, nor *your other grandfather.*

His dilemma had been noted. 'How difficult it all is,' Nicholas remarked. Then he suddenly seemed to relent. 'I should like to hear, some day, about Thibault de Fleury; but not perhaps now. I'm glad that you went. It can't have been easy.' He waited and then said, 'But you want to say something?' He looked patient rather than anxious.

'Jordan de Ribérac threatened the Charetty family,' Tobie said. 'You were to be reared as an apprentice, or you and they would all suffer. Marian educated you, without de Ribérac realising it. She sent you to Louvain with her son, knowing that as Felix's servant you would learn as much as he did. In the end, as we know, she defied him. That was when you were given your scar.' The horse pushed at him, and he ignored it.

'I see,' Nicholas said.

'I thought you should know,' Tobie said. He paused. 'Before we go back. Did you mean to kill Julius?'

Nicholas laid his hand on the prodding nose of the horse. 'I regularly mean to kill Julius,' he said. 'I usually manage to restrain myself, but not then. I had been divining. I was not on very good terms with myself afterwards. But for that, I might have used force against Anna.'

'But you didn't,' Tobie said curiously.

'No. I didn't try to kill her,' Nicholas said. 'I left it to others. I left her in Caffa, knowing that it was going to fall.'

'Knowing?' Tobie said.

'Oh, yes. I spent some time and effort analysing what was going to happen to Caffa,' Nicholas said. 'The Khan would confirm. But I didn't tell Anna. Nor, I'm afraid, the Genoese.'

'I think,' said Tobie, 'that I would have done the same.' He stood looking at Nicholas. He said, 'Despite Astorre, I don't think we are going to be home for Christmas.' It was a grim joke. Christmas was two days away.

On Christmas Day, a hundred men died in the Duke of Burgundy's camp before Nancy, frozen to death by the cold.

On the same day, a short way to the south, an enemy force of eight thousand men scaled the range of the Vosges, and prepared to cross the plateau which would take them to Nancy. Three days after its departure, René's Swiss army also moved out. The King of Portugal, on his way from Paris through Rheims, was then exactly four days away.

IN GHENT, despite some natural disappointment that the Duke was not present, the Christmas festival was extravagantly splendid that year, with bonfires in every street, and skating parties on the canal, and coloured lanterns and bells and the making of pretty snow figures, dressed to look like the lady Marie and her Imperial betrothed. Sugar pastries and wine were sent by the Duchess to all the almshouses. It was assumed that, whether or not Nancy had surrendered, the Duke had retired for the winter.

In the Hôtel Gruuthuse, the Gräfin Anna von Hanseyck (as she still called herself) renounced her fast and began eating again, as if she thought there was something to live for.

In Scotland, Bel of Cuthilgurdy spent the festival with her son, but seemed pre-occupied.

In the Casa di Niccolò, Venice, the director Gregorio and his wife sustained the quiet success of their Bank and their marriage, and tried not to diminish the joys of the season for the sake of their son. Nevertheless, for them, and for a short-sighted Italian in Poland, and a capable monk in Cairo, it was a time for troubled reflection.

In the Hof Charetty-Niccolò, Bruges, the wife of Diniz hid her fears from her sister, cherished her children, and was shaken to find how much she welcomed the arrival, unheralded, of Gelis van Borselen with her son and the doctor's wife, Clémence. Gelis, in her turn, seemed disconcerted by the warmth of her reception, and later, quite unexpectedly, broke into tears. Father Moriz, deploying for once a kindly attitude to his household of young women, found himself in silent contemplation of a number of considerations, none of them to do with the holy season he was supposed to be celebrating. He wished (to God) he had someone sensible to talk to, like Tobie.

In the same town, Anselm Adorne celebrated Christmas by re-opening the Hôtel Jerusalem for the season, and inviting his deserted niece Kathi, her nurse and her children to stay. Naturally, Dr Andreas was also present, but Adorne drew the line at young Nerio, while sorry for whatever reverse he had suffered. He himself had been out of spirits since the departure of his quiet friend from Haddington, the Earl of March's unmarried daughter Phemie. It irritated him when Kathi, on the heels of some tiff with Dr Andreas, began to spend time with de

Fleury's family in Spangnaerts Street. One should never fall out with astrologers.

In Moscow, a philosophical Franciscan made the most of his time and, despite what he had said, occasionally thought, with mild approval, of the soles of his sandals.

Christmas passed.

ON SUNDAY, the twenty-ninth day of December, the Duke of Burgundy's cousin, Alphonse V, King of Portugal, entered the stricken Burgundian camp and rode with his chilled but magnificent train into the grounds of the Commanderie of St John before Nancy. His noble object, all knew, was to implore his cousin to please God and put an end to his fighting. His less noble object, all knew, was to end the French–Burgundian war so that he might obtain French assistance for an urgent small war of his own.

The Duke received him, putting on the table food he could not spare, and warming the gold-lined pavilion with braziers which might as well have been burning flesh and bone. Diniz Vasquez was called to interpret.

The discussions lasted two days. No matter how pointed his enquiries, no one in the company of Captain Astorre was able to discover the exact composition of the royal train. John and Tobie, who had profound reason to dislike the part played in their past by the Vatachino, expressed their frustration. Nicholas, whose concern ran a great deal deeper, preferred not to share it with either Tobie or John.

Finally, a statement emerged. The Duke, to his regret, had been unable to agree to an immediate peace, but had invited his cousin to shorten the war by leading a body of men to defend a pass for him. The King had excused himself, and was leaving immediately for Paris. It was the last day of the year, and the snow had begun falling again.

Diniz reappeared, looking worn, and tramped in his soaked boots and caked cloak straight up to Nicholas. 'He didn't come. Not de Ribérac himself, nor my uncle. The vicomte isn't in Madeira or Portugal. He's got leave to go back to Kilmirren.'

Nicholas looked at him. He said, 'What did you think you were going to do? He is your grandfather.'

'I hate him,' said Diniz. He flung off his cloak.

'I rather wanted to see him myself,' Nicholas said. 'But now it doesn't really matter. You heard the bells ringing from Nancy? It seems some acrobatic friend has managed to climb in and tell them that the Duke of Lorraine is on his way with an army big enough to reduce us to sherbet. It's a pity. Now they will never surrender. But at least Astorre will be able to say he's fought with the Swiss.'

'Oh, Christ,' Tobie said. 'We've no army. Out there, you could hardly count two thousand fit men.'

'It's ironic, really,' Nicholas said. 'I came to find de Salmeton and de Ribérac, and they're both lolling somewhere in luxury while I'm stuck here with you. Well, come on. We might as well make the best of it. Who'll take a wager on what Campobasso is going to do next?'

Chapter 43

FOR ALL THE MEN of the company founded by Marian de Charetty, the acute and mischievous spirit that drew them through the few days that followed was that of Claes, Marian's husband. Claes, the gifted fool in adversity; Nicholas the man, who knew what now depended on him, and dedicated himself to salvaging what he could.

He could not alter the heavy folly of the Duke their commander, deaf to the appeals of his council to recoil and methodically rebuild his army, allowing the advancing forces to enter and reinforce Nancy, in the hope that they would then turn back themselves. René's troops were twice his in number, but these were undisciplined louts, not the drilled Swiss of Grandson and Morat, inspired to protect their homeland at all costs. Once the pay began to fail, they would go.

None could influence the Duke, who derided such counsel and castigated his advisers as cowardly Frenchmen at heart. Nicholas could, however, expect to share the plans and the intelligence of those senior commanders who, weary but loyal, were thus being exposed to useless death. He could take part, with Astorre, in the devising of contingency plans, and he could return, with reservations perhaps of his own, and work over those plans with Astorre and the company. And because, in that lethal cold, the Charetty company was better drilled and cared for and nourished than most, the men responded. They responded to Astorre, whom they reviled and worshipped and trusted. They responded to the knowledgeable orders, the cracking speed, the bawdy jokes of young Claes, who had travelled the world and knew a thing or two. They knew they could depend on their chiefs.

He was forced to sacrifice John, as was inevitable, to the central artillery. They parted with no more than a feinted blow and, this time, a genuine smile.

He forfeited Diniz, unexpectedly, to the Duke, who had become disillusioned with Italians and Flemings and wanted a few soft-spoken, black-haired, reliable Portuguese, or even half-Portuguese, at his elbow. Diniz had looked distraught. 'It's all right,' Nicholas had said. 'You're our strongest weapon. Just keep him from doing anything.'

But while he was speaking, the gleaming blocks of armed foot and the jogging columns of cavalry with their plumes and their banners were already pricking their way across the white hills and through the snow-laden forests, their drums ticking, their commanders' cries frail as claw-marks in the snow. The Lorrainers, the Alsatians, the Swiss, marching to do battle with Burgundy.

ON THE FIRST SATURDAY of the New Year, Charles of Burgundy broke his camp before Nancy and, leaving a holding force to maintain the siege, personally led the residue of his troops to a position just south of Nancy. Before and behind the chosen site were small streams. To the left was a river, the Meurthe. To the right was the forest of Saurupt. The army was then split into three, with the Duke's corps of three thousand in the centre, and those of Galeotto and Lalaing on his left and right. The artillery stood before them all, on the edge of the deep little brook of the Jarville, and facing the way to the pilgrimage town of St Nicholas-de-Port, René's base.

The mercenary company of the Count of Campobasso was not there. That same fourth of January, having been turned down by France, Campobasso cast off his cross of St Andrew and deposited his two sons and three hundred cavalry into the opposite camp of Duke René, where he assumed the double white cross of Lorraine.

Above René's encampment that night, a beacon of assembly glimmered pink in the flake-spattered darkness, and candied his white-humped pavilions. In the Burgundian camp, edged by snow-burdened forest and treacherous swamps, the Duke of Burgundy repeated what he had already said of the Count. He had heard the news. In the right time and place, he would deal with it.

'Well?' said Astorre. The ill-chosen site, the inflexible disposition of the artillery, the lack of good scouts had been a subject of recrimination since dawn, and no one had been able to prevail upon the Duke to amend any of it. Those in the central block, such as themselves, were understandably jumpy.

'Well?' Nicholas said. 'He probably will deal with it, once he's sent for an astrologer. Meanwhile, we know what the chances are. We do what we can. There isn't much option: the bastard has left us nowhere to run to.'

'We've got Metz to run to,' said Thomas. 'Except that we can't cross them damned little tributaries. And Nancy's in the way.'

'We noticed that,' Julius said. With danger, he had come to life for the first time since Ghent. 'Of course, they'd do it better in Poland . . .'

Groans.

'Or Russia,' Nicholas offered. 'Remember, Julius? You trap and saddle a bear, and it carries you right through the swamps, and catches and cooks your fish for you in the evenings.'

'Those were the white bears,' Julius said. 'The black ones did your washing as well.'

'And as for the pink ones . . .' began Robin, carried away. But Nicholas, keeping the grin on his face, had ceased to listen. Bears. Besse, in Iceland. To do something without leave was to do something *with permission of Besse*. In Russia, the Besy were evil spirits. Until he went to Russia, he had not known how close to Iceland it was.

Anyway, it was time to break up the talk and get everyone working. Tomorrow, he knew — they all knew — the confrontation with René must come. It was a Sunday: Mass would be said before dawn by the Duke's chaplain. That was all right, but Nicholas wished it had been someone else. Godscalc, for example. What would he have made of all this? What would he have made of all Nicholas had done, all he had become, perhaps, over these years? There was not very much, he supposed, to approve of, except that he had begun to stop and confront certain things, instead of escaping from them. He had begun to listen in order to learn, instead of to turn the knowledge back for his own advantage.

Going about his business that evening; lying through the short, wakeful hours of the night, Nicholas continued to follow the thread of that thought. It led him to dwell on his tutors: all those men and women who had believed him worth moulding and guiding. Godscalc, of course. But before that — before everyone — Marian, whose company was with him tonight, and to whom he owed everything. And who else from the past? Bessarion; and in his odd way Ludovico da Bologna, whom he now understood. The lecturers, the orators he had listened to, travelling through Germany, in Trebizond, at Louvain. The great men of Africa: Katib Musa, and latterly, the imam Ibrahiim, who had taught him to think about death. Umar, the gentle jurist whose loss he was learning to bear. Brother Lorenzo. Callimaco in Poland, and Gregory. The essential wisdom of Josaphat Barbaro, and of women like Clémence, and Bel, and Eleanor of the Tyrol. The perception of Willie Roger, who had introduced him to music. The strange dominion of Nicholai de' Acciajuoli, who had presented him with the gift of his life. The men around him.

The woman he had just taken again, to where she had always belonged. And the other extraordinary spirit, whom he must not think of, but whose husband was his to keep safe, if he could.

He felt Tobie's gaze, from his pallet, but the doctor did not speak. Instead, Nicholas turned his head in the dark, with a half-smile. 'Thank you. Everything is all right.'

Then it was morning.

JOAN OF ARC had once prayed in the basilica where Duke René heard Grand Mass that Sunday. By eight, the trumpets had blown, and the young Duke, in cloth of gold over his armour, rode his grey mare La Dame through the soiled snow towards Nancy at the head of twenty thousand armed men: foot and cavalry; lances, halberdiers and hackbutters; gunners with their artillery pieces. His banner, representing the Annunciation, was painted with the figure of Gabriel. The snow had stopped, and the cold had lifted a trifle with the coming of day.

There were only eleven miles to cover to Nancy. As they marched, René's men picked off the enemy scouts and dispatched their own to view the Burgundian dispositions. Two hours before noon, the army drew to a halt while the commanders conferred, deferring naturally to René, who was the grandson of that other René, and no fool. The strategy for the day was drawn up.

Just after noon, in the course of a light shower of snow, the Duke of Burgundy's artillery perceived a strong detachment of the enemy advancing towards the double hedges of the Jarville gulley before them. The Burgundian artillery fired, but were unable to align their guns to the greatest effect, and most of the balls flew too high. They began to reload, while the centre and wings of the Burgundian army swung to the right, preparing for orders to wheel.

If any were given, they were not heard. The wood of Saurupt, on the right, emitted two long, mournful bellows and, stretching, flung off its snow. The cries, three times repeated, were from the brazen throats of the bull and cow of Uri and Unterwalden, the two gross Swiss horns which had already shaken the air at the battles of Grandson and Morat. And from the trees which had screened them plunged a yelling horde of enemy horsemen, borne on a cloud of smoke sparkling with hackbut fire. Their own momentum took them shearing into the right flank of the Burgundians, killing Josse de Lalaing; and although his men stood the shock and even fought back, it was not for long, and the Burgundian flank gave way to flight, opening the way to the centre.

There, Astorre's company had already seen the frontal attack under Duke René himself surging over the guns, destroying them, and taking the gunners, John le Grant among them. Another Jarville detachment hurtled into the left Burgundian wing under Galeotto, which held, fighting furiously, until thrown back by superior numbers. Led by Galeotto, now wounded, his company ranged the half-frozen Meurthe until they could cross at Tomblaine and fly north.

Astorre, beset from the front and the side and whacking furiously with his sword, could be heard to shriek that he didn't blame him. The cry *Sauve qui peut!* had gone up, and three-quarters of Charles of Burgundy's force was in flight. The only section still furiously engaged was that which surrounded Duke Charles himself, a frenzied figure on a frenzied black horse. The Duke had taken L'Enfant's attack as a personal affront, to be requited immediately, regardless of injury, death, or what it would cost the duchy in ransom if he got himself captured. The noise was now a continuous thunder, cleft by the dashing of metal. Twenty horns could not have penetrated it.

Nicholas bellowed, 'Astorre?' and saw the ludicrous helm, in a cloud of sparks, turn to acknowledge him. It was time. This was one of the contingencies that had not been hard to envisage. Sick and under-nourished and cold, the disillusioned survivors of the Duke's once-great armies were not going to stand and fight against a fresh force twice their size, which would take none but valuable prisoners. Yet, while the two wings of the main army had fled and the centre was crumbling, his own company was virtually intact, and fighting still as a disciplined unit. He had watched John overwhelmed, but he could still see the serviceable helms and borrowed livery of Diniz and Julius, the battered armour of Tobie, who ought not to be there, and the prodigious plumes of Captain Astorre and Thomas. He knew Robin in his fine-cut bright steel was untouched, because he had never let him out of his sight.

Nevertheless, if they lingered, they would die or be captured. It was time to deploy them, and save them. Nicholas saw Astorre cast one wistful look ahead to where the banner of Gabriel flounced over the massed grey, white and red of Duke René's colours. Given a chance, there might have been real Swiss to fight; and Campobasso's renegade troops to tackle and thrash. But not today.

Through all the madness, the great nobles and the men of his own house had fought to protect Charles of Burgundy, adhering to him, matching his impetuous dashes as he flung his horse from one side to the other. Now the foot and horse of Astorre's company swept up to join them, so that, briefly, a barrier was formed between the Burgundian centre and the host of rearing horses and driving spears that surrounded them. Then they set to engineering a fierce, fighting withdrawal alongside the Burgundian leaders, the Duke in their midst. Shortly, their rearguard covered, they were able to wrench free from the thick of the battle, dividing according to plan, so that it was not immediately clear where the Duke himself was. They carried no colours.

Escape, in that trampled ground full of half-frozen morasses, was never going to be easy. The broken army fleeing before them had only three chances: to strike north and west to the forest of Haye; or north across the tributaries of the Meurthe; or across the Meurthe itself, by the route which led to the Duke's towns of Metz, and then Luxembourg.

That crossing, at the bridge of Bouxières-les-Dames, was the one the Duke was to take, and the honour of racing ahead to secure it fell to Astorre's men. He took half the company with him, and Thomas, leaving Julius to lead one half of what was left, and Nicholas the other. Astorre rode up, his sewn eye scarlet with pride, his sword at the salute, to take leave of his Duke, who lifted his sword in response as he rode. Nicholas saluted the captain as well, raising his arm to the men at his back. Then the little force had spurred off like demons. The bridge was five miles away.

'A happy man,' Julius said, looking after Astorre. 'They'll give him a province to govern.'

'He wouldn't mind that,' Nicholas said. 'He might get a bit bored, once he's trained the cooks and had all the girls.' But there wasn't much time to talk, because the riding was so hard and the enemy troops, now in frank pursuit, were coming up between them and the river. Shortly after that, Nicholas sent Julius's contingent, with Tobie, to try to take the forest route. There was no sense in wasting men. And he didn't like what was happening.

A rout is not a pleasant thing. It was no advantage to be well-mounted when overtaking hundreds of staggering men and packs of riderless horses whose fallen owners were already half drowned in their armour. The plan had been to lead the Duke back through the depleted camp before Nancy, but a group of desperate riders warned them against it. Dying Nancy, swiftly apprised of the victory, had already opened its portals, and sent its people, to the sound of carillons, to hack through the Burgundian tents and carry back anything that could be devoured. The Duke's own household had already gone, taken prisoner in the tents before Jarville.

It was hardly two hours after midday and the light was failing; the skies darkening moment by moment with promise of renewed snow.

There was no word from the bridge. The Duke's brothers, with a small party, rode off in the gloom to discover why, and did not return. A half-crazed soldier, lunging at the Duke's horse, caused it to throw its rider and canter back, in its jewelled housings, the way it had come — the famous Il Moro, prize enough to break up the first wave of pursuit. The Duke was pulled to his feet and stood glaring accusingly after it. His surcoat hung in shreds, leaving the bulk of his magnificent armour exposed, and his florid helmet lay burst on the ground, the golden lion knocked from its crest.

The horse that Nicholas was riding was one of Astorre's best, and he offered it. There was no time to shorten the stirrups. While the Duke was heaved into the saddle, Nicholas strove to catch himself a replacement, using the flat of his sword to fend off competitors. The fear-crazed mare that he stopped would have been hard enough to mount without the encumbrance of half-armour. The pair of strong hands that helped haul him up into place belonged to Robin. Nicholas filled his lungs, and said, 'Give me the sea and Paúel Benecke any day,' and saw Robin grin. Then they turned to rejoin the Duke as the snow started to fall, white as a spear-phalanx from the darkness above, white and pink on the terrain below, where it sank upon the last moments of the retreat and the first of the approaching carnage.

Nicholas had almost caught up with the Duke when his fate finally touched him. At first, he was merely intent on forging his way through to Charles. It was possible to see that de Bièvres, the best and most loyal of men, had taken command of the dozen noblemen still surrounding the Duke, with Diniz and the small band of Charetty soldiers beside them. De Chimay had gone. Someone had found a bright yellow sash and knotted it across the Duke's cuirass: an identification. A man cried, 'My lord!'

Nicholas knew him. The wounded man on the stumbling horse at his side was a squire of the Bastard's — the Duke's half-brother Anthony. The man said, 'I have to find my lord Duke. Is he there?'

'In front. What is it?' said Nicholas. He thought he could guess. He learned the truth as a sick man hears it from his physician. The Duke's brother Baudouin was captured. The Bastard Anthony was missing, and the son who had been with him was dead. They had been waylaid on the way to the bridge of Bouxières, the Duke's only safe exit to Metz. And the bridge, they now knew, was not open, or amenable to being occupied and secured by any company, however gallant, however determined, however well trained. The bridge had been blocked and manned for the last twenty-four hours by the Count of Campobasso and his three hundred mercenaries, avid for ransom.

Nicholas let the man spur off to the Duke. Robin said nothing. Around them, the air was white, the struggling figures grey flecked with white, the cries increasingly muffled. Nicholas said, 'He will have to try to make for the north, over the swamps. I can do no more for him.'

He did not say what he was going to do. He supposed he did not have to.

Robin said, 'I will come with you.'

The bridge of Bouxières should have been impossible to find, but was not. Nicholas rode as if his pendulum hung in the wild air before him: a pillar of light; the spindle of Necessity, whose daughters release souls to new lives, sending them spinning like stars to rebirth.

It was a certainty denied to the others floundering, plodding, hurrying in the dimness all around them. Many were injured, and destined to die, or to freeze in a swamp. Some of the invisible, fleeing army which filled the leagues between the Meurthe and the slopes by the forest knew that to the east and ahead, if they could find it, there was a bridge, a crossing that would take them over the river to safety. Others did not know where they were, or where they were going. No one could tell how close the enemy was, except that its cavalry was north of Nancy, and hence on their heels. And what was pursuing them was not a well-disciplined battle force under orders. It was an excited vanguard of Lorraine and Alsatian knights, some of them hoping for lucrative prisoners, some of them riding the chariots of joy, launched upon triumphant killing. And behind these would be the mountain irregulars, greedy only for the wealth of dead men; apt to kill a man for a button, unless he sported the cross of Lorraine.

A mile short of the bridge, the new dead began to appear underfoot, white as sheep, their blood still fresh on the snow. The first man Nicholas stopped by was a stranger. The second and third were Charetty men.

Robin said, 'It must be over. They would never have run, otherwise.' He cleared his throat. Other riders pounded heedlessly past them, either blind to the signs, or beyond fear. Through the snow, there was no sound of fighting.

'Campobasso's men pursued them to here, then returned to the bridge,' Nicholas said. 'Do you want to come with me?' Then he saw Robin's face and said, 'I'm sorry.'

Before they got to the bridge, they knew that the company Astorre had brought here was finished. Experienced, stubborn old warrior that he was, he was the last man to fall for an ambush. The signs were that he had tried a feint, and tested at least one way of getting across. Then he had, in his ebullient way, simply issued a challenge to battle. Had Campobasso's men been half the number, and battle-weary, he might have carried the bridge. As it was, he had achieved a fine, perhaps a satisfactory fight, and left his mark on the ambushers. There were more Italians than Charetty men among the bodies still piled round the approach to the crossing.

No one had come out yet to deal with the dead: it was more rewarding to trap the rich and throw into the part-frozen water the innocents attempting to cross, or to send out swift bands to round up those who held back. Two men could do nothing to retaliate, or not today. But they could, under cover of flurries of action, and God-given flurries of snow, number the fallen, and make sure that no one was living, and find at last, in the bloodiest heap, a broken-backed poke of red plumes and another of blue, which showed where Astorre and his henchmen had died, as they had irritably fought, side by side. Astorre's sewn eye was shut, but the other was open, fixed round and white in a final, ferocious wink.

Nicholas closed it. After a while Robin said, 'Sir.' And indeed, it was time to go. The hundred men lying here would be many times multiplied by the end of the day.

He did not even remember, afterwards, conferring over what they should do. He and the boy — Kathi's husband — simply turned and rode back to where they judged they might intercept Diniz and the Duke, and the men of their company — his company — who were now in his charge.

It was crazy, of course, because in turning back, they faced the last of the refugees and the first of the oncoming pursuit. It was more ludicrous still when he learned, from someone he knew, that the Duke was still south of Nancy, trapped in the marshy rectangle between streams, and attempting to cross to his old lodging at the Commanderie of St John. If the besieged men of Nancy had raided the Burgundian tents, they would surely have stripped the Commanderie. But there was only one way to find out.

It was only three hours after noon, and Nicholas felt as he had done in the past after many hours of hard riding and hand-to-hand fighting: his sword-hand swollen and aching, his body spent, his mind numb. This battle had lasted only minutes. It was the aftermath which bludgeoned and killed.

About that time, the sky lightened, and the snow stopped. They were then on the northern bank of a pool; part of the deep-trenched stream that took its name from the Commanderie and formed, with its parallel brethren, an icy and unforgiving barrier to the north. Some had successfully crossed: the snowy sides were gouged black by their trail. Others had not. The lighter bodies adhered to the slopes; those more expensively armed had slipped into the trough and lay, submerged or embraced by the water, which was already congealing about them.

On the edge of the pool, one of the bodies wore a bright yellow sash.

Robin cried 'No!' and dropped with a thud from his horse. Mounted, he might have been safe. But the cry and the flash of his cuirass drew the attention of the scavenging soldiers now streaming up to the far side of the ditch. One of them lifted a crossbow and fired, once at Robin, and once at the silhouetted figure of Nicholas, crashing down from his horse. Then someone lifted a handgun.

The bolts struck: the first smashing through Robin's thigh below his half-armour, and the other throwing Nicholas back, half concussed. He saw Robin begin to fall and was struggling to reach him when the hackbut exploded. He would have taken the ball if he could, but it was not aimed at him. Robin screamed as he was hit, and again as he sank to the ground. His fair-skinned face, drenched with blood, turned once towards

Nicholas, in apology, in farewell, in love. Then his shining eyes closed. The next moment, a handgun spoke again, and Nicholas knew nothing more.

AT SEVEN THAT EVENING, René, Duke of Lorraine, rode into his capital city of Nancy through the Porte de la Craffe and made his way by torchlight to the collegiate church of St George to give thanks for his victory. Behind him, on the site of the battle, lay nearly four thousand dead, not yet buried. Among the throng of his captives, he could now count the Bastard Anthony, taken in the forest of Haye, and the Comte de Chimay, the Duchess's captain, and his son.

The one blight on the joy of the evening was the disappearance of Duke Charles himself, whom none had seen since the flight from the battle. The following day, devoted to pillage, the mystery of the Duke's place of refuge continued: polite messengers sent even to Metz returned with negative answers. Overnight, a page produced some story of having seen the Duke slain. It seemed unlikely: one did not harm the ruler of the richest lands in the world when there were so many attractive alternatives. Nevertheless, the following morning, a search party went out, taking with it a small group of the Duke's friends and servants who could, if called upon, confirm his identity. His physician, Master Matteo, was among them, and the young half-Portuguese fellow from the Banco di Niccolò, Diniz Vasquez.

It was again bitterly cold. Diniz, who had not felt warm for a day, rode with the others in silence. The Duke had been alive when Diniz had been captured, but he had not thought of him since. Diniz himself was safe, and would be ransomed, together with those Charetty men who were with him. He found it hard to be thankful. John had gone. No one knew the fate of Tobie and Julius. They all knew about Campobasso's blockade at the bridge of Bouxières, and that Astorre and his company had died there. Also that Nicholas and Robin, who had gone to find them, had not returned.

They were riding past the Commanderie of St John and down to the banks of the stream that ran past it. This had frozen since Sunday, forming at one point a wide pool of ice, humped with bodies. Others lay, pale as sweetbreads, on the rimed mud and frosty meadows about them. All were naked. Some had died from the cold, some from wounds taken in battle, and some had been stripped while alive, and then killed. A man's voice said, 'This is my lord.' He spoke from the edge of the pool, and others dismounted and hurried towards him. After a moment, Diniz did the same, and looked down on the same sight.

He thought he would have known Charles of Burgundy, but he saw only a thickset body in ice, whose profile, half protruding, had been gnawed by some animal, leaving cracked white bone and flesh like congealed wool. When they chopped it out of its tomb, you could also see the original hatchet blow to the head, and the places where a pike had been driven hard: once through the buttocks and once through the groin. That had been done, the doctor said, before death, by those who had robbed him.

They had left a ring, which someone recognised. The body displayed fingernails of unusual length, particular to the Duke; an ingrowing toenail, recently treated; an old wound; and a recognisable fistula on the penis which had proved so infertile these latter years. The Duke's physician and valet expressed themselves soberly as convinced. Here lay the Grand Duke of the West. Beside him, his skull sheared across also, lay Jean de Rubempré, sire de Bièvres.

'You are not shocked,' said a voice in Portuguese. Master Matteo, wiping his hands.

'I have too much else to mourn,' Diniz said.

'Well, perhaps I could prevail upon you to carry this bag,' said the doctor. 'It contains two extra cloaks, although marked, I'm afraid, with the Lorraine cross for security. I should warn you not to slip off, which in these dreadful circumstances would seem to be all too easy. You might not even be missed for some time.'

Diniz stared at the dark face. 'What?'

'Also,' said the doctor, 'you should watch out in particular for Burgundians wounded in battle who may not all have died. I am told that the tower of the Commanderie has not recently been searched.'

Diniz lost his breath. The doctor finished wiping his hands and set to repacking his bag. Diniz said, 'How do you know? Why are you telling me?'

'Men confide in a doctor,' said Matteo. 'Also, I told you, I have heard of you and your company. I did not tell you how.'

'The Vasquez estates?' Diniz said.

'The Lomellini estates rather,' said the doctor. 'My sister married into the family. Slave-owning, of course, and appreciative of those one or two exceptional Africans they have come to know.' He smiled. 'Must I remind you? My name is Matteo Lope.'

'Lopez. Umar,' said Diniz. Tears rose.

'He is dead, I know, but you and your company esteemed him for what he was. Let us call this a gift he would have wished to make. And let me give you a last piece of news. Your John is safe, and a prisoner. But, of course, he needs someone to ransom him.'

'I see I shall have to make an effort,' said Diniz, swallowing. 'But you?'

The man smiled. He said, 'Every Duke needs a good physician. It does not matter which Duke.'

MOST OF THE REFUGEES reaching Metz were in some way injured, or had white toes and fingers, or fevers. All of them were exhausted. They all brought the same news: the Duke had lost the battle, and gone. The reports of what happened then were so contrary that they weren't worth listening to, if you were a doctor, and fairly exhausted yourself, from misery as much as fatigue.

The temporary hospital in the church of St Eucaire was cold, stinking and noisy, and Tobias Beventini had just risen, creakily, from examining a newly sawn leg when someone spoke his name, and he looked up and saw Diniz Vasquez.

He felt the blood flood through his skin. He said, 'I didn't know you were alive.'

In the olive face, Diniz's eyes were enormous. He recited his answer as if he had learned it by rote, on the long, cruel, dangerous journey from Nancy. 'I'm afraid Robin is dead. Astorre and Thomas as well, and their company. John le Grant ought to be safe: he's a prisoner. So was I, but I escaped. I've brought someone with me. He wants a doctor.'

Behind him was a man on the floor, resting against the wall down which he had just carefully slid. 'So that puts you out of court right away,' Nicholas said. 'But I don't mind passing the time of day with another refugee. Are you all right?'

Tobie walked over and stood looking down on him. 'Of course I am,' he snapped. 'So are all the men we brought with us. The only efficient arm, it seems to me, of the entire Bank.'

'We?' said Nicholas. 'Don't tell me that Julius is here?'

In an impatient manner, Tobie dropped down beside him. 'Of course he is. Over there. A picturesque wound in the arm, but nothing to worry about. What's wrong with you?'

'I don't know. My hearing, probably,' said Nicholas. 'You wouldn't like to give me a drink, and then say that all over again?'

He hardly knew, Tobie thought, what he was saying. Below his cap and half-fallen hood, his hair and neck were thick with soiled bandaging, and he held himself like a man with a javelin in him. Diniz, whose eyes never left him, was patched with cursory scars, and looked worn with care.

At his side, Nicholas said unexpectedly, 'I can't joke. I must —'

Until this moment, Tobie supposed, Nicholas had had to suppress everything that had occurred to concentrate on the supreme effort of travelling. Now, for the first time in his life, his composure openly began to give way. Diniz made a movement, but stopped. You could see why. It was no disgrace. This was a place of dying, and anguish. Other men sobbed, some with their heads in their arms; others like this, with tightened lids and heads flung back in a sort of defiance.

It swept aside Tobie's restraint. He did what he might have done all those years ago, and took the lad on his shoulder; except that this time, he was weeping himself.

Chapter 44

KATELIJNE SERSANDERS had to be told. It was natural, in those first hours at Metz, that Nicholas should think of that first, and should take it for granted that he would tell her himself. It was distressing that, at the same time, he should continue, agonisingly, to take responsibility for what was left of the company, assuming the burdens that in the past Astorre, or Marian, or he himself would have shouldered after such a disaster. It was Tobie who had to bring home to him that it would fall to Diniz and to Father Moriz in Bruges to plunge into the work of ransoming prisoners and caring for their families, the salvaging of horses and weapons, the nursing of the wounded, the final assessment of their losses. All of that would be done from the Bank's house in Spangnaerts Street, Bruges, which was not his any longer, and where even his presence would have to be negotiated.

Although less bluntly expressed, the reminder had reduced Nicholas to silence. But when, reviving, he had demanded, grimly, at least the right to go and find Kathi, Tobie had lost patience, asking him scathingly just how fast he believed he could ride, and why Kathi should be left in suspense because of his sensibilities. And he had reminded him, more to the point, that his own wife was in Ghent. So in the end, Diniz went off to Bruges, which was correct, since he was the head of the Bank there; and after two days, Nicholas got himself mounted and rode carefully north, with Julius and Tobie, to Ghent.

Because he was sick, they did not speak to him very much on the journey. Or it was truer to say that Tobie imposed the embargo which kept Julius, with his bursts of anger and misery, apart from where Nicholas rested or rode. The truth was that no one could bear, yet, to talk about what had happened, while there was nothing else worthy of speech.

From time to time, Nicholas thought about Gelis. But this, his return to her, which should have been swift and thankful and joyous, had only a personal significance, compared with the tragedy that was crushing them all. His soul was ripped raw, and the pain was continuous. His mind flinched, again and again, thinking of Kathi.

It had not occurred to him that Gelis might not have waited in Ghent, or that he himself, calling at the palace of Ten Walle, would be hurried into the Duchess's presence, heart-sick and infirm as he was, to report on what he had seen. For, despite the tolling bells, the city enveloped in black, Charles of Burgundy's widow had not yet accepted his death. He might be wounded; a prisoner; fled to some distant spot from which, one day, a courier would come flying. 'Where is my wealth, my kingdom, my empire-to-be? *Je l'ay emprins:* I have dared. I mean to come back and dare once again.'

The Duchess — now the Duchesse Mère — had heard of the Commanderie of St John, and the stream. He spared her the details, telling only of the loss of helmet and horse, so that the Duke rode unrecognised save for his sash. He told of the sash he had seen in the pool.

'But it may have been another man's,' said Margaret of York. 'It may have been retrieved and worn by its owner.'

'It is possible, my lady Duchess,' Nicholas said. 'But I believe there were other signs.'

He was dismissed, with a purse of gold. He did not see the new ruler of Burgundy: the Duke's young, betrothed daughter, who would not believe, either, that her father was dead.

Louis of France believed it. The recapture of Nancy was known to him inside four days; the report of the Duke's death in five. The King had tried, for form's sake, to conceal his transports of joy. Then he had called in his captains from Toul, and ordered the armies of France to invade Artois, Picardy and the two Burgundies. For now, after all, there were only fifteen hundred battle-weary survivors to face.

Ghent shook with the impact of it all: the streets, the courts of the palace were screaming with new reports and fresh rumours. Nicholas forced his way, deaf, through it all. Such information didn't matter to him. It was for the men who still owned a shaken Bank, and a broken army, and had to try to do something with both. He would lay his own plans. The childish outburst in Metz was behind him, and the illusion that had followed. A thinking man keeps his own counsel. *Don't try to piss your woes over me.*

Nicholas left the palace, therefore, blank-minded; stumbling; and joined Julius and Tobie, his keepers. 'And now, bed,' Tobie said. They still possessed the use of Adorne's house.

'And now, Anna,' Julius said.

Nicholas stared at him. Tobie, he was aware, was doing the same. Anna, the vengeful, the deceitful, the sensuous, insinuating Delilah, had gone from his mind. He said, 'What are you going to do? Whatever it is, you don't need us.'

'I need you,' Julius said. 'The Duke has gone. The law courts may not even meet. You and Gelis were Anna's chief victims. Unless you insist, no one may trouble to deal with her now.'

He was probably right. Nicholas said, 'But I don't want revenge. I told you so. You must reach some sort of decision yourself. I'd say, turn her off, and forget her.'

'A would-be murderess?' Julius said.

'Well, what can she do, with no money or standing? Give her a pension and send her abroad. Madeira's a good place,' Nicholas said.

It should have been enough. It seemed incredible that Julius should persist, as he did, until Nicholas grew sick of arguing, and rounded on him. 'Look. Go and see her alone. Tell her what you've decided. For all I know, she may think exile worse than waiting for months to be tried. Then go and tell the authorities.' He paused. Then he said shortly, 'And take a weapon. She's dangerous.'

They looked at one another. Julius said, 'At least, come to the house. At least, be there if I need you.'

Nicholas agreed. He felt mortally weary. He heard Tobie proposing to come and keep him company. Thank you, Tobie. Once it had all mattered so much, and now it didn't. He said to Tobie, just before they left for the Hôtel Gruuthuse, 'Gelis and Jodi are in Bruges. I have to see them. Even if the Bank won't let me into the house.'

'I know,' Tobie said. 'So does Julius. But you made Anna your business. You owe it to Julius to help him finish it. And nobody's rushing to Bruges in one day. You want to be fresh when you get there. If things go well, I'll set out with you tomorrow.'

THE CHAMBER WHERE Anna von Hanseyck was secured was pleasant and large, and not obviously a place of confinement, except for the locked door and the bars on the windows. Marguerite van Borselen, having taken Julius there, returned to talk softly to Nicholas and Tobie in her parlour. She commiserated with them both over their losses, and what they had been through at Nancy. Louis had been devastated. She did not know what they were going to do.

She was too kind to suggest that one of the things they might have to do was cease guarding this woman. But that would be settled today. Either Anna would accept Julius's terms, or she would be taken to justice. Nicholas said to his wife's cousin, 'And have you heard something from Bruges?'

'From Gelis? Of course! You know how silent she is, when her feelings are touched. But she waits for you, minute by minute. The child also.'

'And Katelijne Sersanders?' Nicholas said.

'Ah, that is sad,' his hostess said, with warm sympathy. 'Of course, she is surrounded by family, friends; she is very much loved. She has the children. But it was a strange little marriage, in its way: people look forward to her next choice.'

Nicholas said, 'That was her choice. She will not make another.' He would not have said it, except that he was in no doubt, and others ought to recognise it as well. He was torn between thinking of Kathi, and wondering what was passing between Anna and Julius. He didn't know enough about their feelings for each other. He had always suspected them to be tepid, since it had been, in a sense, an arranged marriage. Julius's vanity had been engaged, and he was man enough to respond to her calculated, experienced lovemaking, although it would never play a large part in his life. Driven by wounded pride, nevertheless, he might go to the most unwise of extremes.

On the other hand, Anna was strong enough to check anything that would frustrate her intentions. With her emotions frozen since childhood, she prized, Nicholas thought, her indifference to men, and the ease with which she could rouse them. Then she had practised the same arts with himself and had failed; but not because he did not want her, or believed her craving assumed. He had felt, even earlier than she did, the signs of something deep-settled between them. He would not let it happen, that was all. And that, she could not endure.

It meant that she would not forgive; that she would make him pay so long as it lay in her power. It meant that she did not care for her own life or her own future. She had none, and she knew it. So he was not surprised when the manservant came to ask if M. de Fleury would object to joining the Gräfin and her husband in the locked room. He apologised for the precautions. Needless to say, Tobie came, too.

Adelina sat in the light by the window. She looked the way Tobie said his grandfather had looked at Montello: fresh and well groomed and aware. She was, after all, Thibault's daughter. Her hair, brushed and loose, was the colour of a ducat seen through red glass. She was smiling. 'I am being sent into exile on a pittance. Your idea?'

Nicholas seated himself on the bed-step. 'I could have asked for your life, but I didn't. This is between you and Julius.'

'I don't mind being hanged by my loving family,' said Adelina. 'I do object to being relegated to tedium because you are too terrified of your own conscience to act. What else should I have done to strike a spark from you? Killed your disgusting friend Ludovico da Bologna as well as Ochoa? I did give away Karaï Mirza: I trust he is dead. And I am sure the

Greek died a noble death in your place: that was a mistake I do regret.' She was flushed. He had expected measured refutations, and possibly threats. He had underestimated her. She had never been interested in saving herself: only in punishing him.

Julius said, 'I don't want to hear any more. You said you had to tell Nicholas something.' It sounded commanding, but in fact he looked devastated, standing with his injured arm by the fire. He had been informed about Anna. He had not, until now, heard it all from her lips.

'I wanted to tell you both something,' Adelina said. Lying back, smoothing the chain of her pendant, she was the opposite of disturbed. She was, Nicholas thought, deliberately reminding Julius and himself of her physical beauty. Tobie, leaning against the post of the bed, gave a snort.

Julius said, 'What is there left that we don't know? You deceived me, and you deceived Nicholas. I'm only surprised that you didn't try to deceive me with him.'

Nicholas shut his eyes and opened them again. By now, he ought to know what Julius was like. He decided he had better say something. He said, 'She made a brave try, but had to make do in the end with Squarciafico. Others, too. But Squarciafico spent half his time in the house.'

'Did you know?' Anna was amused. 'A vigorous man, my dear Julius, but insanely jealous. His men gave Nicholas a hard time at Soldaia before I contrived to contain and then reverse the damage. Are you glad, Nicholas?'

'Because you wanted to preserve me for the gold? Well, naturally, I was glad,' Nicholas said. 'The gold was my carefully planned life insurance. You believed in it. I was lucky I wasn't dealing with Julius.'

The pendant dropped from her fingers. 'Julius!' Adelina said. 'You think my poor cuckolded Julius is *intelligent*?'

Nicholas gazed at her. 'He's here and free, and you're not.'

On the surface, she had calmed. 'That is true. But then, what has he achieved, compared with me? His objective was to become wealthy, and he is poor. Mine was to remind you of the sins of your childhood, and to compel you to regret them.'

'You did quite well,' Nicholas acknowledged politely. He kept his voice steady.

'I think so too. But the *coup de grâce* is still to come. You are very sad, I hear, that your captain and half the Charetty company are dead? This proud little army confided to you by your first wife? How extraordinary,' said Adelina. 'You wouldn't have me, but you forced yourself to take an old woman, provided it brought you her business.'

'No,' said Nicholas, and got up. She raised her voice, and went on. She was smiling.

'And what was she like, when put to her business?' said Adelina. 'A little stiff, and prone to wheeze, but — I am sure — most eagerly grateful. And she knew that to keep such a splendid young stallion, she must spare him more ridicule, if she could. She had the sense, at least, not to complain when, using her in your virile way famed among kitchenmaids, you generously got her with child.'

'She's lying,' said Tobie. 'Come.'

'*Are* you lying?' Julius said. 'How do you know?'

'Anyone going to Dijon can find out,' said Adelina. 'If they know whom to ask, and are sufficiently convincing, and will swear themselves humbly to secrecy. You have a daughter, Nicholas. Are you not pleased? Her name is Bonne.'

The room had become very cold. Nicholas sat. Tobie put his hand on his shoulder. Julius said loudly, 'Bonne is too young.'

Adelina's voice said, 'Bonne is two years older than I told you she was.'

'But she is yours,' Julius said. 'Yours and the Graf's.'

'He adopted her,' Adelina said. 'He was extremely anxious to marry me. He did not care who I was, or what story was told. And he knew I couldn't sully his line, because I was barren.' Her gaze rested on Nicholas, although she spoke to her husband. 'You don't know what Jaak de Fleury did to me. Nicholas could tell you. What Jaak did to me was to ensure that I could never carry a child.' She smiled, still looking at Nicholas. 'Bonne is Marian de Charetty's daughter, by you.'

He steadied then, finding his voice, and causing Tobie's hand to move aside. Nicholas said, 'Can you prove it?'

'I don't need to,' Adelina said. 'You have to prove it untrue.'

Her eyes were glowing, her shoulders straight under the fall of glorious hair. Nicholas stood, and met her gaze, and said, 'I think that is enough. The rest is for Julius.'

'You are running away?' Adelina said. 'She died in a foreign land, for your sake. An old woman, she set out on a journey knowing that she would give birth alone, and that you need never know what had happened — even if she died, as she did.'

Nicholas walked to the door and turned. Tobie had already opened it. Nicholas said, 'If it is true, I ought to know, and I am glad you have told me. If it is false, I shall find out soon enough. I don't think, in leaving you, I am running away. I see nothing in you that I can harm or help any more.'

She did not answer, but he could feel her gaze on the door as he closed it, while the voice of Julius battered at her attention. '*You promised me children . . . !*' And then, darkening, 'So you could sleep with anyone, couldn't you? *Anyone!*'

Tobie said quietly, 'You didn't know about Marian?'

'I don't know even yet,' Nicholas said. They had stopped outside the parlour.

'But you guessed Anna would goad Julius as well.' It wasn't an accusation, or a piece of anxious self-questioning, or a dawning conviction. It sounded helpless.

'I didn't want to come,' Nicholas said. He paused and said, 'If you think it right, you can go back to their room.'

There was a long pause. Then Tobie said, 'No.'

They took leave of their hostess and returned to the house of Adorne, where there was nothing to do. Tobie found a book and sat, seldom turning the pages. Nicholas went briefly to his room, but reappeared to sink into a chair before the handsome Sersanders fireplace. He did not speak. His sombre presence, indeed, seemed to have no purpose at all unless it was to wait out the night along with Tobie. It also demonstrated that, whatever happened, he was not taking it lightly. Whatever happened. Whatever he was allowing to happen.

The news came before dawn, with a hurried, ill-written note from Marguerite van Borselen at the Hôtel Gruuthuse. Mixed with the horror it conveyed was an apology: she and her husband had, after all, been warders of the young woman. Mixed with the apology was a grain of thankfulness: an awkward problem had been solved. Yet who would imagine that, after all these weeks, the Gräfin von Hanseyck would do such a thing?

Certainly, she had been distressed by the interview with her husband. Faced with his revulsion, reminded again of the public ignominy that lay ahead, she had been overcome, it was clear, with despair. Left alone for the merest moment, she had taken her tragic decision. By her own hand, Anna von Hanseyck was dead.

Tobie had leaped to his feet, but the messenger, a man of Marguerite's own, had restrained him. 'I was to tell you, Master Tobias, not to come. The lady is alas beyond help, and her husband has said he does not want company. My lord the Governor will see to all that has to be done, and Master Julius will continue to stay with him meanwhile. My lady's advice is that M. de Fleury should go to Bruges, to her cousin his wife.'

By then, Nicholas was on his feet also, his face gaunt as it had been all night. In reply to Tobie's glance, he made a voiceless sign of agreement and walked away, while Tobie sent off the man with a note and a coin. Then the doctor went and poured two cups of wine. 'Justice,' he said.

'I don't know if it was justice,' Nicholas said. He had again dropped into a seat, his fist to his mouth. He removed his hand. 'It curtailed the damage, I suppose.'

Tobie gave him his wine. '*Did* she take her own life?' he said plainly.

'I don't know. Probably. He probably gave her the dagger. Oh Christ, Julius,' Nicholas said. It was a cry, in a whisper.

'He'll get over it.'

Nicholas thought. He gave a laugh which had exasperation in it, as well as pity and anger. 'In fact, you're right. More than anyone, he probably will.'

'And you?' Tobie asked.

Nicholas rocked his cup, watching it. 'She was graceful, beautiful, clever. We spent a long time together, much of it happy. It was hard sometimes to remember that she couldn't be trusted. She had a sense of fun; she could be understanding, when she wanted to be. She was deeply musical, I discovered. But of course, she used it all for her own purposes.'

'To hurt,' Tobie said.

'She had been hurt,' Nicholas said. Then he said, 'Bonne.'

Tobie said, 'She's in a convent. Father Moriz keeps in touch with her, and will tell her the Gräfin is dead. But I suspect Julius will not want to be responsible for her now.'

'No. I shall. I shall have to look into it all. Is it possible?' Nicholas said. He had not yet tasted his wine.

'It is possible that your wife had a child. It has still to be proved that Bonne is that child,' Tobie said.

'I have to tell Gelis,' Nicholas said to the air.

Tobie hesitated. Then he said, 'Gelis made a journey to Dijon, while you were away.' He did not drop his pale gaze.

Nicholas said, 'She didn't tell me.'

'Because, unlike Adelina, Gelis is someone who does not want to hurt you, these days,' Tobie said. 'But you must have found that out, by now. Will you stay at Spangnaerts Street?'

'Not if it disturbs anyone,' Nicholas said.

'Oh, I think you should get a night out of them,' Tobie said ironically. 'You go to Adorne's, and I'll ask.'

As had been said, Katelijne Sersanders in her loss was surrounded by family and friends, and very much loved. The blow of her bereavement would also be softened, you would think, by the extent of a disaster which had made of her one of thousands of widows, and changed for ever the land she was reared in. She was even thought to be fortunate, being young, with no more than a short married life to grieve over. She was aware of all that. She could not say that, in those weeks of isolation and terror, her heart had been in Lorraine with two men, not one. Or her heart aching for one, and her spirit in bond to the other.

Diniz had brought the news of Robin's death to her uncle's house, and Nicholas's wife had come with him. Adorne himself had ushered them into her room and had stayed, ever kind, ever gentle, while it was broken. Robin had died beside Nicholas, where he would have wanted to be. Nicholas was alive.

In Gelis's face, telling her, there had been no room for relief, only wretchedness on Kathi's behalf. It occurred to Kathi, incongruously, that she at least was spared the task of telling her children. They had loved Robin, but were too young to understand, or remember him. But of course, she would have to send and tell Archie.

There was no recognisable body. She knew there had been wolves. A funeral Mass would be held here, in the church.

Nicholas was going first to Ghent, but after that, would come here directly, with Tobie. Gelis said, 'He will tell you everything.' Then she had paused and said, 'Be gentle. This will be one of the worst things that has happened to him, as well.'

So, living through the unreal days, Kathi waited.

HE DID COME to her first, riding alone to the Hôtel Jerusalem and speaking briefly to Adorne before Kathi was warned and he went, still alone, to see her in her chamber.

She had heard he was hurt, but had not known how much. He said, 'I am so sorry.' It came after a while, as if he had not really thought it necessary to speak. Anyone else might have added, defensively, 'I did my best to protect him.'

She sat down, so that he could. 'Was he happy?' she said.

His expression altered. They talked together so seldom; sometimes she forgot, too, what it was like. He said, 'Like Astorre. They were such fools.'

'I know,' she said. Then she said, 'I made him happy, too.'

His face softened. He said, 'Very few people have the life they deserve. Robin did, from beginning to end. You must be so thankful that you let him go.'

And no one else in the world would have said that. Until that moment, she had not wept.

After a while, he came to her and held her closely and quietly, as if he were comforting a young brother. Then, when it was over, he moved about, awkwardly, and found them both some wine, and would not drink until she did. Then they talked.

It was not much about Robin, or the fighting. It was about her uncle, and the fear for the future that was beginning to stalk Bruges, and Ghent. The future with an exhausted treasury, and no army, and France already inside the barriers. The future, with a girl ruling, betrothed to the son of a German Emperor, while the duchy lay disconnected, its separate parts warring against one another, its rich towns fearful for their independence and resentful of those who, like Adorne, like Gruuthuse, like Hugonet, had helped to raise armies and taxes, steadily holding a course which might pacify the Duke, and yet reserve to the towns some of the sovereignty that they craved.

The foreign merchants were uneasy. Already, there was a move to leave Bruges. Kathi made a small noise of commiseration. 'Poor Tommaso. He was so angry with Uncle, when all he got for the loss of the *San Matteo* was a soothing letter from Callimaco offering friendship, and promising to do his best to extract his ship and its cargo from Danzig. It hardly seems to matter now, except that it must have worsened his debts. He lent the Duke far too much.'

Then Nicholas had said, 'What will you do?'

'I can't tell yet. It depends on my uncle. Stay as long as he needs me, in the first place. And you?'

'If I am allowed, find a house and wait until spring, when David de Salmeton is due to come back. After that, it depends on other people.'

Kathi said, 'After all that has happened? My uncle is not going to send you away. And so far, you have not been rejected, it seems to me, by the others.'

'No,' he said. 'But a long stay might be different.'

She could hear the change in his voice. She said, 'You haven't spoken of Anna. Adelina. You saw her in Ghent?'

'Yes. I didn't want to . . . You will hear soon enough,' Nicholas said. 'She was offered exile, but had the spirit to boast, in the end, of all she did, so that she would be sure to die. Then she did it in her own way, with a knife. She is dead. Julius was there. He is still there. Gruuthuse is dealing with it.'

There was a silence. Kathi said, 'We all played some part in discrediting her. But Gelis said you did give her an alternative. The same choice we gave you. To go east, to build her own business.'

'That was not what she wanted,' Nicholas said.

'She would tell you that. I can't be sorry,' Kathi said. 'Her whole object in life was to punish you for what life did to her. Was it bad? When you saw her?'

For a moment, she thought he would tell her. Then he simply shook his head, and she left it alone.

Before he went, he walked with her to the nursery, where Margaret was battering Rankin, and Rankin was indignantly complaining. 'Pure Adorne as to looks,' Nicholas said. 'But I am afraid that the character is irredeemably Scots.'

Leaving, he was joined at the door by Anselm Adorne. 'Are you going to Spangnaerts Street? Come with me. We shall care for your horse. My barge will take you more comfortably.' His face, though grave, was not unfriendly. 'Diniz told us all you did for young Robin. Poor lad, to die at nineteen. As for yourself . . . We don't know what the future will hold, but I think you should now be free to choose. I shall not stop you from staying in Flanders.'

'Thank you, sir,' Nicholas said. He had promised Adorne a report. He would deliver it. He waited, and added deliberately, 'Berecrofts was a brave man; and a credit to his house and yours.'

Then he went home, to the Hof Charetty-Niccolò; to Marian's house.

ONCE, ON A DARK winter's night, Tilde and Catherine de Charetty had fortified the big merchant's house in Spangnaerts Street against Claes, their late mother's husband. This time, fifteen years later, the porter was primed to allow the same person inside, provided of course he could identify him. It was asking a lot, for the working day was still in full swing, although it was dusk, and the yard and the house were thronged with anxious, short-tempered people, as they had been since the dreadful news of Captain Astorre and the army. The lamps in the house and the yard were all lit, which was some help at least: they made the Bank look welcoming, as it should, and the yard sparkled with frost.

The officers of the Bank had held a short policy meeting that day, after Tobie had left Nicholas with Adorne. In a separate meeting, it had been put to their womenfolk that Nicholas de Fleury might be allowed to join his wife for one night. Tilde and Catherine had agreed. Gelis, wordless, took no part in the decision, nor did the doctor's wife Clémence, still wild-coloured from Tobie's embrace.

They had all required to be told, of course, of the fate of Adelina in Ghent. The report was not quite complete: Tobie had not mentioned the tale concerning Marian's child to her daughters. He did tell the others in private. He suspected that Gelis and his own wife both knew, but it was as well for Diniz and Moriz to be told. No doubt the time would come soon when Nicholas, too, would feel he could discuss it all with them. It affected the Bank.

Then the early darkness had arrived, and the lanterns were lit, and the uneasiness concealed by the glittering lights communicated itself to the children of the Hof Charetty-Niccolò, so that Tilde's baby screamed, and her five-year-old banged a plate until it broke, and Jodi, who had been excruciatingly active all day, threw a fit of temper more to be expected from Lucia than from a trainee swordsman of eight. Mistress

Clémence, with his mother's leave, took the boy out to the back yard, which gave access to the stables, and Catherine's optimistic herb garden, and eventually to the canal gate, for which she had providently brought the key. It seemed to Clémence that a courteous host might lend his barge to a convalescent who had paid him a visit. Doctors seldom gave thought to such things.

So it was with no surprise that, after the ice-breakers had gone, and a vicious competition with snowballs had palled, and close acquaintance with an angry swan had been discouraged, Jodi's attention had been attracted to the sound of a boat crackling up to the bank, to the accompaniment of pleasant men's voices. Then the boat, a private one, drew away, and uneven footsteps began to approach. Jodi said, 'Who is it? Is it the dog-catcher?' His voice was strong now, and not at all shrill. The steps slackened.

Mistress Clémence said, 'It might very well be the dog-catcher. Are you catching dogs, sir?'

It was a clear night. Light from the handsome houses that lined the canal pooled on the towpath and wharves, and bridge lanterns created uncertain scallops in the dark water. The disembarked man was tall, cloaked, and wore a fur hat which shadowed his face. He said, 'If I caught one I'd eat it, I'm so hungry. No, demoiselle. I'm a soldier.'

'From the Lorraine wars?' said Clémence with interest. 'You weren't at Nancy?'

Jodi had become very still. He said, 'My father fought at Nancy. The other boys say he didn't.'

'Maybe I saw him,' said the man. He had come to rest, his face still in shadow, his head a little inclined. 'My troops were in the centre, in the battle-corps of the Duke. We did our best, but we were beaten.'

'The other side had twice as many,' said the boy. 'So I heard.'

'But we should have done better. Do you live near here?'

'Up that lane. It leads to the back. Don't you know?' Jodi said. Clémence smiled, saying nothing.

'I haven't been here for a long time,' the man said. 'You get to know other places well, even though you'd rather stay at home. Then you forget.'

'Shall I take you?' said Jodi. Clémence's smile broadened.

The man said, 'If you want.' He paused, and added, 'I haven't forgotten *you*.' They were moving slowly into the lane. Clémence walked ahead.

Jodi said, 'You were away a long time.'

'I know. I won't do it again. Do you think they'll want me back?'

'I can hunt,' Jodi said.

'That's what I thought,' the man said. 'I'm not bad, myself. I do remember this gate. Jodi, I'm afraid to go in.'

'Why?' said the boy. He turned, and the light from the house fell on the faces of the boy and the man. The eyes of both, which were of the same colour, were shining.

Jodi said, 'I'll take you. They won't be angry. They'll be glad to have you back.' He caught the man by the arm, and started to run, exhorting breathlessly still. He ran to the house, passing Mistress Clémence and bursting through the back door, dragging the man stumbling with him.

'Maman! Maman!' bellowed Jodi. *'Papa's back!'*

PAPA WAS ALLOWED to be back, it transpired, for one night. How much longer depended on the discussion — the examination — the trial — his former partners wished to hold forthwith, it appeared.

Nicholas had agreed to it. After his precipitate entrance, he had managed some social exchanges: a few words with Clémence; a few more with Catherine and Tilde, who had greeted him with a solicitude which might have been genuine, and a caution which certainly was. Gelis was allowed a little longer.

He always knew where she was in a room: it was like surf reforming into a wave. Her face had turned the moment he entered, and she was still looking at him as he was pitched before her by Jodi. When, suddenly smitten by doubts, Jodi had made to retreat, Nicholas had capped him with his fur hat and drawn him into a hug with his mother, during which Nicholas had pressed a kiss into Gelis's neck. He could feel her trembling, but for the moment had himself under control. Jodi, peering upwards, had looked astonished, then thrilled. For the short time that was left, he had shuttled between Gelis and Nicholas in a drunken glaze of satisfaction, his father's fur hat on his ears.

Then the frivolities ended, and Nicholas was alone at a table in what had been Marian de Charetty's room, being interviewed like an apprentice by Father Moriz and Diniz and Tobie. He was not resentful. He understood what was happening. The original cause had been his own fault.

Gelis, who had a right to be there, had absented herself until later. She was one of the great strengths of the Bank. She had also stated, in public, that her investment would remain with the Bank, no matter what happened. In other words, she did not propose to buy her husband out of his banishment. She had made no bargain about her own work.

Father Moriz said, 'Diniz has asked me to speak. We planned some such meeting as soon as we heard you were travelling from Russia. Then, you were coming simply to protect your family from the lady who has now sadly died, and from the man David de Salmeton. We were willing to support you in that, and have, I think, done so. Now the situation has changed. De Salmeton will be absent until spring. You may wish to wait for him. You may wish to take your family and leave, and that decision must be between you and Gelis. We have had to consider what should be done if you stay, and we are prepared to make you an offer.' His short neck was flushed, but his thick German voice remained equable. They had once spent a hilarious, difficult season together in the Tyrol, Nicholas and Moriz and John le Grant. Moriz had never liked his divining. Moriz was right.

You will always be bought, because you will always be worth something to others. It might be true, but Nicholas was not being insulted. He had certain knowledge, certain experience. Adorne had recognised it as well. Nicholas sat and let Moriz detail the limited ways in which, for a negotiable fee, he could make himself useful if he stayed on in Flanders. This, they would make clear, concerned only the immediate period. Anything beyond that must be approved by all the original partners. And, of course, by Anselm Adorne.

'He has already decided to release me,' Nicholas said.

He fell silent, looking at Moriz, who must know, even better than the others, what that meticulously compiled offer had betrayed. Tell me what you are buying and I will tell you what your deficiencies are. Burgundy, to whose fortunes he had committed the Bank, lay now in ruins, and every institution dependent on wealth and stability was endangered, never mind one whose military arm had been shattered at Nancy. Once, they had been able to share the risk with their other houses; but Venice was separate now, and rocked by the Turkish triumphs in the Black Sea and even nearer. Friuli had been overrun last November, and the smoke from burning palaces, so they said, could be seen from the top of the campanile of St Mark. Gregorio and the Ca' Niccolò might survive, but it could not help others.

Nor could aid come from Julius's business, as it stood, vitiated by Anna and only partly restored by what Moriz and Govaerts had done. In Poland, Muscovy, Persia were the openings Nicholas himself had contrived, in order to appeal to Julius's ambitions, and to divert Adelina from her purpose. Trading in Trebizond and within a restored Caffa was possible, even under the Turk. Nevertheless, Nicholas did not think Julius would now go there; and even if he did, and felt generous, the business was too young to help others. There was the gold he himself had promised Anna, of course. But, increasingly, it seemed certain that David de Salmeton had that.

They were waiting to hear him: Moriz, Tobie, Diniz. Behind them, unseen, were the shadows of the others he had offended: John and Gregorio, and the ghost of young Robin. Gelis, he had reason to know, had forgiven him. Julius had never minded what he had done, nor had

Astorre and Thomas. From some houri-laden cloud, Astorre would be watching him irascibly. Get on with it. Tell them.

Nicholas said, 'I can't help you. I suggest you wind down the Bank, and then close it.'

He could feel the shock, then the anger. Tobie said, 'You won't help.'

Nicholas said, 'No one can help. Without Astorre, the army is nothing, and what is left is too small to be viable. Offer it to John, but he would be wasted. As for the Bank, only you know what your reserves are, and how much you will see of the money you have already working for you. I suspect it isn't enough to weather what is coming.'

He didn't spell it out, although he could. He knew enough about business to be sure. Burgundy, the vital balance between France and the German Empire, had gone. He thought of the dazzling riches and power of Duke Philip; of the burning zeal of the Vow of the Pheasant; the hopes of Pope Pius, valiantly assembling his fleet to stop the advance of the Turk; the hopes, even, of Ludovico da Bologna. All ended in a block of ice in a ditch, during a misconceived, squalid fight over boundaries.

Diniz said, 'Can nothing be done?' It was a brave admission. Recently, Diniz, too, had learned to face truths.

Nicholas said, 'You can return to your roots. Dyes may be scarce, and expensive, but you have better sources than anyone. If a new route is found, employ Crackbene. There will always be a place for a good, small money-broker trusted by merchants. You may have to leave Bruges for Antwerp, but you have Jooris, and the goodwill of Veere and of the new Duchess's advisers, so long as they last.' He paused, and said, 'You don't need me. You don't even need Gelis, although you may want her, and she may want to stay.'

Tobie said, 'You remember the business as it was. You and Julius. You could guide them.'

'Them?' Nicholas said.

'What are you going to do?' Tobie said.

'Deal with David de Salmeton. At the moment, if you want me, I'll do what I can. You can't take any decision without a proper assessment. Then the old business will have to be dismantled and the new one constructed. I don't want a fee, but perhaps I can help. After that, it depends partly on you.'

'You won't join us. Would you compete with us?' Moriz said.

'I didn't say I wouldn't join you,' Nicholas said. 'Just that there would be no room for me. And yes, I have come to the point where I should want a business, perhaps, of my own. I don't know where. I don't know yet what is going to happen: no one does. But I do promise it will never compete with you, whatever it is. It may even be able to help you.'

'And Gelis?' Tobie said.

'Why don't you ask her?' Nicholas said. 'Bring her in and put it before her. She owes it to you, as I do, to tell you where she stands.'

'Without speaking to her first?' Tobie said.

And Nicholas said, 'She doesn't need me to help her reach a decision.'

As Conservator of Scots Privileges in Bruges, Andro Wodman spent all his time, these days, at harassed meetings; or waiting to see people who, exhausted, afraid, overworked, did not want to be seen. Adorne, with terrifying concerns of his own, yet wielded his considerable authority to support him. Through days infested with rumour, scraps of genuine news sometimes permeated, and were shared.

That evening, unannounced, the burly figure of Wodman broke into the orderly courtyard of the Hôtel Jerusalem, and asked to see Adorne and his niece. A good deal later, he made his way between lamplit houses and over bridges to Spangnaerts Street. At the Hof Charetty-Niccolò, on being told that M. de Fleury and his wife were both at a meeting, he pushed past the protesting manservant, found the room, and walked in on them all. Diniz Vasquez and the doctor jumped to their feet. The priest, Moriz, gazed at him, frowning. Nicholas de Fleury, who had been putting some point to his own wife, swung round and then stopped, while Gelis did not look up at all, but continued to contemplate her husband.

Then Nicholas threw himself forward. It happened with uncanny speed: Wodman's own entry; the silence; and then the blur of movement.

Nicholas stood before him, incandescent, and said, 'He is alive.'

'Yes,' said Wodman. He held the other man's distended gaze, his own eyes damp.

Diniz said sharply, 'What?'

Nicholas, smiling, did not answer. Wodman looked past him. He said gruffly, 'Robin of Berecrofts. He nearly died of his wounds, but not quite. He is under medical care, a prisoner with John.' Then he said to Nicholas, 'How did you know what I was going to say?'

'I divined it,' Nicholas said. 'Or I didn't. Do you want a pendulum, going cheap, that takes umbrage if you decide not to use it? Kathi knows?'

'Of course,' Wodman said. He was smiling, himself, as Nicholas turned and flung out his arms.

'Oh glory,' Nicholas said. 'What can we do to celebrate this? Pull down the stars.'

Later, when the table was covered with bottles, and one or two of the glasses had fallen, Tobie said, 'We didn't get very far with our planning.'

'What were you planning?' Wodman said. He had earlier won a trial of strength against Nicholas, but was at present just failing to win a wager to drink him under the table.

'It's of no importance,' said Father Moriz, who was sober, but happy. 'Just the future of the Banco di Niccolò. Nicholas was going to tell us what to do.'

'I had told you,' Nicholas said. Gelis and his step-daughters and Clémence had beaten a retreat some little time ago; he couldn't quite imagine why.

'You should go back to Scotland,' said Andro Wodman. 'Stop that bastard David de Salmeton wrecking the country. He's got your gold there anyway, according to rumour.'

'I knew I had to talk to him about something,' Nicholas said. He eyed the floor, which looked more comfortable than his chair, but he didn't want to lose his bet. 'I'll ask him when he gets back from the Tyrol. I'll *go* to the Tyrol. Ever hunted chamois?' It didn't sound right, so he repeated it.

'You just like being a pet of the Duchess,' Moriz said. Moriz had got on particularly well with the Scottish Duchess.

'Well, David de Salmeton failed to become a pet of the Duchess,' said Andro Wodman, giving Nicholas a sharp prod where some of the bandages were. 'Don't you feel you want to lie down? He's not in the Tyrol any longer, he got sent home by Buchan to report on the progress of his peace mission. To stop the war between Duke Charles and the Tyrol.'

'That shouldn't be too difficult,' Nicholas said. Diniz had fallen asleep. He hoped Tilde would excuse him.

'Well,' said Wodman. 'News takes time to travel, in the Tyrol.'

Tobie said, 'Andro? You mean de Salmeton's back in Scotland?'

'On his way there. Not passing through Bruges. You know he's bought your castle at Beltrees?'

Nicholas opened his eyes.

'It doesn't matter,' said Wodman hastily. 'De Ribérac's next door at Kilmirren, and they'll kill each other anyway. Go back to sleep.'

His own eyes were starting to close. Tobie's were open. Nicholas said clearly, 'Go to hell,' and got up, with difficulty, and took himself to bed.

GELIS SAID, 'WHO WON?'

The night was over, and it seemed to be morning. He was in a familiar bed, in a familiar room, and his wife was curled at his back, being familiar. Nicholas gave a jerk of alarmed ecstasy; yelped; swore; and said 'Oh, *Tàte-Dieu,* I'm sorry. I slept all night through?'

'There is a compensation clause,' Gelis said. 'This is it. Does your head pain you?'

'No,' said Nicholas.

'That *is* gallant,' she said.

'I didn't want to discourage you,' Nicholas said. 'From anything, truth to tell.'

'But there are some things you could tolerate better than others.'

'I don't know,' Nicholas said. 'I'd have to try them. *Qui va piano, va lontano*. We could start with one or two possibilities, and then improvise.'

He turned. 'Oh, my sweet,' he said. 'There was a price to pay, but it is paid.'

THEY SPOKE, at intervals, between that waking and the time when they would have to emerge, and step among the people for whom they were responsible, and put to the test what they had learned.

Once, as his breathing slowed, and she lay cradled and quiet in his arm, Nicholas said, 'I am glad my grandfather saw you.'

She turned her head a little. 'Your message reached him,' she said.

'And he sent it to you. He must have liked you. He seems to have been quite a connoisseur, before the paralysis came.'

She was smiling. 'It runs in the family. I wish we could have proved something for you. At least you know what he felt for your mother. Did you know she was a twin?'

'No,' said Nicholas.

'I didn't tell you. I went to your mother's tomb in Dijon. I saw your brother's name below hers. Nicholas? Could *he* have been a twin?'

Nicholas waited. Then he said. 'There was a theory that he was. It can't be proved. And anyway, Fleury and Dijon are French now.' He hesitated, and then said, without looking at her, 'When you were there . . . Tobie thought that perhaps you found out how Marian died.'

'Did you believe Adelina?' Gelis said.

He said, 'I tried to find out for myself. I called on Enguerrand de Damparis — at Chouzy — at La Guiche. No one knew anything.'

'No one told you anything,' Gelis said. He looked down. She went on, 'Clémence and Pasque her nursemaid come from there. It was easier for me, perhaps, to ask.'

'And?' he said. He pulled away a little and eased himself up. It was instinctive. Not to recoil from her, but to spare her contamination.

She didn't let him go, but instead laid her hands on his arm. She said, 'They think Marian did have a daughter. They said it was born dead. I don't think Bonne is yours. She isn't Adelina's. She's just a waif, Nicholas, whom Adelina discovered and used.'

'But Marian did have a child,' he said. 'And died of it. You didn't tell me?'

'She didn't want you to know,' Gelis said. 'If you let it harm you, you'll deny all she did for you.' She broke off, and sat up in her turn, twisting to face him. She put her hands on his shoulders. 'You have come so far. We both have. Three years ago, you were ready to step into mindless oblivion with Benecke. All that has changed.'

He remembered. He remembered the moment when he stood on the jetty at Mewe, and watched the raft with Paúel Benecke leave. He had just heard that Julius and Anna had come. So he had to stay, or leave unprotected all those he cared for. Goodbye, Colà.

But for Adelina, he might never have known about Marian. But for Adelina, he would not be here. And now she was dead. The sheltering tree.

O God! Thou art all-pardoning, Thou likest pardon, pardon me.

The changes the world had seen were far greater than his, and the tragedies, too. He could only grieve on his own account that Adelina was dead in her torment; and Thibault, and stout Ochoa, and the strange Greek whose life had become entwined with his own. Astorre had gone. But Robin was living, and the bright, triumphant spirit to whom he would return. Sometimes, this evening, he had thought he could feel her joy, and he had tried to return it. *Kochajmy się,* my sweet Kathi.

Nicholas said to Gelis, 'You are right. And these things are not for tonight. Tonight is for us.'

'Today,' she said, as he moved.

'Tonight,' he repeated, looking down at her. 'I have not finished yet with tonight. Tomorrow is when we rise and reach our decision.'

She said, 'I think the decision is made.'

She was right, he supposed. There was only one thing he could do, that no one else could do, that would finally repair all he had done. It would not be easy for Gelis and Jodi. It would not even be safe. But there might be ways around that. If she had guessed, she was prepared for that also.

She was here.

The place of the Spindle of Necessity, with its whorl-weight of stars, where a traveller was bidden to choose his new life.

Whoever shall cast love aside, the words ran, *shall lose everything. For by love, laws are made, kingdoms governed, cities ordered, and the state of the commonwealth is brought to its proper goal.* So he recognised; for he was wiser than once he had been.

He gathered her into his arms, and loved her, and thought how blessed he was.

A NOTE ABOUT THE AUTHOR

Dorothy Dunnett was born in Dunfermline, Scotland. She is the author of the Francis Crawford of Lymond novels, a historical sequence set in the sixteenth century; seven mystery novels; *King Hereafter,* an epic novel about Macbeth; the text of *The Scottish Highlands,* a book of photographs by David Paterson, on which she collaborated with her husband, Sir Alastair Dunnett; and six earlier Niccolò novels. In 1992, Queen Elizabeth appointed her an Officer of the Order of the British Empire. Lady Dunnett lives with her husband in Edinburgh.

A NOTE ON THE TYPE

The text of this book was set in a digitized version of Imprint, a Monotype face originally cut in 1913 for the periodical of the same name. It was modeled on Caslon, but has a larger x-height and different italics, which harmonize better with the roman.

Composed by Creative Graphics,
Allentown, Pennsylvania

Printed and bound by Quebecor Printing,
Fairfield, Pennsylvania

DENMARK
Stralsund
Rügen
Rügenwalde
Gulf of Danzig
Oliva
Danzig (Gdansk)
Elbing
Rostock
Greifswald
Wismar
Lübeck
Kolberg
N
Dirschau
Mewe (Gniew)
Marienwe
POMERANIA
Vistula
Graudenz
MECKLENBURG
Stettin
Kulm
0 80 miles
Oder
NEUMARK
Bromberg
Thorn (To

Western Ocean
Baltic Sea
Danzig
Thor
POLA
Cracow
STRIA
HUNG
Buda
Pest
Danube
Belgrade
SER
ALBAN
PORTUGAL
Lisbon
Toled
CAS
Sevill
Tangier
Fez
Marrakesh
Sij
To Audaghost Walata & Mopti
Sea